ED GREENWOOD
P R E S E N T S
WATERDEEP
—— BOOK I ——

FORGOTTEN REALMS

ALSO BY ED GREENWOOD

SAGE OF SHADOWDALE

Elminster: The Making of a Mage
Elminster in Myth Drannor
The Temptation of Elminster
Elminster in Hell
Elminster's Daughter
The Annotated Elminster
Elminster Ascending
Elminster Must Die
Bury Elminster Deep
August 2011

ALSO BY STEVEN E. SCHEND

Blackstaff

ALSO BY JALEIGH JOHNSON

The Howling Delve
Unbroken Chain

ALSO BY ERIK SCOTT DE BIE

Ghostwalker
Depths of Madness

ED GREENWOOD
P R E S E N T S
WATERDEEP
——BOOK I——

BLACKSTAFF TOWER
STEVEN E. SCHEND

MISTSHORE
JALEIGH JOHNSON

DOWNSHADOW
ERIK SCOTT DE BIE

Ed Greenwood Presents Waterdeep Book I

Cover art by: Android Jones

Blackstaff Tower originally published September 2008
Mistshore originally published September 2008
Downshadow originally published April 2009

First Printing: July 2011

9 8 7 6 5 4 3 2 1

ISBN: 978-0-7869-5818-4
620-32298000-001-EN

U.S., CANADA,
ASIA, PACIFIC, & LATIN AMERICA
Wizards of the Coast LLC
P.O. Box 707
Renton, WA 98057-0707
+1-800-324-6496

EUROPEAN HEADQUARTERS
Hasbro UK Ltd
Caswell Way
Newport, Gwent NP9 0YH
GREAT BRITAIN
Save this address for your records.

Visit our web site at www.dungeonsanddragons.com

DEDICATION

Blackstaff Tower
To my grandparents, Mildred and Edward Hayward, for instilling in me a love of history over many summers in New England.

— S.E.S.

Mistshore
Dedicated to the members of WAG, past and present, for bringing me to the party. Most of all to Tim, my husband and friend. You've been there since the beginning, and now, I could never do without you. All my love.

— J.J.

Downshadow
According to Stephen King, writing is a kind of telepathy, where the words that I transcribe convey a thought from my head indirectly into yours. It is this very connection I'm going to try to use right here, right now, when I say this book is for *you*.

Usually, you pick up a book, flip to the dedication page and say "John and Sue? Whatever." But not this time. This time, this book is for you, right there—right now.

(Yeah, I'm talking to you.)

I dedicate this book to you, gentle reader, for having faith in me and in our Realms.

This one's for you.

— E.S.d.B.

Welcome to Faerûn, a land of magic and intrigue, brutal violence and divine compassion, where gods have ascended and died, and mighty heroes have risen to fight terrifying monsters. Here, millennia of warfare and conquest have shaped dozens of unique cultures, raised and leveled shining kingdoms and tyrannical empires alike, and left long forgotten, horror-infested ruins in their wake.

A LAND OF MAGIC

When the goddess of magic was murdered, a magical plague of blue fire—the Spellplague—swept across the face of Faerûn, killing some, mutilating many, and imbuing a rare few with amazing supernatural abilities. The Spellplague forever changed the nature of magic itself, and seeded the land with hidden wonders and bloodcurdling monstrosities.

A LAND OF DARKNESS

The threats Faerûn faces are legion. Armies of undead mass in Thay under the brilliant but mad lich king Szass Tam. Treacherous dark elves plot in the Underdark in the service of their cruel and fickle goddess, Lolth. The Aubolethic Sovereignty, a terrifying hive of inhuman slave masters, floats above the Sea of Fallen Stars, spreading chaos and destruction. And the Empire of Netheril, armed with magic of unimaginable power, prowls Faerûn in flying fortresses, sowing discord to their own incalculable ends.

A LAND OF HEROES

But Faerûn is not without hope. Heroes have emerged to fight the growing tide of darkness. Battle-scarred rangers bring their notched blades to bear against marauding hordes of orcs. Lowly street rats match wits with demons for the fate of cities. Inscrutable tiefling warlocks unite with fierce elf warriors to rain fire and steel upon monstrous enemies. And valiant servants of merciful gods forever struggle against the darkness.

A LAND OF
UNTOLD ADVENTURE

YUSKURL AND THE UNINVITED GUEST

WITH A FLOURISH AND A SMOOTH BOW, THE STEWARD PUT A TALLGLASS of sparkling Thelnroake into the visitor's hand and glided away. A bare breath later, a door half-hidden in the rich paneling of the walls closed behind him, leaving his master alone with this unexpected arrival.

Wealthy moneylenders had an intense dislike for uninvited guests—yet Yuskurl Melmantle rose out of his high backed chair with a smile.

"This is an unexpected pleasure! Well met, Nephew! I cannot help but notice that you are, ah, more *substantial* than when last I saw you. Success agrees with you, evidently. So how, these last few tendays, unfolds the Athkatlan trade in procurements?"

Tarvin Melmantle smiled lazily and patted his belly with a satisfied air.

"Well enough, Uncle," he replied, deftly thumbing one of his rings so a few grains of the powder it contained would drop into his glass and slay any poisons lurking within.

He trusted his uncle wouldn't be offended. The man could hardly have lived long enough to become one of the wealthiest men in Waterdeep without taking similar precautions.

If Uncle Yuskurl was annoyed, no hint of it reached his face. He stood with his own wine in his hand, studying his nephew.

Tarvin's garments were dark and unadorned, but of the finest make and in the latest Amnian fashion, shoulder-cloak falling in rippling splendor from a gilded mask capping the left shoulder. A jewel-hilted blade rode the hip beneath it, and the triple-belted baldric that soared from its scabbard across his nephew's chest held in check a paunch Yuskurl was surprised to see—though in truth, Tarvin had been little older than a scampering lad when they'd last met, only just beginning his first lessons with the Shadow Thieves.

"I arrived in Waterdeep after highsun, took rooms, and came straight here," Tarvin added, raising his tallglass in silent thanks. "As I crossed the city, I found myself a little . . . overwhelmed."

Yuskurl crooked an eyebrow. "How so? Athkatla's hardly a small, slumberous backwater."

Tarvin shrugged. "There's magic here, and the huge mountain towering over everything, and half the Realms gathered and crowded together—on my way to you I saw creatures I'd only heard about, casually striding the streets. I know many a tale of the grand City of Splendors, but . . ."

Yuskurl smiled. "The reality is larger, busier, smellier—and far more dangerous. And a wise procurer learns all he can before . . . beginning to acquire. So you came to me."

He strolled across the room, toward an unbroken row of tapestries. "I must confess that pleases me. What would you know?"

"Everything, Uncle. I know what half the world does, of Waterdeep. That coin is king, and all the world comes here to seek their fortunes. To buy what's rare and precious and can't be had elsewhere, or at least send their wares here to sell. I know about the guilds, the ruling lords Masked and Open, and the nobles—and that nobility can now be bought. Which reminds me; those who keep to shadows are curious as to why you haven't joined the nobility."

Yuskurl Melmantle smiled gently. "Buying a title is like blowing a warhorn to herald a battle, or shouting to everyone to watch you, and heed. I find such wide attention . . . undesirable. Something your guild should understand well."

Tarvin nodded. "They've never managed to gain any lasting hold on power here. You have."

Those words were offered with the ring of praise, but Yuskurl merely nodded. Parting the tapestries, he beckoned.

Tarvin followed that bidding, out through a door onto a high stone balcony where the cool evening air came ghosting past, bringing the clangs and shouts and cartwheel rumblings of a busy city up to them. Not to mention a stink of rotting fish and seaweed.

They stood together, wine in hand, and looked all around, into the deepening night.

Uncle Yuskurl's mansion rose from the landward side of Mount Waterdeep like a solid, defiant stone fist. It was dwarfed by larger and more magnificent walled mansions on either side, sprawling and many-spired palaces. The largest and most gaudily lit were above them, higher on the great city-shielding mountainside, silhouettes against the silver moon.

Tarvin looked up at those lights with the awakening hunger of the professional thief. Grand things, palaces, and they held grander things . . .

His uncle smiled, waving a hand at them. "Hard-blown warhorns," he murmured. "Not my style."

Below them, Castle Ward unfolded down the long shoulder of the mountain. Beyond it lay the harbor. The many flickering lights stretching away along its edge must be never-sleeping Dock Ward, the fabled dark heart of Waterdhavian crime, gateway to the sewers where dread beholders and nameless tentacled things lurked—but what was this dimly-lit wrack of leaning masts and sagging ships, hard by the shore?

"Mistshore," Uncle Yuskurl announced, following Tarvin's gaze. "Now reputedly the most perilous part of Waterdeep. The Watch fear to patrol there. Ship atop rotting, half-sunken ship, lashed together in an unmapped maze of squalor and lawlessness. It's where folk dwell who want nothing to do with the Watch—or dare not show their faces elsewhere in the city."

Tarvin gave his uncle a sidelong look, catching the faintest mockery in the pronunciation of that "reputedly."

"So," he murmured, "what *is* the most dangerous part of the city?"

Yuskurl looked out across the harbor. At its southern end a mist was gathering. The sort of mist that meant rain was falling, in a softly-advancing curtain that would soon sweep across the city.

The breeze around them freshened, rising before the oncoming storm. It brought no more stinks, now, but rather the sharp wet smell of the roused sea.

"In truth, the most dangerous part of Waterdeep," he said calmly, "is wherever most of the Lords of Waterdeep are gathered, at any given time. Yet if you meant to ask me what our most dangerous neighborhood is, that would be Downshadow, deep beneath our feet, where of old Skullport raged and fell Undermountain gave the foolish swift graves. Where monsters lurk, slavery and other unlawful trade is transacted, starving adventurers lurk, awaiting nightfall so they can raid up into Waterdeep, and citizens who've become inconvenient to someone powerful all too often . . . disappear."

"How lyrical," Tarvin commented, as they turned in unison to depart the balcony. "Words worthy of a bard hard at his glib-tongued weaving, setting flesh crawling among simple drunkards listening to him around a dying fire in a dark tavern. You make Waterdeep seem like one vast trap, or battlefield."

"I do?" His uncle's smile was as gentle as ever. "Then you've been made wiser, and my words have done their work."

Tarvin frowned as they returned to the heart of the room, where the chairs faced each other across a central rug that looked to be the pelt of a gigantic snow-wolf. "You'll be telling me tales of ghosts next."

"If you'd like to hear them, by all means. True accounts, mind, every one. Waterdeep has ghosts and wraiths, flameskulls and worse—"

"Haunts that will freeze my blood cold," the young Athkatlan sneered. "To say nothing of horrors a full-grown dragon would flee from, no doubt."

Yuskurl's smile did not change. "You've schooled yourself well. You should last longer here than most Shadow Thieves."

"Is that a threat, Uncle?"

"A warning, Nephew. A kindly warning. You have nothing in Athkatla like the Blackstaff. Or Open Lord Neverember, for that matter."

"We have our ruling families, Uncle—and they have their hired wizards. Five mighty houses are fewer foes to keep track of than twenty-and-one Masked Lords, yes, but their reach is longer and heavier."

Yuskurl Melmantle arched an eyebrow again. "Even here? Is that a threat, Nephew?"

Tarvin sighed, regarding the wolf-pelt under his boots thoughtfully, then replied, "No. I did not come here to threaten or offer insult. And although your wine is superb and your company has thus far been both warm and genial, I did not come here out of any compulsion of kinship. My guildmaster ordered me to confer with you before I, ah, *obtained* anything here in Waterdeep."

"This I strongly suspected," Yuskurl replied, over the rim of his tallglass. "Did he say why he was giving you such an order?"

Tarvin nodded expressionlessly. "He said it might keep me alive."

Yuskurl looked into the depths of his drink. "He is correct in that. Thieves who snatch *things* in this city do not flourish for long."

"So what sort of procurer does flourish in Waterdeep?"

"Those who steal *ideas*, of course. And put them to work outplaying merchants in the market—or swindling them behind their backs."

Tarvin frowned. "That sounds like work. The hustling coin-counting work of a trader, not the skills of . . . my guild."

Yuskurl shrugged. "I unfold Waterdeep before you. I do not control it—no man can—nor condone it. It is what it is: the most wonderful city in the world, awash in riches enough to keep the greatest thief busy all her days. It's called the City of Splendors because it's all *here*—all the splendors of all the Realms come to those docks, or in through the gates as you did. Yours for the taking, *if* you learn how that taking is best done, here."

He sat down in his highbacked chair, but leaned forward in it like a roosting vulture, eyes glittering.

"So, Nephew, do you begin to understand? The city awaits; are you ready?"

Tarvin set his glass down on the arm of a handy chair, smiled, and replied, "I believe I am."

He dug his hand into his belly, and peeled it back like the rind of a fruit. If rinds could curl and slither by themselves, that is; the bulging flesh became a small, many-tailed shapeshifting thing that undulated swiftly up Tarvin's shoulder, revealing the Athkatlan's flat belly—and a wand strapped across it in a sheath.

A wand now out and gleaming, in Tarvin's hand. Rising to menace Yuskurl.

"The taking," its wielder gloated, "begins here!"

Yuskurl Melmantle raised his tallglass for another sip—and calmly thrust his finger into a particular depression in the carved arm of his chair.

Wand, wielder, wolf-pelt and all dropped suddenly out of sight, to the accompaniment of a startled shout from the man who was not his nephew.

A cry that ended very suddenly in the embrace of eagerly-awaiting tentacles.

The longest tentacle thrust up through the hole in the floor, vast and glistening, to deliver a slap of thanks before dropping back down the shaft again.

The wealthiest moneylender in Waterdeep got up and strolled to where he could gaze down, down into the tentacles. Deep beneath his cellars, down almost as far as Downshadow itself.

He drained the last of his Thelnroake. Lovely stuff.

Just for a moment, he caught sight of a white, frantically-staring face among the roiling tentacles.

"You think I wasn't aware of your ruse, Shadow Thief?" he called. "My nephew is left-handed, and so wears his sword at his *right* hip." He shook his head. "No, you'd not have lasted long in Waterdeep."

BLACKSTAFF TOWER

STEVEN E. SCHEND

INTRODUCTION

BACK IN 1966, FASCINATED BY THE FANTASY TALES CRAMMED INTO MY father's study, I started creating the FORGOTTEN REALMS® as the backdrop for my own stories, looking over the shoulder of the swindling old merchant Mirt the Moneylender as he wandered the Sword Coast a mere boot-stride ahead of local authorities and furious rivals.

Well over thirty years passed, and a game known as DUNGEONS & DRAGONS® got invented and soared to wild popularity. The Realms became part of it and literally hundreds of novels, short stories, game products, and articles appeared, all detailing facets of the Realms—building a long, detailed, and complex history for this entirely imaginary place. What I dubbed "Realmslore" started to pile up deeply in some places (such as Waterdeep) and around some characters, such as powerful wizards, who've always held an attraction, and the Chosen of Mystra, servants of the foremost deity of magic, who have an allure all their own.

You may have heard of one of them: Elminster, the sly old meddling rogue. Or perhaps the Seven Sisters, who in the Realms aren't oil companies, priestesses, or princesses (though they sometimes behave like all three), but silver-haired women who share a mother: Mystra herself.

Then there was Khelben "Blackstaff" Arunsun. *The* Blackstaff. The gruff, grim, self-righteous, straight-arrow counterpart to Elminster. A man (?) of as many mysteries as Elminster, but of a very different style. I created him to be "there but aloof from the citizenry on the streets" in Waterdeep, married to Laeral of the Seven Sisters, the two of them providing enough magical firepower to keep the dreaded Mad Mage, Halaster, down in Undermountain, and to prevent all the wizards attracted to Waterdeep's riches or hired by its various ambitious and unscrupulous nobles, wannabe nobles, and guildmasters from blasting the city to ruin every second night as they got into spell-duels with each other, or experimented with a newer, mightier Swarm of Suns spell.

Enter Steven Schend. One of several long-suffering "traffic cops" of the Realms, the staffers who have to rein in not just me, but everyone else with a fun, wild, and crazy idea they want to try out in the Realms, and coordinate the whole ongoing circus. Steven's way of handling the job was to understand why conflicts happen through history—the imaginary history of the Realms. He adopted Halaster (and Undermountain), Khelben (and Waterdeep), the coastal kingdoms of Amn, Tethyr, and Calimshan, and the fallen elf realm of Cormanthyr, and *really* steeped them all in history.

Which is why he was the ideal writer to pen the novel *Blackstaff*, and why he is really the only person who could tell the tale you hold in your hands, *Blackstaff Tower*.

Oh, you're in for a treat. Not a trudge through dusty history, but a tense clash of intrigue in Waterdeep a century after the events of *Blackstaff*. A story built on the secrets of the past that charges boldly into the future.

I couldn't wait to read it, the first time through—and when I was done, I couldn't wait to read it again.

Ed Greenwood
March 2008

PROLOGUE

*The North has sinfully warm days late in the year, which some call elf summers,
that merely bulwark the wary for the inevitable chills of winter to come.*

Malek Aldhanek, *My Travels,*
the Year of the Gem Dragons (812 DR)

20 MARPENOTH, YEAR OF THE AGELESS ONE (1479 DR)

ARE YOU SURE YOU NEED TO DO THIS RIGHT NOW, SAMARK?" THE YOUNG woman's short black hair rippled in the light breeze, never obscuring her bright indigo eyes. "I know it's important, but it's too nice a day. Why spoil our picnic by rifling through that tomb? Stay here, where it's warm and bright."

Vajra Safahr stretched languidly on the blanket. She luxuriated in the sun and playfully clamped her toes on the edge of Samark's robes. "Aren't there *better* things we could do with such a marvelous day?" She let one dusky shoulder slip free from her gray tunic as she leaned toward Samark and winked.

The old man, Samark "the Blackstaff" Dhanzscul, smiled. The smile contorted three parallel scars running from his right cheekbone down to his jaw. "Tempting, lass," he said. "Deliciously so. Hold those thoughts. My task here won't keep me long. Especially with such a motivation putting wings to my aged feet."

Samark turned to face a hillock covered in vines. The flat-sided boulder he approached showed a few graven letters through thick crawling ivies. Samark placed his left hand flat atop the near-hidden **KH**, and the crystal atop the twisted metal staff in his right hand flashed a bright green. He uttered a few syllables and stepped through the stone as if it were air.

The small tomb smelled dank and close. The green light from Samark's staff lit up the tiny space. Dust and cobwebs covered every surface and cloaked the wizard as he stepped inside. Magic crackled in the air, reacting to his presence, but it subsided after he whispered, *"Suortanakh."*

The old man walked down three steps and knelt at the bier dominating the tomb's floor. Complex marks tiled its sides, all glowing a dim blue beneath a spider-spun shroud. The gray carving of a tall man with a full beard rested atop the stone sarcophagus, his hands holding a glass globe atop his chest. After a brief prayer, the old man sent a pulse of magic into the globe held by the effigy. The energy cleared the webs off the glass globe, and it shimmered with emerald-toned magic.

Samark rested his left hand on the glass and said, *"Aegisbiir n'varan colroth aegismiir!"*

His ring and the globe both flashed. The omnipresent illusions of dust and webs dissolved, as did the illusory walls of the tomb. The tomb revealed itself to be the entry chamber atop a long stair that led down into a chamber far more vast than the hillock outside. At the top of the stairs, bright silver bars prevented entry. Samark willed his staff's crystal to glow brighter. The brilliance made the staff's carved metal claw appear to hold a small emerald sun.

Samark leaned heavily on the staff as he walked up to the silver metal bars where the back wall once stood. He placed his left hand flat on a featureless metal plate where a lock might normally appear, and the crystal on his staff pulsed. The bars and the plate grated into the ceiling and floor. Samark shuffled down the stairs. During his descent, he glanced toward the chamber on his left, a gallery of sorts at the foot of the stairs. Twenty-five items rested atop short white marble columns, each amid a bright spotlight. A realistic centaur reared atop the nearest column, carved from a single gourd-sized ruby. Beside it, an undulating ribbon of gold and platinum turned and twisted end over end on its velvet pillow. Beside that, a crown carved from thick bone and set with sapphires seemed to hug shadows to itself, despite the bright light overhead. The rest of that chamber held more than a dozen rods and staves standing on end with no visible supports, as well as eight swords of various makes, all unsupported. Samark walked past the chamber, turning his glance toward the opposite chamber.

Inside this room, a septet of bookshelves all loomed a man's height above his own. As he crossed the threshold of the room, he spoke to the empty air. *"Diolaa siolakhiir. Melkar of Mirabar's Journal. Alsidda's Tome. Te'elarn'vaeniir. Love at Llast."* In response, four books pulled themselves off their separate shelves, floated across the open air, and landed gently in his hand. Tucking the books under his left arm, he turned and walked out to the foot of the stairs and turned toward the far end of the room.

Samark moved slowly down a long hall lined with portraits. As he walked, torches flared to life two paces ahead of him, lighting the paintings and the names embossed in brass on their frames—Rarkin, Strathea, Larnarm, Rhinnara, Phesta, Kitten, Brian, Sammereza, Durnan, Mirt, Ruarn, Pellak, Shilarn, and at least a dozen more. He chuckled as he walked, and muttered, "How many knew the regard with which the Blackstaff held them, I wonder? So few Lords gained Khelben's respect, let alone that of the other Blackstaffs . . ."

At the tunnel's end, Samark entered a tall triangular chamber, two statues flanking him on either side. He bowed his head in reverence, scanning the names of each statue and whispered to each, "Greetings, honored Open Lords. Lord Caladorn Cassalanter. Lord Piergeiron Paladinson. Lord Lhestyn Arunsun. Lord Baeron Silmaeril." Samark stopped, turned to the point of the room, and raised his eyes. "Honored greetings, Open Lord Ahghairon."

This statue gleamed brightest and tallest, its height dwarfing the other four in this chamber. Samark marveled at the workmanship. He sought but never found a chisel mark anywhere on the robes, staff, or even the intricately tangled beard of the bald wizard before him. His eyes darted to the gold ring encircling Ahghairon's left index finger and the sapphires-among-silver amulet resting on his chest—the only things not carved from the marble cliffs of Mount Khimbarr.

Samark set down the books and released his staff, which floated beside him. The wizard wove a complex series of gestures and a longer series of arcane words as he walked sunward around the statue three times. On the completion of his third circuit, he proclaimed, *"Aonaochel. Enakhel adomanth, adoquessir, adofaer. Lakrhel eislarhen aonaoch."* The metal ring and amulet both shimmered and reappeared on Samark's person, albeit scaled down to fit his human form.

Samark smiled, knelt at the foot of the statue, and said, "Thank you, Great Protector. I do thy bidding and that of our predecessors in all your names."

Vajra Safahr sighed as she watched her mentor dissolve into the tomb. She wondered how that old man made her heart beat so fast, and her mother's words returned to her. "Never question love—it makes its own rules each time anew." Waterdeep, Crown of the North, was a tolerant city, but a few still saw their partnership as odd, both due to their ages and because Vajra was a dusky-skinned Tethyrian, not a native Waterdhavian. Even so, none questioned that Vajra Safahr was the Blackstaff's Heir in duty and love.

Vajra rolled onto her back and stared up at the clear sky. After three years in the Sword Coast North, she knew that they had precious few days left before Auril drew a perpetual gray blanket across the skies for the winter months. Vajra could have gone inside with Samark, but she preferred the sun and leaf-scented wind to the dank.

As she lay there, movement seized her attention. A stone arced across her line of sight and fell directly in front of her at the edge of her blanket. She sat up and peered closer it.

The rock spewed a cloud of greenish gas. Vajra scurried back and started a spell to repel the vapors when she felt a sudden pinch. She reached for it and felt a dart in the back of her neck. She turned to see a dark-clad figure rise from the overgrown tomb, his hooded face revealing only a wicked grin as he tucked a blowgun back in his belt.

"She's unable to speak, lads. We should be safe."

The man laughed, and through the roaring in her ears Vajra dimly heard others approach around her. She focused her attention on the laughing man, and willed magic out her eyes. Three bolts of amber energy felled the man in mid-laugh.

Thank the gods Samark taught me how to cast at least one spell without movement or sound, she thought.

Vajra tried to rise but found her legs would not support her. She fell backward as her eyes began to cloud over. She stared straight upward and raged at her body's betrayal. Her foes closed around her, blades drawn. None had seen the business end of a bath house or a razor in some tendays.

"Is she out?" The skinniest of them asked, his pinched face, scars, and patchy beard reminding Vajra of a rat.

"No, she's staring at us. If looks could kill, eh?" The taller man's face bore a beak of a nose, making him the vulture of the lot.

"What do you mean, Rivvol? She's smiling." A pudgy, inquisitive face peered down at her. Realization dawned on the black-haired ferret of a man and he reared back.

Fools should have learned the first time, she thought.

Vajra's contempt for her opponents eked into her smile and spell as she willed more missiles at the three foes. Each of the men staggered back, clutching their faces in pain. One wiped tears from his eyes and kicked Vajra hard in her side.

Another voice from behind the trio said, "You were warned not to underestimate even the apprentice, fools. Now, prepare her and yourselves for the Blackstaff's return."

Vajra wished she could move to see who that voice belonged to. The man's kick turned her away from them, and she stared at the boulder marker of Khelben the Elder's tomb. She tried to move or speak, but failed at both. One of the men picked her up, keeping her eyes directed up and away from himself and his compatriots.

.:⌒:.

Samark the Blackstaff walked out of the tomb and through its covering vegetation as effortlessly as he'd entered it. "I have them, Vajra. Now, where—"

"Do anything but breathe, Blackstaff, and she dies!"

A hook-nosed vulture of a man held his knife at Vajra's throat, his other arm holding her up and pinning her back to his grimy hauberk. Another slovenly rat-faced man, his beard growing only in clumps around many scars, held Vajra's legs and aimed his rusty short sword at her midsection.

A third man sidled alongside Samark, a crossbow at his shoulder. Pressing the point of his quarrel to the side of Samark's throat, he said, "Throw the staff down, old man, and you both might live a while longer. Kessik, grab those books."

The old wizard dropped the books from the crook of his right arm to hold his staff with both hands. "You had better not harm her . . ."

"Shut it, you. And drop the staff!" The vulture's blade pressed closer to Vajra's neck, drawing a bead of fresh blood atop older gore still encrusted on the knife.

"Listen to Rivvol, Blackstaff. He gets twitchy around wizards, and he's likely to kill even one as pretty as that Tethyrian." The speaker moved over next to his comrades, his crossbow always at his shoulder. Kessik let go of Vajra's legs and scurried over to the pile of tomes next to Samark.

"Fine." Samark threw the staff at the ground among the four of them. As he let go of the staff, he clapped his hands, and his form shimmered with cerulean magic. The staff hit the turf right at Vajra's feet and flashed a verdant pulse in all directions. The top of the staff tipped forward onto Rivvol's arm, and he screamed as emerald lightning crackled from the staff into him. He screamed and collapsed, but his dagger fell as well. Vajra collapsed in front of him, her body unharmed by the staff, but her neck gushing blood from Rivvol's knife.

The crossbow's scrape and twang drew little of Samark's attention, but he saw the bolt glance off his protective shield. His face wrinkled in concentration, Samark launched a purple pulse at Vajra, pointing with his other hand to aim a second bolt at the crossbowman. The energy swept through Vajra and looped around to strike the crossbowman. The woman's wounds healed quickly, but the crossbowman's throat opened just as hers had been, and he fell to his knees, his breath and lifeblood bubbling out of the wound.

"Ammol!" Kessik stood open-mouthed. Both his allies had fallen in mere seconds. "What'd that green stuff do to me?" Kessik asked, his eyes filled with terror as he crawled away from Samark, the tomes forgotten.

"Absolutely nothing, boy." Samark said. "It merely undid some spells to reveal your master to me. Now flee, before I become less patient or he decides you're expendable too."

Kessik paused a moment, then turned and fled as fast as he could. Samark barely watched him, his attention focused on the tall, hooded man who had shimmered into visibility when the green energy washed over him. Wearing nondescript olive robes, the man stood with his scimitar drawn, its edge shimmering with red light. The mage's most outstanding features, aside from a very thick, singular eyebrow, were the ornate rings flashing on every digit of both hands. The man's razor-thin salt-and-pepper mustache and goatee framed his sneer.

Samark touched the scars on his own cheek and said, "I wish I could be surprised, Khondar. Your betrayal was inevitable—though, I confess, sooner than I expected."

Khondar "Ten-Rings" Naomal said, "Blackstaff, this reckoning has been coming a long time. I'm glad you know it was me who ended your life and that of your strumpet."

"And how do you plan to do that?" Samark stepped closer to Vajra and his fallen staff. "Far better than you have tried, you know."

Khondar Naomal's response was an angry slash of his scimitar while he uttered an incantation. The blade resonated with magic and a slash of midnight shredded the air between the two wizards. The dark energy shattered the blue shield Samark had around himself, much to the Blackstaff's surprise.

"You've gotten better toys, Ten-Rings," Samark said, "but you've always relied too much on them."

Samark braced himself and summoned energy around his hands and arms as Khondar rushed forward. Ten-Rings chopped downward with his glowing scimitar, and Samark clapped his hands, trapping the blade in mid-chop. Both men stood eye-to-eye, their hatred as powerful as the magic that trapped them together.

"You should have stayed in Sundabar, Khondar. You'd have been the big wizard there, rather than fighting your betters over imagined slights every tenday."

Samark couldn't move or cast without disrupting his active spell and releasing the blade. Luckily, Ten-Rings also could not move without losing his weapon.

Three amber pulses slammed into Khondar's side, and he howled in anger. Taking a quick look to the side, the Blackstaff saw the still-paralyzed Vajra had collapsed facing their battle. Her eyes glowed with arcane power and anger.

Samark chuckled, "Vajra can harm you even when paralyzed, Ten-Rings. Having an ally helps, but having some one who loves you . . . well, that makes all the difference."

Khondar's grin disarmed Samark. "Very true, Blackstaff. I couldn't agree more." The ten-ringed man let go of his scimitar and backed away. "Don't you, Father?"

Samark saw his foe's gaze wander past his own left shoulder toward the tomb. Samark said, "Father? Then you're—"

"My son, and your doom, fool," Khondar's voice rang out behind Samark.

An energy ring blinked into existence around Samark and clenched shut around his midsection, teeth biting into him as it contracted. Samark's last word was a pleading "Vajr—"

Then the spell rent him in two.

Khondar moved quickly behind Vajra and clubbed her on the back of the head with his scimitar's pommel. As he did so, his form blurred and shimmered. Rings faded from his hands, as did his mustache. His hair darkened, and his robes became a black tunic and breeches. The younger man, who shared the singular eyebrow of his father, looked up and said, "She's out at last."

"Thank you, Centiv," Khondar said to his son, as he floated off the ivy-covered tomb toward him. "Your illusions, as always, are excellent. I'm glad Samark's trick only removed your invisibility. It kept him focused on you. Now, stay back. There's going to be power in play here that should keep her from being a bother."

As if on cue, the two halves of the Blackstaff's body sizzled with energy, darkening the gory remnants even further. A tempest of dark lightning crackled out of Samark's remains and arced in two directions—into his staff and into Vajra, who arched her back and legs as if screaming before she fell into spasms. In one breath, the energy cascade ended, and the meadow lay still again. The only sounds were Vajra's uneven breaths and the triumphant howl of Khondar's laughter.

"Rejoice, Centiv! She's the last obstacle we have to conquer, and her secrets will lead to our joining the Lords and ruling the city!"

Vajra lay unconscious, but Khondar approached her warily. He nudged her with the toe of his boot. He gestured and her garments rewove themselves, binding her arms and hands. He looked up briefly and scowled at his son's rapt leer at Vajra. "Centiv, I don't need your help right now. Go chase down Kessik and make sure he cannot talk about this to anyone."

Centiv nodded and cast a spell before he leaped across the landscape in the same direction Kessik fled.

Khondar turned to the remains of Samark. His eyes shone as he reached for the blood-spattered amulet on Samark's chest. He patted down the pockets and body. As he wrenched a gory gold ring off Samark's finger, he muttered, "The power of the Blackstaff lies nearly within reach. Soon, the tower will be mine . . . and I'll gain the secret of long years so far denied humans. I shall become the Blackstaff, and Waterdeep shall know its savior! The rightful rule of wizards is at hand for the Crown of the North again!"

CHAPTER ONE

The Watch is for our people's safety, not solely his Lordship's security or whims, and should be used thusly.

Open Lord Piergeiron Paladinson to a Masked Lord,
Lords' Court Transcripts,
21 Uktar, Year of the Helm (1362 DR)

8 NIGHTAL, YEAR OF THE AGELESS ONE (1479 DR)

THE TAVERN WAS HARDLY HIS FIRST CHOICE OF VENUES, BUT IT HAD GROWN on him after Faxhal first dragged him here last month. Renaer Neverember liked that the usual hateful, conceited social climbers and all-but-nobles that constantly badgered him for his attentions and his friendship rarely came here. This tavern at the edge of Sea and Castle Wards was well-kept and honest, and its patrons were a wide array of Waterdhavians, not just one group or social stratum. Renaer appreciated that, as he did its dark brew and its night black loaves. Atop all that, another small part of it made Renaer agree to meet his friends here repeatedly. Tucked back in the eastern corner away from the doors was a small sheltered nook with shelves on the back wall. Mostly empty, the shelves held a random assortment of broadsheets at all times, though often a few days out of date. Renaer managed to read a few of the more recent issues of *The Vigilant Citizen* and *The Blue Unicorn* before his first friend arrived.

Lord Torlyn Wands tossed a heavy oilskin-wrapped bundle on the table in front of Renaer. "The weather's getting that winter sting to it," he growled as he tugged off his soaked half-cloak. The clasp on his cloak snagged his light gray linen shirt, pulling it out of his belt and exposing his slender yet exceedingly hairy chest.

A few patrons whistled at the young noble, while a passing serving maid ran her fingers across his chest, making him blush. When she looked up and locked eyes with him, she blushed even brighter and stammered, "My apologies, Milord Wands," and rushed away.

Torlyn turned his attention back to Renaer as he tucked his shirt back into his breeches. "Damned shirt! My sister keeps replacing my functional clothes with these 'things that are in style,' and they drive me mad!" He slumped into the seat opposite Renaer and put his boots up on another chair. "Look at these soaked boots! All the trouble to dye the calfskin blue, but they didn't bother to waterproof the blasted things!"

"Ah, the costs of noble fashions and the maintenance of social airs." Renaer smiled, tipping his flagon toward Lord Wands in mock salute. "You have my sympathies, milord. Bad form, really, to not treat the leather well, I agree. I can suggest a few cobblers who can fix those up for you or make you better ones right away."

Torlyn laughed, his irritation at fashion forgotten. "Speaking of better leatherworking, I'm amazed you didn't dive on that parcel the moment it left my hands. I wanted to show you my latest acquisition, since few appreciate a good book more than you." Lord Wands's broad grin was not concealed in the least by his long mahogany locks or full beard. He whispered thanks to the still-blushing tavern maid who brought him a large tankard of the tavern's dark ale, and then Renaer's attention shifted from his companion to the parcel. Two sharp tugs undid the leather lacings and he opened the oilskin wraps around a large book.

Renaer ran his fingers over the ornate leatherworked cover and the bindings, his eyebrows rising in appreciation. He gingerly opened the volume to its initial page and let out a low whistle.

"*The Compleat Dragonhunter?*" Renaer asked, looking up at Torlyn without letting go of the page or the book.

His companion laughed. "Had it for two days now, along with *Gold Amid Dragonfire.* They were hidden among a lot of dross I picked up when I absorbed the last remnants of the Estelmer and Melshimber collections last month."

Renaer chuckled. "You and your dragon books, Torlyn. Are you rebuilding your family's library or gathering a hoard?" Renaer flipped through a few pages, nodded at the good workmanship and calligraphy, and rewrapped the book to protect it.

"Very funny, Ren." Torlyn smiled, swallowed some ale, and asked, "You're one to talk, he who snaps up every book on Waterdeep's past that's been written. Say, did you find *Folk of Renown* yet?"

"No. Well . . . yes and no," Renaer replied. "I found a copy on the market up in Longsaddle last month, but I bought something else."

Torlyn shifted his blue boots off the chair, then stood. From the way Torlyn tugged at the bootcuffs and then shifted how he sat, Renaer could tell Torlyn's clothes and boots were too new and uncomfortable. He noticed Renaer's attention, shrugged, and cleared his throat before sitting down again and asking, "Why? For Oghma's sake, you've wanted that book forever, Ren."

"I know, I know," he answered, amused to see his audience taking the bait. "Instead, I discovered the final pieces for my Savengriff collection."

"You found a complete copy of *A Palace Life?*" The young lord slammed his tankard down in disbelief. The dark-stained table shined with the newest sluice of spilled ale, though neither man cared, save to move the wrapped book to a drier, safer spot.

Renaer leaned back. "I bought all three volumes with an identically bound copy of *Piergeiron as I Remember Him* thrown in for good measure!"

"Nice. 'Tis no wonder you're the new sage of local obscure lore."

"Sage?" Renaer asked. "I'm a mere dabbler and an inveterate reader, 'tis all."

"Still, I'm impressed. The only known library with every mundane work of Aleena Paladinstar and her wizardly husband Savengriff." Torlyn Wands looked down in dismay, then raised his eyes with a smile. "At least my collection still has the only full set of nonmagical books by the Seven Sisters—or at least it will when you return my copy of *Lifelong with Regrets* to me."

"Soon, Torlyn, soon. It's a fascinating read, and I'm grateful for the loan. Laeral's handwriting and her inscription to your great-great-grandfather add a whole new understanding to her." Renaer drank and waved a servant over to their table. "Another round, please, Arlanna." He flipped a taol toward the tavernmaid, and turned back to Torlyn. "When are Faxhal and Vharem due to join us?"

"Patience, Renaer, patience," Torlyn said. "I hear Vharem spent most of his day chaperoning the youngest Phullbrinter sisters in their shopping for the Gralleth feast."

"Ah, what that man does for his coins," Renaer said. "He'll need stronger drink than this, then."

The door to the tavern opened, and two of his oldest friends entered. Renaer stood and waved them over to the table. Faxhal smirked a perfect mimicry of Renaer's own grin back at him. Faxhal resembled Renaer in many ways—broad-shouldered and brawny, clean-shaven, shoulder-length brown hair, square-jawed with chiseled features—but his claim that he was the better-looking of the two urged Renaer to remind him he was shorter and had thus concentrated Renaer's charisma. Vharem wore an expensively tailored night blue cloak in contrast with his unkempt blond beard and scuffed brown boots.

"The Watch is hunting for you again, Renaer. We had to shake a patrol on our way here." Vharem rolled his eyes along with Renaer as he related the news. The tall blond man signaled Arlanna to bring two more tankards as he shrugged his dark cloak open and sat down next to Torlyn. The two men traded nods as greetings.

"What have I allegedly done this time to displease his Open Lordship, my father?" Renaer sighed, rising to let Faxhal get past him to a seat.

The shorter of the two men shook his head, then rushed forward and vaulted over the table, using one hand to catapult himself onto the bench in the corner of the tavern. Renaer grinned and muttered, "Show-off," as he sat down again.

Faxhal said, "Not a thing, so far as we know. It's just a few new shield-lars and their patrols trying to impress their new captain and tonight's valabrar—and unfortunately, tonight's overseer for the Watch in Castle and Sea Wards is Kahlem Ralnarth."

Torlyn choked on his drink and coughed. "How did *that* inbred noble idiot get promoted? What have I missed the past two tendays?"

"Only a marvelous chase across Field and Sea Wards not three nights ago," Vharem said with a snicker. "A dash across the Northbeach is not something I want to repeat before spring."

"Yeah," Faxhal said. "You'd think he'd be grateful we led them right to those smugglers at the Lancecove. Capturing a septet of forgers and smugglers was shine on his sword, to be sure. His promotion from aumarr should have made him more grateful."

Renaer looked up, dropping his sly grin quickly, as he said, "I think he's worried his superiors will regret that promotion if they find out he only caught *them* due to chasing and trying to arrest *us* for assaulting a city official and defiling a holy place."

Torlyn gasped, and Renaer and Faxhal chortled. Vharem draped an arm across Lord Wands's shoulder and whispered, "Kahlem staggered into us after leaving his favorite festhall—er, 'newest shrine to the Red Knight'—and took offense that we happened to be using the midden abutting its wall after a night at Raphen's tavern on Imar Street."

Torlyn's eyes widened, and he said, "Don't tell me . . ."

Vharem nodded. "He pushed Renaer and me to one side, and *this one*"—he jerked his thumb toward Faxhal—"turns and asks, 'What beems to see the broplem, occifer?' as he finished relieving himself on the man's boots!"

"Kahlem's not a bad Watchman," Renaer said, "but his water-headed ideas on how to investigate crimes—"

Faxhal interrupted, "—led the fool to believe we're smugglers too!" He punched Renaer's shoulder and laughed. "Now get ready. I've got time for one drink before we give them the run-around." Faxhal grabbed and downed Renaer's drink in one gulp, and then belched loudly. He pulled two hooded mantles out of his bag and tossed one to Renaer. "Let's give them the old seeing-double bit, yes? I've needed a good run all day."

Renaer marveled at his friend's desire to intervene for him and said, "You know, I could actually let them take me in for a change. Clear the air and settle things with Kahlem?"

To their credit, the four men kept straight faces for nearly two full breaths before snickering. Renaer and Faxhal pulled the stylish dark blue hooded mantles over their heads and atop their black cloaks.

Vharem said, "We'll meet you at the Grinning Lion by the next bell, then?"

Lord Torlyn Wands groaned and asked, "Gods, why does it have to be that place?"

Faxhal asked, "What's the matter with it? Argupt always has a table for us. Besides"—his voice dropped to a whisper—"the food's better there than here."

Torlyn groaned, "It's become a watering hole of late for the Thongolirs, and I'd as soon avoid their ilk until the solstice balls where I've no excuses to avoid them."

Vharem said, "Sacrifices must be made, milord, in the name of friend-ship. Besides, you'd have no problem if the Lady Nhaeran would give Lord Terras an answer on his suit."

"Which, as you're all aware, is an unequivocal *no,* and you know my sister cannot tell him that until after we clear up the debts that Hurnal set up with the money-grubbing old bastard." Torlyn sighed. "My cousin's even opened up our old hunting lodge for rent by hunting parties a tenday at a time. Our family's private hunting lands have become just another asset for him to exploit."

"I'd be happy to help, milord Wands, truly," Renaer said, his face losing its smile as he locked eyes with his friend. Faxhal, for his part, adjusted Renaer's hood so the two of them looked nigh identical.

"Appreciated, but impossible, sirrah." Torlyn shook his head, avoiding Renaer's eyes. He cleared his throat, then chuckled nervously and said, "Be off with ye, nigh-noble rogues. Your sport awaits and the night is young! Vharem and I can't wait to hear about the latest ways you two've found to avoid Watch pursuit."

Renaer and Faxhal looked at each other, sketched salutes at their friends, and bolted for the door. Before they even reached it, Renaer heard Vharem shout, "Ten taols says the Watch comes up empty again tonight! Do I have any takers?"

Renaer looked back once to see Toryln raise his tankard in salute before he was lost behind the quickly massing crowd around their table, all gambling men eagerly betting on successful escape or pursuits.

Renaer and Faxhal found Darselune Street relatively empty. The slate-roofed wood-and-stone buildings across the way had been cleaned by the past night's sleet and ice thawing that day and rinsing soot off the buildings. Ice and frost returned with sunset, and moonlight twinkled on slate and slats alike. The two men passed a carriage tied up in front of the Slaked Sylph, and Faxhal shrugged toward it, his eyebrows rising in question.

Renaer shook his head. "Why actually do something illegal to add merit to their pursuit of me in Lords' Court?"

They jogged across Gulzindar Street, their boots scraping the frost-rimed cobbles on the road. They saw a Watch patrol heading west toward the Field of Triumph, their backs to them.

Faxhal belched loudly, and then bellowed, "Have you no manners, Renaer?" The man grinned and then sprinted south toward the Spires of the Morning, leaving Renaer a few steps behind.

The watchmen spun on their heels and the armar shouted, "There he is! Renaer Neverember, hold! We have a—! After them!"

The broader avenues like Julthoon Street, Calamastyr Lane, and Swords Street glowed brightly in the moonlight due to the diligence of the Dungsweepers' Guild and a lighter shade of cobblestones used on the major roadways all across Waterdeep. As the two men dashed across a carriage's path, they heard their pursuers curses at their path being blocked by that same vehicle soon after.

Renaer kept quiet as the opulent and well-tended buildings of Sea Ward receded. Faxhal was already past the temple to Amaunator, its pink marble courtyard walls glistening with frost and icicles. Looming ahead were the more utilitarian domiciles and row buildings of Castle Ward, though there were exceptions to the common buildings, like the gargoyle-infested Charistor looming three stories tall over the intersection with Swords Street, or the squat white stone of Jhurlan's Jewels with its quaint Old Cormyrean wall merlons atop its roof at Tchozal's Race.

"We'd better split up," Renaer said to Faxhal.

"Last one to Argupt's buys for the night," Faxhal replied, whispering so as not to lead their pursuers to their final destination. "I'll head east up the Walk—you lead some south!"

Both men turned south down Swords Street at full speed, laughing as their pursuers howled their plans aloud. "Head over to the Street of Silks and head them off at Keltarn!"

The two friends pointed ahead and firmed up their plan. Faxhal shouldered an uneven stack of crates stacked alongside the mouth of Elvarren's Lane as he passed. The moldering boxes teetered and fell behind him into the paths of the Watch and a few passersby.

The two saluted each other, and Faxhal whirled off to the east, turning left and racing up Zelphar's Walk. Renaer expected him to run up to Armin's Cut and swing back up to Tchozal's Race to lead a few of the Watch in circles.

Renaer slowed his pace slightly, nearly allowing two young members of the Watch to come within ten paces of him. Reaching into his pocket, he readied his weapons as his ominous target loomed out of the darkness.

Blackstaff Tower seemed to make the night around it darker. No torches lit its windows, nor did any brighten the dark steel and stone of the curtain wall around its courtyard. Renaer raced past the gate, admiring the metal-worked roses and staves that entwined the metal bars. Looking over his right shoulder to make sure they were within range, Renaer tossed a handful of stones at the gates to Blackstaff Tower and immediately doubled his speed, leaving his chasers behind. Suddenly, the night lit up, a sea green glow emanating from the metal gates into the surrounding street. The woman and man slowed, appearing to run but moving only at a snail's pace. Renaer smiled but shook his fascination away and kept running. "I wasn't sure that was going to work. First time I've ever used Blackstaff Tower's spell defenses against anyone."

Renaer dashed left, heading east up Tharleon Street. The Flagon Dragon Inn's three stories dominated that corner, the stone dragons at the base of the walls all gouting fire. He waved at the two dragon-helmed guards at the door as he ran past, and both returned the wave. He'd have to drag Torlyn back here again soon—he liked this place, even if it did cater more to those of less-than-noble class. Renaer jogged into the Silkanth's Cut, ducking behind Rarknal's Whitesmiths and running up the outer stairs leading to the rooftop garden on the adjoining building.

Renaer never slowed his pace and continued to run up to and past the roof's edge, launching himself toward the clothesline that angled over the eastern arc of the cut. He grabbed it and used his momentum to swing himself further up and onto the parapet of a row house. Keeping up his pace, he ran across that roof as well, leaping over the low wall that marked where that building abutted the next. As he ran east across that roof, he headed toward the stone arches that arced over Hoy's Skip below. Since the Spellplague, many of the row buildings had arches to support the buildings.

Renaer deftly ran over the arch as if it were a dry street instead of the ice-rimed bridge it was. He continued south, vaulting over or climbing above the abutment walls among the buildings lining the Street of Silks. When he stopped, dropping into the shadows next to an overlarge chimney, he could look across the street and beyond to see into the well-lit windows of the Smiling Siren festhall.

Renaer waited. The young Lord Neverember heard the Watch stumble past him on the street below, their armar chewing out the new recruits and barking orders. Looking down, Renaer knew he'd run many a scamper with this armar, the bald patch on his head exposing a familiar birthmark.

The balding armar's voice traveled in the crisp winter air. "No, he's not a Shar-worshipper to draw shadows around him! You're just incompetent! Now look down to Keltarn and see if he's heading east. He likes to take Cymbril's Walk, not the Prowl, because the taverns along there like him. We'll head up to Bazaar and investigate parts east. If we don't find him by the Street of Bells, we regroup at the Singing Sword and . . ." The words grew muffled as they moved out of Renaer's hearing range.

Renaer smiled, then something tapped him on the shoulder and he felt his stomach lurch. He turned and found himself facing the tabard of a barrel-chested Watch valabrar standing less than an arm's reach from him, a watchman's rod in hand. In Selûne's pale light, Renaer stood, and said, "At least it was you and not Ralnarth. Well, Officer Varbrent? Am I a prisoner?"

The grizzled older man rubbed his salt-and-peppered beard with the end of the rod, smiling slightly at Renaer. "Nah, but you're getting almost predictable, lad. You've come here twice before. You don't scout too well ahead of yourself or you'd have noticed me waiting here for you. Slow night?"

"Slow enough. I didn't find any other things to lead them toward."

"Like those smugglers the other night? Ralnarth caught a good reward there, he did."

"And we both know he doesn't deserve the promotion, Morrath. He's a bully with coin and a noble name behind him, that's all!"

"Aye, lad, but he's connected in the right places, so he moves up the ladder. Besides, for his faults, he serves a purpose."

Renaer smirked at the Watch captain. "Someone for you to laugh about back at barracks?"

Morrath snorted and said, "No. He's vain, so his uncle's money gets him and his Watchmen better equipment, but ultimately that's only good for the city. Don't worry—we both know why he's got his recruits chasin' you. That'll die down in another day or so, assuming you and your friends stay out of his nose. Kahlem won't bring things to the notice of your father. Not while I'm about."

"Thanks, Morrath," Renaer said, clapping the watchman on the shoulder.

"Boy, your rat-scampers are handy for training the young 'uns or punishing those who've o'erstepped their places. I just wish you or your friends would join the Watch to train them directly. You'd be a farsight better officer than Ralnarth."

Renaer winked and said, "You can't afford me, Morrath."

"Well," Morrath said, "can't blame a man for trying. Just keep yourself from trouble, boy."

Renaer and Morrath both clambered down a stone rose trellis from their rooftop perch. Renaer dropped the last few feet, landing in a crouch onto Swords Street again.

"Do you want to share a carriage?" Renaer asked, but when he turned in Morrath's direction, the man had disappeared. "Well met, Morrath. Have to learn that one some time. "

Renaer stepped out of the shadows at the mouth of Scarlet's Well and flagged down a carriage. The single horse and its young driver both started from his sudden appearance. He didn't blame them, for the area was known to be haunted, albeit by a harmless woman's spirit still weeping bloody tears for her lost love. The boy got over his fear quickly when he saw the quartet of taols Renaer held up. The boy reached eagerly, but Renaer closed his hand around all but one of the square coins. "The rest are yours if you get me quietly to the Grinning Lion in less than two songs."

The boy nodded enthusiastically as Renaer slipped inside the carriage. Renaer found no comfort inside, as the matted cushions provided little relief from the hard bench or lurching ride.

Renaer enjoyed the chases with the Watch, but he bristled when the law enforcers—including his father the Open Lord—flaunted power over him and others. Dagult and Kahlem Ralnarth's abuses of authority showed the people that the Watch did not work always for the greater good of the city—just the whims of officers or the Lords. Worst of all, he didn't know what his father wanted, other than obedience and for Renaer to only act within the limited confines of Dagult's imagination. Renaer heard his father's words often enough—"You're a dupe, a wastrel, and you're throwing money away at every church across the city! I won't have my son waste his life!"

Renaer whispered, almost in prayer, "I want more for my father and for Waterdeep. This used to be a city where dreams came true and gods walked the cobbles. Now, the grime of commerce and greed covers everything, including the once-shining helms of the Lords. The Crown of the North still rules all commerce and politics, but it can't remotely claim to be the City of Splendors. This city needs heroes to bring back its life and luster. But gods know if I have it in me to be one."

Many hours later, Renaer crept quietly up the stairs to his rooms, a task not terribly difficult given the stone steps and carpets. He expected to be alone, but lights still blazed beneath the door to his father's study.

"The man is the Open Lord," Renaer muttered. "Why in the gods' names doesn't he use his offices at the palace?"

Despite his aggravation at the delay in sleep, Renaer smiled. He discovered years ago that he learned more when folk didn't know there were others within earshot. He slipped silently into his room, closed the door, and stripped for bed. Folding his clothes neatly on a side dresser, he shivered from the cold despite the small fire in the fireplace near his bed. Renaer burrowed beneath the furs and quilts, all the while keeping an ear cocked to the voices carried through the chimney shared with the next room's fireplace.

"We've not learned nearly enough, Dagult." Renaer didn't know this thin reedy voice, nor did he like what the man had to say. "She is as stubborn as her master was."

"We know the Blackstaffs have always had access to unknown magic," another unrecognized voice said. "I got her talking about the masked Lords of the past, but she would not say how they controlled them."

The thin-voiced one said, "The secret of long years, of course, is the most profitable of secrets we could glean from her. I always suspected they bargained with elves or dwarves for those secrets."

"Three tendays! That's what you told me! And it's been seven!" Dagult slammed his hand down on a table. Renaer knew his father's temper well, and Dagult's roar meant he was frustrated but not yet angry. That's when he'd get very quiet. "You claimed I would have the Overlord's Helm to help me uncover my fellow Lords' secrets. *That* is what you claimed would make this gambit worth it! Well?"

The second voice joined in again. "We can't get her to focus. She's been mad ever since—"

"Focus?" Dagult snapped. "What do you think you have Granek for?"

The thin-voiced man coughed and said, "Yes, well, his methods are—"

"Only slightly more successful than your magic, apparently," Dagult said. "Now, when are you going to deliver what you promised? You've already received far more reward than what you've delivered in return, but I'm still prepared to bring you into the fold, should you gain results before the solstice."

Just who was Dagult conspiring with here? Renaer wondered. He *never* put more on the table unless he could hang someone with the other end of the deal. And to deal with wizards . . .

"We shall celebrate together before another tenday passes, milord Neverember," the reedy voice replied. "The three of us shall free the city from the Blackstaff's interference for the first time in two centuries—or at least ensure the Blackstaff is aligned in full with the Open Lord's policies."

Renaer heard the door open, and the men wandered out of his earshot. He saw three shadows pass his doorway, and one returned back to Dagult's office. Renaer heard the thud and hiss of another log being tossed on Dagult's fire grate. The bluster and volume had dropped away, and the cold quiet tone chilled Renaer despite the fire and the furs. "Just make damned sure that this never soils my hearth, wizards, or you'll find out I've more power than even your wizards' guild can muster."

Dawn nearly reached his windows before Renaer fell into a fitful sleep.

CHAPTER TWO

It's a trip neither pretty nor pleasant, but delve the sewers if you truly want to learn what goes on in Waterdeep.

Orlar Sarluk, *Down the Drain:*
A Life in the Guild of Cellarers and Plumbers,
the Year of the Worm (1356 DR)

9 NIGHTAL, YEAR OF THE AGELESS ONE (1479 DR)

LARAELRA HARSARD KNEW SHE NEEDED HELP AND NEEDED IT QUICKLY. She looked over the assembled crowds milling around Heroes' Garden. Over the past few decades, each ward seemed to adopt its own unofficial gathering places for swords for hire, where Caravan Court, the White Bull, and Virgin's Square once sufficed for mercenary hiring. The snow-covered hillocks of the garden were already soiled from foot traffic, even though it was barely past sunup. Laraelra wove her way around the statues of heroes of Waterdeep's past. Scanning the crowds, she noticed someone had knocked the right foot off of Lhestyn's statue. Above a skinny man in black leathers, the outstretched stone arms of Lords Oth Ranerl, Tanar Hunabar, and Cyrin Kormallis held only broken blades or sword pommels. Laraelra moved deeper into the Heroes' Garden, searching for strong-backed hirelings but only finding jokesters had stolen the head of Rarkul Ulmaster for the fifth time that year.

If more people respected what it takes to work stone, Laraelra thought, they'd not be so quick to ruin it.

Laraelra had dressed for the weather and the task ahead of her. Her heavy woolen cloak covered her oiled leather tunic, pants, and her seal-skin boots—necessities for mucking about the sewers. The black color of her clothes made her seem even paler in the morning cold. Despite her thick garments, Laraelra hugged herself to stay warm. As she rounded the back-to-back statues of Mirt the Merciless and Durnan the Wanderer, she patted their knees and thought, Milords, help me find men of your mettle before it's too late. Then she spotted the largest group of sellswords in the Garden—or more properly, they spotted her.

"Right here, Milady Harsard!" A stylish young bravo rushed ahead of the pack, his spotless purple cloak flaring behind him. He swept off his large feathered hat and bowed before her.

Behind him thundered a muscled tree stump of a young braggart, his first beard coming in thin patches and barely covering his pimples. "Ignore that fool. I'm your man, Laraelra!" To prove his point, he kicked the bowing man over on his way to intercept Laraelra.

"Hardly," she replied, striding past with a twitch of one arched eyebrow. Laraelra pulled her cloak closer to ward off the breeze and the light snow on it. Scanning the crowd, she looked for men at least her height, then winnowed down candidates by how strong or capable they seemed.

Finally, she approached one man leaning against the statue of some centaur hero. The contented young man was more interested in his roll of sausage and onion than in catching her eye. Blond hair avalanched across his shoulders and brow. Until she got close to him, Laraelra did not see the few days' growth of pale blond beard on his face. When she stopped in front of him, the man was in mid-bite, though he smiled close-mouthed at her around the steaming food.

"You'll do," Laraelra said, "assuming you can focus on a task as much as your meal."

She smiled as the man hurriedly chewed, swallowed, and then choked and coughed in surprise. He stood two hands taller than Laraelra, his shoulders twice hers, and his arms were as large as her legs. Strapped to his back was a greataxe, much-abused but serviceable, like the dagger pommels she saw in his boots. Despite the cold, his cloak was open, exposing well-worn leather armor over a broad chest.

She pressed three silver pieces into his hand and said, "You'll get that much every bell you have to accompany me today, if that's acceptable to you."

The man nodded and coughed a few more times while he tucked the coins into his boot.

Laraelra motioned for him to follow, then turned her back and headed for the copse of trees at the southern end of the Heroes' Garden. "You'll want to finish that before we enter the sewers, I wager."

She half-expected him to stop walking once she mentioned the sewers, but the young man gamely followed her without hesitation.

Laraelra extracted a ring of keys from her belt pouch as she approached the stone hut that covered a sewer shaft among the trees. After she unlocked the access shaft and cracked the door, she turned to her companion. "In case you didn't know, I am Laraelra Harsard. And you are . . . ?"

A broad, beaming smile spread over the man's massive jaw. "Meloon Wardragon, at your service, mistress. What'll need doing this morning?"

Laraelra grabbed a torch off the wall inside the access hut, and lit it as she talked. "I am investigating a problem for the Cellarers and Plumbers' Guild down in the sewers. I simply need you in case anything or anyone tries anything untoward." She raised her eyebrows as she looked Meloon up and down. "You'll be a snug fit in some of the tunnels, so you might want to unbelt that axe of yours ahead of time. Never hurts to be prepared, after all."

Meloon nodded and pulled his axe free while Laraelra descended the rung ladder in the floor shaft.

"Just curious, mistress, but why choose me when all those other swords wanted your attention?" Meloon asked. He wrinkled his nose a bit at the overwhelming smell wafting up the shaft, but sighed and took a few deep breaths to acclimate himself to the odor.

The shaft and tunnel beneath Laraelra added a hollow echo to her words. "Most of those bravos up there dressed to impress and would balk at a morning spent in the sewers. Those who weren't dandies were trying to impress me and get in good with my father. I'd rather have someone who's more attentive to the job at hand. Besides, your boots were already covered with dung, so you're obviously someone who worries more about the work than appearance." Laraelra stepped off the rung ladder to the side of the tunnel before she looked up to see Meloon clambering down. "At least it's warmer down here than it is out on the streets. Wetter, but warmer."

Meloon said, "My father used to say, 'Never trust a man what's not got a little stuff on his boots. If a man's worried about where he's stepping, he's not working hard enough.' Glad to see that wisdom's alive in Waterdeep."

Meloon stepped onto the side ledge that lined the central sluice, and his left boot slipped in slime and slid sideways into the muck. Meloon sighed, looked up at Laraelra, and shrugged, a sheepish grin on his face. Laraelra wrinkled her nose as she smiled at him, then she turned and moved a bit up the path to allow him to shake the offal from his boot.

The pair stood at an intersection of three tunnels, all equally foul in appearance and stench. Walled all around in stone, the passages were twice as far across as Meloon's broad arm span, though the tunnel behind them leading southeast was smaller than the others. Laraelra spotted light flickering at an oval tunnel entrance outside of their torchlight long before she heard the voice.

"If ye and yer new lad're done exchangin' pleasantries, we've need of a strong back, lass!" A gravely voice echoed up the tunnel.

Laraelra darted forward with her torch."Harug, is Dorn still all right?" she called out.

"No, he's far from that, lass," Harug replied. "He's trapped under rubble in a puddle of rising filth."

Laraelra and Meloon moved to the left side of the passage, as the ledge continued only on that side. They turned into the lit entrance of the smaller tunnel, the close confines of which concentrated the stench. The light of their torch merged with that of two others, and they could see the situation.

Part of the side wall had collapsed inward, though the ceiling arch overhead remained intact due to support pillars on both sides of the collapse. Sewage flowed out of the gap in the wall, cascading atop the pile of loosened stones and dirt. A makeshift shield of rocks kept most of it from splashing onto the two dwarves. The mobile one worked to move rocks while the other laid still, his legs trapped beneath the fall.

"About time ye made it back, lass," Harug snapped. "It's getting deeper around me nephew there, and I can't stop the flow long enough to redirect it."

The old dwarf seemed exhausted, his shoulders sagging, but he kept moving, barely facing them before he returned to repairing the crude screen that kept the worst of the sewage off his fallen companion. He kept darting glances up at the dark recess that had opened in the wall above him.

Laraelra's eyebrows arched in surprise and anger, and she felt a flare of heat flush across her face. "Why aren't Parkleth and Narlam here helping you clear rubble?"

Harug turned and shot her a knowing look.

"Those tluiners just left you here?" she said. "Oh, when I get my hands on those parharding wastes of air!"

"How 'bout me first, Elra?" The trapped dwarf opened his eyes briefly and chuckled. "The cowardly bigots can wait."

Her temper cooled, and she dashed toward her old friends. "To be sure, Dorn."

Laraelra knelt by her friend, brushing some mud away from his eyes. She hoped her face didn't betray how concerned she was about the gash on his forehead or the muck rising around him. To hide her worry, she talked over her shoulder at the other men. "Meloon Wardragon, meet Harug Shieldsunder, the most cantankerous dwarf in the city and one of our guild's best tunnel workers. The muddier one here is Dorn Strongcroft, his vastly more pleasant nephew. How can we help?"

"Move yer skinny self out of our way and get the lad to brace his back against that pile," Harug said. "If he can lift that main pair o' rocks for a trice, we should be able to pull Dorn free without the whole thing crushing all of us. Can ye do that, lad?"

"Aye," Meloon said, as he leaned his axe against the wall and ledge. He stepped over and straddled the fallen dwarf, making sure his footing was secure. He squatted and reached behind his back to grab the two largest rocks. He nodded at Laraelra and Harug, who grabbed the groaning Dorn by the arms. The three of them nodded in unison, and on the third nod, Meloon grimaced and lifted, using his legs and arms to pull the weight of the pile off of the dwarf. Rocks and sluice water, now free of the temporary dam, engulfed the tall man, and he gasped at both the stench and the cold water as it soaked him from head to foot.

Laraelra and Harug yanked Dorn free of the rubble, the wet muck making a sucking noise as he slid free. The dwarf himself only made a perfunctory grunt, then his head lolled back as he passed out. Laraelra and Harug pulled Dorn more than three body lengths away from the collapse and up onto the ledge before they stopped.

Sighing in relief, Laraelra called back, "Meloon, you can let go now," and heard him groan as he lowered his burden. The rocks and dirt rumbled slightly as they settled into the space where Dorn once lay. More rocks tumbled from the broken wall, widening the dark gap.

Laraelra focused on Dorn, whose crushed, mud-encrusted legs were twisted unnaturally. She shuddered, remembering the far-lesser pain of a twisted ankle, and she thanked Tymora that Dorn had fallen unconscious from the pain. She needed to keep his wounds clean and determine if any bones broke through his skin. She closed her eyes, focused on the image of a sunbeam becoming a rainbow, and summoned her power. She opened her eyes and spread her fingers in a fan over his legs. The mud shimmered and separated, the water flowing away and the dirt and offal falling off of Dorn's legs in chunks. After a breath or two, she relaxed, not seeing any blood staining his now-dry clothes.

Within the piles around Dorn's legs, Harug spotted the glint of one gold and one silver ring, and he snatched those up. "Delvarin's daubles," he grunted at the sorceress, pocketing the jewelry.

She replied, "You're better off using that digger's treasure to pay a cleric to heal him, Harug, or he'll never walk again. Now why did you send a runner to the guildhouse claiming you needed protection down here instead of a pump crew and an engineer?"

"Fixits always come later, lass. I figured you'd have to bring somebody big enough to help do that more quickly." Harug thumbed toward Meloon, who was busy coughing and wiping the worst of the muck off of his face, arms, and torso. "Oh, and to deal with those, too."

Harug picked up a rock and threw it past Meloon's shoulder to strike a lettuce green mottled lizard in the snout as it appeared atop the pile of rubble. The mastiff-sized lizard's response was a hiss and snap of its jaws, and Meloon punched it in the nose, forcing it back into the darkness. Meloon peered into the wall cavity and said, "There's a lot of noise and movement back here, folks. I think it's a lot more of these things."

Laraelra stood, squaring her shoulders and facing the old dwarf. "Harug," she said, "strap Dorn to a board and get him to safety. We'll take care of those things. When you've heard it's clear, I want you down here to rebuild that wall. Father may favor Rodalun for the engineering jobs, but I don't trust that drunken sot to do it right. Besides, I don't want any others—especially my father—knowing about this breach in the tunnels."

"Finally," Harug chuckled, "I'm glad ye respect dwarves, even if some other Cellarers don't. Thanks, Elra lass." Harug clapped a thick calloused hand over hers and looked in her eyes. Softly, he said, "We owes ye both, lass, that we does."

Laraelra felt the solemnity of the dwarf's promise, and she knew her longtime friend Harug now pledged his life to hers.

Harug's eyes snapped toward Meloon. "Watch them sewyrms, lad. Them lizards're stubborn, but their bite's only half as bad as their tail lash."

Meloon smiled and said, "Thanks!" He stepped over to retrieve his axe, keeping himself between the lizard and Laraelra. In that moment, two sewyrms hopped atop the rubble pile and a third splashed into the sewer stream behind the rocks. Laraelra had to reassess her initial impression of Meloon. She watched his eyes and ears catch everything moving around him and plan his attack accordingly. Sweeping the greataxe as he spun back around, Meloon beheaded one lizard as it leaped at him. The second lashed its scaled tail over its body like a scorpion, slapping the warrior's arm and drawing blood. Meloon grunted and lopped off the lizard's tail on the return swing of his axe. That creature screeched in pain and leaped back into the darkness, out of reach.

Laraelra watched Meloon's axe slide in his grasp from all the water and filth covering him. She stepped closer and cast her spell again. Water and offal slid off of Meloon, his clothes, and axe.

He shook his head and said, "Who did that? I'm grateful, but . . ."

While many still feared magic since the Spellplague, Laraelra reveled in her small and growing sorceries. Even with her paltry few spells, she knew how to winnow down the opposition from lizards at least. Behind Meloon's massive back, Laraelra said, "If you'd move to one side, I'll do more than help dry you off. I can make this battle a lot simpler."

"A skinny little thing like you? A sword's weight could knock you over." Meloon chuckled.

"Don't forget who's *paying* you," she said, and she tried to push by him, but Meloon swept her back with his left arm.

"Unless you've a fireball or two in your sleeves, you'd best leave the fight to me. *That's* what you're paying me for." Meloon swung his axe up and cleanly decapitated another lizard.

The lizards hissed loudly. Three more leaped atop the pile as the survivor jumped down into the sewer stream alongside. The tunnel filled with splashing and hissing sounds loud enough to drown out the near-constant dripping.

"Meloon!" Laraelra said. "We can't pick them off one by one. Pick me up!"

"Hardly time for that, though I'll be happy to oblige later, milady." Meloon smirked as he shoved the greataxe into the rubble pile, reducing it in height but also dislodging and knocking all three sewyrms back behind it.

"Hold me up so I can see into the cavity, fool!" She punched Meloon in the side in frustration. "I'll disable most of them with a spell, instead of us getting overwhelmed by them. Then we can *both* take care of the stragglers, yes?"

"Oh. Why didn't you say so?" Meloon swung his axe one more time to ward off the sewyrms clambering up the pile, then reached around with his left arm, grabbed her around the waist, and held her high up on his torso. "That high enough, milady Harsard?"

"Fine." She muttered a few arcane syllables, breathing deep and thinking of a dragon's head, and a radiant cone of color flashed from her outstretched hands. The brief illumination showed her a deep cavity that used to be a cellar or tunnel, its entirety choked with the green sewyrms. All of them hissed in pain, though most fell unconscious, stunned by the clashing spray of color.

She leaned back against Meloon's shoulder and chest and said, "The few that are still moving are blind and more easily dispatched now. Promise to never underestimate me again and you can call me Elra."

"Done, Elra," the blond man said as he set her down at the edge of the cavity. "You didn't mention you were a wizard."

"I'm not," she said. "I don't tell many people about my hidden talents, given how most feel about magic since the Spellplague. And I'm a sorcerer, not a wizard."

"Doesn't matter to me—for friends or a fight," Meloon said. "We're still striding. That's what matters."

Laraelra smiled, but that vanished when a scream echoed toward them. Before Laraelra could give him an order, Meloon shouldered his way through the loose rubble pile, widening the opening. The two of them clambered up and over into the cavity, haunted by the sounds of their breathing, the hiss of a few sewyrms, and the echoing screams. Laraelra grabbed one of the torches and brought it to light their way.

Meloon's first steps sank ankle-deep into mud. What lizards they found were soon beheaded and shoved out of the way.

"What is this?" Meloon whispered. "Where are we?"

Laraelra said, "There are a lot of hidden cellars, tunnels, and old foundations beneath the northern wards, some of which have been mapped, others not so much. Many places here are decades older than the city around them. As long as they never interfered with the sewers, the Lords and the Cellarers and Plumbers' Guild turned a blind eye to them all. The money that buys these places also buys secrets."

"I can't tell where the screams are coming from," he said, his knuckles white around his axe haft.

"Just up ahead and to the right," Laraelra replied, pointing ahead to an obvious intersection of tunnels. "After a few trips down here, you learn to ignore the echoes and focus on the sources of sounds. Now let's go quietly."

Meloon swept a protective arm to keep her back as he moved ahead. Laraelra bumped into him when he stopped. They stood on the edge of a drop well beyond their torchlight, blackness yawning before them. The pavement fell away here, the walls looking slightly melted, rippling from brickwork to smooth flowstone. Laraelra could see a tunnel entrance outlined indirectly by flickering torchlight far below her and to her right. A woman's ragged gasps and whimpers of pain grew to another anguished scream. The screams echoed up from the depths, along with the murmur of a man's voice.

"Wizards!" The man's spit of disgust and phlegm resounded through the darkness. "You all think you're better than us, but they can't get secrets out of you with magic, so they call on Granek. Wizardry or no, without fingers, you'll be naught but a hard-coin girl after we're done, if you don't yield your secrets."

Laraelra and Meloon paused high above, sharing a look of horror and revulsion as they listened.

"Tell Granek what he wants to know, and we'll stop. For now. Resist, and we'll do worse to your hip than we're doing to your knee."

The woman's ragged sobs and panicked breathing were audible even where Meloon and Laraelra stood far above them. Laraelra hugged herself, her eyes tearing up at hearing the utter hatred in the man's rough voice. She knew people could be cruel, but she'd never heard it so plain. Fear, anger, and her breakfast all warred in the pit of her stomach and she gulped to hold it down.

Meloon paced and smashed the butt of his axe against the wall, loosening stone fragments to clatter down into the blackness. In the firelight, Laraelra could see the anger in his clenched jaw and knew his imaginary target was the torturer down below in the gloom.

"Well?" the man asked, but there was only a long pause. A hollow laugh, a moist crunch, and a deafening scream followed.

Laraelra and Meloon both jumped in shock. Meloon's face shifted to stern resolve. "Can't we help her?"

She nodded, and whispered, "Let's see if there's a way down."

Laraelra grabbed a stone from the floor, cupped it in her left hand, and whispered at it. In a whirl of sparkles, the stone glowed with a steady blue light. She tossed the stone down into the abyss, and it dropped more than five people's heights before it rattled to a stop. The pale azure light revealed a shattered and nebulous system of tunnels, many of which had melted or collapsed together on at least two levels. Her stone's light merged with the outer edges of their torchlight, showing them at least a drop of at least thirty feet.

"No way we can get down there without ropes and hooks." Meloon groaned.

"No," Laraelra said, "but that doesn't mean we can't guess who's doing this."

Laraelra handed her torch to Meloon and pulled a scroll tube out of her belt pouch. She opened the tube and pulled out the parchments within it, flipping through them until she found what she sought. She explained, "My father keeps detailed maps of every sewer connection and tunnel he knows of down here, and he notes who owns the properties above them as well. I've made copies for whenever I need to come down here."

She squinted at the map and motioned for Meloon to bring the light closer.

"If I'm reading this right, we're beneath Kulzar's Alley and Rook's Alley," she muttered, deep in thought. "There's a block of three conjoined buildings up there."

"So who do we go fight?" Meloon asked.

Laraelra stared at the map, then folded it back up sharply. "No one. We can't do anything."

"Who owns this block?" Meloon asked. "We can't let them get away with this!"

"We have to," Laraelra said. "The block is owned by the Neverembers."

"The Open Lord?"

"I doubt it. Lord Dagult wouldn't do this. Even if he would, he's got far more secure locations in Castle Waterdeep or beneath the palace." Laraelra thought aloud, "We could go to the Watch, but who will they believe? The Open Lord or the daughter of a paranoid guildmaster and her hired sellsword?"

"I don't care," Meloon said. "I need to help that woman. Nobody deserves that—servant, coin-girl, or peasant. And if we have to go the palace and confront the Open Lord, well . . ."

"No," Laraelra said. "Lord Dagult's too busy with the city. His son Renaer manages all his properties, allegedly. Let's go pay a visit to and get some answers from Lord Neverember the Younger. Unless you'd like to stay down here a while longer?"

"No," Meloon said coldly. "My axe and I want words with Renaer Neverember."

CHAPTER THREE

Whether a lord knows in his castle what hap or no, his sovereignty makes demands of him for it nonetheless, and any who wouldst gainsay that deserves neither loyalty nor obeisance.

Myrintar Hasantar, *Things a Knight Should Know*,
Year of the Mace (1307 DR)

9 NIGHTAL, YEAR OF THE AGELESS ONE (1479 DR)

"MILORD?"

"Yes, Madrak?"

"Apologies at interrupting your breakfast, but you have unexpected callers."

Renaer looked up from his trencher of fried eggs and potatoes and stared at the white-haired halfling whose face barely cleared the table top. Renaer swallowed and said, "Anyone who knows me would not call on me before midmorn. Who is it?"

Madrak cleared his throat and said, "The Lady Laraelra Harsard, daughter of Guildmaster Malaerigo Harsard of the Cellarers and Plumbers' Guild, and one Meloon Wardragon, sellsword." Madrak's tone left Renaer little question as to his opinion of them.

"I've met Laraelra before at the Wands manse, but never more than to say hello," Renaer thought aloud, "but why she would need a sellsword to come here?"

The halfling harrumphed and said, "They claim to have questions for you about your properties on Kulzar's Alley. They appear to have come directly from the sewers to your door. I took the liberty of receiving them around back at the stables."

Renaer smiled. "Thank you for that."

"No thanks needed, young lord. After all, you'd not be the one to clean up the foyer after such, would you?" Madrak said, and then asked, "Shall I tell them to call another time?"

"No," Renaer said, and he got up from the table. "Odd that the guild-master's daughter herself brings me news of some problem with the cellars or somesuch. It's the sort of thing normally channeled through low-level guild members and servants." Renaer pulled his napkin out of his shirt front and wiped his mouth, then looked down at the butler at his side. "Could you have Bramal bring me the deeds and keys to those properties? I don't know who's renting them at present, if anyone. That way, we'll be able to deal with any problems directly."

"Very good," Madrak replied. "I took the liberty of asking my son to do just that before I came in here. He'll join you around the stables. Now, don't let these strangers take advantage of you. I've heard tell that the cellarers can back the sewers up into one's vaults simply to shake coins loose from an unsuspecting young lord such as yourself."

Renaer chuckled and patted Madrak on his shoulder. "I appreciate the warning, old hin, but I didn't just fall off a dung-sweeper's cart. Let's see what they have to say before we accuse them of trying to separate me from my gold, hmm?"

Madrak snorted and said, "Lad, you just learned to walk a short tenday ago in my eyes. I'm looking out for you as I promised your good mother when she placed your swaddled self in my arms. You've a good ear for sniffing out false-hoods, but your head for business isn't nearly as keen as your love of books."

"And *that* is why Bramal conducts the bulk of the family business as my proxy." Renaer knew that Madrak's son and his children were vastly more capable than he would ever be at keeping track of his holdings, collecting rents, and the like. "I trust you and them, Madrak, but today at least I wish to have a hand in my business."

"Does our hearts good to hear that," Madrak said. "It's high time—"

"The Brandarth holdings were seen to by me, not my father?" Renaer said, and the old halfling flushed.

"I'd never say that, young master," Madrak replied, and he and Renaer said in unison, "for it's not my place nor my concern."

Renaer knelt at his butler's side and rested both hands on his shoulders. "Madrak, you and your family have been at my side since I was born. I know that Dagult would have put you out, save for my insistence and the condi-tions of Mother's will. Never fear. Your family will always have a place in my house—and not just because of the hin-sized servants' passages. You never have to mince words with me, old halfling. I trust your judgment more than my own."

A wry smile appeared on the halfling's lips. "Then you'd best stop leav-ing guests awaiting your pleasure, milord Renaer. Time to start living up to all your potential and being more than a shut-in scholar or a rake-by-night racing with the Watch." Madrak shooed the young man off. He waved a dismissive hand at the cloak rack by the doors leading into the stables. "Oh, and wear that heavy cloak, milord. Auril's blessed us with a biting cold this morn."

.:⌒:.

Renaer grabbed the cloak off its peg and swung it around his shoulders as he shoved open the door. The smell of hay and horse manure wafted around him as he closed the door behind him. He waved to Pelar, the groom, who was brushing down Ash, Renaer's favorite stallion. While all the servants answered to Madrak, not all were halflings related to him. By necessity, the grooms were humans capable of handling the larger animals.

Renaer spotted two strangers standing a few paces to his left by the servants' entrance off of Senarl's Cut. He turned and walked briskly toward the scrawny woman and broad-shouldered man. She stared out at the stream of carts and people heading toward Tespergates at the southern end of Senarl's Cut. She hugged herself, but Renaer couldn't tell if it was from the cold or nervous habit. The young man seemed more interested in admiring Neverember House's carriages and horses.

"Milady Harsard? Master Wardragon?" Renaer asked when they turned to face his approach. "What seems to be the problem today?"

Laraelra spun on her heels and pointed an accusatory finger in Renaer's face. Her face switched from angry to surprised, as if she had shocked herself. "Who's living in Roarke House right now?"

Behind the three of them, the rasp of a sword being pulled from its scabbard preceded Pelar running forward to defend his young master with a shout of "Back away, woman!"

Renaer noticed the blond man with Laraelra—noticed especially his hand reaching for the axe on his back.

Renaer held up both hands and shook his head. "Calm yourself, Pelar. This lady has a lot on her mind. No threats here, right?" Renaer shot a smile at Meloon, whose grip relaxed on his axe hilt.

Laraelra sighed and stepped back. "My apologies, milord. It's been a tense morning." She hugged herself again and stared away. Pelar stopped, sheathed his blade, and slowly returned to Ash's stall.

Renaer exhaled and began again. "I'd invite you in for a warm cup, but the state of your clothes presents a problem for my staff." He smiled at Laraelra's answering blush and continued, "Now why do you ask about

Roarke House? I've got someone fetching me the deeds and details on that property as we speak. Is there a problem with the sewers beneath it?"

"Not as much as—" Meloon started, but he stopped when Laraelra elbowed him in the stomach.

"I just need to know who's living in that building, Lord Neverember," she said. She grabbed some errant black hairs that waved in front of her pale face and pulled them back inside her hood.

"Lord Neverember is my father," Renaer said. "Call me Renaer, but don't expect me to part with my business if the Cellarers and Plumbers' Guild won't tell me why they need to know it."

"This isn't guild business. It's—"

"Someone's torturing someone in the cellars beneath your property, man!" Meloon blurted.

Renaer's jaw dropped.

Pelar stepped forward again, fists up, and said, "Take that back, and apologize to the saer."

Even though Meloon was nearly a foot taller than the stable hand, he stepped back, surprised by the anger in the man's eyes.

Renaer rested a hand on the older man's shoulder and said, "Thank you again, Pelar, but I don't need to be saved from everyone with a cross word for me. Besides, I want to hear what's got these two all wound up and angry with me this morning."

Pelar's eyes never left Meloon's, but he lowered his fists and muttered, "They should show more respect to you, saer, that's all." He dropped his hands, nodded to Renaer, and then returned to brushing the horses.

The door behind them opened and a halfling with his long, dark hair tied at the nape of his neck entered the stables. He juggled a few scrolls, and keys jangled at his belt. He cleared his throat, and said, "Milord, a word. In private." Despite being less than half the size of Meloon, this halfling cowed both him and Laraelra with a stern look when they tried to follow Renaer. Once Renaer was close, he knelt in front of the halfling to block their line of sight to his face.

"What is it, Bramal?" Renaer said. "Do you have the papers on Roarke House?"

The halfling whispered, "No, milord. That's what I came to tell you. They're missing, along with two sets of keys. I didn't sell or lease out the property. The last dealings I had with that house was in renting it this past summer to some guests of Lady Nhaeran Wands. As far as any of us know, Roarke House should be vacant. There're only four people with complete access to those records and keys. You and I are two of them, and the others are our fathers."

"Very well, Bramal, thank you. Don't worry about it, but do give me the other set of the keys to the place." Renaer stood as Bramal put the ring of keys into his hand. "Was there anything suspicious about the deeds on the adjoining properties?" Renaer asked this loudly for his guests to overhear, and Bramal took the hint.

"No milord," he replied. "The Gildenfires remains, as it has for thirteen years, in need of repair and a tenant to do so. We replaced the roof year before last to keep the building intact, but your father insisted we not waste money fixing up anything a tenant might do for us. The warehouse between that festhall and Roarke House has those long-term leases with Houses Ammakyl and Gralleth. At last autumn's inspection, half the warehouse was filled with older furniture and other decorations from the last three times Lady Ammakyl decided her mansion was not quite up to the leading edge of Waterdhavian fashions. The other half, the Gralleths have filled with materials from former noble villas when they absorbed the estates and interests of the Bladesemmers and the Markarls."

"Well, Laraelra? Meloon? Feel up to walking to Roarke House?" Renaer said. "We can inspect the property, and you can tell me more about whatever is 'not guild business.' "

Laraelra had rarely been in this neighborhood, even though it bordered on the Heroes' Garden where she met Meloon earlier. The buildings she noticed lining Skulls Street were better-kept row houses with stone foundations and wooden upper floors, none of which loomed less than three stories high. Once they turned into Rook Alley, the building quality and size plummeted, most of the structures of one or two stories and in ill repair. The roof slates became rough wooden shingles with moss-encrusted gaps, the foundations simple brick rising to knee height and continuing with dark stained wood. While the outer buildings surrounding Rook Alley celebrated the richness of Sea Ward, those hidden within reflected the ill fortunes visited on the city in times past and present.

Following Renaer's lead, Laraelra and Meloon came to a stop on the stoop of an imposing three-story building. The well-kept stone front was freshly scrubbed and cleaned, unlike most other buildings to the south and east. This was one of two stone buildings in the general vicinity, the other being the Halaerim Club directly across Kulzar's Alley. Roarke House's columned frontage seemed ostentatious, compared to the slightly rundown nature of the buildings attached to it. This neighborhood had fallen on bad times in the past decades, and now Roarke House was among a well-tended few. The cleaner buildings here and there along Skulls Street did suggest gentrification might be returning to this part of Sea Ward, but it would be some time in coming.

Laraelra sniffed and said, "Very clean for a vacant place, Renaer. Hiding a rich friend from the Watch?"

Renaer glared at her. "Would I have brought the daughter of one of the loudest mouths in the city with me, if I were?"

Meloon rested hands on both their shoulders. "Hey, I'm sure there's a simple explanation for all this. Can't we be friends here?"

"No," came the simultaneous reply from both.

Renaer put the key in the lock of an ornately carved duskwood door, its surface a relief of stars and crescent moons. The door knocker, lock, and door pull were all silver crescents, as was the decorative end of Renaer's key. The lock clicked, and the door swung easily in silence. Renaer's eyebrows rose in surprise, which Laraelra followed with one arched eyebrow.

Renaer shrugged and said, "Last time I opened this door, the hinges shrieked. Someone's oiled them. Shall we?"

"You're not worried about us fouling your floors here, milord?" she asked.

"Drop the tone, Laraelra," Renaer said. "The walk here cleaned your boots."

The trio stepped into an echoing entry hall, its stone floors and high ceiling dominated by a sweeping grand staircase that hugged the walls of the room as it led upstairs. Overhead loomed a three-stories-high atrium, a glass skylight shining light down to the ground floor. Tiles covered that floor in a continuing pattern of stars, moons, and random pairs of eyes. Two doors bracketed an open archway opposite the front door and beneath the stairs. Additional doors flanked the front wall of the house. All doors were closed, and aside from their footsteps, no sound could be heard.

Meloon let out a low whistle then said, "Why the eyes and moons and stars everywhere?"

Laraelra said, "Roarke House was built by Volam Roarke, an exceedingly devout worshiper of Selûne, right?" She smiled with Renaer's answering nod, and continued. "He financed the restoration of the House of the Moon after the Spellplague collapsed it."

Renaer nodded and said, "The Roarkes had even reached the nobility about seventy-five years ago, but their family fortunes dried up over the years since. By the time they lost their noble status and other riches forty years ago, my grandfather bought their holdings in the city. Last I'd heard, the Roarke clan owned only two inns along the High Road between Leilon and Neverwinter. This place has had about half a dozen long-term tenants over the years. It's only been the past four years that it's been a summer rental. Most of the folk who rented it out never even knew about the sub-cellars."

Renaer walked to the door on the left. "This door leads to the cellars. Now, tell me more about what you saw—no, heard down below. It seems like we'll need to update the maps for the sub-cellars. Wonder if the Rook's Hold was part of what you saw down there?"

"The Rook?" Meloon asked.

"A thief of some repute more than a century ago," Renaer explained. "His hideout was in the subterranean crypts after which Skulls Street outside was named. It sounds like the tunnels and crypts may have collapsed and merged a while back. I never knew they extended beneath this house. They've always been blocked off, or so I was told."

Laraelra chuckled. "Renaer, the amount of things beneath the streets that the city chooses to ignore or not know about would stagger your imagination."

The three of them entered a small stairwell that spiraled down into darkness. Renaer grabbed a torch out of a wall sconce and lit it.

"And I thought I heard you complaining at the last Wands feast that you wanted nothing to do with your father's guild," Renaer said. He took the lead on the stairs, the smoke from his torch rising and stinging Laraelra's eyes. "Why were you poking around beneath the streets this morning?"

Laraelra cleared her throat and lowered her voice. "Someone has to stand up to the bigots in the guild. The dwarves deserve equal pay and equal treatment, and some of my father's foremen will hardly bother with that. Parkleth, one of the worst of them, would have left a friend of mine to drown this morning as a lesson for the dwarves to stay out of sewer work. We only uncovered your house's secrets by accident."

"My—" Renaer stopped dead and glared up at Laraelra. "That's it. We're done here. That's the last insult you get at my expense, when I've been naught but accommodating."

Laraelra's face felt hot as she realized what she'd said, and she slumped her shoulders. "I'm sorry. Truly, Renaer, before the gods, I apologize. I'm tired, angry, and I spend too much time around my father, who's all too eager to blame everything on nobles or the ruling class."

Renaer resumed their descent to the cellars, and Laraelra knew she had to watch her tongue around the young Lord Neverember. His clipped tone told her he was still angry as Renaer said, "I'm neither of those things, really."

"Yes you are, whether you admit it to yourself or not," Laraelra said. "Even without noble title, you're one of the richest land-holders in this city.

When you add your father's holdings to yours, only House Nandar and a handful of others own more properties. Even if you don't acknowledge or use it, that gives you power over a lot of people, Renaer. Now, can we finish what we started here?"

"Not even my father would put up with an accusation of being party to torture," Renaer said. "The only reason I'll continue is to prove this has nothing to do with me and mine." Renaer continued down into the main cellars.

Meloon put his hand on Laraelra's shoulder and whispered, "Maybe it's not my place to say, milady, but I don't think he knows what's going on any more than we do."

"Then we're all in for an education, aren't we?" she whispered in return as both of them joined Renaer in the vast cellar. To the right of the stairwell lay cords of firewood carefully stacked from floor nearly to ceiling. Open and empty earthenware jars rested on shelves to the left, while hooks dangling from the ceiling were empty of the usual smoked meats that might hang there. Across the room was an archway leading farther into the cellar. The trio moved into the next room, where stacked furniture and chests completely filled the right-hand side of the chamber. The long left-hand wall was covered with wine racks, though only a few bottles remained on the shelves.

"Now," Renaer said, "if someone were living here right now, those shelves back there and the wine cellar would be far better stocked, wouldn't they?"

Laraelra waved her hands and said, "Fine. We believe you. Now will you show us where these secret sub-cellars are so we can prove that we weren't lying?"

Renaer approached the wine racks and counted the rows. He reached out, grasped one section of the racks, and pulled. The rack slid out easily and then turned on a hidden hinge to expose a section of the wall behind it. He stepped forward, chuckled lightly, and pressed a small stone on the wall.

Nothing happened.

"Well?" Laraelra asked.

"This should have opened!" Renaer said. "The door leading to another stairwell should be right there!"

Meloon motioned for Renaer to move. He rushed forward and slammed his shoulder into the wall. "Ow! If there's a door there, it's well-braced or locked."

"Or held by a spell," Laraelra said.

In the house above them, shouts filled the air.

"Someone's in here!"

"They've gone down into the cellars! Come with me!"

Renaer shoved the wine rack back into place, and then held Meloon from drawing his axe. He whispered at Laraelra, "Time later to talk on all this. Do you know any spells to help here?"

"Only if you're spoiling for a fight, and they'll only stop someone temporarily," she said. "Nothing that will get us out of here without notice."

"No need," Renaer said, as the three of them rushed back into the front cellar chamber. "I'll explain."

"I hope so, young lord, for you have much to answer for." The white-haired man leaned on a duskwood staff, its presence as much as the speaker's own notoriety identifying him as Samark "Blackstaff" Dhanzscul. The premier mage of Waterdeep, the Blackstaff glowered at them while the crystal atop his staff pulsed a bright purple.

"Indeed they do, friend," said the other man descending the stairs. Bald with a tightly trimmed gray mustache, the man exiting the stairs walked with confidence and strength belying his scarecrow frame. His fingers steepled in front of his face and his prominent eyebrows, the ornate rings on every digit of his hands reminded her of his full name—Khondar "Ten-Rings" Naomal, the Guildmaster of the Watchful Order of Magists and Protectors.

Khondar asked, "Shall I call the Watch or the Cere-Clothiers, Ossurists, and Grave-Diggers' Guild? Your choice, children."

CHAPTER FOUR

I watched a wolf cub challenge his pack leader this morning. The guile and experience of the old wolf won out again, despite the younger's strength and speed. Would that youth did not always rely on bluster and newfound strength . . .

Laeral of the Nine, *Thoughts on Life and Wizardry*,
Year of the Snow Winds (1335 DR)

9 NIGHTAL, YEAR OF THE AGELESS ONE (1479 DR)

KHONDAR SURVEYED THE INTRUDERS CAREFULLY. HE RECOGNIZED THE one at the forefront. Khondar maintained his neutral face, but bristled inwardly at the surprise intrusion. "Renaer Neverember, would you care to explain your presence here? Have you taken to hiding from the Watch here now?"

Renaer spread his arms wide and bowed to both him and the Blackstaff. "I apologize for our intrusion, Guildsenior Naomal. My clients asked to see Roarke House, but there seems to be some confusion as to its current status for tenants."

"I am its current tenant, as of the tenday last. I have a copy of the signed deed upstairs."

Renaer arched an eyebrow at that and said, "I handle all Brandarth and Neverember holdings within the city. And yet, you and I have never spoken aside from pleasantries at parties more than five months ago. Apparently someone on my staff failed to tell me about this transaction."

"Apparently." Khondar disliked this boy more with every breath, since he remained calm and unreadable. Khondar tamped his temper down by focusing on Renaer's companions. The woman he had seen before, but he could not place her face or gaunt form. What made him seethe was the lack of respect for him in her scowl. Beside her, the young blond bear-of-a-man twitched with nervous energy, ready to fight anyone, but he seemed held in check with her hand. Khondar tired of the pretense and asked, "Do you need to see the deed to believe me, lad?"

The Blackstaff interrupted, "My time is short. Surely explanations can wait another time?" He stamped his trademark staff upon the stone floor, its silver-shod end ringing dully. "I'm sure these young people have other matters to which they can attend."

The larger man stepped forward. "No we don't! We need to know—"

The woman stopped him by slipping into his path.

"—if there's anything we can do to make your new home more comfortable?" said Renaer. He turned on his heels, showing Khondar his back as he swept his arms at the walls. "Would you like, perhaps, a few bottles of a lovely Farlindell Red from Tethyr's Purple Hills for these racks? As an apology for our interruption?"

"The only apology we shall need, young Neverember," Khondar said, "is the keys by which you entered this house, followed by your swift exit."

"We have a few questions yet, milord," Renaer said. "My friends Ararna and Pellarm were hoping to purchase this or another house in the same general area. They want assurances that there are no problems with either neighbors or the infrastructure. They don't believe me, as I'm trying to sell them property, but perhaps you could offer a more objective opinion."

Renaer's companions flinched when he said their names aloud, and Khondar knew that Renaer had given them false identities.

"You try my patience, all of you." Khondar sighed. "Such questions will wait for another time, if at all. If you insist on remaining trespassers, the Watch shall be summoned."

"Fine!" said Pellarm. "Maybe they can find out who you're torturing and where you've hidden her!"

Khondar froze, though the Blackstaff's outrage was apparent as he howled at the warrior. "Boy, you delay two archmages in important work with foul accusations! Where is evidence to back your claim?"

"Only what we heard from the street." Pellarm shrugged. "We heard horrific screaming as we walked by—and I for one don't ignore pleas for help."

Khondar smiled mirthlessly as he watched the boy spin his poor lies. He seemed ignorant of just how close to the lion's maw he put his head. "You're obviously new to the city, Pellarm. I'll not waste our time relaying all the sordid ghosts that haunt this and other nearby neighborhoods. That is why we're all in my all-too-empty cellar with neither woman nor tortures at hand." Khondar stepped off the stairs and into the cellar, motioning back toward the stairs. "Now, while I'll happily receive new neighbors at a later date, the Blackstaff's time today is more precious even than mine. Please, *remove yourselves.*"

"Again, my apologies, milord," Renaer said, and he backed up toward the stairs, taking each of his friends by their elbows. "When would be a good time to call again?"

"*Enough!*" the Blackstaff shouted, his patience at an end. He swept his staff in an arc and his other hand wove a pattern in the air. A haze of colors shimmered into existence on the stairs next to the three young people. Renaer and Pellarm both stared fixedly at it, fascinated at its shifting color weave.

The alleged Ararna shook her head and glared at the Blackstaff. "The Watch shall hear of this!"

"Hardly," Khondar said as he finished his gestures and snapped his fingers to get the woman's attention. They locked eyes and his dominating enchantment burrowed into her mind. *You cannot communicate anything you've seen here. Follow your friends and do not come back to this house.* Khondar enjoyed this spell's usefulness in dominating people for days or whole tendays and wiping their memories of its use later. Before he let the spell lapse entirely, he'd find out what she really knew and why they were here, but now was not the time.

As the Blackstaff willed his own iridescent illusion up the stairs, the two young men followed it without hesitation. While the woman had initially struggled against the magic, she followed them as ordered.

After a few moments, the Blackstaff returned to the cellars and said, "I'm sorry if I acted out of turn. Too many questions."

"It got them out of here, and that's all that matters to me right now," Khondar replied. "If the woman hadn't resisted your spell, I'd not have had to waste one on her. Still, should we need to, I can influence her and keep watch on her activities over the next tenday or more."

"Well, not one person blinked as the pattern led them out onto the alley and headed toward Trollkill Street," the Blackstaff said. "I've put an arcane lock on the front door so we won't be disturbed easily now. I'll set up other defenses later."

"They should have been in place already," Khondar said, turning away from his son. "Let's get to work, then."

Samark flinched, looked back upstairs, and then asked, "Shouldn't we ensure they don't talk to anyone? Or at least find out what they know for certain?"

"They may actually prove useful. She cannot say anything due to my spell's enchantment. As for Renaer, his well-known habits for avoiding responsibility and his reluctance to implicate his father should keep him quiet as well. The sellsword . . . well, who's going to believe a sellsword over the Blackstaff and the Watchful Order?"

The Blackstaff's eyes shifted to gray as he spoke, "True, but they could cause problems—like they did here. There's no way they could have heard her, Father." His form wavered, then solidified into Centiv's younger leather-clad form. The pale, balding face melted into one far younger with a full head and beard of chestnut-colored hair.

"Well, they heard *something*, Centiv, and it led them here," Khondar said. "Just open the door, while I figure out what to do next."

Centiv approached the wall and opened the rack-door as Renaer had earlier. His ring flashed bright blue, and when he pushed the rock in the wall, a door recessed into the wall, exposing a well-lit spiral stair leading down.

"I have enough friends and influence to turn the public's trust against them before they can interfere," Khondar said as they descended. "They've played into our hands perfectly. After all, many saw them come here, while we enter and exit invisibly. Should anything get exposed, they're the ones caught on the hook. Dagult will most likely protect his son from the worst of it, which makes the brunt of it fall on that skinny girl and her barbarian friend. Either way, it forces all parties to cover for us, should anything leak out."

"I know I've seen that scrawny woman before, but I can't place her," Centiv said. "She's not a member of our guild, though perhaps she should be, given her resistance to my spell."

"What she should be is grateful I chose to waste that domination spell on her instead of blasting her and her meddlesome friends to ashes." Khondar punched his fist into his other palm. "Now we lose another day before I can get answers!"

Centiv said, "Then that's another day in which we find more folk to rally to our cause—freeing knowledge for the guild from the grasping hands of private mages like the Blackstaff."

"Yes, yes, of course," Ten-Rings said, as they reached the bottom of the stairwell. The chamber they entered was merely another nondescript cellar by all appearances. The elder nodded to his son, who used the staff he carried to tap three stones in succession at one corner of the ceiling. In response, a secret door slid open, the walls and floor unfolding into yet another secret stair. Screams pierced the air.

"That's the only part I hate." Centiv shuddered. "I know we're doing all this for the city's good, but do we really need to torture her to get the answers we need?"

"Unfortunately, we do, lad." Khondar sighed. "Samark and all the Black-staffs keep secrets they should share with the guilds, the Lords, and others. It's how they maintain their mystique, their stranglehold on power—they keep their secrets, even when it harms the City around them.

"We do this only because this woman, like too many, would rather main-tain the way things have always been done." Ten-Rings sneered. "She wants our fair city to stay under the control of the money-grubbing merchant classes and foreign interests. Wizard rulers would never allow Sembian shades to infiltrate the palace. We'll restore things to right, son. We will. We'll clean up this city. All we need are the keys to the tower and its magic. The sooner that outlander bitch gives them up, the sooner her pain will end."

Ten-Rings exited the stair into a tiny chamber only as wide as a staff's length. Set into the wall facing them was a small niche holding a handful of tomes and beneath it a number of vials in a wooden box. He snatched up a vial as he stormed through the open doorway to the left of the stair. A pair of doors lined the hallway on both sides, and all the noise came from the nearest room on Khondar's right.

The woman lay strapped to a rough wooden table, bound spread-eagled with each hand and foot bound to a corner of the table. Her clothes were whole, though rent to expose her limbs and her midriff. Blood dripped or dried on nearly every exposed bit of skin. A large metal clamp encircled her right knee, bending it unnaturally to one side. Obscene black bruising and bleeding around a clamp at her left hip showed that her interrogator had also shattered that bone in his ministrations. Numerous cuts along her arms, legs, and stomach had long since scabbed over. Her face held half-healed bruises days old, and her lower lip was a mass of scabs. She lay senseless, breathing heavily but irregularly, and her eyes were closed. Her short dark hair lay matted to her head with sweat and grime. Blood—both dried and otherwise—coated the table beneath her.

The man standing over her shoved a dirty rag into the pulsing wound on her left forearm as he withdrew a nail, sighing as he did so.

"Has she told you anything, Granek?" Khondar asked, and the man whirled around. Granek was short, stripped to the waist, and covered with hair, dirt, and blood. His graying hair hung loose and long, its receding hairline making it look like his hair slipped to the back of his head. The eye patch over his right eye failed to cover the two scars that crossed his forehead, temple, and upper cheek. He dropped the nail and hammer onto a side table and wiped the blood from his hands onto a rough leather apron and breeches he wore. Granek shook his head and went to a water bucket, raising the dipper to his lips.

"The lass has spirit, aye," Granek said after wiping his mouth with his forearm. "As we'd planned, she had two days to heal before we went at her again this morning. All she's given me are screams and a few insults directed at me mam. Oh, and a few for you as well, Khondar."

"Address him as Guildmaster, dog!" Centiv snapped "Show some respect!"

Granek glared at the younger man and said, "You need me, and I still need to be paid. Gold gets you my respect, as I've done more for you than you've for me. Besides, we're all out on the plank together here. Show some manners yourself, lad."

Centiv's fingers crackled with energy and he began mouthing a spell, but Ten-Rings rested a hand over his fingers and said, "Enough. You should not be so easily baited." He then turned his attention to Granek, and said, "And you should not presume to be more important than you are, hireling, or you shall find out how adept I am at doing magically what you do mechanically. Now, give her this, so we might talk." He handed the vial through the bars to Granek, who snatched it away with anger.

Granek stalked to the woman's side, muttering, "Waste of a good potion, ask me." He opened her mouth, but stopped as Ten-Rings cleared his throat.

"Maybe you should remove the clamps to allow her to heal?" said Ten-Rings. "We already know how well she screams, and don't need to hear it for this discussion."

Granek frowned and tucked the vial into a pouch. He removed the clamp from her left hip, and she groaned. Even Centiv shuddered as Granek removed the knee clamp and her leg moved like its bones were no more than gravel in a bag. Granek retrieved the vial and poured its contents into her mouth, manipulating her throat to force her to swallow. He then pulled the rag out of her forearm, which made blood flow freely again.

Within moments, the blood stopped flowing and the woman's old and new bruises faded beneath her dark skin. She shed the scab on her lip as that wound healed, and her hip and knee returned to their normal positions. Her indigo-colored eyes darted open and she snapped her head up to stare at Granek, then beyond the bars at Centiv and Ten-Rings.

"Does that feel better, Vajra?" said Granek.

"I'd thank you for healing me, but I know you don't do it for my sake. We've danced this dance before, Khondar," Vajra said. "I won't give you the knowledge you seek."

Ten-Rings sighed and said, "To think you came to this city to join my guild—"

"*Your* guild?" she laughed. "Does the Watchful Order know they're your personal servants?"

"Better that than lackeys of the Blackstaff," he said.

Centiv added, "Or whores of the same."

"Centiv"—Vajra shook her head—"so much power stunted by sycophantic adulation. Thirty years here and still no life without Father?"

Centiv's knuckles cracked as he clenched his fists.

"You wizards are all the same—all talk, no action," Granek said. He leaned onto Vajra's recently healed knee, and she inhaled sharply and grimaced. Granek cackled. "Just 'cause you're healed don't mean you're healthy. So tell us what we want to know. Tell us how to enter Blackstaff Tower safely."

She opened cobalt blue eyes and stared past Granek at Khondar. "Ye only need courage and a Blackstaff. Dare ye pick one up?"

"Tell me what the books are for," Ten-Rings said, "and we'll stop the pain. Grant us entry into the tower, and we'll end this once and for all."

Vajra laughed a deep laugh, and then opened wine purple eyes to stare at Centiv. "Why did your father bring you here from Sundabar, Centiv? Did he need a scribe? Or were you just his only child to swallow every lie?"

"Keep this up and you'll part with your life, Vajra Safahr," Ten-Rings whispered. "We saw the Blackstaff's death give you an influx of power. Who's to say that power won't transfer to one of us upon your death?"

"We've been threatened by worse than fools like you who conjure enemies whenever he's denied any desire," Vajra said, glaring at him with sea green eyes. "The enemies you've always seen—from Sundabar to Athkatla to Waterdeep—were all your own fear or your own incompetence. Now, you tell yourselves you do this for Waterdeep. You delude yourselves. You do it for yourselves alone. The power you seek you neither deserve nor understand. Your teachers weep in the afterlife for your failures."

Granek growled and struck Vajra hard in the stomach, knocking the wind out of her. As she fought to breathe, he said to Ten-Rings, "I'll get more answers out of her and tell you later. You'd best go, as all you three do is trade insults."

Khondar shook his head and punched his palm in anger. Centiv stalked out of the dungeon, through the entry chamber, and through the other door past the stairwell leading up. When Ten-Rings caught up to him at the end of the long hallway, the two of them stared at the Duskstaff, which hovered a foot off the floor in the center of the circular chamber

"It took a lot of magic to bring this here," Centiv said, "but with some illusions and Cral's ring, I can make it seem like I'm carrying it. We *could* take it to the tower and see if that truly does get us in. Beyond that, I'm sure the two of us can handle whatever the tower throws at us. It's obvious *she* doesn't deserve the powers hidden away in there."

"I've no doubt, Son," Khondar said, "but patience. She has secrets yet to be slipped, and I'd rather not face that tower without knowing we'll easily exit again. I'll not walk into a trap laid by Samark or one of his predecessors. We've wasted too much time. Go wander a bit and be sure to be seen as Samark. I have a guild meeting to attend. Do make sure the house and these cellars are properly warded this time."

CHAPTER FIVE

Were this humble scribe to note all those who fell before and behind to place such heroes upon their path, this account wouldst be lengthier still for all the blood and bone upon it.

Khel Largarn, *Heroes Legendary and Others Still*,
Year of the Quill (1397 DR)

9 NIGHTAL, YEAR OF THE AGELESS ONE (1479 DR)

SELÛNE AND HER TEARS GLEAMED IN THE CLEAR NIGHT SKY, THE LUNAR satellites illuminating the steam that rose from the mouths of those arguing in the cold night. The figures worked their way cautiously off Heroes' Walk and around to the south along Gunarla's Dash. Their boots scraped the frost-rimed cobblestones. Although they were among the few out on foot in this neighborhood, they did their best to remain in the shadows, hugging the rough wooden walls of the buildings. The moonlight glistened off the tile roofs up ahead, but Renaer couldn't spot anyone standing watch over the alleys. He waved his friends along, but their bickering continued.

"I'm just saying if you're a sorceress, why not conjure a few lights and save us the lamp oil and the smoke?" Vharem whispered.

"Magic is more precious than lamp oil, fool," Laraelra snapped. "Besides, it *also* attracts drifting glow-globes, so it would make it harder to hide. Now would you get out of my way?"

"Why do you need to be right next to Renaer?" Faxhal asked. "Sweet on him already? Fast work, Neverember."

Both Renaer and Laraelra hissed, "Shut up!" Faxhal merely grinned in response.

"Hey," Meloon said in an excited whisper, pointing to his right. "I've been in that tavern. Had my pocket picked, but recovered my loss in the fight after. Anybody else try The Mysticslake?"

"Will you all be quiet?" Renaer said. "We don't want to draw more attention than we already have."

"There's no one else out here, Ren," Vharem said.

"I want to keep it that way," he replied. "Besides, don't you always say that's when you should be more nervous? When you can't see who's watching?"

"What're you so worried about?" Faxhal asked.

Renaer threw his hands up. "We're about to break into a powerful wizard's house—even *if* his ownership of it is suspect—and you're asking me what I'm worried about?"

Renaer paused at the alley intersection. The rest halted behind him, and Faxhal bumped into Laraelra. A lamppost illuminated the north side of Roarke House, the south sides of another of his warehouses, and the slate-tiled Kendall's Gallery. From this angle, the group could see the lights ablaze in the windows of the Halaerim Club across Kulzar's Alley. The windows of Roarke House were all dark. Renaer tugged his hood low and rushed past to the door of the building on his left. Renaer shrugged and then rotated his shoulders a few times, releasing some tension along with a long exhale. He rummaged in his belt pouches for the key he needed.

"I get it," Faxhal whispered. "He's worried because of you. He doesn't know if he can count on you."

"He can count on us," Meloon snapped at Faxhal. "You're the ones late to the party, as I see things. Laraelra and Renaer spent most of the day reading up on the old passages 'neath these buildings. You and he just showed up looking for a free meal and drinking."

"Like we always do," Vharem said. "We weren't expecting a home invasion on Gunarla's Dash. Not that lack of planning makes it any less fun."

"Please, let's keep talking until the Watch finally hears us," Laraelra grumbled.

Renaer grunted as he turned the key in the long-unused and rusted lock, and he pushed the scraping door inward. He turned and nodded at Vharem and Meloon, who both lit their lanterns and brought them up as the five of them shuffled inside. Renaer barely spoke louder once inside. "Welcome to Gildenfires, friends. Watch where you step."

The long-abandoned festhall still had some furniture and décor intact, but all could see why the place had been abandoned since the reign of the previous Open Lord. Scorch marks marred the paintings and half-burned gold draperies along the walls. Massive holes yawned in numerous places in the ceiling and floor.

"What happened here?" Meloon asked.

"A battle among some wizardly patrons," Vharem said. "No one could get any charges upheld, though. These men had so many people scared or bought. Rumor has it they were high-ranked members of the Watchful Order. Because the festhall operators couldn't claim restitution, they went broke and this building's been empty for twelve years. Dagult chose not to fix the place and just had it boarded up."

"Too bad, really." Faxhal sighed. "This place had some great attractions in its day."

"How would you know?" Laraelra asked. "You would have only been twelve or thirteen when it closed."

Faxhal winked at her in response, and Renaer chuckled as he saw Laraelra blush.

"Let's keep moving," Renaer said. He led the five of them past the piles of rubble and around the holes in the floor toward the kitchen. Other than their footsteps on the creaking floorboards, the squeals of rats fleeing were the only sounds.

"So remind me again why we're not out having a fine evening entertaining our new companions?" Vharem asked.

"*I'm* having fun," Meloon said.

"How many times do we have to tell you?" Laraelra said. "Meloon and I heard someone being tortured somewhere beneath this area. We just couldn't get to her."

"So why don't we use the way you two came before?" Faxhal asked.

"We couldn't reach it before," said Laraelra. "The guild should already be at work repairing that breach. Besides, I don't want word to reach my father that I'm—"

"Fraternizing with the high and mighty oppressors of us all?" Renaer smirked, his tone rising to a rough voice with a nasal high pitch.

Laraelra's jaw dropped and she said, "By the gods, that's a pitch-perfect impression of him! I didn't think you'd met him that often."

"Once was enough, I'm afraid," Renaer said. "Your father's rants disrupted a rather pleasant party I attended at the Jhoniron Club last summer down in Castle Ward. As for the impression, my apologies. I don't always realize when I'm mimicking someone's accent."

"You should hear him do Watch Aumarr Krothyn Slakepike!" Vharem said. "His impression's so good, he can get the Watch to abandon their posts by shouting orders in his voice."

"True enough, but now there's enough of us to get caught," Faxhal replied. "It's easier to rat-scamper or avoid being seen with only two or three. This mob's too easily caught, especially the big guy there. I doubt he can move his monstrous feet fast enough to run."

"Don't mind him, Meloon," Vharem said, as he drove an elbow into Faxhal's stomach. "He's just jealous he's the least handsome and shortest one here. He's always been one to pick fights with the biggest guy in the room."

Faxhal spat loudly, landing a gobbet right in front of Vharem's boot. "So how do you know something is amiss? Other than those two *strangers* heard screaming. Bells of Belshaba, I hear screaming in half the taverns every night!"

"Not like this, little man," Meloon muttered, his voice low and serious.

"If you'd heard it, you'd know someone was being tortured," Laraelra said. "Last time I checked, torture was still a severe offense in the city."

Renaer said, "We also saw the Blackstaff and Ten-Rings working together. Willingly. What does that tell you?"

"They're up to something magical?" Faxhal asked.

"Probably," Renaer replied, "but let's look a little beyond the obvious. They acted like old allies, when in fact—"

"Those two can't stand one another!" Vharem said.

"And so?" Renaer spun his questioning eyes toward Faxhal.

Faxhal shrugged. "I don't know. You know full well I'm going to ignore local politics unless it involves pretty women. I make it a point to ignore wizards always, even when it *does* involve pretty women."

Renaer rolled his eyes and said, "One of them wasn't who he seemed to be. Perhaps both of them weren't who they claimed, and they're trying to point blame at targets that no one dares accuse. In any case, the Watch won't believe our word against the supposed Blackstaff, so if anyone is going to do anything to stop them or at least save that woman, it's going to have to be us."

During their conversation, the five of them had inched their way across the creaking and dangerously sagging wooden floor to the cellar door. The floor was stone in the back third of the building where it met the walls and doors. The kitchen yawned off to the right, an icy draft coming down the chimney and stirring the cobwebs at the long-cold fireplace. The party chose the door opposite, leading to the cellars.

Renaer opened the door with some difficulty, its boards having warped over time. He stepped into the stairwell that led down to a small landing before turning into the main part of the cellar. He descended to the landing but stopped and turned to stare up at the rest of them on the stairs.

"Everybody needs to move past me on the stairs. Vharem, bring that lantern closer. Elra, help me look for that trigger." Renaer knelt down on the slab and began scraping at the edge of the upper stairs as the others walked past him.

Faxhal nudged Meloon. "Elra? Have they been getting chummy all afternoon? They've got pet names for each other."

Meloon smiled. "She asks her friends to call her that. Why? You jealous? I'll give you a pet name if you—"

"Will you two *please* be quiet?" Laraelra said as she knelt next to Renaer. "When we find the door to these tunnels, we don't want you two yammering away and giving our foes warning."

"I don't think there's much chance of that," Renaer said. "There are at least three sets of tunnels and chambers we'll pass through to get beneath Roarke House."

"So what're they there for?" Vharem asked. "Your forebears smugglers or something, Ren?"

"Or something. The tunnels were either built by or expanded upon by three or four different ancestors." He pulled off his gloves for a better sense of touch along the wall and step. "One of them was among the earliest guildmasters of the Cellarers' Guild, which explains how they all managed to bypass any mention on official or unofficial maps."

Faxhal, irritated and impatient, asked, *"Why* are they here?"

"Imagine my surprise to find that my great-great-grand-uncle was none other than Kulzar Brandarth."

"The old pirate?" Vharem asked.

Renaer nodded. "Kulzar had been disowned by the family and wasn't allowed to use his family name, but they granted him a house that used to be here. He buried his final treasures somewhere around here, but no one's ever found them in the two centuries since. Of course, the family reclaimed the deeds after his passing, just in case."

Renaer beamed as he and Laraelra both found bricks in the walls alongside the third stepface that each tipped inward.

Faxhal gasped. "We're going after pirates' treasure?"

"Unlikely," Renaer said. "The tunnels were built during the Guildwars for the resistance against the guildmasters' rule of the city. I suspect someone's found part of the tunnels and is using them for a foul purpose."

"Kulzar's treasure might explain the involvement of those wizards," Laraelra said, "but I think the woman they were torturing might be able to tell us what they wanted. If she's still alive."

She and Renaer reached into the hidden trigger points and pressed the stone buttons set into the side of the third step. The upper stairs began sliding silently and swiftly downward, stranding them on the landing but reforming as a new stairwell leading deeper than the Gildenfires' cellar.

"So far as we know, no one's used these tunnels since before any of us were born." Renaer unfurled a parchment from his sleeve, showing a map. "Some of the tunnels shifted or melted together during the Spellplague. They may not be as they're marked. In any case, I'll want to keep the maps of these tunnels current. Vharem, you've got the rope, if we meet any drops?"

Vharem nodded, shrugging his cloak aside to reveal the rope looped around his torso.

Renaer led the way down the stairs, but slowed his pace as the steps grew taller and more difficult to descend. He noticed the tunnel shrank as they descended, and soon all but Laraelra had to shuffle sideways, as the corridor wasn't wide enough for their shoulders. The third landing, which turned them to the right one more time, was partially melted, and the direction the tunnel turned was all a smooth stone ramp.

Vharem unfurled the rope, handing one end to Meloon and the other to Faxhal. Renaer cleared his throat and raised an eyebrow in question. Vharem usually deferred to Renaer's decisions, but he looked him right in the eye and bypassed him, giving Faxhal the rope.

Faxhal clapped Renaer on the shoulder and said, "He wants me going first in case there's trouble, Renaer. No offense, but I'm a little better in a fight than you are. If we meet someone who wants to talk, you're our fellow."

Renaer rolled his eyes but motioned them to continue.

"Why don't I go, then?" Meloon asked.

"Because I need *you* to help me anchor the rope while the others go down ahead of us." Vharem clapped Meloon on the shoulders and braced his feet against the corridor's walls. He'd wrapped the rope around his waist once and fed it through his gloved hands. Once Vharem was braced, Faxhal saluted them, eased his way past his friend, and picked up the rope and Vharem's lantern.

"You can hardly hold onto the lantern and the rope, little man," Laraelra said. "Allow me." She whispered a few words, causing her fingernails to glow a light blue, and slid that blue light onto the pommel of Faxhal's dagger. He smiled, handed Laraelra the lantern, and kissed her hand as she took the lantern from him. He then slipped down the twisting slide, feeding out rope as he went. After a minute or so, his blue light was out of sight.

The rope suddenly wrenched through their hands. It pulled Vharem off his feet, but Meloon braced his feet and stopped them from sliding more.

"Yow!" Faxhal's feet slipped out from under him after the sharp turn in the tunnel, and he slid a ways before he slowed his fall with his feet against the walls. He yelled, "Sorry!" back up the tunnel before he looked below and found himself above a vertical opening in the ceiling of a chamber. He said, "Another drop coming!" up the shaft to warn Vharem, then jumped free, smiling as he slid quickly down more than twice his own height to land on the floor.

The blue light Laraelra placed on him barely reached the ceiling, and Faxhal noticed the opening he'd come through was the highest point in the ceiling—the arc of the ceiling and odd shape of the room made him think of an egg. Stalactites of stretched out and warped brick and mortar hung from the ceiling in places. Faxhal knelt and looked along the floor, easily seeing its uneven slope toward the center.

"Definitely egg-shaped," he muttered. But why such an odd shape?

The only other features in the room he could see were copious amounts of webbing and spiders.

Faxhal tugged on the rope and yelled up, "Nothing down here but spiders! All clear. Send Ren down!"

He untied himself and fastened the line to a small clump of stone beneath the opening. It'll take Ren a little while, so I'll look around a bit, he thought.

Faxhal paced around, finding the room's walls and clearing away the veils of dusty webbing with his sword.

Renaer arrived with a, "Fair day down here, then, friend? Good to have a little light again, that's for sure." He tugged on the rope to signal he was down. "What's the situation?"

"Not much here," Faxhal said, "and the room's warped floor to ceiling like an egg, though I don't think it was built like this. I was just walking the perimeter and clearing away webs to find any doors."

"Well, it'll give us something to do while the others descend."

Faxhal and Renaer stayed together, using their swords to sweep away webs and a few rotting tapestries here and there. Under nearly a solid mound of webbing, they discovered a long-dry cistern, its edges merged with the slope of the wall.

"So what befalls below, gentles?" Laraelra's voice drew their attention up toward her. She descended, a lit lantern floating alongside her while she slid down. Faxhal found himself dashing over to help her down, his hands at her very skinny waist before he even thought about it.

"What exactly are you doing, Faxhal?" Laraelra flinched from his touch and swung slightly to the side on the rope to drop to the ground. She looked irritated and suspicious—reactions with which Faxhal was very familiar.

What wasn't common to him was the nervous feeling of disappointment in his gut. He looked at her arched eyebrows and muttered, "I meant no—nothing. Just, nothing." He stomped toward an unexamined corner.

The three of them diligently and carefully pulled back more and more dust and webs to find the room had once stored old food crates and wine barrels, all since emptied by rats. Faxhal sighed in relief when his probes with his sword finally revealed a door.

Faxhal pressed his ear to the door and listened, but he heard very little.

"Is it safe to drop the rope?" Meloon said. "Are we going to need to climb back up?"

"Unless you found somewhere to anchor it, we'll have to trust in luck that these other corridors can lead us out of here again," Renaer said.

"Could be worse," Meloon said. He tied the rope around himself as Vharem shrugged it off, then braced his feet, and said, "You first, Vharem. I'll jump after you're down."

"You sure? It's a long fall," he said. Meloon answered with a nod. "Very well, friend."

Vharem held the rope on both sides of the loop around his trunk. He slowly played out the rope, sliding down into the chamber, and let himself fall the final few feet to land near what seemed to be a long-dry cistern, its back corner rearing up like a stone wave. He moved forward and waved up to Meloon, who let the rope drop to the floor. As soon as Vharem had gathered the rope, Meloon jumped, landing hard but rolling forward to save his legs from injury. "Whew! There's a jump! You sure we're not in Undermountain, Renaer?" Renaer smiled and offered him an arm to help him up.

"I've scouted a little ways ahead," Faxhal said. "Once beyond these first rooms, there's lots of ways to choose from. Most have no noise behind them, but I didn't open any of them yet. Renaer probably knows what they are, so let's go and let him show us his great brains." He winked at Renaer as the five of them moved through another door and into a very tall but slim door-lined corridor. Renaer took out a small chapbook and flipped pages, nodding as he read and counted out sixteen various doors, eight on each side of the corridor.

The high ceiling echoed their steps back to them. Renaer tried his keys on each of the doors. While some opened into long-empty storehouse chambers, a few opened to reveal melted walls and contortions merging with sewer lines. Laraela shook her head, and muttered, "Either there's older sewer lines we don't know about, or there are breaks in the system we haven't found."

More than half the doors would not budge though, their locks either rusted or the doors jammed by the shifts in the corridor. Faxhal nodded toward one and Meloon and said, "Care to help me knock?" The two men shouldered the door in, and it splintered, falling off its hinge. All they revealed was another warped room with sewage bubbling up in a back corner. After the second of such discoveries, Faxhal gave up helping and just waited on Renaer to open a door with his keys.

The group reached the end of the corridor, which was covered by a carved stone demonic face taller than any of them, its mouth snarling to reveal large fangs the length of Faxhal's forearm. Far above, they could see a light coming through at the ceiling, a vent helping the airflow among the subterranean chambers.

Renaer walked forward, consulted his notes, and reached out to push the demon's head horns closer together on its forehead. An audible *click* followed, and the demon's face moved slightly. Faxhal could feel a draft rushing out the gap, but when he put his hand on the stone to open it, Renaer cleared his throat and shook his head. Faxhal and Vharem exchanged looks and both of them rolled their eyes. Faxhal whispered, "Ren, either let us help or show us what your precious books tell you."

Renaer moved past the others to the nearest door on the right side of the corridor. He reached up, pushed hard on the doorframe, and the stone lintel there slid upward and clicked. Renaer then opened that door and walked through it. "One of the builders had a dwarf's help in some of the stonework. Good distractions and good traps. If we'd used the corridor behind that demon's head, there's at least four pit traps beneath weighted tip-floors. This is the safe way."

"Fine," Faxhal said, "but let us go first."

Renaer opened the door, and Faxhal and Vharem entered the room. After a small tunnel about three paces long, Faxhal entered a small round chamber filled with gold light from an enchanted ceiling. Inside the room was a pair of writing desks and a set of tall shelves heavy with parchments and bound books. The desks held old, desiccated parchments and the ink in the wells had long since dried. Faxhal probed ahead with light toe touches and his fingers ran along the walls, feeling slowly for any triggers or traps. He was especially careful by the only flat wall—opposite the entrance—in the chamber, as it was covered by a bas-relief carving of two trolls battling three Watchmen in antiquated garb. Once Faxhal knew the floor was clear, he examined the carvings carefully and identified one trigger to lock a hidden door from this side and a second to open the door. He left those alone for now and continued checking the chamber.

After one circuit of the room, he nodded at Vharem, who waved the others in. The room became crowded with all five inside, and Faxhal hissed everyone quiet when he heard a voice cry out, "Samurk! Samurk . . ."

"I hear someone crying," Faxhal whispered. "A woman. She keeps muttering a name or something."

A loud snore buzzed through the room, causing everyone to look at each other in surprise.

"We're well beneath both the warehouse and Roarke House," Renaer said. "This is a listening post built earlier for the resistance to spy on guild loyalists to whom they'd rent out the chambers beyond. Everything said, every noise made, in the two lower chambers can be heard here, where scribes used to sit and copy down everything said for use as evidence or blackmail."

Faxhal interrupted, wanting some of the attention, "And there's a secret door in that wall carving there, right?"

Renaer stared at him a moment, then grinned and nodded. "Yes, and it opens to a tunnel that leads back beneath Roarke House and ends in another secret door."

"Why would anyone use those chambers if they knew they could be spied upon?" Meloon asked.

"They didn't know anyone could hear any of that until we gave that away this morning," Renaer said. "According to our records, all of these secret tunnels and chambers were unknown by old Volam himself when he built Roarke House over the existing cellar and foundation. Others found those chambers, linked them to the house, and converted them for their personal use, but they've been unused since Grandfather bought the building decades back. At least, as far as I know." He nodded toward Laraelra and Meloon and added, "You two probably heard things coming from this chamber filtered through some of those links with the sewers."

"Why didn't anyone else find out about the tunnels?" Meloon asked.

"If you don't know to look for something," Faxhal said, "you'll never be bothered to find it. That's why I always keep looking—and getting accused of poking around where I shouldn't."

"Faxhal's right," Renaer said, taking care to keep his voice down, "at least the first part. We can spot the triggers that are almost invisible on the other side."

Faxhal pointed out the lock triggers—the stonework swords wielded by the Watchmen in the battle scene. Renaer checked his journal and began moving the stone swords. Faxhal shook his head when Ren moved the second Watchman's sword. "You just locked the door shut again, chief. Just the two outer swords pushed outward should trigger this door."

Renaer nodded, scribbling corrections in his notes, and he turned toward the group, who stood around a scraped arc on the floor—the door's obvious path on this side. He said, "Everyone, get ready. They may have defenses ready in their cellars, even if they aren't expecting any company from this direction."

Renaer shifted the final trigger, and the door slid in toward them. They looked into a pitch black corridor, lit by the gold light spilling through the now-open door.

"Good." Faxhal chuckled then he drew his long sword out and brandished it in the air a little before he nodded at Renaer. He hoped Laraelra was impressed, and he added, "Been itching for a fight all day."

A sudden twang, and Faxhal snapped backward, a crossbow quarrel lodged in his throat.

"Careful what you wish for, boy," came the hoarse chuckle from the dark.

The thief felt both the impact at his throat and the crack at the back of his head when he slammed back on the stone floor. *I expected that to hurt more,* Faxhal thought. His breath caught in his throat and he found it hard to breathe or move. He lost his grip on his sword and heard it rattle on the stone floor. *Oh stlaern, I never got the chance to tell her how pretty her eyes were . . . or save her from this . . .*

The last thing Faxhal heard beyond his own heartbeat was a plaintive gasp from Laraelra's throat as she looked down at him. *No love poem, but I'll take it,* he thought.

The noise, the smells, the sensations all faded. Faxhal felt lighter and lighter with each heartbeat. Until the heartbeat ended.

CHAPTER SIX

Even on the slowest night, the dark is never quiet in Waterdeep.

Borthild "Steelbard,"
One Season's Nights and Days Waterdhavian,
circa the Year of the Prince (1357 DR)

9 NIGHTAL, YEAR OF THE AGELESS ONE (1479 DR)

LARAELRA GASPED AS FAXHAL ALMOST FLIPPED BACKWARD. HER SIGNAL OF true danger was the spray of blood arcing past her own shoulder. She looked down at Faxhal's fallen body in disbelief, the mixture of annoyance and amusement he triggered in her already shifting to horror.

"Down!" Meloon ripped his axe out of its harness, swinging it up into his hands.

Vharem grabbed Faxhal by the collar and pulled him out of the way. By the time Vharem had his friend behind the door near Renaer, Faxhal had stopped moving and his eyes were open and blank. Renaer pulled out a potion vial from his pouch and looked at Vharem, pleading. Vharem shook his head and reached down to close their friend's eyes. Laraelra couldn't hear everything he said, but she did catch ". . . farewell, little fox."

Laraelra shouted out a spell, and blue light rippled out of her, clearing the darkness from the corridor. They faced two men in Watch garb, one kneeling and holding a spent crossbow while next to him an older man with an eye patch waited with a sword and shield. Behind them both stood Samark "Blackstaff" Dhanzscul, the gem atop his staff flaring red.

Samark waved his hand and red bolts flew from his fingers. Two slammed into Meloon's broad chest, and he grunted but held his ground. Three more arced at Laraelra but skittered around her, feeling like lightning-charged rain on her skin, before they launched themselves back at the Blackstaff.

Laraelra focused, despite the distraction of the Blackstaff's spell, and cast another spell of her own. She pulled up an amber energy that crackled among her fingers until she pointed at Samark and said, *"Drialrokh!"*

That bolt hit its target unerringly—his throat. Laraelra smiled as she watched color drain from the already-pale face of the Blackstaff when he realized he could not speak. The wizard turned and ran, to the surprise and anger of his two guards. The eye-patched one stepped forward, yelling, "Get that crossbow restrung or draw your blade, boy! They'll not be much bother for us, e'en without hisself."

"Meloon?" Laraelra shouted as she stepped back and to the side of the opening.

Meloon jumped into the corridor, swinging his axe wide with both hands, forcing the corridor's two guardians to shuffle back a bit from the door. "Hope I'm bothersome enough, one-eye."

The older man grumbled and spat in Meloon's path, but he and his companion backed up farther from the swinging axe.

Laraelra looked down at Faxhal, caught both Vharem and Renaer's eyes, and whispered, "Avenge him."

Renaer's reached into his wide sleeves and pulled a dagger from each one.

Vharem drew a short sword out of his belt and whispered to Renaer, "Didn't think we'd need these, but thanks for the loan."

The sorceress looked up and saw the younger guard raising his spanned crossbow. She concentrated, waved her hand, and the crossbow quarrel flipped out of the stock just as he pulled the trigger.

Renaer dived and rolled in a somersault, staying low but moving forward. Vharem stepped into the corridor's opening after Renaer, holding a dart in one hand and a short sword in the other. Renaer stopped in a crouch before the guard, adding the momentum of his roll to his two thrown daggers. One missed, sailing past the guard's shoulder, but the second one hit him in his hand, forcing him to drop the crossbow. The guard kicked out at Renaer with little effect. Vharem let his dart fly and hit the young guard in the thigh. He stayed back behind Renaer and Meloon, who parried the older man's blade with his axe.

"You've had good teachers if you're not taking the first swing at me, boy," the gravel-voiced man said to Meloon. "Too bad you gave up your only advantage." The older man stabbed his long sword forward and Meloon brought his axe up, making the blade scrape along his mail shirt instead of piercing it. Meloon countered by swinging the double-bladed axe back down toward the man's side. The older man brought around a shield, and the loud clash of weapon and shield filled the corridor.

Laraelra stood back at the corridor's opening, harnessing her anger at letting the Blackstaff escape as she thrust quicksilver-colored missiles at the two guards. She willed one upon each of them, and the young guard fell over with a choked cry.

"You little traitors'll pay for that," the man grunted, as he stabbed again at the dodging Meloon. "You have no idea what you've stumbled into."

The man backed up the corridor, his features masked in hatred. Meloon pressed forward, and Laraelra could not see his face.

"Granek Ruskelver, I remember you," Renaer said. "You were drummed out of the Watch last year for accepting bribes and conduct unbecoming a Watchman."

Granek flinched, looked down briefly at Renaer, and his singular eye shot him a look of revulsion. "You got no idea how this city really is, rich boy. You'll find out what happens when you trip over the plans of the mighty. I did my job well for Ten-Rings, and no young sellsword's gonna drop me!" Granek swung hard and fast at Meloon, who brought his arm up. The sword scored a long, wound along his left forearm, crossing two thick white scars from some previous battles. When Meloon shoved his axe up to force the blade away, the sword's point stabbed into the mortar in the wall.

Granek's eyes widened as he tugged to free his weapon, and Meloon brought the axe down hard on Granek's overextended right leg. Granek screamed as he fell to the ground, clutching the stump of his leg and groaning. After a few moments, he passed out.

Meloon whispered, "I'm still striding. How about you?"

Renaer stood, noting he and Meloon had both been sprayed with Granek's blood from his leg wound, and blood already covered the floor. Vharem shoved his way past both of them, muttering, "Want to get that wizard before he can cast on anyone again."

Laraelra yelled, "Vharem, no! Don't be a fool!" *I don't think Renaer could handle another death tonight,* she thought. *I don't think I could either.*

Meloon reached out for him and grabbed a handful of his shirt, pulling Vharem short. "Don't let Faxhal's death make you run to your own."

Vharem shot Meloon a look mixed with anger and grief, then shrugged off Meloon's grip, only to find Renaer blocking his path.

"Don't lose your head," Renaer said, his eyes welling with tears. "We will get that wizard, but I don't want to lose another friend tonight. We're here to save someone, not lose everyone."

"Caution is good," Laraelra said, "but we do have to hurry. That spell I hit the Blackstaff with won't last long. I can try it again, but he may have some defenses up against it now. Our best bet is to find and save that woman. We'll avenge Faxhal another night."

"I'll take point. I'm a bit tougher than the rest of you," Meloon said. He kneeled by the fallen young Watchman and ripped off his sleeve, then wrapped his bloodied forearm in one scrap of cloth and wiped off his axe blade with the rest.

Laraelra moved closer and helped him wrap his makeshift bandage around his forearm. She whispered, "Thank you, Meloon. If he'd run on ahead . . ."

"I know," he muttered. "Seen it happen before."

"Don't think that you won't get paid," Laraelra said, "just because we're becoming friends. You'll be compensated as agreed this morning." She put the finishing touches on the bandage and pulled it tight, then smiled at the blond bear of a man.

He returned her smile and said, "Friendships are better currency anyway." From his crouch, he grabbed the empty crossbow off the floor and stood. "Well, what's the plan, Renaer?"

"All we know about the end of this corridor," Renaer said, "is on my maps and notes—and the fact that we've a very angry archmage, or someone powerful enough to impersonate him. I want to get to the bottom of this, but I don't want to die."

"We are *not* leaving without killing him!" Vharem choked. "Don't let Faxhal's death mean *nothing!*"

"He meant as much to me as to you," Renaer said, "but I'm not willing to risk our lives. We can go back and I can hire many more sellswords—"

"And he'll have us arrested for trying to attack the Blackstaff," Laraelra said, "the Watchful Order, or some other trumped-up charge. *And* he'll have this area so well protected we'll never get in again *or* find out who they were torturing or why. We *have* to do this now, Renaer, risks and all. Let's find the woman we came to save—*that* is what Faxhal died for."

The four looked at each other, nodded, and Renaer said, "Very well. Our secret corridor—which they discovered somehow—exits behind a privy. We should turn left and into a corridor lined with doors."

Vharem lined up behind Meloon, leaving Renaer and Laraelra to cover their backs. As the others moved forward, Laraelra felt something touch her foot. She looked down to see a very weak and trembling Granek, whose lone eye locked on hers. "Help . . .," he pleaded.

Renaer stepped over and said, "Even before tonight, Granek, before your lackey killed my friend, you deserved this death. Alone, in the dark, no one to mourn you."

Renaer kicked the man's grasp loose from Laraelra's boot and moved away, taking the lantern with him.

Shadows falling on his form, Granek pleaded with Laraelra, "Lass, mercy."

Laraelra hugged herself, staring at Renaer's back, but she understood his cold anger, remembering her own when she heard his words earlier. She looked Granek in the eye and said, "Nay, before the gods, torturers deserve no mercy. Ask it of Kelemvor when you see him." She snapped her cloak tight around her as she turned to follow Renaer.

.⁙ ▰ ⁙.

They moved quickly and found Meloon and Vharem stopped by the opened secret door, the privy seat still attached to it and turned to one side.

"What's the problem?" Renaer asked.

"No pit," Meloon said, his brow furrowed. He dropped the crossbow and kicked it across the floor, only to watch it disappear through apparently solid stone and clatter loudly as it fell down a shaft. "Hmph. Neat trick, that."

"How did you know that was there?" Laraelra asked.

Meloon grinned. "Saw the seat and knew someone had to have dug one. You dig those enough times, you remember how much work is hidden beneath a lot of dung." He knelt, grabbed a loose rock and scratched an **X** at the near side of the pit. He reached back and said, "Lend a hand, please." He grabbed Vharem's forearm to keep from falling into the hidden shaft and then leaned forward, closing his eyes and tapping ahead with the rock in his hand. When he touched solid rock again instead of illusion, he scratched an **X** there as well, and said, "Haul me back, Vharem, and then everybody, jump past the second mark!"

He got to his feet, took his axe in both hands, and jumped across easily. The rest of the group followed suit. As Renaer landed, a woman's harsh screams rang out around the corner.

The quartet ran around the corner into a slim corridor, two doors lining each side of it. The screams seemed to come from the one on the far right. Meloon started forward, but Vharem bolted ahead of all of them. He ran to the door, reached for the handle, and his hand passed through the illusion. He stumbled forward, off-balance, and Vharem's world went red as fire exploded all around him. The blast knocked him off his feet and threw him back down the corridor. His sword, dislodged from his left hand, bounced across the hall and hit the opposite door. This too exploded in a blast of flame and heat, but Vharem was already down and the explosion passed over him. With the explosion came another shriek from beyond the door.

"*Vharem!*" Renaer yelled, and he rushed to the fallen man.

His leathers and hair all smoking, Vharem tried to talk but just coughed. Much of his long brown hair fell away in singed clumps, and his face and hands were blistered, but he fought to stand again.

Renaer dragged him back against the wall and away from the doorways, saying "Rest here, friend. Catch your breath."

Vharem winced as he flexed his fingers and watched thick, blackened flakes of his skin crack off his hand.

Renaer pulled out a small vial from his belt. "Drink, V." He poured the contents of the vial over his friend's cracked and soot-stained lips, and the cracks instantly healed. The worst blistering on Vharem's face and hands subsided and returned to his normal skin tone. Even his hair began to regrow.

"Wow," Vharem said, looking at Renaer and then the vial. "Who knew healing draughts tasted like clover honey, mint, and zzar all in one?"

"Don't get used to them," Renaer said. "They're more expensive than your usual bar tab for a tenday."

"Didn't you need that for whoever was down here?" Vharem asked as Renaer helped him to his feet. "Help her get back on her feet?"

"I've one left," Renaer said. "Besides, you needed it more. I don't want to lose another friend tonight." Renaer opened his mouth to say more, and then simply hugged Vharem and asked, "Elra? Meloon? Find anything?"

"Look at the marks on the floor," Meloon said. "It's weird that the blasts stay in the doorway and never slip inside the door. They're also not wooden doors, see?" Meloon shrugged toward the farthest doorway Vharem had approached, and the wooden door was now a prison door of metal bars and naught else.

Laraelra's concentration showed her the world she loved—the world of magic. She looked at Renaer, her eyes filled with a sea of stars, then she looked intently at the corridor, the doors, and the floor. "I'm seeing magic all around here. The remnants of the spells Vharem triggered match the auras on those two other doors." She pointed at the doors they had all run past, one on each side of the passageway. "I'm also seeing some lingering but powerful magic. I think it's an illusion of some kind. It's dotting around here, as if it's—"

"Footprints?" Renaer asked.

"Exactly," she replied, snapping her fingers. "You're right, Renaer. Whoever's posing as the Blackstaff only wears his shape. If nothing else, I think he's gone, as the trail heads up the passage and turns."

"Help me!" A voice cried through the first left-hand door.

Laraelra snapped her head in the door's direction, her concentration shattered. She held up her hand and waved everyone away from the door, then tossed some pebbles at the door. The illusory door exploded with flaming fury, but no one stood in its path. Renaer and Vharem found it was a locked wooden door, just like it seemed. The pair kicked it twice before the lock broke and the door swung inward, scraping against the stone floor.

Inside the room, a young woman lay spread-eagled and strapped to a table, blades and other torture implements on the tables around her. Her long red hair matted on the table or to her head with sweat and blood. The gown she wore was reduced to tattered rags, and her feet were visibly injured within iron boots with ankle screws. She saw her three saviors at the door and whimpered, "Please! Get me out of here before he comes back!"

Vharem and Renaer rushed forward, pulling at the blood-soaked leather straps and unscrewing the iron boots. Laraelra wove a minor magic to repair the woman's tattered gown. The woman gasped, "Don't know what they wanted, but they kept hitting me! And my feet! Oh blessed Ilmater, my feet!" She wailed as Laraelra and Vharem removed the boots, but her black-and-blue flesh hardly resembled feet at all, given how many bones were shattered in them.

Vharem asked, "What's your name?"

"Charrar," she replied. "I'm a dancer at the Ten Bells on Brondar's Way."

"What did they want with you?" Laraelra asked.

"I don't know!" Charrar said, but whimpered slightly when Vharem picked her up off the table. "They just kept hurting me, and the Blackstaff just stood there smiling!"

Laraelra started to ask, *When did they bring you here?* but stopped herself. Something didn't smell right here, though the stench of blood was real enough.

Renaer reached into his belt pouch and said, "I've got something that may help."

"Hang on, Renaer," Laraelra said, resting her hand on his forearm and another over the cork-stoppered ceramic tube he held. "Wait, in case someone has lethal injuries, hmm?" She looked around the room and asked, "Where's Meloon?"

A loud, piercing scream came from out in the hall, and Meloon stuck his head in the room to say, "Elra, come look over here. I hear the screaming, but there's nothing here. It's really irritating . . . and repetitive."

Laraelra walked to the doorway, but as she passed Renaer, she arched her eyebrows at him, her back to Charrar. His eyes widened, but he nodded.

Laraelra exited that room and breathed deeply, then coughed. I don't know what's worse, she thought, the smell of blood in there or of singed Vharem out here.

She crossed the corridor where Meloon stood, angry. "I ran down that way while you checked the room. That bastard sealed off the corridor leading out of here with stone. I couldn't find a door, even though I saw scratches where a door scraped the floor for years."

"That's probably an illusion of a solid wall," Laraelra said, "if not a conjured wall itself."

"Did I mention how much I hate illusions?"

"So which room again?" Laraelra asked. As if on cue, the scream pierced the air again. Obviously coming from the room on the far right. "You're right. *Really* irritating." She shared a smirk with Meloon as they approached the room, and Laraelra concentrated, summoning her ability to see magic. The prison-bar door stood partially open from Vharem's disturbing it, and Laraelra looked at the threshold. "There's an illusion set right inside the door." She tapped her toe lightly on the blue-gray puddle of magic, and the screams ended abruptly. Her eyes widened, and she peered intently at the far corner of the room. "This room is clean. No other magic in play that I can see."

"Are you sure?" Meloon asked. He tried to push past her and look in the room himself. He had to stoop, since the doorway was low, and bumped into Laraelra as she turned to leave, knocking her off balance.

She tumbled into the room and said, "Watch it, you—" and fell flat on her back, banging her hip and an elbow. However, before the pain ended her spell, she saw a large gray-silver field of magic above the door. "Meloon—there!"

"What?" Meloon reached down to help her up, and a blood drop plopped onto his outstretched arm. He turned and looked up, just inside the doorway, but he saw nothing. Another blood drop appeared out of thin air and fell onto his shoulder.

"Something's hidden there," Laraelra said, then pointed. "Look at those iron rings in the walls. See if there's a hammock up there. I think it's been made invisible, and it's hiding something inside it."

Meloon poked upward with his left hand. He felt rough cloth and something heavier above that. He pushed harder and heard a low moan. Meloon started feeling around the edges of the invisible cloth, as the woman inside moaned in a foreign language.

"You know what she's saying?" he asked. He found an edge to the invisible cloth. He pulled it open, finding a bloodied and dirtied dark-skinned woman with very short black hair and multiple wounds all over her body. Her eyes were open and staring, but instead of regular pupils, her eyes were dark orbs filled with crackles of red energy. "Whoa."

"Renaer?" Laraelra yelled out into the corridor. "We've got another one here! And she needs help more than Charrar! Hurry!"

Laraelra wanted a closer look at the woman, but if she was right about this, they were in a far worse game than they knew.

Meloon stretched the invisible fabric of the hammock out of the way and rolled the wounded woman down into his arms. As she moved, a chorus of voices—men's and women's both—screamed in pain.

"Selûne preserve her, she definitely needs this more," Renaer said, as he arrived to see the dagger protruding from the woman's stomach. "Hold her, Meloon."

Renaer held her head up, poured the potion into her mouth, and pulled the dagger free. Her body spasmed in reaction to the pain, but the belly wound closed up, as did the lesser wounds on her face and body. She began breathing easier, and her eyes flickered open briefly, but they remained storm-clouded orbs of black. Renaer looked up at Meloon, who just shrugged, but Laraelra pressed in behind them.

"Don't you recognize her?" she asked.

Renaer nodded, but the others shook their heads.

"That's Vajra Safahr—the Blackstaff's lover!" Laraelra said. She didn't want to say more until she knew for certain, but she had the nagging suspicion that Ten-Rings and his associate were trying to steal the power of the Blackstaff—and she wondered how long the illusion-wearer had posed as Samark. Her thoughts were interrupted by Vharem carrying Charrar out into the hall toward them.

"He tortured her too?" Charrar said. "I heard others being tortured down here, but not her." She clung to Vharem, who minded not one bit, and then said, "Get me out of here before he comes back again!"

"Good idea," Renaer said, and he took Vajra into his arms. "Meloon, Elra, see if there's any other way out. Charrar, I'm sorry, but I've no more healing potions. We'll have to carry both of you out of here."

Charrar nodded, but then tearfully put her head down on Vharem's shoulder and sobbed. Vharem held her closer just enough to ease his short sword back into its scabbard.

"What are you doing?" Renaer snapped. "You might need that!"

"And how are we going to fight if we're each carrying someone?" Vharem said. "If we go back the way we came, we can at least block off some passages and hole up until we can all move better. We know what's back there already."

"Yeah," Renaer said, his eyes dropping, "but it's the things we don't expect that kill us."

"The alleged Blackstaff sealed the corridor with some spells or illusions," Laraelra said. "We'll have to go back the way we came."

"What about Faxhal?" Vharem asked, his eyes pleading with Renaer.

"Later," Renaer said, his face cold and impassive. "We'll come back to bury him and mourn later. For now, let's move."

"How do you know where we are, Elra?" Meloon's whisper echoed in the sewer pipes.

"Can't tell you guild secrets," Laraelra replied, as she spotted the keystone in the archway over the intersection. This led into one of the secondary sewer lines beneath the city, and that rune told her they were heading north again. She was trying to get them back to the surface shaft at Heroes' Garden she and Meloon had used that morning. "Hear those picks? That means there're cellarers at work." She motioned for him to turn left, and they saw another light other than the lantern that she held.

Two figures looked up, startled, when the lantern's light came into their tunnel. Laraelra smiled as the familiar gruff voice of Harug called out, "Who delves? Cry out or face blades!"

"Less noise, old daern," Laraelra said. "It's Elra and friends."

When they met up, she moved ahead of Meloon to clasp forearms with both dwarves, thankful to see more friendly faces. It was obvious to Laraelra the dwarves had spent the past day clearing the channel and reshoring the wall.

She looked closely at their work. "Nice secret door you seem to be installing here, Harug." When he scowled at that, she whispered, "It'll be our secret, old daern. Father needs not know."

Harug gripped her forearm and muttered to her in his native Dwarvish, *"Lass, be careful. Best not take this shaft up to the garden. There be folk waiting for ye up there. They don't talk like no Watch I ever seen. Fools forget voices carry down this way as well. Take the next one west up to Shank Alley. That'll leave them like orcs waiting for a gopher that's left its hole."*

Laraelra nodded, then turned as Dorn clapped hands with Meloon. "Dorn Strongcroft pays his debts with friendship!" He spit into his hand and held it out for Meloon to shake, which he did. The young dwarf's eyes widened as he saw the man's weapon. "When that axe needs some work, you come see me cousin in Fields Ward. Ask for the Strongcroft smithy and mention my name. They'll steer ye arights."

"Ow!" Charrar's voice echoed loudly in the subterranean tunnel. She continued her complaints as Vharem approached with her in his arms. "Vharem, aren't we getting out of the sewers soon? I don't like it here!"

Laraelra wasn't sure Charrar could make more noise if she tried, and she watched the woman, wondering what didn't settle in her mind about her. She put her finger to her mouth and signaled for silence. Then she motioned for them to follow, and they inched past Harug and Dorn.

Laraelra let Meloon lead and, as she half-expected, Charrar pointed at the access ladder leading up and yelled, "Hey! There's a—"

Laraelra clapped a hand over her mouth and glared. She whispered, "Someone's lying in wait for us up there, so we're going *this* way. Now *keep quiet.*"

Charrar's eyes narrowed, and she slowly nodded.

When they did finally begin clambering up another surface shaft a while later, Laraelra went first and shoved the sewer shaft cover aside as quietly as she could. Next, Charrar clung to Vharem's neck as he climbed, whimpering as she bumped against each iron rung of the ladder. Meloon climbed up and lowered down a rope. Renaer, the last to leave the sewers, waited while the others reeled the unconscious Vajra up with a makeshift harness on the rope. Laraelra pretended to watch Vharem and Meloon stretching their arms and shoulders out, but she remained watchful of the sulking Charrar, who perched on some crates behind them.

Charrar shifted her position and shoved a barrel to make her perch wider. Two empty crates clattered down into the alley. She flinched away and bumped her left foot into another barrel. She let out a scream and clutched her leg, whimpering.

"Shut it, woman!" Vharem snapped. "You'll draw every cut-purse and Watchman in earshot!"

Dawn was just breaking across the sky, and Laraela could see where she was. Between the smell of fish guts and one particularly gruesome demon's head painted on the back of the tallest building in the center of the alley, she figured out their location. "We're in Shank Alley. That sign faces out on Morningstar Way for the Demondraught tavern."

"If you say so," Meloon said. He turned toward Renaer. "Hey, you're probably tired, and I'm not. I'll carry Vajra for a while." He had hauled her up by rope and held her in the crook of one arm as he coiled the rope up with his other hand. His axe lay on the cobbles beside them.

Renaer shook his head. "No, but thanks. I'll carry her, in case we have to run. I can keep up with you even while carrying her. I'd rather you were ready for anyth—"

"Drop all weapons and surrender!" The shout came from the alley's mouth to the west of them.

"Like that?" Laraelra asked.

CHAPTER SEVEN

A man's home, like a man's wife, holds many secrets from those who don't respect her or know how to hold her in the proper regard.

Rhale the Wise, *Maxims,*
the Year of the Halls Unhaunted (1407 DR)

10 NIGHTAL, YEAR OF THE AGELESS ONE (1479 DR)

"MELOON, HELP ME!" RENAER RAN FORWARD, AND SLAMMED HIS SHOULDER into the tall pile of crates near the alley entrance. Renaer and Meloon shoved the crates over just in time, seeing the surprised looks on the Watchmen's faces as the boxes of seaweed and shellfish toppled upon them.

"Surrender!" Charrar shouted. "Renaer Neverember and company, you're in the custody of the Watch!"

Vharem whipped around, reaching for his short sword, only to find its point at his throat. Charrar stood, despite the apparent wounds on her feet, and she had stolen his weapon. "Charrar, what—"

"Don't embarrass yourself further, Vharem. I'm neither your woman nor your grateful rescued victim. Seems a shame, though, what the Blackstaff'll do to you—such a waste of a good body." As Renaer and Meloon approached, she moved the sword point closer to Vharem's throat. Meloon groaned as he noted she stood on the head of his axe, pinning it to the ground. Charrar called to her compatriots, who struggled from beneath all the crates. "Hurry! We need to get them off the streets!"

Two flashes of quicksilver slammed into Charrar's eyes and sword hand. She crumpled to the cobblestones.

Laraelra stood in the shadows, the same silver color fading from her eyes. "I *thought* something wasn't right about her."

"Run!" Renaer pointed up and to the right. "Go north on Morningstar Way!" His hands, however, waved to the south. Renaer scooped up Vajra and Meloon picked up his axe, while Laraelra grabbed the stunned Vharem by the shirt and dragged him into motion. He stumbled forward, holding his throat, and finally snapped out of it and broke into a run with her. The four of them slipped around the northern side of the Demondraught and ran south along Morningstar Way.

Renaer stopped where Aureenar Street crossed Morningstar near the gray-stoned Stormstar Ride, and he noted that most every building was dark, the street-level shops closed and the homes above asleep beneath their brown-tiled roofs. He whispered, "Vharem, Ravencourt!"

Vharem slowed and hooked arms with Laraelra to help her keep pace with him. Meloon turned, brandishing his axe, but Renaer shook his head. He inhaled a deep breath and let out a piercing whistle. Shouts behind them and sudden movement in the shadows from the debris- and cat-filled Shank Alley told Renaer they'd taken his bait. He launched himself and Vajra forward again, with Meloon running alongside again.

"Why'd you do that?" Meloon asked. "We could have gotten away!"

"I've no doubt we will get away, Meloon." Renaer said. "We lead them on a path of my choosing. I truly doubt they are the Watch—just sellswords wearing the colors. If they're working with that fake Blackstaff, they're up to no good."

"And what does this Ravencourt have to do with anything?" Meloon asked as he followed Renaer's direction further up Aureenar's Arc directly toward one of the Field Ward's watch towers.

"Revenge," Renaer said. He took a look behind to see three figures in pursuit with a fourth trailing behind. He heard the farthest one yell, "They hurt Charrar! Get them!"

Renaer cut a sharp right turn around a whitewashed stone-walled baker's shop, hooking his way into an inner courtyard. While the surrounding buildings were all one- and two-story taverns and shops, the four larger buildings within the courtyard each stood three stories high. Atop the gables on each of them loomed stone ravens. They didn't have time to admire the architecture as they caught up with Vharem and Laraelra, who had stopped, undecided which direction to go. Renaer barreled past them with a sharp "Follow me!" as he ran for the lone shadowtop tree at the far end.

"There's no way out there, Renaer!" Vharem said, though he followed once he heard their approaching pursuers.

Laraelra shouted out a spell, and a cone of bright colors filled the air just as the quartet of pursuers came around the corner. All of them yelled and stopped in their tracks, one of them falling senseless to the street. Laraelra broke into a run after her friends and called, "Who's after us—the Open Lord or the Blackstaff?"

"You'll find out, lass," the lead man growled as he shook his vision clear and raced after her.

Renaer ran to the far side of the tree, where he stopped. Meloon, Vharem, and Laraelra caught up quickly, surprised to see that Renaer had stopped again. "Are we letting them catch up again?" Meloon asked.

"No. You and Vharem should try and clear the alley between the third and fourth buildings there." Renaer pointed at the western buildings a moment. "Elra, a little light here will help."

Vharem and Meloon attacked the debris-laden midden, trying to create an exit. Laraelra sidled next to Renaer as the three remaining pursuers arrived. The three men drew swords out of their scabbards.

"See, friends?" Renaer called. "The Watch *never* draws steel on unarmed foes, only rods or staves. They're our foes' hirelings, be sure."

Laraelra's spell took effect, filling the air with blue light.

The lead pursuer responded, "Only thing folks'll believe is what we tell—Huh?"

The thug fell silent as the outline of the black-barked tree appeared atop the trio. A low moan seemed to issue out of the tree trunk along with a rustle and crackling of nigh-dead leaves and branches. The first man ran forward, intent on Renaer, when black shadows lashed out of the tree to wrap around his sword arm and body. He yelled, and his friends stepped back—too slowly. Leaf-enshrouded black vines lashed out at them too. All three screamed and howled when the vines crushed where they gripped, but their voices grew still as three final vines descended from the tree and looped around their necks as nooses. Branches cracked and groaned as they stretched under the feet of the three, raising them high above the street. With a loud crack, the branches all broke away, leaving the three men to freefall until the nooses ended their falls with the snapping of three necks.

Laraelra watched, morbidly fascinated, as the tree's shadow seemed to shift and not resemble the tree's silhouette but a judge's gavel. She looked at Renaer, who had a grim look on his face. "Did you *know* that was going to happen?" she asked.

"Yes, I expected something like that, but not nearly as dramatic," Renaer replied. "Guess old Magister Nharrelk gets angry if he doesn't claim any guilty souls in a century."

"You led us under that thing, *knowing it could attack us?*"

Renaer turned with Vajra in his arms, locking eyes with Laraelra as he turned. "We were always safe from the Hanging Tree of Ravencourt."

"Why are you so certain?"

"You haven't avoided punishment for any capital crimes in the city, have you?" Renaer said. "Those are the only ones who get judged by the Magistree."

Vharem had watched what had happened even while working to free a passage, and his eyes were goblet-wide and staring at Renaer. "How many times have we led a rat-scamper through here that never happened? And why now?"

"Seven times, friend, all of them successful escapes," Renaer said. "As for them, they were guilty of hanging offenses. Consider it some justice against those who killed Faxhal."

Renaer saw the slight path and kicked-over fence that allowed them to pass up and over a refuse heap. He nodded his approval and began climbing out of Ravencourt while still talking to the group.

"We must go back to Neverember Hall before too many folks question why I'm carrying someone. There's not many people about yet, but that'll change swiftly. Meloon, sling Elra and Vharem over your shoulders. That way, we're simply carrying our drunk friends home from their cups."

Laraelra rolled her eyes and said, "I don't think so. I can stumble home, thanks."

Meloon lashed his axe to his belt and then reached for her. "C'mon, Elra, it'll keep anyone from being suspicious."

She smirked. "Vharem's looking awful, there, Meloon. Why don't you take one arm and I'll take the other? We can walk *him* home, since we're both taller than he is."

Vharem laughed as he threw his arms over the shoulders of Meloon and Laraelra. "It's not as if this isn't closer to a typical end to a night with me and Ren!" As they walked away, Vharem muttered, "Gods speed you to rest, Faxhal, and may the guilty swim in razor-strewn dung for their afterlives."

.:◠:.

The late morning sun shone brightly through the windows at the far side of the room, though the windows facing Mendever Street remained cloaked behind heavy curtains. In the shadows on the bed, a man loomed over Vajra's prone body, his hands glowing green and white. His voice was low and his prayers were barely audible over Renaer's own as he knelt to pray in the sunlight.

"Valkur, speed his path, fill his sails, and calm his seas. Amaunator, light his way and warm his face. Tymora, grant him the luck to be at his reward before his misdeeds are counted in full. Kelemvor, judge him worthy to pass the veils. Gods above, grant my friend the happiness he found so rarely on Toril out among the stars."

Renaer's eyes welled up, but no tears escaped until he turned his head toward the light touch on his shoulder.

Renaer looked up into the peaceful eyes of Wavetamer Garyn Raventree, whose own prayers had ended moments before. "A good prayer, if a bit random."

"How is she?" Renaer asked.

Garyn shrugged and said, "I've healed her, so she's physically as strong as she can be. But mentally . . . I don't know. She's under the influence of some magic I've never seen. Given that she's linked to the Blackstaff, that's not surprising."

"So why won't she wake up?"

"I asked for clarity on her condition, and all I know is her soul now carries twenty or more lifetimes."

"What does that mean?"

"On that, Valkur puts me on still seas, friend."

"Well, thank you for everything, Garyn. I'll be by within a tenday and we'll talk about my debts to you."

"Consider this but payment for our own debts, for the young Lord Neverember has been a staunch friend of Valkur and his faithful."

Renaer stood up, walked over to his desk, and withdrew a small purse, which he handed to Garyn. "In that case, let me pay for some prayers to be sung in Faxhal's name."

"Of course. His ship will sail the stars on the waves of our prayers, friend. While he wasn't the best sailor, he was a good comrade to many of our faithful."

The priest bowed and exited the room just as Madrak came in bearing a pair of copper kettles, their contents piping hot. He poured both kettles into a basin by the window, the steam rising in the sunbeams.

"It would seem that only the lady Safahr has slept well since your adventures began yestermorn, milord. Can we not urge you and your friends to sleep? To eat? At least I can insist you not waste the hot water for your morning ablutions."

Madrak had been starting his normal day just as Renaer and his friends returned to Neverember House. Since then, he'd sent runners to Valkur's temple on Sul Street and another down to the palace to hear of any news or gossip and to notify the Watch or the Lords that the Blackstaff was not who he seemed.

"Later, Madrak," Renaer said. "I want to know what the reaction is to our news before I collapse either into bed or a trencher. Who did you send down to the palace to tell about the Blackstaff—about the duplicity?"

"Varkel. I gave him the Saddelyn pony to make sure he got there as quickly as possible."

"Good. He'll remember every single word spoken to him and around him. Are the others well?"

"Master Vharem is sullenly distraught, but has remarkably stayed away from the liquor cabinet. Mistress Laraelra has been quietly meditating in one corner, while only Master Meloon shows any sense in eating and catching some sleep. Of course, he has placed his filthy boots up on the tables and ruined the tablecloth, but . . ."

Renaer had wandered away from Madrak to approach the bed. Vajra looked vastly better, now that she had a clean robe and had all the grime and blood washed out of her hair and face. Renaer just wished she would wake up and give them some answers to help get them out of this mess.

"The fact that you have the Blackstaff's Heir in your care—however her condition—speaks well for your story, Renaer," Madrak said. "No matter how thickly the lies fly, truth is like a sunlit breeze that scatters them."

"Where did you say the others were?" Renaer asked.

"The dining room, master," he replied. "I'll check with the staff to see what other word is on the streets and meet you there. After you've refreshed yourself and dressed."

The two of them pulled the curtains around the bed closed, allowing Vajra even more warmth and silence to help her sleep. Madrak approached a tall cabinet and pulled on a decorative design between the two drawers, producing a small set of steps on which he stood to open the tall wardrobe doors. The butler began pulling out new clothes, while Renaer stripped off his old clothes and threw them to one side. Renaer splashed the hot water on himself, scrubbing himself clean and thoroughly dousing his head and face multiple times before he put the basin on the floor and soaked and cleaned his feet in it. By the time he was done, Madrak had assembled a new set of black leather pants, green muslin shirt, a black ermine-lined vest, and a new wolf-furred cloak. Madrak withdrew to let his master finish dressing.

As the latch clicked shut on the door, Renaer finished rubbing himself dry with the towel, only to realize he was being watched. Vajra's face stuck out from between the curtains, a mischievous smile on her lips. While Renaer was hardly embarrassed, he was surprised, especially as he watched the woman's eyes shift between normal looking eyes to dark orbs to a pair of mismatched eyes, all as she rambled incoherently. Her facial expressions also constantly shifted, as if she were at war within herself.

"Tasty, just like a good strong lad he carried us all the way wish I could things he needs know protect me is he the Heir can he help something's wrong with the we need help fight Ten-Rings problem is son recover the Dusk owe him pain oh let me play . . ."

With that final reach and one of the most lascivious looks Renaer had ever received, Vajra fell unconscious again, her head and left arm resting on and over the end of the bed. Renaer pulled on his pants quickly and then got Vajra resettled in bed. Even when he lay beside her to pull up the furs and coverlet, she did not respond at all to his presence.

After he finished dressing, Renaer came down to the dining room. As he entered, Vharem turned toward the sound of the door. Laraelra's eyes also opened and locked on his. Meloon's light snore continued as the tall man's chin rested on his chest, his feet on the table, and his chair precariously tipped beneath him.

Madrak entered the dining room, cleared his throat, and said, "Varkel has returned, master. He—"

A blur pushed the door further open and rushed past Madrak. He ran right up to Renaer, his face red with exertion and windburn, his hair slightly frosted from the cold. "Master Renaer!" he shouted, and the noise woke up Meloon, whose sudden start tipped over his chair, and the young blond man fell flat on his back on the floor.

Varkel hardly noticed the crash or Vharem's snickering about it. He started talking very fast. "Master Renaer, they're saying such awful things. I could hardly stand there and listen to them spew such lies about you—what with how well you've been to us all these years. Now mind you, were I not to know that these kind folk were associated with your lordship, I might be inclined to believe—"

"Varkel, slow down," Renaer said. "Take a breath and simply tell me what's news on the streets. What happened when you told them about the Blackstaff?"

"I weren't never getting the chance to, master," Varkel said. "The crowds were so thick, and when they gave the pronouncements, I figured I should highstep it back here right soon!"

"What did they say?" Meloon asked.

The sandy-haired halfling took a deep breath and began speaking very quickly. "Rashemel Steeldrover, the Watchlord of the North Towers, she gave the pronouncements from the steps of the palace, which seemed odd, considering—"

"Varkel! Focus!" Madrak and Renaer said simultaneously.

"There are warrants out for the arrests or information leading to the arrest of Renaer Neverember and any present associates, including Ararna, Pellarm, Vharem Kuthcutter, and Faxhal Xoram, for having allegedly conspired against the Lords' Rule, having knowingly undermined and interfered with the guild business of the Watchful Order of Magists and Protectors, having trespassed upon private property and caused extensive damage thereupon, having caused grave harm to be visited upon the Watch and other persons, and other sundry charges to be visited upon those so warranted at the time of their arrest and summoning for trial."

Laraelra surprised herself when her response was a light chuckle of disbelief. "But . . . that's . . ."

"Fully fabricated and false, I know, but actionable as far as the city's citizens are concerned," Renaer said. "Still, it's another sign that we're in slightly over our heads until we get some help equal to the quality of that stacked against us."

"We better get going, then," Vharem said. "I've a few ideas, Ren—know a few places we can go."

He shook his head. "Thanks, but I've got the perfect place in mind. I meant to take you, Faxhal, and Torlyn earlier, but things got busy."

"They're right, master!" Varkel cried. "You have to flee! Shrunkshanks and I ran as fast as we could, but we've not the speed nor the longest of legs to stay ahead of a battalion of Watchmen."

A loud pounding reverberated from downstairs, a mailed fist against the solid oak door.

Varkel hopped up onto the seat by the bay window, looked out, and said, "There's about a dozen Watchmen outside, and they've brought a battering ram to get through the doors."

"It doesn't look like they're going to use it," said Meloon. "They're talking to someone at the door."

"Nolan has gone down to stall them," Madrak said, "and while he is capable of confusing them awhile, he cannot stop them, should they lose patience."

"Right," Renaer said. "If they're in the front entry hall, we can't go back the way we came." The young Lord Neverember moved to the window to confirm Meloon's observation, talking over his shoulder to the halfling. "Madrak? The garden path?"

"I understand," Madrak said. "I'll fetch what you need." He shuffled out of the room just as a loud boom signaled the end of the Watch's patience.

Renaer sighed. "They've thrown Nolan into the street and started using the battering ram. Here's what we have to do. Meloon, look under those window seats there and there"—Renaer pointed to the bay windows across the room—"and grab as many furs as you can. We'll meet you upstairs once you have them." He put his finger to his lips and then pointed at Vharem. "Can you dash to the kitchens and have Ellial put together some quick provisions for the five of us? Meet us up in the garden. Elra, with me, please."

Renaer motioned for Laraelra to join him and they half-ran out of the room. They turned down the hallway and entered the library. Laraelra breathed in the smell. She loved the scent of tanned leather and vellum and that slight hint of mildew and dust common among old books. Bookshelves lined the north wall from floor to ceiling, but there were large gaps among the books in them. Two tables at the room's center held large piles of books, some opened and some stacked haphazardly. Renaer moved to the large fireplace on the eastern wall. He grasped the corner cornice and slid it upward into the mantle. The nearest bookshelf clicked, and its lower half swung open, revealing a hidden area behind it.

"We'll need these. I don't have time to check which ones, so we'll take them all." Renaer pulled the bookcase open further and he and Laraelra knelt down. Set into the stone wall was a recessed shelf on which were five books bound in black leather with ornate silver clasps. Renaer pulled them out and loaded them into her arms.

"Whose books are these, and why do we need them now?" Laraelra asked. The books thrummed beneath her touch—she could feel there was magic within them. The drumbeat of the battering ram echoed through the mansion.

Renaer shouldered the shelf back into place and headed for the door. "I'll explain later. Right now, we've got to get out of here."

"Let me guess—there's a hidden slide in the walls that'll whisk us to the alley out back?"

"Even better, but we need to hurry."

Loud retorts joined the battering ram's blows as the door started to crack. Renaer heard someone yelling down in the entry hall, "The door's cracking! Get the bar up here now!"

The two of them ran from the library and up the stairs to the third floor. They met Meloon, his arms piled high with various bear, wolf, and ermine pelts.

Laraelra asked, "Renaer, why aren't you carrying something? The rest of us—"

"Fine," Renaer snapped as he opened the door to his room. "I'll let *you* carry Vajra, then, and I'll take Varad's books."

He crossed the darkened chamber to his desk, pulled open the right-hand drawer, and pocketed a large ring of keys. He then moved over to the bed. Vajra lay beneath a heavy fur cloak, which Renaer kept on her as he picked her up gingerly. She groaned and threw an arm around Renaer's neck without coming fully awake.

Renaer whispered, "Head back out into the hall and turn right. Look for a stone rosebud on the wall."

The four of them moved quickly out of the room and down the passage, soon followed by Vharem, who ran up the stairs with two armloads of parcels, from one of which jutted two long loaves of bread. The hallway past Dagult's office ended at a deep curved recess in the wall, stone roses carved in relief all over the back of it.

Meloon chuckled. "First the sewers, then a secret door privy, and now a garderobe. Lovely smells follow our adventure at every turn."

Renaer smirked, and nodded to the sorceress. "Elra, turn that last stone rosebud on the right-hand side toward us, please?"

Laraelra shifted the books into one arm, and she did as directed. Above the pulse of the battering ram, they heard the grinding of stone as a circular stair descended from the ceiling down into the garderobe. A slim pillar of stone rose from the floor of the garderobe to add support to the center of the stairs as well. A chill breeze came down with the stairs, as did Madrak's voice. "Hurry masters and milady, the Watch is almost inside!"

They mounted the spiral stairs, Renaer having to choose his steps gingerly and make sure Vajra's head did not hit anything as they ascended. When they reached the top, they found themselves greeted by Madrak, all wrapped in a heavy cloak. Once all of them were up the stairs, Madrak shoved a metal bench over the stairwell, and the stones recoiled back into place.

"I'm not seeing a way out of here, Renaer!" Laraelra looked over the rooftop garden, its plants in decay or wrapped in burlap to help them survive the coming winter. The entire roof was a meticulously designed garden with tiled paths and a walkway around the perimeter that might have an arbor of roses arcing overhead in summer. With the winter, the terraces and flower beds and arbors were bare mausoleums of dead vegetation. "Do you mean for us to jump down to the roofs of your neighbors?" Laraelra saw the look of excitement on Meloon's face and frowned at him. Despite the strong sunlight, the slight wind made it bitterly cold.

"Be quiet and follow me, all of you. Madrak, if you please. We'll meet you later, if or when you can join us. If Father or the Watch continues to hunt for me, tell him or them I'm off with some lissome young priestess learning about yet another god and its promises—and no hinting at malefic gods this time, mind you."

Renaer and Madrak each winked and smiled at each other, and then moved across the roof. Meloon and Laraelra hurried to keep up with the short butler.

His white hair whipping in the wind, Madrak stopped in one corner in front of a small statue of a kneeling elf maid, her hands cupped as if drinking water. The halfling whispered, "While I pour water into her hands, the gate remains open. Go quickly, and may Brandobaris grant your feet speed."

Renaer nodded and stepped inside the arbor, cradling the still-unconscious Vajra. As Madrak poured water into the statue's hands, Renaer stepped forward and was gone. Meloon stepped back in surprise, while Laraelra said, "Fascinating. Not even any flash or hint of magic."

"Get moving and follow him!" said Madrak. "This only works once a day and only with one stream of water. Now hurry!"

Vharem smiled and followed Renaer's footsteps exactly. "Thanks, Madrak!" he said as he vanished into thin air.

Laraelra stepped under the arbor and along the same path as Renaer. She also rushed into nothingness. Meloon timidly followed suit and vanished just as Madrak's bucket poured the last of its water into the statue's hands.

Madrak smiled as not one drop of water remained to betray what he'd been doing. He quickly walked back to the servants' exit, hugging himself for warmth. He left his cloak on a peg just inside the three-foot-high hidden exit. When he descended through the passage down to the kitchen, he stopped and peered through a spyhole and found exactly what he expected—a cadre of Watchmen bullying the staff for information.

Time to buy the young heroes some time to do some good, Madrak thought. 'Tis about time someone did.

Inside the door, he had left an empty slop bucket to explain what he'd been doing—throwing kitchen scraps onto the compost on the roof. As he had done exactly that, there was no way for anyone to claim he lied. Now he simply had to stall for time and keep the Watch from asking too many questions about his lord.

CHAPTER EIGHT

More has been lost in Waterdeep's City of the Dead than the innocence of youth. Its shadows hold far worse than a chill. Its stones cover more than bones and ossuaries.

Savengriff, *Swords, Spells, and Splendors*,
Year of the Harp (1355 DR)

10 NIGHTAL, YEAR OF THE AGELESS ONE (1479 DR)

KHONDAR NEARLY JUMPED OUT OF HIS CHAIR WHEN AN UNEXPECTED knock on his door disturbed his inadvertent nap. The tome he had been reading before he fell asleep tumbled to the floor. Already, his dream of a wizard in charge of each ward of the city faded to obscurity.

"Who dares disturb me?" he snapped. He picked the tome off the floor as he adjusted his chair. He placed the tome inside his desk and closed the drawer.

"The Blackstaff," came the reply.

"Come in, come in," Khondar said. "I'm honored by the Blackstaff's presence." Behind the closed door, Ten-Rings grimaced at the irony of what he said, given his hatred of the man whose guise his son wore.

The man entered the chamber and closed the door behind him. "Can we talk here?" the Blackstaff asked. "Is it safe?"

"Yes," Khondar said. "One of the few benefits of this poor office location is that a previous tenant set rather durable spells to prevent anyone from hearing anything from without."

"She finally gave up some secrets, Father." The Blackstaff's form shimmered, and the bearded face of Khondar's son smirked at him.

"What are you prattling about, boy?" Khondar said. "She's been out of our grasp since last night—thanks to your and Granek's failures."

Centiv frowned at the reprimand, his shoulders slumping, and he said, "I've already apologized for that. There was nothing I could do, short of being captured myself. I stabbed her to keep her from talking and hid her as best I could in short time."

"They're children and amateurs, Centiv," Khondar said. "You should have just blown them all away." Khondar turned away and stared out his window.

"In those tight corridors? I'd have roasted myself!" Centiv growled. "Not all of us can hide behind so many magical rings to protect us from spells blowing back on us."

Khondar's face blazed with tight-lipped fury, but he kept his temper when he asked, "What was it you came to tell me? How does Vajra spill her secrets now?"

Centiv beamed. "I had a tome and quill magically recording everything said within her cell. I'd hidden it behind an illusion in the cell across from her. After I left Roarke House with those records and books just ahead of the invaders, I used one of my other illusory guises and went to her chambers we keep over on Keltarn Street. I spent much of the night reading the transcript. Vajra had babbled a few things—names, locations, dates, item names, and the like—but we never thought they were anything more than random thoughts or words to stall Granek's next wound. She repeated them at night when Granek and we were gone, as if she were talking to herself. When you look at them all at once, they have a pattern—"

Khondar got up from his chair slowly, glowering, and asked, "You recorded everything?"

"Yes, and when I found—"

"*Everything?* Centiv, you fool! That's now evidence of our direct involvement!"

"I already destroyed the evidence, Father—once I confirmed she spoke the truth."

"What?"

"I found a pattern in a few passages of the transcripts. Each place she mentioned also corresponded to a person's name she blurted out. I've spent the day looking at every place she mentioned and found every person she named. Once my status as the Blackstaff cowed people out of my way, I could search for secret chambers or compartments in their locations. I found a few scraps of parchment hidden in each location. By themselves, the parchment scraps are nothing but trash. But together . . . well, here."

Centiv tossed the dozen fragments up into the air and cast a minor spell on them as they floated. They fell into place as one scrap on Khondar's desk. They spelled a single name: *Sarael.*

Khondar looked up at his son, irritated, and raised an eyebrow in question. Centiv smiled and motioned with his hand to flip the parchment over to reveal Elvish script on it.

Khondar sighed. "You know I don't read Elvish, Centiv. Stop showing off and tell me what you know."

"It says, 'The first heir of his body points the way to a new heir of his spirit. The Tears light the way.' I am certain this refers to Khelben Arunsun, the first Blackstaff. His first son was Sarael Arunsun, whose mausoleum resisted the Spellplague, unlike many others. We simply need to wait for moonrise and visit the tomb of Sarael Trollscourge in the City of the Dead. There, we should find what we seek."

Khondar thought long and silently, his fingers steepled in front of his face, his gold and silver rings all glistening. He nodded finally and looked up at Centiv. "Very good work, Son. I'll send Eiruk Weskur with you in case you run into trouble. He's loyal to a fault and will just assume this is guild business. He'll meet you at the gates of the cemetery at nightfall."

"I don't need his help on this," Centiv said. "I could have done all this without telling you, after all. I might have just brought you the secrets after the fact!"

"Well, you didn't, and this isn't the first time you've had the chance to show initiative and failed me. I'm not going to let your tendency to panic when confronted with the unexpected ruin our plans. Now take Weskur with you and we'll mind-wipe him later if we must. Just get whatever the Blackstaff has hidden in that tomb."

"But I don't—"

"Enough!" Khondar slammed his hands down on his desk. "I will *not* be questioned by my own child! We'll meet at Roarke House when you have the secrets."

Centiv wrapped himself in the illusionary guise of Samark "Blackstaff" Dhanzscul. His illusions did not disguise his anger, though, and he slammed the door behind him. Khondar shook his head. He and his third son shared so much, like the magic that drove them from the superstitious backwater of Sundabar more than two decades ago. Unfortunately, they also shared a temper, and Khondar wondered how much longer their scheme would hold up before someone's temper lost it all.

"Of course, I know that," the Blackstaff told the guard. "My predecessor was the one who created that law. Now step aside. I mean to honor that predecessor's son this night, on the anniversary of his greatest victory. Worry not. Only benefit shall come from blind eyes toward us."

He levitated a large bag of coins at the guard, who took it, then nodded at his younger compatriot who unlocked the gate.

"Come along, Weskur," the Blackstaff said, waving his companion forward.

Eiruk Weskur complied, following the older wizard through the gates. He shuddered despite himself, knowing full well that there were many reasons why people were locked out of the City of the Dead at night. He shivered beneath his heavy wool cloak and hood, wishing he'd not recently cut his black hair to a short skullcap. Still, to work directly with the Blackstaff was worth the discomfort. He just wished he knew what they were doing, as he had only the spells he'd already prepared that day and two wands given to him by Guildsenior Khondar Naomal before he was told to meet the Blackstaff here two bells after sundown.

The two of them left Mhalsymber's Way through the Weeping Gate, so named for an unidentified ghost whose sobs could be heard only on the night of the new moon. Eiruk was glad Selûne shone nearly full and bright tonight, if only to keep that ghost at bay. Inside the gate, the moon shone brighter still, as the interior walls were mirror-smooth and reflected the light, even though they remained worked stone blocks on the street-side. Eiruk had not been in the City of the Dead in quite some time, and he was shocked at how ill-tended it seemed to be. The wide paths, cobbles that had become glazed smooth slabs under the Spellplague chaos, were cracked, and weeds jutted out everywhere along the avenues among the mausoleums. The once-carefully manicured lawns lay untended, rife with weeds and badly in need of trimming. More than a few trees were obviously dead, while others grew out of proportion or unnaturally. The shadowtop in their path looked like a wooden fountain, its trunk shattered and spreading out to fall back and reroot in fifteen different points around itself. That tree proved healthy and strong, even if it did grow over a small tomb, which now lay in rubble beneath its boughs.

Worse yet were the mausoleums and tombs. Eiruk knew they used to hold portals built by Ahghairon the Open Lord himself, allowing more burial space in uninhabited dimensions. The dangers of those portals had been put on display when the Gundwynds buried three of their own shortly after the Spellplague first hit Waterdeep. All those who entered the family's tomb and went through its portal were transformed into trolls or giants. All were maddened by the pains of transformation and rampaged through the city. While they were stopped by the Blackstaff and a contingent of the Watchful Order, no one could be restored, which led to the end of the Gundwynd Waterdeep clan in 1388. Ever since, scouts did extensive magical reviews before anyone entered any of the tombs—especially those warped by the Spellplague. At least a dozen tombs either winked out of existence or exploded in the magichaos of that time, while others morphed or shifted, their stone melting like butter at highsun. Only a handful remained utterly unchanged by that time, and the pair of wizards approached one of those now.

An adamantine statue of a warrior stood proudly atop its blue Moonshavian marble base, as it had since its creation more than three centuries ago. Eiruk liked the look and strength of Sarael the Trollscourge, his face clean-shaven, strong-jawed, and smiling triumphantly, his hair flowing in a breeze and frozen in metal. The warrior wore chain mail from shoulders to toe, his shield resting upside-down on its straight top, the point of the three-sided shield resting on his left knee. His arms held two battle-axes crossed high above his head, and as clouds passed over the moon, reducing the light, a slight blue glow shimmered around the axes. Eiruk remembered an old dwarven forge-magic called blueshine that might explain that. What he couldn't explain was why he was following the Blackstaff as they walked two complete circuits around the base of this small memorial. He had been busy looking at the statue, while the older wizard stared at the marble base. The Blackstaff swore when the moon's light faded, as if he were looking for something by moonlight.

"Watch for any changes or signs on the statue or the base when it's in moonlight," said the Blackstaff. "Tell me immediately if you see something."

With that, the old man pulled his hood close around his balding head. Eiruk peered carefully at the tomb as he walked three circuits around the base, passing the distracted wizard multiple times. As the Blackstaff looked low and at the base, Eiruk looked higher at the statue or their immediate surroundings. On his fourth circuit, Eiruk spotted a hidden blue glow, visible only to his mystically sensitive eyes, and said, "Blackstaff, I see something."

"What is it?" The Blackstaff scurried to his side.

Eiruk pointed and said, "Look there. It points to something."

The Blackstaff sighed loudly. "I've no desire to waste energy on a detection spell or analysis. Just show me where it points."

Eiruk and the Blackstaff stood between the tomb and the northern wall of the City of the Dead. Looking through the wide stance of Sarael's statue, he saw thin lines of magic glimmering in response to the moonlight. Two points led from the axes and intersected with a third line from the point of the shield. When the lines intersected, they became a stronger white beam that pointed directly to one spot on the back wall of a tomb within the shadow of the Beacon Tower.

"There are magic beams directed from this statue to the Ralnarth tomb there," Eiruk said as he pointed.

"Why that tomb?" The Blackstaff wondered aloud. "And what do the beams do?"

"The Ralnarths bought all holdings of the Estelmer clan," said Eiruk, "and I think the Estelmers were allies of the first Blackstaff long ago. That might be the connection. As for what they do, I can see they're conjurations overlaid with illusions, but I can't tell you more. If Vajra were here, she could easily discern these spells. If I may ask, where is your apprentice? She can do this task far better than I." Eiruk hoped he kept his face impassive as he asked. He respected the Blackstaff and his power, but he still pined to be close to Vajra, despite her love for the older man.

"You may *not* ask, underling."

Eiruk became uncomfortable beneath Samark's long and angry stare. He returned his attention and concentration to his spell.

"Show me where the beams touch the tomb," the Blackstaff said.

Eiruk stepped up on the marble dais and crouched to maintain his line of sight. As he squatted, he rested his hand on the cold statue. A stabbing headache suddenly formed behind his eyes and a ghostly shimmer of the lights appeared in normal sight.

"Ah! Very good, Weskur!" the Blackstaff exclaimed.

The Blackstaff moved away to the back of the tomb and began chanting, weaving his fingers through a few simple spells directed at the wall. Eiruk realized that while the statue and his hand were cold, his fingernails glowed the same as the beams.

Eiruk could not discern what spells the Blackstaff cast at the beam's final point, but the younger mage's vantage offered him new insights. Eiruk watched the wizard mutter more arcane phrases, snapping his fingers through spell after spell to no apparent effect and then swear at the wall. The young man had worked briefly with the Blackstaff thrice before in the six years he had been with the Watchful Order, and now he could see that whoever stood before him, it was definitely not Samark Dhanzscul. That older man never swore, even in battle, and always used people's given names. Samark also spoke kindly and respectfully to everyone, from the lowliest servant to the guildmasters and Lords themselves. The contempt Eiruk heard in his voice should have warned him sooner. This person, while a decent enough actor to cow most with his illusionary form, was rash and impatient when faced with the unexpected. As Eiruk watched the wizard move, he detected a shimmer around the Blackstaff and another dark-haired form beneath his skin. He squinted, trying to see the man's face, but he couldn't over the distance with only moonlight.

Eiruk felt a tingling beneath his hand and turned his attention back to the statue. The inside of the shield that rested against Sarael's leg shimmered slightly with the same blue glow as the axes. Maintaining his contact with the statue but moving his hand along the cold metal, Eiruk shifted closer to the left leg and tentatively reached toward the shield with his right hand. He expected to touch cold metal, but instead felt warmth. He felt a throb of heat on his palm, and then the surface yielded and his hand sank inside— but not through—the shield. Eiruk could only feel warm air and the edges of the shield. He smiled, fascinated by the curious magic set by a long-dead wizard, one who truly earned the title of the Blackstaff—an honor for which Eiruk fervently wished.

The open hand of peace and a loyal heart gains you alone entry. Eiruk heard the deep voice in his head and struggled to keep his face from revealing his shock. He felt another stab of pain behind his eyes and heard the voice again. *If ye truly be friend, Blackstaff Tower will welcome you. All others will only enter to gain knowledge in accord with their hearts.*

Eiruk felt a searing sensation in his palm. It ended swiftly, and then he felt stone scrape against the top of his knuckles. A large bundle apparated beneath his touch. He closed his hand, hooking his fingers beneath what felt like leather bindings, and pulled a large parcel out of the shield. As he did so, the light emitting from the statue and the light inside the shield both winked out. Eiruk found no visible mark on his palm, though he felt magic pulsing beneath his skin. He would have to study it later—on his way to Blackstaff Tower for more answers. The leather bundle in his hand was sealed with a complex sigil unmistakable to many Waterdhavians—the wizard mark of Khelben Arunsun, lord of Waterdeep and the first Blackstaff.

"What happened?" The false Blackstaff turned around, angry at the interruption of his activity. "What did you do, Weskur?"

When he saw Eiruk held something, he dashed forward and snatched the leather bundle from his grasp.

Eiruk kept calm and said, "When you cast spells at that spot, the statue's shield here became some sort of portal. I reached in and withdrew this."

The false Blackstaff tore at the leather bindings, ignoring Eiruk and the significance of his predecessor's mark on the parcel.

Inside the surprisingly supple and warm leather wrap were two bundles. One, wrapped in lighter kid leather and stamped with an Elvish rune Eiruk didn't recognize, was round with an obvious bulge on one side. The other was an elaborate scroll tube carved from a dragon's leg bone and set with gold-plated runes and many gems. From the weight of the bundle, Eiruk also knew the tube held far more than the usual few parchments.

Eiruk watched the Blackstaff examine the parcel and tube. The young man resisted the urge to expose the imposter before him. Eiruk knew there was no one here to help him, and his foe's power might be far stronger than his subterfuges. For now, the young wizard held his tongue. Perhaps Maerla Windmantle, another guildsenior of the Watchful Order and one with whom he usually studied and worked, would be able to help. If he could find Vajra, they could expose this fraud of a Blackstaff.

The false Blackstaff looked up at Eiruk. "You should smile, for you've done well. You have the Blackstaff's thanks." The false Blackstaff retied the leather straps and tucked the bundle into his belt pouch. "Let us return to the Towers of the Order and show Master Naomal the fruits of our work tonight."

Eiruk could resist no longer. He had to test the lying wizard as the pair of them headed back toward the Weeping Gate. "As you wish, milord. If I may, will you tell your apprentice Vajra that I asked after her welfare? If she is ill, I'd be happy to visit any apothecary."

The Blackstaff shot a look back over his shoulder at the younger man. "Thank you for your offer, Eiruk, but no matter. Vajra suffers naught. She merely winters with her family down among the hills of Tethyr. She returns with the spring." With that, he pulled his hood tight around his head and said nothing more.

Eiruk worried that this imposter had harmed Vajra. While she only returned his love as friendship, Eiruk knew Vajra would not leave the city without saying farewell.

No, Eiruk thought. Maerla needs to learn of this tonight, no matter how late.

"Thank you, Eiruk," Ten-Rings said. "That will be all. *Return to your room and remember nothing of this night but a long, peaceful sleep.*"

The wizard finished his spell, and Eiruk Weskur walked calmly out of his office and down the stairs toward the younger guild members' dormitories. Once he was gone out of sight, Khondar closed the door, turned around, and said, "Not here." He rested his hand on his companion's shoulder and said, *"Oralneiar."*

The two men disappeared from the Tower of the Order with a chuff of imploding air.

They reappeared in a small, cold room lit only by a meager fire. Two tables flanked the hearth, both piled with scrolls and books. The table farthest from the window held a sculpture of two human hands carved from hematite, rings winking on every digit.

"Show me," Khondar said. "Show me, boy!"

Ten-Rings muttered a few arcane words, and two glowballs flared to life above the tables in his work chamber.

"I wasn't sure what we had, but I recognized both Khelben's mark and the Elvish rune." Centiv's face shimmered back into focus as he dropped his Blackstaff illusion. He reached to the rough table beneath the window and handed his father the tome Samark had brought with him out of Khelben the Elder's tomb. The sigil on the cover matched the one on the kid leather bundle.

Ten-Rings muttered, "That book's protections proved beyond our skills."

His hands out of Khondar's sight, Centiv clenched his fists in frustration against the constant jabs. He had spent eleven days more than Khondar studying the tomes, and he knew the words and letters just swam about, as if he tried to read the book through a foot of wind-shimmered water. When he could catch a recognizable letter or sigil, he could only tell it was a word in Dwarvish, the next in Elvish, another in some form of Draconic. Centiv hated that his father rushed to judge what was beyond Centiv's skills when Khondar's own proved lacking.

"I *know*, Father." Centiv said. "But given that sigils on the covers match, perhaps this can help us with the book." Centiv unwrapped the kid leather to reveal a hand-sized lens of clear amber crystal.

Khondar snatched the crystal away from Centiv with a growl and held the crystal over the first page of the tome. Through the lens, the page swam as usual, but after a moment, both could see the letters stop shimmering and settle into place. Better still, the letters reformed into Common, and both men read the title.

Lore and Awareness of the Dark Archmage's Acolytes: On the Assumption of Power as the Blackstaff or the Blackstaff's Heir.

Beneath the title page were five signatures—*Khelben Arunsun, Tsarra Chaadren, Kyriani Agrivar, Krehlan Arunsun,* and *Ashemmon of Rhymanthiin*—and their wizard marks after them.

Laughing loudly, Khondar threw an arm around Centiv's shoulders, a move from which his son initially flinched before smiling at the show of paternal pride.

"You've done it!" Khondar said. "You've found the way we can make the Blackstaff's power our own! Now if we can just make sure that Tethyrian bitch stays out of the way . . ."

"In a way, I did so earlier today . . ." Centiv's flush of pride deepened as he thought about the report his agent Charrar brought to him the previous dawn. While he bristled at the costs in lives and gold, Centiv was grateful he had had to silence only one agent instead of six to cover his tracks. He marveled at the luck Renaer and his friends seemed to have. They had very nearly caught him, all thanks to that skinny witch's muting spell. Before this was over, Centiv knew he had to rip the secret of that spell from her, both to resist it and to exploit it. With that spell, he might even force his father to acknowledge him as an equal . . .

·:⌒:·

Dagrol, the Watch armar, entered Shank Alley along with an accompanying wizard of the Watchful Order, both of them with their staves at the ready. The five other Watchmen were either in the alley already or at either end, keeping folk from entering and disturbing the scene. Dagrol approached his firstblade and asked, "Who found her, Barlak?"

"He did," the watchman pointed at a young boy taller than Dagrol. Despite the cold, the boy wore no shirt beneath his apron, and his muscles showed Dagrol he was used to hauling around loads of heavy fish. "His name's Karel."

"Talk to him, would you?" Dagrol asked the wizard at his side, who nodded and walked away. "Where's the victim?"

Dagrol's impatience was well-known by his patrol, and the young man nodded up the alley to the left. Dagrol found his best vigilant assessing the scene. Tasmia looked up at him, gray eyes somber and haunted.

The body lay tucked against the rough rear exterior of the Filleted Filliar hearthouse. The woman's body had been shoved roughly behind and beneath large stacks of discarded garbage, fish guts, and other assorted offal. Her body was a mass of welts, scars, and wounds, but Dagrol's eyes fell on two wounds in particular.

A dagger jutted out of her right eye, and a short sword had been driven up beneath her ribs and directly into her heart. The blades were ornately decorated along the hilts.

"You ever seen work like that before?" Dagrol asked Tasmia, who knelt beside the body.

"The killing blows, yeah," Tasmia said. "Standard moves to make sure someone's definitely dead, despite all other wounds. Overly showy blades are all the rage right now among the rich, too. The details on that basket-hilt sword, though, give up our suspect right away."

"Who is it?"

"Well, those arms—the bear's claw atop a diamond, all atop a field with three stripes from dexter to sinister—belong to the Neverembers. Unless you think the Open Lord's killing women in alleys these days, I'd say we need to find young Renaer Neverember. And we'd better do it quickly." Tasmia pulled a rough woolen blanket over the body, and whispered a quick prayer. "Selûne keep her soul safe from the predators that claimed this body."

"Aye." Dagrol nodded, sighing deeply. "Anybody else recognize her?"

"Just me, Dag," Tasmia said as she stood, brushing mud off her leathers. "She's Vajra Safahr, lover and heir of the Archmage of the City. If we want justice served, we'd better arrest Renaer and any accomplices before the Blackstaff finds them."

"Gods help us if that happens." Dagrol shuddered. "If he's like his mentor Ashemmon at all, we'll need a lot more gravediggers."

CHAPTER NINE

No one ever knew what happened to old Varad Brandarth. Many said he went mad. I knew he was mad before the Spellplague, so it couldn't have been that. I suspect he had one or three hidden safeholds of which only he knew.

Elchor Serison, *Sorcery & Trust,*
Year of the Silent Bell (1435 DR)

10 NIGHTAL, YEAR OF THE AGELESS ONE (1479 DR)

RENAER STEPPED INTO DARKNESS. HIS FOOTSTEPS ECHOED LOUDLY. "Kamatar," he said, and fires flared to life in the two hearths on opposite sides of the room.

Vajra stirred in his arms and opened her eyes. Renaer flinched as he saw her eyes waver between the red-black maelstrom orbs and normal eyes of different colored irises. She grimaced, creasing her brow, and her eyes briefly focused into almond-shaped eyes of deep mahogany brown.

"Where am I holding me wait aren't you no a friend carry a vampire's victim?" she said.

Vharem appeared behind them, followed by Laraelra and Meloon. All of them stumbled slightly when they apparated.

Vajra, whose attention shifted quickly to look over the new arrivals. "I don't know . . ." Vajra tapped Renaer on his shoulder and pointed down with her eyes.

"Welcome to Varadras, milady Safahr, everyone," Renaer said, setting her on her feet. Renaer noticed the others looking around the room, but the skies beyond the windows were dark, and snow and ice covered much of their openings. Renaer said, "Palnethar," and torches flared to life on each wall and inside a long hallway leading out of it. Cobwebs covered many surfaces and corners, and the chamber warmed now only due to the presence of the hearthfires.

"Neat trick, Renaer," Vharem said. "You never told us you were studying wizardry."

"Varad taught you don't know where how we'll survive when you are mage?" Vajra said, and while she rambled, she approached and touched Renaer, her fingers glowing with magic. "No he casts not words for any safehouse fine for now don't trust it calm down among friends." Renaer heard her voice change inflections and pitch as she spoke. Her eyes shifted as well, flitting between different colors and shades of gray, brown, green, purple, and a dark blue. Still, she stood steadily, looking around the room and smiling.

"You knew Varad?" Renaer asked.

Vajra's only response was an arched eyebrow and a nod of her head toward Vharem.

Renaer remembered how frustrating it was to talk to wizards who liked their secrets. "She's right, if I understood her correctly," her said. "I'm not a wizard, but I've been studying up on this place and my ancestor who built it three generations ago. He set a lot of magic in place, and most remained stable despite the Spellplague. Mostly, Varadras is just a place to get away. My father has no way of finding me here. The manor house is invisible to those outside of it unless you approach within a certain range."

"So where are we?" Meloon asked. He stood at the nearest window, scraping away some ice and rubbing a window clear. "I only see a lot of trees around us. We're not in Waterdeep?"

"We're about a hundred miles due west of Beliard, the town near the Stone Bridge," Renaer said. While he spoke, he led his friends down the hallway, and more torches lit up as they approached, those in the distant entry chamber snuffing themselves accordingly. Renaer led them past three doors before he stopped, opened a broad pair of double doors, and said, "Dornethar."

Inside that chamber, fires flared to life on three hearths and on six torches set high on the walls. The group entered a carpeted study with shelved books lining the walls. Unlike the other chambers festooned with cobwebs, this room was pristine and cold, though warming quickly. A massive desk of dark wood loomed to the right of the main fireplace, its surface disturbed only by a gleaming ball of dark red crystal and a massive tome lying open.

The five of them rushed toward the hearths opposite or flanking the doors to warm themselves. Vajra, who had followed the group with Laraelra guiding her like a child, rushed over to the right, approached the shelves behind the desk, and pushed in a single tome. Without a sound, the shelves swung inward, revealing a secret passage, and Vajra disappeared into the darkness, chuckling.

"Where does that go, Renaer?" Laraelra asked.

They all moved toward the secret door. Laraelra slammed the set of books she carried on the desk as she passed it, heading into the dark room. She muttered a short series of magical syllables, and her fingernails took on a blue glow as she walked.

"I don't know!" Renaer said. "I didn't even know that was there. It's not mentioned in any of the notes or plans." He repeated the words "palnethar" and "dornethar," but no torches sputtered to life inside the passage.

Laraelra finished casting a spell, and a blue glow filled the room. The small windowless chamber lay revealed as a wine cellar, racks of bottles lining the back and side walls and the left-hand long wall left empty to allow passage without disturbing the bottles. Many racks were empty along the right, but the back wall still held nearly its full complement of bottles.

Vajra stood at the center of the wine cellar holding a bottle of wine and blowing off its mantle of dusty webs. She laughed and said, "Varad kept his best never been here how'd she do never mind we must oh bother let's just drink it no share it not for dining keep clear head." She kept muttering and arguing with herself so that she didn't resist when Vharem eased the bottle out of her grasp.

When he looked at the bottle Vharem's eyebrows rose and he whistled a low unbelieving tone. "Renaer, this single bottle's probably worth a tenday's worth of tavern jaunts! The Surrilan vineyards died out in the drought seventeen summers back—and this bottle's more than eighty years old!"

"So that's good wine, then?" Meloon asked, reaching for another bottle.

"Some of the best," Renaer replied. "Vajra, how did you know this was here?"

The dusky woman smiled, her eyes flitting from purple to gray to blue to sea green. "Varad Brandarth was . . . a good student . . . faithful friend. Stingy with his wine . . ." She reached up for another bottle and wiped the dust and webs off on Laraelra's robes before the sorceress could stop her. She smiled and said, "Pikar Salibuck introduced us. Many secrets shared . . . best was this." She waved an arm around to indicate the room. "Gods, we tried . . ."

As Vajra whirled with her arms outstretched, her eyes rolled into the back of her head, and she collapsed. Laraelra grabbed enough of her sleeve to slow her before her head slammed into the stone floor, and Vharem made a mad dive to catch the falling bottle of wine. Laraelra shot him a look as she tried to settle the unconscious wizard onto the ground.

Vharem shrugged and said, "What? You had her, and we can't have her rolling around on shards of glass or soaking in priceless wine."

Meloon lifted Vajra and headed with the others back to the study. Renaer kept looking around at the contours of the room, nodding to himself, and examining the bookshelf-door and its triggering book.

"Care to explain all that?" Meloon asked as he placed Vajra on a long divan in front of the small hearth on the eastern wall.

"Varad Brandarth and Pikar Salibuck were both wizards of some note decades past," Renaer said. "They had a friend and mentor in common across the years—the Blackstaff, or at least one of them anyway. I think Vajra is possessed or has some memories of the previous Blackstaffs."

"Just realized that?" Laraelra said.

Renaer opened his mouth to respond, and then exhaled loudly and forced his hands to relax at his sides. "We're all on edge with everything that's happened, and we've had no sleep or food. Fellows, let's leave the ladies here while we find some food to go with this wine." Renaer set a bottle down on a side table, and wrestled the other two from Vharem's grip.

Laraelra sighed and said, "You're right. We all need some rest. Then with a brighter day, we can approach this with clear heads. Maybe remember things we're forgetting now. Renaer, I—"

"Offer apologies by watching her?" Renaer said, nodding at Vajra. "Thank you. Stay warm while we go forage some more food."

Meloon grabbed a few furs off the pile he'd dumped in a corner, and gave two to Laraelra and draped another over Vajra.

"Pikar was Madrak's father, by the way." Renaer said, over his shoulder. "When I was a child, I heard loads of stories that are in few histories about the hin sorcerer of Blackstaff Tower. I'll have Madrak share some of them later."

Renaer led Meloon and Vharem out of the room and closed the double-doors. The three men all shivered as they left the warm chamber for the chilly corridor. Renaer led them to the end of the hallway, down a flight of stairs, and into a large kitchen area. Renaer stayed silent, so the hearth fires did not flare up, icy downdrafts alone disturbing the cobwebs at the chimney. Meloon looked out the kitchen windows, only to see the swirl of heavily falling snow. They walked through a large pantry and down another short flight of stairs into a root cellar filled with dried herbs and bushels of potatoes and such.

"Awfully big place, Renaer." Meloon whistled. "Who did you say lived here?"

"Varad Brandarth, my grandfather's uncle. He was a wizard and one of

Khelben the Blackstaff's last students. This place he kept secret from most of his family. My mother discovered the hidden portals leading to it almost thirty years ago. Varadras was empty for more than forty years after Varad died until Mother found it."

"And old Dagult doesn't know about this?" Vharem said. "Seems a piece of property he'd love to get his hands on."

"Mother always thought of this as her secret place," Renaer said, "and she shared it with me alone. Apparently, she found Varad's hidden journals by accident her nineteenth winter, and she hid here whenever she needed. Even though she held few secrets from Dagult, she never told him everything about her family or its holdings. He has never heard of this place. Nor will he."

The young lord led them through the root cellar, tossing an empty bushel at Vharem and then launching a dozen potatoes and half as many onions at him to collect in it.

"So your mother was a wizard?" Meloon asked.

"No," Renaer said as he examined a ring of dried apples before setting it back on its hook. "Neither one of us could read his spellbooks, but his journals are mundane and readable. They recorded most of the words that activate magic around the manor. Even you could activate them if you knew the words."

The trio now entered one room with three archways off of it, all stone walls and ground whereas the root cellar had a bare dirt floor. Their breath clouded the air around them, as it was only slightly warmer in here than outside in the blizzard. Renaer opened one jar the size of his head and sniffed. "Hmph. If we take this up with us, the honey should thaw out by the fire. Good stuff too. Varad kept bees here, and his honey was among the few trade goods that supplemented his stipend from the family coffers."

"If all this was here, why did I need to bring food along?" Vharem complained as he examined a few large crocks of pickles.

"The only stuff Madrak and I keep here are things that won't spoil easily," Renaer said. "Unless you wanted to eat only dried meat, honey, and pickled vegetables, what we brought with us should help keep us fed for a day or so until we return to the city."

"Why wait a day?" Meloon asked. "I think Vajra needs some help."

"I think it's something to do with the Blackstaff's power, not her health. We'll have to ask her when she revives."

"Let me guess," Vharem said. "The portal that got us here only works once a day?"

"Close enough," Renaer said. "Besides, Meloon and Vajra are the only ones who've actually gotten any sleep. We need to eat, rest, and then we'll plan our return."

Meloon smiled and said, "Hey, that's a good idea." He reached up and grabbed a large cured ham covered in dusty white mold. "Let's eat this too, then."

Renaer paused as he entered the farthest larder and said, "Wait a moment. Something's been here since I was here a few months back."

"Probably just a rat or three." Vharem snorted. "Not even wizardry can keep those things out if there's food to be had."

"Bigger than a rat, and I don't know of vermin that stack things to reach high cupboards," Renaer said, nodding toward a haphazard column of boxes atop a chair in one corner.

Meloon looked close at the disturbed dust on the floor and said, "Big feet, too."

"Thanks." A dry laugh answered them from the shadows.

The trio launched into action. Meloon whirled, his axe in his hands. Vharem whipped out his newest short sword on loan from Neverember Hall. Renaer flicked a dagger into each hand and yelled the word *"Ronethar!"* In response, the very air in the room took on an amber glow, illuminating every corner and leaving no shadows in which to hide.

Lying atop one of the high cupboards and peering down at them was a young halfling, now grinning. The hin's bushy sideburns were a chestnut brown, like the curly hair on his head, and he dressed in black, which had helped him hide from them in the dark. Silver rings glinted in his left nostril and earlobe. He rolled onto his back and giggled, swinging his feet down off the high cupboard on which he lay.

"Well, if the gods aren't chuckling!" the halfling said between bites of a raw potato. "Hiya, Renaer, Vharem! Whatchaguys doing here? Who's the big blond axeman? Anybody got any tinder to start a fire? I'm freezing."

The double-doors to the study opened, and a halfling stumbled through them, followed by Renaer, who shoved him forward. Vharem and Meloon, each laden with food, followed.

"Everyone, meet Ellial's son and Madrak's grandson, Osco Salibuck."

Osco recovered from his stumble, cartwheeled across the remainder of the room, and landed easily on a footrest by the fire at the center of the southern wall. The hin gleefully rubbed his hands and buttocks, standing to absorb more warmth from the fire and sighing with pleasure. "Haven't been warm for three days, thank Brandobaris for this," he muttered, and then turned back to the group. "You used to be nicer to me, Ren, when we were the same height," He raised his eyebrows when he noticed Laraelra and Vajra stirring on the divans across the room. He slicked his hair back and jerked his thumb toward Renaer. "We grew up together, you know, and I could tell you stories about him. Why, when he was five—"

"We'd rather hear the story about how you got here," Renaer said, narrowing his eyes.

"Oh, enough about me," Osco said. "What are you doing here?"

"Uh-uh," Vharem said. "This little one's got a talent for avoiding questions—usually because he's filched something or stuck you with his tavern debt."

Osco clutched his hands over his heart and fell on his knees. "Oh, such barbs from one I called fellow and comrade!"

Vharem rolled his eyes.

"Answer me, Osco, or Madrak'll hear where you've been trespassing without invite."

Osco rolled his eyes and sat down hard. "You're no *fun* anymore, Ren. Just because I found out how you get here doesn't mean I'm going to *take* anything. There's no trust anymore."

Vharem cleared his throat, produced three silver forks, and waved them at Osco, who patted a belt pouch and then scowled at the slender human. He crossed his arms and sulked, muttering, "Just needed a place to lie low for a few days. Figured you'd not be here until spring. Sorry for intruding where I'm not wanted."

"Who're you hiding from, Osco?" Renaer said. "And how did you find out about this place and how to get here?"

"You and Gradam are always plotting," Osco said, "and I just made it a point to follow you around, quietlike. I watched you disappear from the garden and you returned the next day, so I figured, wherever it was, it was a safe place. I got Sharal to pour the water for me and ended up here three days ago. Three miserably uncomfortable days, mind you, as there's no fireboxes of wood around here. How'd you guys get this fire going?"

"Magic," Laraelra said. "I know you, little halfling, or at least I've heard of you. Someone matching your description posed as a cellarer and stole a lot of gems a few tendays ago from a client in Trades Ward. My father's still fighting with the Gralleths over that, and the only thing keeping it out of Lords' Court is the indisputable fact that there are no halflings in the Cellarers and Plumbers' Guild."

"You wound me, Lady Harsard," Osco chided, clasping his hands over his heart. "Besides, it could have been anyone shorter than him, as Malaerigo and Lord Chalras can't tell a halfling from a gnome or a dwarf, let alone identify any hin among hin."

"While that might be true," Laraelra said. "I never said which Gralleth was robbed."

Osco grimaced and then shot a wink and grin up at Meloon. "Women with brains. They'll be our downfall in every way, eh?"

Meloon looked down at the halfling and said, "And so the wagons roll, little friend."

"Enough!" Renaer yelled, and everyone started and looked at him. Vajra stirred a moment on her couch before settling back into unconsciousness. "Osco, you're coming back with us tomorrow when we leave. Stay with us, and maybe we can help you with whatever problem had you hiding out here. If you don't want to come back, good luck, but you're not staying here without someone to watch you."

"But it just got more comfortable," Osco whined. He shot a sly glance at the two women and said, "And it just got far better looking than it's been."

Vharem said, "I vote we just chuck him out in the snow. He'll only draw down more trouble on us."

"Oho! Renaer and Vharem are fleeing from trouble?" Osco's face lit up. "Did you get hired to help them out, big axeman, or are you all conspirators, kidnapping the Tethyrian over there?"

"No!" Meloon said.

Laraelra snickered at his shocked look. She snapped her fingers to get Osco's attention and said, "You're very good at deflecting attention off yourself, aren't you, little hin?"

"Yes, he is," Renaer said, "but I know him well enough to know when he's lying. Osco, help us out when we return to the city, or we'll just let Laraelra turn you over to her father and let the taols fall where they may."

"You'd betray a childhood friend, just like that?" Osco said. "Is that why that overgrown hin Faxhal isn't with you now? You left him to his creditors or something?"

Laraelra and Vharem gasped at the halfling, and Renaer felt like he'd been slammed in the stomach again. While others turned away, he met the halfling's gaze, his eyes watering, and Osco realized something truly bad had happened.

"Faxhal's dead, Osco," Renaer whispered.

Osco cleared his throat and said, "Sorry, Ren. Really."

For a few long moments, the only sounds were the crackle of flames in the fire grates. Then Renaer stood, opened a bottle of wine, and took a long drink. He passed it on, and Vharem, Meloon, Elra, and Osco each drank, then held the bottle toward the fire, silently saluting Faxhal. Osco returned the bottle to Renaer, who drained it. "Sleep, friends, and we'll leave come dawn."

Osco, his voice softer, asked, "Ren, why leave at all? This place is stocked well enough to keep us a while. Some of us can hunt for food too. Can't we hide out here until spring?"

"We must help Vajra. She's been tortured for the past month or more."

Osco's curly eyebrows shot up, he shot a glance toward Vajra, and then shrugged. "She looks fine to me. Must not have been too bad. They torture her with feathers?"

"I've had healers cure her body, but they can't repair her mind. She's the Blackstaff's heir, and there's someone back in Waterdeep posing as Samark the Blackstaff. He and Khondar 'Ten-Rings' Naomal, the Watchful Order's most arrogant guildsenior, are up to something, and they need her secrets."

"Why?" Osco asked. "What could she tell them? And why should we get involved in the Blackstaff's mess? It'll just lead to *us* being tortured—the kind *without* feathers!"

Vajra sat bolt upright on the divan, leveled steel blue eyes at the halfling and said, "You know many secrets that lie beneath black stones, Osco Salibuck. Do these deeds for me, and know the Blackstaff rewards his friends well." Her tone was grave and stern, but then she looked quizzically at Osco and asked, "When did your eye get restored?"

When Osco just looked at her strangely, the blue-eyed wizard stopped speaking, and then she collapsed back onto the couch, unconscious.

Osco looked at her, then Renaer, and the others, and said, "Bet she's fun at parties. I've never met her before in my life, so I don't know how she knew my name. And I've *no* idea what else she was blathering on about."

When Vharem shot him a disbelieving look, he pleaded, *"Honestly!"*

"She does that," Renaer said, "but she rarely speaks as clearly. Normally it's like there's a bunch of folk fighting to talk through her. I think if we take her to Blackstaff Tower, it might help her. At least it'd be a safer place for her to hide."

"So how does that make it our problem?"

"Because they knew we're aware that they're up to something, fool," Vharem said as he sliced off a large hunk of cheese from the wheel he'd brought with him. "Besides, if someone else steals her power as the Blackstaff, they could kill Renaer and all of us far too easily. Not to mention anyone else associated with Renaer, like a certain family of hin servants?"

Osco blanched, his connections to the trouble made clear. "Depending on where we can return to in the city, I can probably keep us all hidden from anyone looking for us. Anyone human, at least."

"How can you do that?" Meloon asked.

"Yes, how do you plan to help us avoid being caught?" Renaer said. "We're not even sure who our pursuers are other than Ten-Rings."

"I'll lead you through the Warrens beneath the city. It'll help me avoid others meself."

"Do the Warrens lead anywhere near Blackstaff Tower?" Renaer asked.

Osco's brow furrowed, and he said, "Not that I know of, but I'm sure we can get close."

"Is that easier than using the streets?" Laraelra asked.

"Easier?" Osco said. "Not for you tall ones. Safer? Yes. The Watch and most humans never had much presence in the Warrens beyond a few token gnome and hin Watch. Mostly because the Lords're too big and too arrogant to think that things among the small folk are worth noting. That's why there's a lot of things going on down there that make me gradam think I'm up to no good."

"Well, you skulk in the shadows pretty well," Renaer said, "and you always seem to be in trouble or fleeing from one moneylender to the next."

"And that hardly makes me worse than most of the young nobles and nigh-nobles of Sea Ward now, does it?"

"He's got a point," Laraelra chimed in, smirking.

CHAPTER TEN

Blessed are those enfolded by the Cloakshadow, for their enemies shall see them not, know them not. Things entrusted to the Illusory remain secret, until the time comes to draw back the cloak and reveal what Baravar held dear.

Ompahr Daergech, *Pantheonica, Volume IV,*
Year of the Guardian (1105 DR)

10 NIGHTAL, YEAR OF THE AGELESS ONE (1479 DR)

"MASTER OMPAHR," ROYWYN YELLED, "WE NEED YOUR HELP!" SHE hated trying to talk to the nigh-deaf elderly priest. Even her shouts barely penetrated his awareness.

"You can't have my heart, curse you!" The bald, white-bearded gnome half-sat up against a mound of cushions and pillows at the back of his somewhat sumptuous burrow. His quarters filled the back of the subterranean temple to Baravar Cloakshadow, his honored presence as the elder highpriest of the order apparent from the richness of the trappings about his personal burrow. Ompahr Daergech himself was a frail, wizened gnome who almost disappeared amongst the pillows.

Instead of answering, the young priestess took a helmet off a nearby shelf and handed it to him. It was a curious object—a metal skullcap with two ram's horns mounted over the ears. In opposite fashion from some overdone fighter's helm, the points of the horns went toward the ears and the open ends of the hollowed horns faced outward. The old gnome grudgingly took the helm and grumbled as he put it on. "What are you disturbing my meditations for, granddaughter Ellywyn?" His voice dropped as he realized how loudly he had been speaking.

"I'm Roywyn, Grandsire Ompahr—Ellywyn's granddaughter," she explained in a lower voice, now that he could hear better.

"Well, what do you want, whoever you are?" Ompahr's growl was now more playful. Both she and her ancestor knew each other, but continued the game nonetheless for their own amusement.

"There's someone here bearing your seal—your *green* seal," Roywyn said. Her hands communicated even more to Ompahr that would not be overheard in the tunnels. She knew their guest was wrapped in at least three spells—one illusion, one transmutation, and one divination spell—and that he was impatient and not terribly respectful. His hands also glowed brightly of magic, even though they appeared bare. The child continued talking while her hands flew fast to tell her great-great-great-grandfather all this. "He is a halfling who has come to pay his respects and asks a boon of you." Her final hand-signals elicited much giggling out of the aged gnome, as she explained that if he was truly a halfling, she was a hill giant—after all, he turned down their standard offer of something to eat when he crossed their threshold.

"Send the lad in, then," Ompahr said, "and leave us be." Ompahr's silent hand-signals told Roywyn to stay close but hidden, along with two other priests who could overpower their foe—or at least dispel his active magic and any more he planned to use.

When Roywyn returned, she escorted a male hin. He wore a non-descript cloak and leathers, his hood thrown back, and a pair of short wands tucked into his belt. He bowed, and Omphar looked at him with spell-enhanced sight. He saw who the man was beneath his transformations and illusions—a completely bald man with merged eyebrows and a thin salt-and-pepper goatee and mustache. He noted the ten rings on his fingers—only two of which glowed magically—and saw an additional wand strapped to his inner right forearm. Ompahr didn't know who he faced, but he grinned nonetheless. He hadn't had any fun with strangers in quite some time.

"Greetings, honored Ompahr Daergech," the halfling said as he stood up. "I bring you this—"

"Don't waste my time, boy!" Ompahr roared at him, far louder than he needed for his own hearing. "I'm too blasted old! Show me what you've brought, silly fool of a hin! And give me a name, or I'll call you Puckerpaws and make you match the name!"

The hin coughed once, nervously, and said, "Call me Harthen," and held out his left hand, palm up, to show the gnome priest a rolled scroll closed and impressed with a green wax seal. Written in the old Common trade tongue on the outside of the scroll was, "Take this to Ompahr Daergech or his heirs. They will guide you to your rightful legacy."

Ompahr wiggled his ring finger and the scroll levitated off Harthen's palm. "Hold your palms up to me, Harthen," he said.

Ompahr saw nothing, either on Harthen's palms or on the man's real palms beneath his spells. Well, he didn't find these himself or he'd have the mark on one of his hands, Ompahr thought. I wonder how he found an honest person to do so. The priest wiggled his index finger, and the seal popped off the scroll, the ancient parchment unrolling and brittle edges cracking as it did so.

Ompahr saw an empty scroll for a moment, and he whispered a prayer to his god. "Baravar, draw open the curtains of deceit over this and let me see what secrets we hide from ourselves and others."

Words shimmered into view—words in a strong hand, written in Gnomish. *"Your oath is fulfilled, friend. Give the bearer the right hand passkey, if my marks are on him."* In Ompahr's own hand—written so long ago there was no tremble or waver in his lettering, the scroll read, *"Grant the scroll's bearer the keys of the left hand, if he should come ablustering without the marks to show he passed Khelben's test."*

"So be it," Ompahr whispered. "No marks. No mercy."

"What does it say, wise one?" The halfling asked, lowering his unmarked palms.

Ompahr did not answer for a few breaths, and it amused him slightly to see his guest get increasingly agitated. While Ompahr loved playing games, he suddenly felt tired as his mind washed over memories of friends long fallen and oaths nigh-forgotten. Finally, he snorted. "Well, at least you're as properly impatient as a hin, I'll give you that. Your disguise is lacking, as is your subterfuge, wizard."

"How did you—" the figure exclaimed, then shook his head. "It matters not. Just tell me what the scroll bids, and I'll be back on the streets above where I belong."

"Unless we choose to cancel your magic." Ompahr leaned forward, his hand aglow with his threat. "You'd hardly be able to cast effectively or move easily, once your full form unfolded in my warren."

"Don't threaten me, gnome," the wizard said. "I've bested every challenger I've ever faced in arcane combat or otherwise. Some newcomers digging beneath my streets don't worry me, no matter their age or god."

Ompahr's smile drew tight and thin, his bushy eyebrows rising. "Supercilious shapeshifter. The Warrens have been here longer than ye know. Some existed long before there were human buildings up above us—well, aside from Hilather's Hold and a few temples. We just knew how to hide them better in days past. Once we told the hin about them, though, they invited everybody down here. Our secrets held for centuries among us and the dwarves, but once you tell a halfling a secret, it's a rumor in a breath and a fact by next highsun."

Ompahr's guest drew back, a confused look on his face.

"Did you think the dwarves and humans were the only ones drawn here to this upland?" the old gnome continued. "*Every* race in Faerûn feels the call of this place, one time or t'other, one road or t'other. Not all roads lead to Waterdeep, but precious few lead to more worthy destinations. Magic—not just a good harbor and defensible highland—drew folk here, till they fulfill their purpose on or under the shadow of the mountain. Me, I have a role to play yet. That's why I'm still here after so long—my oath to that scroll and him what wrote it with me."

Confusion danced across his enemy's face, shifting into anger every other moment. Ompahr delighted in toying with the intruder, and he chose to play his hand out in full now and see whether his foe would reach for the prize given or seek out more.

"The scroll talks of keys. Keys to power. I am bound to give them to the bearer of the scroll—save when that bearer brings false face and false name to me. Tell me a name I can believe, and they will be yours."

"Give me the keys, old fool!" His hands fidgeted and two of his rings glowed.

"Yer spells will avail ye little here, boy of ten hidden rings." Ompahr enjoyed the look of shock on the false halfling's face, but continued, making his voice its most serious in decades. "I've not used my sorcery in three times your lifetime, and I can still shrug off your worst with that and the Cloakshadow's blessings."

"I doubt that you understand my full measure, gnome," the man said. "Call me Ten-Rings, then. You'd not be alone in that."

Ompahr chuckled, then broke into a hoarse coughing. The ancient gnome fell back and turned away on his cushions, a wet phlegmy cough ending his seizure. When he regained his wheezing breath, he looked with one eye back at the man. "Ten-Rings," mused Ompahr. "So a senior of the Watchful Order comes scraping for the Blackstaff's power, does he?"

"You know of me, then?" Ten-Rings asked. "Then you know I work toward the city's good, not my own."

"I hear tell of a wizard whose pride and paranoia has him wearing ten rings to hide his magic and show it off at the same time," Ompahr said. "Some of my kin are among your guild, 'tis true, and they speak of your arrogance and magic."

"I am not proud. I simply acknowledge my own abilities. Unlike many others, I do not hide them."

"Why do you seek the keys, then?"

"The city has no Blackstaff nor heir," Ten-Rings said, "and I would put that burden on myself for the sake of the city."

Ompahr snorted and began a great long belly-deep laugh. When he finished, he wiped tears from his eyes and locked them on Ten-Rings. "You might fool others, but orcs make better lies to my face than you just did. You're after power, plain and simple."

"No!" Ten-Rings said. "Our city fares better beneath the rule of wizards like Ahghairon or Khelben, and I willingly shoulder that burden. I only seek to restore the city to its rightful stature again—with the rule of magic as well as law."

"Khelben never ruled outright," the gnome corrected. "And you hardly compare to Ahghairon either, wizard or no."

"I am mighty in magic and wise in the politics of the city," Ten-Rings said, "and I know I can serve the city better than that coin-pincher Dagult."

"That might be, child," Ompahr said, "but that neither makes you Open Lord nor Ahghairon, and I should know. He and I were students in Silverymoon together. I helped him make the first Lords' Helms."

"Challenge me to a duel of wits or spells. I shall prove my worth!"

"I'm too old and tired for such games," Ompahr said, "and a gnome has to be plenty aged to be saying that, to be sure. I have naught to prove, and you need nothing other than that scroll and your bearing it to me."

"Then why bother with this pretext? Why follow an oath to those over a century dead?"

"Across five centuries, I have been many things, but never oath-breaker," Ompahr said. He gestured, and the entire dais on which his pillows and cushions rested rose. In a recess beneath the platform lay a small chest. Ompahr sighed. "Take what I have held for long years, and remember that you took this burden on yourself."

Ten-Rings held his ground, casting a spell or two, and then said, "No protections on it, no illusions, no traps. I thought gnomes kept things hidden better than this." He leaned forward and grabbed the chest, pulling it close to his torso.

"Hidden better?" Ompahr said, "You're the *first* to come looking for it since I took the oath with Khelben twenty-three decades ago, so I consider that well-concealed and protected. May you deserve all that that coffer brings you."

Ten-Rings clutched the strongbox tight to his torso, nodded to Ompahr, and said, "We shall talk again, old one, when I am the city's archmage and you can tell me more of our Firstlord and the city as it once was."

"No," Ompahr said. "I doubt I shall survive to see the year out, with my oaths now fulfilled. Should you need my wisdom, commission a copy of my journals from my temple—if you have both the coin and the shelf space for seventeen volumes of lore."

The old gnome's final smirk and dismissive wave sent Ten-Rings out of the temple of Baravar Cloakshadow in the Warrens.

Roywyn returned and said, "Grandsire Ompahr, do you feel ill?"

The old gnome cackled until he was overcome by another fit of coughing. When he regained his breath, he smiled and said, "Child, I feel better than I have since Caladorn's investing as the Open Lord. Ready my litter and the acolytes. There'll be fireworks on the mountain tonight we have to see!"

"How do you know?"

"Khelben the Blackstaff was the only human I ever knew with a sense of humor to best a gnome's. I swore to hide two coffers and give one to him who asked for it and bore his hidden mark on his palm. Since Ten-Rings did not, I gave him the second coffer, but I never knew what either held. By the gods, I'd even forgotten about them entirely until I saw that scroll! Good thing I used the green seal on the scroll; that reminded me to give him the proper reward."

"But why risk going uptop? The way you talked, I'm worried you don't expect to live long!"

"Pish-posh, Roywyn," Ompahr said with a broad grin. "You think I'd tell *him* the truth? I've got a few more years left in me than teeth, by the gods' blessings. Besides, I may not know all that the Blackstaff had planned, but his pranks were only ever exceeded by Baravar himself!"

In his entire life, Centiv doubted if he'd ever seen Khondar as angry as he was upon his return. Khondar slammed the door and roared, "If I *ever* set foot in the Warrens again in my lifetime, it shall be to *raze them!*"

Centiv hovered over the burden his father set down, only half-listening to the rant. The strongbox's outside was nondescript, a brass chest with iron banding on its edges. He could not detect any magic on the small chest itself, having examined it from every angle and picking it up easily with one hand. Some weight shifted inside but made no noise against the metal. Khondar's tirade proceeded unabated.

"The mongrel races that pollute our city weaken and reduce Waterdeep to a stew of problems. Were we to winnow out all but the most useful of them, we would have no problem restoring prominence and greatness to this city!"

"Father, you're overstating," Centiv said, "and you're losing your focus. Just because some old gnome rattled you doesn't mean—"

"Do *not* accuse me of losing focus!" Khondar raged, grabbing a handful of Centiv's robes. "That gnome laughed at me—despite all I plan to do for—"

"Yes, Father," Centiv said in an oft-repeated litany. "He didn't recognize all you do for us, for the city."

Centiv knew Khondar's temper flared whenever he felt old or belittled. Centiv wondered if Khondar sought the Blackstaff's mantle for the secret of long years, or if it was simply his hatred of Samark. Still, he needed to calm Khondar down and get back to the task at hand. He kept his voice neutral and only fed his father what he wanted to hear.

"Father, you can address those insults later. For now, let's see what that gnome gave you. The work is old and well-done, but I'm no smith. All I can tell you is that there are no spells on the chest itself or its locks. It should open easily and safely. Let's do this, please?"

Khondar's face drained of its red rage, and he exhaled loudly, his shoulders dropping. "Very well. Time enough later to deal with disrespectful dirt-grubbers. Let's see what they kept for our city's archmage."

There was an emblem at the front of the chest and Khondar rotated that sunward until it clicked and the chest's lid popped up. He opened the lid, and inside lay a bundle of red kid leather. Khondar unwrapped it to expose a small garnet-pommeled dagger in a silver sheath set with three more garnets and two large heavy iron keys covered in runes with wolf's heads for their handles.

"Yes," he whispered. "The book you found talked about keys to Blackstaff Tower, worn as amulets rather than wielded, for there are no locks on the tower—just locks in the mind."

Centiv bristled, as Khondar had kept him busy with other errands, collecting spell components and preparations for tonight's work. The elder Naomal had locked up the book, keeping what it said secret from him. He trusted his father not to steer them wrong, but he ached to have that knowledge for himself. Then he could prove his worth to his father and to everyone. "Father," he asked, "of what else did the book talk about? Do we need more magic prepared than those scrolls provide?"

"Of course we will, fool!" Khondar snapped without taking his eyes off the key he rotated in his hands, looking at it from all angles in the late afternoon sun. "We must go back to the Towers of the Order and meditate, then memorize our strongest spells. The scrolls and keys will gain us entry to the tower, but we shall have to win the Blackstaff ourselves."

"But I thought the keys—"

"Khelben Arunsun and his successor Tsarra Chaadren were the last to allow a door on Blackstaff Tower. Since their deaths, none but the Blackstaff, his or her heir, or their chosen guests have entered the tower. Part of that is due to its lacking a door. The keys allow us safe passage through the outermost defenses and make us seem to be heirs to the tower. When used in concert with the scrolls, the keys allow us to unlock other secrets that might normally trap intruders."

"Couldn't we use the Duskstaff we already have? We know we can move that with Ncral's Ring. Having a weapon crafted by the Blackstaff might come in handy."

"Very good, Centiv, and well planned. As it will support your disguise as Samark, I was going to suggest that very thing. After all, we can't teleport inside the curtain wall around the tower, and the book suggested we would need a staff to open the gate. I assume that, should we take it into the tower, we can use it to sense for sympathetic enchantments and track those to the Blackstaff's seat of power."

"So all we need do now is wait for the fall of night and then we breach Blackstaff Tower, to claim its power for ourselves?"

"Yes, my son," Khondar said, looking away from the keys for the first time to focus on Centiv. "And with the power of the Blackstaff and this guild behind us, we should be able to force the Lords into working with us to help restore a more proper order in Waterdeep."

CHAPTER ELEVEN

That old wizard could escape a noose simply by making the hangman disbelieve his head were attached to his neck proper-like! Varad Brandarth weren't called the Shifter for naught, though he never snaked out of his debts neither—unlike some magic-workers I might mention . . .

Jorkens of Waterdeep, *Journal VII*,
Year of Silent Shadows (1436 DR)

10 NIGHTAL, YEAR OF THE AGELESS ONE (1479 DR)

I DON'T WANT TO GET TOO CLOSE. MARAEL SAID SHE'D HEARD THAT Blackstaff Tower drives folk mad who're not supposed to be there."

"I heard it eats the souls of folk who touch it without protection."

"My mother always said Blackstaff Tower stayed strong because of all the ghosts in it."

"Well, you know that if Blackstaff Tower ever falls, so goes the City, right?"

The whispers and rumors flew fast among the Watchmen posted that morning and afternoon around Blackstaff Tower's walls. For the first time in recent memory, the Watch stood guard over one of Waterdeep's oldest landmarks.

"We've been standing out here all day. Why're we here again?"

"You didn't hear? The old man's foreign consort turned up dead!"

"Are we supposed to watch for anyone skulking around the place? Or just guard it?"

"I dunno. I'm not the civilar! I could go for an eel pie right now."

"Stop talking about food. You're making me hungry!"

"So if the Blackstaff's so powerful and this place is powerful, what're we doing here?"

"Jarlon promised the Watchful Order the favor of guarding this place, and he's ordered us here. That's all I know."

"Since when does the Watch work for the wizards of the Watchful Order?"

"Since Ten-Rings and Jarlon learned to scratch each other's back, that's when."

"Stifle it! Here's comes Jarlon. And look who's with him."

"Rorden or no, he looks like a kid begging for a toy from those old men."

"Better not let him hear you say that."

Jarlon, the Watch rorden, walked up the street, and the young Watch officer motioned the guards to let them through the gates. The cordon parted without a word, allowing him, Samark the Blackstaff, and Khondar "Ten-Rings" Naomal to approach. Samark tipped the Duskstaff forward and touched the gates. A ringing sound resonated through the gates, and the ironwork writhed and twisted, the iron rosebushes and staves shifting out of the way to unlock and open the gates. The ringing stopped, and only the slightest of protesting groans accompanied the sound of the gate's hinges.

Once they passed through the open gates and were inside the curtain wall, both men turned to face the Watch. Samark addressed the guard captain. "Thank you, Rorden Jarlon. We appreciate your men's vigilance. Thank you all for keeping watch over my tower from those who attacked my heir during my absence. Now, you may disperse, as your services are surely needed elsewhere."

The watch commander nodded, then shouted, "Stand down, men! Convene back at the Tharelon Street post!"

The two dozen men and women of the Watch did not linger, though a few muttered as they fell out of formation. Not a one cast another look back at the forbidding stone wall or tower that they would all swear made them feel colder than the chill winds did.

The two wizards stood stock still until the street around the tower's wall was empty. The gates closed and locked, the ironwork reweaving its tangled rose briars across the bars and lock. Only then did the two men turn and walk to the tower.

Khondar forced himself to breathe deeply, keeping his excitement to himself. He'd dreamed of making Blackstaff Tower his for decades, and his dream was at hand—as was the constant reminder of the one who'd stolen his dream. "It still makes me shudder how well you ape that bastard Samark in tone and voice," Ten-Rings said softly.

"Well it's easier than trying to duplicating some of his spells," Centiv whispered. "Now are you sure we have the proper precautions?"

"I have Krehlan's rings, you have the Duskstaff, and we each have a key," Ten-Rings said, reaching into his cloak and removing a large parcel. "We should be safe from immediate defenses. Once we've breached the tower, we simply have to find the true Blackstaff and claim its power for our own. Do we have appropriate cover?"

"For all anyone knows or perceives," Centiv bragged, "you and the Blackstaff have taken to walking a circuit or two around the tower, talking low between ourselves, since I addressed Rorden Jarlon. Should anyone bother to try and listen in, we are currently discussing rumors and gossip among the Watchful Order. That illusion should give us about half a bell's worth of cover and also cloak our physical presence and voices. It ends with the two of us entering the tower anyway, so we won't be seen in two places at once."

"Good planning, Son," Khondar said, clapping a hand on his shoulder. "Here are two spells you must cast on the walls, while I work on our protections." He handed him a scroll tube with two scrolls, both slightly heavy from the gem-encrusted sigils and heavy metallic inks. In turn, he opened a tube of his own, withdrawing the first of numerous scrolls. The two wizards intoned the phrases from the scrolls, and wisps of smoke rose from the vellum as the sigils disappeared. While cloaked from outside view, the two wizards' forms and the tower wall before them glistened with magic sparks of a variety of colors. Eventually, the sparkles stopped whirling around them and shimmered into translucent fields of blue-green energy. When that happened, Khondar cast his fourth spell, the scroll consumed itself in white smoke, and the stones and mortar glowed with the same energy—as did the two keys that hung on cords around their necks. He nodded, and the two men stepped forward into the walls of Blackstaff Tower.

Khondar stood just inside the wall he'd just passed through and smiled. He'd expected much of the interior of Blackstaff Tower, and this did not disappoint. Instead of a common stone tower with defensive spells flaring to life, this was special. The walls became lost amid a sea of floating stones and random architecture, from flagstones to arches and statues to doors floating free in a dark night lit from behind, as if they now floated among the Tears of Selûne trailing behind the moon. The only stable feature here was a set of stone steps spiraling up into the night, though no mortar or stones lay between each successive step.

Khondar and the illusory Blackstaff each stood upon a patch of solid flagstone floor, but while they entered within a hand-span of each other, they now stood more than a man's height apart, and Khondar actually had to look up and behind himself to spot Centiv. When he did so, he also saw something coming out of what appeared to be a bright red nebula.

"Son, watch out!"

A blast of red energy slammed into Centiv's back, but his aura held firm and the energy ricocheted off to blast some of the stairwell free. A giant hand made of lightning reached around from behind him and wrapped its crackling fingers around him. While a portion of his protections burned up and the pressure was enough to keep Ten-Rings from using his spells, the aura held. Centiv spat out a spell at the hand, making it fizzle out.

"Thank you," Ten-Rings said, and he returned his attention to his bracers, clasping each with the opposite hand. The gems glowed as he thought about his rings that gave him the ability to move objects from afar and the ability to control the elements. He smiled as the rings blinked into view on his hands, replacing Krehlan's shield rings. Khondar hadn't been sure the transfer would happen inside Blackstaff Tower, but the proper rings gleamed on his index fingers. He used their magic to move his stone platform well away from Centiv and toward one of the few patches of wall still floating near them. Once in motion, he withdrew one more scroll from his sleeve and read it.

Centiv tried to disperse any and all illusions around himself, but he still floated aimlessly in a night sky. All his actions managed to do were to set his platform to spinning him upside-down. Centiv noticed Khondar moved farther from him, and asked, "Father, where are you going?"

Centiv's control over the Duskstaff faltered, and the Duskstaff rocketed off the platform away from him. Centiv tried to grab at the staff, but he did not leap off of his only solid perch. The Duskstaff, free of any control, flew straight through a black tear in space and disappeared. His voice quailed as he shouted, "Father, I've lost the Duskstaff!"

Khondar ignored Centiv and continued reading from the scroll and waving one hand in an involved casting.

Centiv tried to dispell the illusions again. "Father! I can't dispel any of this—they're *not* illusions!"

As both mages wove spells of dispelling frantically into the void, rips appeared in the air around them. Out of the rifts flew a wild snarl of translucent blue imps and a shriek of glowing red gargoyles. The creatures descended upon the two wizards' platforms and attacked their protective magic auras—the gargoyles vomiting fire, the imps spitting ice. Just as the attackers reached Khondar, two silver pulses expanded in the air around him and dissipated like smoke rings. Khondar heard the creatures jabbering but could not understand them.

"The shields are holding!" Centiv yelled. He drew a wand from his belt, blasted a gargoyle with orange missiles. "I thought you said the spells would make the tower accept us! These things are speaking Elvish, saying, 'Neither bears the mark. Neither is an heir true!' What went wrong?"

"Don't you have any stronger spells, boy?" Khondar asked, his aura filled with the white smoke of the consumed scroll he had cast. He waved his hands, and white light shimmered around every imp and gargoyle around him. Many froze in place, and with their wings no longer beating, they fell into the void around him or clattered, paralyzed, on the stone platform where he stood. Khondar smiled—until he saw more opponents flowing out of the void.

Centiv snapped his fingers through a quick spell and he and his stone platform appeared in eight different places, hovering at different angles. As the imps and gargoyles spat and clawed their way past the illusory Black-staffs, two wands flew down the stairs, leaving trails of silver sparkles in their wakes. Weaving paths through the fray, the wands settled into the hands of Ten-Rings.

"Your mirror images will only delay them so long," Khondar said. "You've always relied too much on the misdirection and tricks of your illusions. Time you learned and used real spells, like a real man!"

"Those illusions helped keep you alive and safe and in power at the Watchful Order!" Centiv shouted, as a translucent gargoyle shattered against the blue shield. "They were good enough when you needed them! At least I've never had to rely on items, like you and your rings! And my lies were only spells, not actual treason to guild or city!"

"Everything I've done has been for Waterdeep!" Khondar said, brandishing the wands. "I'll supplant Dagult and return Waterdeep to the proper rule of proper wizards!"

Khondar waved, and the blue shields that wrapped him unfurled and became a wall that shoved all the confining imps off of him and his stone platform. He gestured with his opposite hand, the sapphire on the ring glowing coldly. The corded key around Centiv's neck drew taught and snapped, and the key flew into Khondar's palm.

Khondar looked at Centiv, smiled coldly, and said, "Prove yourself now. Tame Blackstaff Tower, boy! If you can, we'll rule as Open Lord and Blackstaff. If you cannot, you're no son of mine!"

With that, Khondar wrapped the two wands and the key in his cloak and stepped back through the wall of the tower.

Centiv's shout of "No!" fell upon silent stone.

His anger at his father's betrayal vanished as Centiv realized he was alone. The translucent gargoyles and imps all turned to him and smiled. They became more transparent until all had disappeared. The strange void in which Centiv floated began to shrink as the stones assembled and came together as a chamber. There were still holes in many places, and Centiv himself stood as if the eastern wall were the floor, but it appeared to be a standard chamber.

"Father, *no!* Don't leave me!"

"O-ho, someone's fallen into another web of yours, old man."

The voice took Centiv by surprise, its lilting tone arising very near him but without a person attached to it. A light green fog rolled down the stairwell, and Centiv thought he heard a low growling like a wolfpack on the hunt. A tendril of fog slipped ahead and touched the illusory robes Centiv wore as the Blackstaff.

"That form is not yours, boy," said a harsh whisper.

Centiv recognized it as Samark's voice. The illusion he wore of Samark's form shattered. Centiv stood with his own form and face in the humble blue robes of a Watchful Order mage.

"Congratulations, little illusion-weaver. You and your sire are the first unwelcomes to darken the doorstep of Blackstaff Tower in more than a score of years." Another deeper voice he didn't recognize. It was a man's voice, spoken from the air before him. As he stared, Centiv saw a face coalesce in the green fog—an angry face clean-shaven save for dark sideburns, and long dark hair that swept past shoulders barely manifesting out of the mist. Other beings partly or fully phased out of the fog, their bodies alternating between translucent fog and seemingly solid features. Within a breath, Centiv found himself being watched by multiple fog-forms.

"We've been bored without playthings," said a lissome half-elf with dark hair and a shock of light green at her temples. She whispered into his ear, wrapping her fog-self around his body and teasing his face with a kiss as cold as the night air outside. "No offense, Sammy, but he's prettier without your face on him. Reminds me of one of the Estelmers from times long gone."

"He's not one of your conquests, Kyri. He's a shapestealer, an intruder, and a traitor to Waterdeep. It simply remains to be decided how he shall be punished." The voice, far away from Centiv, drew his attention to an older woman kneeling on the stairs and drawing a bow on him. He wove a shield in the air before him but hardly expected that to do more than delay things.

"I'm not a traitor!" Centiv shouted, and he turned to follow his father's example by fleeing—only to find all but the patch of floor on which he stood to be less than solid. In every direction he tried to move, the stones either tipped and floated off like loose stones as light as feathers or dissipated as illusions. The tautness in Centiv's stomach wrenched another knot tighter. He leaped for what appeared to be the outside wall—only to collide with the same solid spot on which he was now trapped.

"The pack has been hungry since the Night of the Black Hunt more than two-score years gone," said the male half-elf, his open robes exposing a lightly haired chest of wiry muscle beset with a multitude of sigil tattoos. "Set them loose on him perhaps?"

"Ashemmon speaks true. The pack is hungry." Centiv started as the first face he saw returned at his shoulder, speaking directly into his ears. "And we know what you visited upon our heir, false one."

"I did nothing!" Centiv howled. "It was Father and Granek!"

"Every Blackstaff and heir is tied to this tower," said the darkest, deepest voice. "What you did to Vajra is inexcusable . . . and inhuman." Samark's face, almost white in anger, wisped before Centiv's eyes. "Your lack of moral courage had you stand by while others did her ill. That brands you villain, Centiv Naomal. If I still had a body, I'd share some of her pain with you."

As Samark spoke, the stones on which Centiv stood rolled up and clamped hard around his feet. He screamed as bones in his feet ground together, and he fell backward, his feet still imprisoned.

"Oh wait," Samark said softly. "I *can* share something."

"We are none of us powerless, limited though we are to the tower," said the deepest voice. "We are merely limited until our heir can rise to the fore and face off our second hapless victim."

"Victim?" Centiv asked, panting hard in panic and in pain as the stones continued to press on his ankles and feet. His leather boots began to rip at the stones' edges and blood appeared there. Centiv swallowed. "My father betrayed me and fled!"

"Some of us are familiar with that," the first voice muttered.

The mists wrapped more thickly around the half-prone man. The tattooed half-elf knelt by his face but did not face Centiv. It spoke toward the voice and said, "Krehlan, you let that anger go a half-century ago. You and Khelben made your peace." He then turned back to Centiv and said, "The incantations your sire used allow you to penetrate the walls of the tower.

What they also do is set into motion contingencies laid long ago by Arun's Son and Tsarra Autumnfire."

The bow-wielding shade on the stairs said, "You and your father fell into a trap for those who would abuse the Blackstaff's power. The lens only works truly for the one marked by Sarael's tomb. It was neither you, weaver of lies, nor your sire."

"No, Tsarra," Samark's ghost said. "Whose trust did Khondar betray, Centiv? Who found the lens and the scrolls?"

"Weskur? Marked how?" Centiv's attention ricocheted about the room as all the shades began talking rapidly. "Why him? Why not me?"

A disembodied voice glowered all around him. "What I hid in Sarael's tomb could only be retrieved by one who respected others above the self. And he would be marked invisibly with this." Bright green phosphors laced in the air before Centiv's eyes to create the webwork of lines in Khelben's wizard mark.

"So another is marked as heir," Krehlan said. "Why is he not here with you?"

"It's obvious," Ashemmon said. "They betrayed the heir in their greed. They found what they wanted and ignored the signs. They walked the wrong path. As Ten-Rings cast certain spells on himself alone, those spells now compel him to complete his unwitting new course."

"Whatever his previous motivations, he must seek out keys that will pierce the veils around Ahghairon's Tower." The deepest voice manifested a face larger than all the other phantoms. Centiv recognized it from several statues and paintings. He faced the shade of Khelben Arunsun, the first Blackstaff, and he was angry.

"The secrets there are far more dangerous than those here," Kyriani's shade said. "I'm glad we're left a plaything, myself." The dark-haired half-elf materialized atop the prone Centiv, and the stones beneath him pulled at his robes, ripping them and exposing his chest.

"Do you think there's a chance he might actually succeed and harness some of Ahghairon's magics?" Tsarra's shade said.

Samark's shade shook his head. "They have the books I'd planned to show Vajra to teach her more about those very fields—Melkar's journal and Alsidda's Tome give him more than enough information on how to penetrate the magic around it, if not Ahghairon's Tower itself."

"Tymora always leaves a chance. He may pierce the initial veils, given the power we sensed in him, though how far only chance knows for certain."

"But entering those fields is a capital offense!" Centiv shouted. "He'll be killed!"

"If the Watch is up to its mettle as in times past," Ashemmon's voice mused, "aye."

"Indeed," whispered the shade of Khelben Arunsun.

With that, all the shades dissipated into mist again, though Khelben's dark eyes remained locked and glaring on Centiv for long moments after the rest of his spectral form was gone. His voice made Centiv shudder to the core of his being.

"There still remains the matter of what to do with you, little illusion-caster. No doubt it shall be uncomfortable at best."

CHAPTER TWELVE

The Spellplague-warped Pellamcopse remains tainted after decades. Its mutated guardian and the denizens of the wood protect their home fiercely, but the Blackstaff tells us the Pellamcopse Haunt, in his own way, protects Waterdeep as well.

Arn Gyrfalcon II, *To Walk Lands Afflicted,*
Year of the Wrathful Vizier (1411 DR)

10 Nightal, Year of the Ageless One (1479 DR)

"WELL, I don't know about you, but I'm bored," Osco said after having paced around the warm study a number of times.

"If you'd spent last night fighting an archmage and corrupt Watchmen, then fleeing through the sewers before coming here, you'd be tired too, little man," Meloon mumbled as he lay before the fire.

Osco wandered past the large fighter and bent down to whisper in Vharem's ear. "Hey, V, want to explore this place with me? There's some interesting stuff here—and I'm not talking about the wine cellars, though those *were* a good find."

"I don't steal from friends," Vharem said, opening only one eye. "They know where to find you."

"You used to be more fun, V," Osco said. "There were a few locks I wanted you to help me with."

Renaer sleepily rolled over on his couch and faced Osco. "If it's any of the doors in the tower, I've their only keys—and they're all magically locked besides. There's things up there you shouldn't disturb, Osco. Things I know to leave well enough alone."

Osco sulked as he walked to the table and buried his frustrations beneath a flurry of eating, consuming what remained of the large ham and the bread. In between bites, he mumbled, "Just because I wasn't up all night doesn't make lying around all day dull as dwarves."

Vajra, who had remained unconscious most of the day, rose slowly from the divan and said, "The hin speaks true. We must get to Blackstaff Tower. It has chosen a potential heir. I need to become Blackstaff before that path—and my mind—dissolves. I have need of Varad's books and counsel." With that, Vajra vanished.

The only sounds in the room were the crackles of fire and the snorting chuckles of a halfling with his mouth full. The others staggered up from dozing as Osco said, "Guess someone's disturbing things anyway, chief—and I doubt she's gone to the kitchens." With that, he dashed out of the room and cut left down the corridor.

Vharem asked, "Where'd she go?"

Renaer threw off his furs with a growl. "Varad's books are either here or in the tower!"

By the time the whole quartet roused themselves from beneath their furs, Osco's movement had lit up all the torches back down to the entry chamber. Renaer snapped "Stlaern!" as he pushed past a tapestry and through an open doorway mostly blocked by the wall-hanging. Vharem, Meloon, and Laraelra followed him into the stairwell that led up into a high tower. A blizzard howled outside the slim arrow-slit windows. Ice and snow pelted the tower.

They ignored the smaller landings and doors as they raced past two upper levels and found Osco at the third landing, waiting for them in front of a door.

"Well," Osco said. "Saer, 'I've got the *only* key to the tower rooms,' I can hear her rummaging around in there."

Renaer scowled at him and reached into his belt pouch to withdraw a silver key. Osco's eyes widened, as the key was a true work of art. Pure silver with some light runes around the bow end of it, the key's tines were table- and trap-cut emeralds of various sizes.

"Weird key," Osco muttered. "No wonder I couldn't pick the lock."

Renaer unlocked the door and opened it. The five of them entered a chamber that seemed larger than the tower in which it was housed. Renaer noted it was devoid of cobwebs and cold, unlike the lower rooms, and very orderly. Not a single book lay out on any of the three tables, nor were any stuffed haphazardly atop a shelf. The only things on the tables were rows of wooden rods, ivory wands, and other components laid out as if someone were planning to craft something.

In the center of the circular room lay a rune-inscribed circle painted in a variety of colors, twelve different runes in each of three successive circles. At the center of the circles, the floor was painted black. Stars glinted inside that void, and Vajra levitated cross-legged above it with a massive spellbook in her lap. She nodded at the group's entrance.

"How did you get up here, Vajra?" Renaer said. "Varad's tomes said none could enter this chamber without his key."

"I've been here before, youngling," she said, her voice and demeanor far older than she seemed. "The Shifter held few secrets the Blackstaff did not share. Now hush." Silence muffled the room. The only sounds heard now were Vajra's mutterings and the sound of her turning the vellum pages of the spellbook. After a short time, all but Laraelra withdrew from the room to sit on the steps outside the room.

"—really hate wizards, aye." Osco's voice returned as he stepped out of the room. "Was she this much fun to be around earlier too?"

"I liked her more when she needed to be carried," Vharem muttered.

"Could be worse," Meloon said. "If she's getting her head together, that means we might have a fighting chance against Ten-Rings and his fake Blackstaff. I say we keep helping her, and she'll be able to help us."

"I certainly hope so," Renaer said. "If she knows so much about Varadras, she probably knows how to use the portals. I just hope she doesn't use them alone and leave us stranded here another day."

"So where would we end up if we used them?" Osco asked.

Renaer sighed, thinking a moment. "The portal from my garden only leads here—to the receiving hall. There's three command words that take anyone standing on the mosaic back to Neverember Manor, Ordalth House, or a stone circle in the middle of the Pellamcopse north of the city. If the mosaic is used, it can't be used again for at least half a day until its magic restores itself."

"The Pellamcorpse?" Osco blurted. "Why would anyone visit that monster-infested place?"

"It wasn't always as it is now. In Varad's day and before, it was a pleasant little woods good for hunting game within a short walk from the Northgate. The Spellplague corrupted it. I've only read about that link, never used it. Varad's book talks about the arrival point being a place of worship older than the earliest settlements of Waterdeep. I think he tapped into older magic there to make this portal network of his stable."

"Um, are we supposed to know what and where Ordalth House is?" Meloon asked.

"It's a marble four-story grandhouse in Castle Ward, close to Diloontier's & Sons Apothecary."

"You forget," Vharem said, "not all of us study history, the names of buildings, or wander every street and alley in the city."

Renaer smiled and nodded. "Fair enough. We'll go to Ordalth House and Osco can get us into the Warrens from there. Then we'll get as close as we can to Blackstaff Tower without being detected and hope the gods are with us as we dash to the tower. I hope Vajra's presence will get us through its gates."

"Lots of hopes in that plan," Osco said. "Trust in us, not the gods, Ren. We can be counted on more often."

"Tymora'll help us," Meloon said.

"You rely on luck a lot, big guy?" Osco asked.

"I'm still striding," Meloon replied with a wink.

"Well," Vharem interrupted, "I hope that luck's with us, as milady wizard and our friendly sewer-sorceress are done with whatever they were doing in there."

The door thundered and all four heard both women cry out. Meloon shoved the door open and Renaer stepped to the side, his daggers at the ready. Inside the room, a column of green energy roared, Vajra hovering at its center. Lightning crackled off of her, and she spasmed with each pulse leaving her hands or feet. The magic circles above which she hovered absorbed some of the magic, but random bolts arced across the room.

Osco yelled, "Down!" and shoved at Vharem's knees, knocking him out of the path of a blast heading out the door. The halfling looked at Vajra, then yelled to Vharem, "I agree with you—I liked her better unconscious too!"

From behind the open door, Laraelra said, "Just before this started, she dropped that wizard's tome, her eyes went all black, and green lightning crackled all over her. Then she said, 'Chartham, ye stand as traitor,' and slammed me into the door. I can't stop her!"

"Chartham?" Renaer asked.

Vajra's head snapped toward him. Her gray eyes widened and she spoke, her voice deeper than usual, "Slay my heir, would you?" She raised a hand, and Renaer dived behind the table to his right as lightning exploded where he had stood.

"Blackstaff!" Renaer yelled. "You're dead, Krehlan! Let Vajra go!"

The energy in the room dimmed, but Vajra remained focused on Renaer. "Dead? Let who go?" She stared at him, then down at her own outstretched hand, and finally down at her body. "But—oh, we're not in the tower. In an unreadied heir . . ."

With a snap of her fingers, the lightning storm ceased, and Vajra settled down on the ground. Her head kept twitching left and right, and Renaer saw her eyes shimmering in many colors. Her eyes widened as she saw Meloon helping Laraelra up with one hand, his other holding his axe. As Renaer approached her, she nodded, murmuring something he didn't catch.

"What did you do, Ren?" Vharem asked.

"Chartham Dellenvol killed Krehlan Arunsun, the Blackstaff, over fifty years ago," Renaer explained. "When Vajra said his name, I guessed she might be possessed by Krehlan's spirit. He was the one who was Varad's friend too. All I could do was make him notice he wasn't in the past and hope that'd do something. Guess it did."

"And here I thought reading all those books would never help," Osco said.

Vajra balled her fists and closed her eyes a moment. When she looked up at Renaer, her deep brown eyes stayed focused and alert. "Thank you," she said. "Can we get to Blackstaff Tower soon? The power is . . . unstable. I need to claim it before it claims me . . . or another usurps it . . . and with it, the city. And my life."

"Very well," Renaer said. "Let's go."

Renaer led everyone out of the chamber and down the stairs. As they descended, Renaer said, "We can use the entry hall to teleport directly to another house I have closer to Blackstaff Tower—one the Watch may not know I own. From there . . ."

Osco nodded and said, "We'll improvise."

They entered the receiving chamber, and Renaer said, "Everyone stand on the carpet at the room's center—where we arrived—and hold onto each other. Do we have what we'll need?"

When the others nodded in agreement, Renaer stepped onto the carpet with them. He opened his mouth to speak the command, but Vajra's hand shot out to hit him in the chest. Her eyes were black storms afire with green energy, and she yelled, *"Uarlaenpellam!"*

Renaer shouted, *"No!"* as the six of them vanished—

—and reappeared in ankle-deep snow and a wailing wind. The sky was open overhead, though dark and frigid, and they saw they stood at the center of a stone circle, its ancient arches holding back the thick, dark forest that surrounded it.

"Quality place, Renaer," Vharem said. "Very top coin, this. Roof needs work, though."

"Nice, Ren." Osco snorted. "The one place we don't want to go—"

"I didn't do it—she did!" Renaer grabbed Vajra by the shoulders, hoping for an answer.

She smiled, looking past Renaer at Meloon, and said, "Find something that's been safe here—an ally for today and in times yet to pass. Find your fate." She pointed at the stones to the east, and fired five amber missiles from her fingertips. One lanced through a stone arch, disappearing but leaving a wake of sparks, while the others splashed onto the stones and lit the entire circle with a yellow glow that pulsed upward as a pillar of light. With that, her eyes rolled up into her head again and she fell into Renaer's arms.

"So much for help from the mighty wizard," Vharem said, "or for avoiding notice."

"You know," Osco said, "if all it took was so much fainting, my Aunt Delalar could be considered a wizard."

"What'd she mean?" Meloon asked. He took Vajra from Renaer's arms and hefted her almost effortlessly into his own. "Where's this ally she mentioned?"

"Out there. The quicker we find him, the sooner we can head back to the city." Renaer stomped angrily through the archway and into the forest in the direction of Vajra's missile. The trail was easily followed as the orange sparkles it left behind still hung in the night air.

It was not yet midnight, but the night was icy. The blizzard and its cloud cover at Varadras had not yet drifted south to this area. Selûne and her Tears sent moonlight filtering through bare branches bedraggled by glowing mosses. Lichens and mosses glowed underfoot. The spongy deadfall and undergrowth crunched and crackled as the friends' steps cracked the frost and snow.

"Where are we?" asked Meloon. "I don't recognize the trees or the scent of this place."

"The stars look right for the Sword Coast," Vharem said, "but I can't see much beyond the trees."

"It's odd," Laraelra said. "All the magic around here seems tied up in knots instead of flowing. See?" She pointed ahead and the orange sparkles whirled around like angry gnats and then splashed into a large tree, which quivered in response.

"This place is as far from a normal forest as Undermountain is to a cellar," Osco said. "They say it's a haunted place filled with dead wizards, spell-warped animals, and worse. No one goes through the Pellamcorpse unscathed. The only good thing is that no undead walk here."

"Osco, would you be quiet?" Vharem said

"Would you *all* be quiet?" Renaer snapped. "Or do you want to attract more attention than Vajra's magic already has?"

"I'd say that's a moot point," Laraelra whispered, pointing down the vine-choked trail toward a clearing, where a shadowed figure blocked their path.

Tall and wide-shouldered, the cloaked figure hunched over on one knee in the center of the clearing. In the moonlight, they could see clouds of its breath curling from beneath its hood. The figure lifted its hooded head, and the moonlight caught a bright patch of white hair on the darkly bearded chin. Little else was visible beneath that hood.

"Khelben?" Renaer whispered. "But he's been dead for more than—"

"Is this the ally we were supposed to find?" Meloon asked. "Doesn't look too friendly."

A snarl cut him off, and the figure leaped straight up, clearing the height of the trees, and his arms threw the cloak wide. Huge black wings threw it off and a massive cat-headed man with raven black wings flew around the clearing. Various white sigils stood out on its torso and arms as if tattooed or bleached into its black body pelt. A long tail lashed behind the figure, its movements swift and angry.

"Oh stlacrn," Osco whispered. "The Nameless Haunt!" He looked around for shadows in which to hide, and quickly slipped behind Meloon, who was handing Vajra over to Vharem with one arm while unbuckling his axe.

Laraelra whispered, "I never expected . . . he's beautiful."

Vharem said, "Yeah, like a knife's edge—and far more dangerous!"

While his voice should not have carried across the distance, everyone heard the creature equally well when it spoke. "Intruders," he snarled, "have you come to steal our power?"

The cat-man's hands gestured, and his claws and pinfeathers glowed green. The forest shifted around them, trees sliding backward with groaning, clattering branches. The six heroes found themselves standing in a clearing with the creature diving toward them. He smiled, and his fangs gleamed in the moonlight. The cat-man broke out of his dive and landed in a crouch nearby. "Good," he said. "We've been bored."

"Forgive our trespass," Renaer said. "We come as friends. We mean you no harm."

The Haunt laughed. "You couldn't harm us if you tried, boy. But since you've come as friends, I'll be polite and warn you." His claws wove a spell, and suddenly there were seven identical images of the Nameless Haunt standing in a semicircle, spreading around them. All of them smiled their fanged grins, and said in unison, "Run." With that, the figures leaped toward the group.

Laraelra stood her ground, launching two quicksilver bolts at the images. An illusory Nameless Haunt dissipated under the assault, and the other roared as the silver colored missile slammed into his wide feline snout.

Meloon ran forward, leaped into the air, and swung his axe with a roar. The blades passed cleanly through two more images, popping them like soap bubbles. Meloon landed and rolled along the ground, coming back up in a crouch behind the creature, his axe at the ready.

Vharem carried Vajra back to the trees as quickly as he could, preceded only by Osco running full out. Renaer held up a long sword and backed away, trying to provide cover for them to get their vulnerable friend away from danger.

The claws of the four remaining Nameless Haunts all glowed silver-blue. They raised their arms and wings in unison, and then snapped all sixteen limbs straight out. Shadowy webs shot out of eight pairs of wings and claws to entangle Osco, Meloon, Vharem, and Laraelra.

Meloon whirled with his axe and stumbled out of the dark patch. He encountered no resistance. "Hey! It's nothing!"

Laraelra stepped to one side, her hands cupped together. She finished her spell and unleashed a dazzling display of colored lights over the cat-man and his shadow web. Her magic wiped those images away.

Osco jogged forward, a slight whistling at his side, and whipped his sling upward. The stone bullet easily pierced the head of his feline attacker, and the mirage dissolved.

Renaer stepped forward to help Vharem and Vajra, but yelled, "Hey!" as he found the shadow webs solid, unlike the others. The dark cocoon containing Vharem and Vajra quivered and large batlike wings unfurled from its surface and flapped the cocoon skyward. The sole remaining Haunt flapped its wings and hovered over the clearing, chilling everyone with the cold downdraft of his huge wings. While the dark cocoon flapped off to the east, the Nameless Haunt looped high skyward and then dived toward Laraelra.

Quicksilver bolts flashed from her fingers and streaked straight for his wings, stunning him and turning his glide into a tumble. Laraelra turned and ran, but the Haunt rolled out of his fall and pursued, loping along on his arms and legs like a cat. She reached the trees just ahead of the Haunt, who shoved her into a large tree.

Laraelra vanished.

"No!" Renaer and Meloon yelled, and they broke into a run, brandishing sword and axe.

The Nameless Haunt turned toward the roaring warriors. He gestured, a slight glow of magic on his claws, and a large pit groaned open in their path. Renaer, unable to check his speed, fell in. Meloon leaped, swinging his axe, and landed on the far edge of the pit. He sank his axe into the frozen turf, his weapon holding him up at the edge of the pit. "Climb up me, Ren!"

he yelled, but Renaer lay stunned at the bottom of the pit. Meloon shifted around, using his free hand to grab at frozen grass and turf at the edge to pull himself out.

The area went dark around Meloon as the Nameless Haunt glided down to crouch over where Meloon scrambled out of the pit. The cat-man sniffed, growled low, and extended one claw at Meloon's axe. His touch turned the axe's wooden haft to dust, and Meloon yelled as he fell backward into the pit.

Sniffing and growling, the Nameless Haunt looked down into the pit. He called down to the men. "Nameless shall take wizards to talk. You and your friends stay here."

His head twitched to one side, as if he caught a scent, and he lashed his wings back, slamming Osco Salibuck on both chest and back, driving the wind out of him. The Nameless Haunt stepped over to the gasping halfling and picked him up by his cloak and collar, sniffing at him more intently. Osco struggled for breath, made even harder as his cloak pulled taut, pressing the clasp against his windpipe. The cat-man's yellow eyes widened, and he smiled.

Osco winced. "Stop! Don't eat—"

"HappylittlemanPikar! Nameless joyous!" The cat-man pulled the halfling into an embrace and licked his face, then pulled back with a growl. "You are not Pikar, though your scents are similar. Who are you?"

Osco, finally breathing normally, struggled against the creature's greater strength, and said, "Pikar? You've got me confused, saer. I'm Osco Salibuck."

"Osco did not have this." Osco shuddered as the cat-man's claw popped out in front of the halfling's left eye. "He also had a beard and stank of bad pipeweed."

"Sounds like me great-gradam. Hey—you knew him? And Pikar *was* me great-gradam! Say, how old are ye?"

The Nameless Haunt cocked his head, considering Osco's words, and the lightly furred face held a quizzical look. "You are a friend of the Blackstaff?"

"Aye!" Osco nodded, still squirming to break the creature's grip. "At least until you made off with her! Where'd you take her?"

"Home." He carried Osco over to the pit's edge, holding him over the edge as he looked down on the two men. "You are friends with the Blackstaff, too?"

Meloon nodded. He seemed awkward and insecure without his axe.

Renaer rubbed the back of his head and said, "Yes, and if you've—"

The Haunt gestured, and the pit filled up from below, raising the two humans back up to stand even with him. Renaer still held his sword, but he dropped it when the Haunt tossed Osco at him. The cat-man held up his hands and said, "Peace, then. We too are friends of the Blackstaff. We shall go to my home. We carry you, yes?"

"I can walk on my own," Meloon huffed.

The Nameless chuckled, shaking his head. "You cannot reach our home by walking. You need wings."

"Do you vow on the Blackstaff not to harm us? Or those you captured?" Renaer asked.

"Aye. All are safe. We go now."

The Nameless Haunt spread his arms, but Meloon shook his head. "I'm not going with that thing. Not flying."

The cat-man seemed puzzled as he looked to Renaer, Osco, and then back at the cross-armed Meloon.

"Meloon, come," Renaer said. "We know we can't fight him, and he's offered us hospitality. Let's go."

"You go. I'll follow on foot." Meloon picked up Renaer's sword and looked at the cat-man. "Which way do I need to go?"

One claw extended to the northeast. Meloon nodded, then turned and started walking that way. The Nameless Haunt launched a quick spell at his back, which froze Meloon in mid-stride. He swept his left arm back to hold Renaer back, and said, "He is scared to fly, we think. We go now. Easier. Come."

The cat-man wrapped his left arm around Renaer's shoulders, and Renaer threw his right arm around the Haunt's massive shoulders, above the joints where his wings sprouted from his back. The Haunt shrugged Renaer off the ground and walked to collect the frozen Meloon, wrapping his right arm around Meloon's waist and carrying the paralyzed warrior like he would a large log. He then flapped his wings and took to the air.

Renaer had only ever been this high in the air with a solid tower beneath his feet, and his stomach warred with him as he saw the ground drop away. He gulped and breathed deeply, and the cat-man snorted. "It's easier to not look down. Look up, groundling. Look up."

The Nameless Haunt flew high into the air, and Renaer looked up. The clouds had parted and he could see Selûne brighter and closer than ever before. The Haunt swooped up and over, and Renaer let out a slight gasp of surprise that became a deep laugh as they rushed to the ground. "I never knew flying felt so free! So alive!"

"Hey!" Osco yelled. "What about me?"

The Nameless Haunt snatched Osco by the shoulders with his foot claws. After a moment of wailing and howling, Osco started laughing.

Renaer called down to him, "What's so funny, Osco?"

"You ever have such a view, Ren?"

"Never."

Renaer's worries about the others faded as he focused on the experience of flying. The Nameless Haunt's strange combination of feathers and fur and strong scent mattered little, though Renaer was glad the creature's hard muscles held them aloft rather than fought them. He looked down and around and smiled. Osco was right—to see the world from on high was breathtaking. The moonlit trees were silver and white, and they flew high enough that Renaer could make out the entire southern half of the Pellamcopse. They passed over a small clearing, and Renaer saw a six-legged bear with a white mane leap upon what looked like a deer with two heads. Nearby, a tall collection of conifers stood out above the bare deciduous treetops, though their needles were a blazing red and glowing slightly in the moonlight.

"Amazing," Renaer whispered.

The Nameless Haunt purred. "There's more to see when it's not winter."

As they swooped around the red pines, three tentacles lashed out of the treetops toward them. Renaer saw numerous fanged maws dotting the wide flat limb and he tried to free his sword. The Nameless Haunt growled out a spell, and brilliant light shone down from his eyes. The tentacles snapped out of sight beneath the tree cover. The Nameless said, "The buarala hunger, but they shun light. Much more dangerous beneath the trees."

The quartet flew in silence after that, and Renaer kept his eyes open despite the wind and cold. He loved the sensation of flight and enjoyed the expanded view all around. He could see the Crown of the North far off to his right, and a few fires dotted the night to the south and the east of them and the forest.

"Travelers bringing goods to Waterdeep before winter?" he said.

"Fools should hurry," the Haunt replied. "We scent blizzard coming fast. Two suns or less."

"Speaking of fast, are we there yet?" Osco asked. "It's chilly down here!"

The cat-man looped lower and down to the right. " 'Tis a short flight yet. The forest pulled me far to answer the call."

Renaer asked, "So the Pellamcopse's magic drew you to us? Or was it Vajra's spell?"

"No spell. The Pellamcopse asks us to go to any magical intruder—and helps us do so. Vajra is the one marked by Blackstaff?"

Renaer nodded.

Osco's questions came quickly through his chattering teeth. "Why do you look the way you do? Did a Blackstaff do this to you? Did Khelben curse you to haunt this place?"

The cat-man's growl-like chuckle vibrated against Renaer's side. "Khelben was a friend—and more. The Spellplague made us. We had to become as we are to save our love. We protected Blackstaff so she could guard Waterdeep."

Renaer noticed the cat-man's eyes tearing as he talked, but he cleared his throat with a rumbling growl and then focused on their flight, not saying a word.

For the rest of the flight, the only sounds were the flapping of the creature's wings and Osco's incessant chatter.

". . . big baby—scared of heights. He'll be sorry he missed this view! Hey! Ren, did you see those green owls down there? And those perytons? This forest has some of the nastiest critters alive down there."

⁚⌒⁚

They arrived at the Haunt's treetop lair with the stars still bright. The cat-man spread his wings wide, and they came to a soft landing on a balcony formed from three parallel tree limbs. The lair looked like what Renaer had read about elven tree settlements—platforms and rooms shaped out of or into massive trees. The only difference was that Renaer couldn't see any stairs or ways to reach this height without flying. Renaer guessed they were higher than even a five-story building in North Ward.

The Nameless Haunt ushered them into a large chamber, and Renaer gasped at the warmth in what appeared an open-air room. The cat-man set Meloon properly on his feet and relinquished the spell on him.

Meloon said, "Well, which—Hey!" The blond warrior reached back for his weapon, only to find it missing, and he looked around in confusion and anger, scratching his head about how he arrived here.

"We are sorry to enspell you," the Nameless Haunt said to Meloon. "We only wanted to reunite friends more quickly." He motioned to the rear of the chamber, where Vharem, Laraelra, and Vajra sat or lay inside cells within the massive tree trunk, the bars thick thorn-laden branches. The cat-man gestured and the bars all spread wide, allowing them to exit their cells. While Vharem and Laraelra got out quickly, Vajra remained unconscious.

Osco cackled happily and asked, "What happened to you guys?"

"That cocoon dumped me here in this cell along with Vajra," Vharem said. "The place is warm and there was food—but it's still prison!"

"For your own protection." The Nameless flexed his claws, cocked an eyebrow, and asked, "You wish to fight us, boy?"

Vharem fumed, but Renaer intervened. "No, we don't. We just didn't know what you wanted with us, why you attacked us, or why you abducted our friends."

"Wizards more apt to talk than warriors," the Nameless explained. "We only take warrior because he carried her." He pointed at Vajra. "She sick? Nameless know Samark healthy. Did someone kill Blackstaff?"

Renaer nodded.

The cat-man's face glowered, and Renaer suddenly understood the tales of how fearsome Khelben's glare could be, especially now when mixed into leonine features. The cat-man returned to stroking Vajra's hair and face, whispering to her. "She has not been to tower? She needs help to understand her power." He uttered a few quick syllables and his palms glowed as he stroked her head.

Vajra's eyes snapped open, black orbs with storms of green energy. The Haunt shushed her like he would a baby, and continued to stroke her head. Crackles of lightning surged from her eyes, then died down to normal hazel-colored eyes rimmed with tears. "Raegar . . ."

"Tsarra love mistress wife . . . we are glad to see your eyes again." He purred in return.

"It hurts to see you this way, Raegar. What you and Nameless did . . ."

"Had to be done. Now why do you haunt this lass? You belong in tower, as we belong here."

Vajra sat up and looked around. "We're in the Pellamcopse?" When the cat-man nodded, she said, "Vajra wasn't readied. The power transfer happened outside the tower. Someone killed Samark. Why are we here though?"

The woman's eyes clouded to black again, then shifted to cobalt blue eyes. Vajra sat up straighter, her shoulders squared, and raised an eyebrow as she stared around the room. The cat-man bristled slightly, his wing feathers ruffling.

"I brought us here," she said. "Nameless, you've guarded something well for some time, but it needs to return to the city."

"As do you, Khelben. Spirits hurt Vajra."

"I realize the dangers more than you, familiar friend. Let us attend to our task and we'll visit again when we have more time." Vajra's stern voice whispered something only the Haunt could hear, and he nodded.

The cat-man and Vajra both cast the same spell with their left hands, their right hands remaining tightly grasped together. Their magic opened one wall of the room, revealing a small chamber.

"You four men need to see who she'll allow to wield her," Vajra said. "Her time for sleep is over."

"So what befalls here?" Laraelra asked, stepping up and blocking the opening. "Why not me?"

"You shall wield something far greater, girl, should you prove patient enough."

Vharem, Osco, Renaer, and Meloon entered the small chamber, finding it close and small for all of them. At the center of the room was a tree stump, and embedded in it was a beautiful silver axe with a rune-carved double-bladed head, its haft wrapped in blue dragonskin and a star sapphire winked at the pommel's end. The exposed edges of the blades all glowed with a shimmering blue radiance, lighting the chamber.

Renaer stepped forward, whispering, "Azuredge." When he grasped the axe's handle, he pulled hard once, twice, and gave up after the third tug didn't release it. Renaer was crestfallen as he stepped back and let Vharem try. "This axe is legendary. Its wielder is always a great defender of Waterdeep. Ahghairon the first Open Lord himself made this as a tribute to the Warlord Lauroun more than four and a half centuries ago."

"Well, it's useless if none of us can pull the thing free from this stump," Vharem said. "Why do wizards always muck up good weapons by sticking them in things that need a prophecy or destiny or something to get it free?" The slender man grabbed the axe's haft, but rather than pulling, he held it and his eyes wandered and his face lost its color. After a moment, he let go, as if the axe were painful.

"What happened?" Renaer asked.

His long-time friend looked at him, opened his mouth, and then closed it, shaking his head. "Not for me," he whispered. "Told me so."

Meloon, who had been awestruck when he entered, stepped up, but Osco leaped up onto the stump to straddle the axe's handle and pull on it as hard as he could. His efforts were useless, other than to make Vharem chuckle and Renaer and Meloon smile. The halfling opened his eyes after another strained attempt, and shrugged. "Had to try, didn't I? I get the feeling this thing's meant for the big guy."

"That thing probably weighs as much as you do, Osco." Renaer said. "If you'd drawn it, how could you have used it?"

"Fetch a fair price for the gems, the silver, the dragonskin," Osco ticked off items on his fingers to Renaer's gut-wrenching horror, and then giggled when he saw Renaer's face. He winked at Vharem and said, "I'm not sure. Has he always been *this* easy to tease?" Osco hopped off and clapped Meloon on the calf as he walked out of the room. "Go to it, big man."

Meloon reached over and grabbed the haft of the axe. Blue flames flared around the axe and the warrior. Renaer and the others flinched back, but Meloon stayed transfixed and seemed unharmed by the blue fire.

A bitter wind whistled around Meloon, who found he stood alone on a wooded plateau, seedling trees and shrubs slapping his knees in the wind. He whirled around to the familiar sight of Mount Waterdeep. But all else was strange. No city, no roads crossed the plain where he stood, and the mountain lay bare and untouched by any hand but nature's.

He stood near a crossroads, and he turned toward a rider's approach. Astride a stallion was a woman clad in chain mail, her face framed by the metal garb and a few stray red locks. She stared down at Meloon, her cerulean eyes freezing him in place. She broke eye contact first and stared east, down the lone dirt path. She looked again at Meloon, then directed her eyes west, down toward the deepwater harbor. Meloon could see a log palisade on the mountain spur where Castle Waterdeep would be, and he could see the Spires of Morning, recognizable as the great temple to Amaunator, even though it was still being built.

Meloon asked, "Am I fallen into yesterday? Is this Waterdeep in the past?"

"Will you fight?" the blue-eyed warrior asked.

Meloon nodded. "If the cause is just."

"Or the pay is right?" She cocked an eyebrow at the sellsword's common phrase.

Meloon shook his head. "Take only honest pay from honest folk, or you repay coin with guilt."

The woman smiled, then tossed a double-bladed axe to him. "If the Black Claws descend upon us, how do we protect the city?" She stared to the east, a cloud of dust rising beyond the trees.

Meloon looked east, then west toward the temple and further down the plateau at what he knew as Dock Ward and she knew as the city. He saw the limited trails, the heavier forest to the northwest, and the cliffs to the east.

"The walls protect the docks and the southern city?" Meloon asked. She nodded, and Meloon pointed with the axe at the trees along the trail. "I'd use my axe to fell the trees and block the trail. That forces any attackers into smaller units among the trees or around the whole plateau to attack along the roads to the south. Either way buys you more time for more defenses—or more ways to pick off the enemies. If you have to, set fire to the undergrowth—the smoke will slow them further, and it shouldn't harm the trees much."

The woman smiled and brought her shield up—a serpentine dragon wrapping vertically around a sword resting point down on a green field.

Meloon's eyes went wide, and he said, "Did you copy that from my memory?"

The woman's face became unreadable, as she shook her head. "This is my family's crest. Why?"

Meloon pulled his shirt open to reveal the same emblem—the dragon over the sword—tattooed over his heart and beneath a hairy chest. "It's my family's mark of old. The Wardragons of Loudwater. I was told many Wardragons originally settled Waterdeep, but I'd found none in two years in the city."

The woman dismounted and grasped Meloon by the shoulders. "You found me. You are not only worthy, you are kin. Know me as Lauroun, once-warlord of this place. Now, together, we can both be her defenders." She grasped his hand around the axe and brought them both up, her eyes framed above the blade. The axe burst into blue flames that matched her eyes.

.·:⌒:·.

Meloon's eyes focused on what he held in his hand. The runes on the axe head flashed three times, and the entire axe flared with blue flames. Meloon whispered, repeating the voice he heard in his head, "May the weapon be as worthy as its wielder, its wielder as worthy as the weapon . . ."

Meloon blinked and saw the last of the flames wink out as his normal eyesight returned. He came out of the room carrying Azuredge.

Vajra smiled a tight, thin smile, and said, "Good. Wield her well, warrior." She looked back at the cat-man. "When dawn breaks, the magic that created and tied you here should open. We need to redirect it, pulling us home." She reached up with a glowing hand and rested it on his cheek. The Nameless Haunt snarled in pain as she sent magic into his head. She muttered, "I'm sorry for it all," and collapsed into the cat-man's arms.

"We are too, Blackstaff." The Nameless stood and carried her out onto the balcony overlooking the forest. The light of dawn lit the eastern horizon. From their high vantage point in the tallest trees of the forest, everyone could see the distant slopes of Mount Waterdeep and the city huddled around it a few miles to the west.

The Nameless Haunt settled Vajra into Renaer's arms and began weaving a complex spell. He seemed to pull more and more light from the horizon and onto the balcony with them. After a few moments, he turned and said, "Stand here and face the mountain. I'll send you home."

"Thank you for everything," Renaer said. "If there's anything—"

"Not for us," the Haunt said. "Get her to her tower. She needs to touch the true Blackstaff soon. Then all may be better." He looked at them all, then shot a quick look at the eastern horizon and ruffled his wings. "Go now . . . to where we became. Help her and our city. Tell her we love her always. And be her friend, for a Blackstaff's life is lonely too."

The Nameless Haunt's wings spread full, scattering magic all around and over the group, his black feathers edged and glistening with red-gold energy.

Vajra stirred in Renaer's arms and said, "Farewell, love." Tears fell from her hazel eyes and streamed down her cheeks.

The sparkles swirled into a ring of light that settled around and over the six of them. Renaer watched as the air around them grew hazy. The haze shimmered, then a flare of light on its eastern face lit up the entire globe. The silver ring expanded from their feet, rising up around them and above their heads. Renaer closed his eyes and felt his stomach flip, and he had a brief sensation of flight again.

When he opened his eyes, he stood in a small fenced garden, winter bare and frost-rimed. Before him were not the trees of the Pellamcopse but the seaward slopes of Mount Waterdeep. Night still reigned in the skies overhead, but the first rays of dawn lanced beneath the heavy clouds that drifted above from the western sky. What bothered Renaer more was the fact that he stood alongside Osco, but the others had disappeared.

CHAPTER THIRTEEN

In efforts to avoid the worst of the Second Pestiliars, those who could afford it built upward, scaling the mountain and building upon it, as old protections kept them from burrowing into Mount Waterdeep. Mountainside was borne of panicked nobles and a need for cleaner air.

Kuldhas of Waterdeep, *A Walk in My City,*
Year of Azuth's Woe (1440 DR)

11 NIGHTAL, YEAR OF THE AGELESS ONE (1479 DR)

RENAER DID NOT OFTEN COME TO THIS AREA OF MOUNTAINSIDE, BUT HE knew the cobblestone road he faced was Mandarthen Lane because of the bright blue doors on every building and the white-stone tiles on the roofs. He also knew most folk, who disliked the abusive Mandarth noble clan and its whaling-derived riches, referred to it as the "Ambergrislide." Below them, Osco and Renaer could see the morning shift change of the Watch on the west wall, as lights bobbed along the length of the walls, new watchmen climbing the tower stairs with torches.

Osco smacked Renaer behind his knees, causing him to fall and land hard on his back. Before he could yell at the hin, the halfling's hairy hand covered his mouth, and Osco's face came close with his index finger at his mouth, signaling quiet. Renaer relaxed, but fought the urge to cough, as a foot patrol of Watchmen wandered past them. They were close enough that Renaer and Osco overheard snatches of conversation.

"—said there's an extra bonus in our pay if we can catch them without the Watchful Order's interference!"

"You ever had to chase him? Renaer Neverember's a greased fish that slips the net every time."

"When it don't matter, maybe. Now, with the murders in Ravencourt, he'll be caught. And he's got friends. They'll be easily enough caught, and then—"

"What? He'll come for them? Anyone who'll do what he did to the Blackstaff's heir isn't worried about retribution and hardly cares what happens to others!"

A third rougher voice growled at the chattering Watchmen. "Less jabber, more seeking, fools!"

"They'd stand out too easily up here," the first voice said. "There's no one awake and on the streets but a few servants heading downslope to fetch mornfeast for their masters."

Renaer could now make out the Watch patrol passing directly in front of their position on the other side of the iron-rail fence. If they looked even an arm span in their direction . . .

In the distance, Renaer heard some commotion, and Osco whispered, "Somethin's disturbed some dogs."

A few breaths later, the shadowed pack of four Watchmen started, as a horn sounded a few streets over.

"Let's see where our fellows need our help!" said one of the Watchmen.

They ran east and up over the slope of the mountain, leaving Osco and Renaer behind them. The two of them exhaled in relief, their warm breath clouding the air around them.

"Sorry, Renaer," Osco said, brushing snow and frost off the human's cloak and vest. "No time for warning. How you humans avoid trouble with such poor eyes and ears is beyond me."

"I suspect avoiding trouble's not on our agenda today," Renaer said. "You heard them and that horn. How much would you wager they've spotted some friends of ours and sounded the alarm?"

Osco beamed a broad smile. "Haven't had a tussle with the Watch in four days myself. Let's see if we can trip them up without them being the wiser, eh? We'll head up Gorarl's Way and over to Tybrun Ridge, right?" With that, the halfling slipped through the wide rail fence and scampered off into the shadows.

"Osco!" Renaer whispered harshly, but not too loud to draw attention. "I meant we should—grrr!"

Renaer got up and found he could not slip between the rails as the hin did. He found the gate and eased it open with only some noise from its hinges. He headed in the same direction as the halfling and the Watch, and he found it easy to know what direction to travel by seeing the scuffs in the mostly undisturbed frost on the street. He just hoped they'd reunite with their friends before anyone got caught.

Laraelra slipped and began to fall as the ground under her proved too icy. She felt someone catch her, but she could not see with the rising sun lancing in her eyes. Shielding her face, she realized that Vharem stood behind her, and he kept his feet despite the ice. "Thank you, Vharem," she said.

"Any time I can help damsels in distress." He grinned.

"Any idea where we are?" Laraelra asked as she regained her footing and looked around. The two of them stood in an open court that sat higher on the mountain slope than most of its surrounding one- and two-story buildings. In the shadows of the buildings, untouched by the rising sun, furred creatures stirred and stretched. One or two dogs slipped into the sunlight and approached the two humans, growling and apprehensive.

"Stlaern," Vharem whispered. "Elra, back out of here as calmly as you can, but quickly."

She tried but found her way blocked by another growling dog, a Moonsharran mastiff. "Where are we?"

Vharem did not answer. He reached into his belt pouch and withdrew three large hunks of dried venison, which he now waved to spread the scent. He whispered, "I'm going to toss these. Then we run."

The court exploded with color and light and numerous yelps. Laraelra grinned as Vharem turned to find her casting her spell. She clapped her hands together as if brushing off dust, and said, "Or I can take care of a pack of dogs with a simple spell."

"You didn't get them all—run!" Vharem threw the venison to her right. His aim was true, and the mastiff caught the largest hunk of meat in his jaws instead of lunging at the sorceress. Other dogs now fought over the unclaimed meat as Vharem and Laraelra ran out of the enclosed court and into the small street.

Vharem looked left, saw a number of folks heading east toward them with hands raised to see against the rising sun. Two wore Watch colors. Vharem pulled her to the right and the two ran. No other steps disturbed the morning frost on the streets in this direction. Laraelra realized they were up in Mountainside, racing down the northern slopes of Mount Waterdeep. This road ran parallel and just one block east of Tybrun Ridge, the slope edge of the mountain. She recognized no buildings, as she'd rarely entered Mountainside.

"What was that?" she whispered.

"Wildhound Court," Vharem said as he steered them to the right and onto a wider street that curled back north almost immediately, but ran lower on the slopes. "Whenever dogs get loose up on the mountain, as they do when drunken nobles stagger home in early morn, the dogs get drawn to that court and form a wild pack, no matter how good-tempered they might be normally. Oftimes, folk who wander into it at night are found dead by full morning. It has something to do with some old curse left over from the warlords' time or something. Here!"

Vharem pointed, and he and Laraelra swung left into another court that had an exit opposite them. He rushed them both toward a baker's window just opening for morning business. He flipped a few coppers toward the young apprentice and said, "Fresh bread, and hurry."

The entire time they stood there, Vharem never stopped tapping his foot.

"Do we have time for this?" she asked in a fierce whisper.

"We've got to let those Watchmen go by."

"But why are you nervous now?" Laraelra asked. "You weren't even this twitchy against that fake Blackstaff two nights ago."

"I was sure he didn't know me or carry a grudge," Vharem said. "There's a few Watchmen up here who really don't like me, and I need to get both of us out of here. We need to find the others. Why didn't we arrive together?"

"I don't know," Laraelra said, "but don't worry. We'll find them."

"I'll worry. I've played some pranks on the Watch up here."

The apprentice baker reappeared with two piping hot loaves, which he handed over nervously, apologizing for the slow service. Vharem handed one to Laraelra and moved to keep on walking, when the court exit was blocked by a Watch patrol. One of them pointed, and the rest chuckled. Vharem and Laraelra turned on their heels to leave the way they had come, only to find the Watch armar blocking their way.

The tall man, whose remaining long black hair was tied behind his shaved scalp, rubbed his head and smiled at Vharem without saying a word. He simply pulled his signal horn up to his lips and blew. The high, clear sound echoed in the court.

"Oh parhard," Vharem and Laraelra swore.

Meloon's eyes remained clouded, the haze of silver replaced by a full blue glow. He saw Lauroun's face again, her cerulean eyes, hawklike nose, and strong brow beneath a chain mail headpiece. She smiled at him, and mouthed the words he heard in his head. *Home again. Good.* Meloon tightened his grip on Azuredge, the axe whose voice spoke to him.

A small hand at his belt steadied him before he fell forward, and he shook his head to clear his eyes. Meloon found Vajra smiling up at him. Her brown eyes became purple and she licked her lips while looking at him. The eyes shifted again to sea green, and she said, "Listen to Lauroun. She'll never steer you wrong." Her gaze darted to the magical axe, and she said, "Nameless's portal only works when the first rays of dawn strike the place where he was born. Alas, we alone arrived on target. The others are near, scattered by some whim of magic attached to this mountain. Perhaps the Godstair interferes . . ." Her voice trailed off and Meloon followed her gaze to the peak of Mount Waterdeep. When she turned back to look at him, her eyes were brown again. "We have little time and must get to the tower. They can meet us there."

"No," Meloon said.

"Don't argue with me, warrior. Why not?"

"Because you faint. A *lot*. And I can't fight *and* carry you. So we find the others first." He looked around and found that the cobblestones on which they stood were scorched in the shape of a cat's head. "Did we do this?"

"The Spellplague did a century ago," Vajra said, her hazel eyes shining with tears. "It robbed me of both husband and familiar in one magical blow. The magic marked the city forevermore, even though they have changed the stones seven times in and since my lifetime."

"Vajra?"

"Tsar—Unh," Vajra said. "Fehlar's Bones, this hurts! They keep pushing out of my head!"

"Yet another reason why we need the others," Meloon said, looking out from the intersection in which they stood. The crossroads led straight along the ridge of the mountain to the south, but zigzagged away from their meeting point down the slopes to the west, east, and north. As he looked down to the city, a brief flash of colors flared up in a court south and east of them, and he pointed. "There!"

Meloon turned to help Vajra along, but she sped off ahead of him, running faster than he thought possible—he had to run full out to catch up. He wished he knew the names of the streets, but they headed down toward the flash, and Meloon's speed showed him why all the roads were switch-backed and zigzagged. If they ran roads straighter in Mountainside, carts or horses would easily get out of control or run too fast down the mountain and shatter legs or goods along the way. During the run, Meloon heard a horn and noticed a number of shutters disturbed by it, as well as some folk either heading toward the sound or away from it.

By the time Meloon caught up to Vajra, she stood outside a court and was casting a spell at the backs of a Watch patrol. The two men and one woman all fell asleep before their bodies slumped to the cold ground. She looked back at him as he arrived and slid to a halt on a patch of ice.

She wore a serious mien, and her gray eyes held no humor. "Come. Our comrades await."

Meloon and Vajra entered the court, and Meloon's stomach growled as he caught the scent of fresh bread. He ignored it and beamed as he spotted Elra and Vharem—and the watch armar past them. Just as Meloon focused on the oddly mussed and frizzy hairstyle of the armar, the man's eyes rolled into the back of his head, and he fell forward, unconscious. Behind him, a grinning Osco Salibuck stepped out of the shadows, his sling dangling from his right hand. Moments later, Renaer appeared in the alleyway behind the halfling.

Everyone entered the courtyard, saying nothing but surveying the four downed Watchmen, then the large covered well at the yard's center. The folk who lived and worked in this stories-tall court had opened their windows or doors when the horn sounded, and they yelled out their upper windows and into the streets. "Young Neverember and his friends assault the Watch at Trellamp Court! Murderer on the loose 'tween Sulvan's Way and Three Lords' Crossing!"

"We're innocent!" Renaer shouted. "We've killed no one!"

"Aside from that one-eyed Watchman and his flunky," Vharem whispered to Osco.

An elderly matron of doughy countenance leaned out her window and cackled at Renaer. "If ye're innocent, stay and explain why the Watch lies at yer feet, laddie!"

With more than a few folk yelling into the streets, a warning bell sounded in a nearby temple tor, and the sounds of boots approached.

"Parharding bells." Renaer groaned, and then said, "This way, everyone!"

The six of them sped out of Trellamp Court, racing down Sulvan's Way as if gods themselves dogged their steps.

CHAPTER FOURTEEN

Pave your path through life with kindness to others and every step forward will reward you with soft landings and little resistance. Pave it with anger or force to others, and your every advance will be hard fought.

Bowgentle, *Meanderings*,
Year of the Bright Star (1231 DR)

11 NIGHTAL, YEAR OF THE AGELESS ONE (1479 DR)

THAT WAY!" RENAER SAID, KICKING A BLOCK OUT FROM BEHIND A WAGON wheel, and Vharem did the same on the other side. "Down Shyrrhr's Steps and northeast on the Garmarl's Dash over to Windless Way!"

The two of them pushed the wagon and sent it careening back down the street to slow any pursuers and distract any observers. They caught up to Laraelra and the others dashing down a short stairwell linking them to an alleyway behind a slate of rowhouses. They looped around a pair of adjoined buildings and a covered well, startling three scullery maids filling buckets there. With Osco in the lead, the group slipped over to the brick-paved Windless Way.

Laraelra stopped dead and rasped, "Osco, stop!" She looked for Meloon, Vajra, Vharem, and Renaer, and spotted another Watch patrol in pursuit behind them. Luckily, the morning sun rose into the Watchmen's eyes, which helped conceal the fugitives. Laraelra could see both Vharem and Renaer keeping their hands in front of their torsos, hiding their directions from the Watch, and pointing her to their right, to the south.

Laraelra held back, letting Osco, Meloon, carrying the swooning Vajra, and finally Vharem and Renaer past her, as she hid behind the side of an apothecary shop. Once everyone was past her, she let the Watch close a little more before she cast her spell, unleashing an explosion of magical colors over them. Of the quartet, three fell unconscious and the armar went blind. She smiled at the effectiveness of her magic and ran to catch the others.

Renaer had led the rest of them down the dark-bricked Windless Way. As Laraelra reached them, they darted onto a black cobblestone alley and into a tiny bricked courtyard. Three doors faced out onto the court, and the south-west-facing upper windows of the three two-story homes were still shaded from the morning sun. Renaer pointed at the door on the far left and said softly, "A friend lives there. He should be able to hide us from the Watch for a nonce."

When Meloon approached the door and raised a fist, Renaer whispered, "Stop!"

The burly man raised an eyebrow in question, and Renaer reached up and used the door knocker—a crude iron sculpture of a bird's head set atop a large plate of iron. The knocker oddly made no sound, but within a moment, a window overlooking the door on the upper floor opened.

"Who's there?" The voice preceded the night-capped head of an older man with a close-cropped gray beard, who fumbled to put spectacles on his long nose.

"Parlek, it's me!" Renaer said. "Let us in, please!"

The older man leaned out, squinted down at Renaer, and gaped at them and at the prone Vajra in Meloon's arms.

"You're wanted for murder, boy," Parlek replied. "Give me one reason to trust you and your friends there."

"I'll give you three—*The Annals of Kyhral*. You'll finally complete the set! The volumes are yours in exchange for safe haven."

The old man's face brightened. "Finally! I knew I'd gain those volumes from you one day, boy!" The old man practically cackled with glee, then caught himself and said, "Er, well, that proves you are who you say, as you're the only one in the city with those volumes. And for you to part with them means you're either desperate or innocent—or both. Come in, all of you."

The man waved, a light bout of sparkles drifting off his hand, and the door below unlocked. As Renaer opened the door, the older man above closed the window.

"We'll be safe here, temporarily," Renaer said, escorting them all into the row house.

They entered a snug antechamber, then walked through a slim passage-way to the front of the house and an equally slim stairwell leading upstairs. Down those stairs came a bowlegged old man wrapping his robes more tightly about himself.

Renaer gestured up and said, "Everyone, Parlek Lateriff—sage, sorcerer, and smith of the highest order."

"Stop basting my ego, boy." The old man stopped in midstep, grabbing the railing in surprise. "I wasn't sure . . . but it is! You've got her! That *is* Vajra Safahr, isn't it?"

Renaer nodded. "What exactly are we accused of doing now?"

"The usual, when they want someone caught without having to explain much—murder, dissent against the Lords, and more. Surprisingly, there are specific charges that tell more, if you know how to listen." He motioned them all up the stairs and continued. "The fact that you're protecting someone you're accused of murdering should help your case—or harm it, if they claim you used your connections with many temples to resurrect her so you could kill her again."

Renaer sputtered, "But . . . why—who?"

Vharem smacked him between the shoulders and said, "He's stuck. Lemme help."

"Who's accusing us of all this?" Laraelra said.

"And who might you be, lass?" Parlek asked.

"Laraelra Harsard, daughter of—"

Parlek's eyes widened and he interrupted her, "Malaerigo Harsard, who claims his daughter has been bewitched into helping a murderer and offers a reward for her rescue. Interesting. Interesting."

Laraelra groaned. "On a brighter day, Father'd not be such a fool."

"Yes, but your own reputation for cool-headedness serves you well. More folk than your loud-mouthed sire believe your involvement is both voluntary and honorable."

Laraelra got a small smile out of that.

"What did you mean when you said the charges tell more?" Vharem asked.

"You disappeared yesterday morning from Neverember Manor. Too many people saw you go in, and none saw you come out. Without someone telling your side of the story, your accusers filled the streets with gossip to support their claims. What'd you do to get on the wrong side of Khondar Naomal, Renaer?"

"How did you know he was behind it?"

"Those slinging the most accusatory statements all had ties to the Watchful Order, and to him specifically. I have some guilded friends who want to know what's going on, since most of them aren't buying the story. The Watch—or at least those few you've shamed in your nightly pranks—believes the rumors and search hard, as do some Order apprentices. Otherwise, most of us use our heads as other than hatracks and wait for the truth to come out at Lords' Court."

"Thank the gods for that," Renaer said.

Parlek led them through a small room toward a doorway in the far wall. "Don't touch anything—especially *you,* Osco Salibuck!"

There were two work tables, on which were fine smiths' tools, vises, and some works in progress—a bracer, a headdress, and an amulet. Above the tables and set on slim support rods were two long planks, on which were gems small and large of various colors. Across from the tables were shelves overflowing with books and scrolls.

Everyone passed through the room quickly. Renaer held onto Osco's cloak, and Vharem held onto the hin's tunic. However, while Renaer and Vharem were broad-shouldered, they were not as large as Meloon. In order to avoid dislodging things from the shelves on his right, Meloon bumped into the table on the left as he passed it, and he knocked its shelf over, spilling its contents on the table and floor.

"Parharding stlaern it!" Parlek swore. "It's going to take forever to sort all that out again! You've ruined my work for the next tenday!"

Meloon blushed and muttered, "Sorry," but whispered back at Renaer, "What's he got all that for?"

"Parlek makes a living by creating replicas of jewelry pieces for nobles," Renaer said. "It allows him to afford better books and time to study on all things ecclesiastical."

While Parlek groaned and shot glares at Meloon, the others gathered up everything that fell off the shelf onto the table.

"You big ox!" Parlek snapped. "I'll never finish that tiara in time!" He pointed at a half-finished headdress of filigreed silver webworks, half its fake gems in place. The parchment on the table illustrated the finished piece, but that was half-covered in loose gems.

Osco hopped up on the stool, produced a lens out of his back belt pouch, squinted to hold it close to his right eye, and began picking small gems up to examine them. "It'll be less than forever and certainly not a tenday, but it'll still take some time. Settle back, gentles, and let me show you glass from class. *Ooo,* nice work there! Almost didn't see the seam."

Laraelra swept all the loose gems together, gestured at the jumbled pile of fake and real gems, and uttered a few syllables.

"Hey!" Osco yelled, as all but the single gem in his hand spun away from him, glowing. The gems glistened and spiraled into eight separate piles—two blue, two red, two clear, and two green gems, one each of fake and real gems. The fake gems easily outnumbered the real gems by ten to one, as there were only two or three real gems of any color.

Parlek gasped, looked at Laraelra, and back at the piles, and both of them smiled.

"It's a minor magic of mine," Laraelra said. "Separates out components and puts like with like."

"I might pay you to teach it to me, lass, but another time," Parlek said. He motioned them forward toward the door behind him. "Let's get out of my workroom and into my parlor. *Please*." The last word he pleaded, looking directly at Meloon, who gingerly side-stepped his way through with Vajra.

They entered a moderate-sized room flooded with morning light. Two couches and four chairs hugged the walls of the room. Parlek motioned them all to sit, himself taking a seat by the window and the light. They all sat and Renaer said, "Sorry for the disruption of sleep and home, but we need to know everything you've heard."

"Too much," Parlek said. "Tell me what you know and I'll try and fill in the rest."

Meloon chimed in with, "All we know is Khondar and somebody posing as the Blackstaff want us dead because we kept them from killing her. They stuck a knife in her gut!"

"Those two hated each other for decades," Renaer said. "I suspect Khondar killed Samark or had him killed, and then had a trusted lieutenant wear an illusory shape to divert attention or sow confusion."

"We don't know who the illusion-weaver is," Laraelra added, "but they must have enough information to steal the Blackstaff's power. When Vajra's cogent, she talks about getting to Blackstaff Tower before someone takes its power."

Parlek listened to all of them, nodded, and said, "You're right in that you need to get her to the tower—her place of power. I suspect that'll help her just by being there. As for the illusion-wearer, that's probably Khondar's son, Centiv. He's good with illusions, and one of the few that ring-wearer would trust—at least as much as he trusts anyone." He whistled. "You sure pick enemies, Renaer, that's for certain." His gaze happened upon Osco, whose hands shot up into the air to show he didn't have anything in hand despite having passed by a silver serving set on the sideboard.

"The gods' honest laughs," Osco said. "They found all this trouble by themselves!"

"What can you tell us about Ten-Rings?" Renaer asked.

"Once I realized he was the one slandering your name," Parlek said, "I asked friends who know the city's wizards. Naomal only picked up that name about eighteen years ago when Sarathus died and Khondar failed to become Ashemmon's apprentice and heir for the third time. Before that, he'd been a middling wizard with a brief stint in the Watch-wizard corps.

In less than a year, he was a power in the guild with his new affectation of a ring on every finger. I heard he searched spellplagued areas in Neverwinter Woods and found some artifacts—including the Jhaarnnan Hands." Parlek smiled, happy to impart his knowledge. "The four sources that discuss them say the items are from Memnon in Calimshan, though all disagree as to their origin. One says they were made by the great djinni lords, one says efreeti, and the third by their wizard servitor-proxies. The fourth insists demons worked to undermine the djinn-rule of the time and made them to do so."

"By the gods, man!" Osco said. "We're hunted! Less story, more information!"

Parlek frowned and said, "Of course, you're right, you're right. The Jhaarnnan Hands are a matched set of gold bracers and sculpted stone hands, which allow Khondar to swap out magical rings he wears with those on the Hands. I assume he wears a ring on each digit to disguise when he changes rings."

"So if we find these hands, we can strip him of power?" Meloon asked.

"Doubtful, but decreasing his power should keep you alive." Parlek shrugged.

"Don't suppose you've got a way to just blink us over to Blackstaff Tower, do you, old man?" Renaer asked, winking at Parlek.

He laughed and said, "Even though magic's more stable in the city, Renaer, there's very few of us who would dare to teleport to Blackstaff Tower—even if we could."

"So we're on our own," Vharem sighed.

"I think you'll find that the only folk who're pursuing you in the streets are the ignorant or those corrupt few who seek to curry favor with those more corrupt above them." Parlek rose and approached another door, which he opened to reveal another set of stairs leading down. "These are the outside stairs leading out onto Firegoad's Gambol. If you're lucky, you can take that down to the Talltumble Stairs, which should get you to Castle Ward. From there, you've a bit of a run to Blackstaff Tower. May the gods whisk you along, friends."

They left Parlek's home and emerged onto a slate-colored brick street that was starting to bustle with activity. When a few folk took note of them because of the unconscious woman in Renaer's arms, he quickly explained, "She's sick. We're looking for the nearest shrine to Tymora."

The fact that she was hooded and heavily wrapped against the cold kept most from recognizing who she was. Some helpful folk pointed out directions, while others shunned them, but they made their way to the top of the Talltumble Stairs as most folk ended their mornfeast and got on to work in the city.

The Talltumble Stairs clambered down the eastern slope of Mount Waterdeep to provide a way for the Watch and others to go up or down into Mountainside. The name came from how folk lost their balance on the shallow steps and oft-tumbled down a bit of the mountain slope. The name remained, even after the Stonecutters' Guild reworked the stairs from one complete straight run to a number of angled stairs with four resting platforms along the way.

The party made its way down the first set of stairs to the Lovers' Landing, so named for its use at night by amorous nobles of Mountainside. The only others on the stairs were merchants carting goods in packs, heading up to the High Market to sell their wares. No one gave the party much notice, focused as they were on simply keeping their balance and their wind while trudging up the steps with their heavy packs.

The party continued to the Dragon's Spout, the informal name for the second landing, at which there was a magically maintained fountain with clear, fresh water. The stone fountain—a carved dragon's head— once topped the Dragontower of Maaril, but that edifice had rocketed skyward during the Spellplague and exploded high over the city. The only piece to have survived was the dragon's head, which was put to use at this fountain.

Osco whispered to Vharem, "Hey, V, is this going too easily or is it just me?"

"No, it's not just you," Vharem said, his hand resting on his sword hilt, as he looked around at all those approaching them.

The group paused to drink at the fountain, and Renaer passed Vajra over to Vharem to stretch out his arms and lean over for a drink. With the group clustered around the fountain, Osco snapped to attention and hopped up onto the fountain's surrounding ledge. "Something's wrong."

"What makes you say that?" Meloon asked.

"It just got really quiet, and those two people on the far side of the fountain haven't stopped talking." He unfurled a whip at his belt and snapped it out into mid-air—and suddenly the air shivered around them.

Within a breath of Osco's whip-snap, nine young wizards wearing the gray robes of the Watchful Order surrounded him and his friends against the fountain.

"How the gods did he know?" A young mage yelled as he came into sight.

His companion lurched over, howling and holding his face. He glared at Osco, the welt on his cheek fresh and bleeding. "You'll pay for that, halfling."

All nine of the gray-robes held wands, aimed at Laraelra and her friends.

CHAPTER FIFTEEN

Regrets? I haven't wasted my time or energy on them for seventy winters, and I'll not start now. All I do lament are missed opportunities, ignorant fools, absent friends, and good wine spilled.

Kyriani "Blackstaff" Agrivar, *A Life Relentless*,
Year of the Fallen Friends (1399 DR)

11 NIGHTAL, YEAR OF THE AGELESS ONE (1479 DR)

IT SHOCKED EIRUK WESKUR THAT THESE ACCUSED MURDERERS TRAVELED so brazenly with an injured person, but he held his wand on the large blond barbarian while Sarkap called out, "Renaer Neverember and company, you are to come with us to answer for your crimes!"

Eiruk knew all of the gray-robes had wands to either paralyze or slow their foes down, but he didn't trust Mauron or Ulik to not have more potent magics at hand. The pair of them were fanatic followers of Guildsenior Naomal, and they followed his every command. While Eiruk respected the wizard, he could not put his finger on why he felt increasingly nervous around him.

Some of the younger apprentices seemed scared even while leveling wands at Renaer and his friends, but the Naomal-loyalists seemed happy to provoke a confrontation, including Sarkap.

"Put down your weapons and throw yourself on our mercy!" Sarkap said.

Eiruk hated working with these bullies, but his tutors tasked him with cloaking them with illusions to take their targets unawares. Eiruk just wanted answers. He'd only heard about the murder of Vajra that morning and was still numb. She'd been his friend—and now she could never be more than that.

Renaer held up his hands and said, "As you can see, we can't be guilty of someone's murder—"

"Silence!" Ulik yelled. *"Riarlemn!"* His wand fired a blue-gray beam, but Renaer leaped forward and down, avoiding it, and it struck the dragon's head fountain to no effect.

Renaer answered the attack with a dagger, stopping his roll forward but letting the dagger fly as he did so. The ornate hilt of Renaer's dagger stuck out of Ulik's arm, his blood staining the sleeve, and the young man howled as if mortally wounded.

Eiruk watched in horror as his companions unleashed spell-missiles on every member of the party, including the wounded woman. Her hood fell back as she grunted in pain from the missiles her bearer failed to shield her from. Eiruk's jaw dropped. It was Vajra—alive!

His head and heart revolted. Eiruk been ordered to capture her murderers, but here the supposed murderers were protecting her.

"Stop!" Eiruk yelled, but few were listening. They were all trained in the Art, but most had never been in a magical fight. Thus, the apprentices panicked or, like the bullies Mauron and Sarkap, took advantage of the situation to abuse others. Luckily, those brutes focused on those who fought back, not the helpless like Vajra.

Eiruk heard Renaer yell for them to stop, but no cooler heads heard him. Laraelra Harsard unleashed a well-aimed blast of colors that knocked out Mauron and blinded two others, but Raman paralyzed her with a bolt from his wand. Renaer's friend Vharem Kuthcutter, who had set Vajra behind the fountain, slashed an angry wound across Ulik's arm, making him drop his wand. The bully of the third-year dormitories fainted at the sight of more of his own blood. The halfling wielded his whip effectively and managed to trip Gharill, bouncing the wizard's head off the cobbles.

Despite surprise and their better numbers, some younger Watchful Order apprentices panicked, running from the fight when challenged with a blade. The few who remained either missed or aimed only at the biggest target—the blond man named Meloon. However, Eiruk saw the blond man step in front of spells and heard him yell, "Protect Vajra!"

That's when Eiruk made his choice. He focused on the remaining three Watchful Order attackers. He wove his spell carefully, and two of his compatriots fell asleep, slumping to the ground, while the third whirled around to face Eiruk in disbelief.

"Traitor!" Sarkap screamed. "Ten-Rings will kill you!" His attention on Eiruk, Sarkap didn't even see the halfling's whip lash out, wrap around his leg, and pull that leg out from under him. All he saw were the cobblestones rushing up at him to send him to oblivion. Eiruk smiled grimly when he saw two broken teeth fly out of Sarkap's mouth.

Renaer sighed and said, "Thanks, friend," though Vharem, Meloon, and Laraelra all glared at Eiruk with suspicion.

"I did this for Vajra," Eiruk said. "They said you killed her, but I saw—is she all right?"

"She will be, if we can get her to—" Laraelra said

But Vharem interrupted her. "We're *not* murderers. Why not call off your dogs?"

"I tried, but . . ." Eiruk noticed that some of the wizards were stirring, so he said, "Let's go. We'll talk on the way!"

Renaer nodded and picked up Vajra while Meloon unhooked a massive axe from his back, its edges glistening with blue energy. The axe reminded Eiruk of something, but he didn't have time to think yet.

·:⁀:·

Once the others were past him and down the stairs to the next landing, Eiruk lay a spell down to slow pursuit—he savored the irony of using it to help, not hinder, Renaer and his friends. As he turned to follow the others, Eiruk found Vharem sticking close to him, a naked blade in his hand. "Give me one reason, wizard, and I'll hurt you worse than your men hurt my friends."

"All I care about is *her* safety," Eiruk said, pointing at Vajra. "If that's your goal, we're on the same side."

Yells drew Vharem and Eiruk's attention behind them on the stairs. Two apprentices had reached the steps where Eiruk's spell lay, and both slipped as if grease coated the steps. Both fell off the stairs and rolled a bit down the slope of the mountain. Vharem smirked slightly and lowered the point of his blade, but Eiruk knew it would take more to gain the man's friendship.

The last wizard on that patrol, a fourth-year named Phalan, lit up the morning sky overhead with green fire. The fireball exploded, and emerald sparks showered down onto Eiruk, Vharem, and the others—but no bystanders on the stairs.

"Stlaern," Eiruk swore. "This spell will draw every patrol right to us—Watchful Order and Watch alike!" He and Vharem reached the next landing, halfway down the slope.

The seven of them, their bodies sharing bright green auras, took refuge behind the only cover they had at this landing. Northspur Rock, like other massive boulders on Mount Waterdeep too large to move out of the way, jutted out of the landing constructed around it. Eiruk joined the others behind the massive house-sized rock, shielding them from immediate view.

Only then did he realize they were backed into a corner against a sheer cliff of exposed rock with no way out but the stairs.

"*Good* leading, Elra." The halfling's voice dripped with sarcasm. "I *love* being cornered."

The chorus of "Be quiet, Osco!" at least gave Eiruk the halfling's name.

"I am Ei—" he started to introduce himself, but he gasped as Vajra woke to his voice. Instead of the intense brown eyes he loved, she stared at him with lettuce green eyes that reminded him of Samark.

"Eiruk Weskur," Vajra said. "You may accept Ainla's son, friends. He can be trusted, now that his path intercepts ours."

Eiruk's stomach felt like it dropped away. Vajra didn't know his mother's name—but her mentor did. "Samark?" he asked.

Vajra nodded. "All of us . . . we need your help, son."

"Help's what ye need all right," said a gruff voice. The speaker was a squinting, much-scarred man with a patchy scruff of a beard, a rusty chain shirt, and a large number of friends behind him. Only then did Eiruk remember that Northspur Landing was also a mercenaries' gathering place. The leader growled out to his followers, "Boys, I hear there's a price on their heads taller than a tavern. Whatsay we capture these folk before the Watch does it for free? Or before some of them angry wizards yonder steal our bounty?"

Eiruk gulped as they all turned to meet the voice. A score of grizzled sellswords raised weapons.

CHAPTER SIXTEEN

While I might map all the unseen pockets of magery about the city, I cannot predict the effects visited upon those who trod upon them. Northspur Rock alone has blessed or cursed many a guardsman on the mountain, whether they knew it or no.

Khelben "Blackstaff" Arunsun,
On the Matter of Magecraft and the City,
Year of the Stalking Satyr (1179 DR)

11 NIGHTAL, YEAR OF THE AGELESS ONE (1479 DR)

SELLSWORDS CLOSED IN ON THE PARTY FROM BOTH SIDES. VHAREM counted at least nine men closing in on them from the far side of the rock, all armed with drawn swords, cudgels, or maces. Laraelra shouted a spell and blasted them with a silent maelstrom of colors; while many of them howled and grabbed at their eyes, only one fell unconscious. Osco jumped up onto the Northspur Rock and scattered caltrops among the men, the sharp metal barbs slowing their advance.

Between Laraelra and Vharem, Eiruk Weskur swept his arms up as he intoned a spell, and a cloud of glittering golden sparkles erupted among the mercenaries closing in on them from the rock's southwest side. All but two of them clutched at their eyes and yelled about going blind. Like Vharem and his companions' green glows, the mercenaries shone in gold light.

Vharem clapped Eiruk on the shoulder and nodded his thanks. "That helps, but we're still trapped. Come, Meloon—Osco's got the right idea. We need the high ground to tackle a lot of them!"

Vharem scrambled up the rougher side of the Northspur and found the halfling whipping sling stones down on the heads of blinded mercenaries and cackling with glee. "I liked the sneaking-about plan better, V!"

"Me, too." Vharem sighed, as he showered the larger crowd near Vajra and Renaer with caltrops of his own.

Meloon clambered up the rough outcropping, his axe dangling from his wrist by a strap. Once Meloon stood next to him atop the rock, Vharem saw the bright blue flames suffusing the axe head.

Atop the Northspur, Vharem saw how dire a situation they were all in. Four of them were hemmed in between the rock and the cliff face by twenty sellswords. From above and below, wizards flew in their direction.

"What do you think we should do?" Vharem said. When he turned and looked up at Meloon, he saw the axe's blue flames filling the man's eyes. Meloon didn't respond other than to swing his axe with both arms, his actions forcing Vharem to fall back onto Osco. Meloon swung the axe in a wide circular arc, twisting his body as he did so, and the blue flames became a pulse of magic that flashed out in all directions. The four wizards flying up from the city and the pair flying down the mountain all dropped out of the sky, trailing light blue flames as they fell.

Lying atop the Northspur, Vharem looked down at his oldest friend and knew he had to help him.

"Vajra!" Vharem yelled, and she stirred, her eyes a blur of shifting color and energy. "Blackstaff, we need you!"

She glowered at him, her eyes focused points of cobalt blue. Her head scanned around and she growled as she got her bearings. "Northspur, good," she said. She began a complicated spell, her voice a low whisper, but her hands never stopped moving. The ground beneath the four of them began to glow.

Renaer whispered, "Everyone get close and ready. I don't know what she's doing, but that glow's staying tight around us. Vharem, get ready to join us or head out. You know where to meet us."

Osco whipped a sap down at a half-blinded cutthroat who moved toward Vajra, and the man crumpled, falling atop another blinded sellsword. Vharem saw a bull of a man shake his head to clear his vision, and then raise a rusty battleaxe, aiming at Laraelra. Vharem pierced the man's arm with a thrown dagger, forcing him to drop the axe. Laraelra's quicksilver bolts hit him in the chest and head, and he died before he hit the ground. Eiruk Weskur reached past Renaer and cast his spell, entangling the other dozen or more sellswords to the southwest in thick, gray strands of spiderwebbing. The gray tangles blocked off that escape, but it also hindered the sellswords. Curses, swear words, and the futile struggles of the sellswords shook the webs from within.

Meloon drew up to his full height with Azuredge, then he chopped the Northspur rock. The boulder shot blue flames at the eight sellswords on the northeast approach. Those eight flew out of the way like a shipwreck thrown by a wave.

Vajra continued her spell, and Vharem watched the ground beneath them, while still solid enough to stand on, grow transparent. Renaer gulped as he saw a huge pit yawning beneath them, even though it remained solid ground beneath his feet. Vajra's eyes darted up at Vharem, then back at Renaer, without halting her spell.

"Osco, get ready," Vharem said, "and . . ."

Renaer yelled with Vharem "Jump!" as Vajra said, *"Sruahiil!"* and those inside the circle of transparent rock began to slowly sink through it.

Osco stood atop Northspur and said, "You are mad if you thi—hey!"

Vharem grabbed Osco by the belt and yelled, "Elra, catch!" He flung the hin to her in the glowing circle. The halfling nearly collided with Laraelra, closing his eyes at the expected impact, but his plummet became a slow fall in unison with her.

Osco laughed when he opened his eyes, hanging upside-down above the flinching sorceress. He yelled, "Come, V!"

Eiruk sank alongside Renaer, and he grabbed Vajra's face with both hands and kissed her gently. He said, "Stay alive and stay safe, Vajra," then jumped outside of the glowing effect. "I'll remain behind to explain the situation—hopefully, I can at least keep the Watchful Order off your backs. Speed of gods to you, friends."

Vharem noticed that Vajra's face contorted in shock and surprise, but the stone-face returned almost instantly.

Meloon shook his head as the flames snuffed out on Azuredge and in his eyes. "What happened?" he said.

"Later!" Vharem said. "Jump!"

Meloon looked down at the others, all of whom were nodding or gesturing him forward. He leaped off the Northspur and laughed as he entered the spell's effect, sinking slowly just above shrieking Osco.

Vharem braced himself to follow suit, but his last glance around showed him a young wizard with hateful eyes casting a spell from the steps. The wizard's attention focused on Vajra, and Vharem saw lightning crackling in his palms. Too far for a dagger throw, Vharem thought, and no time. Just do it. He'd do the same for you in a heartbeat.

"Renaer, Vajra!" Vharem yelled. "Down!" He leaped directly into the path of a lightning bolt. Vharem spread his arms and legs wide, and his world went white and silent as the lightning overwhelmed his senses. He could not breathe, but he felt his body seize from the energy. He hoped his spread limbs would deflect any extra energy into the Northspur or the mountain rather than his friends.

Vharem could tell he was floating down slowly, and someone grabbed him beneath his arms to pull him close—Meloon, judging from his grip and the size of his hands. His hearing returned, and he heard Meloon shouting, "Vharem? *Vharem?*"

Vharem tried to whisper, "Stop yelling, big man," but he couldn't catch his breath. His sense of smell returned and he could smell acrid smoke surrounding him. Haze still covered his eyes, and it went pitch black. He gasped, jerked his arm, and his body exploded with pain.

As Vharem groaned against the pain, Meloon said, "Vajra just closed the shaft above us, Vharem. You're not blind."

Vharem tried to speak, wheezing for breath. The effort it took to choke out words, and a lightening feeling in his chest told Vharem to hurry. "We made it?" Those words alone forced him to cough, and the tightness in his chest and head faded.

"We're all right," Meloon said. "You saved us all."

Near Vharem's head, blue light flashed, and he could just barely discern the shape of Azuredge casting light all around him. He tried to wheeze a response, but he couldn't breathe, so he just gripped his friend's hand. He smiled, and the light in his eyes grew brighter as the pain disappeared. He shuddered, and then relaxed into death, his hand falling from Meloon's while they drifted down deeper through the mountain.

.:⌒:.

Renaer could not shake the image out of his head—his oldest friend, yelling at him with resolve in his eye, his body crackling with lightning. He held onto Vajra and sank slowly, silently. He could hear Meloon talking above. Vajra conjured up six pairs of glowing eyes, each surrounded by seven stars, to add to Azuredge's light. Renaer tried to speak, but only coughed, and he could now see Laraelra's tear-slick face, which told him what he dreaded.

"I had to open the shaft to save us all, not just the one," Vajra whispered. "I'm sorry."

Renaer looked away and set his jaw, clenching his fists to fight for control of his emotions. His face quivered only slightly when Osco whispered, "Oh stlaern it. Not V . . ." The halfling punched fist to palm numerous times.

Silence filled the rest of the descent, as the party watched the shaft become a bricked construction, not just a spell-slick hole bored through the mountain. Renaer realized this shaft—or at least some of it—had been built long ago. Vajra—or one of the Blackstaffs in her head—had known about it and used that to escape.

The party settled to the ground, and Meloon and Osco rushed over to help Elra with Vharem's body. Renaer shrugged Vajra out of his arms, since she seemed conscious and lucid. Once her feet stepped onto the stones of the tunnel, Vajra's entire body pulsed with silver light. She grimaced, groaned, then sighed in relief. She opened her eyes again, and almond-shaped mahogany eyes looked into Renaer's. He nodded, then rushed to help the slowly falling Meloon settle Vharem's body lightly on the ground. Renaer fell to his knees and silently prayed while clutching his friend's lifeless hand. *Kelemvor, god of death, if you be kind at all, welcome him to rewards unending for his sacrifice. Welcome and honor him, as I know we must let him pass from this life.*

Vajra hugged each and every person as they surrounded Vharem's prone form. She then knelt down to whisper a prayer over Vharem's body. "We shall always remember and honor your sacrifice, noble rogue." She wove a spell that cocooned Vharem's body in magical blue-gray energy. "That's the best I can do for you now, but we'll pay homage to you soon."

She rose, brushed off her robes, and said, "It's easier for me to maintain control the closer we get to Blackstaff Tower and the things in which our power flows—like these tunnels. No enemies block our path any longer. These tunnels haven't been traveled by other than spiders and rats in many moons. Most folk forgot about these tunnels once the Blackstaff and the Lords stopped being the most congenial of friends. That's what Khelben used them for—secret meetings with the Lords so they could travel unseen and unmolested." She gestured and the floating eye-lights now merged into the stonework, placing their glows into the mortar.

Vajra headed down the dusty and webbed tunnel, its mortar seams glistening just enough to provide lighting for the path outside of Azuredge's blue light. Renaer remained frozen, his face impassive in the glow of the magical coffin around his lifelong friend. The others paused, and Renaer could feel their indecision and conflict of staying with Renaer or going with her. In silent answer, a grim-faced Renaer picked up the cocoon and wordlessly walked after Vajra. The three others followed in silence.

The group walked a while before Vajra stopped, reached over, and traced her fingers on the mortared wall. Her finger left a brighter trail of white behind it, and she drew an odd rune along the bricks. Without even a protesting groan or scrape, the wall parted. Vajra stepped through the doorway and torches erupted into life on every wall, their flames flaring wide as they burned up the huge clumps of spiderwebs atop and around them. Renaer and the others followed and they entered a small antechamber with a small desk and chair set into the rock wall. To their left, two tunnels yawned before them, inside of which no torches flickered. Across the room lay a small set of steps leading directly into a blank brick wall.

Vajra stood in the room, confused a moment by the three directions. A brief flash of silver in her eyes, then she nodded. She turned back and said, "Come, friends. All you have to do is step on the stairs, say the word *nhurlaen,* and you'll be brought to my study, safely."

"You sure we're safe?" Osco asked.

"Doesn't matter, Osco," Meloon chuckled. "Better to be in the home of a friend than at the blade of an enemy, right? Besides, who wants to stay down here in the dark?"

"Are we?" Renaer asked. "Friends, I mean?" His tone was cold and distant, tinged with regret. The ache he'd fought against now filled his chest. Both of his oldest friends lay dead, and all to help this stranger get to this place. Renaer could keep the anger out of his voice no longer. "Are you friend enough to me to be worth the *costs?* Worth the *friends lost?*"

Vajra sighed, walked over, and placed one hand on Renaer's cheek, the other over her heart. "I've been nigh-incoherent the past few months because the power granted to me was not properly assimilated. Two others paid with their lives—two debts I can never fully repay, save with lifelong amity to surviving comrades. I cannot replace your lost friends. Nothing can, Renaer Neverember. Even if you'd not done all you have, ending my torture and saving my life would have made us lifelong comrades."

"Are you sure Ten-Rings ain't already the Blackstaff?" Osco said. "We been one step behind him all the time."

Vajra looked down at the halfling and said, "Blackstaff he is not, little man. The tower would tell me, as it has told me things during our walk here. It guards itself well, even from those with power enough to breach its outer defenses. However, he may yet be a danger to us and the city, given the power that he stole from here."

"Ten-Rings got in here?" Meloon asked. "Or was it the imposter Blackstaff?"

"Aye, both," Vajra said, "but Blackstaff Tower conquered them, rather than the opposite. We shall discuss and attend to their fates later. But for now, please, come—help me to become the Blackstaff for certain, so we may all find our true paths."

Vajra stepped onto the stone platform. Her eyes flashed with energy. The brick wall ahead of her receded. The stones formed a spiral stair ahead of her, and all could see and hear the magical torches flaring to life further up the stairs. Vajra took three steps up and said the word, *"Nhurlaen,"* and vanished.

After a pause and a shared look among themselves, Renaer set Vharem's coffin on the chamber's desk, rested his hand on it in silent salute, and said, "Good luck, friends." He then followed Vajra and disappeared. Within a few breaths, Laraelra, Osco, and Meloon repeated the procedure, leaving the chamber empty only with the glow of Vharem's coffin and the torchlight.

The torch flames flickered and sputtered, the only sound until a thin, reedy voice called out, "Father? Have you come for me? The ghosts . . . they left me in the dark. Help me. I did it all for you. I did it all for you . . ." The voice fell to sobs as the torches flickered out, restoring the all-encompassing darkness.

CHAPTER SEVENTEEN

Khelben the Elder built that tower like he carried himself—rod-straight like his back, stone as black as his scowl, and bristling with magics unguessed. Only the most foolish would ever attempt to steal into the forbidding tower, let along steal from it.

Drellan Argnarl, *My Walks through the City of Splendors,*
Year of the Lost Lady (1241 DR)

11 NIGHTAL, YEAR OF THE AGELESS ONE (1479 DR)

OSCO STEPPED OFF THE STAIRWELL AND GAPED. WHATEVER HE'D expected to find inside Blackstaff Tower, it wasn't this. He stood at the top of a staircase opening into a large ten-sided antechamber, corridors leading off in eight different directions, magical green torches flickering every twenty paces or so. The only other feature was a stone statue of a rearing griffon directly opposite the stairwell against a blank wall. At the center of the room stood Vajra, her back to him.

"Vajra?" Osco asked. "Where'd everybody go?"

Vajra turned to him, a lone tear running down her cheek. While she looked in his general direction, Osco knew her eyes didn't focus on him. "I'm sorry, friends, for what we now must endure. I thought it safe, but the tower seeks to prove us worthy to walk its halls." Her form shimmered as she sobbed. "I'm sorry . . . and may Tymora bless you with good luck." As her voice wavered, she faded into a wispy miasma of green mists, leaving Osco alone to contemplate which direction to follow.

"Parharding wizards," Osco swore under his breath. "So . . . we do this by the numbers, as if it's any other place we're casing." Osco started on the first corridor on his left, scanning carefully for any traps or hidden dangers. After he'd gone thirty paces, he discovered doors on alternating sides of the corridor every six paces beyond the first green torch. Scanning down the seemingly endless corridor, he noted seventeen doors before he stopped counting.

Shaking his head, Osco returned to the original antechamber. He chose the next corridor that arced off in a slightly different direction, and repeated the whole process. His eyebrows rose when he found the exact same dimensions and features in that corridor. He looked, but did not spot any of his own footprints, as these corridors were suspiciously devoid of dust. "Hmph. So much for the easy way of tracking."

Curious, Osco took out a small hunk of chalk and marked the first door on his left with an **O** beneath the lock. He retraced his steps back to the antechamber and chose the third corridor. All the details remained the same as the first two, though Osco growled when he approached the first door to find no mark on it. Scratching his head and scanning further down the corridor, he spotted his mark on the third door on the *right*. "So, you want to play games with me, wizard? Send me down the same corridor and shuffle the doors? Fine." Osco rubbed his hands together, then unbuckled his lock picks from the back of his belt, and said, "Let's see what's behind our marked door, then."

The lock appeared clean, unlocked, and without any traps, so Osco opened the door to find himself in a small room, a cot against one wall, a rug at the room's center, and a set of shelves holding a handful of books. Atop the shelves was a statue of a cat made of ivory with sapphires for eyes. Osco's own eyes widened, and he carefully scanned for traps around it before picking it up and slipping it into his backpack. He muttered, "Well, after all, the biglings always take from the hin, so we're due a donation on our parts."

Osco walked around the room, tapping the stones in the corners. He found no hidden doors there. He flipped up the edge of the carpet to expose the trapdoor he assumed would be there. It was.

Osco opened the trapdoor, only to find his view blocked by a cloud of greenish mist. He poked a dagger through and stirred it around, making the mists swirl but not dissipate. He dipped the dagger lower and lower, and his hand felt no shift in temperature or other danger. He leaned his head in, but mists blocked his sight. He whistled low. From the sound he could tell he was in a larger room than before, but could not tell how big. He whispered a prayer to Brandobaris, the halfling god and Master of Stealth, and dropped a copper, counting the ticks before he heard it stop. When it hit a solid surface, Osco knew it had struck stone and it wasn't more than a typical corridor's height. He rolled himself through the trapdoor, holding onto the edge and dangling uncertainly within the mists. Another whispered prayer of, "Brandobaris, may the risks I undertake in your name lead only to great rewards," and Osco let go. He dropped into the mist, and his stomach lurched when he realized he'd dropped farther than expected. Just as he started to shout in surprise, he landed outside the mists—

Back in the original antechamber.

"Parharding wizards," Osco grumbled, and he stalked into the fourth corridor.

Osco wiped the sweat from his face, then rubbed his hands dry again on his cloak. This lock was tricky, and it was his third attempt at picking it. He'd spent what he thought was at least two bells opening doors, finding hidden doors, and picking the locks on chests. The locks were getting more and more difficult, but Osco liked the challenge almost as much as he liked what he'd filched so far from those locked chests and secret rooms. His pockets, pouches, and bag all bulged with easily fenced goods and gems he'd found along the way. What drove him to distraction was his constant return to that ten-sided room.

Osco had found this room through a series of six locked and hidden doors, though they all shared similar locks, which made them progressively easier to pick. In fact, he actually found that when he looked closely, the lock itself started showing scratches from his own picks before he even started working on the locks.

"Hmph." Osco smiled. "Any advantage given is one step up a hin needs to get eye-to-eye with the biglings, who take advantage of us." With the latest lock picked, Osco pushed the door open into the largest chamber he'd yet found.

Green flames flared from the tops of crystalline pillars almost twice his height, six of them placed around the octagonal room in front of each wall save the one through which he came and the wall opposite that entry. The chamber held two statues, and Osco smiled when he realized this seemed to be a chamber honoring two halflings, rather than the usual human-scaled statuary. The bases were at least as tall as the statues themselves, their plaques identifying the statues. He walked up to the marble statue on the right and gasped. The figure was clad in wizard's robes cut for a slender half-ling, and he held a staff also cut to his size, the staff crowned by the carving of a lion's head. He'd seen paintings and drawings of this broadly smiling hin, but never such a lifelike representation, complete down to a dimpled chin still carried by his familial line. Osco's hand rubbed his own dimple as he read the tall base of the statue: *Pikar Salibuck. Friend of Two Blackstaffs.*

Tamer of the Three Fires of Harland. Vanquisher of Huillethar the Devourer. He Stood Tall in Art and Life.

"Thank the gods the Blackstaff remembered to honor me great-grand-father," Osco said. "Too bad we only get some backwater chamber buried deep away from everything else. No respect, really."

He turned on his heel and gasped as he saw movement. The marble statue he now faced was far less friendly. A dark scowling grimace seemed to darken the marble from which it was carved. Here was a halfling with long hair bound behind his head and an eye patch over his left eye. He wore older-cut leathers and a cloak and a hin-sized scimitar at his belt. Osco's eyes widened when he realized the statue's details even included the bulges and hints of daggers in both boots and sleeves. Around the statue's feet were bulging stone bags of carved coins, a pile of gems, and, oddly, a penguin. The living Osco read the inscribed plaque as the first line recarved itself anew with two words added to the end of that line. It now read: *Osco Salibuck the Elder. Agent of Khelben. Ampratines' Friend. Infiltrator Extraordinaire. No Fear Hindered Hin.*

Osco groaned at the pun on the plaque, but smiled as he liked the idea that two members of his family—including the man after whom he was named—were remembered by the bigling wizard everyone remembered. As he stared up at the statue's dimple, his hands fell against the bulging pouches on his belt, and he paused. He looked at both statues and how they had been remembered.

"Stlaern it!" Osco yelled, and he began pulling all his treasures out of his bags, pockets, and pouches. He threw them on the ground in front of the one-eyed halfling's statue, which made the honor plate glow green. From out of the plaque stepped an identical phantom image from its statue. The ghost of Osco Salibuck the Elder dusted its arms off and smiled at the very startled Osco, exposing three missing teeth with his grin.

Osco fell back in shock, and then scrabbled backward on all fours like a crab, his breath caught in his throat. He didn't mind ghosts, when he didn't know who they were, but family was another story.

The grizzled and much-scarred face chuckled, "Heh. You done better than I did, lad, the first time I darkened Khelben's door and helped meself to some of his things."

Osco felt more weight in the few pouches in his cloak, and he fished out four small cat's heads carved out of onyx. He tossed them at the ghost, as if to ward him off, and the ghost held his distance. The one-eyed halfling stalked over to the opposite statue and stepped through it, saying, "Wake up, son. Family's come a-visitin'."

STEVEN E. SCHEND

The ghost trailed greenish smoke, but it drew out more smoke that soon collected into the visage of Pikar. While Osco still hated the fact that he was trapped in a room with two ghosts, Pikar's smile comforted him a little.

"Great," Osco said as he stood. "I realized that the test is in not stealing from a friend, rather than taking what's owed me. That's not going to have me haunted now, is it? You'll back off, now that I've thrown all that away."

The one-eyed ghost crouched down by the ivory cat statue and raised his eyebrow over his eyepatch. "Ye sure ye want to just toss this away?"

Osco the Younger nodded vigorously, and the elder ghost let out a low whistle. "Worth a fair piece, all this stuff."

"So're friends, and I lost one already today." Osco sighed. "Don't need to lose another. And I sure as sunrise don't want to be a ghost down here the rest of my days."

Pikar's ghost floated closer and put an ephemeral arm around Osco, saying, "We're proud of you, great-grandson. It is tough being friend to the Blackstaff, but the road's an exciting one, and one filled with treasures vastly more valuable than gems."

"Oh joy," Osco muttered. "Lessons from me family what died helping the Blackstaff. That'll motivate me to keep helping Vajra. What'll it get me at best but a statue down here with you ancestors?"

"What makes ye think we're family, boyo?" Osco the Elder's ghost chuckled, and it began to morph, his features and clothes shifting to greenish hues and growing. He grew to twice his original height and the eyepatch dropped away. His long hair unfurled, and his hair grew slightly longer and darker, a widow's peak forming at the top of his forehead. His mustache and sideburns grew together to a full beard with a recognizable lighter patch at the chin. Osco saw the similarities between the Nameless Haunt and this ghost and nodded.

"S'pose I'm to be honored that the oldest Blackstaff chose to test me?" Osco said, placing his fists defiantly on his hips and looking up at the phantom's impassive face.

His only answer was one slightly cocked eyebrow as the wizard-ghost conjured up a pipe shaped like a loredragon, placing it in his mouth and lighting it with a jet of flame from one finger.

"So are you wondering how I knew?" Osco said, nervously pacing about the chamber, kicking now errant-gems into the corners. "Simple. Nobody but nobody puts gems in chests where you can find them. They hide them in plain sight if they've loose gems. Seen some in vases with dried flowers, others in a fish tank. Best place I ever saw were emeralds slipped into tubes set into the legs of a table—those were tricky to find."

Osco realized he had paced around the chamber while he talked, and the ghost did nothing more than puff on his pipe and remain facing one direction. His eyes did trail on Osco when he was in front of him, but he never made any move to turn and watch him when he walked behind.

"Say something, ye parharding spook!" Osco threw a handful of the gems through Khelben's head. Each made a small hole in his features, trailing wisps of green smoke. When the mists coalesced again, the ghost's front had shifted toward him. Osco found it even more unnerving to have the ghost of an archmage smile at him.

"Silence always makes hin nervous, I have found," the ghost said, with a wink, "and they tell more than they should. That seems the same since my time. When did you realize this was merely a testing, not an actual looting of Blackstaff Tower for your benefit, Osco Salibuck?"

"Well," Osco said, "Vajra'd said something about the tower testing me, and it didn't stop me. Not all hin're greedy *and* stupid—count on dwarves for that. I figured the only way to help myself is to not help myself, and when I saw those statues, I figured out that all these temptations were just that—to tempt me away from where I'm supposed to go."

One eyebrow rose over the wreathing cloud of smoke from his pipe. "Oh really? And where is it you are supposed to go, little halfling, filcher and spy?"

"This way," Osco said, walking directly through the green ghost with a wicked grin. He felt the wall a moment before triggering the secret door, and stepping through. Where the door deposited him was unexpected, windy, bitter cold.

And Osco wasn't alone there.

CHAPTER EIGHTEEN

Tonight I test my theories under the darkmoon. I have the keys, I have the will, and I have the knowledge. Tonight, I shall penetrate the innermost sanctuary of Ahghairon himself, and tomorrow, I shall penetrate the old wizard's secrets.

Melkar of Mirabar, *Journal*,
Year of the Shattered Wall (1271 DR)

11 NIGHTAL, YEAR OF THE AGELESS ONE (1479 DR)

THE GORECLIPSE SHEDS ITS CRIMSON LIGHT OVER FAERÛN ONE NIGHT every 784 winters, and it also sheds light on many a legend. Learn, too, that those things that suffered 'neath Ahghairon's hand unlock many secrets. Should ye gather as many 'neathmountaineers he battled when Selûne and her tears wept blood in his lifetime, ye shall then gain the Tower Impregnable."

The words from his studies haunted him and goaded him on. *I need more keys,* Khondar thought, *and Dagult has them. He doesn't deserve them—no one untouched by the Art deserves them.*

On his best day, Khondar "Ten-Rings" Naomal was one to avoid in the streets, his kindest face a glowering warning to those in his way. Today, even the dogs and cart traffic stayed out of his way as the wizard stalked his way up the Street of Silks to the Palace. Despite the strong highsun glare, the wizard's disposition wove the cold of the early winter more tightly around him, and folk shivered with his passing.

Khondar passed a steaming food cart, its vendor hawking hot buttered payr nuts, the smell of which reminded him of Centiv, who loved the snack. Khondar's step and face tightened as he thought of his last view of his son in Blackstaff Tower, the fearful face, as green mists and blue imps swarmed over him.

I just need those keys, he thought, *and I can re-enter Blackstaff Tower as the Open Lord, not an intruder. Then my son can find himself my most favored of children again.*

What snapped him out of his reverie were the overheard rumors. "They say the Open Lord's son killed the Blackstaff's heir!"

Khondar's attention snapped back to the nut vendor, who passed on the latest gossip to his customers, a pair of servants wearing the star-headed mace atop the green banner seal of House Korthornt. One of them responded, "Aye, his love of history has got the better of him, what he tries to steal the secrets of Blackstaff Tower itself." The woman elbowed her companion and whispered a response Khondar did not hear. Still, he smiled as his distracting rumors kept the gossips busy and everyone's attention away from him. That would make this easier, and also serve to keep the current Open Lord off his guard—an advantage Khondar would exploit.

Ten-Rings had fled Blackstaff Tower last night, slipping invisibly back to Roarke House to recover his energy. He tried to sleep, but to no avail, so he buried himself in research all night, specifically the books from Samark. The items they took from Samark's corpse glowed with a new light after Khondar's trip through Blackstaff Tower. He now saw a minor enchantment he'd previously ignored as merely a signature of sorts by the items' makers. He realized each of these was a key. Ahghairon and anything he himself enspelled acted as a key to pierce the fields around his tower—and Khondar already had five of the six keys he needed in the amulet, the ring, the dagger, and the two wands he pulled from the grasp of the Blackstaff's Tower.

That realization forced him through the streets on a frosty morning with flurries in the air. All that time he and his son had researched spell fields and protections around Blackstaff Tower had paid off—and now the Ten-Ringed Wizard would pierce veils unbroken for centuries. He would claim far greater prominence as Ahghairon's Successor and the new Open Lord. All he needed was one last key—and he knew that more than one was in Daugult's grasp. First he would take the keys from him, then the Open Lord's throne, and then the city would see the munificent rule of wizards again.

Khondar turned slightly off the main street toward the palace, but he stopped to stare at Ahghairon's Tower. The slim stone pinnacle rose four stories high. It had a conical roof and very few windows—a very plain and most common of wizards' towers. Were it not for its location or its builder's prominence in Waterdeep, few would ever give it a second's pause—until they noticed the slight glow around it and the skeleton that floated within that glow at street level. While most others had never known much about the failed invader, Khondar smiled. One of the books Samark brought out of Khelben the Elder's tomb named that invader—Melkar of Mirabar. Why Samark sought the book was unknown to Khondar, but he learned from it nonetheless. He reread it in the early morning, seeing it in the same new light he now saw the items he claimed from Samark.

Melkar had failed more than two centuries before because he misunderstood the legend. While many still talked of Ahghairon and his deeds to this day, those tale-spinners corrupted things in the telling. Details were lost and secrets obfuscated, either by accident or design. Most Waterdhavians learned "The Ballad of Battle Ward" by repetition and sing-alongs at taverns in any ward, its simple refrain praising Ahghairon's holding the line against Halaster and his pet demons. Most people assume that this long-ago battle involved only two demons and Halaster himself, as few bards bother to learn more than nine verses of the song, three verses per battle. Khondar knew that Melkar believed in that, which is why he only penetrated the first three barriers around Ahghairon's Tower when he attempted his entry. The legend he'd learned suggested the number of keys should match the number of monsters Ahghairon fought during the Goreclipse, a celestial event where Selûne went fully eclipsed and dark but the Tears of Selûne were stained red.

Khondar's deeper researches and his torture of Vajra taught him that he needed not three—the number of foes assumed by most—but six. That clue came from *Love at Llast*, a rather insipid volume of love poems with the full version of the ballad written in with footnotes detailing what spells Ahghairon used against them. Khondar knew he needed six keys—one for each of the five demons to pierce the barriers, and a sixth key representing Halaster to enter the tower itself. According to the poet Malek Aldhanek, Ahghairon slew the demons on the very spot he built his tower, sealing an otherworldly portal with their blood and sinew.

Khondar felt the two keys he carried with him—the ring and the dagger—thrum with power as he passed Ahghairon's Tower. "Soon," he whispered, "soon, I will claim that as my own. For now, my power is enough to force the Open Lord's attentions—and to claim from him something he's taken for himself." He masked his eagerness and impatience as he mounted the long and deep steps leading up to the palace.

Standing in the central reception hall of the palace, Ten-Rings drifted over to one of Ahghairon's more amusing creations—and one more easily noticed if moved or lost. Resting on a chest-high base, the crystal globe contained a miniature diorama of Waterdeep as it had stood when Ahghairon founded the Lords of Waterdeep. The weather depicted in the globe had accurately predicted the weather as seen at highsun the following day for more than three centuries. Khondar stared into the massive crystal ball, watching the snow swirl around its confines. As he peered closer at Ahghairon's Tower within the globe, a page approached and cleared his throat.

Standing at attention, the sandy-haired lad had the usual face-rash of early adolescence but the stance and voice of someone trained in diplomacy and courtly manners. "Milord Naomal, I am Milluth. Please forgive my delay. It took us some time to track down the Open Lord, as he oftimes strays from his official schedule, much to our dismay."

"Never mind that, boy," Khondar said. "Just take me to him."

"I can't do that, milord," Milluth replied. "Milord Neverember is in a meeting and cannot be disturbed. If you'd care to make an appointme—"

"No," Khondar said, putting magical compulsions and spells behind his clipped whisper. "You'll find you can, Milluth. Let us go find and interrupt your precious Open Lord."

Ten-Rings was grateful the alcove in which Ahghairon's Globe rested kept any from seeing him cast the spell on the boy, whose glassy-eyed response revealed the spell held him in thrall.

Milluth quickly crossed the chamber, leading Ten-Rings out of the palace proper and to the southeastern tower of the palace—the Parley Tower, where the Lords met with any envoys or ambassadors from lands east of Anauroch. As they crossed the courtyard, Khondar noticed the clouds growing darker overhead and Ahghairon's Tower looming beyond the curtain wall of the palace. He knew it would snow before too long, and he wanted to be inside, preparing his spells and meditating before it did. The pair crossed to the heavy door with its pair of flanking guards. Milluth led them through the door, across the entry chamber, and up three levels. As they climbed, Khondar planned his next move, and with a thought, two rings among his ten blinked with light, and were replaced with a different pair of rings. He looked at his hands and smiled, confident in his protections and magic.

They stopped at the landing and the ornate double doors that topped the stairwell. Flanking the doors were two pairs of guards—two in Lords' livery and two bearing badges with a raven holding a silver piece in its mouth. Khondar recognized the badge and smiled grimly. As Khondar and Milluth approached, all four guards put hands on their weapons but did not draw them. Khondar whispered a spell, unleashed it ahead of the boy, and paralyzed all four guards. He pushed the boy forward and said, "The door, Milluth."

When Milluth hesitated, Ten-Rings concentrated and willed the boy to forego knocking and simply open the doors. Milluth's hand jerkily reached for the key ring at his belt, and he unlocked the doors and opened them in one smooth motion. Khondar cast one spell on himself, in expectation of trouble.

Inside the room, wide windows covered with expensive glass let in much light and allowed guests a good view of Castle Waterdeep, the spur of the mountain, and southern Castle Ward. Dagult sat facing the doors with his back to the windows, both allowing his guests the view and showing he worried little about having his back exposed. Many described Dagult Neverember as a "lion of a man," and Ten-Rings could see how he earned that ascription. His pumpkin-brown hair flew around a furrowed brow, deep-set dark eyes, and an angry mien like a mane. He looked every bit the impressive and forceful ruler, even when taken by surprise. He wore a gold velvet overtunic emblazoned with the Lords' mark, and his black linen shirt and black-bear pelt cape broadened his already-wide shoulders impressively.

Chairs shrieked as people shocked by the intrusion stood or shoved their chairs back from the door. Khondar's reaction was equally swift. From the guards outside and at least two old acquaintances at the table, Ten-Rings knew this was a Sembian trade consortium—Concord Argentraven—meeting with the Open Lord. He rushed to the table at one man, half-risen from his chair, and he punched him hard in the throat. The man fell back into his chair, choking, and Khondar put his left fist to his mouth, uttering a low syllable. Ice erupted into the man's mouth, surged out his nose, and engulfed his entire head.

"What is this?" Dagult yelled. "Guards!" as he snapped a dagger out of his sleeve and into his hand.

Khondar saw all the other delegates in the room had minor weapons in hand. Their attention was on Khondar and his victim, who had suffocated in the ice and now wore a different face than the white-bearded one he wore moments before. The corpse had no beard, but his skin and hair were varying shades of ash gray. It told those assembled much.

"A shade!"

Khondar turned to face the assembly and said, "Forgive my intrusion and attack, milords, but haste was the best course of action here—lest our Open Lord and you be further duped by a cunning shade seeking to undermine our fair city."

Tradelord Amhath Dessultar cleared his throat and said, "How did you know that he wasn't who he appeared to be? I've known Markall Silverspur for more than thirty years, and you dispatched—"

"—a traitorous being who'd impersonated him for more than three years."

"How can you know that?" another Sembian howled, one Khondar had never met.

"Because," Ten-Rings replied, raising his rings, "it's my business as a Guildmaster of the Watchful Order of Magists and Protectors to know."

"Not good enough, wizard," a third Sembian said. "Explain or hang." The woman was the only person without a dagger at hand. She held a small diamond-studded rod in his direction, and her eyes crackled with magical energy thanks to a diadem at her brow.

Khondar glowered at the woman, then said, "I slew Markall Silverspur years ago in Yhaunn when I caught him blackmailing my guild and stealing thousands from our coffers. I had heard of his recent rise in fortunes and rumors had placed him in the city again. Whether grave-risen or replaced by an imposter, the man's insults were enough to garner a second spot of revenge on my part. Just how well did you all know Markall?"

Khondar fought a smug smile as he let that news sink in, the coin-grubbers wondering how much gold or influence they'd lost to hidden subterfuges of the now-dead shade.

"Khondar," Dagult said in a low voice, "I trust what brings you here is of the utmost importance to disturb these negotiations."

"It is, Open Lord Neverember," Khondar replied, sketching a barely respectful bow. "It is only a surprising gift of fate that I was able to prevent the shades from gaining any foothold in trade or other concessions with our fair city. After all, we welcome fair Sembia and its trade, not its insidious back-shadow rulers."

"Watch whom and what you accuse, Naomal," Amhath said. "We know each other and do business, but we are hardly friends."

"True enough," Ten-Rings said. "My business with the Open Lord is crucial for the city's welfare and must be private."

Khondar had been pacing around the table, past the slumped shade corpse, and when he finished talking, he stood at Dagult's right shoulder. He touched him on the shoulder, and the diamond ring on his right hand flared bright. When everyone's sight cleared, both the wizard and the Open Lord were gone.

Madrak ran his feather duster over the collected bric-a-brac on the ledge around the bay window seat in Dagult's office. As he brushed away a tenday's accumulation of soot and dust, he gazed out the window at the light snow falling.

"Auril," he whispered, "be kind to the young master, and use your snows to hide him from his foes, who seem to lurk closer than he knows."

Madrak hopped off the window seat and was picking up dishes and remnants of meals half-consumed off the three tables, the desk, and the floor when four feet suddenly appeared on the carpet in front of him. He stepped back, startled, and looked up into the cold gray eyes of a wizard glaring down at him. Dagult's back was to him, and he seemed to be sitting in a phantom chair. The halfling butler stepped back just in time as the very surprised Dagult let out a roar and fell solidly on his back. The stream of invectives and swear words coming from Dagult as he rose were directed solely at the wizard, who Madrak learned was named Naomal or Khondar and who had questionable parentage concerning lower animals and even lower planes.

Madrak cleared his throat and said, "Er, welcome, milords. Would you care for anything to drink?"

Years of practice kept any hint of amusement or terror off his face as the halfling flicked his glance from Khondar to Dagult. The wizard, however, made his disdain and dismissal of both Madrak and his master quite plain, at least to the butler's eye. Dagult, as usual, blustered and abused those under him privately, despite all his public demeanor painted him an unmatched diplomat and shrewd negotiator.

"By all the gods, when I tell you to stay out of my office when I'm not here, I *mean it!*" Dagult, having risen to his feet, aimed a powerful kick at the old halfling, who ably dodged the attempt and retreated through the hidden door just barely tall enough for him in the office wall.

"Thrice-damnable halflings!" Dagult roared after the retreating butler's door clicked closed. He spun back to Khondar and said, "Always rooting around, sneaking about the house through secret doors I can't fit through."

"Good help is hard to find, indeed," Khondar said, and he found himself remorsefully thinking of Centiv, left to his fate inside Blackstaff Tower. He paced the room to cover his sudden emotional response, and remembered his goal. The key! Unfortunately, getting a word in edgewise around Dagult proved difficult.

"But they're not nearly half as presumptuous as you, Ten-Rings! Our agreement was that no one would ever see us associated together! You've now given any foes a link between us and a suggested past history. Kidnapping me in front of witnesses won't bode well for your trial." Dagult's voice had started loud and barking, but by the time he finished his sentence, it was a cold, hard whisper with an edge of steel to it. "Abduction and threats against the Open Lord is a punishable offense, after all."

"Don't threaten me, little Open Lord." Khondar smiled as Dagult's face paled and his fists clenched at the insult. Ten-Rings continued, keeping him even more off-balance. "You don't have enough power to challenge me, even if that sword at your side truly holds all the magic it allegedly did in the hands of your predecessors. Frankly, I doubt you're able to draw it, and you just wear it to impress."

"That might be, Guildmaster, but what I do know is this—You assaulted me, my aide, my guards, my guests, and slew a member of a trade delegation. Even if they did not see your flashy abduction of me from the Parley Tower, many saw you enter the tower just before the panic began. Tongues are wagging now, even as we speak. No one can turn rumors and gossip into coins like Sembians. Should anything happen to me before I explain myself, all manner of hells will empty upon you and yours. And you have only yourself to blame for that. Beyond all that, there's this matter you seemed to have skillfully dumped into my son's lap. While the boy needs some challenges, I'll not see him swing for your activities, wizard."

"Hmph. Well, be that as it may, we both have our secrets and our sins. You, I'm sure the people would love to learn, have a knack for acquiring things, if only so you can gloat in their having. I sensed it last time I visited here—you keep true magical items of the Lords here, while leaving fakes behind to keep anyone from looking for them." Khondar's theory got its proof by Dagult's face going ashen again. "I'm looking for a key, Dagult. Do you have it?"

"You'll need to be more specific, Naomal." Dagult sneered, trying to regain control of the conversation. "I have hundreds of keys to hundreds of properties, secret places where only the Lords walk, and keys to every tomb within the City of the Dead."

Khondar glared at him. "Where have you hidden Ahghairon's Key? The one on display in the Ruby Hall at the palace was false—I could sense it! Now show me the real key!"

"If your information is accurate, wizard," Dagult said, "and you can sense fake constructs, you should be able to find it yourself."

Khondar walked around the room, angrily at first, but then secretly delighted that Dagult had given him the excuse to examine the room closely. Like the rest of Neverember Manor, the room was richly appointed with thick carpets and wall hangings in Dagult's favorite red hues. Ten-Rings skipped over all the bric-a-brac in the windows, sensing no magics from them, but his senses sang of magical auras against the back wall. He paced back and forth, seeming to admire a painting hanging there, and he spotted a stone out of place in the corner seam of the wall. He pressed it, and the painting and part of the wall recessed and slid out of the way, revealing a shelf with a number of items on it. Dagult's sigh of defeat was audible across the chamber.

Khondar reached in and picked up a small brass key, the handle of which was Ahghairon's swirling whorl of a wizard mark. It thrummed beneath his touch, and his wizard sight told him this was the genuine article. "What ever did you need Ahghairon's Key for, Dagult?"

"That key identifies and unlocks any door, known or unknown or however barred, when it passes nearby. When my wife died, she left me nothing—gave everything to the boy. I used it to search this entire mansion, finding out every secret door, every compartment, every possible place she might have hidden money, or every place my son might have hidden things from me. I kept it because it amused me to do so and because I'd never know when I might need it again."

"Well, I need it now." Khondar said, dropping the key into his belt pouch.

"That is not yours to hold," Dagult said, his hand on the dagger that rested on his desk. "Return it or find yourself in deeper trouble than even you can imagine."

"No, I don't think so, little man." Khondar laughed. "Should anything happen to me, your son dies." The wizard let that sink in, and while he knew Renaer and Dagult were estranged, he counted on fatherly attachment to stay his hand. Khondar found himself amused by some of the other things in Dagult's hidden cache, from a small metal dragon sculpture that breathed fire when you pressed its foot claw, to a small silver necklace dripping with thumb-sized sapphires, to a singular silver bracer with two palm-sized sapphires set in its guard. He left the recess open and wandered closer to Dagult's desk, where he spotted a gnarled hunk of phandar wood and gasped with what he saw through his wizard sight.

"You have a piece of the Staff of Waterdeep?"

"That? It's just a idle hunk of worrywood I rub when I need to relax."

"Hardly, Dagult, and forget bluffing me. Few can sniff out lies better than I can." What Khondar left unsaid was that the power in this isolated piece of wood tied into greater magic than he dared dream of. While inert on its own, it joined with eleven other fragments to create a fabled artifact tied directly to Waterdeep. Khondar picked up the lump of wood and tucked it into his belt. "I believe the Watchful Order is better prepared to protect this item of Ahghairon's making, rather than leaving it lying about holding down a pile of parchments."

"Put that back, wizard. I don't care if I can't use it. That staff is better kept apart."

"The Staff of Waterdeep saved the city twice!" Khondar whirled and glowered at Dagult.

"And nearly destroyed it! That stays here, or I'll have you and every member of the Watchful Order loyal to you rounded up and imprisoned *at best.*"

Khondar considered Dagult's threat and, seeing no doubt or hesitation in his eyes, bowed deeply. "Enjoy your tenure on the throne, little conniver-merchant. Soon Waterdeep will see Ahghairon's heir rise to take Waterdeep back to the heights it deserves. I shall restore the City of Splendors, and there shall be a reckoning upon those deemed *less than loyal* to me."

With that, Khondar teleported away, the chuff of imploding air being the only sound in Dagult's office until the gnarled piece of ironwood fell loudly back on the desk, knocking over a wine goblet. Dagult watched as the wine soaked into the parchments, causing the ink on the message to bleed and run. The red wine made his hand-scrawled Lords' coat of arms—the torchlike seal of the Lords—blur into a mass of black ink. Dagult shivered, but he could not tear his eyes away from the spreading stains.

CHAPTER NINETEEN

In her long-held guise as Khelben Blackstaff, Tsarra Chaadren held the Spellplague at bay the first time it struck Waterdeep. Its resurgence from Undermountain forced her unveiling by shattering her illusory guise amongst a crowd of nobles outside the palace. This led to the two long Retributive Years when Khelben's foes descended upon the city, ne'er expecting the half-elf to bring them to heel like misbehaving hounds.

Maliantor of Waterdeep,
My Eyes Open Always: Memories of the Blackstaff,
Year of the Enthroned Puppet (1416 DR)

11 NIGHTAL, YEAR OF THE AGELESS ONE (1479 DR)

MELOON STEPPED OFF THE STAIRWELL AND SWALLOWED HARD. WHATEVER he'd expected to find inside Blackstaff Tower, it wasn't this. He stood on frost-rimed grass in a tiny clearing, surrounded by a forest and a starlit sky. Behind him, the stairwell's stone steps descended under a small hillock. Only one other friend was here with him. Vajra hovered at the center of the area, standing upside down from where Meloon stood, the top of her head even with his eyes. The floating patch of stone on which she stood seemed to be the floor for her, as her hair and robes all fell toward it.

Vajra turned to him, a lone tear running down her cheek. While she looked in his general direction, Meloon knew her eyes didn't focus on him as she said, "I'm sorry, friends, for what we now must endure. I thought it safe, but the tower seeks to prove us worthy to walk its halls." Her form shimmered as she sobbed. "I'm sorry—and may Tymora bless you with good luck."

As her voice wavered, she faded into a miasma of green mists, leaving Meloon alone to contemplate what to do. He looked more closely at the trees, the pattern of the woods, and found it slightly familiar. Intrigued, he climbed the nearest tree, securing Azuredge to his back before doing so.

He climbed to the top of the tree, confused as it seemed to grow beneath him. When he reached the crown of the tree and looked out onto the forest, he gasped. Dotted in amongst the trees and various clearings were landmarks of Waterdeep—Mother Marra's House, Pamhael's Inn, the Stag and Hawk, Zarlhard's Swordsmithy, the Open Lord's Palace—and others he didn't recognize, like a tower shaped like a dragon, a trio of towers joined at the top by arching walkways that met a solitary tower above them all, a huge mansion he'd seen in ruins down in Dock Ward, and a noble's villa, its curtain wall keeping much of the forest at bay from its six buildings. As there was a slight glow coming from the windows of the villa, Meloon decided to head there, investigating the Stag and Hawk which lay along that direction too.

Meloon clambered down, dropping to the forest floor the last ten feet from the lower branches. He expected a cushioned fall from the usual woodland deadfall, but it felt like he landed on hard stone. Hearing a noise behind him, he leaped and rolled to his left, narrowly avoiding an arrow that now jutted from the ground where he landed.

"Thanks be to the Lady Who Smiles," Meloon whispered as he came up into a crouch, readying Azuredge in his hands. He looked at the arrow and tried to judge the direction from which it came, but the arrow itself dissolved into green sparks as he watched.

Meloon rubbed his chin and decided to continue on his original plan. Whoever was stalking him could follow him, and he'd catch him or her later. For now, he'd head for the light at that villa. Above him, there were only stars in the sky and no moon, so the two brightest lights came from his axe and the villa.

He jogged through the forest, taking a zigzag path to avoid the archer. Frustrated at feeling so exposed, he whispered, "I wish this axe wouldn't be so bright. It's giving me away." With that, the flames on the axehead snuffed out, leaving Meloon wide-eyed and in relative darkness.

Another arrow thunked into the tree ahead of Meloon, and a woman's voice came from it. "She listens to you, despite your callow nature, boy. Do *you* listen to *her?*"

Meloon kept running past that tree, not recognizing the voice. He heard another twang of a bowstring behind him, and the next arrow zipped by his left shoulder, grazing his leather armor. He turned hard to the right, grabbing the vine-covered tree and swung himself around to face his attacker. "Some light would be good now, axe!"

Azuredge flared, its blue fires lighting up the woods around Meloon and revealing the attacker. She stood almost as tall as Laraelra, clad in leathers, and her long hair was pulled tightly back and bound with a silken cord, revealing slightly pointed ears. She held her bow in her left hand, but her right was weaving a spell. What Meloon found most curious about her was the green hue in everything—her skin, hair, clothes, and weaponry.

"Who are you?" he asked. "Why are you attacking me? And where are my friends?"

"You're in no position to demand anything, boy," the woman said. She finished her spell, and all around her in the shadows among the trees, huge eyes reflected Azuredge's blue fires. Eight new eyes, each larger than his fists, stared at him, and he heard a loud growling coming from all sides. One of the creatures stepped into the light, its golden mane and fur glistening. Meloon judged this lion to be at least three times his size. He gulped and tightened his grip on the axe.

Patience, Meloon, a voice said inside his head, its soft tone melding with glimmers of light within the runes on the axe's head and haft. *She is Tsarra. Talk, don't fight. Move toward the light.*

Meloon saw Lauroun's face in his mind's eye, and her eyes matched the shimmer inside the runes of his axe. Meloon stared at the axe for a moment, then his eyes darted at the gigantic lion approaching and baring its fangs.

Tsarra stood back, drawing another arrow into her bow. "Well, warrior? Surrender or a hopeless battle? Which would you prefer?"

"Neither, Tsarra, thank you," Meloon said, and he backed away, ducking behind a large tree to break the charge of the lion. When it hit the tree, Meloon turned and ran toward the villa and the light.

Behind him, he heard arrows striking the trees and the roar of the lions. He felt more than heard their heavy footfalls in the forest around him. He focused on his first goal—the Stag and Hawk tavern mysteriously moved within this grove. When two arrows struck the trees on either side of him, he marveled at his luck that they'd missed him—

Until sprays of webs came from each arrow. Within a step, sticky arm-thick spiderwebs filled the path before him. Meloon tried to turn, but his feet slid out from under him. A spray of dead leaves covered the lower webs as he rolled to the right. He could see his path to the Stag and Hawk cut off.

Behind him, Tsarra uttered a swear word only his grandfather still used. Meloon got up, only to find his path blocked by two of the lions. He turned back to find the other two lions and the webs preventing escape down his previous path. He tightened his grip on the axe and said, "Come on."

He stepped toward the lion in his path, swinging Azuredge, only to see the lion grow more and more transparent. By the time he closed with it, the lion had disappeared. He broke into a run again.

Arrows sprouted thorn bushes, slinging more webs, and even a few gouted fires or noxious gases when they hit. Meloon charged past all of them, calling behind him, "Tsarra, it's obvious you could easily stop me, so why don't you?"

"Haven't had a good hunt in ages," she said, suddenly beside him. "We rarely get to play here."

"Here?" Meloon asked, dodging away from her and out into a clearing on the western side of the noble villa. "So I'm still in Blackstaff Tower? And since when do wizards use bows or hunt?"

He took a quick look behind to see where Tsarra was, but spotted no one behind or beside him. He picked up his pace, arcing around the clearing to the front of the villa. He ran through the open gates, only to skid to a stop on its cobbles. Tsarra leaned against the villa's corner. On one side of her was the servant's entrance tucked to the side, and on the other the main entrance in proud, overdone details of metal banding and highly polished pharnal wood. Light streamed out beneath both doors and the windows high above.

"Wizards don't, but I do," Tsarra said, as she leaned on her bow.

"Did you hunt down my friends too?"

"Hardly," Tsarra said. "There are others tending to your friends."

"Let us help. You're guarding Blackstaff Tower. Let us help Vajra, and we can all help Waterdeep."

"Did she tell you that?" Tsarra nodded toward Azuredge.

"She who? The axe? No. But she has said a few things, like your name. I'm sorry I don't know who you are. I'm not a history student like Renaer."

"I used to be a Blackstaff. You're a sellsword. If we promised you a fortune in gems, would you help the other guardians and me rout the other invaders out of the tower?"

"No."

"Why not?"

"They're my friends. We're here to help the city, not ourselves. I thought that was what Blackstaff Tower was all about too."

"Very good, Meloon Wardragon," Tsarra said. "There's more to you than a great physique and a magical axe. I expected you to fight my harassment long before you ever got here. If Lauroun"—and here the ghost nodded toward Azuredge—"honors you with advice, listen to her. You're both defenders of Waterdeep now, and that's rarely the easiest path on which to walk. Are you certain you choose this?"

Meloon smiled and said, "And so the wagons roll."

"So be it, warrior," Tsarra said. "How do you know which door to choose, then?"

Meloon laughed and winked at her, then strode past her and through the servant's entrance. As he crossed the mist-enshrouded threshold, he heard Tsarra's ghost mutter, "Brawn and some brains when he chooses. Just like you, husband . . ."

Meloon's third step took him through the mists and into a decidedly cooler place.

And again, not where he expected.

CHAPTER TWENTY

I worry for our son, my love. His temper is as yours was, though he has not my mother's gifts to protect him. Krehlan climbs to your example, but 'tis such a fall from so high . . .

Laeral Arunsun, *Lifelong with Regrets,*
Year of the Wrathful Eye (1391 DR)

11 NIGHTAL, YEAR OF THE AGELESS ONE (1479 DR)

RENAER JUST STOOD AND STARED. AFTER ALL HE'D READ ABOUT Blackstaff Tower, he'd not expected this. No one else was present other than Vajra, and the room itself was tiny with barely room for Vajra and him to stand face-to-face. Its walls were made of some chilling, white energy. Touching them felt like brushing a hand against glacial ice. Pushing his hand farther through, Renaer quickly lost all feeling in his hand. The room's featurelessness frightened Renaer, as he rubbed his hand to restore feeling to it.

"Vajra, what's going on? Where's Vharem? And the others?"

Vajra turned to him, a lone tear running down her cheek. She looked past his left shoulder and said, "I'm sorry, friends, for what we now must endure. I thought it safe, but the tower seeks to prove us worthy to walk its halls." Her form shimmered as she sobbed. "I'm sorry—and may Tymora bless you with good luck." As her voice wavered, she faded into a frail cloud of green mists, leaving Renaer alone.

He turned back to the stairs, only to find them gone. The white walls dissolved into mists that slowly rose and cleared. Renaer gasped, finding himself at an intersection among rows upon rows of bookshelves. In every direction, books rose on ancient wooden shelves up to a ceiling more than three times' Renaer's own height. He let out a low whistle, turned, and walked into another row, only to be faced by the same scene—thousands of books of all conceivable sizes and bindings.

Renaer reached out at random, grasping a red-leather bound folio off the shelf and opening it to its title page. The rich smell of vellum wafted over him as he read in elegant script "An Archmage's Life at Court, by Vangerdahast Aeiulvana." The scribe's notation at the bottom marked this as a personal copy for Khelben Arunsun, penned in the Year of the Crown, 1351 DR. More astonishing were brief scrawls of "Enjoy!" written by Azoun IV, and another hand writing, "Now you owe me your next," followed by an elaborate rate **V**. Renaer replaced the book with reverence, knowing this tome alone would cost him a month's worth of rents.

Renaer turned and grabbed a more modest brown leather book bound by straps. He gingerly undid them and opened *Wanderings with Quill and Sword* by Mirt the Moneylender, penned in the Year of the Bridle. Renaer's eyes widened as he realized the book had been copied that same day 130 years in the past! He put the book back and wandered down the rows of books, less frequently taking books down for identification as much as absorbing the variety and breadth of the tomes in Blackstaff Tower.

When Renaer turned down his twentieth row, he stopped in his tracks, startled by the appearance of someone in the library. More than ten feet overhead, a man stood on thin air at the high shelves, reading. The man's olive robes and hood hid his features, but Renaer noticed that his green boots showed no wear and tear on their soles.

"Forgive my intrusion, master," Renaer said. "Do you know where I might find Vajra Safahr or my other comrades?"

The figure barely twitched, though the man's left hand began a spell. Renaer watched carefully, but neither moved nor interrupted him. When the spell finished, a brief cloud of sparks surrounded the man's hood. "How did you know?"

"Know what?"

"Not to fear the spell. Most folk would have dodged for cover behind the books when they noticed my working a spell. Are you simple, fearless, or some combination thereof?" The man's tone was haughty and condescending, a combination that set Renaer on edge.

"Even if I can't cast spells," Renaer replied, "I know how to identify which spells mean property or personal damage, and which ones simply mean the caster desires information for which he is too uncouth to ask directly."

The wizard's head snapped toward him, and he pulled his hood back, glaring at Renaer. "The merchant class has grown ruder since my time." The man's hair, skin, and eyes were all varying shades of green, his hair and neatly trimmed full beard a lighter mossy green than the rest of him.

"No ruder than you, ghost." Renaer said. "Now that you're done trying to distract me, why not test me? That's what you're here to do—test me to see if I'm worthy to accompany the Blackstaff inside her tower?"

"She's not the Blackstaff yet, nor are you protected by her hopes and promises," the ghost replied, and he descended to the floor to face Renaer as if he walked down invisible steps. "As for testing, let us commence with something simple. Who am I?"

"Krehlan Arunsun, son of Khelben and Laeral. You were never simple in life, and I doubt you are after death."

The ghost's eyebrows furrowed, but then rose and he chuckled. "Levity in the face of danger. You're a rare one, boy. How did you know me? I was dust before your father's birth."

"I assumed the most likely candidates to haunt Blackstaff Tower were those who bore its burdens," Renaer said, "and as Krehlan's silver hair from birth made him the only Blackstaff with one solitary hue in beard and scalp, it was a simple guess."

"Fairly deduced, Renaer Neverember," Krehlan said, and he smiled at Renaer's surprise. "Now, how do I know your name, if I have been dead and a ghost for two lifetimes or more?"

Renaer stopped and thought, then replied, "I know your previous spell won't reveal my name to you. While you might have been one of the many spirits possessing Vajra over the past few days, only two managed to stay in control for more than a moment or two, so I suspect you never overheard my name. Thus, I'm left to consider that a Blackstaff would know the identity of anyone who walks inside the tower, whether such detection and identification magic can be felt by the target or not."

"Well, which is it?"

"The last. I've read Maliantor's *Eyes Open Always,* which is considered the definitive tome on life in Blackstaff Tower in the fourteenth century. She talked about the Blackstaff knowing the location, identity, general mood, and intent of anyone inside the tower's walls, simply by his or her magical ties to the stones. I doubt that ended with your death, since at least a part of your spirit seems to remain here."

"And how do you know I'm not fully haunting the tower, awaiting resurrection?"

"You once penned a treatise on elven *kiira* based on your study of the *kiira n'vaelhar* worn by Tsarra, Kyriani, and yourself until the Year of Staves Arcane. I've read it, and you describe how *kiira* create a spirit template to hold and personify knowledge within them. They're less the actual person's spirit than a permanent illusion. You obviously did something with the gem and the tower, as your image retains the green of the gem, even though you've not worn it for sixty-four years."

Krehlan nodded, then waved Renaer toward another intersection of shelves. "Very well. You're at least as smart as most of the agents who've trod the halls of the tower in the past century. Why don't you avail yourself of the library? Discover things you'll never again have the chance to read?"

"On any other day, this labyrinth might have kept me enthralled for ages. But not today."

"How can you resist? Surrounding you are books for which any wizard, sage, or halfwit would give both his arms and read using his feet! All you need do is reach out and read them."

Renaer sighed. "I've already lost two arms because of Ten-Rings. Their names were Faxhal and Vharem. They were friends. My right and left arms, according to some. They are dead and gone, and all I can do is make sure they didn't lose their lives in vain."

"So what will you do?"

"Use what I already know. Your parents taught me that." Renaer fought off a smile when he saw the shocked look on the ghost's face.

Krehlan regained his composure and asked, "How did they teach you? You weren't alive in either of their lifetimes, and Father's spirit occupies another of your friends just now."

Renaer waved his hand around, gesturing at the books. "I've read any and all histories I can find about this city and its heroes. Your parents wrote at least seven books between them about the Waterdeep of their long lifetimes, and I own and have read five of them. I've even read Malchor Harpell's *Two Mages' Legacies* and Savengriff's *Swords, Spells, and Splendors*. All of them taught me much about Khelben and how he thought, not to mention a few choice quotes that apply."

Krehlan's left eyebrow rose, and he said, "Indeed?"

"No, that one doesn't apply." Renaer laughed as he walked past Krehlan and faced the nearest bookshelf. "Your father said, 'The door to truth opens with knowledge. The door to knowledge opens when you admit you do not understand.'" Renaer paused as he realized the shelf ahead of him now glowed slightly—or at least around the decoration on the spine of a massive hand-thick tome. He reached forward and said, "I don't know how to escape this room, but I'm willing to learn and accept such learning."

He reached out, grabbed the decoration, turned it, and the entire bookshelf opened outward as if it were a door. Renaer stepped through it, despite the icy cold draft coming from it.

Behind him, Renaer heard Krehlan mutter, "Stlaern. Took me seven years to realize that secret, and he figures it out in less than a day. He'll do just fine."

CHAPTER TWENTY-ONE

The golden-haired half-elf Ashemmon carried his mother's grace, his father's guile, and Art both learned and innate. Many said the fifth Blackstaff outshone all but the first in statecraft.

Sarathus Hothemer, *Blackstaves: Their History,*
Year of the Forged Sigil (1459 DR)

11 NIGHTAL, YEAR OF THE AGELESS ONE (1479 DR)

Laraelra found herself at the top of a stairway. Behind her, a chamberlain announced in a loud voice, "The Honorable Guild Master Malaerigo Harsard and retinue."

Laraelra was shocked to note her friends were gone, and she was on the right arm of her father, his other arm attached to Yrhyra, his latest companion, a giggly and short but buxom auburn-haired lass several years younger than her. Malaerigo held tightly to Laraelra's arm, leading her into one of her most hated arenas—a noble's feast. She recognized the green-marbled setting as the Ralnarth noble manse off of Vhezoar Street.

Laraelra found herself wearing a summer-weight gown of deep purple with black and red highlights, her boots replaced by heeled shoes of crimson that made her ankles ache in three steps. Her long black hair no longer hung loose and straight down her back, but was up high above her head in an elaborate Mulhorandi headdress. Her dress was immodestly cut and tight, its front dipping far lower than Laraelra liked, as she normally disguised her slender-to-gaunt figure in layers of clothes. Yrhyra in contrast reveled in the attention her nearly exposed and more curvaceous front garnered her.

Malaerigo also had dressed up beyond his usual attire, slicking his normally unkempt brown hair back on his head and shaving, which exposed the line of moles down his right cheek. Laraelra knew this was an illusion, despite all the evidence—including the proper smells and sounds—merely because her father had always been too cheap to own such well-tailored clothing of red silk and black leather.

Laraelra looked around the crowd surrounding them, not resisting the hold her father had for now. She searched for familiar faces—specifically those with whom she had come to Blackstaff Tower. Perhaps they might have answers. While Malaerigo whispered this or that wrong someone in the crowd had done to him, Laraelra spotted Vajra off to one side.

When she made as if to close with Vajra, Malaerigo held her wrist. He continued smiling broadly and nodding at passersby, but his harsh whisper chilled her. "Child, don't shame me in front of these folk. You'll go where *I* direct, not where you will."

Even for an illusory duplicate, Laraelra felt the all-too-familiar anger at her father's intransigence. She considered exposing the illusion for what it was, but decided to manipulate it to uncover its true purpose.

"Father, I merely sought to steer us away from another dreadful encounter with that coin-sucking Amnian harpy, Lady Kastarra Hunabar."

As expected, her father's face paled to an ashen gray as he scanned the crowd and spotted the large olive-skinned woman with blond hair heading their way. Laraelra managed to steer them behind another crowd of folk behind Vajra.

"Vajra?" Laraelra said. "Milady Safahr?"

Vajra turned to her, a lone tear running down her cheek as she looked straight into Laraelra's eyes. "I'm sorry, friends, for what we now must endure. I thought it safe, but the tower seeks to prove us worthy to walk its halls." Her form shimmered as she sobbed. "I'm sorry—and may Tymora bless you with good luck." As her voice wavered, she faded into a puff of green vapor, leaving Laraelra adrift in a sea of politics, people, and pageantry—three things she avoided as much as possible.

"What are you doing talking to the Blackstaff's heir, Daughter?" Malaerigo said. "Like every wizard, she tries to pry secrets out of every honest man's brain. Never trust anyone touched by magic, especially those in power."

Laraelra stopped and stared at her father, wondering how he had forgotten her own abilities.

"Wizards are icky, Mally," Yrhyra cooed at him. "I don't let them use their wands on me now that I got you."

"Hush, Hyra." The guild master's grip on his daughter's arm tightened. "What does that Tethyrian bitch know about you or about our guild? Is that why she was talking to you—trying to muscle in on my control through you? That's *exactly* how our oppressors operate, you know . . . stealing secrets and—" In a heartbeat, Malaerigo's visage and voice shifted from angry diatribe to pleasing sycophancy. When Laraelra responded to his turning her around, she saw to whom his smiles went. "Why, Lord Gralleth, how marvelous to see you! I hope you're happy with the solution we came up with for your property on River Street. Here, my lovely daughter will keep your son from getting bored while we talk business."

Malaerigo nearly shoved Laraelra into the arms of the younger Lord Gralleth. While she was relieved to be away from her father, Laraelra now despaired as the adolescent and far-shorter Rharlek Gralleth boldly placed his cheek against her exposed cleavage, smiling lecherously as he lisped, "A pleathure to meet you, lovely lady. Let uth danth and you may tell me all about yourthelf."

Unlike most other women in the party, Laraelra did not find Rharlek fascinating or attractive, despite his social and financial prominence. She saw him as he was—a squat, poor-complexioned boor with bad teeth, worse manners, two left feet, and a wasted education. Still, she had something to learn here, so she continued to play along.

"Milord Rharlek, I hope nothing is amiss at your mansion on River Street. It's such a marvelous example of modern Tethyrian architecture—definitely something to gentrify Trades Ward, if I may say so."

"You may, my dear," he replied, readjusting his too-tight grip on her hip. It took some work for Laraelra to keep them even barely in step with the dance, not that Rharlek noticed either the beat or the other dancers. "No, there'th nothing wrong, unleth you count thievth coming up through the thewerth."

Laraelra kept her interest from her face. "Surely my father has put the guild to work to prevent any such incursions ever again."

Rharlek nodded. "Yeth, but we're more interethted in where they came from, becauth they theemed to have keyth to many lockth in my houth."

Laraelra gasped, "Oh my goodness!" both to this and to Rharlek's exuberant entry into the next dance atop her right foot. She knew the younger man wanted her to ask what was stolen so he could brag about his family riches, but she took another tactic. "I'm glad no one was hurt by the intruders. Isn't it awful, the lawlessness in the city? You'd think the Blackstaff or someone could do something about that."

With musicians playing an exuberant dance, the pair whirled about the room. Laraelra nodded at a number of other women, all of whom would gladly be in her shoes, no matter how often their feet were trod upon. Her smiles were met with scowls or outright fury, and one woman even stormed across the floor toward them. Laraelra carefully timed her minor magic and prestidigitated the front of the woman's dress beneath her left foot. The youngest Lady Korthornt sprawled forward with a scream, her sliding fall knocking four other dancers down with her.

Rharlek did not even see the woman tumble on the dance floor, but with unexpected deftness, he maneuvered Laraelra into a double-whirl off the floor and through a side door from the hall. With a flick of his wrist, he spun Laraelra onto a divan, and he closed the doors behind them. Before he turned around, his hair lightened to golden blond and lengthened until it nearly reached the floor. His back remained slender but grew taller, and his garish purple velvet outfit became a wide-necked robe of scarlet. The man turned around, and Laraelra saw a variety of sigils and designs tattooed in black and blue across his chest, shoulders and neck, as his torso was exposed down to his lightly haired navel. The man's face was clean-shaven with hawklike features, and while she imagined he could be severe, she found his smile kindly and pleasant.

"You're good, but you overreached there. Do you know where?" he asked.

"Excuse me?"

"What did you do wrong back there? Loved your very deft use of magic on that silly woman. Unless someone specifically watched your hands, no one would think anything other than the clumsiness of an angry, over-wined young woman. Brilliant, really, save for those who watch and truly see."

Laraelra reviewed the last few moments of the encounter and sighed. "I should not have mentioned the Blackstaff. That tells him what I'm more interested in, rather than having him lead me to what he's wishing to tell me."

"Exactly," the man said, as he settled down next to her. "And the rest?"

Laraelra shook her head, stiffened her back, and put her hand out. "I am Laraelra Harsard, and I would know what you are called, master."

"Heavy-handed, lass, but fair," the man said. "And correct in asking what I'm called. We of the Art should never give out names if we do not need to. I have been called Blackstaff in my day. What would you call me?"

Laraelra paused, looking the man over, and said, "You answer also to Ashemmon, don't you? The only unbearded male Blackstaff other than Samark. You look remarkably well, given that you died fifteen years ago."

"Insightful, yet not intrusively so. You shall go far, once you get past your fears."

"Oh? Which fears?"

"Your father's disapproval. The disdain and jealousies of others."

"But I don't—"

Ashemmon held up his hand and said, "Each of you is being tested to see what kind of folk you are, and if you are worthy comrades or agents or merely acquaintances of our dear, damaged Vajra. Your patience and adaptability were found adequate, my dear. However, you failed to confront your father's comments, nor did you face your rivals fairly in there."

"I see rather deeper than that, master. You were known as a political being, Ashemmon, so you know that public arena was not the place for any confrontation with my father. His temper is explosive, regardless of context, and it was more politic for me to swallow my confusion and deal with him when it would not disrupt either his or my plans. As for the jealous women, what I did was the least of what I could have tried—and certainly far better than she treated me at my first noble feast years back."

Ashemmon smiled and nodded. "True, very true. You've my admiration for recognizing when to confront and when to prevaricate. You'll be a splendid help in teaching Vajra to be more politic. I doubt she'll listen much to me. Or Khelben. She's too much like Kyri."

"This was all a test to see if I could help Vajra?" Laraelra asked.

"We know you can do that. We've been watching. We want to know how you might help her in the future. I think you will be a good friend to the Blackstaff."

Laraelra flinched as she realized the colors of her surroundings had been bleaching away, the blond and scarlet on Ashemmon's image slowly shifting to greens.

"I don't know if I'm worthy of such attention," she said. "Besides, my father would explode if he thought I was to work directly with the city's *oppressors,* as he's always called those in and of power."

"He's aware of your talents, is he not?"

"He must be, as I'd inadvertently cast spells on him before I understood what I could do. Most days, I think he chooses to ignore what he knows and operate as if I'm just a tool for him to manipulate for his political games. I don't know if I deserve to—"

"Poor child." Ashemmon's shade became more and more translucent as he spoke, fading almost to invisibility. "Like me, you were so often told your limits—what you could not be—that you fail to see what you *can* be. I see a future unimaginable for you right now—power and privilege with a price, but honor throughout. You and your friends share a noble goal. Do not despair. Do not abandon that dream. We shall not judge. But we shall be watching."

By the time Ashemmon's form became transparent, so too did the Ralnarth manse. Laraelra felt an icy cold draft whipping around her, and she shivered, thinking of her low-necked gown. She hugged herself, and found she was again clad in her heavy wool cloak and her usual beltarma and robes. Her hazy surroundings whipped around with another blast of wind, and where she found herself was as unexpected as her first location inside Blackstaff Tower.

CHAPTER TWENTY-TWO

The Art that is true magic cares not a whit for the hands that wield it. It sings in the heart that embraces Art for her own sake, not the sake of power.

Zahyra Ithal, *Annals of the First Vizera, Volume XXI,*
Year of the Burning River (-159 DR)

11 Nightal, Year of the Ageless One (1479 DR)

Unlike her companions, Vajra had been to Blackstaff Tower many times before. She knew to expect the odd architecture, the guardians, and the dissociation when teleporting from one stair to another. She knew she stood in the entry hall of Blackstaff Tower, regardless of how it looked. Free-floating architectural details filled the room, from arches and statues to doors and torches set into walls that were mere patches floating in space. The rest of the air was filled with elements from the royal court at Faerntarn in Tethyr, the lonely hills where Samark died, and her childhood home at Shelshyr House. The most dominant feature here was a set of stone steps spiraling up through the center of it all, and at the foot of them stood Samark.

Vajra's heart leaped, and she tried to dash forward to where he stood, but he shook his head. "You are not whole, darling Vajra, and you are not Blackstaff. Not yet. We must test you, heal you, and then you can move around the tower."

Another ghost wisped into existence before Vajra's eyes—Kyriani Agrivar, a mischievous half-elf spirit of a former Blackstaff. "You and I share two things—we assumed the Blackstaff's power without proper preparation, and we fight wars in our hearts. Until we settle the latter, the former can never be attained." With that, Kyriani simply shuffled sideways, lay down catlike on a divan that floated by perpendicular to Vajra's floor, and drifted off, leaving the young woman alone again.

"We'll allow you one brief moment to address those with whom you arrived," Samark said, "and then all will be called to testing, for Blackstaff Tower is no place for the unwary, the unwilling, or the unwise."

Samark and Kyriani both cast spells, and Vajra saw Osco upside down on a gray stone platform, Meloon standing to her right on a patch of grass, Renaer on her left on a floor near a wooden shelf, and Laraelra alone stood eye to eye with her, though a gap loomed between them. Vajra looked down and saw Vharem's cocoon far below in a dark tomb alongside a number of other sarcophagi.

Vajra looked up again and locked eyes with Laraelra, a lone tear running down her cheek. She spoke to them all, knowing they could hear her if not clearly see her. "I'm sorry, friends, for what we now must endure. I thought it safe, but the tower seeks to prove us worthy to walk its halls." She sobbed. "I'm sorry—and may Tymora bless you with good luck."

Once she finished, her friends faded from view, though the chaotic environment did not. Indeed, it became even more confusing when she saw two more images of herself floating on the platforms with Kyriani and Samark and one closer to her, alone. The closest image was Vajra as a young girl, weaving illusionary fairies in the air. With Kyriani stood a ram-rod stiff figure of Vajra, standing at a bookstand and reading a wizard's tome. Her other image lay with Samark on a hastily conjured bed of cloud, and the sounds of their shared passions drifted to her ears.

"What do I do?" Vajra asked.

But no one answered her. Kyriani simply stared straight at her, while Samark ignored her in favor of the ardorous image of her. This pained her, as she ached for one more moment with Samark. But this situation held its own message. Vajra fought to remember what she could about Kyriani.

Despite the greenish shades of both Samark and Kyriani, Vajra knew Kyri had purple eyes when she was alive. The half-elf was once one of the *tel'teukiira*—the Moonstars, as humans called them. Kyriani saw the second Blackstaff—Tsarra Chaadren—and her heir die in battle against a coven of vampire-wizards in the Stump Bog. Kyriani honored her friends by taking up the Blackstaff and risking her own sanity to carry its power back to Waterdeep.

What else? As if Kyri could hear her thoughts, the half-elf's eyebrows rose and the ghost idly scratched one of her pointed ears. Vajra furrowed her brow in concentration. Kyri was a half-elf, and there lay a clue.

Kyriani Agrivar had been the daughter of a human wizard and a drow. Vajra remembered weeping the first time she read of Kyri's constant battles to reconcile and merge her warring natures of darkness and light, and how she'd twice been split into separate bodies.

"That's it!" Vajra exclaimed.

"What is it, dear?" Kyriani asked.

The other Vajra on the platform behind her muttered, "Shush. I must study this."

"I've got to reconcile myself—change my self-image," Vajra said. "For so long, I've seen myself as different things, and they're all here." She pointed at the various platforms and images of herself around the room. "I'm a child and a sorcerer, Tamik al Safahr's youngest girl, and the only one born with magic. I'm the Blackstaff's heir, and I must study and learn more and more to be worthy of this honor. I'm a woman desperately in love despite the differences between us."

Kyriani asked, "So why are all those separated?"

"For the same reason you warred within yourself—we get so used to compartmentalizing ourselves and our images of self that we splinter what should be whole." Vajra wept as she saw the image of her long-dead father pick up her child-self and toss her high in the air. "I was fourteen when my father died defending Darromar from assassins. My sorcerer's spells weren't enough to save him, and he and my aunt died for my failures. I had just begun my wizard training with her, and I turned my back on sorcery that day, since it was the wizardry she taught me that helped us save Tethyr's Queen Cyriana and King Errilam."

"Ignoring an essential part of you creates holes in you," Kyriani said.

Vajra nodded, then turned her gaze on Kyriani and the image behind the green shade. "I see myself there as the wizard, the Blackstaff's heir, the capable student. But never a master. I'll never learn enough magic and wizardry to deserve the honor of being the Blackstaff's heir."

"That's a problem, then." Kyriani laughed. "Since you've got to accept being worthy enough to be the heir *and* to be the Blackstaff. Who filled your head with this nonsense?"

"I did," Varja said, casting an embarrassed eye toward the ardor-fueled meeting of Samark and herself. "I came to Waterdeep to learn foreign magic, as is required of any student of Tethyr's Court Vizera. If we challenge the Tethyr Curse and survive for a winter, we may return and enter her apprenticeship, in hopes of serving the Crown directly. I joined the Watchful Order and expected to return to Tethyr three summers ago, but . . ."

"Yes?" Kyri pushed her.

"I never thought love could overpower me," Vajra whispered. "It's a more demanding magic than any Art I'd known. It drove me to his side, and he fled, thinking it improper. Samark was like me."

"How so?"

"We were both so afraid at first. We ignored it, and you know how it is when you don't answer love's call."

"Afraid not, dear." Kyriani giggled. "I never resisted." She winked, and Vajra found herself both blushing and slightly jealous of the woman.

Vajra fell silent, searching her head and heart for the key to reconcile these fragments of herself. Samark's ghost winked out from the divan where he and her other self lay. He reappeared before her, his robes and composure restored. He reached out, and his cold touch ruffled the short hair on the nape of her neck. "Still questioning, my heart?" he asked.

She looked into his green eyes, remembering them as the sea green they were during his life, and she wept.

"I regret what happened to you in our name, love," he said.

Vajra's head snapped up at his words and she gasped. "No, you don't."

Samark and Kyriani suddenly floated free of any platforms, and all of them began to shift around the chamber.

Vajra kept her eyes on Samark and spoke with confidence. "You said it after we finally admitted our love. 'Only regret what is left undone, what is left unsaid. Regretting what has happened that cannot be changed is wasted energy.' Stop questioning and just accept—that was my test." As she spoke, she relaxed. Taking a deep breath and wiping away the tears on her cheeks, Vajra chuckled. "The answer's been so simple and in front of me so long." She concentrated, snapped her fingers, and a Blackstaff shod with silver on both ends appeared in her hands. "Even the heir can summon a simple Blackstaff."

Vajra looked over the room and saw all the sides of herself drifting near and far. She resolved to change that.

"I'm ready now." She closed her eyes, resting her forehead on the staff, and whispered. "I am Vajra, daughter of Tamik al Tamik el Safahr, paladin proud, and Parama yr Manshaka, mother beloved. I accept the gifts with which I was born, the Art in my blood as sorcerer. I am Vajra, apprentice to Mynda and the Princess Zandra, the Court Vizeras of my homeland, and I am worthy of their praise and teachings. I am Vajra, heir and lover of the Blackstaff Samark Dhanzscul, and our love and our magic completed me. I am Vajra, I am worthy, and I am unified."

Vajra opened her eyes to find her other images missing and the entry chamber gone. She now stood in the private library of the Blackstaff, though she focused little on the books surrounding her. She looked upon the true Blackstaff, no longer hidden in its smoked-glass cabinet but floating free before the massive fireplace. The true Blackstaff was a massive entity of rune-inscribed duskwood, made black by years of use, melded with veins of silver metal rune-carved. Atop the staff was a large axe head in the shape of a snarling wolf's head, its eyes aglow with green magic.

Drawn on the flagstones beneath the true Blackstaff were six circles, all aglow with runes and magic. Each circle held the silvery wizard mark or sigil of each Blackstaff before her, and each of them hovered above their marks, staring at her. Vajra had met all but the last and eldest in her three years at Blackstaff Tower, but the first Blackstaff usually only manifested by locking doors or appearing as forbidding eyes whenever she sought to explore more of the tower than he thought wise. Today, she faced every spirit of the tower. She quailed inside, but breathed deep and steadied herself. She would face these spirits in chronological order, from the most recent at the outer circle to the oldest Blackstaff at the center.

Khelben spoke, his bass voice thundering. "When the Blackstaff was forged, it was made by the will of my father, myself, and our goddess. Since that time, the assumption of the true Blackstaff has gained its rituals. Step forward, make your claims, and be the Blackstaff, if you so dare."

"By what right do you claim the Blackstaff?" asked Samark, his kindly smile muted for the seriousness of the ritual.

"I claim it by responsibility, for no one stands as the Blackstaff, and Waterdeep needs one to stand for Art, for order, and for good."

With her answer, the shade gestured, and the outermost circle around the staff disappeared, allowing Vajra to step closer to it.

"By what right do you claim the Blackstaff?" asked the shade of Ashemmon.

"I claim it by inheritance, for I am the last heir."

"No, child, you are not. Another has been recruited."

Vajra stopped, the litany in her head disrupted. She stared at Ashemmon's shade in disbelief, then searched her memory. She nodded and smiled. "It's Eiruk, isn't it? Even with Khelben possessing me, we all felt it when he touched us—Khelben's mark is on him."

"Aye, lass, good deduction. He may be your heir, should you choose, though he himself is yet unaware of his potential and his gift."

Vajra hesitated, then said, "He is a good friend, but his feelings run deeper for me than mine do for him. Until I can face that more evenly"— Vajra cast her eyes back at Samark's ghost—"let us leave Eiruk in peace. The Blackstaff needs less passion and more thought at present."

Ashemmon's shade began again. "By what right do you claim the Blackstaff?"

"The Blackstaff before me bound me to this power, this tower, and this time and place."

Again, the ghost gestured and the circle barring her from moving closer disappeared.

"By what right do you claim the Blackstaff?" said the image of Krehlan.

"I claim it by power, having been born of Art with sorcery in my veins."

Another circle gone.

"By what right do you claim the Blackstaff?" said Kyriani's spirit.

"I claim it by knowledge, having learned of magic at the feet of the Grand Wizard of Tethyr's Crown, the Court Vizera and my aunt, Mynda Gyrfalcon-Thann."

Kyri winked at her as she skipped around the circle, the magical barrier dissipating with each playful step.

"By what right do you claim the Blackstaff?" asked the ghost of Tsarra Chaadren.

"I claim it by love, having earned the trust and heart of Samark, the Blackstaff before me."

"By what right do you claim the Blackstaff?" came the stern question from Khelben, the greatest and oldest of the Blackstaffs.

"I claim it by pain, having endured much in its service, having lost friends and lover."

Khelben smiled grimly. "Girl, you have not yet known hurt or loss."

With that forbidding omen, Khelben swept his hand around, and the final barrier between Vajra and the true Blackstaff was gone. Vajra was sure she heard the wolf's head on the staff snarl a warning at her, but her heart pounded in her ears now.

All six of the Blackstaff spirits hovered near, creating a new circle around Vajra and the staff. They joined hands to seal the circle behind her. When they all linked, the floor pulsed with silver and green energy, filling the room with light.

Taking a deep breath, Vajra said, "I, Vajra Safahr, take up this burden willingly, humbly, and with all I was, am, and ever will be."

Her right hand closed about the metal-and-wood amalgam. It felt warm and inviting. The only sensation she felt was a centering, a grounding, as much of her tension slipped down through her body and into the stones beneath her. She shuddered as she expected some explosion of power when she touched it, but she felt nothing new other than a reduced pressure in her head.

She looked at Samark and Khelben, who stood together, surprised. Samark's shade said, "Darling, you've been carrying the full power and knowledge of the Blackstaffs within you for months. It came to you when I died, as it does to the Blackstaff's heir. Alas, since you didn't come to the tower and touch this staff to ground that power, it wreaked havoc with your mind. For that, I'm so sorry. Our spirits remain here in these stones, available for counsel and help, but never to walk the city again."

"You mean I was as powerful as any of you all the time I was Ten-Rings's captive?" Vajra felt her temper rise, but let it go when Kyriani raised her hands before her.

"No, dear heart. You carried fragments of our spirits, pieces of our knowledge, and only some wisps of power—enough to let us send you aid to keep you alive."

"I don't understand."

Krehlan stepped forward and said, "Woman, when the Grand Mages of Rhymanthiin and I dissipated the *kiira n'vaelhar* that held the spirits of my father, Tsarra, and Kyriani, we bonded its magic to this tower and its sister in the Hidden City. When someone takes on the mantle of the Blackstaff or its heir, a template of their spirit, their intellect, their knowledge, becomes part of the Blackstaff and its place of power. What you had to endure was all that knowledge without sorting or grounding it properly in ritual. While Ashemmon and Samark assumed their power easily inside the tower, you had neither the benefit of a Blackstaff in hand to hold some of the power nor the tower itself to ground it. You held all our spirits and knowledge, but our collective lifetimes and awareness overwhelmed yours."

Tsarra, impatient at Krehlan's long answer, broke in. "We drove you mad because the tower is what should hold twelve centuries of life experiences. That's why Krehlan merged the gem with the tower—so it could be your advisor, rather than have the Blackstaff be a slave to the copied minds of those who came before her."

Khelben cleared his throat, silencing all the others, and placed his hands on Vajra's shoulders. "It is your time now. I see my blood and Gamalon's blood in you, and I know Waterdeep is safe. Go now and be the Blackstaff. Reach out with your feelings, find your friends, and go forth. You all have work to do this day. We shall be here to help if you need us."

With that, he disappeared, and the others did as well, filling the room with greenish mist. The last to dissipate was Samark, who embraced and kissed her before dissolving, leaving Vajra with tearful eyes in the chilling mist.

Vajra cleared her throat, and then did as Khelben bid. She realized her companions stood in chambers below, each of them tested by the spirits of the tower. She knew how to manipulate the tower so that all the doors they opened would lead to where she was. With concentration, she even could listen in on what they were saying. Vajra knew the secret words that locked and unlocked score upon score of mysteries within this tower. She realized she had no new knowledge of magic or spells, but she knew where to find information and hidden lore to do so. She knew the location and nature of every magical item within the walls of the tower, and some made her shudder with their power or what they held at bay.

Vajra could see another tower—N'Vaerymanth—in her mind's eye, its layout the same as this, but the city over which it looked was far more orderly, far more magical, and she vowed to visit Rhymanthiin, the Hidden City of Hope, when the time came.

All this and more awaited her as the Blackstaff. It was time to let her city know.

CHAPTER TWENTY-THREE

The original splendors of Waterdeep were Ahghairon's secrets, which keep us safe today and always, despite the predations of lesser so-called lords."

Agnan Crohal, *Tales Told Tavernside*,
Year of Daystars (1268 DR)

12 NIGHTAL, YEAR OF THE AGELESS ONE (1479 DR)

KHONDAR STOOD AND STRETCHED IN THE MORNING SUN FLOODING through his windows. He walked over to the western window. Guards dutifully walked the parapets of the palace, and he could see from this vantage that breakfast had been laid out in his office in the easternmost tower. With a mere thought and a blink of magic on his left index finger, the Khondar became a beam of light and lanced across the distance, reappearing among a gasping group of courtiers, visiting envoys, and various sycophants and servants.

The room proudly displayed the Lords' Arms and the Seal of Waterdeep in massive tapestries on opposite walls. Marble floors and intricate wood-inlay walls gleamed with the polish of human effort, not magic. The palace no longer catered to outlanders or nonhumans, and the city was richer for it and for the rule of mages. Khondar looked out the window to see many tall ships in the gleaming harbor, wizards from many lands coming to this great city and the rebirth of magic.

All around the table, applause scattered and then grew as people cheered his arrival. Above all, he heard Centiv the Blackstaff sing out in pride, "All hail the Open Lord! Long live Khondar, destroyer of the Shadow Thieves, the Dark Brotherhood, and the Cabal Arcane! All hail the Restorer of an orderly and lawful city! All hail the Open Lord!"

The tall doors leading into the chamber slammed open, and Renaer Neverember led a group of dirty, ragged-clothed halflings into the chamber. The female wizards in the crowd fainted at the sight of the lecherous midgets. Renaer loosed a crossbow quarrel at Khondar, who altered the bolt into a magic missile that returned and slammed into Renaer's chest. Centiv cowed the rabble that followed him by making the floor seem to fall open into spiked pits. The rebels fell to the ground, insensate, and Khondar reached down to hoist Renaer up by his now-filthy shirt.

"Why do you resist our rightful rule?" Ten-Rings demanded. "Why do you not let the wizards rule?"

Renaer smiled a cat's grin. "Because the Blackstaff and the Open Lord serve the city, not the other way around."

Khondar Naomal tossed in his sleep, his dreams of power driving him. He rolled over, pulling his furs and covers closer to him. The small fire in the hearth kept the room above the freezing temperatures outside, though the room could hardly be considered warm.

The spell-fields Ten-Rings established around his new home kept out all magical intrusions but those he desired. Wards protected all the doors and windows, and some of Centiv's more ingenious illusions cloaked the entire third floor, where Khondar now slept. Those magical protections muted all noise coming through walls and windows, allowing him rest despite the nearby belltower off the Fanebar or the noise and occasional tumult in the street outside the inns and festhalls in the vicinity.

Normally, he would not have heard the voice on the wind in the Crown of the North that frosty morning. The fact that it launched him out of a sound sleep both irritated and frightened him as soon as the message was delivered. He growled, *"Blast* that woman!"

Khondar threw back the furs with a growl, launching himself out of bed and over to his worktable. With a snap of his fingers, the fire on the hearth blazed up, increasing the heat in the room. He took a quick survey of the table and sighed with relief. All six keys were in place—Ahghairon's Amulet, Key, and Ring; the sheathed dagger his research told him was Anthaorl's Fang, a gift to a long-since-dead loyal watchman from Ahghai-ron; and the two wands he'd plucked from the clutches of Blackstaff Tower. He breathed a sigh of relief and reached for a ceramic dome on the corner of his desk.

He lifted the cracked blue cover to expose a crystal ball the size of his fist. "Show me my defenses," he said.

Mists filled the center of the globe and showed swirling images of various rooms and doors, each aglow in shades of pink, ochre, and ash. Khondar exhaled in relief as his survey showed no spells had been disrupted, but he vented his fury. "That bitch bypassed my wards without disrupting them!" He muttered in harsh whispers to himself. "Bah—it matters not! Blackstaff or no, I'll soon have power over her and the entire city!"

Khondar settled on to a cushion next to the hearth, his spellbook on a low stand before it. Time was of the essence, and he needed every spell prepared for the coming battle for Ahghairon's Tower—and control of Waterdeep.

CHAPTER TWENTY-FOUR

With Open Lord Caladorn at her side, Kyriani's proclamation from atop Blackstaff Tower was necessary to acknowledge her legitimacy in the role of the city's archmage. The Blackstaff's proclamation became tradition when the son of Khelben took up the mantle in the Year of Lost Ships and as his long-time friend Ashemmon did in Ches of this year.

Paerl Nhesch,
Architects Arcane: Waterdeep and the Sword Coast North,
Year of the Dog-Eared Journal (1424 DR)

12 NIGHTAL, YEAR OF THE AGELESS ONE (1479 DR)

THE CROWN OF THE NORTH AWOKE AT DAWN WITH A WOMAN'S VOICE carried on the snow-laden winds. Her voice echoed through every alley, every privy, every bedchamber, every hearth house, and every nook and cranny within the walls of Waterdeep. Even those places guarded by spells and prayers heard this proclamation. Few folk recognized her voice, but more than a few had heard this oath, or versions quite similar, more than a few times in the past decades—each time a new Blackstaff stood atop the tower to declare the assumption of power.

"Know this, now and hereafter, the Blackstaff has fallen in service to the City. Mourn Samark Dhanzscul and honor his memory. Yet the Blackstaff has been taken up once more. I am Vajra Safahr, and I am the seventh Blackstaff of Waterdeep. Hear my solemn vow—I shall protect the city, its citizens, and its future from all those who would see it harmed. I act as Magic's eye, hand, and heart for the Lords and for the good residents of the city. My predecessor Samark Dhanzscul died due to the predations of power-hungry men. I and my friends shall avenge him, and I shall strive to be worthy of Waterdeep's friendship and respect. Know you that she already has my protection and my loyalty."

As expected, those in the immediate vicinity around Swords Street and upper Castle Ward threw open their shutters to glimpse this event personally.

Those farthest off with a high vantage point saw five figures at the top of Blackstaff Tower, four standing in an arc around a solitary figure holding a massive staff almost half-again as tall as she was. The tower gleamed and pulsed with silvery energy in every mortar crack in the tower and its curtain wall. Folk nodded, remembering this happened each time the tower found a new master. Talk flitted about the gathering crowds that the tower had never accepted anyone unworthy of being the Blackstaff—even if she were "but a slip of a girl."

⁙⌒⁙

Atop Blackstaff Tower, Vajra turned back to the group assembled around her. "I am very glad to see all of you survived. I know now, moreso than I did before, that you are worthy allies and friends to the Blackstaff. And I'm sorry for all you've suffered and lost in my and Samark's name. Now, I can do more to help us all—and hurt those who so richly deserve it." Vajra stepped forward, and stamped her foot once on the roof.

A flash of light and the five of them stood in a library, surrounded by walls of books save one wall with a massive fireplace. The ceiling rose higher than three men's heights, and book-laden shelves covered every span of the walls, some even floating without floors to support them. Globes of light shimmered brightly and zipped around the books and shelves to put lights over every person's head.

"There's quite a crowd growing outside right now," Vajra said. "More than a few have dozens of questions, not the least of which have to do with my being declared dead and Renaer accused of my murder."

"Can't say I'm surprised," Renaer said, "given how Ten-Rings managed to pin every ill he's done on others. Shouldn't your announcement take the wind out of the Watch's sails? Keep them from bothering to capture us?"

Vajra chuckled and said, "And did your obvious innocence ever stop some less-than-objective officers from chasing you?"

"Fair point."

"I'm all for a little banter to lighten the mood," Osco said, "but don't we have an over-accessorized guildmaster to stop from conquering the city?"

"Listen to you, little halfling," Laraelra said, "talking like a hero. I thought you only got involved in things with profit."

"If that one takes power, there won't be much profit to be had in a city run by magic-users. All that energy goes to their heads, makes 'em crazy." When Laraelra and Vajra shot him hard looks, he stammered, "Yourselves excluded, goes without saying."

"He's right, though," Meloon added, smacking Azuredge's haft into his palm. "Ten-Rings must be stopped."

Vajra reached up and touched him lightly on the arm, her head not even reaching his shoulder. "We will, Meloon. But first we must marshall our energy. To do that, I'll need Elra's help."

"How do you know that nickname?" Laraelra asked.

"I wasn't completely unaware of what was going on around me, and I hope I can call you that and more. I have a favor to ask, and it's not one I ask lightly. I would have *you* be my heir."

Laraelra stared at Vajra, awestruck by the suggestion.

"You can do this, Elra," Vajra said, leaving the true Blackstaff to hover next to Meloon. She placed her dark hands around Laraelra's lighter, trembling hands, and looked deep into her eyes. "I wouldn't ask this if I didn't sense you could handle the responsibility. I need someone I know and trust. Someone with a good head for intrigues." And no romantic inclinations toward me, she added to herself. "We don't have much time. There are very few spellcasters I can trust in this city, and you are one of them. Please help me so we can all help Waterdeep."

"But I'm no wizard," Laraelra whispered. "I'm barely even a sorcerer!"

"Neither Tsarra nor Ashemmon were wizards, and they served nobly," Vajra said, "and I need one touched by magic to be able to carry one of these against Khondar." She snapped her fingers and a smooth Blackstaff shod with silver on both ends shimmered into her grip.

"You can't expect us to face him directly," Meloon said. "He's ten times more powerful than any of us. I'm not afraid of him, but I'm not stupid either!"

"That's another reason why it's important for her to become the Blackstaff's heir. You all know the stakes and the location of our foe. I'll best help you by remaining here in my place of power, sending power and aid through my heir. I cannot do any of this without your help, Elra. Without you, Ten-Rings may get away with it all, and we'll have to fight from the shadows to take back our city."

"Sounds good to me," Osco muttered, and Renaer smacked him lightly on the head.

"Will you shoulder this burden, Elra?"

Laraelra gulped, her palms sweating profusely. Thoughts of her parents raced through her head, urging her not to be seduced by the promises of power. She also hesitated as she recalled Vajra's instability over the past few days. The two women locked eyes. Despite having been nearly comatose for the past three days, Vajra's eyes held no hesitation, no doubts, only confidence and power. Laraelra heard her father's voice in her head, complaining that she was a traitor for allying with those in power, but she knew in her heart that Vajra and the power she promised needed to be held by those who wanted and needed Waterdeep to be a better place, not just a more prosperous one.

"What do I need to do?" Laraelra said.

Vajra waved her left hand, and a rune-inscribed circle appeared on the floor around them. The three men backed away, leaving the women inside the circle alone. "Sit. Calm yourself. When you're ready, all you'll need to do is take my hand in one hand and the staff in the other. I'll do the rest."

Laraelra and Vajra settled cross-legged within the magic circle, the Blackstaff floating horizontally above the floor between them. One intoned syllable from Vajra and the runes flashed green. A translucent emerald dome enclosed them. Laraelra heard only her own nervous heartbeat.

Vajra spoke in low tones, facing down at the staff and the circle, and her voice was a chorus again of male and female voices. Laraelra would later swear she saw eyes and partial faces within the dome's energy as she listened. She didn't understand what Vajra said, but she knew she spoke Elvish. When Vajra faced her again, her eyes shimmered and shifted, the colors swimming from blue to purple to gray, brown, hazel, and green. The Blackstaff held out her right hand and placed her left hand atop the floating staff. Laraelra exhaled, shook her shoulders, and let go of her fears.

With a silent prayer to Tymora, Laraelra gripped Vajra's right hand with her left and closed her right hand over the Blackstaff. She winced, but she merely felt a buzz in her head and a warmth in her palm, as if the staff were a living thing. Vajra's palm was just as sweaty as her own, but her tiny hand held power—as did her eyes. Laraelra felt rather than saw three pulses of magic pass from Vajra's eyes into her own. After the third pulse, Laraelra found she gripped the Blackstaff alone, and she felt its power simmering just inside the duskwood staff's surface.

Vajra cast a final spell, dissipating the energy dome over them, and said, "For as long as you and I concur, you are an heir to the power of the Blackstaff. That won't provide you with any more power at the present time, other than the ability to safely carry and wield a Blackstaff. In days to come, we'll talk more of you learning from me and from the tower."

Laraelra gulped, realizing this meant more time with the ghosts inhabiting the most formidable fortress on the Sword Coast. She started to ask, then coughed nervously, swallowed, and tried again. "How can we stand against Ten-Rings? He's powerful enough to destroy all of us with one spell."

"Once you get to Roarke House, simply say the word *gehrallen,* and my power will be added to the battle," Vajra said. Laraelra smiled, realizing she understood what was to come without having to utter it aloud. She nodded and shifted the Blackstaff to her left hand, resting one end on the ground. "So what next?" she asked.

Vajra seemed distracted for a moment, as if she were listening to something no one else could hear. When her attention snapped back to the group assembled around her, she said, "Forgive me. That's going to take some getting used to. I can hear and see what folk are doing anywhere inside or within a step or two from the walls around the tower. Watch commander Delnar Kleeandur just demanded the surrender of all of you. He wants you to come to the palace for questioning and a possible trial. At least he has the sense to be courteous."

"I'll go," Renaer said.

"What?" Meloon said. "They'll hang you!"

"Doubtful," he said. "The main charge is for the murder of Vajra, who's very much alive. I want to clear all our names. Also, if I'm keeping the Watch busy, they can't get in the way of what the rest of you have to do. I'm less use in a fight than the rest of you, but I can talk our way out of the false charges Ten-Rings dumped on us."

"A sound plan," Vajra said. "Say the word *traeloth* when you step onto the stairs, and they will deposit you at the entry chamber. When you exit the tower, the gates will wrap around you, but not let anyone else enter. Advise anyone trying to do otherwise to desist, as the Blackstaff is not receiving any more visitors today." Vajra hugged Renaer and kissed him lightly on the cheek. "Thank you again, friend, for all your help. We'll discuss things at length later at your home—matters of days past and the future."

Renaer sketched a salute at the rest of the group and headed for the stairs.

Vajra gestured, and a trio of rings appeared in mid-air in front of Meloon, Osco, and Laraelra. "Those should help you all survive the coming battle with Khondar. Consider the rings my thanks. Now, here's the rest of the plan . . ."

CHAPTER TWENTY-FIVE

. . . and every citizen shall have his say, be it in open Court or in private with the Open Lord.

Ahghairon, *Lords' Writ, Volume II,*
the Year of the Haunted Haven (1039 DR)

12 NIGHTAL, YEAR OF THE AGELESS ONE (1479 DR)

RENAER'S STEPS AND THOSE OF HIS WATCH ESCORTS ECHOED FROM THE marble of the floor to the peak of the dome that loomed over the Lords' Court. He held his head high, neither flinching his eyes away from those who met his nor looking at any beyond those in his path. After the trial at Blackstaff Tower, this held little fear for him.

He stood at the center of a semicircular table's arc, his father straight ahead of him and in full regalia as the city's Open Lord. To see his father reminded Renaer that father and son shared much in looks and manners. Long brown manes tumbled past both their sets of muscular shoulders, though Dagult's hair tended more toward pumpkin while Renaer's locks were almost a chestnut brown. Both men preferred to remain clean-shaven, though Renaer's stubbly chin bespoke his past few days of hard pursuit and toil. They both wore clothes of good solid workmanship and tailoring, but while Renaer's clothes were subtle and simply better-made than many of those around him, Dagult stood out, a blazon of color and sartorial excess in his black velvet cloak, ermine-lined vest, red Shou-silk shirt, and the Aglarondan hip boots of deep crimson leather. Dagult's face wore an expression of deep disgust and impatience.

To each side of Dagult sat three gray-robed and gray-helmed Lords. As usual, they appeared identical in form and stature, regardless of whomever wore the helm and robes. No details of gender, girth, or infirmities could be discerned through the robes, as the Open Lord Ahghairon had designed them long ago.

Behind the Lords loomed a giant bulldog of a man, Lord's Champion Vorgan Drulth, looking uncomfortable in his formal uniform as the Open Lord's personal bodyguard. Renaer noted he wore metal sleeves over each of his index fingers, both sharp as claws, and other weapons bulged conspicuously from his boots, sleeves, and belt.

Dagult opened the proceedings by unfurling a scroll and reading it to the court. From the corner of his eye Renaer noticed a quill untouched by any hand, scribbling away the transcript onto a thick tome at a stand in a side alcove.

"Let this Lords' Court be convened on the matter of the death of Samark Dhanzscul, the Blackstaff; the murder of Vajra Safahr, heir of the Blackstaff; and the deaths of Ramok of Red Larch, Jarlan of Waterdeep, and Baentham of Luskan," Dagult said. "Given that the accused is my own son, I have an obvious conflict of interest here. I therefore recuse myself from this proceeding's judgement, but stay in accord with the traditions of the Lords' Court."

Dagult stepped back, handing the scroll off to a masked Lord who had entered the chamber behind him. The same dark robes and helm enshrouded this Lord as they did the other six. The seventh masked Lord stepped into Dagult's place, sat down, and intoned in a hollow, toneless voice, "The accused stands before us. How does he plead to his Lords?"

"Innocent of all charges, milords," Renaer said. Gasps erupted among his guards, the packed gallery of observers, and also from a few of the Lords themselves. Renaer continued, "I beg my Lords' indulgence, but could you identify the last three names you noted?"

The masked Lord on Renaer's far left stood and pointed at him. "They swing from the shadowtop in Ravencourt, as the tree refuses to give up its dead. We have more than two handfuls of witnesses claiming you led them there to their deaths, and either you or your pet wizard cast the spell that slew them."

"Hardly, but thank you for identifying them. I knew not their names."

This elicited a fresh set of gasps from the gallery and even one shouted, "Hang him too, then!" before the presiding Lord pounded a gavel on the table.

Renaer continued, keeping the proceedings in his favor. "In fact, I am not guilty of any deaths laid before me this morn. Four fell by others' hands and one is not dead, as you all may have heard with her pronouncement at dawn."

"That can be faked," the accusing Lord said, sitting again. "And if not by your hand, all others died at your orders."

"No," the fifth Lord said. "I was on the streets this morning. I saw Vajra atop Blackstaff Tower. Only a Blackstaff true could hold the staff with the wolf's head, make the tower glow silver, and send that pronouncement throughout the city." The Lord's helm turned in Renaer's direction, and asked, "I would know, young Neverember, if Vajra be not dead, who lies in the Castle's crypts with your weapons in her heart and eye?"

"You will probably need the Watchful Order to dispel some illusions on her body," Renaer said. "As for who it is, I suspect it might be an agent who failed my foes—a woman who called herself Charrar. I lost two daggers and a short sword over the past few days due to haste and peril. It would have been an easy matter for my foes to gather and use them."

"And those strangers were party to their deaths?" A new Lord chimed in, pounding a fist on the table in emphasis.

Renaer paused, thinking his way through his personal library. "If my Lords would have their staff consult Quallon of the Six Fingers' book *Ghosts and Spectres Vengeful*—or their own court transcripts from multiple incidents between 1268 and 1300—they will find ample evidence that Magister Pallak Nharrelk's ghost judged and sentenced those men, not I. His presence beneath and in the Magistree killed those men, for they were unpunished for previous crimes."

"What prevarication is this? Centuries-old scrolls cannot help your cause!"

"They will," Renaer said. "Ravencourt's three-centuries-old shadowtop is all that remains of the House Nharrelk noble villa. Buried beneath that tree is a magister of the city who was slain by the corrupt Guildmasters who overthrew the Lords for a brief time two hundred years ago."

The presiding Lord flinched at that and paused, but said, "This court shall recess to test the accuracy of the defendant's statements. Until we reconvene, you are a prisoner and shall—"

As the other Lord was speaking, a court aide had approached another of the Lords and whispered to the side of the helm. That Lord nodded once, twice, and then held up a hand to interrupt both the aide and the presiding judge. "My aide Urlath supports what the accused has stated. The Hanging Tree of Ravencourt, while inactive for more than a century, has been deemed a rightful arm of the Lords' Justice and thus none can be held accountable for deaths caused by it save the victims themselves."

"What of sworn testimony from a guildmaster that you are responsible for torturing young women in hidden cellars beneath a property of yours?" said another Lord. Renaer found it irritating that all the Lords spoke in the same hollow, nondescript voice.

Renaer had to fight off both the lurch of fear in his stomach and a smile, admiring the deftness at which Ten-Rings covered his own tracks. He paced a moment, collecting his thoughts, and then said, "What we do on our own properties to consenting peoples is our own affair, a code to which each of you Lords, if unmasked, would attest. What we do to those unwilling is actionable, I agree. I'd like to face my accuser in open court and send the same charges at him, for he seeks to place his crimes on me. I proclaim Khondar Naomal of the Watchful Order, the mage oft-called "Ten-Rings," a traitor to the city and one of two persons guilty of the crimes of which I am accused and more. I would accuse another, but he remained cloaked behind illusions. His co-conspirator walked the streets as Samark "Black-staff" Dhanzscul for at least this last tenday, if not longer."

Tumult erupted both on the floor of the Lords' Court and up above in the gallery of witnesses. As the presiding Lord tried to gavel the crowd into order, Renaer yelled, "I demand a private audience! It is my right as a citizen of Waterdeep to plead my case to the Open Lord before any trial or sentencing is final." With his first statement, Renaer himself quelled the crowd to a watchful silence.

"The Open Lord recused himself from these proceedings," the presiding Lord said.

Another of the Lords spoke up. "Regardless, it is the boy's right as a citizen."

Five other Lords nodded in agreement and looked to Dagult. The one closest to Dagult said, "As it is our right to hold the Open Lord accountable for judgments he proclaims in our collective name."

The Open Lord readjusted his ermine-lined vest and his heavy amulet of office on his chest, and said, "Very well. Guards, provide us our escort. I shall lead the way."

·:⌒:·

Lord's Champion Vorgan and three guards led Renaer through the back of the Lords' Court chamber, down a slim hall northward, and through a series of stairs and turns until he wasn't sure of his orientation. By the time they reached a set of double-doors, Renaer knew he'd not seen this place before, despite much time spent in the palace over the years. Dagult, ever in the lead, opened the doors, let his son inside, and then closed the doors again, saying to Vorgan, "Remain here, in case of need."

Renaer looked around this private office, sumptuous in its appointing. "The Chamber Emerald. I've heard of it but never seen it." Renaer went around, touching the silk wall hangings of a green dragon in flight flanked by an outward facing pair of black-pelted pegasi with green feathers and manes. "Can't quite remember—this was built with money from a noble family from Impiltur, right? They lost their fortune a few decades later, leaving this as their only surviving legacy. Didn't they lose all their family and fortunes with the Spellplague?"

"Enough scholar's games, Renaer," Dagult said. "You have your private audience. Don't waste my time and yours reciting what you know of House Khearen."

"You know these charges are false, Father," Renaer said. "You know I can prove my innocence beyond what I've already said out there in open court. I'm just here to save face—yours, in fact."

Dagult, drinking from a goblet, spit out wine in surprise and coughed. "What are you blithering on about?"

"You're in this too, Father. I just didn't want to expose you before your fellow Lords."

Dagult spun toward Renaer, his face purple with fury, but before he could unleash his temper, Renaer simply said, "Roarke House."

Dagult deflated and took another breath before he said, "I don't know what you're talking about, boy."

"You're the only one who had access to the deeds and keys to all our holdings, Father," Renaer said. "You gave or sold Ten-Rings that house in return for something. What were you promised for his doing the dirty work?"

"Careful, boy," Dagult said. "You can still be punished by my hand, officially or simply parentally."

"Don't even think to try it," Renaer said, "or I'll simply start asking questions out there as to how Ten-Rings the Traitor got hold of a house owned by the Open Lord. That alone shall lead even dim-thinkers to other questions. And worse answers." He knew his father was shaken by these accusations, even if it didn't show on his face. The fact that he paced without looking at anyone or anything in particular told Renaer volumes.

Dagult took a few breaths before he said, "Don't threaten idly or without proof, Renaer. It's unbecoming. Besides, you're dealing with wizards here, boy." He paced away from Renaer. "They obviously got to your precious hin, charmed him into selling them Roarke House, and then wiped his mind of the memory later. We see at least one case a month like that in court."

Renaer slammed his hand against the desk. *"Don't lie to me!"*

The doors to the chamber burst open. Vorgan and the armed Watchmen entered. Dagult shook his head and waved them back. They closed the doors behind themselves after they looked around, seeing only the two men in the room.

"You have a share of my temper," Dagult said, "as much as you have your mother's wits."

"Father, her wits are what undid you. Them and your choice of agents."

Renaer tossed a small pouch at Dagult, who opened it to find a blood-spattered eyepatch. He turned his back on Renaer to stare out the window of his office, only allowing his son to see him crush the pouch and patch. "Granek worked for you on more than one occasion before and after he was drummed out of the Watch. No longer. As for your cover earlier, one of the reasons I trust Sambral to collect my rents and manage my affairs is simple—he seems to be nearly immune to any mind-affecting magics. I am sure you know how many hedge-and-penny wizards and sorcerers try to weasel out of their rent by bending the brains of the collectors."

Dagult froze, his back to Renaer, and then sighed. Without turning to him, he said, "What is it you want of me?"

"I want all charges dropped and a public apology issued for me and my friends. I also want an end to this harassment by certain members of the Watch," Renaer said. "We both know they're more needed elsewhere than they are chasing me and my friends every night."

"Fair enough," Dagult said. "Provided you actually favor me with your presence when I ask for it. For the past two years, the only times I've seen you are when the Watch arrests you and drags you to me."

"I'll not appear simply at your summons," Renaer said. "A meal shared and scheduled once a tenday here at the palace, and I'll bring the wine."

"You do have your mother's penchant for good wines." Dagult chuckled. "Aye. Done."

"I also want independence," Renaer said. "You're the Open Lord, so live here at the palace. Conduct your affairs from here. Leave me Never-ember Manor. I'm planning to restore its original name of Brandarthall in Mother's honor. I can oversee the Neverember business, if you wish, or you can find someone else to manage your holdings—openly or in secret. I only wish to manage what Mother left me—her wealth and her family's holdings, which far outstrip what you cobbled together with her money and family's connections. You can even pretend that I'm simply a wastrel son living off his father's money, if you choose to continue that tale. We'll both know who's the larger land holder in Waterdeep—and we'll both know each other's measure. I'll keep your secrets, if you keep out of my affairs."

After a long pause, Dagult said, "Done," but he remained unmoving before the large window.

"Am I free to go, then?" Renaer asked.

"One thing more—do you know where Khondar Naomal is now? Or his illusion-slinging lackey of a son?" Dagult turned to face him. "They, at least, are traitors, and the city shall demand blood."

"I don't know what happened to Centiv," Renaer said, "but my friends were going to face Ten-Rings before he tried to broach the shields around Ahghairon's Tower."

"*What?*" Dagult's surprise was genuine. "Guards!"

The three Watchmen burst in.

"Summon all forces and surround Ahghairon's Tower!" Dagult screamed. "*Now!* Get a runner to the Watchful Order and get us their most powerful to stop one of their own guildmasters from high treason!"

"Why the panic, Father?" Renaer asked. "It's not like Khondar'll be able to penetrate all the shields. He's under a compulsion to do this, and Vajra believes it to be a suicide run. Thus, the city will get its blood after all."

"I helped raise you, so I know *you're* no fool," Dagult said. "Few know how to penetrate those shields, but those who tried unleashed all manner of magic. Ahghairon's magic helps protect this city and keeps spells more stable here than elsewhere. Should something disrupt that, the only magic left here might be mundane commerce."

Renaer finished his father's thought. "And there's too much coin to be taken from wizards and their ilk to let that happen."

Dagult spun around and spread his arms as if to say, "Of course!" His smile faded when he said, "Another thing we do know is that any intruder who penetrates those fields far enough, a Walking Statue—yes, a monolithic guardian of the City—teleports in from gods-know-where to attack the intruder."

Renaer started to ask where the problem was, but stopped and gasped. "That statue hasn't been summoned. Ever. It could very easily—"

Dagult and Renaer uttered the same conclusion together. "—bring a patch of the spellplague back with it!"

Renaer ran for the door, heading for the same destination as the Watchmen.

.:⌢:.

Dagult walked quickly back to the Lords' Court, its gallery now emptied as folk chased the commotion outside. "Where is Renaer?" asked the presiding Lord.

"He is free to go, by my hand and by Code Legal," Dagult said. "We shall have our answers on those other matters soon enough. Come, our best view of a traitor's end may be from the East Tower."

"What happened in there?" another Lord asked.

"My son has become a man, and worse yet, a hero. Something this city has not seen in some time."

CHAPTER TWENTY-SIX

The only thing the Watch may count on among lawbreaking-wizards is this—corner them where they live, and they are loathe to loose spellwork that damages overmuch.

Ahghairon, *Works and Woes (Volume IV)*,
Year of Azure Frost (1057 DR)

12 NIGHTAL, YEAR OF THE AGELESS ONE (1479 DR)

MELOON, OSCO, AND LARAELRA APPARATED ONTO THE STOOP OF THE Halaerim Club on Kulzar's Alley. They breathed a sigh of relief. No shadows at their feet showed them the invisibility Vajra wrapped around them stayed in effect.

"Eugh," Osco whispered. "Hate that. Always leaves me guts in an uproar."

"We must be as quick as we can," Meloon said. "Catch the bastard before he's ready for us or any opposition—or before this spell fades."

Laraelra held the Blackstaff out in both of her hands, paused a breath, and then said, *"Gehrallen!"* She sighed in relief as the Blackstaff suddenly grew much heavier. The duskwood staff was replaced by a larger staff of twisted black metal topped with a clear crystal. The duskstaff's crystal glowed slightly, and Laraelra heard Vajra, though none of the others could.

Ah, good, she said. *Elra, you'll be able to hear me, and I can cast spells through this staff as long as you hold it. This ought to even the odds against this wizard.*

Laraelra smiled and said, "I'm ready. Let's go."

Meloon and Osco moved ahead, and Laraelra stepped forward to cross Kulzar's Alley. For the third time in as many days they stood at the threshold of Roarke House.

"Ready?" Meloon asked, hefting Azuredge, the blue runes shining brighter than the golden sunshine rising behind them.

"No," Laraelra said, her voice intermingled with Vajra's. "Let us."

She leveled the duskstaff at the door, and a blue-black beam erupted from the globe. Laraelra saw four separate flashes of energy as the beam punched through and dispelled Ten-Rings' defenses. A massive hand of energy formed from the beam, and a blue-black fist punched down the door to Roarke House. A brief shimmer around them all, and their shadows fell across the threshold.

"I suppose this means we can enter," Laraelra said, turning to Meloon and Osco. She smiled. "After you."

She heard a voice in her head from Vajra. *Don't be overconfident, Elra. I can only cast spells and counter those I'm expecting. Ten-Rings is predictable when it comes to his outer defenses, but his spells in combat may be less so.*

The trio moved cautiously into the star-and-moon covered entrance hall, Meloon in the lead. He stepped toward the cellar door, and Laraelra hissed at him, shaking her head. She whispered, "Even if he flees that way, Harug and his friends have some surprises behind every way out down there. What we need to find is probably upstairs." She pointed up the stairs that spiraled up the outer wall and overhead.

"I'll scout ahead and disable any traps or locks I find along the way," Osco whispered. "Just don't expect to see me easily, thanks to this ring." With that, Osco hopped up the stairs silently, slipping into a shadow and vanishing from sight.

Meloon dashed up the stairs after him, Laraelra following. Energy flared out of the crystal, enveloping Meloon and then Laraelra in protective spells, though Laraelra still felt nervous heading into unknown territory. They reached the first landing and paused at the first ajar door. This floor had a number of doors off this hallway while the stairs continued up, winding along the wall. Laraelra barely noticed the ball of flame bouncing down the stairs ahead of them when Meloon grabbed her and forced her through the door. He shoved her inside and kept his shoulder to the door as explosive gouts of flame scorched the wall alongside the partly open door.

"Thanks, Meloon," Laraelra gasped. "How did you—"

"Just lucky, I guess," Meloon said, and he dashed out the door and up the stairs toward the next level.

Laraelra followed, looking up the winding stairwell that led to the third and fourth floors of Roarke House. Dominating the stairwell atrium and facing east on the front wall of the house was a massive stained-glass mosaic filled with crescent moons and stars. She spotted a figure on the stairs ahead of and above Meloon—Khondar Naomal in olive green robes and a bear-pelt cloak, as if he intended to go out in the cold quickly. Elra cast a spell at him, and the purple dart caught him in the throat. His hands stopped glowing and his current spell dissipated, allowing Meloon the chance to catch up to Ten-Rings. He swung the axe and shattered some kind of magical shield around his target, but the mute wizard held his right fist toward Meloon, and a ring on his thumb pulsed with gray magic. As if he'd been shoved hard, Meloon fell backward, rolling down the stairs until Laraelra broke his fall.

On her knees, Laraelra leveled the duskstaff at Ten-Rings, and Vajra's illusory image settled over hers as the Blackstaff cast a spell Elra had never seen. A flurry of tiny feylike beings flew out of the staff's crystal, and they zipped around Khondar, each trailing snowflakes, glowing embers, a high-pitched buzz, and a light green mist. The faeries harassed his remaining shields and unleashed fire, ice, sound, and poison gas upon him. The faeries managed to pierce some of his defenses. He roared in anger. Meloon shook his head clear and got to his feet.

Khondar looked down at his foes and chuckled. "They sent you two to stop me? Is the new slip of a Blackstaff too tired to face me? Or too afraid?" He squinted and saw the duskstaff in Laraelra's hands. "Ah, so she works through you, scrawny creature. Well, we can't have that. *You cannot hold the staff.*"

Horrified, Laraelra was unable to stop her grip from opening, despite Vajra's voice in her head screaming, *No!* While in a slight daze, Laraelra willed her freed hands into casting a spell, and a cone of blinding colors flashed out of them and up the stairs to envelop the wizard.

"An apprentice's spell, easily thwarted," Ten-Rings said, behind his magical shield.

"Kept you distracted, though," Meloon said as he swung the massive blue-edged axe and let it go. The axe flew straight at the wizard, easily slipping through his spell defenses. Khondar's left arm went up and he lowered it, the wide sleeve torn and darkly wet with blood.

Ten-Rings howled in anger and pain, but his attention was now on the axe, which landed on the stairs beside him. "Ha! You've given me another key, foolish barbarian. The First Lord Ahghairon made Azuredge himself. You've sealed my victory!"

But when Khondar reached for the axe, the blue sapphire set in the pommel flared with light. The axe twisted in Ten-Rings' grasp, as if it tried to get away from the wizard's touch.

"She won't work with anyone but a wielder she's chosen," Meloon said, drawing his little-used short sword from his belt. "A wielder worthy to defend Waterdeep."

"I'm *far* worthier than you, boy!" Khondar yelled, as he stepped backward up the stairs and away from Meloon and Laraelra. "You'll not keep me from my destiny!"

"They kept you from noticing me, Dumb-Rings," Osco said, his voice coming from behind the wizard.

Khondar twisted to see who spoke, and the halfling became visible as he drove his two daggers into Khondar's back, eliciting another raw howl from the wizard. More than twice his foe's size, Khondar's backhanded slap was more than enough to send Osco tumbling down the stairs and colliding with his friends.

Khondar panted, in pain and blooded by the attacks, but he still limped up the stairs by leaning on the railing. His free hand moved furiously, preparing a spell. "I've no time for this or for you. My destiny awaits, but I neither want you three to escape my wrath, nor do I want to damage my house overmuch."

Ten-Rings cast his spell as Laraelra lunged for the duskstaff on the stairs below her, but she could not wrap her hands around it and only shoved it along.

All three of them yelled as the world flipped, and they fell upward.

Meloon grunted as he slammed into the underside of the stairs above him, but Osco and Laraelra, who were closer to the railing, fell up toes over brows all the way to the top of Roarke House. They lay stunned and groaning against the skylight four stories above the hard marble floor below. Ten-Rings stood at the railing, his feet hooked to its underside, while his robes and cloak fell upward. Strangely, the duskstaff made no noise at all when it fell upward to cling to the jagged perch under the stairs near Meloon.

"I'll not waste another spell on you lot," Khondar said, but he held onto the railing with white knuckles. He gritted his teeth as the red gem on his left forefinger ring glowed with regenerative magic, and his wounds closed.

"Khondar, catch!" Meloon yelled from above him.

The wizard's attention snapped upward, and he saw the warrior using his short sword to flip something at him against the pull of the reversed gravity. The duskstaff flipped end over end, and reflex brought up Khondar's arm and hand to catch it or fend it off. The staff settled against his palm with a crackle, and Khondar's eyes went wide as he remembered what happened when unworthies touched a Blackstaff.

The explosion blew Khondar up the stairs and through the stained glass window, launching him out across Gunarla's Dash and onto the roof of Kendall's Gallery. From his odd vantage point, Meloon could see the wizard laying stunned. Meloon and his friends remained pinned helplessly by his spell. I've got to try to get them before the spell ends, Meloon thought, or they'll fall. Maybe I can reach Elra's staff . . .

Meloon strained against the spell's pressure, sat up, and lashed his belt at the twisted remnants of the stair's railing. It caught, and Meloon yanked hard to pull himself down before the belt came loose again. He stood on the stairs, hooking his feet on the railing as Khondar had done. He looked up and saw his friends stunned atop the house. He called to them without response.

Meloon worked his way up along the railing, bridging the gap in the railing carefully toward the open window. By the time Meloon reached the breach to look out, Ten-Rings stood atop the far roof, glaring at him through the shattered window. Meloon could see two flashes of blue and green light on Khondar's fingers. The axe spun in his grasp, but the wizard held Azuredge over his head with some effort. He yelled, "Revenge can wait, but victory cannot. *Rekarlen!*" and was gone.

Meloon howled, "No!" but was heard only by passersby in the alley outside, drawn out by curiosity and the noise of the battle in the early morn. He felt his stomach flip again, and his feet landed back on the stairs. He watched the slightly stirring Osco and Laraelra began their long fall to the floor below.

CHAPTER TWENTY-SEVEN

Step back, secure your goods and children, then sell tickets or place bets. Your choice.
Savengriff on what common folk could do about spell battles,
City of Mages, Year of the Starving (1381 DR)

12 NIGHTAL, YEAR OF THE AGELESS ONE (1479 DR)

KHONDAR "TEN-RINGS" NAOMAL REAPPEARED AT THE APEX OF THE conical roof of Ahghairon's Tower. He halted a moment, assured that one of his rings would keep him aloft. His regenerative ring had healed his wounds, but he growled in discomfort from the aches in his back and arm, exacerbated by the axe that spun in his hand and fought to be released from his grip. He held it immobile with both hands and whispered, "Calm yourself Azuredge. Help me uncover the secrets of your maker. That's all that matters now—the tower and its secrets."

Khondar scanned the dingy rooftops and thick cooksmoke, the sprawl of Fields Ward and Mountainside, and the filth of the harbor and its morass of wood that was the Mistshore. He surveyed all and smiled grimly. "Soon, those secrets will make all this mine, and it will shine under wizards' rule. I shall restore its glory, and they shall call me the Inheritor of Ahghairon!" He looked down at the twitching axe and said, "And we shall find you a far better wielder with whom you can defend the Wizard-City of the North. For now, open the door."

The winds whipped light snow around him as Khondar swung the axe down on the magical field and the crest of the tower's roof. The impact sounded like a thunderclap, and blue fires suffused the fields all around the tower. Khondar flinched, then realized the effect simply merged Azuredge's magic with the fields, harming him not. He laughed and slowly sank through the first magical field up to his waist. "Thank you, idiot and axe both, for your unwitting help!"

Khondar threw his cloak back behind his shoulders. From beneath the bracer on his right forearm he pulled one of the wands he'd stolen from Blackstaff Tower. He dropped the white ash wand point first onto the surface of the fields, and it lit up the second field with gold energy and emitted another thunderclap before it sank into the magic. The wand remained half-embedded inside the translucent field, the magic fading to a light yellow color. Khondar sank through the fields, the biting wind only reaching his head, shoulders, and heart outside the fields. He smiled, feeling only elation at his impending control of the city.

His grin faded when he saw opposition headed for him. "The fools would try to stop me. It is now time to show them Ten-Rings was ever their better."

"Hang on!" Eltalon Vaundrar's voice rose from its usual mutter to warn his companions as the graying wizard steered his flying carpet through some crosswinds. They dipped close to the near-empty market, its open spaces given over to sellswords or cart races as winter set in and wares for sale were no more 'till spring. Maerla Windmantle and Eiruk Weskur clung to the edges of the flying carpet, their faces serious as heartstop. Eltalon said, "The Blackstaff didn't warn you or us in time, boy!"

"Look at Ahghairon's Tower!" Eiruk Weskur pointed, and the three of them saw the plume of blue fire that surrounded one of the most sacred magical sites of the city. "He's not just robbing me of memories or honor—he's out to steal Waterdeep's greatest secrets!"

"Of that, I'm hardly surprised," Eltalon said. "Maerla, once we're in range, hit him with a cacaphonic burst while I try a feeblemind on the bastard. Eiruk, hit him with whatever you have. We may only get one or two passes to stop him."

Eiruk gritted his teeth and hugged himself as they flew into the wind and the biting flurry. He kept his attention on the tower as the three of them slalomed around chimneys and taller buildings. Once within range, Eiruk cast the most powerful spell he had with the longest reach, and a ball of fire streaked out of his palm toward Ten-Rings. The fireball engulfed the top of Ahghairon's Tower.

Khondar's smile faded, even though the flames washed around him harmlessly. An apprentice-level spell, he thought, one easily ignored. Ten-Rings willed his blue-stone ring away in favor of another, which he activated the moment it arrived. Additional defenses fell into place around him.

With his other hand, Khondar cast a spell behind the southward side of the tower. A massive hand formed from magical force appeared and hovered out of the approaching guildmasters' sights. Ten-Rings held his concentration to maintain the magical hand. He felt but ignored the buffeting and blasting maelstrom of noise around him—Maerla's spell, no doubt. One of his rings protected him from what he knew would be Eltalon's standard mental attack. He saw them now—Eltalon, Maerla, and Eiruk—on the flying carpet speeding toward him—and their doom.

Khondar willed the magical hand alongside the tower and outward. The magical construct grabbed for the flying carpet as it flew past the tower's roof, and the hand succeeded at crumpling it in its grasp. Two figures jumped free of it and floated to the ground slowly, the wintry wind pushing them apart and farther away from the tower. Eltalon, unfortunately, found his right ankle pinned in the massive hand's grip. Despite the awkward position at which he floated above the tower, Eltalon unleashed a cone of grayish waves of energy at Khondar, but to no avail.

"Eltalon, you fool," Khondar said. "Wasted energy, that spell. My own spells easily thwart that exhausting magic—and soon, I'll claim more magic *and* the Open Lord's Throne. I'm doing this for the betterment of the city and its wizards. You'll see! And then we'll discuss if you're still worthy of serving as a guildmaster in *my* city."

The hand carried Eltalon away to the far side of the tower and lowered him out of Khondar's sight. Khondar heard the brief yell when the hand dissipated, dropping Eltalon unceremoniously into the crowd gathered below.

Khondar cast a spell barrier above him, not to close off any egress of his but to prevent being attacked from behind.

"Tymora, let me be in time. Let them have survived that." Meloon dashed down the stairs to the front entrance hall of Roarke House. When Khondar's spell ended, Meloon had landed safely on the stairs and Osco had managed to twist and grab at the railings and lintels as he fell, slowing his descent. The halfling hung overhead, yelling "Ow! My arms!"

Just as Meloon ran past, Osco's grip slipped. However, with no useful magic at hand, Laraelra fell the entire height of the house from its skylight all the way to the hard marble floor below. She lay still in a pool of blood.

Meloon reached her side and yanked the ring Vajra had given him off his finger, putting it on Laraelra's hand. Vajra promised it would heal him once a day from great wounds. Its red gem glowed, and she began breathing more regularly. Meloon looked over at Osco, who sat up groaning a pace or two away, "Let's not do that again. Ever."

Laraelra opened her eyes and smiled up at Meloon, touching his arm. "Ten-Rings?" she asked.

"Gone," Meloon said, "and he took Azuredge with him. At least that Blackstaff of yours gave him a good blast out of here."

Laraelra sat bolt upright and snapped, *"Gehrallen!"* The duskstaff appeared in her hands, and she sighed happily as her hands closed around it.

The crystal atop the staff glowed, and Vajra's voice said, *Thank the gods. You must move fast! Ten-Rings has breached Ahghairon's Tower.*

"Don't worry, folks." Osco chuckled. "I think I might know how to slow him down."

⦂⌢⦂

Renaer ran out of the palace in time to see two of three wizards of the Watchful Order fall as slow as feathers to the ground. The winds outside the palace whipped a light snow, but this discomfort didn't stop crowds from gathering in a thick circle around Ahghairon's Tower—at a respectful distance. None wanted to be *too* close to the semi-visible blue fire shields that still held a skeleton floating in their midst, the warning for the past three centuries that Ahghairon's Tower was sacrosanct and not to be disturbed.

Renaer ran over to a friendly face and helped Eiruk Weskur avoid landing on his head, the winds having spun the feather-light spellcaster upside-down. Eiruk settled back onto his feet and nodded at Renaer. "Thanks. I take it you've cleared your name, then?"

"Aye," he replied. "It's now fairly obvious who's causing all the mayhem, isn't it?"

"Vajra sent a message to us at the Towers of the Order, exposing Ten-Rings's and Centiv's treason. We were supposed to capture him before he tried this, but we were too late. I don't understand why he's so brazen to do this in broad daylight, do you?"

"I think Blackstaff Tower has much to do with that," Renaer replied. "The ghosts of the tower set some spell on him, compelling him to try and breach Ahghairon's Tower. Even if they hadn't, he might have done this anyway before Vajra rallied all her energy as the new Blackstaff against him."

STEVEN E. SCHEND

233

"Where are the rest of the guild wizards?" Eiruk wondered aloud, looking to the east toward the Towers of the Order. "They swore they'd follow either by air or foot."

"Could be some are more loyal to Ten-Rings and hope that by delaying, they'll be in position to garner favor from him in his new position." Renaer smacked his fist in his palm. "Waterdhavians are nothing if not practical, adapting to every changing situation, Eiruk. You know that."

Maerla Windmantle came up behind the two young men, sidling in between them briefly for warmth. "Well, there'll be many a former member of the guild by nightfall, once we determine who stood with Ten-Rings in his treason. Eiruk, stay here, while we try and bring him down from there yet again." With a few words, Maerla launched herself skyward, arcing toward the top of the tower.

Khondar smiled as he felt the magic of this place and its protections wash over him. He thought the fields would have had dangerous magic trapped between them, but he encountered nothing so far. As he looked up, he saw the matronly Maerla launching spells at his barriers to no avail. They would not hold for long, but Ten-Rings knew that he only needed to pierce another field or two before he was out of reach.

The sapphire amulet on Khondar's chest flashed as he drew its necklace over his head. Ten-Rings laid the amulet and necklace to rest on the magical barrier, and another crack of thunder echoed across Castle Ward. Khondar did not hear much of the outcry from below as he sank deeper into Ahghairon's magical defenses.

Khondar was so enraptured by the magic all around him that he failed to notice the sparkles that rose around him until they became a swarm so thick they could not be ignored. He looked up and saw a more solid form taking shape—a long-sleeping defense had awakened, changing the tower beneath him as its stones shifted and slid into place. Khondar blanched in fear, but he laughed when he realized this defense held no danger for him either.

"The tower accepts me! It takes me as its rightful heir, not an invader!" No one but Khondar heard his howls—at least no one outside the tower and its fields.

Osco pushed open the door, and Meloon helped Laraelra walk into the room. She leaned on both the duskstaff and Meloon, having nearly died in her four-story fall. She smiled at him and Osco, and whispered, "Thanks. Let's find his secrets and get them out of here before someone else has the same idea."

"Gods, I thought wizards were supposed to be smart," Osco said. "Ten-Rings had this great bedroom big enough for seven hin, and he slept on a cot in his secret workroom behind it. See?"

Osco stood on his toes and reached a hand up into the left side of the chimney to trigger a switch. A door popped open in the stoneworked mantle, revealing a smaller chamber beyond with a cot, two worktables, and a small bookshelf heavily laden with books.

Laraelra resisted the temptation to sit down and begin reading, but instead hobbled over to the farthest worktable. She pulled away a small green cloth, and found a pair of hands carved from russet sheen. On each of the fingers and both thumbs gleamed a ring. Laraelra started to cast a spell to examine the magics or determine which rings were magical, when Vajra's voice came out of the staff. *Don't bother, Elra. The Jhaarnnan Hands are obviously magical, as are most of Khondar's rings. Gather those and the books, and I'll bring you home.*

"We'd better find a way to seal this place up," Osco said, "or looters'll pick it clean. After all, there's two big holes in the front of the place—and I haven't had the chance to root around much."

Vajra's voice rang out from the staff. *Good thought, Osco. Thank you.* A spell flashed out of the duskstaff and they could no longer hear the howling wind coming up through the atrium from the smashed stained-glass window.

Meloon and Osco shrugged and looked at Laraelra, who held up the sculpted hands and said, "Wards of some kind. Meloon, could you take these? Osco, grab that small chest down there." She gathered the books off the desk, and said, "We're ready, Vajra."

The staff said, *You boys better hold on to Elra now.*

The air glistened and shifted, growing darker amid a vortex of snow and magic. Within that vortex grew solid stone, and the tower itself groaned and scraped loudly as a massive shape formed four stories above the street. Folk below gasped and pointed as the conical roof of Ahghairon's Tower collapsed and shifted, the tower widening at its top to reform as crenellations and a more solid base for the statue that now loomed overhead.

The summoning spell abated, and the air above Waterdeep filled with the screeching roar of a massive stone griffon. The Walking Statue that had long waited in reserve to protect this tower spread its stone wings wide with a clatter of carved slate feathers and reared on its powerful hindquarters, its talons digging into the new stone crenellations that formed its perch.

The Walking Statue froze in place, its rearing form and spread wings now making Ahghairon's Tower taller than the minarets in the palace and the tallest structure in Castle Ward by far, save the towers of the castle set high on the mountain.

Standing in the shadow of the tower, Eiruk Weskur looked up at the statue and knew it was almost three times a normal griffon's size. His studies and experiences with magical beasts told him something else: while it might be a magical statue, it acted like a real griffon. Eiruk knew that its preening display was more a show of its power and virility, rather than any attack. In fact, its paralysis and lack of any attack posture gave him hope.

"It's not attacking," Eiruk whispered, smiling.

Beside him, Renaer saw the same clues and said with him, "Because he can't get in."

Maerla Windmantle flew over the two men, pulling her gaze away from Ahghairon's latest wonder to land next to her most-prized apprentice. "Eiruk, what do you two know?"

"The statue's not in any offensive or defensive posture, mistress," Eiruk whispered. "Khondar must not be any danger to the tower or its fields!"

"That might be the reason, but don't assume more than you can prove. Ten-Rings might simply have already been accepted by the tower, and he's controlling the statue. Let us see how this plays out. Keep your wand at ready. If spells start to fray or go wild because this thing brought magichaos with it, we'll need all the help we can get to contain a rebirth of spellplague—especially since Ten-Rings has disrupted one of the city's places of power."

"And here you are." Vajra's voice shifted in the wind, even though she stood directly in front of them, her hands on the duskstaff as well as Elra's. Osco, Meloon, and Laraelra shivered in the cold wind atop Blackstaff Tower again.

"Can't you bring us anywhere warm?" Osco complained.

"Not until we've stopped Ten-Rings. Meloon, put the Jhaarnnan Hands down here, please."

"I don't suppose you'd let us try any of those rings out?" Osco asked.

Vajra's voice alone carried enough snap to cure Osco of that notion. "Be content with the gift you have, Osco Salibuck."

"That ring with the blue gem—what does it do?" Meloon asked.

"It looks like a spell-storing ring or one that triggers a pre-set teleport," Vajra said. "Why?" She barely looked at Meloon as she prepared the Jhaarn-nan Hands with some spells.

"I want my axe back," Meloon said as he snatched the ring off the sculpted hand, placed it on his own, and said, *"Rekarlen!"*

The warrior vanished as the shriek of a stone griffon rang out across Waterdeep.

Khondar looked closely at his hand, admiring the rings he had collected over the years but focusing on his newest acquisiton. The sapphire ring of Ahghairon gleamed bright, as if carved and set only yesterday instead of four centuries ago. He felt the power of the ring thrum on his finger, and it resonated strongly when he crouched and pressed his hand flat against the next barrier. Again, thunder pealed within the barriers and all throughout the city, but Khondar had stopped laughing. His destiny was at hand, and he was but one barrier away from the tower's surface.

Few had been this close to Ahghairon's Tower since the fabled wizard's nine apprentices sealed it after his death. Only those few possessed by the ghostly Aghairon's Cloak ever broached the barriers or the tower, and none of them retained any memory of what wonders the tower held.

Khondar held his breath and stopped to savor the moment as his form slid through yet another barrier. He whispered, "Ahghairon, hear me. I am Khondar 'Ten-Rings' Naomal, master of the Watchful Order of Magists and Protectors. In tribute to you, I would bring glory and power back to your city. I humbly approach your tower and take up your mantle with all the respect and honor I have. Allow me to serve your city as its Open Lord as you did."

Ending his prayer, Khondar touched the final barrier.

Meloon blinked into existence standing knees deep among blue flames. He lost his balance but soon realized the flames were neither hot nor harming him. Meloon steadied himself atop the flat tower. He saw Ten-Rings within the magical fields directly beneath him. The wizard knelt upon other fields inside, resting a blue ring against a field that pulsed with the same energy, and he apparently hadn't seen Meloon's arrival.

The warrior turned and spotted his axe. He stepped close and grabbed the haft of Azuredge, which now lodged between the toe talons of a massive stone griffon. Meloon tugged at it, and a shriek sounded louder in his ears than the grinding stone of the talons as the statue reacted in pain.

Meloon readied himself to pull Azuredge loose from the magical field, bracing his feet on either side of the embedded axe. In his head, he heard the axe's voice—

Patience, warrior. Vengeance sweetens with patience.

.:⌒:.

Vajra, Laraelra, and Osco stared out over Castle Ward from atop Black-staff Tower, amazed at the massive form of the stone griffon. Their argument continued despite their combined wonder.

"Ten-Rings had Azuredge?" Vajra snapped. "Why didn't someone tell me that earlier?"

"You didn't ask," Osco said. "So what's your plan? Can you blast Dumb-Rings by blasting those hands?"

"Something like that." Vajra sent her silent instructions to Laraelra, who nodded, then approached the halfling from behind.

"What do you need me to do?" Osco asked, then stepped back in surprise as Laraelra drew her dagger and dragged a long cut down the length of her index finger. She dripped blood onto the Jhaarnnan Hands and said, "He who has caused me pain, find him through this magic. Find his scent and bring him to ground."

"Just do the same and repeat what I'm saying, little man," Vajra said, "and think of Ten-Rings while you do."

Before Vajra even began her litany, Osco slashed his forearm and repeated with her, "He who has caused me pain, find him through this magic. Find his scent and bring him to ground."

Vajra nodded her thanks, and the duskstaff whirled across the roof and into her hands. With a thought, she exchanged it with the true Blackstaff, and an eerie glow surrounded the metal wolf's head at the staff's end. In her mind's eye, Vajra could see the hidden library of the Blackstaff clearly, even though she remained outside the tower. Four phantom shapes, none distinct enough to be named, hovered around an image of a translucent wolf. The chorus of voices didn't identify which of the former Blackstaffs worked with her, but they told her, *We can lend you some aid for this, which bulwarks our works of old. Be swift though, for this expenditure weakens us all for a time.*

Vajra smiled, and sent back a silent response, *Better to thwart this enemy now. If he is not stopped, we'll be weakened for far longer.*

The Blackstaff loomed almost a full yard taller than the young woman, but her magic and her will stood taller still. Vajra raised and then drove the true Blackstaff hard onto the stone atop Blackstaff Tower, the impact sounding like a giant's hammer blow. She focused and whispered *"Yaqrlueiehar qapeoirl suakr."*

The eyes on the staff's wolf-head glowed green, while Osco and Elra's wounds and eyes glowed white. The energy leeched out of all eight points, and a pair of ephemeral wolves made of white and green energy stalked around the Jhaarnnan Hands, drinking in the scent and magic of their prey. They leaped off the tower and loped their way across the skies above Waterdeep, heading toward Ahghairon's Tower. Unearthly howls filled the air and frosted the clouds across which they raced.

Vajra finished her spell and said, "May this be enough to stop the traitor—and serve to discourage those who would follow his example."

"Actually, I think ol' Dumb-Rings will be discouraged enough when he realizes he doesn't have these." Osco grinned wide as he produced a rune-covered key and a garnet-covered dagger out of his belt pouch. "The fool didn't notice they were gone during the tussle at Roarke House. Guess my fingers must be magical too, eh?"

Vajra and Laraelra stared in shock at the halfling, then giggled, working their way up to exhausted laughter among all three.

Khondar pulled the sheathed dagger off his belt and pressed it against the final energy barrier, but he felt more resistance than usual. He pressed it point first, then flat against the field again, and only sparks arced up his hand and forearm in response.

Khondar pulled the dagger from its sheath and screamed in anger. The blade was simple steel, and Khondar realized the gem in the pommel was an opaque red jasper, rounded and smoothly cabochon cut rather than the rose-cut garnet it was earlier. The blade held the carved words in trade Common, proclaiming the blade "Osco's Luck."

Khondar Naomal found a dry, hollow laugh escaping his lips despite himself. He reached into his belt pouch to withdraw his final item. "Perhaps Ahghairon's Key could force the final barriers open anyway," he muttered, and then realized the key he held was an ornate one to be sure, made of silver with three emeralds for its tines. It was no simple iron key like thousands of others throughout the city, but it was also not the key he needed. Some power hummed within it, but it was not a magic that would help him now. With that realization, the last glimmers of hope flickered out in Khondar.

He looked up through the fields, knowing he could still escape while the previous keys stood in place, and he paled in disbelief.

"You should be dead, boy!" he yelled.

The blond barbarian stood atop the final field, his hands around the blue axe. "I'm still striding, Ten-Rings," he said. "How do the wagons roll for you now?"

Meloon smiled, eyes locked on Khondar's, and brought his left hand up toward his face. Khondar could see the ring on his hand—for it matched the mundane one on his own left hand. His stomach tightened into knots as he cast a spell to fly out of the fields—

—and then he heard the unearthly howls as if they were on his heels.

Meloon's focus on Khondar broke when the first howls drifted his way. He swallowed hard when he saw the magical wolves racing toward him. He wasn't afraid of the wolves, but now that he looked out over the city, he realized just how high he stood above the streets—and his stomach lurched in fear.

He clutched Azuredge's haft as strongly as he could and looked to the west, on the chance some kinder fate wait in that direction. He stared into clouds black as night and a howling wind driving snow and ice their way. Despite it being near highsun, torches and lights blazed on the castle and palace ramparts.

Meloon looked back in time to see the wolves bring their own clouds and cold trailing them as they loped around Ahghairon's Tower. The warrior's fear faded as he realized the wolves paid him no mind, focusing all their dark green stares at Ten-Rings, who had begun to rise out of the fields.

Have faith, kin mine. Face fear and take the leap.

The voice both calmed and shocked him. Meloon looked down at Ten-Rings and knew he had to act fast to stop him. Khondar paused to pluck small items out of the magical fields and saw the wand floating in the energy field near his left foot.

Meloon reached down and grasped the wand with his left hand, keeping his right on the axe. Khondar let loose a roar of anger contrasted with the pale look of fear on his face. Meloon froze, holding both items in his grasp, and Azuredge twisted so her handle pointed out. *Hold and take your leap of faith, my kinsman.*

Meloon swallowed hard, whispered, "Lady of Smiles, I need your guidance," and stepped backward off the fields and the tower.

With the wand in his left hand and the axe handle in his right, Meloon spread his arms above him, wand and axe dragging against the magical fields. They slowed his plummet only slightly. Meloon wondered if the look of horror on his face matched that first look on Khondar's face when he slid past, pulling away the two outermost keys for Khondar's escape. Any other thoughts soon left Meloon's head as the ground rushed up far more quickly than he liked.

Faith is tested in leaps, not steps, Meloon. Azuredge's voice was calm as ever.

To his surprise, Meloon's racing heart slowed and he calmed as well. "So I've heard," he said, and he looked down as he heard the crowd below scream and yell at his descent. Oddly, the first person he noticed as he approached was Renaer, who pointed at him. Meloon yelled, "For Waterdeep!" and expected to slam into the cobbles of the palace courtyard a breath later. Instead, he slowed to a stop as his weight disappeared and he floated the last few lengths down the tower. He blinked, and then looked down to see the ground a mere fingers-breadth away. He laughed and stepped down, turning to see Eiruk Weskur standing behind him, his hands in casting readiness.

"Meloon, watch out!" Eiruk yelled.

Meloon turned to see Khondar's furious face right before him. He lurched backward, pulling the wand and Azuredge with him. The magical fields snapped with thunderous booms. The recoil knocked Ten-Rings off his feet, but more importantly, the fires around the tower snuffed out.

"The wolves are trailing magic and building another spell field around the tower," Eiruk said, his eyes wide with wonderment. "They're sealing themselves in with Khondar."

The translucent white-green field completely encased the tower and all its subsequent magical fields, coalescing from top to bottom like a snow-drift built in reverse. It closed completely around and beneath the talons of the stone griffon atop the tower. The field shimmered and faded to near-invisibility. The populace watched as the wolves flew sunward around the tower, seeking the traitor Ten-Rings.

Khondar heard the howls, and he heard the claws scrabbling against all the other magical fields. The two wolves clawed their way past the first two barriers through the tears the barbarian's plummeting escape had created. But rather than close with him directly, the wolves each dodged into the spaces between the barriers, harassing and howling at Khondar with only air and energy between them.

Khondar tried to fly straight out, using the tears in the outer barriers to escape, but the fields slowed him, as if he flew through thickening syrup. The tears sealed before he could leave. He lunged toward the fallen Meloon Wardragon, only to see Renaer Neverember and Eiruk Weskur drag the barbarian back to safety. Ten-Rings slammed face-first into the second barrier. He tried to concentrate, but the increased howling distracted him.

Ten-Rings concentrated on his bracers and tried to will his spell-storing ring to him, but no transfer happened.

That Blackstaff bitch found a way to disrupt the Jhaarnnan Hands? Impossible!

He imagined more tortures he would visit on her. Now that Meloon had taken Azuredge away, the wolves closed on him.

Khondar flew up from the base of the tower, using one of his rings to call up an earth elemental from the courtyard stones at the base of the tower. One of the wolves simply grew in size and savaged it to rubble in less than a breath. The second wolf swooped up and ate Ahghairon's Amulet. That barrier slammed shut again with a thunderclap, and Khondar realized to his horror that the barriers that penned him in meant nothing to the wolves. They dived through the tower itself if their paths took them that way. The first wolf flew above and gobbled up the wand floating in the third barrier. When the wand snapped in two in its jaws, the sound echoed, as if it were a century-old phandar falling in a storm.

The howling wolves flew three passes while Khondar flew one circuit up and around the tower, and one last thunderclap told him one of them had removed Ahghairon's Ring from the fields.

Ten-Rings slipped up to the top of the tower and unleashed a chain of lightning bolts, engulfing both creatures, but the energy served only to make the wolves seem even more solid. One wolf bit and slashed at Khondar as it flew past, dislodging the bracer he wore on his left wrist and swallowing it whole. The wizard did not initially feel his wounds, but soon screamed in pain as he realized it had stripped flesh from his arm along with the bracer. He pulled his wounded arm in close and readied a spell with his undamaged hand.

"I'm Ahghairon's heir! You things should be hunting down *my* enemies!"

Khondar "Ten-Rings" Naomal unleashed a dazzling flurry of colored orbs from his right palm, the iridescent blasts from the orbs temporarily scattering the image of one wolf. The second wolf slipped around the tower and came up from below the wizard. It clamped its jaws down on his extended right hand and chewed. The wizard screamed and pulled his arm back. All he retrieved from the wolf's jaws was half his bloodied sleeve and his muscle-clad bones. No bracer, no skin, and no rings. Khondar's last coherent thought as he descended into madness was—I'll need that skin more than they will . . . for spell components.

The cloud of white and green energy drifted around the tower, slowly becoming a spectral wolf again by its third circuit. It chased Ten-Rings four full orbits around the tower before it snapped its jaws closed over his left hand, stripping it of flesh and rings. Khondar blasted the wolf's head off, as many green missiles crackled off his skeletal right hand, but again, the green-white cloud drifted away slowly, lupine features growing back together slowly. The other wolf attacked from behind, snatched Ten-Rings up in his jaws, and worried him left and right, tearing his cloak off his shoulders and rending his tunic to tatters before letting him fly. Khondar fled.

Items clattered onto the cold, snow-covered stones at Vajra, Laraelra, and Osco's feet. The bracer she'd seen Khondar wear, along with a handful of rings, appeared, covered in blood.

"They started with the left hand and arm, I see," Vajra said, dispassionately.

"You mean . . . those wolves . . . ?" Laraelra asked, swallowing hard and gagging as more bloody bits arrived to stain the rapidly falling snow. Laraelra staggered over to the tower's edge and retched. She wiped a hand across her mouth, then pulled at the trap door atop the tower. It opened easily, and she said, "I can't watch this. I'm sorry."

Osco kept his stomach from rebelling, but he too retched when steaming remnants of Ten-Rings's gore-soaked tunic and breeches landed with wet splats atop the pile around the Jhaarnnan Hands. He followed Laraelra into the tower, casting a sad eye back toward Vajra. "You coming?" he asked.

The Blackstaff shook her head without turning.

The Black Hunt delivers what it brings to ground, Vajra recalled reading, but she never realized that the wolves and the Black Hunt magic would be involved when she set her spells into motion. The bloody rain of rent garments continued, followed by the clang of the second bracer and the tinkling of five metallic rings. Vajra steeled herself and swallowed, whispering, "The Blackstaff is as hard as stone."

She thanked Auril silently for the heavy snow that now swirled around, as it helped blanket and deaden the strong smell of spilled blood.

Inside her head, Khelben's voice said softly, *Birth and death always come with blood. Waterdeep has seen a traitor's death and a Blackstaff's birth—and perhaps more still.*

Some mothers dragged their fascinated and bloodthirsty children away, while other Waterdhavians pushed forward or joined the crowd to watch the gory display. People cheered as the wolves clamped onto opposing limbs and pulled. The only things hindering people's views of the carnage were the constantly changing flight of the chase and the onset of winter's first blizzard.

Renaer, Eiruk, and Meloon smiled grimly when Khondar's eyes locked on each of theirs in succession as he passed by while flying from his tormentors. The wizard's brief pause allowed a wolf to catch him again and rend the last rings from his left hand—along with the rest of its flesh. The young Lord Neverember, Meloon Wardragon, and Eiruk Weskur were among the few folk who remained in place, watching this spectacle wordlessly. They were also among the very few who did not begin taking wagers as to which body part would be next to be damaged. They simply waited to see that justice was done. By the time the wolves charged in opposite directions to tear the body of Khondar "Ten-Rings" Naomal in twain, glow-globes shed light down on the snow gathered deep across their shoulders.

EPILOGUE

For Waterdeep to remain the City of Splendors, it needs heroes and folk of valor to carry her banners higher than commerce or politics. Splendor is not a right but a privilege, and one that must be earned by courage, not bought by coin nor conjured by magic.

Aleena Paladinstar, *Of Fathers, Faiths, and Fortunes,*
Year of the Hidden Harp (1403 DR)

20 Nightal, Year of the Ageless One (1479 DR)

The light of Selûne and her Tears reflected off a fresh snowfall as the private carriage dashed past Ahghairon's Tower.

"Ugh," Lady Nharaen Wands said. "I can't stand that new horror the wizards unleashed." She looked away, pulling her mink-lined hood closer to shield her eyes, but Lord Torlyn Wands could not tear his eyes away.

The now-skeletal remains of Khondar "Ten-Rings" Naomal continue to fly within the spell barriers around the tower, his skull ever turning to spot his pursuers. Also within the barriers lurked two spectral wolves, ever giving chase. Torlyn smiled grimly as the wolves flew in opposite directions around the tower, only to have Khondar's skeleton explode as the wolves tore him in two different directions at once. Lord Wands knew that the skeleton would reform and the chase would be on again—forever a warning to those who sought to abuse Waterdeep's past and its magic.

A good sign for our times, Torlyn thought. *The past watches and warns us always, and we can't ignore it. Still, we have to keep moving forward—and perhaps we'll be deserving of the gifts of the past in the hopes of a brighter future.*

A short time later, the carriage halted at Roarke House, and Torlyn said, "This is my stop, sister. You go on and enjoy the Gralleth ball. If our business gets concluded early enough, Renaer and I will be along."

"Can't I come with you, Brother?" Nhaeran asked. "With Hurnal being found dead, are you sure it's safe for either of us tonight?"

"We're both safe. Our cousin died because of his own dealings with Khondar Naomal. Even if the old wizard hadn't killed him to get at the Blackstaff, Lord Thongolir and his men might have done so rather than just reporting their finding his body." Torlyn smiled, and his reassuring touch on her arm calmed his younger sister. "So go to this feast with a light heart, but don't expect me before highmoon."

"I shall have to set up a number of ladies with whom you can dance when you arrive, Brother," Nhaeran teased.

Torlyn shut the carriage door and shook his head as he approached the door and knocked.

Madrak, Renaer's halfling butler opened the door and waved him in, smiling. "A pleasure to see you again, Lord Wands. This way, please."

Renaer watched from above as Torlyn, the last of his eight guests, arrived. He smiled and finished adjusting his new tunic and jacket before he headed downstairs to the dining hall. According to Madrak, the early arrivals had quickly guessed who had summoned them here to Roarke House, given the presence of the halfling servants and cook staff from Neverember Hall. Still, as requested, all the hin begged off providing any more details when asked by simply replying, "The master will tell you when he's ready."

Renaer entered the room, and Madrak and the three other halfling servants withdrew, closing the doors behind them. Renaer strode to the head of the table and raised a goblet, toasting all.

"Friends, good health, good deeds, and good fortune to us, those we hold dear, and our city!" He looked on each of them and was glad all were now healthy and healed from their recent adventures.

After the nine of them drained their goblets and filled them again, Renaer strode to the sideboard and pulled a long chest out of the lowest drawer. "I asked you all here tonight—at the sight of our foe's failings—to thank you all for your help in these past tendays and to beg one more indulgence on my part." He placed the large box at his end of the table, opening it and withdrawing its contents one by one.

He passed each of them a small box, which opened to reveal a gold signet ring marked with a crescent moon and a star. "Look inside them as well," Renaer said. Inside the band, beneath the signet, a smooth garnet glinted in the light.

Osco snorted. "What's all this?"

"I want you all to join me in restoring the city to what it should be—the

City of Splendors. We need to be heroes like those who used to fill this city. We need to bring hope and honor and trust back to the streets."

"And we need rings for this?" Eiruk Weskur asked. "One would think after Khondar's fall, you'd not want anything to do with rings for a while."

"Not particularly, no," Renaer said, "but I wanted a badge or symbol of some kind for us. When I had those rings made, I was thinking I might try and restore the Moonstars, who were former Harpers and personal agents of the Blackstaff."

With that, every other head in the room turned to Vajra, whose silver-shod Blackstaff rested upright of its own volition next to her chair. She finished what she was eating and wiped her mouth.

"You're not personal agents of *mine*," Vajra said. "That was more than a century ago. I'm happy enough to call you friends and staunch allies. Nor am I a leader of folk—at least, not yet. Know that while Renaer and I talked about this, I am not the driving force behind the idea—Renaer is—though you're all welcome to use the name of the *Tel'Teukiira*. I know those who came before you would be honored. I will happily work with you, but my responsibilities force me to remain apart from your group for now."

"I remember most of them Moonstars dying at the Stump Bog fighting some group of vampires or something," said Harug Shieldsunder. "Year of the Fallen Friends or something."

Parlek Lateriff said, "That's right. Many did. But not all. The most significant change from that battle was the death of Tsarra, the second Blackstaff. The *Tel'Teukiira* are a dubious group to follow, Renaer, with a less-than-charmed legacy left behind."

"Why not be the Red Sashes?" Osco piped up. "Isn't that where you were going with the hidden red gem, Ren?"

The only response he got from Renaer was a sly smile as he lifted his goblet to his lips.

Torlyn Wands snorted and said, "Depending on whom you ask, the Sashes were either the agents of a rogue Lord, a lawless band of brigands who thwarted the Watch from ever changing Dock Ward, and even some who claimed they were demons hiding in the city and slaying those who dared try and send them back to their home planes."

"Well, I don't want to be linked to that!" Meloon said, slamming his mug down. "What's all this about linking us to some old group long-dead? Not all of us have our heads stuck as much in the past as you do, Renaer."

"I'm hardly stuck in the past," Renaer said, placing his goblet back down quietly as he got up. "It's more about honoring the past efforts of those who kept Waterdeep a good . . . nay, a great place. But above all, it's not the name we call ourselves as much as that we acknowledge the past while forging a new way for the future. Change is all around us, and it's inevitable. I just want us to make the city change for the better, whether we use old names or new."

"Count the Wands as allies in secret," Torlyn said. "I for one love the idea of aiming for a better city—one filled with heroes and magic like my ancestors built, rather than the one the Spellplague did, full of mistrust and fear. Old Maskar would have loved this."

"I'll do it," Laraelra said, "provided we can honor Vharem and Faxhal with posthumous membership in this group of ours."

"Already done, but thank you for bringing them up, Elra." Renaer paced around the long table, touching her shoulder as he passed. He raised his goblet and said, "To Vharem Kuthcutter and Faxhal Xoram, to lives of friendship and honor, and to fighting for what is right and true. May the gods smile on all who thrive or fall while pursuing such lives."

Everyone drained their goblets and mugs and Renaer began again.

"Vharem and Faxhal are both interred in a tomb Harug and I converted from one of the storerooms in that hall of doors beneath us. Their sarcophagi each bear the crescent moon and star. That's why I want to use Roarke House as a base for this group. I don't want this place to only be half-remembered as a house of a traitor. I want it to hint at but not confirm that our group is indeed here."

"But if you want us to be heroes and inspire folk, why operate in secret?" Osco asked. "Other than to keep your cards close to the vest?"

Again, Renaer's only answer was a sly grin.

"Mirt's Mysteries," Vajra giggled. "Well done, Renaer. We approve."

Harug also grinned beneath an ale-foam-soaked moustache.

Meloon looked at Vajra and Renaer, and said, "Huh? What's she talking about?"

Parlek smiled as he said, "It's an old idea of the Lords, attributed to Mirt the Moneylender, from whom all the modern usurers take their name. 'If you want people to talk about things in Waterdeep, suggest that folk keep it a secret. It'll be on everyone's lips without your ever having to utter a word.' "

Eiruk and Meloon started talking over each other, soon joined by Elra and Osco and Harug. Only Parlek, Vajra, Torlyn, and Renaer kept their council as everyone fought over what to call themselves and why. They argued long into the night, never deciding on their group's name, nor attending any solstice ball, but cementing friendships that would last years. Renaer had no doubt that these comrades would help him foster new changes. He looked forward to seeing increased valor and bravery on the mean streets of Waterdeep for the first time in a long time.

GLOSSARY

Armar—Second officer's rank in the Watch (equal to a sergeant)

Aumanator—God of the sun, dawn, light

Aumarr—Fourth officer's rank in the Guard (equal to a captain)

Castle Ward—the heart of the city, home to governmental buildings (the Palace, Castle Waterdeep)

City of the Dead—walled cemetery for the city against its eastern cliffs

Civilar—Generic term for officers above armar-rank and below senior commanders

Crown of the North—Waterdeep's common title/honorific (since the Spellplague)

Daern—Dwarven term for "familiar"

Delvarin's Daubles—Dwarven term for "digger's treasure" (ala "finders-keepers")

Dock Ward—the southernmost and oldest ward on land, filled with warehouses and danger

Downshadow—the undercity that was once the uppermost levels of Undermountain (the city's dungeon)

Field Ward—the ward between North Trollwall and the new city walls, home to many demihumans

Guard—the bodyguard and external army/guard for the City and Palace, supplementary to the Watch

Hin—racial name that halflings call themselves

Mistshore—the former naval harbor filled with wrecks and debris, now a dangerous floating slum

Mountainside—north/northeast faces of Mount Waterdeep, homes for those of rising fortune & the rich

North Ward—the northwestern ward filled with nobles, Waterdeep's "old money" neighborhood

Orsar—Fifth officer's rank in the Watch, envoy to guilds, noble houses, etc.

Rorden—Fourth officer's rank in the Watch, in charge of a Watchpost, barracks, or five to six patrols

Sea Ward—the northeastern ward for nobles and social climbers, the "new money" neighborhood

Shieldlar—Third officer's rank in the Guard (equal to a lieutenant)

South Ward—the southeastern ward of the city, home to caravan drovers, carters, and many adventurers

Taol—the common trade-coin of Waterdeep

Trades Ward—the eastern ward abutting the City of the Dead and home to scribes, business folk, and guilds

Valabrar—Fifth officer's rank in the Guard (equal to a major)

Undercliff—newest ward at the base of the eastern cliffs and includes subterranean links up to the city

Warrens—subterranean territories beneath Dock and Castle Ward, home to smaller demihumans

Watch—the police force for Waterdeep

Zzar—Waterdhavian wine that tastes strongly of almonds

MISTSHORE
JALEIGH JOHNSON

INTRODUCTION

AT ITS HEART, THE FORGOTTEN REALMS ISN'T GEOGRAPHY, IT'S PEOPLE. Those "people" may be dragons or elves or scaly shapechanging monsters rather than humans, but good writers bring characters to life in front of our eyes, making us see and care about what unfolds in their lives.

Waterdeep is a whole bunch of people dwelling together, all striving to carve out lives and riches for themselves (sometimes out of each other). A relative few of them are wealthy, and live in splendid mansions in Sea Ward and North Ward. Most of them are hard-working, "caught in the middle" types, who dwell all over the city.

And then there are "Those Below." The poor, the outcasts, the misfits, the shunned. In Waterdeep, they may literally be "Below," under the surface wards of the city, in the Warrens or Downshadow. Or they may dwell in the mean streets of Dock Ward, or a fog-shrouded, eerie neighborhood that has been slowly growing in the "home" Realms campaign (the Forgotten Realms game I run, at home) for some years: an unmapped, rotting, water-logged backwater of lashed-together, sinking, mildew-shrouded boats at the northern end of the Waterdeep's inner harbor.

A corner of Waterdeep much whispered about by the fearful, who believe all manner of sinister half sea-monsters, half-humans lurk in its sagging riggings and rotten cabins. Creatures with webbed fingers, gills hidden under high-collared robes, and sly, stealthy tentacles waiting to throttle or snatch.

Welcome to Mistshore.

The book you hold in your hands opens in the Year of the Ageless One. A hundred years on from its beginnings, Mistshore has become part of Waterdeep. Not a part many Waterdhavians would care to visit, mind you.

A place you can safely venture into, in these pages, to see and smell it without actually risking a dagger between your ribs, or the suspicious glare of the Watch if you should happen to prudently flee wildly back out again.

It's a journey you'll make in good hands. Jaleigh Johnson knows Waterdeep, and can make us all feel and taste Mistshore. From my few paragraphs of description, she has made this damp, fish-stinking, mist-shrouded, sinister neighborhood come alive.

"Alive" because she brings us not just a rotting chaos of ships, but people. Real people: Icelin, and Ruen, and Cerest, characters who have problems and personal mysteries, too. Not to mention officers of the Watch whose lives and careers we can understand, whose heavy boots thud with the ring of believability. There's the beauty of it: without ever risking humdrum, this book makes the fantastic believable. No marching armies, lost princesses, or glittering throngs of nobles this time (oh, we'll see those in other novels, no fear, and they have their powers and places, too).

Jaleigh brings us some of the folk who dwell behind the tattered curtains and shuttered windows of the mean streets of Waterdeep, a city of a thousand tales.

Here's one of them. A darned good one. Enjoy.

Ed Greenwood
March 2008

PROLOGUE

Dear Granddaughter,

I leave today on a new adventure. Faerûn calls to me, and I find I must answer her gentle whisper. You are too young, as I write this, to understand such a call, or even to speak the name of your homeland. All I can tell you about Faerûn is that it is a vast, lively, and aching world. The adventures found on her soil incite equal measures of bravery, recklessness, glory, and tragedy. I have learned much of adventure, and much of Faerûn, in my life.

I hope to be able to return to you one day, to spin you tales of the places I've been and the people I've met. But the decision is not mine. It is in the hands of the gods. I can only write you this letter, before you are old enough to read it, to tell you not to be afraid for me, or for yourself. Leaving you behind was the hardest battle I have ever fought, but I believe you will have a far better life growing up in my brother's house than traveling the dusty roads with me. Brant can give you the home I never made for myself. Your parents would understand. Someday, you will understand as well. I expect Brant will keep these correspondences from you until you are of an age to comprehend them, but I will write diligently, my dearest one, so you will know you are never alone in this large world.

Night rises around my quill, and so I will close. There are many dreams I wish for you to realize. I beg that you remember two things: The past is part of us; it shapes us irrevocably, but never allow grief and regret to rule your heart. The second is that I love you, more than my own life. I act as I do out of love, and if I have acted wrongly, or hurt you by my absence, please believe the wound was unintentional. Adventure attracts the foolish as well as the mighty.

Someday, you will go forth into the world and find your own adventure *waiting. I want this for you, above all things, granddaughter. The world is spread out before you, and life is meant to be lived. Be well, and be happy, Icelin.*

 Your grandfather,
 Elgreth

CHAPTER ONE

22 ELEINT, THE YEAR OF THE AGELESS ONE (1479 DR)

ICELIN PRESSED HER BACK AGAINST THE WARM CHIMNEY AND WATCHED AN island of rock drift across the sky. Like a roughly hewn barge, it cut through cloud wisps and shrugged aside winging seagulls on its way to some unknown destination, far across Faerûn.

If any living beings walked upon its surface, Icelin couldn't see them. Tiny lightning bolts chased each other across the rock's surface, flashing bruise purple and deepest black. They might have belonged to some other-worldly creatures at play. Icelin ignored them. She was far more interested in the events unfolding below her tucked-up perch on the rooftop.

Dawn had come, and with the first rays of sunlight, the city of Water-deep came alive.

She heard the wagons first. The commerce of South Ward turned on the spokes of caravan wheels. Merchants carting goods in from the trade routes formed a jagged line that funneled through the south gate from Caravan City. The scent of animal sweat, spices, and earth saturated the air, like threads in a familiar tapestry.

From her vantage, Icelin couldn't see the lines of traffic moving up and down The High Road and The Way of the Dragon. But the huge dust clouds they caused drifted up from the streets to mingle with the dawn fog. The dry air stung her eyes.

Voices shouted from the alley below her. A rear door opened. Icelin caught the sharp tang of yeast in new bread. A tired-eyed woman of middle years stepped into the alley, lugging a bucket of soapy water. She emptied its contents into the alley and glanced up to where Icelin sat. She threw a careless wave and turned to go back inside the bakery. Icelin smiled and waved back.

Most of the buildings, including the bakery and her great-uncle's sundries store, fronted The Way of the Dragon; behind they hitched up together against the darker shades of Blacklock Alley. Icelin preferred the quiet of her high perch, especially at dawn, when the rougher alley folk had gone abed or collapsed with a bottle.

Across the alley another door opened. Light spilled from the House of Dust, an affectionately named tavern where much of the caravan traffic ended up at the close of their long journeys. The tavern keeper, a man named Sintus Farlhor, shuffled through the door, sweeping out the leavings from the previous night's business. Muttering and cursing under his breath, he beat the broom against the wall to loosen the dust.

Icelin watched the man impassively. She lifted a bulky sack from a nook behind the chimney and placed it on the ledge next to her. The small lump of burlap had been tied tightly with a leather cord.

"Not sleeping again, lass?"

The voice made Icelin jump. She hadn't heard her great-uncle's approach.

"I thought Waterdhavians considered it virtuous to rise before the dawn," she replied, and she pressed an ivory finger to her lips. "Hush, now. I'm on a mission of deepest revenge this morn."

"Oh, is that all, then?" Brant came to sit next to her on the ledge. He was dressed for work in breeches and a double-pocketed vest of moss green, exactly the shade of the sign over his door. Brant's General Goods and Gear catered to the wagon folk, just like everything else in South Ward.

Brant pressed a mug of something steamy into her hands. Icelin inhaled the sugar and cinnamon in the tea and nodded her thanks, but she refused to be distracted.

"I heard Farlhor was at it again last night," she said, nodding to the tavern keeper, who had not yet noticed them.

"Shouldn't believe everything you hear." Brant loosened the ties on Icelin's sack and wedged a finger in to touch its contents. He brought the brown substance to his nose and gagged. "Gods, Icelin! You aren't ten years old anymore."

"My poor great-uncle," Icelin said, "you have never appreciated the subtle art of revenge." She put an arm across his thin shoulders. "Watch now. I promise you'll enjoy the spectacle."

"Whatever you say, lass." Brant swiped her tea and took a sip for himself. He wiped his other hand on the shingles.

Three stories below them, Farlhor finished his mad beating of the broom and seemed about to storm back inside the tavern when the door opened in his face. A bouquet of blonde hair and lively chatter spilled out.

"Her name is Eliza," Icelin said for her great-uncle's benefit. "She is sixteen this winter."

The girl was small but compact. Her brown arms showed a slight definition of muscle, but not so much as to make her unattractive. She was built well for barmaid's work, with animate features and friendly brown eyes.

A shutter closed over Eliza's face when she saw Farlhor. She started to back away, but the tavern keeper put himself in the path of escape.

"You're late," he said. He slammed the door, sealing them both in the alley. "I told you to be here before daylight."

Roughly, he grabbed her wrists, hauling her away from the building. The angry glaze in his eyes softened, became something more personal and far more sinister.

"Gods' teeth!" Brant hissed, slamming the tea cup down on the ground. He leaned so far over the ledge Icelin had to grab his belt. "I know that girl's father. Son of a whore! He better not touch her."

"I don't think he shares your sensibilities, Great-Uncle," Icelin said. She lifted the sack and let the cord fall away. In one motion, she upended the vessel of sweet revenge and emptied fresh dung into the alley.

The cow pies showered down on Farlhor, turning the tavern keeper into a mosaic of straw and animal filth.

Farlhor let out a lusty, inarticulate cry of rage and instantly released the barmaid's wrists. Eliza, who had missed the worst of the dung, bolted down the alley and disappeared around the corner of the tavern. Icelin hoped the girl would be smart enough to find a new place of employment.

"Oh, that was glorious," her great-uncle said. He rocked back on the ledge. "I wouldn't have appreciated the story nearly enough if I hadn't seen it!"

Icelin smiled. But she wasn't done with Eliza's tormentor.

"Sintus Farlhor," she said. Her voice echoed off the surrounding buildings, carrying to the tavern keeper's ears. "Heed me."

Farlhor tried to look up at her, but there was dung in his eyes. Icelin wondered what he could see of her. Her voice was strong, almost masculine—her great-uncle claimed that was because she used it so frequently—but her body was small. She had a thin, pale face curtained by long strands of unruly black hair.

"There are no fouler men than you in this city. But darker still are the eyes that watch this alley," Icelin said. "If you want to tryst here, let it be with yourself and not the girls under your care. If you forget, I will rain more than animal filth on you."

"Who are you?" Farlhor yelled, trying to sound fearsome. He squinted at her. "I know you! You're Brant's little she-witch! Come down here, then. I'll crack your bones." He reached for his broom.

"Will you, now?" Icelin said. Her voice was very soft.

She could feel Brant's eyes on her as she started the spell. No words came to her lips, not at first. Instead she hummed, finding the tune of an old song. She could recall it without breaking her concentration on the magic. The rhythm of the song steadied her until she was ready to cast.

The words and gestures felt foreign to her at first. She used them so seldom that recalling each aspect of the spell was a chore. Patiently, she worked her way through the complex patterns.

When she was done, the air crackled. Farlhor's broom snapped in half.

The tavern keeper shrieked and dropped the broken pieces. Cursing, he grabbed for a pouch that hung around his neck. The trinkets inside were meant to ward off harmful magic, but Icelin knew for a fact that they were owl pellets and painted stones, sold at the markets as arcane charms.

Rubbing his precious forgeries, Farlhor opened the door and darted through it into the safety of the tavern.

Icelin leaned back against the chimney, breathing hard.

"Icelin—lass!" Brant grabbed Icelin's shoulder as she swooned, but the faintness passed quickly enough. Then came the nausea, but she mastered it as well, swallowing and gulping air like a drowning swimmer.

It had been too long since she'd used such magic. She hadn't been properly prepared. The spell was not difficult, but she had worked herself up into a fury before the casting.

"I'm all right," she said. She squeezed his hand. "I'm just weak."

"You shouldn't have spent yourself like that," Brant scolded her, his good humor forgotten. "It's not like you to be so careless."

"You're right." Icelin grinned and pulled back her sweat-soaked hair. "But revenge is such a demanding creature. You have to be patient, day after day, until your chance comes in a wondrous spark of inspiration. The stableman down the south end of the Way; his son has a devious heart the equal of my own."

"I find that hard to imagine," her great-uncle said dryly.

"He selected the dung personally: aged one day inside a fat, cud-fed cow. I'm told she has loathsome intestines."

"Oh, I hope that's so," Brant said. "But you didn't need to use magic, Icelin. The dung was enough."

"I know." Her gaze flicked briefly to his. "Eliza and I used to play together as children."

"I remember," Brant said. "I don't fault your feelings. But you could have given Farlhor over to the Watch if you feared for her safety."

"Yes, and you know precisely why I didn't." Icelin leaned her head back against the chimney and closed her eyes. "Hush, now, while I bask in the sweet glory of my victory."

"Perhaps you should take to sleeping on the roof always," Brant observed. "Up here, you seem to have command of the whole world."

"If by world you mean Blacklock Alley, then I'll warrant you're right." Icelin didn't open her eyes. "I will reign over it as queen—or witch—and never have to sleep again. The Watchful Lady, I shall be, with her raven-black tresses and bloodshot eyes."

"We all need to sleep sometime, lass," her great-uncle said seriously. "Tell me truly: are the nightmares getting worse?"

"No. They are what they are."

"It's been five years, Icelin. Maybe, if we found you another teacher, he could help. You clearly still have the ability. It's only the control you lack."

"No," Icelin said. "I don't want to get into all that again. Today was a lapse. I lost my temper. It won't happen again."

She stared down at the alley, refusing to meet Brant's eyes. After a breath, she felt her great-uncle take her hand. She leaned sideways and allowed him to gather her up. They sat together, silently, against the backdrop of the awakening city.

"You never knew my Gisetta. But when you were humming that song, you sounded just like her," Brant said quietly.

"The music calms me," Icelin said. "The rhythm it makes in my chest. . . . Spells are just like music, only more. And more frightening," she added. "But the song braces me." She looked up at him. "You used to sing it to me. 'Give me eyes for the darkness, take me home, take me home.' " She knew Brant liked her singing voice. It was the only untainted gift she could give him, so she sang in his company as often as she could.

Brant patted her shoulder. "We should go below," he said. "The day has started without us, and you've an appointment with Kredaron after highsunfest."

"I haven't forgotten." Icelin said, wrinkling her nose.

"He's a respectable merchant, Great-Niece," Brant said. He always called her "great-niece" when duty and responsibility were involved. "You made a contract, and you have to honor it."

"It's not the honor part that I'm dreading," Icelin said. "But you're right. The price is more than fair, for one afternoon's work."

"What's he having you guard?"

"He wants to sell jewelry—family heirlooms, mostly—to boost his coin while he establishes his spice business. He's offered me first selection of the pieces before he sells them. All I have to do is ensure their security before and during the transaction."

Brant whistled. "That is generous. You remember what I taught you about appraising?"

Icelin shot him a wry look.

"Right, of course you do." Brant offered a hand to help her up. "You'll do well by him. This will be a good day."

"Assuming everything goes smoothly." Icelin plucked up the discarded cup, got to her feet, and drained the rest of her tea in one swallow. Brant sighed at the gulping noise.

Icelin wiped her mouth. "Yes, Great-Uncle, I slurp my tea and will therefore never be a proper lady." She widened her eyes. "Didn't I horrify you with that revelation a long time ago?"

"Can't an old man hope for a miracle?" Brant smiled. "In with you. The least you can do is meet Kredaron in something more than a dressing gown."

"Anything to make you happy, Great-Uncle."

.:⌒:.

The sun was warm and high in the sky by the time Icelin got out of the house. She and Brant shared a small, neat set of rooms above the sundries store. Her great-uncle had few possessions, and Icelin had no great desire for baubles. The space was more than adequate for them both.

As promised, she'd shed her dressing gown, and even washed her face. But then Brant had cornered her in the kitchen and forced her to eat some bread and a bowl of the simmer stew he'd prepared the night before. He claimed she never ate enough. Her usual chores were after that—washing the windows and sorting coin from the previous day's business—before she had to prepare for her afternoon meeting with Kredaron.

She'd braided her hair and put on an ankle-length dress of light linen—brown, of course, so it wouldn't show the dust. One had to measure beauty against practicality in South Ward. Clouds of dust were everywhere on the dry days, and the mud slowed traffic when the rains came. But she had tall boots for those wetter occasions.

Crossing the High Road, Icelin wove among carts and shouting drivers until she reached Tulmaster's Street. She slowed her pace and walked in the shade of the crowded old stone shops and warehouses. The cries of cattle and horses mingled with the constant chatter of people coming and going on the busy streets.

Icelin knew the way without marking it. She knew that two streets north sat Shureene's Clothiers, and after that The Lone Rose, a flower shop that had been vacant since the winter but still smelled of fresh blooms. New violets grew in boxes outside the empty shop's windows. Someone had been watering them, though Icelin knew the shopkeeper had left the city months ago, with no expectation of returning.

This perpetual motion of travelers and traders, old and new settlers making their marks, left a strange mixture of restlessness and comfort in the city's inhabitants. Change could come in a day, yet commerce carried on. There was always more coin to be made and more to be lost. Icelin had been born to this function; it was the one thing you could always count on, according to her great-uncle.

Between the flower shop and the Inn of Spirits were two condemned warehouses. Icelin turned off Tulmaster's before she reached them, opting instead for Caravan Street to take her to the designated meeting spot.

The Watch claimed the warehouses were not dangerous, but Icelin had heard rumors, whispers that Spellplague workings had made the buildings unstable. Icelin avoided such places, as did all sensible folk in Waterdeep.

The city had been lucky—or gods-blessed enough—to escape much of the destruction that came in the wake of the Spellplague, an event that Icelin only comprehended through her great-uncle's stories. The explosion of wild magic had swept through Faerûn decades before her birth. Icelin and the rest of the younger folk had been spared the phenomenon and many of its aftereffects.

Icelin glanced at the sky. In the distance, she could still see the floating rock mote and its lightning play. One could get lost watching the strange islands drift over the city.

She blinked and saw the impression of a tower: white stone buried in sand. The spire appeared grown from the rock itself. Icelin shivered and looked away. When she looked back, the tower was gone. She must have imagined it.

That was another reason folk were quick to come and go from the city. All over Faerûn, the Spellplague had made life an uncertain notion at best. At times you couldn't trust your own eyes. And the strange, deadly spell ravages always seemed to spur people in one of two directions: to the cities, for relative comfort and security; or to the wilds, so that the travelers might comprehend some small piece of this changed landscape. Whatever strangeness had been wrought in Waterdeep by the Spellplague, Icelin wanted nothing of that outside world and all its upheaval.

Quickening her pace, Icelin tucked up closer to the familiar buildings, structures that didn't change shape or sprout new heads.

She reached the end of Caravan Street and a small, open square between buildings. Portals had been cut in the side of the nearer building, and folk leaned out to serve handpies and cold drinks to laborers and passersby. Wooden benches lined the square, and a handful of people sat at tables and sipped while they conducted private business.

Kredaron sat at the far end of the square. He was an aging man, with white hair that curled at the ends and papery skin that had seen the sun too often. He carried a rolled bundle of silk close to his chest. He rose and waved when Icelin caught his eye.

"Greetings, Kredaron," Icelin said, taking the seat across from him. "I hope you haven't been waiting long."

"Not at all, lass," the merchant said. His voice sounded soft and reedy. "I appreciate you coming. I trust Brant is well?"

"Yes, and he sends his greetings," Icelin said. She spread her hands. "So, where is this trove you would have me safeguard?"

Kredaron smiled. "Brant said you didn't enjoy wasting time—how rare in a young person. To business then, but if I may: would it be rude of me to ask for a small demonstration of your qualifications?"

"Not at all." Icelin's polite smile held. She listened to the sounds of the square. After a breath, she put her hand on the warped tabletop and made a gesture against the wood grain.

Light glazed her fingertips, and a warm glow spread across the table. No one sitting nearby could see the light except Icelin and the merchant. When the light faded, Icelin took a moment to gather her wits. There was no nausea, just the edge of weakness that came with every spell. Fortunately, she'd eaten heartily before leaving home—her great-uncle had seen to that—and barely noticed the pull.

She focused on Kredaron. "There are three occupied tables behind me. One is a lad and lass, roughly six summers my junior. They are lovers planning how best to tell the lass's father that she is with child, and they not yet hand-fasted. The second is a gnome sitting alone. He talks to himself, lives in the Warrens, and thinks it's too warm this Eleint day for being out of doors. The third table bears two women, pocket-thieves, who until a breath ago were very interested in your roll of silk. I've since disguised it to appear as if you're holding an ugly and very sulky dog, wrapped in a silk blanket. We should be undisturbed."

Kredaron shook his head in admiration. "Brant didn't exaggerate. You are remarkable, lass. Did you determine all that with your magic?"

"No," Icelin said, chuckling. "Mostly I listened to their conversations. Folk reveal more about themselves when they feel they are unobserved than most magic could tell you about their entire lifetimes."

"True words," Kredaron said. His forehead wrinkled. "You have an extraordinary memory, to note so much detail."

Icelin's smile twisted ruefully. "My means of living is spellcraft, but it is not my only gift. If you would know my full qualifications, you should be aware that my memory is flawless. I can recall any piece of information I am confronted with, no matter how trivial."

Kredaron smiled uncertainly. "That's quite a statement. I would dismiss such a claim entirely, especially coming from so young a person, but you don't seem to take any joy in the admission."

Icelin lifted a shoulder. "I only speak of it when it's necessary to the task at hand. Whether you believe me or not, you should know what you're getting when you hire me. Would you care to test me?"

"I would, for curiosity's sake," Kredaron said. "How?"

"Spread out your pieces," Icelin said. "I've shielded the table from prying eyes."

"As you say." Kredaron unrolled the span of silk on the table in front of her.

Icelin looked at the spread for two breaths and then back at Kredaron. "Cover them," she instructed.

He did as she asked. When the pieces were safely hidden, so that not even their shapes could be discerned in the wrappings, Icelin folded her hands on the tabletop.

"I am by no means an expert," she said, "but by my estimation your heirlooms would easily bring in enough coin for you to establish a presence in the spice market, perhaps even secure property for a small shop. You have three opals: one in a silver ring, thumb-sized; one in a clawed brooch; and one alone, ripped from its setting by some force. There is a ruby with a well-concealed flaw, and a silver braided neckpiece, like a spiderweb but with links missing. You shouldn't have any trouble repairing them; the damage is minimal. The gold chains are problematic—one is a clever forgery, but nested with the others it appears just as fine. I would of course remove that one before trying to sell the lot.

"You won't have trouble with fakery when it comes to the matching circlets. Those chains are genuine, and the diamonds they hold are the star items of your collection. But I didn't have to appraise them to know that. Your displaying of them in the exact center of the collection shows your pride. The sunlight catches the stones and sets them aflame with color.

"There is magic swirling in all the pieces," Icelin said, "of varying degrees. It would take further study to determine how much and of what type."

"What about the bracelet?" Kredaron asked her. "The charms on the chain, what were they?"

"The charms were a lock and key, both tarnished, a tiny slipper, and a rose," Icelin said. "The rose was pink topaz. There was no bracelet. Shall I keep going?"

"How long could you recite them?" Kredaron asked, fascinated. "Will you remember the pieces tomorrow, or is this just a mind trick you've mastered?"

"I will remember them tomorrow and every day for the rest of my life, if it serves me," Icelin said. Kredaron was right. She felt no joy in the admission. "Since it likely won't serve me beyond this day," she added, "I will put the knowledge away, find some dusty corner where my memory has space—there's always space, of course—and there it will stay. Once I've put a recollection like that aside, it's difficult to find again, since I don't have a ready use for it. It's much like locating a single crate in all the warehouses of Dock Ward. It may take hours, days, but I can remember them all."

Kredaron shook his head. "Well, lass, you are a wonder, which is rare in a city full of them. You have shown me your skills. I am assured of success in this transaction."

Icelin inclined her head. "Then let us proceed." When he'd spread out his items again, she laid a finger on a cameo brooch. The figure was of a thin woman sheathed in lace. The piece was smooth with age, but the detail was still astonishing, from the creamy relief to the oval background. She'd briefly touched the magic in the piece, but that was not her reason for choosing it. Her interest lay in its value to a jeweler.

"May that be my payment, Kredaron?" she inquired.

"You have excellent taste," said the merchant. He lifted the brooch for her inspection. "It's not the most valuable, nor the most ostentatious of the lot. But there is history here, I think."

"You *think?* You don't know the origins of the pieces?"

"Not all of them," Kredaron admitted. "They came from my father's family, and he's been gone a long time. I don't even know who the woman is, so I haven't formed any particular attachment to the piece. You may have it with my gratitude."

Icelin slid the brooch into the coin-purse fastened around her neck and tucked the pouch away in her dress. Kredaron ordered them light wine from the vendors. The glasses were just being poured, the wine's buttery color glowing warm in the sunlight, when Kredaron's buyer arrived.

CHAPTER TWO

ICELIN WAS SURPRISED TO SEE THE GOLD ELF APPROACH THEIR TABLE. SHE didn't know what sort of man she'd expected to be interested in Kredaron's pieces, but this one was an anomaly, even among the varied folk of South Ward.

The elf was unusually tall. Not gangly, but thinner than he should have been. He was dressed in a tailored, deep blue doublet with a subtle river of silver thread ornamenting the shoulders. The cloth was only marginally above workman's material, however. She recognized the style from what Brant sold in his shop.

He buys for resale, Icelin thought, not for his own collection. Yet his style and carriage suggested he had at least some means of his own.

When her eyes reached his face, Icelin took care to keep her expression politely blank. His own features were impossible to read. The right side of his face appeared robust and healthy, the color enhanced by his dark clothing. But the left side was a patchwork of burn scars.

Puckerings of deep red skin quilted his forehead and all the way down to his jaw. From what she could tell, his left eye appeared to see normally, but it moved slightly out of concert with his right. The strikingly blue orb in the left socket looked like it was being chewed up by the field of angry red. Part of the elf's ear on the scarred side was missing, skewing the pointed end. The disfigurement caused a jarring, asymmetrical appearance to his face.

An elf, but not an elf, Icelin couldn't help thinking.

"Well met, Kredaron." The gold elf bowed to the merchant and took a seat at the table. Icelin watched in silence while the pair conversed. The merchant did not introduce her, but she hadn't expected him to. Kredaron's buyer was well aware that her purpose in the transaction was security. Icelin watched him closely, but she could detect no deception in him when he bargained for the jewelry.

It was well into late afternoon by the time a price had been decided for each piece. Kredaron chose the type and denomination of coin, and the elf agreed to his terms. Through it all, Kredaron was calm and eloquent. Icelin had no doubt his new business venture would do well, and she was glad of her small part in bringing that about.

When they were alone again, Kredaron beamed at her. "I thank you, Icelin, for all your help."

"It was my pleasure."

"Cerest is a good businessman," Kredaron said. "He has always dealt fairly with me, but it never hurts to ensure the success of a transaction."

"You've had dealings with the elf before?" Icelin asked, surprised.

"Oh, yes." Kredaron wiped perspiration from his brow. The sun baked the dusty streets during the day, though it would be cold once night fell. "Cerest came young—a relative phrase for the elf folk—to his trade in Waterdeep. A handsome eladrin and shrewd bargainer—he was born to be a merchant."

"Handsome?" Icelin said. "Then how did he come to be . . . as we saw him today?" She knew she was rude to ask. It was none of her affair, but she couldn't fight her curiosity.

Kredaron must have sensed her discomfort. He chuckled. "Don't worry, you're not the first to gossip about him. There's been wild speculation about Cerest's scars and his business dealings," the merchant said. "I first heard of him when he was buying antiques from the poorer upstarts, like me. I had little to sell back then, but he treated me politely, never made me feel as if I were less a man for having little wealth. For that I was grateful. I didn't realize then what he was truly seeking."

"But you know now," said Icelin. She considered, remembering how the elf had examined each of the pieces. In most cases he'd passed over the fashionable items in favor of the older pieces—the ones that sparkled with magic. "He is not a jeweler or an antiquities dealer, is he? He's hunting for treasure."

"Exactly right," Kredaron said. "Magic in all forms draws Cerest's attention. Of course magic is unstable at the best of times, but Cerest knows his market well. Folk seek magic trinkets now more than ever. They trust them. And I think solid objects sit better in their hands than spells cast by strangers."

"I can see how they would be justified in their fear," Icelin said. She stared at the tabletop, her eyes following the swirling patterns in the wood. "So Cerest buys and resells the magic items?"

"And anything else of value he can get his hands on, these days," Kredaron said. "He had a good eye and a bright future in the city, or so I thought."

"What happened?" Icelin asked. "Was it anything to do with his scars?"

"I don't know how he received them," Kredaron said sadly, "but I've heard he has spent most of his accumulated wealth trying to repair the worst of the damage. The whole affair is mystery and rumor. He disappeared for a time and left his business in the hands of his employees. When he returned, he was as you saw him today. He never spoke of what happened to him, and none of the clients who relied on him has dared to ask."

"What do you think it was?" Icelin asked.

"I think he dabbled too closely in dangerous magic and paid the price," Kredaron said. "We'll likely never know the full story."

"But if he deals honorably in business, why should he be judged for his appearance?" Icelin said. "Whatever mistakes he made, his scars have more than paid for them."

"You are right, of course," Kredaron said. "I shouldn't have doubted his character. But if I had not"—his eyes twinkled—"I would never have met and conversed with you. So you cannot fault me too harshly."

"True, I cannot," Icelin said, smiling.

The merchant glanced up as evenpeal sounded. The bells in Castle Waterdeep's turrets could be heard all across the city. "I've kept you too long. My apologies. May I escort you home? It will be dark soon, and I don't want your great-uncle to be distressed at your absence."

"Thank you, but I know the way well. I can be home before gateclose," Icelin assured him.

She parted ways with Kredaron at Caravan Street and headed in the opposite direction, back to The High Road. As she walked, she slipped the brooch from her coin-purse and examined its surface in the dying sunlight.

The woman in lace had a stunning profile, and the blue agate of the cameo gave her face an ethereal quality. Her delicate eyes held secrets Icelin could not begin to guess. Pressed silver bounded the piece in a teardrop design, forever capturing the woman's enigmatic beauty.

"You are an elegant lady," Icelin murmured dryly, "just as I am not. But I am practical, as many elegant ladies are not. You will keep Brant and I well fed, though I hate to part with you."

She slowed when she approached The Way of the Dragon. Normally, she would have cut between buildings and walked the alley, but dusk was imminent and the brooch too precious to lose to thieves. On impulse, she decided to stay on the Way and stop at the butcher shop at the end of the street. Brant would be glad for fresh meat, and they could afford the luxury, just this once.

She picked up her pace, excited at the prospect of surprising her great-uncle with a sumptuous meal. She was so absorbed with her thoughts and plans that she didn't hear the first scream. She heard the second; the sound made every hair on her neck stand up.

It was not unusual for horses to neigh and cry on the Way. The caravan traffic brought animals that were in as many and varied conditions as their handlers: robust, sick, starving, even dying.

But everyone in South Ward knew the sound of a mad horse's scream. It was the scream that caused drivers to bring their carts to a dead halt in the middle of the road. Mothers yanked children up into their arms, and anyone who stood on foot near the dusty Way found cover with haste. The crowded road was unforgiving to those who walked it unawares.

Such was the man cutting across the Way twenty feet in front of Icelin. He walked with his head down, shoulders hunched. Impossibly, he didn't appear to have heard the horse's scream.

The animal, a brown velvet streak in the sunset gloom, reared and broke from its handlers. A coil of rope dangled from its neck. It bolted down the Way, heading straight for the man.

People were screaming, Icelin among them, but she was running too. She charged down the Way, her hair flying, and launched herself at the man's back.

She had a brief impression of orange sunlight and a horse's hooves flashing over her head. Four deadly clubs, poised to strike, Icelin thought. She closed her eyes, waiting for the weapons to come down and crush her skull.

Cerest Elenithil had never been in South Ward on foot before. He'd never liked the notion of walking here, having no strong desire to plod among draft animals and caravan lords. But he'd had two exchanges in the Ward today, and one of them had required his wagon to haul the goods. It was a simple transaction of silver for two antique tables.

The seller had insisted the markings on the edges were arcane. Cerest had sent three of his men to confirm the claim and transport the tables, leaving him alone to conduct the affair with Kredaron. If he'd had more men—or more wagons—he might not have had to breathe the dust and detritus of Caravan City at all. Perhaps, if one of those tables did have arcane powers, he would never have to breathe here again. But after years of merely scraping by in the City of Splendors, Cerest doubted his luck would be running that high.

So when the elf found himself crossing The Way of the Dragon after evenpeal, he paid no particular attention to the traffic around him and the shouts and conversations of the predominantly human throng. He wanted only to get back to his men and his wagon.

A few folk ceased their chatter when he came near. They met his good eye and then quickly looked away, not wishing to offend him. He was dressed near enough to nobility that they paid him deference, but they could not keep their reactions to his scars in check.

Cerest wanted to be home, back in his stone house with its quiet garden. None who served within those walls would ever remark on his disfigurement. He'd seen to that a long time ago, at the point of a sword.

"I'm tellin' ye, that horse won't take a whip crack more than a fly's arc from its rump," he heard someone saying. "'It's not right in the head. Too jittery."

Cerest turned, and so didn't hear the horse master's reply. The damage to his left side was immutable. There were too many scars to salvage his hearing in that ear. Sound simply died when it came to him from the left.

"Clear the way! Move!"

The scream came at him from the right, and a shower of black suddenly exploded in Cerest's face.

Blinded, Cerest lost his balance as a dead weight slammed him from behind. The force knocked him completely off his feet, and he went down on his stomach in the dirt. Numbness shot up both arms. Cerest thought he heard bones crunch. The weight landed on top of him and stayed there.

For a long time Cerest tried simply to breathe. The air had been completely knocked from his chest, and a black curtain blocked his vision. He could hear more shouts and screams now, all filtered to the right. The effect unbalanced him. He felt sick to his stomach.

Breathing through his mouth, Cerest forced his arms to move. He levered himself up and slid the offending weight off his back. He turned and sat down in the road, ignoring the pangs from his protesting bones.

When he looked up and saw the black curtain again, he realized it was a woman's hair, dangling loosely from a ruined braid. She pushed the strands out of her face and massaged her neck gingerly.

Gods, a human lass had brought him low in South Ward. There was no pride left in the world.

"Are you all right?" the girl asked. She appeared to be about twenty, with milk blue eyes and pale skin. He recognized her. Where from?

Kredaron—that was it. She'd been his security. He'd tried not to be insulted by her presence and ignored her during their transactions—a gesture that had been rendered pointless now she'd planted her rump on top of him and ground his bones into the dirt.

Cerest coughed. "I think you broke my back."

"Oh no. You wouldn't be hacking like that if I'd done any such thing; you'd be screaming," the woman said, and she offered him her arm.

Cerest reluctantly let her pull him up. She was a petite thing, half a head shorter than he. Something about her seemed oddly familiar, but he didn't think he'd ever seen her before.

"Why?" he asked.

"Why what?" She cocked her head.

"Why did you almost break my back?"

Her expression slid from tight concern to full-blown incredulity. She pointed over his shoulder. "I hoped to do you a favor, and that's why."

Cerest turned and saw the carnage for the first time.

A broken wagon was twisted around a crushed archway that had once been a storefront. Blood splattered the otherwise pristine windows. A dead horse lay among the wreckage. The tall stud had been brought down near the wagon. An arrow jutted from the beast's neck. Foam still dripped from its lips. Its eyes were open, frozen in half-crazed fear.

"It went wild and broke its reins," the girl explained. "Everyone could see it going, but the fool with the whip didn't. He won't last long in South Ward with a whip hand like that, and neither will you, the way you wear your head so low on your neck. You have to look *up* when you walk, or else you'll be trampled." Her words crowded together. She shuddered, clearly unsettled by what had happened.

"I didn't hear it," Cerest said. "I don't hear well, from the left side." He turned back to the girl. "My deepest gratitude," he said. "You saved my back, and the rest of me, such as I am." He smiled wryly. "My name is Cerest Elenithil. We met earlier, though not formally. May I know you?"

The girl hesitated. "My name is Icelin Tearn."

"Icelin Tearn," he repeated. The shadow of familiarity snapped abruptly into a picture—a memory—and the elf lost his breath.

He was not often caught so completely off guard, but at that moment, Cerest simply stared at the woman before him.

Framed by swirling dust clouds and the curious onlookers who'd come to see the accident, she was a vision, a ghost given life.

Memories surged through him, phantoms he could draw from the air: Elgreth, the fire, an opportunity lost forever, or so he'd thought. Yet here she was, standing before him like a small, dark angel.

Icelin Tearn, he thought. You are all grown up. I would never have known you.

An awkward silence had settled between them. Cerest recovered himself and hurried to fill it. "You must allow me to repay my debt. Please, I would like to escort you home. The Way of the Dragon is no place for a girl to be at night."

Cerest was careful to maintain a cordial manner. He didn't want her to realize how off balance he was. Did he imagine that she looked at him strangely, or was it just his scars that unsettled her? Before he'd been maimed, it had been effortless to charm people, in business or in his bed. Now it was more difficult to get folk to trust him.

"That's not necessary," said the girl. "I know the way well, and I like to walk."

An error. He'd been too forward. Cerest cursed himself. She was being cautious now, businesslike, just as she had been with Kredaron. He would have to snare the rabbit carefully, or she would run.

"I'm afraid my home is a far walk from here, but I have a wagon somewhat closer." He offered a mock wince. "I've learned my lesson. I shall never leave it to go on foot in South Ward again. I will retrieve the wagon and come for you here. Please, I could have you home to your family very shortly, and it would ease my mind to know you hadn't suffered any injuries preserving my poor neck."

"You're very kind, but I'm afraid I can't."

She was starting to edge away. Cerest could see she didn't trust him. He sighed inwardly. This was going to be more difficult than he'd thought. Ah, well. Perhaps his scars would serve him in this case.

He slipped his hand over her nearer wrist, as if it were the most natural gesture in the world, and not an intrusion in her space.

"Does my appearance unsettle you so much?" he asked, pitching his voice low.

That gave her pause. She flushed attractively. "I'm not troubled by your face, but by your sudden interest in me. You showed no such attentiveness before."

"Perhaps I am enchanted by the woman who just saved my life."

Her eyes narrowed. "Your hands are cold and dry, when any other man's should be shaking and clammy. You don't seem the least bothered that there is a dead animal reeking in the street behind us, an animal that almost killed you in a grisly fashion. You look as serene and collected as if you were hosting a dinner party and I had suddenly become the honored guest. Please let go of my hand."

She jerked away and immediately began walking in the opposite direction. Cerest had to admire her quick wit. She would be difficult, just like Elgreth had been.

"Wait, please." The elf matched her stride easily. "Icelin. Icelin, listen to me. Please don't run away. I don't want our acquaintance to start like this."

"We have no acquaintance," Icelin said curtly.

Oh, but you're wrong, Cerest thought. You don't know how very wrong you are.

He allowed her to pull slightly ahead of him before he fired his next shot, "Don't you remember me, Icelin?"

That stopped her cold. She spun to face him. "What did you say?"

"Of course you wouldn't. I shouldn't have expected . . ."

"Stop it." But she was looking at him now, her eyes raking his features, searching for something recognizable. No one had ever looked at him so intimately after he'd been maimed. His heart sped up. Gods, she was beautiful, more beautiful than Lisra. . . .

She raised her hand to her mouth. Her chest heaved up and down. "Gods, no, it can't be. No. I'm sorry, I have to. . ."

She turned and fled, cutting down a back alley. Two carts jammed the way. She slid underneath the closest, ignoring the shouts of the drivers who had to steady their horses.

Cerest watched her go. He was too shocked to follow. What had caused the reaction in her? A breath ago she'd been grinding his teeth in the dirt and giving him a dressing-down for carelessness, and now she was a frightened waif running away from him as fast as she could.

He laughed out loud, startling the men who'd come to clean up the horse gore. Icelin was a strange woman and fascinating. Gods, he was almost glad she'd run. It made everything more exciting. Now he had to know her better.

He wanted to keep her forever.

The elf turned and broke into a run down the Way. He had to find Riatvin and Melias. They were better trackers.

His men would get her back. Now that he'd seen her, he didn't want to lose her again. His hands trembled from an excitement that was almost sexual. Come back to me, Icelin. I'll explain everything. I'll *make* you remember.

Cerest's men were waiting for him at the wagon. Riatvin and Melias were gold elves, like himself; Greyas was the only human who served him. Cerest sometimes thought that, despite the inferiority of Greyas's race, the human understood him better than most eladrin. On a more practical level, Greyas was the only human who possessed tact enough to avert his gaze from Cerest's scars. A burly man with black hair sprouting from his head, chest, and nose, Greyas looked anything but tactful. He was sorely out of place between the two smooth-skinned elves.

"I need you to retrieve someone for me," Cerest told them.

"Deal go sour?" Greyas asked.

"The deal is in progress," Cerest corrected. He turned his attention to the elves and described Icelin in detail. He would never forget her face now. "You two go and find her. Bring her to the house. Hurry!" he snapped. "She moves fast, but someone will have seen her on the streets. Question them if need be, but discreetly."

The elves nodded and took off, moving like glowing streaks through the crowd.

She won't outrun them, Cerest thought. "Greyas, I want you to find out where she lives."

"How?"

"Go to Kredaron. He'll still be in the ward." Cerest's mind raced. An idea started to unfold. "Ask him politely where Icelin Tearn dwells. Apologize, but tell him you bear unhappy intelligence. Tell him that Icelin has stolen the jewels he sold to me. Ask him to please give an inventory to the Watch of the items in the transaction, as I had no time to make a record of them before I was robbed. That will remove Kredaron from the situation and assure him that I have no ill intentions."

"Do *we?*" Greyas asked.

Cerest looked at him, but his mind was still occupied with other things. "Find out if she has any family left. If she does, that will be problematic for what I intend."

"You want me to remove the problem?"

That was why Cerest employed Greyas. He was unlike most humans, just as Cerest was different from other elves. His tone was businesslike; he passed no judgments, nor offered any reassurances on the consequences of Cerest's actions. For all his human frailties, Greyas was an instrument that cut quickly and without emotion. Cerest needed more men like that, but for now he could not afford them.

"Yes," he said. "Remove the problem, but do it tastefully. I don't want Icelin to suffer more than necessary."

Icelin ran all the way back to Blacklock Alley, pausing only once for breath and to see if she was being followed.

Rustling movements disturbed one of the trash piles in the alley. Icelin nearly swooned. But it was only a small gray dog, snuffling through the garbage. It raised its head, sniffed the air around Icelin, and went back to foraging.

Shaking, Icelin pressed a hand to her stomach. She was nearly home now, but she couldn't go to her great-uncle like this. She glanced in one of the glazed shop windows. Her hair stuck out crazily from her braid; her dress was caked in dirt from her tumble with the elf. She couldn't let him see how wild she was, how terrified. And what if the elf still trailed her?

Leaning against a building, Icelin hid herself in the shadows. She would wait, for a while at least, to make sure the elf wasn't coming for her. In the meantime, she tamed her hair as best she could and tried to relax.

Cerest and his scars floated in her memory. Gods, did the elf truly know her? Had he been there five years ago? She hadn't known the names of any of the folk involved, except Therondol. She hadn't wanted to know their names or faces. How could she carry them in her memory and survive? Nelzun had been bad enough. Her teacher.

Don't blame yourself.

She heard his words again. They haunted her. If the elf came after her for what she'd done, she could hardly blame him, could she?

Icelin pressed her forehead against the cool stone building. She would ask her great-uncle. Brant would know. He'd raised her, protected her, even after what had happened. He would know what she should do.

Icelin stepped around the side of the building and glanced at the sign above the door. She saw with some surprise that it was the butcher's. "Sull's Butchery," it stated, in blocky brown letters over a painted haunch of meat.

I didn't even notice where I ended up, Icelin thought. A dangerous lapse, in Blacklock Alley. Well, she'd wanted meat. . . . Maybe the everyday chore would calm her. Anything was better than being in the street alone.

A bell jangled loudly when she entered. Icelin gritted her teeth at the sound. She wanted to be home where it was quiet and safe.

"Be right out!" The bellow sounded from somewhere in the back of the shop, a cross between a lion's roar and a ram's gravelly tenor.

A breath later, a giant human figure crowded the doorway. He carried a half-carcass of deer, dangling by a metal hook. Grunting, he heaved it down on a covered portion of counter at the far end of the room.

"Sull?" she inquired. She half hoped the imposing man wasn't the name above the door.

"That'd be me." He turned to give her a friendly smile, exposing a wide gap between his two front teeth. Red, frizzy hair covered his head, ending in two massive sideburns at his jowls. A shiny bald circle exposed the top of his head. "What can I do for you?"

"I need some. . . ." she trailed off, watching him wipe the animal blood on his apron. The streaky red stains reminded her of the dead horse.

"Aye?" He looked at her expectantly. "Are you all right, lass?"

"I'm fine." Icelin swallowed. "I'd like two cuts of boar and one of mutton, if you have them."

"I do, and you're welcome to 'em. Just let me take care of this beauty." He took a long cleaver from a padded pocket in his apron and cut into the carcass on the counter. "Lass a little older than you is comin' in for this one." He took a fistful of salt from a jar on the counter and sprinkled it like snow on the cut meat. "Aw, you can make a hearty stew with deer or boar, and that's the truth. I got my own seasonin's—best recipe you'll find at any fine inn. Most folk have me prepare 'em in advance, tenderize 'em, let the juices mingle a while. Delicious."

The big man reached into another apron pocket and pulled out three small jars. "Peppers, some ground-up parsley, and more salt. Nothin' fancy. The key's in the quantity. I'll show you what I mean. It's best on the raw meat, when it's drippin' just a bit."

The bell at the door jangled again as the butcher headed for the back room. "Be right back," he hollered.

Icelin turned. A pair of gold elves stood in the doorway. They were dressed in servants' liveries. Neither paid her any attention, but Icelin felt sick in her gut.

They were Cerest's men. She knew they were.

CHAPTER THREE

THE SHORTER OF THE TWO ELVES TOOK UP A POSITION BY THE DOOR. THE other came forward to lean an elbow against the long counter.

They all move like dancers, Icelin thought, as if the ground beneath them could be measured and controlled through their feet. Would they fight the same way?

Pinned between them, Icelin weighed her options. She could run, but they would be on her before she reached the street. If she screamed, would the butcher come to aid her?

The last thing she wanted was for harm to come to him or his shop. She couldn't use her magic for the same reason.

"Your master is persistent," she said, stalling for time. If she could just get them to move, take the inevitable fight to the alley. . . .

The elf at the counter regarded her coolly. He said something to his companion in Elvish. Sharp, elegant words to match their looks. The other elf nodded.

"You know, that's terribly rude behavior," Icelin said. She crossed her arms. "Talking as if I'm not in the room. If you're going to execute a successful kidnapping, the least you could do is be straightforward with your intentions."

The pair exchanged a glance. Icelin couldn't tell if they were amused or annoyed.

The elf at the door looked her over. "You've a blunt tongue," he said in Common. "I don't suppose if we were 'straightforward' and asked you to come with us, you'd cooperate without resistance?"

"Ah, if only a woman's intentions bore any degree of predictability," Icelin said, smiling. "Let me think. If I kick and scream and conjure fire to boil the flesh off your lovely cheekbones, does that count as resistance?"

"I believe it does," the elf said, genuinely amused now. "But I think you're bluffing."

"You think I don't have magic? I suppose I don't give much of an appearance of sorcery." Icelin reached up to grasp the coin-purse at her neck.

"Hands at your sides!"

Her head cocked, Icelin obeyed. "But I thought I was bluffing," she said. "The pouch is too small to hold any useful weapon."

"*Mefilarn stowil!*" the elf at the door said sharply to his companion. "Make her hold her tongue, Melias."

"Your friend's right, Melias, I do talk too much. And that's a fault to reckon with," Icelin said. "But don't interrupt me now, I've only just got going. The pouch can't contain any weapon deadly to you. So what am I keeping in here, if not some dark magic that you both fear?"

"Empty it," Melias commanded.

"Not here," Icelin said, "in the alley. We can have a nice, quiet conversation—"

"Sorry to be so long!" Sull's booming voice cut through the tension in the air like a saw grating on wire.

"Watch your hands." The butcher tossed a pair of bundles wrapped in brown paper onto the counter next to Melias. "Seasonin's, I was talkin' of." He uncapped the jar of salt again and poured a fistful into his large hand. He gestured at Icelin and sprayed salt across the counter.

"Large crystals, that's what you want," Sull said. "Not ground as fine as for a noble's table in North Ward—that bleeds the flavor out—but try talkin' sensible cookin' to a noble, eh? The salt's what teases the tongue. You put some pinches of this on the fire while your boar meat's simmerin' in my spices, the whole thing'll be so tender it falls juicy onto your spoon. Make a man weep unashamed pleasure, that's the truth." He looked at the elves as if he'd only just remembered they were there. "Sorry 'bout that, gentlemen, I like to blather. What can I get the pair of you?"

"Nothing," said the one by the door. "We didn't see anything worthy of our master's tastes. The lass and we are leaving."

"Aw, shame, that," the butcher said, looking crestfallen. "This is prime meat, you know. Here now, maybe you'd like this cut instead."

The red-haired giant turned, yanked the meat hook from the deer carcass, and swung it in a downward arc. The hook sank into the countertop, the curved metal trapping Melias's delicate wrist against the wood.

Screams of elf fury filled the shop.

"Told you to watch your hand," Sull admonished. He threw his handful of salt at the elf by the door, grabbed Melias's head in his other hand, and slammed the elf's skull against the countertop.

Blood poured down Melias's face. He fell back over the counter, his hand still pinned awkwardly under the hook.

The elf by the door took the salt in the eyes. Crying out, he drew his sword and scraped a hand across his face.

Stunned by the violence, Icelin almost didn't react in time. Reaching into her neck purse, she chanted the first simple spell that came to mind. The elf at the door brought his blade up, but Icelin got to her focus first and hurled a handful of colored sand into the air.

A flare of light consumed the sand and shot at the elf's face. Luminous colors filled the small shop; Icelin covered her eyes against the brilliance.

She heard the elf fumble his sword, but he didn't drop it. Instinctively, she ducked. Wood splintered from the wall.

"Run, lass!" The butcher yelled at her.

Icelin broke for the door, stumbling over her dress. The noise betrayed her. The elf dived at her from the side and caught an arm around her waist. They went down together, arms and legs tangling.

Pain lanced along Icelin's flank. The elf's weight pinned her to the floor. She kicked out viciously, trying to find a vulnerable spot. He forced her arms against her sides and put his boot on the back of her head. When she tried to move, he pressed down, hard. Icelin thought her skull would crack from the pressure.

She heard him groping for his sword. He dragged the blade over to them and brandished the pommel. He was going to knock her out, Icelin realized. The fight had come down to kicking and screaming after all, but she was still going to lose.

The elf's head snapped to the side. Steel clattered on wood, and he pitched forward, sprawling heavily on top of her.

Her arms free, Icelin heaved the elf off and kicked his sword across the room. She raked the hair out of her eyes and felt moisture on her back. She could smell the blood.

"It's not yours." The butcher stood over her, clutching a mallet in his hand. "For tenderizin'," he explained.

"I think you killed him," Icelin said. She rolled the elf onto his back and put her hands over his heart. "There's no beat. What about the other?"

"He's breathin,'" Sull assured her.

Icelin had to see for herself. The butcher had strewn Melias across the counter next to the dead deer. Blood and bruises darkened his temple. His chest rose and fell intermittently. He would need healing soon, or he would join his friend.

"Why did you kill him?" Icelin demanded. Fear shook her voice. How had everything gotten so out of control? This could no longer be a private matter. The Watch would have to be called, if someone hadn't already heard the commotion and summoned them. She would be questioned; Gods, she would have to go through all that again. . . .

"Lass." The butcher was speaking to her. She'd almost forgotten he was in the room. "I had to, lass. Beggin' your pardon, but I was eavesdroppin' just now. These two, or whomever they serve, meant you harm. No man sends his own men—men he knows might be traced—after a person unless he plans for that body never to come home. After they'd trussed you up and made you gentle, they would have killed me for witnessin'. I'd be just another abandoned shop."

Icelin felt light-headed. "I have to go home," she mumbled.

"Best to wait for the Watch."

"The Watch be damned!" She lowered her voice. "Forgive me, but my great-uncle—he must know about this. I'll bring him back here—"

"Wait! What if there are more of them out there?"

More? She couldn't comprehend it. She was one small woman squirreled away in a shop, in a city full of folk much larger and darker. Why would someone want her so badly?

Cerest's scarred face appeared in her mind—the puckered red skin, the ruined ear.

"He wants revenge," Icelin said. "There's no other explanation." She glanced at Sull. The butcher looked extremely uncomfortable. "You know who I am," she said. It wasn't a question.

Sull cleared his throat. "Aye, I know. I recognized your face when you came in the shop. Someone's after you because of that business?" He shook his head. "It was years ago."

"He has burn scars all over his face," Icelin said flatly. "He recognized me too."

Sull sighed and nodded. "Go then, to your great-uncle. I'll speak to the Watch. But you'd best be runnin'."

Full dark pressed down on the city by the time Icelin reached her great-uncle's shop. The place was closed up, and there were no lamps burning in the second-level rooms. Brant always left a lantern in her bedroom when she was gone after dark.

Icelin fumbled her key in the lock at the back door. Sometimes her great-uncle lingered downstairs after closing to review his accounts. Meticulous in his records and his housekeeping, Brant never let anything stray out of order. That patience and painstaking attention to everything—including his great-niece—made her love him all the more.

Icelin stepped into the dark shop, leaving the door ajar for Selûne to light the entryway. The shadow of a tall wooden plant stand caught her eye as she groped for a lamp. The piece of furniture had been moved slightly away from the wall, and the vase of lilies that had been displayed on it lay overturned on the floor. Water funneled through cracks in the floorboards.

Water, not blood. And no other earthly thing was out of place in the room.

But Icelin screamed anyway, screamed and dropped to the floor, clutching her hair and sobbing. In the dark, she crawled across the floor of the shop, feeling her way, fighting the dread bubbling up inside her.

Someone had already been here, seeking her. But how had they known? *How?*

"Great-Uncle," she whispered. Her fingers found a rack of boots, then a stand of belts. Long, leathery softness caressed her fingers. She crawled on, her skirts collecting dirt and dust that her great-uncle should have swept outside at the end of the business day. She found the broom in the next corner; the worn bristles reminded her of insect legs.

She reached the front of the shop. Clear glass jars lined the counter, each filled with a different herb or spice.

"Salt, mint, comfrey, basil." She named each one out of habit, stopping before she reached the wall. Selûne's glow poured in a window and over her shoulder. She put her hand tentatively into the beam of light and followed it down to the floor. At the edge of the light, her hand found her great-uncle's chest.

Brant lay on his side, tucked against the back of the counter. There was very little blood; he'd clutched most of it in and made gouge marks in the wood with his other hand where he had held on. The sword thrust had been quick and precise, slipping right between his ribs.

When she touched him, his eyes fluttered open. Icelin could see he was already going. She had no time, no breath to explain that he'd been killed because of her, no time to say anything of meaning.

"Great-Uncle," she choked.

His eyes widened when he recognized her. He let go of the wood and grabbed for her, catching hair and dress and skin all together. He pulled her close.

"Get out of here," he said, his voice a terrible rasp.

"I'm not going anywhere," Icelin said. "I'm not leaving you."

"Get . . . the . . . box." The words came out broken by gasps and blood dribbling from his lips, "The floorboards, by the bookcase. Take it with you. Should have . . . been yours . . . before."

"You've given me everything I've ever needed," Icelin began.

"No!" He said it so viciously Icelin flinched. He held her tighter. "I lied, Icelin. I loved you, but now he's going to. . . ." Brant started to sob. She had never seen him cry before, not even when he spoke of his dead wife, Gisetta.

"I won't let him," Icelin said. She put her forehead against his. His lips moved, but she could barely hear what he said next.

"Run. Leave the city. Make something . . . new . . . better. Don't blame yourself. . . ."

"Shh, Great-Uncle, please." Icelin held his hands, but they'd gone boneless in her grip. He had no more strength.

"Rest now. I . . . I'll s-sing to you," she promised him. He could still hear her voice. Haltingly, the words came.

> *The last falling twilight*
> *shines gold on the mountain.*
> *Give me eyes for the darkness,*
> *take me home, take me home.*

"Do you remember, Great-Uncle?" she asked. She cupped his wrinkled cheek in her hand. His eyes stared glassily up at her. He nodded once. She felt the moisture at the corner of his eye.

"You always remember," he said. "I'm sorry . . . for that too." He closed his eyes, and his head slid away from her. She lost him in that last little breath.

Icelin curled protectively around the still-warm body, cradling her great-uncle's head in her hands. She stayed there, hunched, until she couldn't feel anything except a burning ache in her legs. The pain was the only force that kept her sane. As long as it was there, she wouldn't have to feel anything else. She would never leave that floor. She would stay there until the world withered away.

Moonlight still bathed them when Icelin heard the shop door close. She raised her head and saw the butcher's bulky shape crammed in the doorway. He seemed brought to her from another time, another century, one in which her great-uncle wasn't dead.

"Sull?" She didn't recognize her own voice.

"It's me, lass." The big man knelt beside her and lifted Brant's head from her lap. "Are you all right?"

"My throat hurts," she said.

"You were singin'."

"Was I?" She hadn't been aware, but now she thought of it, she could recall every song. Of course she could. She would remember them and the look on Brant's face when she sang. She would carry those memories with her until she died.

"You always remember. . . ."

"Icelin, you need to come with me," Sull said. He took her hands. She was dead weight, limp as one of his carcasses, but he pulled her to her feet easily.

"He told me to leave the city," Icelin said. She might have laughed at the jest, but she didn't want to alarm Sull.

"I think he was right," the butcher said. He took her chin in his hand, forcing her to focus on him. "I've been to the Watch, but that elf bastard got away while I was gone. Guessin' he wasn't hurt as much as we thought. Ransacked every damn tool and stick of furniture in the place before he left, as if you were a mouse he was trying to scrounge up. Maybe to him that's what you are, but the Watch thinks differently."

"They've never liked me," Icelin said, and this time she did laugh. She could feel the hysteria bubbling up inside her. "Small wonder, I suppose. I'm the she-witch of Blacklock Alley, didn't you know?"

"Lass, that's not it," Sull said. "They've instructions to bring you in."

"For what?" she asked incredulously. "I didn't kill anyone!"

Not this time. . . .

"It's not like that," Sull said. "You're wanted on suspect of jewel thievery. The one who placed the request was named Kredaron, actin' on behalf of Cerest Elenithil."

"Kredaron?" Icelin closed her eyes. "Of course. That's how Cerest found out where I lived. So it's suspicion of thievery, unless they can prove I'm a murderess as well."

"I didn't tell 'em you were comin' back here. I told 'em I left you unconscious in my shop. But they'll check this place soon," Sull said. "I can get you out before that."

"Why should you care what happens to me?" Icelin said. Her voice held a bitter edge. "How can you be sure I'm innocent?"

Sull's brows knitted in a dark red line. "You and your mouth might be famous in this ward, but now's not the time to let loose on me," he said. "If he was alive, your great-uncle would give you a smart slap for takin' that tone with your elders. Brant Tearn was a fine man, he raised a good girl, and that's plenty of reasons for me to bother with you."

He left her at the counter and roved about the room, lighting a small lamp and placing it on the floor away from the windows. He selected a pair of swash-topped boots from the rack and tossed them to her.

"Put those on," he said. "You'll need new boots for the road, and a pack." He pulled one down off the wall. It was a nondescript brown mass of buckles and straps. "Blankets and ration bundles. Where did your great-uncle store 'em?" he asked.

"On the shelf behind you," Icelin said. She watched him collect some flint and steel, a compass, a weathercloak, and one of the belts. He put them all in a pile next to her.

"Don't wait for me; start puttin' it on," he told her. "I have a friend at the gate. He doesn't respond well to moral causes, but he can be bribed, so it suits me well enough. Stop lookin' at him, lass. We have to move!"

"Where do you think I can go, Sull?" He paused long enough to look back at her. "I have never trod on soil that wasn't Waterdeep's. My only family lies on this floor. Where would someone like me find a kind place in the world?"

Sull opened his mouth to answer, but the silence stretched.

Icelin nodded. "Exactly. I can't leave. I have to hide, at least for now."

But where to disappear to? Cerest's men had tracked her easily, and the Watch now joined them.

"You'll have to leave Blacklock, that's a certainty," Sull said. "If I knew your face, others will too, and they'll be watchin' for you."

"So, I leave the Alley," Icelin said. She picked up the pack and the belt and put them on. The rations she took as well. No telling where her next meal would be coming from.

Reaching over the counter, she took out the knife Brant had kept for emergencies. He hadn't been able to get to it when they came for him. She used it to cut a slit up her skirt. She needed to be able to run full stride if it came to that.

"There is a man I know in the Watch," she said. "Kersh. Fortunately, he *does* respond to moral causes. I think he'll help me, or at least be able to give me some information about Cerest."

"Help *us*, lass," Sull said. "I'm goin' with you."

Icelin shook her head. "You've already gotten yourself in enough trouble on my behalf. What about your store?"

"Stone and timber," Sull said, shrugging. "It'll be there after I've seen to you. This man," he said, and he knelt to touch Brant's shoulder, "he was known in South Ward. Like I said, he's a good man, and so is his kin. I'll be goin' with you lass, so it'd be best if we don't waste time arguin'."

Icelin looked at the butcher in the flickering lamplight. He still wore his bloody apron. He'd tucked the mallet and several wicked-looking cleavers into a leather harness that he draped sash-style across his broad stomach. Even had she not known what he could do with those tools, he was a fearsome sight to behold. Yet he handled her great-uncle's body with infinite gentleness. He tucked Brant's arms against his body and laid a blanket over him. Icelin swallowed the emotion rising up within her.

"All right, then, we'll go together," she said. "But you'll leave me at the first safe place I find. I'll sort the rest out on my own." She paused with the pack in her hands. "Wait. I need one more thing." She remembered her great-uncle's cryptic words. "Something he wanted me to take. He said it was near the bookcase."

"Could have been gibberish he was talkin'. A dyin' man might say things that don't make much sense," Sull said.

"No, he was very specific. He said it was in a box."

"If you say so. But we don't have time to be solvin' riddles, lass. What do you need?"

Icelin thought about it. "A sledgehammer," she decided.

Sull blinked. "Wasn't expectin' that."

"Over here." Icelin went behind the counter, where a narrow stretch of floor fronted a bookcase containing her great-uncle's favorite volumes. They were bound in leather, with red ribbons draped over the spines. He loved to read them on slow days. Tipped back on his wooden stool, he'd lay the pages open on his lap. When she was a child, Icelin had perched on the counter to listen to him read to her.

"I need to break through these boards," Icelin said. She wanted to smash them with her bare hands, to howl out the rage boiling inside her. But she would need her hands, her whole body's strength, in case she had to cast spells. "Do you think you could break them?" she asked Sull.

The butcher hiked up a leg and brought it down against the floorboards. The old wood splintered and gave way.

"There's dirt here," Sull said. "I don't feel anythin' else."

"Let me in there." He made way for her to crouch over the small hole. She felt with both hands in the musty darkness.

"Hurry, lass," Sull urged her. "Someone will have heard that noise."

"Found it." The box was small and narrow. She could feel the ridges of some kind of scrollwork running along the outer edges. When she brought it up, Sull's gasp drowned out her own.

"Bring the light," Icelin said.

Sull held up the lantern. The box shone, eclipsing the moonlight in the glow of flame.

"Is that—"

"Gold," Sull confirmed. "Or I'm no judge of beef. A small fortune's worth of it, at least. You have a dragon's hoard of mysteries about you, lass, and that's a certainty."

"Let's hope this is the last one," Icelin said. Escape was her greatest concern. She had no time to ponder what the box contained or why her great-uncle had concealed it from her. She buried it at the bottom of her pack and blew out the lamp.

Cerest didn't bother to light the lamps in front of his Sammarin Street home. He bypassed the front entrance of the blocky stone structure, with its single tower braced against the main building. He headed instead for his private garden.

He'd spent the largest share of his hoarded coin here, where he could be among the wild things and the quiet. It was his place to think, and where he often met the two women whose company he sought now.

Moonlight cast milky shadows over the cobblestone path leading to the small gladehouse. It was not as grand as those found at a high noble's mansion. The long sheets of glass that formed the circular cage were expensive and fragile, but they ornamented his most exotic blossoms: panteflower, with its bell shape and dark red stems; yellow orchids, the most fragrant; and all the rose varieties he could afford.

He lifted the latch on the door and stepped inside. The elf women were waiting, perched on stone benches on either side of a long rectangular pond. A fine layer of green scum covered the water. He would have to tend it when he was alone. Cerest looked forward to such tasks, but the Locks would have to come first.

Ristlara and Shenan, the Locks of North Ward, were sisters, or so they claimed. Privately, Cerest wondered if they were lovers. Not that it mattered, as long as they came to his bed.

Both had fiery gold hair, bronze skin, and moss green eyes. They were too beautiful and knew it, but they were also the richest pair of professional thieves living openly in the City of Splendors. That position demanded respect.

The Locks had defined the market for rare antiquities in the city, and Cerest knew what pleased them best: magic, the older the better. Their private mansion resembled more of a museum, stocked with artifacts either stolen or recovered from tombs across Faerûn, all of it carefully tagged and catalogued. It was a concise history of thievery that covered almost two centuries.

The sisters were mostly retired, preferring to commission their raids among the eager treasure-seekers who passed through the city. They were still rabid collectors, and to date, Cerest was their most successful contact. But for all his dealings with the sisters—both in the bedchamber and out of it—he'd never been invited to see inside their residence.

With this venture, Cerest vowed, things would change.

"Clearly, *you* don't see the need to maintain your business contacts, Cerest, since we haven't heard from you this tenday, but my sister and I were hosting a dinner party when you dragged us away to your swamp." Ristlara leaned back on the bench, crossing her shapely legs and scowling at him. She looked like a bronze sculpture against the stark gray stone. Her hair was upswept and bobbed at the back of her head, giving her face and neck a long, elegant line.

"Let him speak," Shenan told her sister. The older elf wore her hair loose, almost wild, and was as sedate as her sister was furious.

"Ladies, I appreciate you coming on such short notice," Cerest began. "You know I wouldn't have contacted you after such an inexcusable absence—roused you from tea with boorish human muck-rakers—if it wasn't important."

"How did you know who we were meeting?" Ristlara demanded.

Her sister smothered a chuckle with the back of her hand. "Those are foul words to use, Cerest," Shenan chided him. "The humans led a legitimate expedition—a feat you have not achieved in some years."

"Digging in farm fields and wastelands where no real magic has dwelled for a century, you mean." With a melodramatic flourish, Cerest slid onto the bench next to Ristlara. He pulled the bronze she-cat onto his lap. "No thank you. I don't take up after the spellplague's leavings. Your lovely human pets are wasting your coin, sucking you dry like parasites. I have something better for you," he said against the squirming female's ear.

He felt her face grow warm against his cheek. Cerest nuzzled her neck until she stopped thrashing. "Are you interested, Ristlara? Or should I be coddling your sister?"

"Will it make us a lot of coin?" Shenan asked.

"Darlings, you won't believe me when I tell you," Cerest said. "I've found Elgreth's granddaughter."

Ristlara turned in his arms. Their faces were inches apart, but she'd stopped flinching at his scars a long time ago. "Are you jesting?"

"Not a bit."

"Have you spoken to her?" Shenan asked. She eyed Cerest shrewdly. "Will she work with us?"

"Not yet," Cerest said. "She needs time. I made a terrible first impression, I'm afraid."

"Poor Cerest," Ristlara cooed. She tipped her head back against his shoulder, so he could not help but catch the scented oil in her hair, or notice the full effect of her cleavage in her green lace gown. "Did you frighten her away? Did she think she was seeing a mask and not a face at all?" She reached up to touch his melted skin.

Cerest caught her wrist before she could touch him. He laid his other hand casually around her throat. For a moment, the elf's eyes widened fearfully. The irony of where she sat only then dawned on her.

The Locks were well aware of the change in Cerest's demeanor since his disfigurement. One of his former servants, a retired fence named Tolomon Shinz, had been unable to keep from staring at Cerest's scars. Cerest had been too ill at first to respond with any censure, but later, when the immediate pain and horror had abated, a general wildness of temper took its place.

He was known to react with violent outbursts to any insult, real or perceived, and so when Tolomon Shinz had looked too long at his crooked ear one Kythorn morning, Cerest had reacted decisively . . . most would say harshly.

Cerest had since mastered his emotions to such an extent that he could ignore most people, no matter their reaction to his deformity. But that didn't change the fact that Tolomon Shinz was entombed beneath Cerest's fish pond, and Ristlara's shapely toes dangled above the water scant inches from where his skull was decomposing.

The pretty elf, staring up at him while his hand noosed her neck, was most likely wondering, if only for a breath, if a similar fate awaited her. Ristlara's uncertainty was Cerest's power, and the elf reveled in it.

Shenan cleared her throat, and the tense breath passed.

Cerest relaxed and pushed the golden bitch off his lap.

"I was insensitive to Icelin," Cerest admitted, continuing their conversation as if nothing had happened. "Too greedy for my own good."

"You made the same mistake with Elgreth," Shenan reminded him.

"That was different. We had history between us. I expected more from Elgreth. But Icelin—"

"How lovely. It has a name," Ristlara purred.

"I think he's smitten, Sister," Shenan said. "I wonder if the lady will feel the same."

"She will," Cerest assured them. "I'm eliminating all her safe places. The life she knows is ending. When she has nothing left, she'll come to me gladly. I will be the only one who can protect her."

"And we will turn a tidy profit besides," Shenan said before he could. "It is a tempting offer." She swept a hand down beside the bench to caress one of the rose blossoms. She took hold of a thorny stem and severed it from the bush with her nail.

"Shall we agree to be partners again?" She offered the rose to Cerest.

Cerest took the flower and clenched it in a fist. Blood welled where its thorns pierced his flesh. Shenan watched in fascination as the droplets ran down his golden skin.

It was just the sort of poetic, gruesome gesture she preferred. In bed, she was no different, her nails digging blood trails into his skin until he cried out.

Dangerous, sadistic cats, these two. Cerest couldn't help adoring them both.

"We are in agreement," he said. He held out the bloody rose and watched Shenan kiss the stem.

Glass shattered behind them. Cerest turned, his hand on his sword hilt.

Melias lay sprawled in the doorway of the gladehouse. He'd collapsed against the structure and shattered the fragile door panel with his weight. Blood trailed from a blunt strike to the elf's head.

Cerest crouched next to the dazed elf. Melias's pupils were huge. His mouth moved, but the words that came out made no sense. He'd suffered too much damage to his head to live.

"Melias." Cerest shook the elf, trying to get him to focus. Melias whimpered, and his head lolled to one side.

"I think you might be in for more of a game than you thought, Cerest," Shenan commented.

The small elf crouched next to Melias and cradled his head in her lap. "Dearest," she cooed in his ear. "Who did this to you?"

"She . . . ran," the elf murmured. He was looking past Shenan, up at the gladehouse ceiling and through it to the stars. "We're dead . . . butchered . . . us." A slack, vacant smile passed over the elf's face.

"Yes, my sweet. Unfortunately, she did." Shenan took the elf's chin and forehead in her hands and jerked his head to the side. The sharp crack echoed off the gladehouse walls.

"You take too many liberties, Shenan," Cerest told her. "He was my man. I wanted him questioned."

"It was a kindness to end it," Shenan said, rising to her feet. "Pain is only alluring when there is the possibility of surviving it."

"I have to leave," Cerest said. He headed for the main building, leaving Melias's body concealed in the gladehouse.

The death of his men complicated matters with the Watch. They would not easily believe a waif of a girl could overpower two armed elves. How in the names of the gods *had* she done it?

She must be more powerful than I imagined, Cerest thought. The idea gave him a thrill of excitement and trepidation all in the same moment.

So much the better he declaim her a murderess, Cerest thought. He would tell the Watch that his men had been killed trying to retrieve his stolen property. They would have no proof to the contrary, as long as Icelin kept running.

The she-elves trailed behind him. "Do you intend to track her down by yourself?" Ristlara said.

Cerest stopped at the door to his house. Another idea occurred to him. On the surface it seemed perfect: efficient, clean, and with no way it could be traced back to him. But could he trust the Locks?

When he turned, he addressed Shenan. "Those human muck-rakers you're employing—how many are there?"

"Seven," Shenan said. "But they can muster the strength of twelve or more for longer expeditions. Why?"

"What say you put them to a different use, something that might actually end in profit?"

He could sense Ristlara gearing up for a fight, but Shenan's look was speculative. "How much of the profit would be for us?" she asked.

"If I get Icelin—unharmed—the percentage will twice exceed what you take now," Cerest promised.

Shenan smiled. "You truly are smitten," she said. "We'll bring the men. I want to watch this spectacle."

CHAPTER FOUR

Watchman Kersh Tegerin turned off Copper Street, crossing a footbridge linking Dailantha's Herbs and Exotic Plants to Breerdil's Fine Wines. A small, man-made stream ran under the bridge. Breerdril and Dailantha spent a small fortune to keep the water enchanted to appear midnight blue.

Kersh counted the paces from one end of the footbridge to the other. It was a habit from childhood that he'd never quite broken. Meren, his old friend, used to tease him for it.

The bell for gateclose had rung long ago, but he still had a little time before he needed to join up with his patrol. Kersh wasn't looking forward to the night's work. The word had gone out when he'd left the barracks: the Watch had orders to bring in Icelin Tearn for questioning.

How in the names of the gods did the girl get herself into these situations?

Kersh nodded to the lamplighters as they passed him on the street. The trio of men waved back, their iron reaching-hooks resting against their shoulders. They were sooty standard-bearers. The soft glow of flickering lights followed in their wake.

This time of night always made Kersh think of Meren, and tonight the feeling was heightened. They'd been on patrol together ten winters ago and had become fast friends. Meren had been young and, with all the wisdom of youth, had believed the quiet streets of North Ward held no threat for someone as spry and as skilled as he.

Meren learned differently, and Kersh lost his first real friend in Waterdeep. Kersh remembered the day vividly. The boy had had no kin, but his former employer had come with his great-niece to claim the boy's body.

Icelin had been only a child at the time, but Kersh had never met a person who acted as she did. Bristling with opinions and outlandish teasing, she had seemed a fully formed adult merely lost in a child's wrappings.

Kersh remembered how, in the midst of his grieving, this strange child had walked right up to him and greeted him by name, as if they'd been friends for all their lives. Later, Kersh learned that she'd memorized the names and faces of almost all the Watch officers, simply by passing through the barracks when she'd escaped her great-uncle's sight.

After their first meeting at the funeral, she visited him regularly. She told him stories about Meren—silly, adorable boy, she'd called him—and his time working for her great-uncle in his sundries store. No detail or behavior escaped her memory.

Their friendship had continued, and Kersh had watched the odd child blossom into a lovely, confident woman. But he never forgot the affection with which she'd reached out to him all those years ago. It had been a balm to the terrible grief. The only being she paid more attention to was her great-uncle. She trailed his heels as if he were the center of her vast playing field.

So when the order came down that Icelin was to be taken for thievery and questioning for Brant's death, Kersh knew something was terribly amiss. Icelin was in trouble. And if Kersh knew her at all, he knew she wouldn't prefer the idea of surrendering to the Watch.

After the lamplighters had passed by, Kersh slid to a crouch on the bridge. Directly below his feet, between two of the bridge's supports, stood Icelin herself.

She was knee-deep in the perfect, midnight blue water, her thin frame concealed by the shadows. Behind her, a huge man emerged from a metal grate at water level. He crouched beside her, hissing at the cold water. Kersh had never seen the man before, but the small bridge barely concealed his massive frame. If the lamplighters came back this way to chase an errant flame, they would spot the pair in a heartbeat.

"Icelin, what web have you gotten yourself caught in?" Kersh said through his teeth. "And why meet here, bare-bottomed to the world?"

"Hello, old friend," Icelin said, "lovely to see you too. I'm afraid the risk was necessary, as I'm a bit pressed for time."

She shivered with cold and had deep circles under her eyes. Her hands gripped the bridge pilings as if for support. There were dark stains under her fingernails. Kersh suppressed a gasp.

"Icelin, what happened?" he demanded. "The patrols are getting your description as we speak. We're supposed to bring you in—subdued, if necessary."

"Then it's fortunate I'm a master of subtlety," Icelin jested. "Stand up and pretend to enjoy the night, you dolt, so no one looks under the bridge."

"This is serious," Kersh said, but he did as she asked. "How can you be so reckless?"

"I am taking this situation *very* seriously, my friend," Icelin said coldly. "Brant is dead. I assume you heard that too. He died in my arms."

"I'm sorry, Icelin. Who did it?"

"You'll recognize the name. Cerest Elenithil."

Kersh started. "The one who wants you brought in?"

"The same," Icelin said. "Obviously, he has a grudge against me that demands attention. Setting the Watch on my trail was an expedient way to corner me. I need a place to hide from him, somewhere the Watch won't readily find me."

"Unless you're sitting with the gods, there's no such place," Kersh said. "All the patrols have been alerted, and if that wasn't enough. . . ." He didn't know how to say it.

She did it for him. "They all remember Icelin Tearn. I have no illusions about my reputation among your fellows."

"Told you we should have made a run for it." The big man spoke up for the first time.

"Who's that?" Kersh wanted to know.

"Sull's my butcher," Icelin said, elbowing the big man into silence. "There must be somewhere we can go, Kersh."

Kersh hesitated. "You could come in with me."

"Hah."

"I'd speak for you," Kersh insisted. "My word doesn't carry as much weight as a swordcaptain's, but I know your character."

"The Watch has no desire to help me," Icelin said. "And I will not sit idly in a dungeon cell, waiting for them to deliberate my fate, while Brant's murderer plots my demise."

She stopped speaking. Kersh heard a soft sob, then silence. He waited for her to gather herself. He had never seen her fall apart before, not in all the years he'd known her.

"Kersh?" Her voice sounded strained.

"I'm here."

"What if—I know this will sound like lunacy—I could find a guide, someone who knows the city well and could hide me for the time being? Just until I figure out what to do about Cerest." Her voice grew stronger. "There is one person I can think of who would be perfect for the job."

It took Kersh a moment to realize where she was leading him. "Absolutely not!" he hissed. "You're right. You're talking lunacy."

"Who are we talking about?" the butcher wanted to know.

"Kersh used to work a night watch in the dungeons," Icelin said. "He told me a story once after several goblets of wine of a famous rogue he made the acquaintance of. A man named Ruen Morleth."

"He's nothing special, except he stole a fortune in paintings from a noble in North Ward, a great collector of odd and obscure art," Kersh said. "Brought the largest bounty on his head I've ever seen offered in the city."

"So he was caught?" Sull said. "Doesn't sound like a very good thief to me."

"Exactly. And he'd been imprisoned for some years," Kersh said. It was a stupid story. He couldn't believe he was reciting it now. "He asked me to get his hat back from some guards who were dicing over the thing." Of course Icelin would remember the whole tale perfectly, damn her. "I don't know why he bothered. It was the ugliest hat I'd ever seen."

"Kersh said the rogue offered to tell him a secret if he got his hat back," Icelin added. "So Kersh, being the curious thick-head that he is, set out to win the hat back from the guards. Fortunately, our Kersh has a good hand at dice. Tell him how grateful the rogue was, Kersh."

"I gave him back his hat, and he informed me very solemnly that he believed the secret of my parentage involved a tavern wench and several barnyard animals, and did I want to hear more?"

"Sounds like a lovely fellow," Sull snorted. "But you can't blame him for being angry over losing his hat."

"Oh, but you see, Kersh didn't tell the rogue that to get his precious hat back, Kersh had to gamble away half his wage for all the month of Ches," Icelin said. "The rogue got wind of it though, and this is the important part. Go on, Kersh. Tell him what Morleth said."

Kersh sighed. "He apologized, told me that he appreciated my looking after his hat, and said that if I ever needed a favor in return, I should go to Mistshore."

"Mistshore?" the butcher echoed incredulously. "That's the worst section of the city. He wanted to send you to Waterdeep's bowels to reclaim a favor?"

"At the Dusk and Dawn Inn," Kersh said. "I was to inquire at the dicing rounds."

"Those were his exact words," Icelin said.

"You would know." Kersh rolled his eyes.

"Except it's bollocks and cream," said the butcher. "Even if you were to brave the journey to the harbor, how's this thief goin' to be any help to anyone when he's locked in a cage?"

"He's not in a cage," Icelin said. Kersh glanced down and saw her leaning against the slime-clad piling, looking like a smug queen surveying her holdings. "He escaped not six nights after he got his hat back. He's the only man who has ever escaped from Waterdeep's dungeons."

"You think because he offered me a favor he'll help you hide from the Watch?" Kersh shook his head.

"And the elf," Icelin reminded him. "All I need is permission to call in your marker."

"Icelin, he's dangerous—dangerous and strange. You don't want to get tangled up with someone you can't trust, not when I'm here to—" he stopped, cursing under his breath.

"I would trust you with my life," Icelin said softly. "But folk have been turning up dead around me today, and I don't want you joining them."

"Then what's the butcher doing here?" Kersh asked, a little sullenly.

"Noisome baggage, but I can't shake him," Icelin said. "Please, Kersh. Give me your marker and let me be gone."

Reluctantly, Kersh reached into his coin-purse and pulled out a pair of cracked dice. They fit comfortably in his hand, clicking softly together. It had been years since he'd examined them, but for some reason he always carried them close. He handed them down to Icelin's cold fingers.

"Thank you," she said.

The butcher leaned in to look. "Are those bosoms where the sixes should be?"

"They are," Kersh said. "He handed them to me, clasped my left hand between both of his for a breath, then he nodded, like he was satisfied with a shift in the weather. He said, 'enjoy a long life, friend,' and smiled like he was having some jest. But I could have sworn, by any god you'd care to name, that he was serious—relieved, almost. That part of the story I never told to anyone, not even you, Icelin."

Kersh went about his patrol as usual that night. When he was finished, he headed back to the barracks to report to the rordan on duty.

Icelin was his friend. He would lay down his life for her, and he would not sit idle while she wandered the most dangerous paths of Waterdeep.

Mistshore was a product of neglect more than anything else, but it had grown into a rotting infection on the back of an already struggling city.

Waterdeep's harbor had become a steadily growing source of pollution and despair over the last century. The water had turned murky brown, and the breeze that blew off the harbor was rank with filth.

Ships had been scuttled haphazardly on the north shore of the old Naval Harbor; their owners were dead, gone, or content to leave them to the poisonous waters. One atop another, they'd gradually stretched wooden talons out into the brown harbor, forming their own private continent. The landscape on this strange plain could shift dramatically from day to day, with old wreckages dropping off into the depths and fresh tangles being added to the pile.

No one knew who it was that first discovered you could live on the floating, twisted wreckage—if living was what it could be called—but since then the newly christened Mistshore had become a beaching ground for wreckage of a different sort: the poorest, most desperate folk of Waterdeep.

Mistshore had earned such a dark reputation that the Watch patrols rarely visited the place. Their efforts to restore order on the battered harbor had earned them several slain officers and grief from the rest of the city, who preferred that Mistshore be left to its own devices. Kersh thought it comforted them in some way to have all the worst elements in the city confined to one area. As long as the violence didn't bleed over into the other wards, the people were content.

But Icelin was striding right into the center of the chaos. Worse, Kersh had sent her there.

Kersh entered a low-ceilinged building that housed the Watch garrison. Passing through with a wave to comrades he recognized, Kersh kept going, ascending a short flight of steps to a separate complex. Torches clung to the walls on either side of his path. The soot piles they left on the stone gave the air a dense, pressed-in feeling.

Or maybe that's your conscience prickling you, Kersh thought. He knew Icelin was innocent; it was the elf that worried him. Icelin would need the protection of the Watch, whether she wanted to admit it or not.

Turning down a south hall, Kersh stopped in front of an iron-bound wooden door. He rapped twice on the solid planks.

"Come."

The gruff voice sounded much deeper than Taythe's—the rordan who worked the night watch. Kersh felt a sinking in his gut.

He entered the small office. A broad table dominated the center of the room, lit by flickering candles that dribbled pools of white wax down the table legs.

A gray-haired man stood hunched behind the table, surveying a crinkled map spread out before him. A bronze, boxed compass sat at his right elbow. He looked up when Kersh entered the room.

Kersh swallowed and immediately saluted, tapping his forefinger against his temple. Gods, he'd come looking for a superior officer and found the commander of the Watch himself.

The Watch Warden of Waterdeep, Daerovus Tallmantle, surveyed Kersh through steely, narrowed eyes. A gray moustache draped the lower half of his face. In Waterdeep he was known as the Wolfhound, and Kersh could well see why. He moved around the table with a graceful, predatory air, despite the years on his body.

"Well?" the Warden asked, knocking Kersh from his stupefied staring. "What have you, lad? Don't lurk in the door. Close it behind you."

Kersh shut the door and came to stand in front of the table. Now that he was here, before the Watch Warden, he felt even more the betrayer. Icelin would never forgive him.

"I have news," Kersh said, "on the whereabouts of Icelin Tearn."

The Warden nodded. "Your patrol spotted her?"

"Not my patrol," Kersh said, "myself alone."

"Did you apprehend her?"

Kersh felt his throat dry up, but he was an honest man. "I did not. I spoke to her, and I let her go."

The Wolfhound sank slowly into his chair. He leaned back, crossing his arms. "So you've a tale to tell me about why you acted thus. Out with it, lad."

Kersh had expected fury from the Watch commander. He hadn't counted on the man's cool-eyed assessment, which, by its sheer weight, was harder to bear than any shouted censure.

"I believe Icelin Tearn has been wrongfully accused of theft," Kersh said. He relayed to the commander the whole tale, as Icelin had told him from under the bridge. He didn't have her gift of memory, but he thought he recalled the details as near perfect as he could manage.

"Do you believe her?" the commander said when he'd finished. "Do you think this elf, Cerest Elenithil, is responsible for Brant Tearn's murder?"

"I do," said Kersh. "I believe he has a personal vendetta against Icelin, and that she needs our protection."

"You have no proof that your friend isn't spinning her own tales," the commander pointed out. "Her name is known in this barracks, and among many in the Watch."

Kersh felt a flare of indignation. "That does not exempt her from our protection, should her claims prove true."

"You don't believe the murder of a Watchman should warrant our enmity?"

Kersh felt his face flush with shame and something else. Righteous indignation, he might have called it, though he'd never thought himself capable of such emotions. However you termed it, the wrongness sat bitterly in his mouth. "There was no murder," he said. "It was an accident, as all involved are aware. Blame the gods if you will, but no man or woman should be punished for the fell magic that has gripped this city since the Spellplague."

The Warden gazed at him steadily. Kersh felt his heart hammering against his ribs, whether from anger or fear of a reprimand, he couldn't say. He'd never been so bold before.

"As it happens," the commander said softly, "I agree with you, lad."

Kersh offered a quiet prayer of thanks. "I want to take a patrol into Mistshore." He spoke faster, planning it out in his head. "I should never have let her go. She could be killed—"

The Warden held up a hand. "Before you break ranks, lad, and start leading your own patrols, hear me out. You say she intends to seek out this thief, Ruen Morleth?"

"That was her intention when she left me," Kersh said.

"Then our solution resides with him."

Kersh kept his mouth from falling open with an effort, but he couldn't keep his tongue from moving, not now that it had got going. "He's an escaped criminal; he's not to be trusted with her safety. How can you consider such a thing?"

The Watch Warden almost smiled. Kersh could see the quiver in his moustache. "Ruen Morleth has never escaped from anything in his whole life."

This time Kersh did gape. "You know where he is?"

"Indeed. He is a fine thief and as crooked as they come, but he's also smart. Ruen Morleth is a survivor. He has contacts in Mistshore and the Warrens, and probably other places we aren't aware of. We made him a generous bargain: his freedom in exchange for access to those contacts in Mistshore. With Morleth as our agent, we can work within Mistshore, and none of our own men need die. It's a bargain both sides were more than willing to make."

"Why are you telling me this?" Kersh asked. He felt hollow, betrayed by his own ignorance.

"Morleth is many things, but he won't harm your friend," the Warden said, as if sensing his distress. "We'll contact him immediately. When he finds Icelin, he'll bring her in, and I'll see to her protection personally until this matter can be resolved to your satisfaction and mine," he said.

"How will you find him?" Kersh wanted to know.

"We'll attempt magical means. But as you know, such methods don't always function well within the city," the commander said. "Fortunately, we have other ways to get information into Mistshore. Go outside the door, lad, and call down to the commons. Then come back. I've work for you yet."

Kersh hastened to obey. He had no idea where the night would lead him. But when the Wolfhound spoke, he found himself eager to follow the man.

·:⌒:·

When he was alone, Daerovus Tallmantle spoke to the empty air. "You heard, I expect."

A figure stepped into view from nowhere and crossed the room. The train of her fine crimson cloak was last to appear from the empty air.

She had gray hair to match the Watch Warden, but hers was a frizzy mass gathered into a hasty tail at the back of her neck. Her spectacles rode low on her narrow nose, held in place by a sharp upturn at its end.

"Will you want me to contact Morleth?" his assistant asked.

No one in the Watch or the Guard knew that the Warden employed the small woman as his spell guard. Tesleena had been with him for years. She never seemed to mind staying in the shadows while he conducted the affairs of his post.

"Yes. See if the girl has made contact," Daerovus instructed. "If she has, we'll have to move carefully. We don't want to lose her. If all goes well— and I expect nothing less—she'll be brought in safely. I want this Cerest Elenithil summoned as well. Then we can determine guilt and innocence."

"And if Ruen Morleth is forced to aid us in this, you'll have the opportunity for a clear test of his loyalty," Tesleena pointed out.

"He will honor his end of the agreement," the Warden said, "or he knows we will hunt him down. But," he conceded, "I would just as soon know for certain that our contact in Mistshore is secure."

"Then I will leave you." The gray haired woman bowed briefly and vanished into the invisible world all wizards seemed to gravitate to.

Daerovus sighed and rubbed his eyes. "Where are you tonight, Morleth?" he said aloud, and chuckled. "You have no idea what interesting encounters you have in your future."

CHAPTER FIVE

ICELIN HAD SEEN JAW-DROPPING WONDERS THROUGHOUT HER YOUTH IN the City of Splendors, and just as many sights that had convinced her of the worthlessness of some folk. She had never seen anything that inspired such measures of both emotions as when she first set eyes on Mistshore.

Adjusting the hood of her long cloak so that she could see a farther distance, Icelin took in the sprawling mass of wood, rigging, and moving bodies that swelled the harbor.

The place reminded her a little of Blacklock Alley: twisting, narrow corridors, broken here and there by the half-exposed bellies of ships that had been turned into living quarters or hawking grounds for vendors selling food and ale, or drugs and flesh. Torches lined the walkways. Small boys pushed past her with buckets of water, which they emptied onto the path. The saturated wood kept the torches' sparks from erupting into fire.

The wind blowing in from the sea was cold, and plucked uncomfortable holes in Icelin's cloak. The air reeked of fish, stale sweat, and a prevailing, sunk-in pollution that arose from the harbor itself. Tainted forever, the brown, salty sludge clung out of stubbornness and spite to the wreckages of Mistshore, determined in time to drag the structures down into the depths.

Icelin stopped to make way for a grizzled man in a tattered cloak hauling a hissing, spitting cat under one of his arms. He paused long enough to offer her an open bag of half-rotted fruit that had obviously come from a refuse pile. Flies buzzed around the brown apples and pears.

"Copper a dozen," he hissed, sounding just like the cat. He smiled at her, exposing an empty mouth and a scar across his gums.

Icelin started to shake her head, but the man was already moving off, a look of fear crossing his face. Icelin turned around to see Sull towering over her. His own cloak did little to hide his bulk, but the hood kept his bright red hair under wraps.

"You're going to draw more attention to us with that scowl than you would if we were both running around here stark naked," she said.

"I don't like this place," Sull said. He kept a hand on her shoulder, his eyes constantly moving among the crowd. "Shifts under my feet."

Icelin looked down. The rough walkway, reinforced to hold large numbers of plodding feet, was still a slanted, groaning mess. The wood had rotted or broken in places, allowing brown water to seep through when the wake kicked up. Anyone not minding his feet ran the risk of tripping and falling into the polluted harbor. Sull's weight made the rotting planks creak and bow.

"We'll find better footing closer to shore," Icelin said. "We only have to be out here long enough to find the Dusk and Dawn."

The structure they stood on now was at least a hundred yards across and roughly the shape of an octopus. The central head was marked by smoke plumes rising in massive clouds to the sky. The largest concentration of people gathered around an immense, controlled bonfire. Wooden paths branched off at odd angles from this single head, ending at other wrecks and sail-covered remains of ships that would no longer be recognizable to their former owners.

"Should never have come here," Sull muttered. He eyed the controlled devastation like a fish that had suddenly flopped onto the dock. Icelin knew she wore a similar, gaping expression.

They moved through the crowd slowly. Sull's presence soon warned away any eyes that lingered on Icelin, so they stayed unhindered except for the occasional vendor.

A woman carrying a tray of brown glass bottles stepped into Icelin's path. Each small vial had a cork stopper and a crudely inked label. She brandished them like a barmaid passing out ale mugs. Icelin could see down the cleavage of her low-cut dress. Water stains blotted the peaks and valleys of its hem.

"Need a pleasure draught, young one?" the woman said, "or something a little more fatal?"

Sheer curiosity drove Icelin to pick up one of the bottles. She ignored Sull's disapproving grunt.

"That's a good choice, that is." The woman took the vial from Icelin and popped the cork. "My own special brew. Call it Grim Tidings." Her laughter boomed over the crowd. "Completely odorless," she said, holding it under Icelin's nose, "unaffected by alcohol or sugar, so you can put it in your lord's tea or strong drink, whatever his pleasure. Course, it won't be pleasurable for very long!"

"So it's poison," Icelin said.

"Should bottle the harbor water," Sull said. "It'll get you the same effect."

The woman laughed again. "Oh, you've got a nasty one here, don't you? He your bodyguard?"

"You could say that," Icelin said. A gust of wind kicked up. Icelin buried her freezing hands inside her cloak. "Why aren't there more fires?" she asked. "You'll freeze to death out here in the winter."

"Some do," the woman said, and shrugged. "You won't find much heat on the fringes, 'cept from the torches on the paths. Didn't used to be that way, and whole ships'd go up when some poor drudge was careless with the cooking embers. Only fire allowed now comes from the path torches and the Hearth," she said, pointing to the thick smoke plumes. "Largest fire pit offshore anywhere in Faerûn."

Icelin heard the unmistakable note of pride in the woman's voice and marveled at it. "Who built the Hearth?" she asked.

"Same person who pays the boys to empty water buckets on the walk-ways, I expect," Sull said.

The woman nodded. "The gangs do it. The children are their children. The ones that enforce the rules are their enforcers."

"The gangs rule here?" Icelin said.

The woman chuckled. "You're round as a newborn babe, aren't you? No one 'rules' Mistshore. We're lucky to keep it floating. Everyone takes a little chunk of power, but no one wants it all. Who wants to be king of a rat heap? The ship's already sunk; we just haven't got the sense to get off. So we keep it floating, make coin, and everyone's happy." She smiled sardonically. "My power is bottles. So buy one or don't. But every breath I spend flapping with you, I lose coin. So what'll it be?"

Icelin took out a handful of coins. "Is this enough for the vial?"

"Not by my measure, nor any self-respecting poisoner." The woman sniffed and raised her nose a notch in the air. "More silver, young one."

"Perhaps we'll shop elsewhere." Sull took Icelin's arm and started to lead her away.

"Hold on, now, fleet-foots!" The woman scuttled around until she was in their path again. "Let me look a little closer at that handful of coins, I didn't get a good glance the first time."

"Count quickly," Sull said. "We're in a rush."

"Ah, there's the extra silver. You got it right." The woman scooped up the coins, buried them in the bosom of her dress, and handed Icelin the vial in exchange. "Enjoy," she said, and moved off.

"What was that about?" Sull said when she was out of hearing.

Icelin shrugged. "The way I see our situation, we have two weapons: your butchering tools and my magic, which is unstable under the most ideal circumstances. What can it hurt to have a vial of poison?"

"Just stay away from my tea," Sull murmured. "Why is your magic unstable anyway? From all I've heard, Waterdeep's the best place for wizards. They come in droves, sayin' somethin' about the city is better at keepin' the wild magic under control."

"That may be true in most cases," Icelin said. "Not in mine."

Icelin saw a break in the crowd at the end of the walkway. She started in that direction, as much to end the conversation as to get out of the throng. She felt Sull jerk the back of her cloak.

"I don't want to speak of this—"

"Hush, now. Look at the water." Sull pointed to a spot thirty feet out in the harbor.

Icelin looked, and through the wavering torchlight saw a faint, glowing shape pass close to the surface. Against the dark harbor, it shone as white as dust off a moth's wings. For a breath, she thought the shape looked human, writhing and clawing through the water. But that couldn't be. . . .

"What was that?" she said when it disappeared.

"A reason to get back to shore," Sull said. "And there's another." He pointed ahead of them, where two men faced each other on the narrow dock. Both held rust-covered knives. Cursing and grappling, they fought while a crowd watched. Some of the nearby vendors pulled out coins, calling for bets as to whose throat would be slit first.

The bigger of the two men shoved forward, driving his blade into the smaller man's thigh. Blood poured down the man's bare leg, and he stumbled backward into the water. Crimson flowed to join the torchlight dappling the harbor.

Icelin pulled against Sull. "We have to help him!"

"Too late," Sull said. "Look."

The flash of glowing white came again, just as the man went under in a swell of wake. His head broke the surface once, and he screamed, screamed until he was choking on the terrible water. He disappeared again beneath the waves. This time he did not resurface.

Icelin stood frozen. Her legs felt weak under her. She looked around for a reaction from the crowd, but the bettors and the gawkers had broken up. The crowd kept moving, the vendors kept hawking, and those that did stand by to watch wore vacant expressions. Icelin wondered how much of the vendors' drugs they had coursing through their blood, to be immune to such a strange, violent spectacle.

"What is this place?" she said. But she wasn't really talking to Sull.

"These are parts of the city you're never meant to see, lass," Sull said, patting her shoulder.

"And what of you?" Icelin demanded. "What have you seen of this kind of death? How can you just stand there and do nothing?"

Immediately she regretted her words. She had no cause to attack Sull. None of this was his fault.

"I'm sorry, Sull," she said. "That wasn't right."

But the butcher merely shook his head. "I been in my share of troubles, doin' things I'm not proud to tell you about," he said. "But this"—he spat in the water—"this is unnatural, even for Waterdeep. I didn't mean to patronize you, lass. My aim is to get you out of here safe. ""Keepin' our heads low and out of other folks' path is the only way to do that."

She knew Sull was right, but nothing about this place made sense to Icelin. The people—scarred by disease and wounds suffered from fights like the one they'd just witnessed—wandered around like refugees from a nonexistent war. Where had they come from? And what horrors had they seen out in the world that made them want to stay in a place like Mistshore?

They passed a crude signpost driven into the side of the walkway. Dock beetles scurried over its painted surface.

"Whalebone Court—Dusk and Dawn, appearing nightly," Icelin read. She followed a painted arrow to an open space near a pile of rocks. Here the wood had been reinforced several times over with new planks and a fresh coat of paint. The footing still shifted, but Icelin no longer felt the queasy up and down motion that had accompanied all her other movements.

Twelve wooden poles jutted out of the platform like exposed ribs, six on either side. From a distance, they vaguely resembled the carcass of a whale. Men moved among them, tying off ropes and securing the flaps of a bright red canvas.

"Puttin' up a tent," Sull said. "Think they intend on having a show?"

"Make way!" A stumpy man with a blond, pointed beard shouldered past Icelin. He wore a red velvet coat to match the canvas. He hauled an armful of knotted rope whose ends kept sticking in the gaping planks. Cursing, he jerked them free and moved on.

"Is this the Dusk and Dawn?" Icelin called after him.

"Working on it," the man shouted back. "Should have been open an age ago." He threw down an armful of rope. "Aye, I'm looking at you, Grazlen. Now get moving with that! Every breath you waste costs me coin."

Icelin and Sull moved out of the way. While they watched, the men hauled two more long poles out of the water where they'd been floating against rocks. Five of the men moved together to stand the poles vertically in the center of the platform. The bearded man stomped over and put his hand around the base of each.

Icelin saw his lips moving, the rhythmic song of magic she knew so well. Light flared at his fingertips, and the poles snapped to attention like wary soldiers, rigid upon the platform.

"Bring down the red!" the man in the red coat yelled. He spat on both his hands, rubbed them together, and shimmied up the poles.

The men below unfurled the canvas to its full length, securing all sides with the rope. The man in the red coat took an end and climbed to the top of the long poles, draping the canvas over them. That done, he slid to the platform, and watched as the men dragged the canvas over the rest of the exposed poles.

While the men tied the ropes to the platform, the man in the red coat removed a crumpled parchment sheet and a slender nail from his breast pocket. He spread the parchment out flat and pinned it to the canvas.

The sheet fluttered madly in the breeze, and Icelin could just barely make out the writing. "Dusk and Dawn," she read. And below that: "Time of Operation—Dusk until Dawn. Proprietor: Relvenar Red Coat."

"Open for business," the man in the red coat shouted.

Icelin looked around and saw that a small crowd had gathered with them to watch the proceedings. They filtered past in clusters, pushing and shoving to get into the tent.

Sull shook his head, chuckling. "I thought I'd seen everythin'. But a moveable feastin' hall I'd not expected!"

"It makes a certain sense," Icelin said. "You were right about the planks. They're too unstable to support a permanent structure this far offshore, not without stronger magic or more coin, or both. With a tent, he can move his operation whenever he likes and still be in the most crowded area of Mistshore."

"So it goes in fair Waterdeep," Sull said. "Commerce moves ever forward."

"Let's go in," Icelin said.

Sull sighed loudly. "And so it goes with all young people. Stridin' in headstrong, not carin' a bit if they're walkin' into certain doom."

Icelin threw him a bland look over her shoulder. "What kind of body-guard talks thus?"

"A smart one," Sull replied.

Relvenar "Red Coat" made a quick round of the card players in one corner of the tent before heading past the dicing area. All the gambling areas were marked off with paint on the floor. There were no tables and no chairs, and the only bar to speak of was the mass of ale kegs and crates of foodstuffs hauled in every night. The setup suited him just fine. The only thing about him that bore any frills was his bright red coat.

Dancing lamplight cast large shadows on the tent canvas. He paid an aching amount of coin to the gangs to keep the private lamps, but it was worth it not to have his patrons stumbling or knifing each other in the dark.

Relvenar moved to the back of the bar, where the wind teased the loose canvas and the smell of the harbor mingled with food and drink. He counted the kegs to make sure they would have enough for the night's crowd. He knew he should keep a larger stock, but transportation was cumbersome in Mist-shore. The Dusk and Dawn had all the problems of a normal tavern mingled with the worries of a ship's captain. Relvenar wore the dual roles as well as he could. Business was good, and his ship—such as it was—was intact.

The sound of fingernails scratching the outside of the tent brought Rel-venar to a halt in his inspection of the kegs. The scratching moved along the canvas, and a shadow loomed suddenly in front of him. Relvenar recognized the slender, agile shape, with a bulky top where a hat might be perched.

A very ugly hat, Relvenar thought. But business was business, and this client didn't enjoy being kept waiting.

Casting a quick glance around to make sure he wasn't being watched, Relvenar huddled down and crawled under the loose canvas. Outside in the clear air, the smell of the rank harbor hit him square in the nose.

Relvenar brushed a hand in front of his face, as if he could banish the stench. He shivered in the cold night air. "Didn't think you were going to show," he said to the figure leaning casually against a wood piling. The man stood easily, his arms crossed over his stomach, unbothered by the cold and the stench. He did not look happy. But then, Relvenar had never seen Ruen Morleth wear any expression except for a kind of blank coldness.

It's the man's eyes, Relvenar thought. There's too much wrong with them.

"Is she here?" Morleth said.

"Came in right after opening," Relvenar said. "Her and a big fellow. Keeps pretty close watch."

"How unfortunate for your cut-purses." Morleth produced a folded bit of parchment from inside his vest. "Send them to this location."

Relvenar took the parchment but didn't look at it. "What if they don't want to go? I'm not forcing any trouble in my establishment. If folk don't feel safe, they won't come back. I'll have to close down."

"I have a difficult time imagining your clientele feeling 'safe' anywhere in Mistshore," Morleth said. "Don't worry. These two are lambs; they'll go wherever you tell them. They *want* to find me." For a moment, Relvenar thought he read amusement in the man's features. Morleth turned, his worn boots making no sound on the platform.

He's almost too frail to be a proper thief, Relvenar thought. Light on his feet, but it's like he's a wisp. All bone, hair that's as fine as dark spider's silk. . . . The lass was the same way. They both looked like brittle spiders, apt to break in a harsh wind.

"I wish the lass luck handling you," Relvenar said, and bit his lip when Morleth paused. He looked back at Relvenar, holding his gaze until Relvenar shifted uncomfortably and looked away. When he looked back, Morleth was gone.

"Just like a spider," Relvenar muttered, shivering in distaste.

Cerest paced the dark street behind his home. The night was slipping away. Where were they?

He had already entertained a visit from a Watch patrol, and endured a polite but firm summons issued by the little bitch in charge. He was to give testimony against Icelin Tearn, before the Watch commander of Waterdeep himself!

Cerest knew they could have nothing with which to charge him. His men had been careful. The trails he'd left pointed to Icelin as a thief and now a murderer.

But what if he was wrong? Cerest leaned against the wall of the alley, his hands rubbing reflexively over his scars. The puckered texture of the burns helped to focus him, to remind him of how far he'd come.

All he had to do was find Icelin. Once he had her, he could leave the city if necessary. Baldur's Gate was thriving and swelling with more folk by the day. He and Icelin could start over there, disappear into the crowded cityscape, and make their fortune.

Everything would be exactly as it was before. When Elgreth had been alive, Cerest had had bright hopes for his future prominence in Waterdeep. Elgreth and his family were going to take him all the way to the circles of nobility. Even when he'd been scarred, Cerest hadn't been afraid of being shunned. He'd held onto the hope that Elgreth would save him . . . But then the man died, and all Cerest's dreams had died with him.

No. He wouldn't let it end tonight. He would find Icelin and make her understand the kind of man Elgreth was, and all that he owed Cerest. She would pay his debt, or he would kill her for raising his hopes all over again.

The crunch of booted feet broke the stillness. Cerest tilted his head to the right to hone in on the sound.

Ristlara strode out of the shadows, her golden hair caught up in a black scarf. Behind her stood four men of various heights, shapes, and degrees of armament.

"You're late," Cerest said.

"How would you know, standing there so oblivious to all the night?" Ristlara sniffed. "It's a wonder you're still alive, Cerest." She nodded at the men. "We had to move slowly, in smaller groups. We'll meet at a location I've designated, if you're prepared?"

"I am." Cerest pulled up the hood of his cloak. "You told them Mistshore?"

She glanced sidelong at him. "Yes. Shenan will be there to meet us. Are you certain your information is accurate?"

"It is." What coin Cerest hadn't spent on his garden, he'd used to garner information from one of the low ranks in the Watch. His pride wouldn't let him confess the amount to Ristlara. The Watch was notoriously hard to bribe. They acted swiftly and decisively to cull betrayers from their midst.

He hadn't been able to get Icelin's exact destination, but the thick-head he'd spoken to had been savvy enough to know that many eyes were turning closely to Mistshore this night. All that remained was for Ristlara and Shenan's muckrakers to find her out, wherever she was hiding.

"How many did you bring?" he asked Ristlara as they walked, slipping from shadow to shadow on the broad street.

"As many as you could afford," Ristlara said. At Cerest's scowl, she added, "With you, Greyas, Shenan, and I, we are twelve strong. I've divided everyone into groups of four. Our searches will be more effective that way, given the layout of Mistshore. All the 'muckrakers' are human, so Icelin will not see them coming this time."

"Good," Cerest said. He remembered poor Melias and felt a flare of regret. If they were to work together, Cerest would have to teach Icelin control and restraint. He'd done it before, when those that served him had first witnessed the extent of his scars. Icelin had already demonstrated she could look at him without seeing the marks. There would be plenty of time for her to learn what else pleased and displeased him.

CHAPTER SIX

ICELIN SAT ON THE FLOOR ACROSS FROM SULL, WHO NURSED ALE IN A glass the length of his forearm.

Working Ruen's dice between her fingers, Icelin said, "I think we should join them." She nodded to a pair of men throwing dice near the rear of the tent. A third man stood beside a painted board with chalk markings. The dice clattered off the board, with one man hurling curses at the numbers, while the other threw back more ale and collected the pile of coins on the floor.

The other tent patrons were more subdued, playing cards or huddling in circles with their own drinks. Lamplight glowed all over the room. Icelin's eyes were already watering from the smoke and the stench of so many unwashed bodies packed into the close quarters.

Sull eyed the dicers. "How do you want to play this, lass?"

"Try the game, I suppose," Icelin said. "Might be we'll have to give them some coin before they'll help us."

"Do you even know their game?" Sull asked skeptically.

"I've been watching," Icelin said. She yielded to the smoke and closed her eyes. "They roll pairs. Highest roller gets to buy points on the board—one copper per point, up to two." She opened her eyes and pointed to the dice board, where the man running the game was putting up marks with a stubby piece of chalk. "He can use those points to add or subtract from his next roll. Lowest roller that round picks a target number. They both roll again. The closest person to that number wins the pot. But if the winner isn't the man with the points, the low roller gets the pot plus all the copper his opponent spent on points to the runner—the man at the board. Side bets could be—"

Sull thunked his glass on the floor. "You could tell all that from across the room?"

"I memorized the numbers being rolled," Icelin said. "The rest was just putting together the rules of the game."

"They've been rollin' since we came in. How many numbers did you memorize?"

"All of them."

Sull nodded slowly. "Is this somethin' you do often, breakin' down dice games for your own amusement?"

"Not if I can help it," Icelin said. The numbers were already crowding her head, putting a dull ache at her temples. She rubbed them absently. "The problem is that I memorize everything I see and hear. I can't not."

Sull raised an eyebrow. "How long have you had this gift?"

A gift. That's what everyone called it. Icelin was long past being amused by the notion. "Almost ten years now."

It had also been ten years since the headaches started. The blinding, heavy pain came whenever she was in a crowd, or had too many facts vying for space in her head. Schooling had been a chore. Brant had taken on the task of teaching her himself, but they'd had to move slowly. She was quick and eager to learn, but there was only so much information she could be exposed to in a day, before the load threatened to overwhelm her.

Not until she started studying the Art did she discover how to bind away the information in her mind. Nelzun, her teacher, had shown her how, and had saved her going mad from the constant headaches.

It turned out storing information was no different than storing a spell once you'd memorized it from a book. Icelin had simply set aside a specific place in her mind for the facts to rest until they were needed.

"Picture your mind as a vast library," Nelzun had described it at the time.

"No vault can hold all of what rattles around in my head," she'd complained. But her teacher had only smiled indulgently.

"Once you have walked the halls of Candlekeep, with permanent wide eyes and slackening of the jaw, you may feel quite different," he'd said. "But let us stay in more familiar territory. Picture a building like your great-uncle's shop, but with an infinite number of levels.

"Follow a winding stair, up and up until you reach the place where magic dwells. Can you see it? Be playful, be mysterious, whatever suits your nature."

Icelin remembered squirming. "But I don't see how—"

"A red, plush carpet, so soft you can sink your feet right in." Her teacher had carried on as if she hadn't spoken. "Gold brocade curtains that shine in the sunlight, a fireplace covering an entire wall. And on the others: row upon row of bookshelves—empty now—but soon to be filled with the wonders of the Art. Everything you will ever learn or discover will be housed on these shelves.

"Picture a large wingback chair with leather cushions. Draw it before the fire and find upon the seat a single book—a very old, worn tome. The leather is cracked, the pages heavily browned by fingerprints of students who long ago became masters. Open the book. See what secrets lie inside."

When Icelin had opened her eyes, her teacher had presented her with a book exactly like the one he'd just described. It was to become her first and only spellbook. Icelin had been fascinated, and had loved her teacher from that day on. She would have done anything, mastered any spell, to please him.

Better that she'd never opened that imaginary room in her mind. She hated the thought of it now.

"Come on," she said to Sull. Distraction was better than a locked door for keeping memories at bay. "We're wasting time."

She approached the group of dicers and cleared her throat. No one paid her any heed. She cast a pointed look at Sull.

"New player, lads!" the butcher boomed.

Three heads turned to regard Icelin with a mixture of curiosity and annoyance.

Hesitantly, Icelin let her hood fall back and held out Ruen's dice. Suddenly she didn't feel so confident. She felt exposed, naked under the gazes of the rough men.

She cleared her throat again so her voice would be steady. "I've been told these are lucky dice," she said. "Do you gentleman mind if I throw with them?"

"No outsiders," one of the men snarled. "You throw our bones or none, girl, 'less you'd like a private game." He leered at her.

Sull stepped forward, but the man who'd been chalking the board spoke up.

"You're not welcome at this game," he said, watching Icelin closely. His eyes fell on the dice she held. "You should try the shore. There's a woman there, prostitute named Fannie Beblee. Give your dice to her. She'll get you what you need."

"My thanks," Icelin said, and to Sull, "Let's go."

The men resumed their game while she and Sull headed for the tent flap. She glanced back once and saw the man in the red coat watching them from behind the makeshift bar. He looked away quickly.

When they were outside, Sull said, "Awfully accommodatin' fellows. Oh yes, I feel much more secure under their direction."

"You think it's a trap?" Icelin said dryly.

"I think I won't be puttin' my cleavers away any time soon," Sull said.

"Aren't you the least bit curious?" Icelin asked, picking her way along the unstable wooden path to the shore. "About this Fannie Beblee? Or Ruen Morleth?"

"Least it gets us to shore," Sull said, "and off this stinkin' water."

"And we'll be able to fight better on land, assuming it is a trap," Icelin said.

"Now you're thinkin'." Sull clapped her on the back.

The shore, for all its stability, was not in much better shape than the floating parts of Mistshore.

Crude tents and lean-tos had been erected all along the shoreline. There must have been hundreds of the structures. Fires crackled in crudely dug pits, for there was little to burn here. In most cases a pot or spit hung over the flames. The meat on them was meager, consisting of rodents or small fish.

The people moved around in a sort of forced communal camp, talking or sleeping, huddled together for warmth. Icelin heard snores, hushed whispers, and a baby wailing in the distance.

She bent to speak to the nearest woman, who was stirring a pot of fat white beans in a watery broth. The lumpy mixture and its smell turned Icelin's stomach.

"I beg pardon, but I'm looking for someone," she said.

The woman ignored her and kept stirring the pot. The slow, rhythmic task absorbed her entire attention. Icelin might as well have been a fly buzzing in the air.

Sull put in, "Her name's Fannie. She's a friend of mine—"

Tinkling coins interrupted him. Icelin had pulled two silver pieces—nearly all of her remaining coin—from her neck pouch, drawing the woman's gaze from the pot as if by a mind charm.

"She's a prostitute," Icelin said, handing the woman the silver. "Fannie Beblee."

The woman curled her fingers in a claw around the coins. She pointed with her spoon to a spot south along the shore where two fires burned, one next to the other, then went back to stirring. The tents behind them were tied shut.

"Thank you," Icelin said. She straightened, but Sull remained kneeling next to the woman. Her expression had not altered throughout the whole exchange. Her eyes were lifeless, rimy pools sucked down in wrinkled, parchmentlike skin.

"We have to go, Sull."

The butcher reached into his apron and pulled out a small wrapped packet. He tore one end off and emptied the contents into the woman's soup pot.

The woman's stirring hand froze. She gazed up at Sull with a mixture of fear and hope swimming in her eyes.

"Not poison," Sull said, "but salt. Keep stirrin', and add this to the mix when it's ready." He drew out another packet and handed it to her. "Pepper grounds, and a few other spices I added to make a seasonin'. Works for potato chowder, so why not beans?"

But the woman didn't seem to be listening to him. She opened the second packet and touched her tongue to the edge to taste the spices. Her eyes filled with tears. She seized Sull's hand and kissed it.

Sull's face turned bright red. "Oh, er, you're welcome." He stood up quickly, tripping over his own feet.

Icelin took the big man's arm to steady him, and they drew away from the fire. For a time, neither spoke.

"I would never have thought to do that," Icelin said. "I would never have guessed that she'd want spices. I just assumed coin would move her."

"Coin's more valuable, but easily stolen," Sull said. "Salt and pepper don't amount to much, but if I'd been eatin' that bean slop for as long as she has—and I'll wager my stock of good steaks that's all she gets—I'd be cryin' for somethin' to flavor it with."

"You really enjoy cooking, don't you?" Icelin said. They'd reached the closed tents, but she hesitated to approach. She felt like an intruder.

"Always have," Sull said. "My father taught me to hunt game. This was, oh, long before we came to Waterdeep, and my mother let me watch the right way of preparin' it. She was forever making up her own recipes. Lot of them amounted to a burnt tongue and watery eyes, but she could make some of those dishes sing. I learnt all the best fixins from her."

"Does she still cook?" Icelin asked.

Sull shook his head. "Ah, she died. Year or so after we came here. Birthed a second son for my father, but she was too old for it, and she didn't live to see 'im. The little one followed her."

Icelin nodded. "I'm sorry. What about your father?"

"He found another wife and lives, still," Sull said, "but doesn't know much of where he is or who he is, most days. He'll be gone by the winter, I think." He nodded to the tent flap. "You can't put this off forever, lass. Best get it over with."

"You're right." Reluctantly, Icelin approached the closest tent. She called out, "Fannie Beblee. Are you in there?"

For a breath or two, there was no movement or response from within the tent. Then the cloth flap shuddered and was torn aside by a small brown hand.

The woman who peeked out was so tanned Icelin could barely distinguish her from the darkness of the tent. She peered at Icelin through muddy brown eyes. Her hair hung in graying, lank halves from a part in the center of her scalp. Sand grains sparkled in the tangled locks.

An angry dust devil, Icelin thought.

"Did you call Fannie Beblee?" The woman spoke in a rush, shoving the two names into one.

"I did," Icelin said, stepping forward. "We were sent here from the Dusk and Dawn. I have something to give you."

The woman's jaw hung slack. She clicked her tongue against the roof of her mouth. "You come from Whalebone Court. A criminal's alley, that is. What you bring me from there that's any good?"

Icelin held Ruen's dice up to the firelight so the woman could see.

"The bosoms are on the bottom," Sull muttered.

Fannie took the dice, pressing them between her two hands. Her face lit with a wicked smile.

"You bring me cursed dice," she said. "The boy is cursed."

"Ruen Morleth?" Icelin said. "What do you know about him?"

"The world is cold to him," Fannie said, "even old Fannie Beblee. So why not be cold right back to the world, eh? That's his way."

"Is that why he's a thief?" Icelin asked.

"A damn good thief!" Fannie shook a finger at Icelin and Sull. "He gave me this." She worked the strings of her raggedy cotton dress.

"That's all right," Sull said hastily. "We don't need to see any of . . . ahem . . . whatever you got under there."

Fannie shot him a scandalized look. "You think I'm going to give you this show for nothing?" She propped a hand on her bony hip and stood on her knees, swaying back and forth. "You pay, then we talk, big fellow. But later. I'm busy now." She waved a dismissive hand.

Icelin didn't have to look at Sull to know his face was bright red again. She bit her lip hard to keep from laughing.

"*This* is what I mean." Fannie pulled a leather cord from around her neck. Attached to one end—which had been buried in the bodice of her dress— was a tiny quill. A black crow feather, the quill had been stripped of its barbs, and the shaft appeared to have been dipped in gold. There was no longer a hollow end for the ink to reach parchment. So far as Icelin could see, the quill was for decoration only, and served no functional purpose. Yet Fannie gripped the gold shaft like a writing instrument, her tiny brown fingers fitting perfectly around the tip.

"It's . . . lovely," Icelin said. "Ruen gave this to you?"

"From his collection," Fannie said proudly.

"Collection?"

"Darzmine Hawlace's collection. They say he is mad—Darzmine, not Ruen—but he is not. Smart was the word. Hoarded items of power, disguised as art. Ruen was smarter. He knows art and power too. Knew just what to take from old Darzmine."

"So this is one of the pieces Ruen stole, the theft that got him imprisoned." Icelin looked at the quill with new eyes. "What is its power?"

Fannie's smile broadened. "I show you, but only you." She waved Sull away. "He don't understand."

Icelin and Sull exchanged glances. Icelin nodded at the water. "Wait for me over there. If trouble comes, I'll scream until my lungs burst."

Sull hesitated, and nodded. Icelin watched him stride down the shore to where the brown water lapped at the sand.

"What wouldn't my friend understand?" Icelin asked. But the woman didn't seem to hear her. She squatted in the sand and bent close to the fire. By the light, Icelin could see her tanned skin hanging in tiny ripples off her neck. She must have been almost fifty winters old. How long had she lived out here, alone?

Fannie looked up to make sure Icelin was still watching, whistled like an angry bird, and went back to her work.

Icelin realized she was sketching a picture in the sand. The gold quill matched the fire in color and movement. Remnants of the crow feather quivered in time to Fannie's scrawling.

"Here it is," Fannie said. "Now look. Move, girl."

Icelin hiked up her skirt and crouched in the sand, bending her head close to the prostitute's. The figure she had drawn in the sand was a hawk. She could see the predator's talons and curved beak. For a sand drawing, the picture was remarkably vivid. The depression where Fannie had placed the raptor's eye almost seemed alive.

Icelin gasped. The bird's head and body were rising, drawing sand and separating from it at the same time, as if they'd been buried and not merely a sketch. The thing took on shape and mass before Icelin's eyes. She had seen castles forged from sand or mud, but she'd never imagined the childish images coming *alive*.

The bird shook out its wings. Sand flew, catching a shocked Icelin in the face.

"Is it real?" she whispered, afraid to disturb the air and cause the sand-bird to disappear.

Fannie laughed. "No, no. Magic tells it what shape to take, and magic holds it together. Won't last long, but it makes a pretty art. Turtles," she said, chewing her lip. "I like turtles better. They don't move so fast, and the shells make them last longer."

Icelin reached out to touch the slender bird's wing. When she pulled her fingers back, they were glazed with sand. The bird did not react to her touch. It spread its wings as if for flight, and collapsed into a pile of sand.

"See," Fannie said, disappointment heavy in her voice, "they try to fly and fall."

"That was amazing," Icelin said.

"Aha! I knew you would understand," Fannie said. "He will like you, poor man."

Abruptly recalling why she was there, Icelin sobered. "You mean Ruen. I need to find him. I was told that you could help me."

"Oh, I can," Fannie said. Her gaze turned shrewd. "But what can you give to Fannie for helping you?"

Icelin didn't know what to say. She was rapidly running out of coins, and she suspected a woman like Fannie had as little use for them as the woman and her bean pot.

Inspiration struck her. "My friend, the one you sent away"—she waved an arm to get Sull's attention down the beach and motioned for him to rejoin them—"is the finest cook in Waterdeep."

"Is he?" Fannie watched Sull with renewed interest.

In truth, Icelin had no proof that Sull was any good in the kitchen, but she hoped Fannie wouldn't know the difference.

"Sull," she said, when the butcher approached, "I wonder if you would be willing to cook a meal for Fannie, as payment for telling us where to find Ruen Morleth?"

Fannie nodded eagerly, but Sull was looking around at the barren camp.

"Be happy to," he said. "But I've got no tools here."

"I have them!" Fannie scurried back into her tent like a mouse going to ground. She came up with a small black frypan, which she handed to Sull. "You cook for me with this."

Sull scratched his sideburns. "I suppose I could do a little fishin'," he said slowly. "Don't know what I'll catch that's not contaminated."

"Just try. That's all I ask," Icelin said, and turned back to Fannie. "Sull will cook for you, but we haven't much time. I need you to set up a meeting for me with Ruen. Can you do that?"

"Ah, I do one better for you, since you cook for Fannie." The woman pointed out to the harbor. "You find him out there. He takes a little raft out every night, to catch his own fish. You take a boat, go beyond Whalebone Court, and you find him. You'll see his light on a sagging pole. Only he goes out far enough to waltz. You'll find him."

Sull shook his head. "I don't like the sound of this," he said. "You're not going out there alone while I'm here cookin'—"

"It's our bargain, Sull," Icelin said firmly. "Besides"—she lowered her voice—"if it is a trap, at least you'll be on the shore. If Fannie is involved, you'll want to keep her close by. If I'm attacked or kidnapped, she can help you find me."

"That's not a comfortin' thought," Sull said.

"We don't have our choice of comforts tonight," Icelin pointed out. "It's either this or we run on our own, and I don't like those odds."

Sull sighed. "If you're determined to go, be wary, and signal me with one of those bright color spells if somethin' is amiss. I'll come runnin' across the water if I have to."

"I know you will." Icelin touched his cheek. He blushed mightily.

She turned to Fannie. "Do you know where I can borrow a boat?"

Fannie sniffed. "I know where you can steal one."

I suppose I'm officially a thief, Icelin thought as she rowed out into the harbor.

On the shore, she could just make out Sull, dangling a driftwood pole he'd constructed in the water. He kept his head bent, shoulders hunched, trying to ignore the sounds coming from Fannie's tent.

Her latest customer had arrived in a tiny rowboat, which Fannie had offered to Icelin as soon as she'd gotten her man safely out of sight inside the tent.

Icelin prayed she'd be out and back without incident, and the man would never know she'd taken his boat.

The way was slow going. More than once Icelin had to turn the boat around and row in the opposite direction to avoid a shelf of rock or ship debris. Small wonder this section of the harbor had fallen into disuse. Any sound ship entering the area would soon have her hull scraped raw.

She rowed past Whalebone Court and the Dusk and Dawn's red tent. Behind them, she could see the distant glow of the Hearth fire. The sound of raucous laughter and clumsy lute music drifted along the water. At least here, there was some semblance of normal life, even celebration, in Mistshore.

Icelin left the noise behind and rowed out into the dark water. She didn't know how she would come upon Ruen Morleth, or what she would say when she did. Why he would dwell alone in the putrid harbor was a mystery to her, but she didn't have long to ponder it. In the distance, she saw a sagging light, just as Fannie had said she would.

It bobbed faintly—a lantern, she saw as she approached—on the end of a long, bending pole attached to a raft. There were no other boats so far out in the harbor.

When she got close, Icelin heard voices. Two shapes stood out in the weaving lantern light. She could not make out their features, but the profile of the nearer one was short and rotund, his head hairless. The other held a fishing pole as tall as his body. He was very nearly as slender as the pole. Icelin also noted that the man either had a very misshapen head, or was wearing a floppy hat.

Icelin stopped rowing. She lifted her oars carefully out of the water and listened to the voices.

"I'm a clever man, Ruen. You could do worse."

The tall man cast his line into the harbor and answered, dryly, "Oh, I'm aware of it. I could tread the catwalks of Mistshore with a viper around my neck. Come to think of it, the snake might not be so bad, if I walk lightly. No, I don't think I need a partner, Garlon, especially one who sells his own brother to the Watch."

"How did you know about that?" The other man's voice squeaked like a guilty child's. "That was family business, got nothing to do with you and me. Come on, Ruen, you know you can't go it alone forever. You already got caught once. Admit it, you need a man to front you. You're too well known in Waterdeep."

"This isn't Waterdeep. This is Mistshore. We're dancing on the city's bones out here. Leave, Garlon, before I decide you'd make a pretty skeleton."

"But, I rode out here with you. You have to take me back to shore!" The man whined so loudly Icelin's ears ached.

"Yes, but you see, the fish are biting now. And if I move, I'll lose my spot."

"There's no one out here but us!"

"Are you sure about that?"

Icelin stiffened. She waited, crouched low in the boat, but no one called her out. Ruen must have been jesting.

"I was trying to do you a favor," Garlon said. "Word is you've still got a pretty pot of that treasure you stole from Darzmine Hawlace sitting around. I could move it for you. I know people."

"Ah, now we come to the true reason you're soiling my raft with your boots," Ruen said. "What makes you think I didn't dump the lot?"

Garlon scoffed. "You enjoy giving presents to whores and dealing with piss pushers like Relvenar, but you're not stupid. You kept some treasure back for yourself. All I want is a little piece."

"No."

Garlon spat on Ruen's boots. "To the Hells with you then." He strode to the opposite end of the raft. He paused at the edge. Icelin could feel him weighing his dignity against jumping into the fetid water. She felt a pang of sympathy, but it disappeared when she saw Garlon reach for something at his belt. He slid a dagger noiselessly from its sheath. Her heart sped up.

"What say you, Ruen? Last chance. Row us back to shore, and I'll buy you a drink while we discuss our partnership."

"Turn around," Icelin said, but no sound came out of her dry mouth. Her eyes bored into Ruen's back, willing him to turn and look at Garlon.

"Do you mind keeping quiet, Garlon?" Ruen said. He twitched his pole in the water. "You're scaring the fish."

"Course, Ruen," Garlon said, his voice dropping. "Not a squeak." He snapped his arm back, and forward, so fast Icelin couldn't see exactly when the blade left his hand.

"Watch out!" she screamed.

Ruen pivoted, his slender shadow seeming not to move at all. He dropped his pole and tore the spinning dagger out of the air. Flipping the blade to his other hand, he hurled it back at its owner.

Distracted by her scream, the fat man spun toward Icelin as if he'd been jerked by a string. His eyes widened when the dagger stuck in his chest. For a breath he swayed in time with the lapping water. Then he reached up, clutching his own weapon hilt. Icelin turned her head away from his staring eyes.

Silence, and then Icelin heard an *umph* followed by a loud splash. She looked back. The spray of water caught the moonlight and fell back into the harbor, which had swallowed up the fat man.

When the noise died, the scene returned quickly to normal. The moonlight settled onto the gently rippling water. From a shocked distance, Icelin saw Ruen pick up his pole and sit at the edge of the raft, his back to her. He cast the line into the water.

Numbly, Icelin picked up her oars. She considered rowing back to shore. Maybe he hadn't heard her shout, or maybe he didn't care that she'd just seen him kill a man, albeit in self-defense. Icelin gripped the oars. She forced herself to move the boat forward.

He came into focus at the opposite end of the raft, sitting cross-legged and dangling the pole near the water. He looked something like Sull in that pose, his shoulders hunched, trying to remain oblivious to the world around him.

Icelin rowed her boat up to kiss the raft, but Ruen never stirred. She wasn't brave enough to step aboard, but she had to get his attention somehow.

Icelin took the dice out of her pouch and tossed them onto the raft. They skittered across the wood, bounced off Ruen's back and came up double bosoms.

"Yours, I believe," Icelin said.

CHAPTER SEVEN

For a long time, Ruen didn't move. Icelin thought he must not have heard her. But eventually he turned, and his profile caught the lantern light.

He looked to be in his early thirties. His hat, which appeared much older, was as ugly a thing as Kersh had claimed: brown leather and so creased the edges of the brim were flaking off.

Beneath the hat his black clad body looked like a scarecrow, so slender Icelin thought he must be half-starved. His cheekbones were two carved, triangular hollows; intermittent beard stubble graced the contours of his jaw.

A scarecrow, Icelin thought, except for his eyes.

His eyes were red-brown, their deep centers forming pools of muddy crimson when they should have been black. Either his eyes were a defect of his birth, or else . . .

Icelin had heard stories of such oddities from the children in Blacklock Alley, back when she was only a child herself. The boys talked in menacing whispers about the plague-touched, the spellscarred—men and women who'd been brushed by the deadly fingers of spellplague. Most died from the exposure, but a few managed to survive its curse. They were never the same.

Some emerged deformed, their bodies twisted into hideous shapes by wild magic. Others bore their scars in less obvious places, but developed strange new abilities: powers of the mind, magic that even the wisest wizards on Faerûn had never seen. It was said that a strange blue radiance often accompanied such displays of power, but Icelin had always thought these were fanciful stories that bore little truth.

Somehow, looking at him, Icelin knew Ruen Morleth was spellscarred. She remembered Kersh's warning about the man being strange.

"You know, it's impolite to eavesdrop on strangers' conversations," Ruen said, speaking for the first time. He picked up the dice and looked at them. "Stealing is generally frowned upon, as well. These aren't yours," he said.

"I didn't steal them," Icelin replied. "They were given to me by a friend. He told me you could help me."

His eyes traveled up and down her body. Icelin worked hard not to flinch under the gaze. "You look capable enough. Why should you need my help?"

"I'm being followed by someone who wishes my death."

He raised an eyebrow. "You think that's a compelling argument to me?"

"It sounds a bit dramatic, I know, but it's been a fine motivator for me," Icelin said. "I'm in no rush to die."

"Death is a common occurrence in Mistshore."

"So I see."

Ruen removed his pole from the water and laid it on the raft. "On the other hand, if you knew a likely fishing spot, you'd catch my interest. What's your name?"

"Icelin," she said. She held out a hand, but he showed no interest in taking it.

"Where did you get these dice?" he asked.

"From Kersh. I believe you two knew each other while you were . . . er—"

"Imprisoned. You can say it, I'm proud of the distinction." Ruen stood up. At his full height, he was well over six feet, which only accentuated his odd slenderness. "I remember Kersh. He retrieved my hat for me. Quite a service, under the circumstances."

"You gave him your word you'd repay him," Icelin said.

"I did. But I don't see him hiding behind your skirt. My debt is to him. I owe nothing to you."

Ruen removed a dirt-speckled rag from his belt and began cleaning his pole. Leather gloves stretched taut over his long-fingered hands. He seemed content to ignore her.

Icelin was at a loss. Of all the things she'd expected from the man, blunt refusal had not been among them. But why shouldn't she have foreseen this? Kersh tried to warn her. Sull tried to warn her. The man was a thief. She'd had no reason to believe he'd be honorable in any dealings with her.

But Kersh's story . . . the man's gratitude at being treated kindly, the quill he'd given to Fannie—he could have sold it for a handsome profit, yet he'd made the powerful magic item a gift to a prostitute so she could draw pictures in the sand. None of what she'd heard equated to the aloof man before her.

"I'll pay you for your services," she said finally.

Ruen glanced up at her. "You don't look as if you have anything I need, or enough of the coin I'd demand."

"I have this." Icelin took the cameo from her neck pouch and tossed it to him.

Ruen caught it and held the piece up to the lantern. His muddy crimson eyes mingled with the gold light. "You steal this?"

"Does it matter?"

"No. What do you want for it?"

"I need a hiding place, for myself and a friend. We're being pursued by the Watch as well."

Ruen cocked his head. "Why all the interest?"

"Let's just pretend I'm a criminal," she said with a half-smile. "A notorious, irredeemable scoundrel. Would that be near enough to your understanding?"

"Are you?"

"Am I what?"

"Irredeemable?"

Icelin's humor evaporated. "Probably," she said. "Will you help me anyway, in exchange for the jewel?"

Ruen put the pole away and walked to the edge of the raft. He cocked a boot on the bow of her boat and looked down at her. There was no discernible expression on his face. It made his eyes so much more disturbing. They were distant and menacing at the same time. Icelin suppressed the urge to put an oar between them.

"I'll hide you for one day," Ruen said. "After that we renegotiate the price or go our separate ways."

"One day—that piece is worth at least ten!" Icelin said.

"Then find someone who'll keep you from the eyes of the Watch for a tenday," Ruen said. "I'm sure there are lads everywhere in Mistshore hopping eager to take on the job. I don't mind at all dispensing the honor to them."

Icelin ground the oars against their moorings. "I have your marker! You're honor bound to help me, with or without payment."

Ruen smiled. "You're very passionate, my lady. Hold to that. It'll take you far in the world."

Icelin contemplated bludgeoning the man with an oar, just to wipe the mocking grin off his face, but she decided against it. She had one night; it was best not to waste it. "Fine. We have an agreement." She snatched the cameo back and put it in her neck pouch. "You'll get the payment after my night's over."

He tipped his ugly hat. "Whatever you say, lady."

So it was done. Icelin was going to ask if he'd like to follow her back to shore, when below them, the light she and Sull had glimpsed earlier reappeared, gliding across the water like a fresh oil slick. Icelin lost her train of thought watching it. The humanlike apparition drifted past them and out into the harbor, moving fast. Several breaths later it illuminated a large, misshapen structure Icelin had not known was there.

It was difficult to make out many details in the dark, but by the apparition's light it was the strangest shipwreck Icelin had ever seen. The vessel had been boosted straight up on its bow, the length of it seeming to dance upon the air. Something, an even larger structure, was propping it up in that odd position, like two lovers embracing on the lip of the sea.

The apparition floated right up to the mass and joined with it, illuminating the whole before evaporating into darkness.

"What was that?" Icelin said, stunned.

Ruen looked out into the darkness. "The Ferryman's Waltz," he said. He looked at her askance. "You've never heard of it?"

Icelin searched her memory. Ferryman sounded vaguely familiar, an echo from her childhood. Her mind cycled back, peeling away the layers of invisible brick she'd used to close off the memories, until she could visualize ships: dozens of cogs, rakers, and greatships lined up in the harbor. Brant had taken her to see them; they'd gone for a ride on one. Icelin remembered the greatship was so large she could barely make out the fish leaping along the keel.

"*Ferryman*," she said. "It was a ship, a converted passenger carrier. A merchant of Waterdeep built it to hire out for pleasure-sailing, a way to say 'look at what a big toy I have.' She recited her great-uncle's words exactly. It brought a profound ache to her chest. She could picture his eyes sparkling as he told her the story. Quickly, she raised the mental wall again. "I never knew what became of the ship."

"Destroyed, in a tangle with a leviathan," Ruen said.

Icelin's eyes widened. "A sea monster, invading Waterdeep harbor?" It sounded too mythical to be real. "I thought we were supposed to be protected here, shielded from attacks of the Art and—"

"You mean spellplague," Ruen said. "Maybe that's so. But who's protecting Waterdeep from those scarred by the plague? No keeping them out. Even those that get dumped in places like Mistshore can cause their share of trouble." He nodded toward the Ferryman's Waltz. "Locked together in a lover's waltz. Poetic, don't you think?"

"You mean a wizard did this?" Icelin said. "To summon this creature . . . He'd have to be mad."

Ruen lifted a shoulder. "Perhaps it's just a story. Whether it's true or not, something draws the sea wraiths out to the wreckage. There's wild magic there. That's why they glow as they do. Ordinarily, you'd never be able to see them in the water. I'd bet any amount of coin the plague still thrives at Ferryman's Waltz, and the wraiths are drawn to it like moths."

"Sea wraiths," Icelin said. So the Waltz was the source of the strange apparitions. "None of this feels real." Her gaze swept the Waltz and Mistshore: Whalebone Court and the Dusk and Dawn's red tent, the Hearth fire and all of the other structures. They blurred together in the darkness just beyond her sight. She caught Ruen looking at her. "What?"

He shook his head, as if he couldn't believe what he was seeing. "You're just a child," he said. "You don't know Waterdeep at all. What are you doing out here?"

"Conversing with thieves"—Icelin spread her hands—"fearing for my life and virtue, all of that."

"Why should you fear for your virtue?"

"Oh, I'm not afraid of *you* taking it," she said. "I don't trust myself. I'm afraid I'll have to offer it up to every lad in Mistshore to get them to help me after your contract runs out. This night was expensive enough. I shudder to think what the price will be day after tomorrow."

"So you're not afraid of me?" Ruen said.

"You mean because of Garlon?" She squared her shoulders. "I think he had his fate coming to him."

"That's bold," Ruen said. He tilted his hat to see her better. "Considering how pale you were when you rowed up to my raft, I would have thought you were a terrified mouse."

Icelin swallowed. "I've had fresh perspectives on terror tonight. Nothing you can do will frighten me."

"Truly?" He moved so fast the next breaths were a blur.

His hands encased both of her wrists. He hauled her out of the boat, onto her back on the raft. The hard planks knocked the breath out of her. He forced her hands above her head and half-straddled her.

"What about now?" Ruen said. He'd moved like a demon, yet he wasn't even breathing hard. His crimson eyes were so close they filled her vision. He didn't wait for a reply. He put his head on her chest.

Icelin bit back a whimper, but he made no other move to touch her.

"I hear your heartbeat," he said, lifting his head. "It's a wild bird." He smiled. "Are you certain you aren't scared?"

He knew she was terrified, and Icelin hated him for that. She could do nothing about the wild hammering in her chest, so instead, Icelin forced her rigid body to relax, one muscle at a time. It was the hardest work she'd ever done. "You know," she said, pleased that her voice did not shake, "if it's my virtue you're after, I should confess I gave it away a long time ago."

"How unfortunate," Ruen said. "Who was the lucky lad? Another thief?"

"A stable boy, actually. We did it behind the chimneystacks on the roof of my great-uncle's shop. He was two years older than me."

"Was he handsome?"

"Not really, but more so than you. We were outside all night, and I took sick the next morning. These are much lovelier conditions." She met his gaze, forcing a look of bored expectation. "Well? Are you going to do this or not?"

"You've got hard nerves, lady," Ruen said, "but you don't know this world. If I was any other man you'd be raped and robbed and bobbing in the harbor by now."

Icelin felt annoyance flare above her fear. "You're right, I don't know much about the world. In the last five years, I've rarely been out of my great-uncle's shop. I would love nothing more than to be there right now, but my great-uncle is murdered, and that shop is a tomb. Everything I once trusted is gone. I tell you truly, I have no one left to put my faith in, except a criminal. The irony of this could fuel many comic ballads, I'm sure. I may be naïve to you, but I have a sharp tongue and more than half a wit and if you can keep me alive long enough, I will find a way to pay you for the services you render me, if it takes all the blood in my body to do it."

They gazed at each other, their faces inches apart. Something like admiration passed over Ruen's face. He started to speak, but suddenly his face was illuminated by a brilliant, arcane light.

Icelin looked down, and saw the source coming from the space of water between the boat and the raft. A second apparition glowed from the water, but this one shone clearer, and its form melded into a twisted mockery of a human face—

"Watch out!" Ruen shouted. He hauled her up, but it was too late.

The sea wraith burst from the water in a shower of wet and light. The force of its appearance blew the small boats into the air.

Pressure, then fire shot up her right arm, but Icelin didn't dwell on that calamity. She felt her body leave solid ground—she was flying, the world tilting—and then the fetid water closed over her head, blocking out all sensation except cold.

Frantically, Icelin kicked in her bulky skirt, propelling herself to what she hoped was the surface. She came up gulping air. Nothing but cold blackness surrounded her. Ruen's lantern had been extinguished.

Raising her hand above the water, Icelin chanted, praying all the while that the weakness she knew would come would not render her unable to swim.

Light burst from her hand, transforming her arm into a makeshift torch. Nausea hit her hard in the gut. The queasiness in her belly combined with the stench and motion of the harbor proved too much. Icelin turned her head and retched, spitting water and filth. Her throat burned, but she forced herself to ignore it.

By the light of the spell, she saw a crooked gash running from her elbow to the middle of her forearm. There were splinters in the wound.

Ruen was swimming for his raft, which had been flipped upside down. He reached it, hoisted himself up, and pulled a knife from his belt. The thin blade bore a coat of rust. It was a not a weapon at all, but a gutting blade for fish. Icelin watched, incredulous, as Ruen brandished the rusty blade confidently at the sea wraith. The apparition swooped down from the clouds to hover above the water.

He's completely mad, Icelin thought. The knife would not put a scratch on the undead horror.

A glint of silver on Ruen's left middle finger caught Icelin's attention. He'd removed his glove, and she could see a ring glowing with arcane power, illuminating his pale flesh.

The glow spread down his arm, then flowed across his body like a weird, sped-up river. The light died away, except for where it illuminated the gutting knife. A single strand of silver lit the blade, eclipsing the rust.

Icelin swam to the raft, searching her memory for some spell that might aid Ruen. She hadn't used magic to defend herself in years. The spell in Sull's shop had been a harmless light trick. Gods, could she bring herself to remember how to call fire and ice? If she could, would it affect the wraith at all? She'd never faced anything like it before. Nelzun had purposefully guided her training to suit a woman traveling alone on the streets of Waterdeep.

While her thoughts spun and her arm burned, Ruen moved with preternatural speed across the raft. His knife blade flashed, cutting into the creature where its shoulder might have been.

Icelin saw no wound, but she heard an unearthly screech issue from the wraith.

The apparition twisted away, blasting through Ruen's body in its incorporeal form. For a breath, Ruen appeared to be treading water as the ghostly mass enveloped him. Then it passed, and the thief fell back onto the raft. Icelin was close enough to see his muscles twitching from the brutal exposure to the wraith's body.

She grabbed the raft with both hands and hoisted herself up next to Ruen's prone form. The wraith circled above their heads, as if trying to decide which of the two posed the greatest threat. Icelin swung her glowing arm back and forth, trying to keep the creature's attention away from Ruen.

She could recall no spells, nothing to harm or to kill. She'd buried them all long ago, vowing no living being would be hurt by her hand again.

But the memories were there, if she wanted to find them. The arcane power, locked away in the topmost tower room of her mind, like a princess in a tale. She needed no spellbook to find them, only the will.

She could picture her teacher's words of admonishment. This thing before you isn't alive, he would say. It has no warmth, no compassion. It seeks only death. When confronted with such creatures as this in the world, you have no choice but to deal death first.

The wraith, finally distracted by the waving light, swooped low across the water, its face inches from the rippling current.

It was coming at her from the right. Icelin braced her feet, certain she'd be knocked from the raft if the thing hit her.

A sharp arc, and the wraith was up and over the side of the raft—

Suddenly, Ruen sprang up between them. He'd only been pretending to be injured. He planted the gutting knife in the wraith's chest and held on.

The wraith thrashed and screeched and lifted Ruen off his feet. For a scant breath, they hung suspended over the water. Ruen jerked, tearing ghostly flesh. He jerked again, and the wraith spun, flipping the thief over its body to shake loose his grip.

The move worked. Ruen's fingers slipped from the knife, and he plunged into the murky water. His hat floated to the surface, but Ruen did not reappear.

Alone on the raft, Icelin at last found a spell. Calmly, she waited for the wraith to circle again. She watched it come, a ghastly glowing arrow running parallel to the water. Ruen's fish knife protruded from its chest, but the light had faded from the blade. As the creature glided closer, Icelin saw the blade and handle crumble, sprinkling ashes over the water.

This time the wraith would not be distracted from its prey. Ruen was either drowned or too far down in the water to help her.

Trembling, Icelin extended both hands out from her body. Pressing her thumbs together, she chanted the dusty words and prayed that she would not be burned alive.

"Begone!" she screamed.

Nothing happened. The cone of flame that should have spread from her hands manifested as a feeble yellow sparking at her fingertips. The palms of her hands grew faintly warm, but the heat soon died.

"Get down!" Ruen shouted from somewhere to her left. Icelin was too shocked to react. She saw the wraith bearing down on her, but she couldn't think or move. There came a rush of air, and the creature enveloped her.

Light blinded Icelin. She closed her eyes, but it was all around her. Cold. A bitter, biting freeze crawled over her skin like wet snakes, immobilizing her limbs. She tried to take a step. Her boots scraped the raft. She opened her eyes, desperately seeking escape.

Hollow eye sockets stared back at her. Ghostly flesh clung to the wraith's lipless mouth. It was nothing more than a parody of a human face, but the body was smothering her, freezing her to death. In the faint gray light between consciousness and oblivion, her teacher's words came to her, propelled from her memories with a life all their own.

"If, gods forbid, you ever have to fight a monster in the wilds, remember that it does you no good to think like a human woman. Each being responds differently to magic, and some can resist even the most potent spells."

"How will I be able to survive," Icelin remembered asking, "if I'm too weak to fight?"

"By being smart before you are powerful," her teacher said. "Certain creatures owe their existence to magical perversions. They are drawn to the Art, and can be distracted by it. Remember that."

Sucking in a ragged, painful breath, Icelin choked out the simplest spell she knew, one that always worked and never caused her pain. Long ago, she'd used it to mend tears in her clothing.

An invisible pulse of energy engulfed her hands as she finished the casting. Every successful spell she'd ever cast brought the sensation. Her teacher explained it away as one of the physical effects of magic on the body. Since the Spellplague, arcane energy was in a constant state of flux, manifesting in different forms for different wizards. This was hers.

According to Ruen, the wraith was a slave to the spellplague. Her distorted spell energies, however slight, might be enough to get its attention. Icelin prayed her simple spell would be enough.

Arcane energy sparked inside the wraith's incorporeal form. Whether from surprise or some other effect, the creature recoiled, forcing her out of its body.

Icelin stumbled back, but she was too weak to steady herself. She managed one feeble breath before she fell into the water.

After her brush with the wraith, the harbor actually felt warm. Icelin tried to swim, but her arms were still clutched into tight claws at her sides. She couldn't get her limbs to function.

Black spots popped in front of Icelin's vision. A part of her mind urged that drowning would be a better option than returning to the surface to face the wraith. Her lungs disagreed. She expelled her breath in a rush of bubbles. Above her, she could see the wraith's darting light. It was back in the water again, disoriented, searching for the arcane energy it craved. But the creature and its light were growing smaller the farther she sank.

At first she didn't feel the arm that encircled her chest. The burning was too painful for her to notice anything. It jerked her upright, and Icelin felt herself smashed against a hard wall. The wall moved, drawing her to the surface. Whenever Icelin thought she would slip, the arm would pull her back from the abyss.

She broke the surface gasping, choking foul water when she tried to suck in air. Her muscles were on fire. But she was alive.

Ruen was treading water directly behind her, holding her afloat with his right arm. The wall she'd been crushed against was his chest. The light spell on her arm still functioned. She could see the wraith making mad, swooping circles all around Ruen's raft.

"What did you do to it?" he demanded. "Its senses are blinded."

"I'm not sure." Icelin coughed and spat water. "We have to get away from here."

She felt Ruen shake his head. "Won't get far without a boat," he said. "Drive it away. Use your magic."

The wraith burst into the air, spraying them with water. Its attention refocused on the swimming pair. A high-pitched scream rent the air, and the creature dived at them again.

Ruen dragged her underwater, and they barely dodged the attack. When they came back up, the wraith had circled around for another pass.

"Cast your spell," Ruen ordered her. "Make it a good one. You won't get another before it kills us."

"You don't understand. I have no magic." Icelin tried to swim away from him, but he pinned her against his chest.

"Your glowing arm suggests otherwise," he said.

"It's also bleeding. Let me go!"

"Listen to me." He raised his left hand in front of her face. Icelin remembered the silver band. It rested on his finger, its light dull. "Everything this ring touches grows in strength, including magic. As long as our bodies touch, your spell should work."

He didn't wait for her to respond. He put his glove back on and folded her left hand under his.

Icelin felt a tingle of electricity coming from the ring. She searched her memory again. The fire spell was gone, but there was another. . . .

"When I cast this, I will likely lose consciousness," Icelin said. She fought to keep her voice steady.

Ruen tightened his grip. "You won't drown—you haven't paid me my fee yet. I'll hold you up, only work your spell!"

Icelin blocked out his voice, the icy water, the wraith's screams. She waited for the creature to glide close to the water again. When it was in her line of sight, she muttered the spell.

Burning pain erupted behind her eyes, a side effect Icelin only vaguely remembered from her early lessons. She had not cast spells of this magnitude for years. Her body was not ready for the shock.

Fighting oblivion, Icelin thrust her free hand above her head. The arcane pulse came again, strong and sustained. This time, the spell was going to work.

A stream of white vapor unfurled on the air like a sheet. It snapped and coalesced into a savage-looking spear, which shot across the water, trailing ice shards in its wake.

The magic impaled the wraith through its eyeless head. Unholy screams shattered the air. Ice flew in all directions. The force of the magic drove the creature back a full ten feet, and the light in its body flickered and died. The wraith collapsed in on itself, disappearing into the water without creating a wake.

For a long time, there was no sound except Icelin and Ruen's breathing. Icelin saw her breath in the wake of the cold spell. A fine layer of ice rimed the water in a straight line to where the creature had been. She watched the shards flake off like so much paint.

"That's i-impossible," Icelin said. Her head swam. "Never should have been so much, so big."

"It was my ring," Ruen said. "I told you it would strengthen the spell."

"Oh, well." Icelin felt unconsciousness looming. She was more than ready for it. "That's nice, isn't it?"

CHAPTER EIGHT

RUEN RETRIEVED HIS HAT AND SWAM TO HIS RAFT, DRAGGING THE senseless girl behind him.

"You live up to your name," he said, grunting as he lifted her onto the deck. The ice had melted, but he could still feel the brittle chill in the air, a chill that had nothing to do with the wraith's presence.

Ruen put a hand on Icelin's chest to make sure she lived. She breathed deeply—the sleep of exhaustion. Her light spell flickered and died, leaving him only moonlight for navigation.

He knew magic taxed a wizard's strength, but he'd never seen a spell affect anyone the way the ice spear had wracked Icelin's body. He'd felt her trembling in pain.

He held his ring up close to his face but found no answers from the plain silver band. It no longer glowed with power.

"Did I push too hard," he murmured, gazing down at Icelin. "Or are you more than what they told me?"

He reached into the pouch strapped beneath his right arm. Inside he kept only two items: the ring, when he wanted it hidden from prying eyes, and a black *sava* piece—a pawn. He drew out the piece and palmed it. It took several breaths for the pawn to warm to his flesh and attune to his identity.

"Tesleena," he spoke aloud, and the pawn's answering flicker told him the magic connection was functioning. "I have the girl."

"Is she unharmed?" The tiny voice issued from the pawn as if across a vast distance.

"She's well enough, but unconscious," Ruen said. "We fought a sea wraith in the harbor. You owe me a new boat."

"You *what?*" Tesleena's voice shot up an octave. "Your instructions were—"

"Not well received by the undead," Ruen said. "I wouldn't be worried. Your little girl killed the thing with one spell."

"She used magic to fight?"

There was something in Tesleena's voice Ruen didn't like. "We can talk about it when I hand the girl over," he said.

There was a long pause. "Very well. Where can we meet?"

Ruen glanced at the shore. "I'll contact you."

"Wait."

Ruen severed the connection by dropping the pawn back in his pouch. Let the Warden's pet curse him. He needed to get back to shore. Then he would find a safe location to drop the girl. The Watch would find her easily enough from his instructions. He had no intention of meeting them face to face.

He gazed down at the sleeping girl. She was a hardy thing. Already her color was coming back.

Better she remain unconscious. He didn't want her kicking up a fuss when he left her. Betrayal was much easier with the eyes closed.

·:⌒:·

"Did you see that?"

Shenan's fine eyes were just visible above her scarf. The watching elves stood in the shadow of Whalebone Court, near the water's edge.

Cerest followed the elf woman's gaze out to the harbor in time to see the spell erupt. It was nothing more than light from this distance, but Cerest felt a thrill of excitement.

"It's her," he said.

Shenan looked at him. Torchlight reflected off her burnished skin. "How can you be certain?"

"You heard the people whispering. No one goes out in that direction. It's Ferryman's Waltz."

Shenan looked around. People were hurrying across the planked pathways. They cast nervous glances out into the harbor, as if they expected the light to notice and follow them.

"It's possible," Shenan admitted. She turned and made a subtle gesture against her chest.

A pair of men standing twenty feet behind them on the pathway slowed. One of the men signaled back, and both turned around and headed for shore.

"We'll intercept them when they come back to land," Shenan said.

Cerest nodded, but he didn't move. He watched the light until it went out.

.:⌢:.

His big hands buried in his sleeves, Sull pulled the cooking pan off the fire and placed it with a regal flourish in front of Fannie.

"My lady," he drawled, "your mystery fish is prepared."

Fannie clapped her hands once and proceeded to scrape the hot meat off the pan. Juggling the steaming hunks of fish, she popped them in her mouth one at a time, pausing only long enough to spit the bones onto the sand.

Sull watched her gulp down the food and hastily put Icelin's fish, which he'd already cooked, on the other side of his body. He wanted to make sure Icelin ate some proper food before they moved on, and Fannie looked too ravenous to be trusted.

He'd cooked the blind, horned fish to a blackened crisp to boil away as many of the toxins as possible. Afterward he'd tasted the fish—crunchy, but edible enough. Not his best work, but Fannie didn't seem to mind.

They heard it at the same time, the sound of a raft scraping over sand. Sull jumped up, Fannie right behind him.

A man stumbled up the shore. He carried a bundle draped over his shoulder. Sull didn't recognize it for a person until the man strode into Fannie's camp.

"Lass!" he roared, and to the unknown man, "Put her down."

"Gladly." The man dumped Icelin unceremoniously into Sull's arms and kept on walking.

The butcher lowered Icelin gently to the sand and looked her over for wounds. When he saw her arm, his face turned an ugly crimson. "Who are you? What'd you do to her?" he demanded. He lowered a hand to the closest cleaver on his sash.

"Hello, boy," Fannie said when the man approached her fire. "You in trouble again, Ruen, eh?" She grinned, but Ruen didn't return her smile.

"Get her awake," he told Sull. "We need to move. Half of Mistshore probably saw the battle in the water, and the rest saw me coming in to shore. We'll have eyes on us, and worse, if we don't get moving."

Icelin stirred. Sull put a hand under her head to support her as she sat up. She looked groggy, as if she'd been asleep for days, but otherwise Sull couldn't see anything wrong.

"Lass?" he said, turning her chin toward him. "Are you all right?"

She blinked. "I think so. It was the spell." She looked around. "Where's Ruen?"

"Don't worry about him," Sull said darkly. "We're leavin' just as soon as I see to your arm."

"But—"

"Hsst!" Fannie scuttled around her tent, cocking an ear to listen. "Someone comes."

Ruen kicked sand onto the fire, dousing it instantly. "Friendly or not?" he hissed to Fannie.

"What's friendly here?" The woman snorted. "You go now."

With Sull's aid, Icelin got to her feet. "Where are we going?" Icelin asked.

"Just be quiet and follow me," Ruen said. With a nod to Fannie, he moved away from the camp, crouching low to weave among the tents. He fumbled in a pouch as he went, but Sull couldn't see what he was after.

Icelin kept close enough to whisper to Sull. "We were attacked."

"By the elf?" Sull asked.

Icelin shuddered. "Worse, by the gods. A sea wraith. I'll tell you the tale later."

They moved slowly, Sull jogging along impatiently in the rear. Finally, he called out, trying to keep his voice low, "Faster, damn you. They'll be catchin' up."

But Ruen didn't seem to hear him. He passed the edge of the tent encampment and stopped, listening to something on the air.

"This way," he said, and began running.

Icelin hurried to follow. She could hear them now, the sounds of running feet pounding against the sand, gaining ground with each step.

They circled a caravel that had had its hull split in two. The jagged wood opened a dark maw into the ship's interior. Icelin thought Ruen meant them to hide inside, but suddenly, Ruen stopped short and cursed. He shoved her behind him and reached for a weapon at his belt. He'd forgotten the fish knife was long gone.

"They're herding us!" he shouted to Sull, just before the men jumped them.

Two figures leaped over the side of the ship, landing on either side of Ruen and Icelin. One had bright, corn silk hair, the other was dark and compactly built. Ruen skidded on the sand to avoid plowing into their sword points. He dropped into a crouch and swept out with his leg, catching the two men at the ankles. He hit so hard Icelin thought she would hear the bones in his leg crack. But they did not, and the two men stumbled and fell.

"Behind us!" Sull drew his mallet and cleaver. He charged a second pair of men coming from the rear. Before they could reach for weapons, Sull cut a wicked gash across the first man's arm. He backed off a pace, clutching his arm and shredded shirt.

His companion came in low, dodging Sull's swinging mallet. He wore dirt-caked traveling clothes and a hooded, threadbare cloak. He brought a broadsword up to halt Sull's advance.

Sull was no trained fighter, Icelin knew. But what he lacked in skill, the butcher made up for in sheer ferocity. He twirled the cleaver once, letting the bloodied weapon dance in his hand. He smiled at the man with the sword, and the whites of his eyes were huge in the campfires' glow.

"Come on, dogs!" he shouted, stomping the ground, feinting left and right between his two opponents, letting his size intimidate the men and keep them on the defensive.

Caught between her companions, Icelin wrenched a loose board from the ship and swung it at the dark, burly man before he could rise to his feet. The plank hit him in the chest; a protruding nail tore into his skin. The man screeched in pain and fury.

"Run!" Ruen barked at her. The man with corn silk hair brought his sword down in an axe chop. Ruen dodged, and the blade buried itself in sand. He rolled away and came up practically between the man's legs. He snapped out a fist, connecting just below his attacker's ribcage. The blow would not trouble the man, Icelin thought. She had seen the glint of mail through his thin shirt.

To her shock, the man whooped out a breath and bent double. His sword dropped, allowing Ruen to come in around his guard. He locked an elbow around the man's neck, jerking sharply to the left.

The loud crack sent a sick coldness through Icelin's body.

"Beware, lass!"

Icelin turned in time to see Sull's mallet fly from his hand. The butcher fell back, clutching his arm against his chest. Blood dripped through the gaps between his fingers.

Horrified, Icelin dropped the board and started to run to him.

She felt a presence rise up behind her. She'd forgotten the dark-haired man. She tried to spin, but the sand slowed her. Large hands grabbed Icelin around the waist and slammed her sideways into the caravel's hull.

Icelin felt the breath leave her body in a rush. Her head hit an exposed board. Stars burst in her vision. She tried to call a spell, but her mind wouldn't function. She collapsed back against her attacker's chest. He manhandled her to the ground, pinning her arms in front of her while he fumbled for a piece of rope at his belt.

Icelin struggled wildly. Sand raked her wounded forearm. The pain was unlike anything she'd felt before, but she had to keep her hands free. She had to have magic. She wouldn't let them take her. . . .

Somewhere behind her, she could hear Sull snarling, his cleaver whistling in his hand. The dark-haired man wrenched her hands together, tying off the rope. Ruen leaped to his feet and started toward her, but was distracted by another figure coming out of the night. This one was tall, agile in motion. The moonlight revealed a face covered in puckered scars.

"Bind her mouth!" Cerest cried. "She is a wizard." He noticed Ruen and drew a sword. "Shenan!"

Icelin could see no one else, but a breath later, magic erupted behind Cerest. Icelin smelled the burning, and chemical heat seared her eyes as an arrow streaked through the night, aimed at Ruen.

"Acid!" Icelin cried.

The dark man grabbed her by the hair, jerking her head back. She couldn't see Ruen, could only make out the night sky and the distant flakes of starlight visible through the clouds. She heard the arrow impact wood, hissing as the spell fizzled out.

The dark-haired man used his teeth to pull off one of his dirty leather gloves. Stuffing it in her mouth, he looped more rope around her head, binding the glove tight to her face until she choked.

Icelin felt herself lifted, tossed over the man's shoulder. He moved off into the night, around the ship wreckage, away from the sounds of fighting. She could not see if Cerest was following.

Icelin squirmed and tried to scream, but she could force no sound through the gag. They moved out of the campfire light, and the night grew pitch black. She could see nothing of her surroundings except the dark-haired man's broad back.

She prayed Ruen would help Sull. Over and over she begged the gods that they would escape. But even if they did, Cerest and his men would be gone in the night. Sull and Ruen would have no idea how to track her.

Abruptly, the man carrying her stopped. Icelin felt his hands leave her. She heard him fumbling with something. Metal clicked against metal: a door lock.

Now was her opportunity. She might not get another. Bracing herself, Icelin threw all her weight to the right.

She toppled off her captor's shoulder, raising her bound arms in front of her. She hit the ground hard on her stomach amid the cries of the dark-haired man. He recovered from his surprise and immediately crouched, grabbing her ankle so she couldn't run.

Icelin grappled with the gag at her mouth, tearing away leather, rope, and hair that had gotten caught against her face.

Her captor was on top of her now, trying to wrestle her hands down, but it was too dark for him to get a proper grip on her. Wherever they were, there were no torches or lanterns nearby to provide illumination.

Icelin thrust her elbow into the man's ribs. The pressure on her back slackened. She ripped the gag aside and screamed at the top of her lungs. The shrill sound pierced the night, and even the dark-haired man shrank back in momentary fear.

Several things happened at once. Her captor recovered and pushed her onto her side, backhanding her across the face. Dazed, Icelin flopped onto her back. She tasted blood on her lips. Her face felt hot. At the same time, footsteps were approaching rapidly from somewhere in the distance. Icelin's heart lurched—had Ruen and Sull come for her?—until she heard Cerest's voice.

"Strike her again, Greyas, and I'll split your tongue down the center," the elf promised. "Shenan, would you mind?"

"Of course," said a new voice, feminine, and as peacefully melodic as Cerest's. How many had the elf set upon her? Icelin thought. Hopelessness seized her, and with it came a hysteric frenzy.

She struck out, and by chance caught the dark-haired man in the throat. Icelin screamed again.

"Sull! Ruen!"

"Quickly, Shenan," said Cerest calmly over the noise.

Icelin heard the honeyed voice speaking in an even, arcane rhythm. A cold mist stole over Icelin's mind. Her body felt heavy, and her eyes burned as if she had not slept in days.

"No," she cried. But the word came out slurred, feeble. Icelin trembled, fighting to stay awake, but it was no use. She went limp on the cold ground, and all the melodic voices receded.

Ruen's fist glanced off jawbone, and the latter of Sull's opponents turned his full attention to Ruen. His arm still dripped blood freely from the wound Sull had dealt him. Ruen tipped his hat to the side and smiled before launching a flurry of numbing blows to the man's torso. The ring on his hand burned silver; Ruen felt its magic coursing through his bones, propelled on by his natural speed.

In his peripheral vision, he noted the tracks Icelin's captors had left in the sand. They were not the tracks of the Watch. He'd known it as soon as the ambush hit them. If he hadn't thought it was Tesleena's party pursuing them, he could have outrun the men easily. He should have known when she didn't answer his summons through the pawn.

Sull dodged a thrust from his opponent's broadsword. The butcher was quick enough, but the sword still whistled close to his ear, too close for the man to last much longer in the fight.

Ruen aimed his next blow at the man's sword arm, putting all the force he could behind the punch. The man's arm spasmed; his sword fell from nerveless fingers. Ruen punched again. The man went down and did not rise.

Sull threw his weight backward to avoid another sword thrust. He landed on his backside in the sand. Scooting away, he kicked sand, spraying the air and creating a meager shield between himself and the flashing sword.

Ruen came at the man with the broadsword from behind. He grabbed the man's shoulder and turned him. Locking a hand on his wrist, Ruen twisted until the bones cracked. The man's sword fell to the sand to join his friend's. Ruen jammed his elbow into the man's throat, and he fell, unconscious next to his companion.

Ruen looked briefly to see if Sull was bleeding more than necessary and, satisfied he wasn't, began disarming the unconscious men. He took a dagger from one of them and slid it into his belt. He much preferred the fish knife—it was his favorite—but the wraith had stolen that from him.

He stood up and saw a red blur charging at him. He managed to dodge the bull rush, but Sull's fist still found his cheek. One side of Ruen's head erupted in pain.

Ruen danced back, retaining the presence of mind to raise the dagger before Sull could come at him again.

But the butcher seemed uninterested in continuing the attack. Instead, Ruen saw tears leaking from the man's wild eyes.

"You damn fool!" Sull bellowed. "You let 'em get away."

"I saved your life," Ruen said calmly. He tucked the dagger away and rubbed his jaw. "She wouldn't have wanted me to let you die."

Sull hiccupped and seemed to consider this. His eyes were still furious. "You led us right into their trap. Do you have any idea what they'll do to her? They'll—"

Ruen shook his head. "They want her alive. They took a lot of trouble to remove her from the battle unharmed. We can track them now."

"How?" Sull demanded.

Ruen crouched next to the smaller of the unconscious forms. He nudged the man, but he did not stir.

"We wait for one of these to wake up," Ruen said. Sull made a noise of displeasure, and Ruen finally looked up at the big man. "They won't get far—look." He nodded to the horizon, where gray, pre-dawn light was giving way to sunrise. "They're not stupid enough to move her out of Mist-shore while it's light. With the Watch patrols out, they'll be seen. We'll question these, rest and move on."

"What if they won't tell us anythin'?" Sull asked, glancing pointedly at Ruen's fists.

Ruen shrugged. "We'll have to be convincing." He got to his feet. "Help me move them inside the ship's hull. We'll be sheltered there."

Together they hauled the bodies, the dead and the unconscious, through the torn gap in the ship. The interior smelled of must and mold. Driftwood and the tattered remains of hammocks were piled in one corner. Rats scurried out of the lumpy mounds.

Ruen sat down on a pile of rigging next to the bodies. Sull moved around the ship with an air of ripe impatience. Ruen watched the chests of the unconscious men rising and falling. He had beaten them severely. He did not know when they would regain sense, and if they would be in a fit state to answer any questions.

Sliding forward, he removed his glove and reached across the closest man's prone body. He pressed his hand against the man's open palm. He wasn't sure what drove him to do it—he always avoided touching people when he could help it—but he needed to know. He ignored Sull's curious expression.

Faint blue light outlined the cracks between his fingers. Ruen curled his hand under the man's, but he didn't think Sull could see the light. The man's hand stung with cold; it was like pressing his palm flush against a frozen lake. He'd expected some degree of chill, but not this. The feeling repulsed him. Ruen removed his hand from the unconscious man's and put his glove back on.

"What are you doin'?" Sull said.

"Checking for signs of life," Ruen explained. He turned his attention to the other man. "We'll need to question this one. The other won't survive. I hit him too hard."

"I didn't see you feelin' for a life beat—"

Sull stopped. The man's eyelids had twitched. A breath later they opened, and the man let out a rough moan. He focused on Ruen and the butcher with the bloody cleaver in his hand. His eyes widened.

"Welcome back," Sull said, smiling cheerfully. He seemed to have forgotten Ruen's odd behavior. "We've a few questions for you."

Icelin knew she was dreaming. The scene was familiar. Barefoot, she walked on green grass, up the side of a wide, rocky hill. Shafts of sunlight shone on her white dress. There were wildflowers blooming, gold and purple, all around her feet.

She stopped at the crest of the hill. A stone tower rose up before her. A single window had been cut into the curve facing her, a dark and unblinking eye. The western side had caved in, leaving a gaping hole into which birds flew and nested. Their cries were the only sounds on the hilltop. But Icelin felt she was not alone.

There were other figures moving up the hill toward the tower, indistinct shadows darting in and out of her field of vision. She tried to grasp them with her eyes, but they had no more substance than the wind brushing her cheeks.

I will follow them, Icelin thought. It seemed the most natural thing in the world to stride across the grass to the gap in the immense tower. She put her hands on the exposed stone. Warm from the sun, bleached with age, and ribboned with thousands of miniscule cracks, the stone held secrets. Someone had told her this.

"All the ancient places of the world hold secrets. Who knows what manner of men walked here, be they beggars or kings—men who now lie in dusty tombs, their memories husks. Will the stones remember who touched them, when you lie beside these somber lords of the earth?"

Icelin remembered the words vividly, but for the first time in her life she could not recall who said them. The thought was vaguely disturbing, but she pushed it to the back of her dreaming mind.

She had entered the tower now. The stones blotted out the sun at her back. The tower's wood floors had long rotted away, leaving the interior open from earth to sky. Crushed grass and the remains of a small human body were strewn on the ground.

Icelin tilted her head as far back as she could, taking in the circle of blue rimmed by blackened stones through a gap in the ceiling. The tower had been damaged by fire; she could see the soot stains streaking the walls. Had this small human been the only person to die here? How had it come to be?

She felt tired now. Icelin sat down in the middle of the tower, still staring up at the sky. The shadow shapes moved around her, but she wasn't afraid of them. She felt that if they would only be still, she would be able to name them. It was the same with the tower—a living presence that, if she knew its name, would open its secrets to her and welcome her inside. Unnamed, it cast an immutable shadow over her dreams, dominating everything.

"Have you found anything?"

The voice, so loud in the peaceful place, made Icelin jump. The shadows flitted closer to her, and Icelin felt their urgency. Something was happening. The stones around her changed color and became bright orange and blue like storm clouds. The sun pouring through the tower roof was too hot, too hot.

She looked down at her skin and found it melting off her bones. She was burning alive.

CHAPTER NINE

ICELIN AWOKE TO DARKNESS AND MORE SHADOWS MOVING AROUND HER. This time she felt real terror, for she knew where she was. The gag stank in her mouth, and voices floated around her.

Cerest was there, somewhere in the darkness. She heard him say, "We'll wait for gateclose. Bring her, if she's awake. Be careful of her arm."

Icelin looked down and saw the clean bandage tightly wrapped around her injured arm. There was a dull ache where the pain had been.

Two pairs of rough hands grabbed her shoulders and hauled her to her feet. The dark-haired man stood to her right. Her captors guided her over to the center of a large, rectangular room.

Icelin looked up, just as she'd done in her dream. Timber beams crisscrossed above her head. Tin sheets formed parts of the walls. Wooden crates lined the whole building, some stacked as high as the ceiling.

A warehouse, Icelin thought. She felt the floor slope down sharply; the ground the warehouse was built upon had shifted over the years. There was a good chance they were still in Mistshore, near the harbor.

In the center of the room, Cerest and the female elf stood talking. The two men guiding her sat her on a crate before them. The dark-haired man removed her gag.

Cerest faced her, a cloak hood tucked close around his face. He appeared to be keeping his distance from the human men. Did he fear their reaction to his scars? The thought came unbidden to Icelin, and she wondered why the murderous elf would be bothered to care how others saw him. He nodded to one of the men.

"Wait outside," he said. "Greyas, you remain here, but step back so we may talk."

With the men dismissed, Cerest focused his attention solely on Icelin. "Hello again," he said softly. The female elf—Shenan, he'd called her—brought a lantern close and handed it to Cerest. The elf held the flickering flame close to her face so he could see her clearly.

"What do you want?" Icelin asked.

To her surprise, the elf went down on one knee in front of her, so that he was looking up into her face. She supposed he meant to appear non-threatening, but Icelin found the effort he took more unsettling than comforting. He angled his body so that the unscarred portion of his face was most visible.

"I would like," Cerest said, "for you to tell me how much you remember of your childhood."

The question was so bizarrely out of context with the situation that Icelin didn't immediately answer. Cerest, intent on her expression, seemed to take her silence as defiance. He frowned.

"Icelin," he said, at the same time gesturing to the dark-haired man—Greyas, he'd called him. "I know you don't trust me. That's to be expected. You don't remember who I am." He smiled. "But I have known you for a very long time. Gods, I *named* you. I remember the night you were born—"

Icelin lunged at him. Shenan caught her by the throat and pushed her back, but Icelin's gesture had the desired effect. Cerest stopped speaking and stood back a safe distance. He regarded her with wounded curiosity.

"Why do you behave this way?" he asked. "I've not hurt you, and I don't intend to."

"You killed Brant," Icelin said. Her throat burned. "All your lies, no matter how prettily spoken, won't change that."

"I'm not lying," Cerest said. "Brant cared for you. He was a good man. I know that." When Icelin only stared at him, he went on, "But I think you'll discover Brant had his share of secrets, especially where you were concerned. I'm confident he acted to protect you, but in doing so, he short-ened his own life."

"Master." Greyas stepped forward again, dragging a smaller figure. Icelin pulled her gaze away from Cerest's face to see who it was. Her heart dropped.

Fannie stood in front of Greyas, looking like a doll in the man's muscular arms. While Icelin watched, Greyas placed a hand on either side of Fannie's head. Fannie quailed, but he did not exert any pressure on her skull. He didn't have to. Fannie stood utterly still, held in place by the mere threat of what he could do to her with those large hands. She was gagged, as Icelin had been. Her eyes were huge above the scrap of dirty cloth. She looked beseechingly at Icelin.

"We took her at the same time we took you," Cerest said. He motioned for Greyas to bring Fannie into the light. He pushed her, stumbling and barefoot, into the small circle of illumination.

"Shenan," Cerest said, and the female elf stepped forward, taking Greyas's place at Fannie's back. She patted the woman on the shoulder, whispering comforting noises that made Icelin's skin crawl.

"What do you remember of your childhood, Icelin?" Cerest repeated the question slowly, glancing meaningfully between Fannie and Icelin.

"I am an orphan," Icelin said. She met Fannie's eyes, trying to silently reassure her. "My parents were killed when I was barely two summers old. Brant, my great-uncle, raised me."

"Your great-uncle," Cerest said. "What about your grandfather, Icelin?"

"My grandfather is dead. I have no other living family," Icelin said. "Why are you asking me these questions? If you want to revenge yourself on me, let this woman go and have your pleasure! What more can I possibly give you than my life?"

Cerest's brow furrowed in confusion. "Revenge?" he said, sounding almost amused. "My dear girl, far from it. I have no quarrel with you. What gave you that notion?"

"I—" Icelin turned away. Her mind raced. He wasn't after her. She'd been wrong this whole time. He hadn't been in the fire. . . .

Relief and fear vied for control of Icelin's emotions. She hadn't injured the elf. But if it wasn't revenge he sought, why had he killed Brant? Why had he hunted her so diligently?

"Shenan," Cerest said quietly.

Fannie's muffled scream snapped Icelin back to the present. She looked up in horror to see the female elf holding Fannie's head back by the hair. She placed a gleaming dagger blade against Fannie's arched neck. Blood welled where the blade pressed flesh. The dagger was so sharp, one slip and Shenan would slice open the prostitute's throat.

"Answer my question, please," Cerest said. He sounded like a father coaxing a child. "I think it important I hear this tale, so that we understand each other."

Icelin swallowed. She looked at Cerest, letting him see the undisguised hatred. "I studied magic under the tutelage of Nelzun Decampter, a skilled wizard," she said. "My great-uncle paid out most of his savings to apprentice me to the man because Decampter specialized in handling wielders of unstable magic. Such was mine. I studied under Nelzun for three years and acquired a reasonable level of skill in the Art."

"A reasonable level—did Nelzun believe you had the potential for greater power?" Cerest asked.

Icelin's jaw clenched at the eager light in his eyes. "Yes. He wanted me to travel with him, to test my skills out in the world. But I had no desire to leave my home. That mistake cost Nelzun his life."

"What happened?" Cerest said.

"First tell her to move the dagger," Icelin said, looking at Shenan but addressing Cerest.

Cerest nodded to the elf woman. Shenan appeared disappointed as she removed the blade from Fannie's throat.

"Nelzun took me into the city to test my powers. He wanted me to be able to defend myself in the rougher districts. None of the spells I was to cast that day were dangerous, and Waterdeep is more stable than many cities when it comes to magic going awry." Icelin knew she shouldn't care what the elf thought of her, but the need to explain, to justify what couldn't be justified, clawed at her.

"We were in Dock Ward. A fight broke out at a tavern as we were passing by, and the brawl spilled into the street." Icelin could see it clearly in her mind: the shattered door, the man being thrown into the street. Another pair of men followed, brandishing weapons. She'd thought . . .

It didn't matter what they'd intended. She never had the chance to find out.

"I ran toward the fight. I left Nelzun. When I saw the man about to be attacked, I cast the only spell I knew that would hurt. I'd never called the fire before, but Nelzun had showed me how it was done."

"To summon fire to your fingertips is one of the easiest attack spells to master, because you cannot burn yourself, as real flame would."

Her teacher's words, Icelin thought. But he'd never given a care to what might happen to him if things went wrong.

"The spell ran wild?" Cerest asked. He touched his face, rubbing the scars thoughtfully. "The fire spread?"

"I can still remember how high the flames soared," Icelin said. She was dimly aware of wetness on her face. She reached up with her bound hands and felt the tears. It didn't matter. They had already seen how weak she was. "There was a boardinghouse—old wood, and a dry season—next door to the tavern. The fire took the roof first, caving in the ceiling on the people inside. Five people on the topmost floor were killed instantly, including a Watchman who'd been investigating a woman's disappearance. The people below escaped—miraculously, I thought." She took a shuddering breath. "Until the spell ended, and I realized Nelzun wasn't with me."

"What happened to him?" Cerest asked. But Icelin wasn't listening. She recited the tale automatically, numbing her mind to the most painful part of all.

"Nelzun had gone into the boardinghouse to save the rest of the people inside. He got them all out, and then he collapsed outside the building. I tried to get him to take healing, but he said he'd breathed too much of the smoke, that healing wouldn't save him. He spent his last breaths telling me not to blame myself."

Icelin looked up. The warehouse was utterly silent. Greyas stood somewhere in the shadows, unseen, but probably listening. Nothing seemed to exist outside the dim circle of lantern light: it was only herself, Cerest, Shenan, and Fannie. She glanced at the two women and was horrified to find them both looking at her with pity in their eyes.

Gods above, she'd never thought to be making a confession before two monsters and a terrified prostitute. She'd never imagined such beings pitying her.

"I understand now," Cerest said. "You believed I escaped the boardinghouse fire, horribly scarred and out for revenge against the lass who'd maimed me."

Icelin nodded.

Cerest smiled gently. "You have nothing to fear from me, Icelin. My scars are from a different fire. Like your teacher, I see great strength in you. I want to help you harness your gifts—"

"Never!" Icelin's shout shattered the stillness. "I swore I'd never pursue magic again."

Cerest and Shenan traded glances. Icelin couldn't tell what passed between them.

"She is untried, Cerest," Shenan said, voicing her thoughts aloud. "You have led us on a fool's chase." Her tone was mild, but she tightened her grip on the dagger.

Good, Icelin thought. Let them slay each other and have done with the whole business. For the first time in her life she felt grateful for being inadequate.

"She can learn," Cerest said. "She's already had a wizard's training, which is more than Elgreth had."

"Elgreth," Icelin said, surprised, "you knew my grandfather?"

"It's true," said Cerest. "Elgreth was my best friend."

"No. You're lying again," Icelin said. His words cut her. This couldn't be. Her family would never be connected to a murderer.

"You don't know your family as I do, Icelin. Your grandfather was afflicted with a powerful spellscar. Did Brant ever tell you that?"

Mute, Icelin shook her head.

"He should have. The scar gave Elgreth substantial abilities," Cerest said, "abilities that I believe you also possess."

"That's not possible. You have to be exposed to the spellplague to bear such a scar," Icelin said. "I have never been outside Waterdeep's walls."

"You were too young to remember—"

"I remember everything!" Her body shook with suppressed fury. "I possess all my memories, whether I want them or not. And you, sir, are not among them."

Out of the corner of her eye, Icelin glimpsed movement. A slender shape flowed down the sloping floor toward them. Icelin thought it was a snake moving in a crooked line, but as it drew closer, she recognized the metallic smell. The substance pooled in a thick circle at her feet.

Cerest recognized it at the same time. He drew his sword.

"Greyas!" he cried. But there was no answer from the shadows. Cerest looked down at the blood pool and cursed. Shenan shoved Fannie away and brandished her own blade, moving into position at Cerest's back.

Icelin used the distraction to slide off the back of the crate, putting it between her and the elves. She heard Fannie stumbling for cover, but Cerest was no longer paying her any attention. He was watching the shadows intently.

"Show yourselves!" He shouted.

Tense, Icelin waited, but there came no answer from the shadows.

A breath passed, and a sound like beating wings came out of the darkness. A huge metal cleaver buried itself deep into the crate where Icelin had been sitting. The handle quivered from side to side.

Icelin reached up and snatched the weapon. As soon as her fingers touched the handle, the attack came.

Sull leaped from behind a crate, charging into the circle with a loud roar. The sight of the red-haired giant hurtling across the warehouse was enough to break apart Cerest and Shenan. They dived for cover, and Sull placed himself squarely in front of Icelin. He grabbed the cleaver from her and sliced her bonds.

"Get back!" Sull shouted as he parried a blow from Shenan's blade with his mallet. The dagger left a deep gouge in the wood.

Icelin backed away, seeking cover. Cerest broke to follow when another shadow moved—a large burst of darkness that came from above.

Ruen dropped from a column of stacked crates, landing behind Cerest. He grabbed the elf around the throat, dragging him away from Icelin.

"Greyas!" Cerest shouted, twisting to shove the man off. "Rondel!" He spun. Icelin saw the instant the elf locked eyes with Ruen.

For a breath, Cerest froze like a frightened deer. Icelin heard him mutter, "Spellscarred," before he went for his sword.

Ruen stood before him, unarmed and at ease. His knees slightly bent, he all but danced on the balls of his feet. Cerest thrust with his blade, and Ruen jumped back. The thrust never came close to his flesh. The elf swung again, and again Ruen dodged, this time finding an opening to punch Cerest in the gut.

The elf stumbled back. His sword wavered; he didn't know whether to attack or defend.

He has no notion of how to fight an unarmed man, Icelin realized. It would be more to his advantage if Ruen had a weapon.

The thief, on the other hand, appeared to be reading Cerest's attacks before he made them. He danced back, sweeping his foot out in a kick that connected solidly with Cerest's knee. The elf had his full weight propped there; he went down with a cry of fury.

This wasn't desperate street fighting. Icelin observed Ruen's measured stance, the balance between rest and motion. He stayed suspended between the two, almost floating, until Cerest's attack came. Only trained, disciplined warriors fought this way, facing whirling steel with an air of serenity and absolute comfort in the strength of their bodies.

Ruen Morleth was not a thief, or at least, not *only* a thief. He was a monk, a warrior trained in unarmed combat.

A loud pounding sounded outside the warehouse door. Icelin tore her attention away from the battle. Ruen and Sull must have sealed the door from the inside when they'd entered the warehouse. Cerest's men—gods knew how many had come running at the elf's shout—were trying to break down the door. The flimsy wood and rusted iron wouldn't hold for long.

Not this time. She wouldn't be caught again. Icelin took a deep breath and searched her mind, cycling through spell after spell in the vast tower library.

Wind. Force. Her teacher had shown her how the spell could be used if she was ever jumped in Blacklock Alley.

Good enough to seal a door. Spellbooks opened and flew before her mind. She discarded the safe spells, those that would do no harm. She threw them all into a dusty corner and pictured a black book, something fearful and dangerous. Yes. Those were the spells she feared most, but they were the only ones that would aid her friends.

Then it came to her: a black tome with a gold spine. The words were written in faded ink, as if her mind were instinctively trying to protect itself from the deadly power in the words. She forced herself to visualize them clearly. Her heart tripped rapidly in her chest. She thought of a song to calm herself, chanted in time to the music, but her voice quivered. She was no monk. There would be no serenity for her in this fight.

The spell manifested in a burst of energy. Icelin's hair blew straight back from her face. The hot wind made her eyes stream. She lifted her hands, and the wind rose, spiraling outward to the door in a contained funnel. The force of it grated against the wood, forcing the door tight into its frame. The pounding ceased.

"Ruen! Sull, let's go! I can't hold it for long!" Icelin screamed above the wind.

Sull turned, his mallet tangled with Shenan's dagger. He kept barreling into her, knocking her off balance so she couldn't cast a proper spell. "Hold on, lass. We're comin'!"

Icelin heard a loud thud. It sounded like someone had been thrown into a pile of crates. She was too focused on the spell to see whether it was a friend or a foe.

The breath burned in her chest. Too hot, she thought. The air thickened, and sweat poured down her face. The spell was too strong. It was happening just like before, but this would be much worse. She could feel the heat building. Paint bubbled on the warehouse walls.

Gods, don't do this to me. Not again.

Five years fell away like scales. She was losing control; the spell was slipping away, taking on a life of its own. Icelin was powerless to stop it. She could hear the screams coming from the boardinghouse. So many people, trying to get out. . . .

The wooden door buckled in its frame. Frightened shouts rang out from the other side. Icelin fought to contain the wind, to keep it caged in its deadly funnel.

Flames burst into being and flew along the funnel's rim. Icelin could do nothing but watch them, a dozen restless sprites spiraling through the air. Pain shot through her after each flame appeared, as if they were being torn from her body.

Icelin dropped to her knees, and the funnel burst. Freed, the fire shot in all directions. The deadly flame arrows buried in crates or ricocheted off the tin walls.

Everyone in the warehouse would be a target, Icelin thought wildly. She couldn't end the spell; the magic became unrecognizable once the spell went wild. She had no way to contain it now.

Through a haze of smoke and pain, Icelin felt a presence behind her. For all she knew, it could have been Cerest or one of his men, come to stick a dagger in her back. Somehow, she knew it was Ruen. The thief crouched behind her.

"Can you walk?" He had to shout to be heard above the roaring wind.

Icelin shook her head. The slight movement made her vision swim.

"I can't touch you," Ruen said. "My ring will enhance the spell. It could kill us all."

"Where's Sull?" Icelin said. "Fannie—she's here too." She couldn't see them through the smoke. The crates were on fire, the blaze spreading to every corner of the warehouse. Soon the ceiling would collapse, just as it had done five years ago.

"Sull and Fannie are fine," Ruen said. "The others fled in fear of your spell."

Relief flooded Icelin, bringing with it a sense of peace. This was justice, she thought. I will die here and never hurt anyone again.

"Go," Icelin said. "Get out of here. Make sure Sull gets to safety, and your marker is paid. That's all I care—"

A wave of energy shuddered through Icelin's body. She felt the last vestiges of the spell inside her explode outward. The door and part of the wall blew apart, but Icelin didn't hear the grinding, tearing metal. The force of the blast deafened her.

"How convenient," Ruen said. He was still shouting, but his voice seemed to come from very far away. He had his hands at her armpits, dragging her to her feet. "You made us a door."

"You shouldn't have . . . done that," Icelin said. She swayed on her feet. A beam broke away from the ceiling, trailing a sheet of flame all the way to the ground.

"We've got to run," Ruen said. He took her hand, yanking her behind him. "Put your arms around my neck."

"But the ring—"

"Do it!"

Icelin wrapped her arms around him. Ruen lifted her onto his back and sprinted to the gap in the wall. Icelin felt as if she were flying. More beams dropped around them, but Ruen found a path through as if by magic. The fire and smoke were everywhere, but he kept running.

Suddenly they were through. Cool air hit Icelin's face. It was daylight.

The twisted opening spat them out onto a small dock behind the warehouse. Parts of it burned with the building, but Ruen didn't stop to see if it would hold their weight. He charged down the narrow platform all the way to the edge and jumped into the water.

The impact shook Icelin loose from Ruen's back, but he stayed beside her. The cold water shocked her limbs into functioning. With Ruen's aid, she swam to the surface.

"We'll stay in the harbor," Ruen said when they'd caught their breath.

"Swim underwater as much as you can," he told her. "They'll be watching to see if we survived. We've got to find cover."

He dived down. Icelin followed, keeping a hand on his flank so she wouldn't lose him in the murky water. As far as she could tell, they were headed roughly in the direction of the shore.

They surfaced in a thick stand of brush about thirty feet from the dock. Sull waited in the weeds.

"I saw you go off the dock," he said. "Fannie slipped away. No one's watching that I can see."

Icelin was shaking by the time she got out of the water. When she came within reach, Sull pulled her against his chest, hugging her so hard Icelin couldn't breathe.

"I'm all right," Icelin said weakly. She patted him on the back.

"Thought I'd lost you, little one," the butcher said roughly. He released her and mopped his eyes with his apron. Ruen stood a little apart, scanning the area. The warehouse continued its slow collapse, but they were clear of the devastation.

"Let's get out of here," Ruen said finally. He moved away, crouching low along the shoreline, not waiting for their reply.

"Where are we goin'?" Sull asked. He led Icelin by the hand, half-supporting her. "She needs rest."

"Back into the water," Ruen said. He waded in up to his waist. "Keep her head up. She'll be fine."

The water felt colder. Icelin's teeth chattered, but she swam with Sull's aid, following Ruen into the harbor.

They swam clear of the dock and out into open water. The sky was gray and overcast. In the distance, deep blue clouds threatened rain, but the day was still too bright. Icelin felt horribly exposed. At any moment, she expected shouts to go up from the shore.

"Don't worry," Ruen said, seeing her expression. "We're going under." He took in her chattering teeth and general state of disarray. "Sull, you'll have to tow her if she slows."

"I can make it," Icelin said, but she slurred the words.

"We'll stay under until we reach the wreckage," Ruen said, nodding to the floating mass of Mistshore's main body. "We should be able to swim under the docks and footpaths. Ready?"

Icelin nodded, and they dived. Sull kept one arm around her and used the other to swim close to Ruen.

They swam for what seemed like an eternity. After a time, Icelin simply floated in Sull's grip, concentrating on keeping her breath in her body.

When she felt she could bear no more, Sull angled upward to the light.

They came up under one of the wooden pathways. There was barely room for their heads underneath the rotting planks, but the sound of the waves lapping against the pilings concealed their gasping breaths.

Icelin could hear footsteps echoing loudly just above their heads. "Where are you taking us?" she whispered.

Ruen put a finger to his lips. He disappeared beneath the surface, leaving her and Sull to tread water.

"We should swim back to shore," Icelin said. "I don't like this." She expected Sull to echo the sentiment, but the butcher shook his head. Water plastered his red hair over his ears.

"I wouldn't have found you without him," Sull said. "He tracked you. Persistent as a demon, he was. Ghosted into that warehouse and took out the meanest of the elf's men without a sound."

"But why?" Icelin said. "He never wanted to help me. He could have left you on the beach to die."

"Maybe he is everythin' you thought he was," Sull said.

Ruen broke the surface a few feet away and waved a hand. Icelin experienced a renewed shock of weakness as she slogged through the water. "We're here," Ruen said.

"Where?" Icelin asked.

"If you can hold on for a little longer, I'm taking us someplace safe," Ruen said. "Nine feet straight down there's a figurehead: the Blind Mermaid, they call her. She sticks up from the sand, so you can't see her fish half. She's buried along with the rest of the *The Darter*."

"*The Darter?*" Sull said. "You mean she was part of a ship?"

"She still is," Ruen said. "But she has a more important job now. She's the guardian of a door, a secret door we're going to need. So we'll be paying her a visit." He raised a hand to forestall more questions. "When I go down, you'll follow a few feet behind. Don't be afraid of what you see, or how deep we go. Just keep following me."

Icelin nodded, but her hesitance must have shown. Ruen scowled and shook his head impatiently.

"This is important," he said, speaking to both of them. "You can't turn around. Once we go down, it's all the way. Or you'll drown. That's how they keep out the ones who aren't supposed to be there."

Isn't that us? Icelin thought, but she didn't give it voice.

"We'll follow you," she said. She'd decided to trust Ruen Morleth once, and now Sull seemed convinced of the man. He'd saved her from the fire, risking his own life to do so.

They dived. The water seemed darker here, a creature stretching out inky black arms to envelop them. When they got to the bottom, Icelin and Sull stayed back. Icelin pushed her drifting hair out of her eyes and strained to see what Ruen was doing ahead of them. Craning around his body, she saw the figurehead.

The wooden mermaid was covered in a shawl of seaweed, the thin, green streamers trailing behind her like a living cloak. Buried to the waist in sand, the mermaid stared up to the surface through her sightless eyes.

Ruen put his thumbs to both her eye sockets and pushed. The wooden orbs disappeared inside her skull, and Ruen backstroked furiously, propelling himself away from the figurehead.

Light burst from the mermaid's eyes, beams of illumination that spilled over her wooden sockets and down her rigid face like tears. The rotting wood glowed golden, suffusing, impossibly, with life.

The mermaid's skin turned white, and her hair moved in the water, shifting colors from brown to blue-green. She uncrossed her arms from in front of her bare breasts, brandishing a trident in one hand, and a glowing green orb in the other. She turned her head at an odd angle to regard them. Though her body now throbbed with life, her eyes remained vacant.

She doesn't really live, Icelin thought. She's a construct of some sort. A guardian, Ruen had said.

"Welcome to the Cradle," the mermaid spoke. The words reached Icelin's ears clearly, magically propelled through the water. "Those who seek entrance, come forward. But do no harm in Arowall's house, or face a slow death in Umberlee's embrace."

With those cryptic words, the mermaid lifted her arms, crossing the trident in front of her. The orb flashed green, and the trident glowed in answer. She brought it down in one swift stroke, driving the weapon into the sand covering her lower half.

A deep rumbling echoed beneath them. Awestruck, Icelin watched the sand roil, parting on either side of the mermaid's body. Contained by magic, the tempest of sand and water swirled around the mermaid and revealed her glossy silver tail. Beneath the webbed fin, a dark space yawned.

Lit by spheres of magical radiance, the narrow passage led into the hull of what looked like an ancient sailing ship. The wood around the animated figurehead was rotting and caked with barnacles, but somehow it remained intact.

Ruen swam for the passage; Icelin and Sull followed quickly. Icelin's chest ached to draw breath, and as she swam down the dark tunnel, she realized what Ruen meant about not turning back.

The sand was already swirling behind them, sealing off the entrance. The mermaid resumed her frozen pose, her sightless eyes betraying nothing of what lay beneath her fin. There was no way out behind them. It was death or forward.

CHAPTER TEN

CEREST PACED IN FRONT OF THE BURNED-OUT SHELL OF THE DOCKSIDE warehouse. He stopped long enough to kick a smoking timber against the tin wall. A rattling crash brought down a rain of ash and smoke.

Ristlara and Shenan stood a little way off, looking anxious and unamused by his outburst.

"Come away, fool," Ristlara said. "The Watch is sure to bring a patrol. We won't be seen here with you."

"Tell your men to regroup. I want to know how many we lost." Cerest already knew Greyas was gone. Greyas, Melias, and Riatvin. Now he was entirely dependent upon the Locks and their hunters. The idea galled him, but what choice did he have?

"She walks with two companions now," Ristlara said. "The big one is an oaf, but he's strong; and I'll lay odds the thin one is a monk, and quite powerful. Think, Cerest," she said, putting a hand on his arm. "How can you be certain she possesses the powers Elgreth did? Shenan says she is an untried child."

"Can Shenan deny the evidence of her eyes?" Cerest waved an arm to encompass the devastated warehouse. "My untried child did this. The men may have slain Greyas and the rest, but *she* brought the building down. You heard her, Shenan; it wasn't her first display of such power. She is more than Elgreth ever was. While she is alive, I will have her."

Ristlara and Shenan exchanged doubtful glances. It infuriated Cerest. How dare they show such disrespect?

"Where do we search now?" Shenan spoke up. "The trail is cold."

"They can't go far," Cerest said. "If she is as unstable as I believe, she'll turn up again. Until then, we wait."

Cerest rubbed his face. He needed to rest. If his own body sought reverie, Icelin would be near exhaustion.

We'll both rest, Cerest thought, and tonight—yes, it would be tonight—we'll talk again. He would help her work through the trauma of the past. She had been scarred too—not physically, but the pain was there, a raw wound that only another, equally scarred being would understand. Those scars would be the link that bound them together. They would make each other whole.

"Cough it out, there's a good girl."

Sull smacked her on the back, forcing up more of the loathsome harbor water than Icelin thought possible for anyone to swallow.

She crouched on the floor of the lowest deck of *The Darter;* Sull and Ruen stood on either side of her. Behind them, a wall of water stretched weirdly from floor to ceiling, kept from rushing into the cabin by an invisible magical field that faltered and sprayed jets of water at random intervals.

In front of them, a trio of large, armored guards stood with drawn swords, the unfriendly ends pointed at each of their throats. The one pointed at Icelin bobbed uncertainly as she threw up around it. Icelin tried to appear as contrite as she could, under the circumstances.

"Where are we?" she asked when she could speak again.

"I told you: this is the back door," Ruen explained. "They'll check our weapons here." As he said it, the guards stepped forward, divesting Sull of his sash of butcher's tools. They took nothing from Ruen but the ring on his finger. Icelin saw his jaw tighten, but he said nothing.

Icelin allowed them to take the pack off her back without resistance. She saw one guard's eye linger on the gold box buried at the bottom.

"What's in it?" he asked.

"An heirloom," Icelin said, "bequeathed to me by the last of my family."

"Open it," the guard said.

Icelin looked at Sull uncertainly. He knew what she was thinking. She'd not yet opened the mysterious box, found buried beneath the floorboards of Brant's shop. Who knew what it might contain?

"Arowall's rules state that no one may lose their possessions while under the protection of his hospitality," Ruen said. Icelin wondered whether his words were for her benefit, or the guard's.

The man glared at Ruen and spat on the deck. "I know the rules better 'an you, Ruen Morleth." He looked at Icelin. "I said open it, girl."

Icelin took out the box and laid it in her lap. She ran her fingers along the edges until she found the clasp. Thank the gods it wasn't locked. Releasing the catch, she lifted the lid.

Red velvet lined the inside of the box, but it was frayed and soaking wet from their swim. Nestled in the small space was a stack of folded parchment sheets, tied together with a black ribbon. The parchment and the ribbon were dry and perfectly preserved, obviously via some magical means. "Icelin" was inked on the top sheet.

"They look like letters," she said. She traced her name and felt a stab of disappointment. She had hoped Brant's words would be on the pages, but she didn't recognize the thick, black script proclaiming her name so boldly.

"Some heirloom." The guard sniffed. His fellows chuckled.

Icelin clutched the letters and tried not to let her anger show. It would be foolish to provoke these men.

Ruen laid a hand on the closest guard's arm. Immediately, the other two raised their swords.

"Step back," the largest of them warned.

"My apologies," Ruen said. He smiled easily and removed his hand. "I couldn't help but notice how cold your friend's skin is."

The guard he'd touched paled. Reading the mocking light in Ruen's eyes, he gripped his sword as if he might strike out at the thief.

"Get on with you," he said, his teeth gritted. "Though if it were up to me, I'd stick your head through that wall and let you breathe seawater."

Icelin quickly sealed the box and stood up. She wished she could read whatever was in the letters, but this was not the place. Palpable tension thickened the air. She had no idea what Ruen had done to offend the guards, but they stared at him now with murder in their eyes.

"You know the way," the guard said, still eyeing Ruen hatefully. "He's expecting you."

"You know this Arowall fellow?" Sull asked when they were past the guards. "I hope he likes you better than that lot."

"Arowall was captain of *The Darter*," Ruen said, "a pirate vessel for twenty years. When his ship finally went down, he'd strung it with so many magics salvaged from old cargo that the ship stayed intact. It drifted into the harbor and stayed here, resistant to water and, mostly, to time."

"What is *The Darter's* purpose now?" Icelin said.

"Without a ship, Arowall had to turn his hand to another profession," Ruen said, running his hand along the wall.

"The Cradle?" Sull said, echoing the mermaid's words. "Sounds awfully harmless for a pirate."

"Not exactly," Ruen said. He pointed ahead, where another pair of guards flanked a door at the opposite end of the ship. "Fighting was Arowall's second favorite activity, so he created a shrine to the sport. He died years ago, but his descendents—one of them is the man we're going to see, he goes by Arowall too—have been keeping up the business, and they turned *The Darter* into a secret passage to their domain."

The guards opened the portal and Ruen ushered them through.

Icelin's mouth fell open in shocked amazement.

She'd expected to enter another cramped cabin, but instead she beheld a tunnel through the seawater. It extended eight feet above their heads, reinforced by another magical shield. Water beaded and dripped on their heads in a steady drizzle. The air reeked of salt.

"They drain the water periodically," Ruen said, "so it doesn't flood the passage."

"Don't look sturdy to me," Sull said.

"It isn't." Icelin pointed to the stutters in the shield. The sensation of walking on water unnerved her. She kept her eyes off her feet. "Was the shield here before the Spellplague?" she asked.

"Yes," Ruen said. "The enchantments held. Most people who come to the Cradle come from Mistshore, walking above water. Only the lucky souls who can't afford to be seen entering the Cradle use this entrance now."

"Who?" Icelin asked.

Ruen shrugged. "Maybe a young noble. He wants a night of fun but doesn't want his face known in Mistshore. Long as he doesn't mind a swim, this is the way he comes."

The tunnel began a gradual, upward slope. At the end loomed another water wall.

Ruen passed through the opening first. Icelin followed, with Sull bringing up the rear.

Behind the wall Icelin could tell they were in the belly of another ship. The hull had been reinforced several times over. No visible magic greeted them beyond the water wall. A ladder led up to the main deck, and Icelin could see a square of dull sunlight above. The breeze blowing down the ladder was cool and smelled strongly of rain. She couldn't see anything beyond the opening, but she heard muffled voices.

She turned around and noticed for the first time the pair of guards standing on their side of the wall. One of them, a young man not much older than Icelin, stepped forward to speak to Ruen.

"Arowall sends his greetings, Ruen Morleth, and I bear a message. If you wish his protection, the cost will be the same as when last you came here. Can I tell him you will fight in the Cradle?"

"Yes," Ruen said.

"No, he won't," Icelin interrupted. "Ruen, what is this? We're not here to fight. You told us you were taking us someplace safe."

"Safety comes with a price," Ruen said. "Haven't you learned that yet? Fighting is Arowall's business. So if we want to stay here, that's what we do. Tell your master that I'm in," he told the guard. "Expect his champion to fall tonight."

"Bold words," the guard said. His face split in an involuntary grin. "Bells has no equal this past tenday."

"Bells?" Sull said. He snorted. "The champion is called Bells?"

"Death knells, that's why," said the guard. "They nicknamed her after she sent that poor bastard Tarodall into the pool. She hates it, but everyone likes a good nickname, you know."

"We need time to rest," Ruen said.

"Arowall says if you're committed to fighting, you can stay here in safety for the day," said the guard. "Fight's tonight, after gateclose."

"Give him my gratitude," Ruen said. The guard nodded and climbed the ladder. His partner followed, leaving them alone in the cabin, which reeked of mildew and the general stink of the harbor. Icelin found she was growing used to the smell. She wrinkled her nose. Likely because she was soaked in it, she thought.

"You've been here before?" Icelin asked Ruen when they'd arranged themselves on the floor near the back of the cabin.

"I only come here when I need protection," Ruen said, "when I'm desperate enough. We're safe here for the day. You should both sleep." He looked at Icelin. "We'll need whatever spells you can muster if things don't go well tonight. I see no way Cerest could track us here, but I want to be prepared."

"You said one night, and then we'd renegotiate the price for your aid," Icelin said. "The cameo can't possibly cover all you're doing for us."

Ruen laughed. "That, my lady, is the most profound understatement I've yet heard you make."

Icelin bristled. "You don't need to throw it in my face. In fairness to me, I hardly expected to be menaced by the undead, ambushed by a dozen men, interrogated by an insane elf who knows more about my life than I do, which, considering my powers of recollection, is distressing in the extreme. Then you drag me underwater, half drown me, and where do we end up? Back in Mistshore, in the teeth of gods alone knows what type of men, with only a warm place to sleep as consolation." Her brow furrowed. "Come to think of it, that's not terribly awful under the circumstances."

"You talk a lot," Ruen said.

"Only when I'm under immediate threat," Icelin said. "Keeps me calm."

Ruen nodded politely—a ludicrous gesture, considering his previous attitude toward her. And he was letting the subject of his payment drop like it was nothing of concern.

"Why are you doing this?" she demanded. "In case you hadn't guessed, I have no idea where this little adventure is taking us. You'd be wise to get as far away from me as you can. I don't have any coin to pay you, now or later. The Watch will have secured all my great-uncle's possessions. We didn't have a great deal to start with. I have nothing to offer you at the end of this long tunnel."

There, she'd admitted it. He would abandon them now, Icelin was sure, but at least she'd offered him truth. She heard Sull, already snoring softly in the opposite corner. Gods, she hoped she could keep him safe. She would give anything if he would abandon her to her fate too.

Ruen looked at her for a long breath. Icelin couldn't guess what he was thinking. The man had no range of expressions she could measure. He wasn't cold, exactly. Removed, was more like it. His eyes curtained his emotions.

Ruen reached into her pack and pulled out the gold box. The feathery designs caught the dim light from above and sparkled.

"You can give me that," he said. "Keep the letters."

Icelin considered. "What about your friend's protection?" she asked.

Ruen's eyes hardened. "Arowall is not a friend. He won't give us aid unless I fight in the Cradle. You heard the guard. His champion's been on a streak for a tenday; his crowd will be getting restless for new blood. No matter how much they may like Bells, they love an upset even more."

"So if you beat his champion, you help his business," Icelin said. She was beginning to understand the stakes. "You have to win his aid, not buy it."

"Yes. If I can win, we can negotiate with Arowall to hide us all, maybe for days."

"Then . . . we are agreed?" Icelin could hardly believe it. "You'll stay with us?"

He kept his eyes on the box. "I'll stay with you."

"You have my deepest thanks," Icelin said.

Ruen slid the box away into her pack. "Keep it hidden for now. And don't thank me. We made a bargain, and I'll keep it."

And with that, he was removed again, aloof. For those few breaths, he'd seemed like a normal man. Now he was the scarecrow—a blank face and a floppy hat, which he seemed always to hold onto, no matter how many times they'd been dunked in the harbor.

Icelin leaned back against the hull. With her immediate concern assuaged, she could feel her body relax. The frightened energy that had kept her moving was beginning to ebb, and she could feel the effects of the wild magic on her body.

To say that she was more exhausted than she'd ever been in her life would be a vast understatement of what was happening inside her. She felt like a child coming around from a long illness—or descending into one.

Every time she cast a spell, her energy returned more slowly. She'd never felt that strain before, not during her most arduous lessons with her teacher. What would the implications be if she was forced to cast more spells?

Ruen was right. She needed sleep to recover as much strength as she could. Her eyes burned, but she couldn't drift off. Restless questions flitted through her mind: Cerest, Ruen, the letters, her family. She couldn't settle on which mystery baffled her most. To distract herself, she picked the easiest.

"Why did the guard recoil when you touched him?" she asked Ruen. She vividly remembered the shocked, frozen look on the man's face.

"Because I have cold hands," Ruen said. He shrugged dismissively.

"No, that was what you said about him."

"Did I?" Ruen leaned his head back and closed his eyes. "You have a good memory."

"I have a perfect memory," Icelin said.

"I know. Sull told me." He opened one eye. "Nothing to brag about there."

"Nothing to—"

No one has ever said that to me, Icelin thought. The observation was so simply, absurdly true, an echo of everything she'd ever tried to tell people, that she started to laugh. At first out loud, then under her breath, until tears streaked her cheeks.

The wave of grief shocked her with its intensity. She slid down the curving wall, curling into a tight ball. She covered her head with her hands, trying to be silent, unwilling to cry out her misery in front of her companions.

She heard Sull stir in his corner, but Ruen said, tersely, "Leave it. Go back to sleep."

He thinks if Sull comes over, that will be the end of me, Icelin thought. I'll be howling, and bring every damn guard above and below the water running to throw us off the ship. He was probably right.

Wiping her eyes, Icelin took out the box again and removed the stack of letters. She wanted to read them. Even if they weren't in Brant's hand, they were the closest link she had to her great-uncle.

She removed the ribbon and unfolded the topmost sheet, the one bearing her name.

> *Dear Granddaughter,*
> *I leave today on a new adventure. Faerûn calls to me, and I*
> *find I must answer her gentle whisper.*

Granddaughter. Icelin mouthed the word. The letters were from Elgreth. She read the rest of the letter, hastily scrawled in the same bold writing. There was no mention of spellscars or powerful abilities, just a farewell from an aging adventurer setting off on another journey.

Elgreth was my best friend.

Cerest's words haunted her. Did she really want to know the man who'd been friends with the monster that hunted her now?

She held the letter, staring at it but seeing Cerest's scarred face instead. She folded the parchment and laid it beside her with the other letters. They beckoned to her, silently, but her arms felt weighted to her sides. She couldn't focus her eyes. Sleep, so elusive, was claiming her at last.

You speak to me of adventure, Grandfather. Icelin sighed. I know the word. I've already had enough for one lifetime.

Ruen waited, alert in the dark hold. He watched the square of dull sunlight above him turn steel gray, and then the rain came with full force. The air in the hold grew chilled, and a puddle formed at the foot of the ladder. The rain did not abate until the sky began to darken and the gateclose bell was near to sounding. Through all the weather changes, his companions slept, the butcher snoring in intermittent gulps and wheezes.

Icelin lay on her side, twitching now and then in the throes of some dream. If not for those small movements, Ruen might have thought she was a resting corpse. Her face was pale, her cheeks etched with dark circles where exhaustion had worked on her.

Before the past night's ordeal, she might have been beautiful, in a fragile, glass-blown sort of way. Grief had certainly left its mark on her, but the unstable magic she wielded had drained her more than any emotional trauma. She was dangerous, to herself and those around her, anytime she used the Art.

Yet, what choice did she have, if she had any hope of survival?

With that thought in mind, Ruen took out the *sava* pawn and softly called Tesleena's name.

"Before you speak a word, I want you to relay your exact location and that of Icelin Tearn." Tesleena's voice was colder than the air in the hold. She sounded like she hadn't slept in days.

"Are we having a rough time, darling?" Ruen said, smiling to himself. He was going to enjoy this more than he'd thought.

"Is the girl safe?" Tesleena repeated, louder.

"She is," Ruen said. "I'm glad to see the Warden's ankle-nipper has her priorities intact, even if she is a liar."

"You haven't been deceived, Ruen. You were only told what you needed to know—that Icelin is wanted by the Watch—"

"And a fair number of other interested parties," Ruen interrupted, "as I discovered last night. Had I possessed this information beforehand, we might not have strayed so dangerously close to death. What business is this, Tesleena? If you won't speak truth, I'll wait for Tallmantle's word. I give you nothing until then."

There was a long pause, during which Ruen imagined he could hear Tesleena planting her pretty fist into a wall, assuming wizards did such things. Perhaps she blasted it with fire instead.

"Icelin is being pursued by an elf, Cerest Elenithil," Tesleena said finally. "I assume you've gathered that much?"

"Yes."

"He claims she stole property from him, but he has yet to appear before the Watch to give personal testimony against her. And now he has disappeared to Mistshore, searching for her. We have information that Icelin confided to a Watchman friend of hers that the elf had a personal grudge against her. I have men questioning Cerest's contacts in the city, but there's little information to be had about him. We've determined he was not born in Waterdeep, but he came to the city at a young age. His conduct in business is without fault, but the details of his private life are sketchy. He was the second or third son of a noble house, but he was not raised in a state of wealth or privilege. Nevertheless, he would have been significantly above Icelin in station. The only event which might link them happened five years ago, at a boardinghouse in Dock Ward."

"It wasn't the fire," Ruen said, before she could relate the story he'd overheard in the warehouse. "The elf wasn't scarred by Icelin's hand; he admitted as much. He wants her for another purpose."

Stunned silence met this pronouncement. "Has Cerest encountered the girl? You gave your word she was safe!"

"She is," Ruen said. "I can keep her away from Cerest, but I need to know how many men are after us."

"Ruen, by the gods, *bring her in* and the Watch will see to her safety. This is beyond your skill or caring. Why do you delay?"

"Perhaps you've turned me into a loyal Watch dog—officer—after all," Ruen said blithely. "She's safer with me, and she pays better. I'll be in touch when you have more information for me to work with."

He clenched the pawn in a fist until the magical connection died.

"What do you think?"

Daerovus Tallmantle pushed out of his chair and leaned over the desk. "I think you owe me new furniture."

Tesleena looked down at the desk. Her fingernails had left deep furrows in the wood. She waved a hand impatiently, and the marks smoothed out and disappeared.

"I'd wager Icelin Tearn wishes she had your control in magic, if not in temper," the Warden commented.

Tesleena nodded, but she didn't seem to be listening. "We'll track her from the warehouse. Her unstable Art will make her easy to find." The sorceress winced. "For Cerest, as well."

"All the more reason to step up our efforts." Daerovus took a sheet of parchment from his desk drawer and handed it to Tesleena. "Take this down, if you would. It's an order for a second, smaller patrol to join the first in Mistshore. These men will not be wearing Watch tabards."

"How will Ruen know them?" Tesleena asked.

"You heard him. Ruen has no intention of cooperating willingly with our search," the Warden said. "Since his release from the dungeons, he's been sullen but resigned to his role as an agent. Something changed last night. He's regained some of his old arrogance. He hasn't shown such spirit since the night we captured him." The Warden looked thoughtful. "Icelin Tearn has lit a fire in him. Time will tell if that will work to our advantage."

Tesleena sniffed. "I don't see how it could possibly be to the good. He was going to be our eyes in Mistshore. We should have known his defiance would win out over sense."

"He still might be of use," Daerovus said.

The outcome of Icelin Tearn's ordeal would be revealing in more ways than one, if everyone involved survived.

Ruen slid the *sava* pawn away in his shirt and checked to be sure Icelin was still asleep. After sleeping through the butcher's heavy snores, he was certain it would take a cannon blast to wake her.

He looked up at the hatch. The square of sunlight had disappeared. A sliver of moonlight spilled down the ladder in its place. He could hear bodies stirring above decks. They would be coming to ready him for the Cradle in another bell.

Automatically, he felt for his ring. He'd known the guards would confiscate it, but he still felt naked. Whatever else came of the fight, his body was going to hurt like unholy fire after it was over. He just hoped the old man wouldn't let him die.

The dream took her again.

She stood in the center of the ruined tower, looking straight up at the sun burning through a gap in the ceiling. Her skin tingled. The hair stood up on her arms. She didn't like this place. The shadows moved when she wasn't looking. Frightened whispers—the footsteps of folk who'd walked and died here a century ago—made it impossible to hear her own thoughts. She turned in a circle, searching for the gap in the wall, but something impeded her.

I am a child, Icelin thought. Her limbs would not move properly. She stumbled and fell, scraping her knees on rock.

She started to cry. Her knees hurt. The sun burned her neck. It was so hot in the tower. Why didn't someone come to pick her up, to take her away from this place?

"Icelin," said a feminine voice. She didn't recognize it, but it spoke with enough urgency to make her turn. Icelin tried again to stand and was suddenly knocked from her feet.

"Get her out!"

The shadows were shouting at her. It was too hot. Icelin looked up, and her body burst into flames.

CHAPTER ELEVEN

I CELIN AWOKE SHIVERING, BUT HER BODY POURED SWEAT. HER BODICE was saturated. She buried her head in her hands and waited for the dream fear to subside.

In the panic and grief of the night before, she'd almost forgotten the nightmare. After the boardinghouse fire, she'd been terrified of seeing the faces of the dead in her nightmares. But she only ever dreamt of the tower. It was a perversion of the tower Nelzun had created for her. She thought she'd left it behind when she'd left her great-uncle's shop, but the tower had followed her, to the warehouse and now here.

Drawing a slow breath, Icelin forced away the frightening images. Her heartbeat resumed its normal pace, and she drifted for a time, meditating, summoning the energy she would need to call her magic for another day. The words of the spells were there; she had no need to memorize them, but the power required concentration.

When she was finished, she opened her eyes and looked around, blinking in the darkness. Slowly, she recognized her surroundings. The ship's hold— their sanctuary for the day.

She longed to cover her head and sleep for days on end. The cold combined with the raw emptiness in her stomach forced her to a sitting position. Her hair, stiff from multiple dunkings in salt water, stood out in snarls all over her head. And the smell . . .

Icelin groaned. The smell was coming off her body.

Seeing she was awake, Sull ambled over to sit next to her. The butcher looked and smelled as unkempt as she.

"How do you feel?" he asked tentatively. His face was pale under his red hair.

"Food," Icelin said. She tried to run a hand through her hair and ended up getting her fingers stuck. Cursing a streak that would have made Brant blush, she yanked her hand free. "Food," she repeated, and smiled for Sull's benefit. "Succulent lamb's stew, to start, with fresh vegetables smothered in butter. Sharp cheese melted on bread slices. For the main course"—she scrunched up her face, pretending to give the matter grave consideration—"nothing whatsoever that includes fish." She waved a hand imperiously. "That's my order. Off with you."

Sull's deep chuckle filled the hold. "Ah, thank you, girl. I was worried you'd lost your good humor forever." He shot her a look of chagrin. "As to the food: the waterskins are fine, but the rations are soaked. I don't think they're fit to eat. But I found this next to me when I woke up."

He handed her a loaf of crusty bread. Icelin tore off a hunk and bit into it, expecting the worst. Surprisingly, the bread was flavorful and chewy inside. She took several more bites and a swig from her waterskin and immediately started to feel better.

"Where's Ruen?" she asked, noticing for the first time that the thief—monk, she reminded herself—was not in the hold.

"Don't know," Sull said, but I heard a lot of activity going on up there. Must be near fightin' time."

Icelin listened to the footsteps clattering above them. Sull was right. The voices were building into a dull roar. She wondered how many people would be present for the fight. Her earlier apprehension returned in full.

Ruen meant to win them protection by fighting in the Cradle. But for how long could they realistically hope to stay safe? Icelin had never met Ruen's contact, but already she didn't trust the man. If Cerest offered him coin enough, Icelin had a feeling he would betray them in a heartbeat.

"Sull," she said.

The butcher slanted her a look, his mouth puffed up with bread. The sight made Icelin smile and twisted her heart at the same time.

"If Ruen succeeds tonight, I want you to leave us. I trust Ruen to take care of me, and I don't want you in anymore danger on my behalf."

"Aw, don't go startin' that foolishness again." Sull wiped the crumbs from his mouth with an angry swipe. "Doesn't matter what that thief's done, you need me looking out for you, unless"—he hesitated, his face reddening—"unless you think I'm slowin' you down." He clenched his hands into fists. "I know I'm not much good in a fight."

"Sull, that's not what I—"

"I know it!" His face crumpled. He looked near tears. The sudden shift in mood caught Icelin completely off guard. "I know you're worried about me gettin' hurt on your account. It isn't fair—me strappin' myself to you, makin' you worry. Selfish is what it is."

"Selfish?" Icelin said incredulously. "You've risked your life over and over for me. I'm the one who's selfish and no good in a fight. Without you, Sull, I'd be lost." Icelin felt dangerously close to tears herself.

"But it isn't for you," Sull said, his voice barely audible. He dropped his head in his hands.

Feeling helpless, Icelin scooted closer to the big man and put her arm around his shoulders. "I don't understand," she said. "What do you mean, Sull? If not for me, why are you here?"

Sull sniffed loudly. He wiped his eyes but wouldn't look at her. "I love my shop," he said. "Always wanted one of my own, ever since I was a lad."

Guilt stabbed Icelin. "I'll get you back to your shop. I promise."

"No!" Sull roared. He jerked away from her as if he'd been stung. "Serves me right if the place burns to the ground. Let me finish, lass, I beg you."

Icelin nodded, staying silent.

"I love my shop," he continued, each word a trial for him. "In the early days, all the folk knew me. Once I got established in the neighborhood, I helped others just startin' out. Wasn't anything to it, I just liked 'em and wanted 'em to have the same chance I got. So I gave meat to the baker and the blacksmith, kept 'em fed over two winters so they would have coin to spare for their wares. I spent the summer helpin' Orlan Detrent put a roof over his cow pen. Hot as the Nine Hells, it was, but we laughed over a pitcher of ale afterwards."

"That's wonderful," Icelin said. "They were lucky to know you."

Sull's eyes filled with fresh misery. "Not so lucky. You put me too high in your heart, lass, and I don't deserve it. I made friends with a lot of folk, so when Darthol and his boys came to the neighborhood, they knew to come straight to me."

"Darthol?" Icelin hadn't heard the name in years. Darthol Herendon had conducted a brief but lucrative extortion operation in Blacklock Alley and other parts of South Ward. Icelin remembered Brant had insisted on escorting her everywhere she went during Darthol's brief "reign." Her great-uncle hadn't wanted her to cross paths with any of Darthol's men, though Icelin suspected he'd paid a substantial amount to ensure her safety. Fortunately, they'd been spared any lasting strife. Darthol's body had been found in a garbage heap one night. Folk thought he'd been stabbed to death by one of his own men.

"I didn't know you ever encountered him," Icelin said. "I'm sorry for it. That was a dark time for many of us."

"Darker than you know," Sull said. He wasn't crying now. He looked old and sad. "I was cleanin' out the shop one night. I like to work late, when the streets are uncluttered, but I was being quiet so not to rouse folk. They didn't hear me at first."

The words hurt him. Icelin squeezed his shoulder. "You don't have to tell me," she said.

But he went on. "I had the big wooden washtub outside the back door, couple of candles lit so I could see. My cleavers were all in the tub, needin' a good scrub. I'd just picked up the rag"—he mimicked the gesture, lost in his tale—"when they came around the side of the shop, draggin' old Orlan by his bare feet."

"Oh, Sull," Icelin gasped.

"He wasn't dead," Sull said, "least not then. Face was covered in blood and sort of mashed in, but his eyes were open. He stared at me the whole time they were beatin' him, beggin' with his eyes for help. Somehow, I was stuck. I couldn't get my arms out of that washtub. I had my hand on a knife, gods forgive me, and I couldn't raise it up out of the water." He looked at his shaking hands, seeing a weapon that wasn't there. "I could have planted it in that son of a whore's back before his boys were ever the wiser. Worst of it was, Darthol knew I was there all the time. He beat poor Orlan to death in front of me. He *knew* I didn't have the guts to stop him."

"You were frightened, and rightly so," Icelin said. "Even if you'd killed Darthol, his men would have slain you."

"I wasn't afraid," Sull said. "Not for my life, anyway. All I could think was that they'd take my shop. Everythin' I'd worked for—I didn't want to lose it." Finally, he looked at her, but his eyes were bleak, unfocused. "The years haven't changed me any. You'd think they would have, but they haven't. I'm still selfish. When you came into my shop, and those elves were after you, I wasn't really aidin' *you*. I'm not so noble. All I could see was Orlan's bloody face, the whites of his eyes bulgin' out when he died. Whenever I look at you, I see him. You have to let me stay with you, Icelin. I know it's askin' too much. My burden's nothin' to do with you. But if I leave you, I'm never going to see anythin' but Orlan's face."

He started to cry then in earnest. Icelin laid her head on his shoulder so he would not have to see her. They sat that way for a long time while the big man sobbed quietly. Above them, the voices rose and fell, but that world seemed a thousand miles away from the cramped ship's hold.

Icelin reached for Sull's hand and found it waiting for her. "Sull?"

"Yes, lass?" He sounded remote, drained.

"Please stay with me." Her voice shook. "I'm selfish too, and frightened. Will you stay with me, until it's all over?"

He sighed deeply. "I'll stay. Thank you, Icelin."

Icelin felt his big body relax slowly, the knotted muscles loosening. The misery was still there, but she could feel him burying it.

When she lifted her head, Ruen was coming down the ladder. Their eyes met for a breath, and Icelin knew, though she could not read his crimson gaze, that he'd heard every word of Sull's confession. She nodded minutely. He mirrored the gesture.

"Thank you for the bread," Icelin said. "I assume you left it for us?"

Ruen nodded. "I couldn't arrange a bath for you. Perhaps if I win the tournament. Something to hope for, eh?" He wrinkled his nose.

Icelin glowered at him, but Sull said, "Tournament? You mean you have to fight more than once?"

"I'm a new entrant," Ruen said. "I'll have at least three matches before I get to fight Bellaril—Bells." He picked up Icelin's cloak and pack. "Keep these close," he said, handing them to her. "They're ready for us."

No matter how intense her apprehension about the Cradle, Icelin was grateful to climb the ladder out of the oppressive ship's hold.

On the main deck, night had fallen. Stars canopied the harbor, and the remnants of the day's rain glimmered on the wet wood. Torches lined the deck, lending smoky illumination to a sight Icelin could not have imagined in her wildest fancies.

The Cradle perched on the water, bounded by a loose circle of four half-sunk ships. The vessels listed at various angles, half supporting each other, their masts crisscrossing in a vast web work of rigging and wood. Rope bridges hung suspended from the main masts, allowing foot traffic to flow between the four ships. Figures swarmed the bridges or climbed, monkey-like, on the rigging to find a better vantage point for the activity.

On each of the four ships, wooden benches were bolted in rows to the deck, creating a sort of graduated seating on the listing surfaces. These rough seats were already packed with people, and the unlucky few who couldn't find a bench were perched on the rails, their feet dangling above the water. All told, there must have been hundreds of people crowded on the ships.

In the center of the Cradle, water was allowed to flow freely in a sealed off pool. Wooden platforms, not unlike Ruen's raft, had been arranged at various points, so it was possible to cross from ship to ship without touching the water. Four guards arranged themselves on the outer fringes and took charge of distributing weapons.

Icelin watched a pair of men walk out onto the platforms. Both carried the same weapon: a spiked ball and chain. To her shock, they bore no shields and wore no armor. The crowd screamed and pounded their feet when the fighters faced each other and swung the chains like deadly pendulums in front of their bodies.

"Gods above," Sull said, shaking his head. "I'd never have believed such a sight if I hadn't seen it with my own eyes."

"The platforms are stained red," Icelin said, half to herself. "What happens if they fall in the water?"

"Nothing, if they can get out fast enough," Ruen said. "They stock the pool with blindfin, shark, eel, and whatever else they can find that's vicious enough."

Icelin flinched as the combatants leaped at each other. The spiked balls whistled through the air, thudding sickly into flesh. The crowd cheered wildly. Both men fell back, clutching gaping wounds to the leg and flank.

"The winner will bleed to death before he claims his prize," Icelin said.

Ruen shook his head. "He only has to stay on his feet. Once the victor is confirmed, Arowall authorizes the winner to receive healing."

"Where is Arowall now?" Icelin asked, leaning close so Ruen would hear her over the crowd.

"You won't see him until after the tournament," Ruen said. "He watches the matches from there." He pointed to the largest ship in the circle.

In the Cradle, the combatants were already tiring. The heavy weapons were difficult to maneuver under the best of circumstances. On the water they were clumsy and shook both men's balance. The taller of the two swung with both hands. His opponent dodged back but tripped on an uneven board. He went down on his knees at the edge of the platform.

Sensing victory, the man still on his feet leaped across to his opponent's platform. Frantically, the man on his knees tried to scramble away, but there was nowhere left to go but into the water. Hurling the heavy weapon at his opponent, the man dived into the water.

The crowd went crazy, piling against the rails to see if the man would be devoured by sharks.

His head popped up a few feet away, next to another platform. He hoisted himself up, and for a breath it looked like he would make it. But the taller opponent had been watching, biding his time.

As soon as the man's shoulders came out of the water, the taller opponent swung the ball, releasing it to fly across the water.

The ball impacted between his opponent's shoulder blades. Blood spurted, and the man lost his grip on the platform. Jerking, he sank into the water.

Icelin thought the wound hadn't been very deep, but then she saw the water churning, the flash of a gray fin.

"Gods," she said, "how could he leave him for the sharks?"

"It was a clever move," Ruen said. He watched the man intently. "He'd already taken a wound to the thigh. He couldn't jump from platform to platform, which is what his opponent was counting on. Essentially, he had one shot, and it turned out to be a good one."

"Do they always fight to the death?" Icelin asked.

"No," Ruen said. "You have the opportunity to yield, but many don't. The winner's purse is too tempting, and the crowd doesn't like a coward."

A guard approached their group. "I'm to escort you down," he said to Ruen.

Ruen turned to follow the guard down a ladder. "Stay at the rail where I can see you," he told Icelin and Sull. "This will likely take all night."

"Good luck," Sull said doubtfully. He stood shoulder to shoulder with Icelin at the rail. Both were too tense for conversation.

There was no formal announcement when the fighters came into the Cradle—no names, no mention of how many victories each entrant had won. The crowd cheered their favorites and jeered others, according to no pattern Icelin could see.

She waited for the crowd's reaction when Ruen entered the Cradle. Would they favor him?

After what seemed like an eternity, she saw his old leather hat bob into view as he came up a short flight of stairs to the platform on the far side of the Cradle. Hushed murmurs ran through the spectators when they caught sight of him. He removed his hat and handed it to one of the guards standing at the bottom of the steps. When he returned to the platform, he raised both hands in the air, like a conductor readying his minstrels. He bowed low—Icelin could have sworn he winked at her as he straightened.

The crowd erupted in wild applause.

"Seems they like 'im," Sull said. "We should take that as a good sign."

Icelin nodded absently. She was waiting to see Ruen's opponent.

" 'E's a stick, this one," wheezed a man standing at Icelin's elbow. "Maltreth's gonna break him, you watch now."

"Oh, really," Icelin said, her temper prickling. "The crowd doesn't share your opinion."

"Ha!" The man slapped the rail. "Don't jingle your coins on this bunch. They're only cheering the poor bastard 'cause they know what's coming. Crowd loves to see the little ones get squished. Borbus!" he shouted across the deck. A pudgy man with skin the color of prunes looked up. "What're the odds on the skinny boy?"

"Ten to one, Sheems," the man shouted back. "There's a side bet says the sharks get to cut their teeth on 'im."

"You want in on that?" Sheems said, turning back to Icelin.

Icelin didn't bother to reply. She was watching Ruen stride confidently out to his starting platform. He waved to the roaring crowd, a lopsided grin stretched across his normally expressionless face. Icelin had never seen him look that pleased with himself.

"Gods give me strength," she murmured. "Tell me he's just playing the crowd, Sull. If he doesn't keep his wits, he'll get his head bit off out there."

"Among other parts of 'im," Sull said, pointing to the other side of the Cradle.

A man stepped away from the guards and climbed the stairs. He was not as big as Icelin had feared, but his musculature far outstripped Ruen's wiry frame. He carried a long, barb-tailed whip in his right hand. On his left, he wore a pair of polished brass knuckles.

The guard holding Ruen's hat stepped forward, raising his sword to silence the crowd. He then turned to Ruen and said something that Icelin and the watching crowd couldn't hear.

Icelin saw Ruen shake his head. The guard's face scrunched up in confusion, and he said something else, more emphatically this time. Ruen shook his head again. The same lopsided, complacent grin was still plastered to his face.

The crowd was starting to get restless, stamping their feet and whistling. This seemed to galvanize the guard, who waved a hand at Ruen as if to say, "good luck," and walked back down the stairs.

Maltreth, the man with the whip, assumed a crouched stance on his platform. Ruen stood, weaponless, with his arms loose at his sides.

"He was tryin' to get Ruen to take a weapon," Sull said, nodding to where the guard stood at the base of the stairs. A whip dangled from his right wrist. "Guess Ruen didn't need it," Sull said uncertainly.

The guard raised his sword again, and an ear-piercing whistle sounded from somewhere above their heads. It must have been the starting whistle, for Ruen's opponent immediately charged forward, leaping from his platform to the one floating adjacent. He swung his whip and snapped it above the water.

Shouts and wild applause erupted from the crowd.

"He's a peacock," Icelin said. "Strutting around like that's a waste of energy." She switched her attention to Ruen, but the man still hadn't moved.

He stood, his arms at his sides, watching Maltreth with a bored expression. "Oh, that's perfect," she murmured.

"What?" Sull said. Icelin noticed he was gripping the rail as hard as she. "What's he doing?"

"Baiting him," Icelin said, "drawing him in. But he can't keep it up for long. The whip has reach. The barbs will tear him open."

Maltreth jumped again, and this time when the whip cracked, the edge of Ruen's platform splintered.

"That's done it. He'll have to move now," Sull said. "What's he waiting for?"

"I don't know. Oh, gods, he wouldn't go that far, would he?"

"What?"

"Move. *Move!*" Icelin shouted, but the crowd drowned out her voice.

Crack.

"Maltreth takes the first bite!" Sheems yelled gleefully from next to her.

Sull cursed. Icelin gripped his hand. A dark stain soaked through Ruen's sleeve. The barbs tangled in cloth and flesh.

Ruen staggered back, clutching his injured arm. He slid to his knees amid thunderous applause from the crowd. They might as well have been foaming at the mouth, Icelin thought.

Maltreth grinned at Ruen. He let the whip sway in his hands, swinging it back and forth like a skipping rope. The force was not enough to dislodge the barbs, but the whip pulled and tore new gashes in Ruen's skin.

He's waiting for Ruen to make a move so he can pull the whip out, Icelin thought. No matter what Ruen did, the wound would tear open when the barbs came out. Why had he let himself be hit? Icelin had seen Ruen fight. He could have dodged the blow easily.

She saw Maltreth take a step forward, then another, and suddenly Icelin wasn't paying attention to Ruen anymore. She was focused on Maltreth's shuffling steps, and remembering the way Ruen had dodged Cerest's attacks in the warehouse. Maltreth was far less graceful than the elf. His body was painfully readable.

"It can't be that easy," Icelin said.

"What?" Sull repeated, with a look of anxious annoyance. "If you're going to map out the battle, lass, at least let me in on the outcome."

"Watch," Icelin commanded.

Maltreth shuffled another step and jerked the whip. Ruen howled in pain. Icelin couldn't hear the sound, but she saw his face twist in agony. The whip hadn't come out of his wound. He pivoted toward her, and Icelin saw what she'd been hoping to see. She grabbed Sull and pointed.

Ruen wasn't holding his wound, which continued to bleed freely. He was clutching the slack end of the whip. Maltreth couldn't see it. He gave in to the cheering crowd and turned his face up, smiling in smug satisfaction. As soon as his attention left Ruen, the monk yanked the slack end of the whip with all his strength.

Maltreth's body teetered, his eyes bulging as the whip left his hands. He stumbled to the edge of the platform, but instead of pitching into the water, he jumped, using his forward motion to get him across the water.

He landed on Ruen's platform. The monk had already steadied himself in anticipation of the extra weight. Ruen tore the barbs out of his arm and threw the whip across the Cradle. Blood dripped copiously from his wound, but he ignored it and turned his attention completely to Maltreth.

Now he's within striking distance, Icelin thought. No more reach weapons to deal with. For Ruen, the match had not truly begun until now.

Maltreth, for his part, looked furious. Ruen had humiliated him in front of the mob, and now he was down to one weapon.

Raising his fists so Ruen could not help but see the brass knuckles, Maltreth came in low, aiming for a quick jab to Ruen's ribs.

Ruen dodged, grabbed the man's wrist and twisted it away from his body. The crowd collectively winced and sat back in their seats. Their reaction might have been comical had Maltreth's arm not been dangling at an odd angle to his side. He staggered back but kept his other fist raised to defend himself.

The crowd waited, tense, for Ruen to finish him off. Maltreth was outclassed in a fistfight with the monk and everyone, including Maltreth, knew it.

Ruen kept his distance and spoke to Maltreth. They couldn't hear the words, but Icelin could see the guard at the base of the stairs preparing to draw his sword.

"He's offering him the chance to give it up," Sheems said. He'd been subdued ever since Ruen turned the fight around. "Crowd won't like that."

He was right. Jeers and booing came down from the crowd. People on the rope bridges stamped their feet, spitting at Ruen and sending dust and debris raining over the crowd.

Egged on by the violence of the outburst, Maltreth shook his head and spat at Ruen's feet. He charged, swinging his functioning fist for Ruen's head.

Twisting, Ruen caught Maltreth around the mid-section in a series of quick punches Icelin had trouble following with her eyes. When he ceased, Maltreth folded, collapsing to the platform. He was unconscious before his head hit the wood.

And just like that, it was over. The guard drew his blade and pointed at Ruen. The crowd cheered the newcomer's victory.

So it went throughout the night. Icelin and Sull stood at the rail, watching combatant after combatant enter the ring. Ruen fought three more times, and each time he took no weapon, but managed to disarm his opponent and end the fight with his fists. Sometimes it took longer, and he collected wounds over various parts of his body. He never showed it in his face, but Icelin could tell the injuries were taking their toll. Ruen wasn't moving as fast, and his punches were easier to track.

"He's going to be worn out for the final match," Icelin said. "How many damn fighters are left? It must be almost dawn."

"They're down to it now," Sull said. "Ruen's got where he needs to be. I heard Sheems say the winner's purse is a big one, on account of how long Bellaril's been champion." He leaned heavily against the rail, looking as anxious as she felt. "She won't give it up easy. Still, he's got this far. If he can hold out, he'll get healin' at the end of the match."

Icelin wondered what this Bellaril would look like. As reigning champion, she was only required to defend her title against the winner of the tournament, which meant she would be rested and, more importantly, she'd probably been watching the entire tournament to get a measure of her opponent.

Icelin saw Ruen climb back to the platform. He was still moving slowly, but his muscles were loose. He looked as relaxed as he had during the first match.

At the other end of the Cradle, the guards parted to admit a stout figure with a wild mane of strawberry blonde hair.

Bellaril was a heavyset dwarven woman with ruddy skin and large blue eyes. She wore plain brown breeches and a white vest cross-stitched with leather cord. Her face was as devoid of expression as Ruen's when she ventured out to her platform. She nodded to Ruen, and he returned the gesture.

Instead of cheering Bellaril, the spectators stamped their feet, and several of them produced small hand bells, waving them furiously above their heads. The din was shrill and loud enough to drown out Waterdeep's own great bells.

The guard raised his sword for quiet and approached the combatants. He spoke to each of them in turn. Bellaril answered his query regarding weapons with a shake of her head.

"Fist to fist, then," Sull said when the guard left the platform without distributing weapons.

This did not reassure Icelin. As soon as the guard was down the stairs, Bellaril darted forward, jumping nimbly from her platform to Ruen's, landing as far from him as she possibly could in the small space. The dwarf looked up, meeting Ruen's gaze and smiling.

CHAPTER TWELVE

WATCHMAN TARVIN SURVEYED THE VIBRANT EMBERS AND ASH CLOUDS of the Hearth fire with one hand raised to shield his eyes against the wall of heat. It reminded him briefly of the burned warehouse he'd seen on the shore—or the smoking skeleton of a boardinghouse.

The metal basin from which the Hearth flames ascended had steep sides, but the bottom of the structure sat several feet below the walkway, allowing easy access.

The setup was ingeniously designed and protected the surrounding structures from damage quite well. The basin's inner shell had long ago turned an oily black color. The smells of cooking fish, meat, and the occasional spice were everywhere, but did nothing to mitigate the nauseating odor of the bodies gathered around the fire for warmth or sustenance.

There were no benches near the outside of the basin. People sat on the crude walkways built around the pit, cradling children in their laps or leading the elderly by the arm.

A pack of young girls, the youngest no more than five years old, was selling cooking spits for a copper a foot. Tarvin bought two from one of the older girls and shooed the rest away.

He leaned close to the child's ear when he paid her and asked in a confidential whisper if she'd seen a particular young woman walking by the Hearth.

"Black hair, white skin like a ghost's," he said, and he saw the girl's eyes widen. "Not a real ghost," he said quickly. "There's a man with her—tall, with red hair all over his head. Have you seen anyone like that passing this way?"

The girl shook her head. Tarvin gave her the copper coins and sent her off. He scanned the crowd a second time, his eyes coming to rest on a woman sitting alone near the edge of the fire. She was wrapped in a thin, dirty cloak, trying to blend in with the crowd.

In need of some amusement, Tarvin crouched next to the woman. He smiled when she averted her face. She had straight, drab brown hair and a tiny hooked scar on the bridge of her nose.

"Can I buy you dinner, pretty lass?" He held up his newly acquired spits, twirling them like batons.

The woman looked at him, but she didn't smile. "What are you doing here?" she demanded. "This is my territory."

"Lovely Deelia, I'd never infringe on your authority. I was just doing some independent scouting," Tarvin said. He made a vague gesture to the outer rim wreckages.

"You'd better hope she's not out there," Deelia said. "That's gang territory."

"Yes, it would be a shame if they dragged her off, had their fun, and didn't leave any pieces for us to find," Tarvin drawled.

Deelia shot him a look, but she didn't comment. Tarvin knew she didn't want to be out here anymore than he did. But the Warden had spoken, and the Watch had answered the Wolfhound's call. Icelin Tearn would be found and hauled in from Mistshore on the end of a leash if need be.

"Foolish to come down here," Deelia said. "This place'll eat her alive. What was she thinking?"

"She's afraid of the wolves," Tarvin said. "Us," he clarified when Deelia only stared at him.

The Watchwoman shook her head and turned her attention back to scanning the crowd for Icelin. Tarvin wanted to tell her not to waste her time.

The crowd huddled closest to the bright flames was mostly made up of women and children. Tarvin had thought this would be the first place she'd run to, with the late season darkness running cold and the wind colder still on the harbor. If the gangs hadn't already caught up to her, she'd need light, warmth, and especially food, if she hadn't had time to gather any. But so far, his search had come up empty.

"Did you know Therondol?" Tarvin asked abruptly.

"No," Deelia said. If she was surprised by the change in topic, she didn't show it. "I came to the Watch after his time."

"That's right. I'd forgotten how many years he's been gone. You'd have liked him, though. Steady, but he had eyes that could cut, you know? You could never lie to the man. I don't know why that made me like him, but it did. He was smarter than all the men in his patrol, but he never looked down on anyone."

"He sounds just like the Warden," Deelia said.

"Better than," Tarvin said. "But all that's gone, so no use dwelling on it, eh?"

Deelia shrugged. "Why are you out here, Tarvin? The Warden didn't send you. You should be on patrol in South Ward."

"What does it matter? We're all looking for the same woman, as if there wasn't a whole city of more worthy folk to mind."

"You'll be reprimanded," Deelia said.

"Be worth it, if I get to bring her in."

"Good luck to you, then," Deelia said. "Now either leave me, or stop talking."

Tarvin didn't get a chance to reply. A pair of women sat down directly in front of them, too close to their personal space to allow any private conversation.

Tarvin exchanged a glance with Deelia. After a breath, one of the women half turned to face them. Her left eye was swollen shut. Blood crusted the seam.

"Are you Serbith?" she whispered, addressing Deelia.

"Yes," Tarvin said, ignoring Deelia's sharp poke to his ribs. He loved to irritate her.

"Who are you, then?" The other woman turned. She had an open sore on her lip.

"I'm her bodyguard," Tarvin said without hesitation.

"Wasn't part of the deal, her bringin' another pair of eyes," the woman said. As she spoke, Tarvin found himself unable to look at anything except the ugly sore. "Never mind then, no hard feelings. I brought the goods. Let's see your coin."

"My bodyguard has it," Deelia said sweetly.

Tarvin smiled. "Of course. But I want to inspect the goods before I pay a copper."

"You hear that, Mabs? He wants to count fingers and toes," the woman with the swollen eye said.

"Oh, he's got 'em all, no mistake there." Mabs laughed and unwound a thin wrap from her shoulders.

Deelia hissed out a breath and a curse, but Tarvin kept his composure.

The baby was naked and new, probably only a handful of tendays old. His lips, fingers, and toes were blue from the cold. He should have been wailing his discomfort for all Faerûn to hear, but he was too underfed. He didn't have the strength to cry.

"How long has he been off his mother's milk?" Deelia said. Her mouth was set in a grim line.

"Never been on it," Mabs said. "It was the mother's fourth, so her teat's all dried up. But he's the best of the lot. Lord Theycairn's gettin' his coin's worth, don't you worry."

Tarvin stiffened. Lord Theycairn was a nobleman recently widowed. His wife had died in childbirth, but the family insisted the babe, a boy, had survived. No one had yet seen the child in public.

Deelia said abruptly, "I am satisfied." She removed her cloak and handed it to Mabs. "Wrap the child in this, please." She waited until it was done, then went on, "If Lord Theycairn should happen to have interest in . . . other children—"

"Lookin' to stock his larder with heirs, is he?" Mabs chortled. "We can do that. The other girls and us, we got just as many go in the harbor as not, on account of how we can't feed and clothe 'em all. But we could save back the best of 'em for you to inspect."

"That would be acceptable," Deelia said. "Could you remain here? Someone will be coming with your coin."

"Thought you said your bodyguard had it?" Mabs looked at them suspiciously.

"Lord Theycairn sent us to ensure you kept your end of the bargain," Deelia said quickly. "Serbith has your coin and will come to collect the babe. She knows nothing of us."

Mabs scowled, but she finally nodded. Her suspicion wouldn't keep her from taking the promised coin.

Deelia took Tarvin's arm and hauled him to his feet. When they were out of earshot, Tarvin said, "What was that about? I'll wager this Serbith is Lord Theycairn's washerwoman, or some such. If we'd waited, we could have caught her buying babies in Mistshore."

Deelia looked pale and angry. "And risk that baby being one of the discarded if the deal went badly? Better that one becomes Theycairn's heir. I'll report to the Warden when we see him next. We have to see about getting some food down to the prostitutes, at least those on the shore. You're right, there are more important things going on in Mistshore tonight than Icelin Tearn." She shivered. "I hate this place. Babies in the harbor—godsdamn bloody mutilated part of the city. That's all it is. A leech."

"Nice to see you again, Morleth," Bellaril said.

Ruen inclined his head. "It's been a long time, Bells."

The dwarf's expression darkened. "You know better than to use nicknames with me, Morleth. That's going to cost you."

They were circling each other now. "You don't like being called 'Bells'?" Ruen said. "I'd have thought you would have embraced the nickname. Your fans certainly have. Or are they plants by your master, to drum up support for his champion?"

He lunged, aiming a fist at the dwarf's face. The blow glanced lightly off her jaw, and Bellaril was already ducking under his guard for a jab to his midsection. Ruen fell forward into a roll. He tried to snag Bellaril's ankle as he passed, but she jumped out of the way.

Ruen sprang to his feet, his arms out in defense, but the dwarf kept her distance. He could feel the burn in his ribs where she'd jabbed him. Quick punches, just enough force to give pain. She knew exactly where and how hard to hit him. That was the damnable part of this fight.

"I did warn you," the dwarf said. "What is it you need from him this time, Morleth? Protection? Coin? Whatever it is, it won't be worth it." She moved in again, throwing a quick succession of punches, all aimed low where he had trouble defending. Ruen took another blow to the flank, but he caught the dwarf a heavy blow to the shoulder that had her backing off.

"I need a place to hide," Ruen said. He took the reprieve to catch his breath. The air burned against his cracked ribs. "There're two others with me. I assume he's seen them?"

"A bird and a butcher," Bellaril said. "Not the sort of company you generally keep. He'd love to hear the tale behind it."

"I'll happily throw the fight and tell it to him," Ruen said, "but I think he wants me to win."

The dwarf's swings faltered. Ruen got in another blow, a numbing shot to her arm. He pressed forward, but Bellaril kicked, catching his knee.

Ripples of pain shot up Ruen's leg. He wobbled, gritting his teeth to keep from collapsing to the platform. Breathing fast, he stepped back, unable to press his momentary advantage.

"Give this up, Morleth," the dwarf said. She massaged the feeling back into her arm while he seethed in pain. "It doesn't matter if Arowall wants me to lose. The title is mine. I'm not letting you or him take it from me."

"If you think so little of my chances, come ahead," Ruen said, opening his arms.

The dwarf shook her head. "I'm not to be baited like that, Morleth. I was giving you a chance." She dodged to the side when his fist came in, hooking an elbow around his arm. Securing her hold, she squeezed.

Ruen felt the bones snap. His mind momentarily blanked, but he kept his feet, largely by holding onto the solid dwarf. When he looked into her face, he could see she'd put very little effort into the attack.

"I'm the only person in the Cradle who knows how much pain you're in," she whispered. "I know how many of your bones are broken, and if I wanted to, I could drop you to the floor or the sharks. You can't win without your ring, and you know it." Her eyes softened. "One last chance, Morleth. Give this up."

"I have a better idea," Ruen said. He licked blood from his lips. The ribs must be broken, not cracked, he thought. "How about a side bet of our own?"

"You're mad," Bellaril said sadly. "What is it you want? Why are you fighting for those two?"

In response, Ruen jerked the dwarf close. He wrapped the palms of both his bare hands around hers. Bellaril's eyes widened in shock. She had not seen him remove his gloves. They lay discarded on the platform.

Ruen did not attempt to strike her. He waited a breath for her to see the blue light, to realize what he was doing, then he whispered against her ear. When she drew back, her expression was unreadable.

"Fine," she said, breaking his hold. "It's a bet. I'll try not to kill you, Ruen Morleth, but I make no promises."

"Fair enough." Ruen set his feet. He didn't trust his speed anymore. He would have to work on the defensive.

She struck at him again, hitting his jaw, his collarbone, his shoulder. Each time her fist glanced off a bone, Ruen felt himself come apart a little. She left him his legs. Aside from the blow to his knees, he could remain upright and maneuver enough to dodge the worst of her attacks. It wouldn't last. She would bring him down soon.

He took another blow to the shoulder, but this time he snagged her arm before she could dance back. Immediately, she began punching with the other, struggling to free herself. Ruen absorbed the blows, letting his weight shift against her. She stumbled, off balance by the sheer dead weight of him.

Ruen brought his good knee up, planting it in her stomach. She gasped and bent double, but he struck again before she could fold. Wildly, she clawed at him, but he kept pressing down with his weight, until they were both crouched on the platform.

He forced his knee across her throat, pinning her. Choking, she tried to sit up, but he kept her down. Her reach wasn't great enough to get around his long legs. She could keep punching him in the gut, but Ruen was beyond the pain.

The dwarf snaked an arm up, grabbing his leg. She twisted viciously, no longer concerned with his balance. Ruen bit his lip; blood filled his mouth. The Cradle wavered, the faces of the crowd blurring into indistinct smudges. He kept Bellaril down with his ruined leg. She hissed and sputtered and cursed him.

"You'll never . . . stand," she said. "Your legs are ruined." Her voice was nothing more than a whisper. He'd cut off her airway. If he could hold on long enough, she would lose consciousness.

"Maybe you are the better fighter," he said, as her body went limp. "The only thing that separates us is where we keep our pain."

He looked up. The crowd was on its feet, screaming and stamping at the turn the match had taken. Icelin and Sull were still watching from across the Cradle.

Directly behind him, the guards were clustered around a figure coming up the stairs. Long, meticulously trimmed gray hair fell across his shoulders. His face was pale, his skin wrinkled but not yet taken heavily by age. He might have been a handsome figure, but his eyes were yellowish, his jaw tight, as if some hidden strain were working on his mind.

The man stopped ten paces from Ruen. His gaze moved from the crowd to Bellaril's unconscious body and finally to Ruen's face. He raised his hand, and the Cradle noise died instantly.

"You know the rules, Morleth," he said, his rich voice pitched loud enough for the crowd to hear. "Stand and declare your victory. *Stand*, or forfeit."

He's playing the scene for all it's worth. A part of Ruen had to admire the man's gall. Whatever the outcome, there'd not be an empty seat in the Cradle after tonight.

Ruen slid his knee off Bellaril's prone body. He felt the grating of bone against bone, the pull of muscles and tissue twisting in ways nature had never intended. He shivered. Cold sweat stood out on his skin. The blood was still hot in his mouth.

Best to do it all at once, Ruen thought. It was the only way he would be able to gather the strength. One quick thrust to his feet, and the bastard would have to give him healing. The crowd demanded the rules be obeyed. Even the master of the Cradle couldn't deny the crowd.

Ruen closed his eyes and breathed. "Keep the pain locked away," he murmured. He pushed it all—the broken bones, the torn muscles—to a far corner of his mind, a box whose lid he could fasten tight and push away from conscious examination.

He waited until the pain was safely contained, then forced himself to stand.

Icelin covered her ears against Ruen's scream. She knew the cry was involuntary. He would probably never remember uttering such a sound, but she would forever remember the terrible, animal whimper that followed the scream. She'd known his wounds were severe, but now she was terrified he might have killed himself just by climbing to his feet.

He swayed. Icelin dug her nails into the rail, willing him to stay upright. His head lolled to one side; blood dripped in tiny rubies from his lips. But he stood, facing the tight-lipped man and his retinue of guards.

"I stand," she heard him say into the silence of the Cradle.

Arowall didn't react. He stood, watching Ruen with amused curiosity. A smile played at his lips.

"No," Icelin hissed. She grabbed Sull's arm. "No, *no!* He's going to wait until Ruen falls."

Sull cursed. He grabbed Sheems by the back of the neck and hauled him aside. "He can't do that! Tell me he can't."

Sheems cowered in the face of the butcher's livid expression. "Rules aren't clear on how long he has to stand. Depends on the master's mood. Makes for a good show—" He caught himself when Sull bared his teeth.

Icelin reached for her neck pouch, frantically searching its contents for a spell focus.

Sull grabbed her shoulder. "Lass, I appreciate the sentiment, but that's a good route to getting us killed."

"He's going to fall, Sull. Where in the Nine Hells is that wood!" She searched her memory to unearth the spell. "It's not an attack," she assured him. "He just needs to stay upright."

Magic for simple tasks. She could hear her teacher's words. *"The spells you'll use most often in the early days are spells to imitate simple tasks. Don't let the ease of their use make you complacent. A servant, unseen, should never replace your own two hands."*

A servant unseen. An invisible hand to keep him standing that would escape the master's notice. Icelin's fingers closed on the focus in her pouch. She didn't bother to pull it out but chanted the spell, her will centered on Ruen.

"Go. Hold him," she chanted, mixing the plea with the arcane phrases.

A swirl of brilliant gray mist shot from her fingertips. The loop of magic descended from the deck of the ship to the platform, taking on shape, if not substance, as it went. The crowd shouted in warning and awe.

"Gods-cursed magic!" Icelin clutched her head, feeling the familiar pain behind her eyes. Sull tried to support her, but she shook him off. She had to see how the wild spell would manifest, and control the damage if she could.

The gray mist coalesced into a human shape. The unseen servant was now a woman in a flowing dress, her colorless hair drifting around her face. Arms swathed in ghostly lace encircled Ruen's body from behind. The spectral lady stepped forward, taking Ruen's weight against her chest.

"I know that woman," Icelin said, aware that the crowd and the master of the Cradle had turned to look at her in a great collective. She drew her hand out of her neck pouch. The focus she held was not a piece of wood, as she'd thought when she cast the spell. It was the cameo she'd been holding for Ruen. The woman's face gazed serenely back at her from the portrait—and from the platform behind Ruen.

Arowall regarded Icelin with interest. "You're building a fine and dangerous reputation in Mistshore, my lady," he called out to her. "I daresay some of the poor folk will be glad when you leave us."

Icelin heard the threat behind the words. "Believe me, sir, I will be equally relieved to escape this place, and I apologize sincerely for trespassing on your hospitality." She pointed to Ruen. "But I need that man alive, and I wonder if you will have it so."

There were titters from the crowd. Arowall looked up sharply, gauging the reactions. "I adhere to the rules of the Cradle," he said. "Ruen Morleth has not fallen." He flicked a glance to Ruen, who was watching the exchange with half-closed eyes. "But if your spell fails, will he keep his feet? That is the issue at hand. Your interference is grounds for his immediate disqualification."

"No," Ruen spoke up, his voice thick. "She interfered without my consent." He looked at Icelin, but his eyes were unfocused. Icelin wondered if he truly saw her at all. "Drop the spell," he said.

"You'll die," Icelin said flatly. "He'll feed you to the sharks."

Angry shouts arose from the crowd, surprising all three of them. The people stamped their feet. Refuse showered the Cradle, and the rope bridges swayed above their heads. Arowall's guards formed a protective wall behind him.

"The people have spoken," Arowall said when the noise finally died away. "If Ruen Morleth stands, he will be declared champion. Is this acceptable, my lady?"

"Yes," Ruen answered for her. Icelin shot him a withering look. "Drop the spell. Now."

Icelin raised a hand. She could feel the crowd cringing back in their seats, but the gray lady did not explode into fire like the spell in the warehouse. She melted away, leaving Ruen alone on his feet.

Icelin leaned forward, her hands on the rail in a death grip. Ruen faltered, steadied himself, and stood still. His posture was straight. All eyes in the Cradle watched him.

"Our new champion," Arowall said.

The crowd bellowed its approval. The wooden ships shook in their ancient moorings. Icelin thought the whole of Mistshore must be hearing the tumult.

The master turned and dropped a steel vial on the platform ten feet away from Ruen. "Accept your healing, champion." He ascended the gangplank to the largest ship and disappeared below deck.

Icelin vaulted the rail, landing at the edge of the Cradle. She ran out onto the nearest platform, crossing to Ruen's in three quick jumps, just as the monk started to fall.

She caught him at the waist and guided him to the ground. She heard Sull lumbering behind her, and a breath later he put the healing vial in her hand.

"Don't move him," Icelin said when Sull would have picked Ruen up. "We'll do it here." She pressed the vial to his bloody lips.

Ruen opened his eyes and drank. As the healing liquid poured down his throat, he sat up and moved away from her. "You made a spectacle of yourself again," he said, but he didn't sound angry. "Hundreds of people know your face now, to say nothing of your troublesome nature."

"Yes, but thank the gods for them. At least Arowall respects the crowd." Icelin put the vial aside when Ruen finished drinking. "He must be furious with me. He'll give us nothing now, I suppose."

Ruen laughed. His eyes looked clearer, more brown than red, as the healing potion took effect. "He's not angry, or he won't be for long. You gave the crowd a show they'll be talking about for a tenday. Even if he wanted to kill us, the man knows how to play his part. I'm the declared champion. The crowd expects to see us again. Come to think of it, your interference might have been the best part of the whole spectacle." He winced and fell silent.

"What is it?" Icelin asked. "Are you still in pain?"

"The bones are reknitting," Ruen said. "Stings."

Icelin ran her hands over his sleeve and across his torso. "You're right, they're mending," she said. "Gods above, she must have broken every rib. How could she hit so hard?"

"Don't let her height fool you." Ruen retrieved his gloves, took what was left of the healing draught, and poured it down Bellaril's throat. The dwarf was already stirring. When the liquid hit her tongue, she spluttered and opened her eyes. "She's much stronger than she looks."

Bellaril sat up and looked around at the crowd filtering off the ships. Icelin thought she must be looking for her master. She didn't realize he'd left her unconscious on the Cradle floor.

"Suppose I owe you congratulations," Bellaril said, offering a hand to Ruen.

"It was a good fight," Ruen said. "You're still too merciful, Bells. You should have taken my legs first."

"I won't make the same mistake twice," the dwarf assured him.

"Merciful?" Icelin said. "She broke practically every bone in your body."

"He knew the rules," Bellaril said. "No magic allowed in the Cradle."

Icelin decided not to tell the dwarf about her miscast spell. "Why would Ruen need magic to protect himself?"

"You didn't tell her." Bellaril snickered, her eyes alight with humor. "Well, that's interesting, isn't it?"

Ruen glared at her. "The ring I wear is magical, as you've already seen," he said to Icelin. "I told you it amplifies whatever it touches. I can shift that focus, a little, according to my will."

"He means his bones are sticks," Bellaril said. "Can't you tell by how thin he is? Without the ring to strengthen the bones, he's going to get pulped in any fight."

"Arowall knew that going in, didn't he?" Icelin said. "He knew how hard it would be for you to win."

Ruen shrugged. "He can't fix his own game. Like Bellaril said, there's no magic allowed in the Cradle. That's the rule."

"But he made you stand longer than was needed," Icelin said fiercely. "He wanted you to fall."

"Maybe, maybe not. He can't break 'em, but sometimes Arowall tries to bend the rules," Bellaril said. She stood. "He's a twisted creature, make no mistake."

"Why do you serve such a man?" Sull spoke up.

The dwarf looked at the butcher for the first time. "He pays me well. I don't want for anything, and I like the crowd's attention. Might be I'm a bit twisted myself." She shrugged.

"We should be going," Ruen said. "He'll be waiting for us. Coming, Bells?"

Bellaril's face hardened. "Don't have a choice, do I? You won the side bet."

"What did you win?" Sull wanted to know. They climbed the gangplank and joined an escort of guards.

Ruen smiled cryptically. "You'll see."

CHAPTER THIRTEEN

UNLIKE THE SPARSE SHIP'S CABIN THEY'D SLEPT IN, AROWALL'S QUARTERS were carpeted with blue rugs that looked as if they'd been meticulously cleaned. The furniture was dark wood; a desk and matching chairs were arranged in one corner of the room. Arowall sat at the desk. A guard stood behind him.

In the middle space, a couch and another small table sat against the hull. Fist-sized globes of magical light floated along the ceiling. The portholes had been blacked over. There was no seeing in or out of the ship.

Icelin could sense the tingle of enchantments protecting the hull. This room must be where the master's more interesting audiences take place, she thought.

Their escort indicated the chairs for Icelin and Ruen, then returned above.

"You fought well, Bellaril," Arowall said, waving a dismissive hand at the dwarf. He looked at Ruen. "I'm pleased you survived, Morleth." He reached into his desk drawer and pulled out a familiar ring. He handed it to Ruen. "Yours, with my thanks."

Ruen took the ring. He slid it on his finger and covered it with the glove. "These are the people I wanted you to meet," he said. "Icelin you already know—"

"Of course," Arowall said. His gave Sull one disinterested glance before turning his full attention to Icelin. "My pleasure, Icelin." He held out a hand.

Reluctantly, Icelin took it, surprised at how warm his hand was. She'd expected a cold, clammy grip. He held her hand for a breath and released it.

"Well, Icelin, your champion has won in the Cradle," Arowall said. "You've earned the right to ask for what you need. If it is in my power, I will provide it."

Icelin exchanged a glance with Ruen. He nodded.

"I would request protection," she said, "for myself and my two companions. "We are hunted by the Watch and a party of elves and men. You've given us a place to rest, but we need concealment during the day. If you hide us, we will leave at nightfall and not trouble you again."

Arowall inclined his head. "Easily done. I have a place where you could be concealed quite well"—he leaned forward—"if you've the stomach for it."

Icelin met his calculating gaze. "What place do you speak of, sir?"

"He calls it the Isle," Ruen spoke up. "A half-sunk ship behind the Cradle."

"I appropriated it some years ago to take care of a minor inconvenience to my operation," Arowall explained.

"What sort of inconvenience?" Icelin asked, knowing instinctively she would not like the answer.

"Mistshore is a unique entity in Waterdeep," Arowall said. "We welcome all folk, no matter how desperate or murderous, so long as they've coin to spend. Unfortunately, being such a large enterprise, the Cradle attracts its share of . . . lesser beings."

"The diseased, the starving, the scarred," Ruen said. "The beggar folk, shunned even among the damned."

"We used to dispose of them—discreetly," Arowall said. "It was a mercy, I assure you. Their conditions were affronts to nature; whitewasting and darkrot, godscurse and worse. A few here or there were never missed."

"I wonder why you stopped," Icelin said sarcastically. The man's callousness knew no bounds.

"Some days I wonder that myself," Arowall said.

"Don't let him lie to you," Ruen said. "He knew that mass murders would not go unnoticed for long, no matter what sort of folk were dying. He devised a surprisingly merciful solution."

"I took them in," Arowall said. "They live on the Isle now, in relative comfort and, more importantly, out of sight of normal folk."

"No one goes there," Ruen said. "They're afraid of catching something."

"I know I would be," Sull muttered.

"Don't worry," Ruen said. "If he intends to send us there, he will provide us with disguises and spell protection against the sicknesses."

"Absolutely," Arowall said. "I would not send you off unprepared. You will have your disguises, which I daresay will continue to serve you after you've left us."

"Then we are agreed," Icelin said. She stood and extended a hand, but there was no warmth in her eyes. "We thank you for your hospitality."

He smiled and leaned forward to kiss her fingers. "You are not easily unsettled, my dear," he said. "I admire your nerve."

He looked past her shoulder, his brow furrowing in consternation. "Bellaril, you may go. I have no further need of you."

The dwarf shifted uncomfortably. "There is a matter I must discuss with you, Master. It concerns Ruen Morleth, and a wager we made during the fight."

Her master raised a brow. "I have the distinct impression I'm not going to like this, Bellaril."

"It was my doing," Ruen said. "I made a side bet with Bellaril. If I won the match, she promised to accompany us for three nights—to whatever destination Icelin names—as a bodyguard."

"And you agreed?" Icelin said, looking sharply at the dwarf.

"I did," Bellaril said. "No offense meant, lady, but at the time I believed I could win the fight."

"You discovered differently," Arowall said. He kept his voice even, but Icelin saw his cheeks flood with color. "Your arrogance will be the death of you yet."

The dwarf said nothing, only bowed her head.

"I will honor the wager," Arowall said, rising and coming around the desk. He towered over Bellaril. "Take her, but don't be gone long, little one," he said softly "And don't displease me again."

"Yes, Master," Bellaril said.

Icelin turned to leave, but Arowall held up a hand. "Morleth, a word with you in private, if you please?"

Icelin started to speak, but Ruen shot her a quelling glance. "I'll be along soon," he told her.

"If you say so." Icelin nodded to Arowall and climbed the ladder. She wondered if she would spend the rest of her life passing from the belly of one strange ship to another.

.:◠:.

"Well," Ruen said to Arowall when they were alone. "What is she?"

"Your friend is a human girl and nothing more," Arowall said. "I detected no concealment magics, nor modifications to erase her memory. No wizard, in the Watch's employ or any other, has tampered with her."

"Why is she so powerful, then?" Ruen said. "Is it the spellplague?"

"You already know the answer to that," Arowall said, waving an impatient hand. "She is spellscarred, just like you; and like you, her powers are debilitating. But her condition is perhaps more serious."

"In what way?" Ruen demanded.

"I can sense the spellplague as clearly as you smell the rot coming off the harbor. I have met few individuals living with so strong a taint in them. To put the matter bluntly, you and that girl are rotting with spellscars; but while you can live with brittle bones, Icelin is dying."

"What?"

"Gods' breath, haven't you touched her yourself?" Arowall took in his expression. "If you did, you'd doubtless find her frigid."

Ruen lowered himself into a chair, in the way a cat sinks into a wary crouch. "Why is she dying? Explain."

"I am only speculating, of course, but I believe that whatever ability Icelin gained as a result of her brush with the spellplague is interfering with her magic. Her spells go wild more often than they succeed. Am I correct?"

"You are," Ruen said.

"Then, in effect, every time she casts a spell, her body wages war on itself—the spellscar fighting the ordered forces of magic. Her scar must be a powerful talent, to cause such a chaotic reaction. What is it, exactly, that Icelin can do?"

"That's for her to say." Ruen stood. Tension hummed in his blood. His body must be readjusting to the ring, he thought. He held up his hand. "Is there any magic like this ring that can calm the forces in her, make the spellscar sleep?"

Arowall smiled. "That's why I like you, Morleth. You think of it as a living thing, just as I do. It surrounds the city, weaving into the wood and stone. Folk think they're safe here, but they breathe the plague every day. They just don't realize it. You and I are the only ones who know how doomed the world is."

"You've spent too long in the harbor rot," Ruen said, "and you're wasting my time. If you can't help me—"

"There is no magic that can stave off the spellplague forever," Arowall snapped. "You know that as well as anyone."

"She's stronger than she looks," Ruen said. He turned away from Arowall. "Stronger than you."

Arowall laughed. "Yet I would not trade places with her for the world. My men will bring your disguises. Bring them and Bellaril with you when you return to the Cradle to fight for me. I'll give you a tenday before I hold another tournament. A tenday, Morleth. You've tried my patience more than any other man and lived. Don't displease me again."

Ruen nodded. A question burned on his tongue, but he did not ask it. He climbed the ladder and left the ship, but the thought haunted him.

How long does she have? He'd have to touch her—the bare skin of her hands—to know for sure. He could touch other parts of her and get impressions, but they wouldn't be as strong.

He'd never known why it had to be so specific a touch. The monks of his order believed the hands were the links that most strongly connected mortals to the world. A warrior's hands could take a life; a midwife's could bring a babe into the world. Ki manifested through the hands.

It didn't matter. He would never touch her. His hands—his whole body—were abhorrences, mistakes of nature. The gods alone were supposed to know how long a being had left to live, not mortals.

Especially not a cutpurse from Mistshore.

.:⌢:.

"Everywhere we go has a name," Sull said. "Mistshore, the Hearth, Whalebone Court; now it's the Isle." He gazed at the latest jumbled wreck of a ship. This one, a cog, had been hollowed out, the decking torn up to form one high-walled chamber at the bottom of the ship.

"There's a ladder here," Bellaril said, stepping onto a short gangplank off the raised dock. She pointed to a rickety ladder laid against the inside of the ship. It descended into the cog's belly, disappearing from sight. "That's our way down."

"We're at the nether end of Waterdeep, yet they still get around to namin' everythin' here," Sull babbled on. "Unsettlin', that's what it is." He shot a quick glance at the ladder. "Unnatural."

Ruen handed Sull a rolled bundle of cloth. "Put it on," he said. "You'll feel better once you're protected. Arowall said even the stench is blunted by the magic."

"Why does he have these?" Icelin said, taking her own bundle and unrolling it. A simple cloak of layered rags, it hardly looked like it could stop a swift breeze, let alone be magical.

"He's never told me, but I suspect he uses them for spying," Bellaril said. "His own man poses as a beggar, then the master sends him wandering around the Cradle. Folk try to ignore him. They don't see him as a real person, with ears and a tongue that can tell what he's seen."

"So after he's done spyin', the guards grab him and throw him on the Isle, just like a staged play," Sull said, shaking his head. "Everyone serves a purpose. Tidy little business he keeps. Too bad someone hasn't killed him." He ignored Bellaril's narrowed eyes.

"He's offered us shelter," Icelin said, trying to head off the confrontation, "such as it is." She donned her cloak and felt a warm wave as the magic flowed over her. "How do I look—any worse than before?"

Sull turned green in the face. He looked like he might gag. "You could say that, lass. I wouldn't go searchin' for any mirrors if I were you."

"Some gallant gentleman you are," Icelin said. "Let's see yours, then."

Ruen and Sull and Bellaril donned their cloaks together. Icelin knew instantly when the magic had taken hold.

"That's . . . effective," was all she could think to say.

Open sores blossomed from Bellaril's and Sull's faces. Yellowish fluid seeped from the bulging skin. Sull's red hair turned gray and lifeless, and his skin had a distinctly wasted tinge. Ruen looked no better. His red eyes sank into his skull, and his already gaunt face looked skeletal. Icelin could see the crooked blue veins just below the surface of his skin.

"No one will recognize us," Icelin said. And indeed, she did feel better. Cerest's gaze would never linger on creatures like this. "We'll be safe, even in broad daylight."

"If we're so well disguised, why do we need to stay here at all?" Sull said. "We can walk about Mistshore as we wish."

"No," Ruen said. "They'll start searching magically for such disguises, if they haven't already. I don't want to test the limits of the cloaks in daylight. At night, perhaps. Besides, we need to sleep sometime, and I'd like to be as protected as possible."

And I'll be able to read grandfather's letters, Icelin thought. It was fast approaching dawn. She had until nightfall to find some clue as to the nature of Elgreth's relationship with Cerest. She had no idea if such knowledge would aid her in defeating the elf, but she had to know the truth. She had to know if Elgreth had been Cerest's friend.

"Dawn is coming," she said, putting her hands on the ladder rungs. "Let's get this over with."

She descended the ladder. Shapes moved below her—brown humps that stumbled and pushed each other out of the way in the small space. The farther down they went, the more she could distinguish the babble of voices.

"All at one end, you know better than to crowd the stage, Hatsolm, you old fool."

"I want to be able to hear the music this time. I'm a full ten feet back. You mind your own seat; it's wide enough to demand your full attention."

"I'm not fat, you imbecile!"

The voices died when they reached the bottom of the ladder. Icelin could see dozens of rag-cloaked figures angling for a space at the far end of the ship's belly. They all stopped what they were doing when Icelin's foot touched the ground.

A tense silence followed. Icelin stepped forward, raising a scarred hand in greeting. "W-well met," she said.

"Well met." A man with a crooked back ambled over to take her hand.

It was like greeting a skeleton. His fingers had no meat. Real sores peppered his arms and bare legs. Icelin swallowed hard and tried not to pull her hand away.

"You look like you could use a rest, friend," the man said eagerly. "I'm Hatsolm, and I won't bother you with the rest of the names for now, just you remember mine. Taken together, we're the Drawn Cloaks. Lovely and mysterious-sounding, isn't it? I came up with the name myself. Come and sit over here. We've some food and drink to spare."

Icelin let herself be led over to the others. Hands patted her on the back and guided her to a seat on the ground. Immediately, a cup of water was pressed into her hand, and a bowl of some unidentifiable substance appeared in front of her. Similar treatment greeted Ruen, Sull, and Bellaril.

Icelin sniffed the food and looked at Sull. Her mouth was already watering, but she wanted to be sure the meat wouldn't kill her. Sull sniffed his own bowl and nodded slightly. Icelin scooped up a handful of the stewlike substance and ate.

She tasted stringy meat and hard potatoes, liberally seasoned with grease that pooled at the bottom of her bowl. Not a king's feast, by any standard, but it was more substantial fare than her body had taken in days, and did much to clear her head and soothe the raw churning in her belly. She'd been so hungry, her hands shook when she brought the food to her mouth. She looked at Hatsolm, unable to speak, grateful tears standing in her eyes.

"Yes sir, that's what they all say." He chuckled. "Now then. Where do you come from?"

"We . . . don't hail from Waterdeep," Icelin said quickly. "We came in on a caravan. Our village was dying. Everyone was leaving, so we thought we'd come here, to start anew."

Hatsolm nodded gravely. "Aye, that's the story among many of us. And here we are"—he waved his rag-draped arms expansively—"in Waterdeep mighty, a city that looks precious little like a city and smells a bit like the rotting bowels of a once-fine ship. Alas, the bards, how cruelly they exaggerate!"

There was a smattering of applause and rude gestures from the beggar folk. Shouts of, "Save it for the real performers!" had Hatsolm throwing up his hands and laughing.

"Eat hearty, all of you," he said, and he waddled off to find his own bowl. "We're fed and clothed and grateful, and the troupe's comin' in. What more could kings ask for?"

"The troupe?" Icelin said. But Hatsolm was gone, and the others were immersed in their own conversations. The temporary distraction of their arrival had passed; the people seemed to be waiting for something. They kept shooting glances at the bow of the ship, but Icelin saw nothing except a stack of rotting crates. Rats weaved among the loose boards.

"Surely Arowall doesn't provide food *and* entertainment for 'em," Sull said. "Not when he'd just as soon be killin' 'em."

They looked to Ruen, but the monk shrugged. "They seem in high spirits, which is more than I expected. Perhaps one of them is a musician."

Hatsolm came around again to collect their bowls. Icelin tugged on his rag cloak. "Are they waiting to see a show?" she asked politely.

He grinned. "Aye, lass, the best in Waterdeep, though we're the only folk knows it. Sit you all right here and see what there is to see." He patted her arm and settled back on the ground.

A crow flew over their heads, descending into the ship to pluck a rat from one of the crates. The bird was large and sleek, with oily black eyes that watched the beggars even as it snapped the rat's neck. Icelin cringed.

The sun had risen outside the ship, but a shadow fell across Icelin and the rest of the crowd. She looked up; more crows were flying in an uneven formation, clustering close and snapping at each other as they dived down into the belly of the ship.

Instinctively, Icelin ducked. The birds flew over her head and landed on the rotting crates. The air filled with restless caws, but a hushed silence had fallen over the beggar folk. Every face, including Hatsolm's, was tuned in rapturous attention to the crows.

"What's going on?" Icelin whispered to Ruen.

"Halt your lips, you ungrateful lot!" shouted a voice that made Icelin jump.

A crow's head stretched, its black feathers shrinking into pale flesh. The bird stood up on two spindly legs, which lengthened and shed more feathers. The creature shook itself, and was suddenly not a bird any longer, but a boy, a boy grown from the body of a crow. The ungainly creature hopped up on one of the crates and surveyed the crowd.

"Are we the show this night or not?" the boy demanded. He looked to be about eleven years old—human—with greasy black hair tucked under a brown cap. A crow's feather rested behind his ear like a quill. His eyes shifted around like restless insects, never settling on one object. "Answer me, dogs! Are we the entertainers?"

"Ho!" A chorus erupted from the beggar folk. For a breath, Icelin thought she was back in the Cradle.

"They're new arrivals, Kaelin, not true Drawn Cloaks," said Hatsolm. "Give them a chance."

The boy regarded Icelin's group with interest, his gaze fixing on each of them in turn. "They're false fronts," he said.

Ruen glanced up sharply. He'd avoided eye contact with the boy until that instant. "We're refugees, the same as any person here," he said. "What of you? What do you have to say for yourselves?"

The boy hopped from crate to crate, his arms spread. "Do you hear, friends? He wants to know who we are."

The crows flapped their wings in a grim chorus, and suddenly the air was full of feathers. When the black shades fell away, a dozen men and women stood where the crows had been.

Icelin gasped. The crates were gone, transformed into a wide, foot-high stage that stretched from the port bow to the starboard. The boy pranced from one end to the other, pulling lit torches from a bag at his hip. He placed them in sconces at the edges of the stage. Their fiery brilliance lit up the suddenly shadowed hold. It was as if all the sunlight had been sucked from the ship, replaced by torches that gave off light but no heat.

"They can't be real," Icelin whispered to Ruen. "It's wizardry. Illusion."

"Complex magic that can transfigure and interact by itself, all for a crowd of beggars?" Ruen said. "No one would take such trouble."

"Then what are they?" Sull asked.

It was Hatsolm who answered. "Ghosts," he said.

CHAPTER FOURTEEN

A WOMAN STRODE TO THE CENTER OF THE STAGE AND PULLED A LUTE from her back. She began to play a lively tune for a pair of jugglers that somersaulted onto the stage. They tossed a dizzying handful of colored balls into the air and caught them before they gained their feet. Hatsolm laughed and clapped. The beggars were enraptured.

"They're such a motley troupe," Icelin said. "Shouldn't they be haunting a playhouse?"

"That's the charm of it," Hatsolm said. He leaned closer so his voice wouldn't carry to the stage. "They've never said, but I think the whole group was lost in a shipwreck. I'll wager they're chained to it still, so they seek out the audience that's closest. Before we came, they said they performed for the crows. After we arrived, they took the shape of the crows and performed for us. Isn't that lovely?"

"They sound friendlier than the sea wraiths, but are they dangerous?" Icelin asked.

"Not so long as you fix your attention on them and keep your tongue between your teeth," Hatsolm said pointedly. "They don't like to be interrupted."

"Of course." Icelin gave up and fell silent. She sat back against the hull and watched the boy, Kaelin, flitting through the crowd. He straightened a cloak here, shushed an errant tongue there, and teased an old woman who called him her boy. He seemed excessively fond of touching everyone. Icelin didn't know if they could feel him, but all the faces turned up eagerly at his approach.

The jugglers bowed and ran offstage, leaving behind a trail of balls that burst into sparkling fireworks. When the light spots faded from Icelin's eyes, the lute player was back, changing her tune to something mournful. It took Icelin a breath to recognize the tune.

> *The last falling twilight*
> *shines gold on the mountain.*
> *Give me eyes for the darkness,*
> *take me home, take me home.*

Icelin's heart stuttered in her chest. It was the same song she used to sing for Brant. The woman on stage looked directly at her while she strummed the lute.

"What's wrong?" Ruen asked. He reached out but stopped short of touching her with his gloved hand.

"Nothing," Icelin said, "I'm cold." She wrapped her arms around herself.

Ruen continued to watch her intently. Icelin kept her eyes forward, but she couldn't look at the woman's face. The song was painful enough. She stared at the bard's feet and tried to blank her mind.

She felt a weight across her shoulders. She looked up, off balance as Ruen pulled her against his side. His arm, hidden under the cloak, was draped across her shoulders. He was staring straight ahead.

"Ruen," she said, fighting a smile, "your arm seems to have fallen on me in a suspicious gesture of comfort."

"Is that so?" He still wouldn't look at her. "I suppose your virtue is distressed by this turn of events?"

"Terribly. I believe I will expire from shock."

"Better than expiring from the cold. Why is the song bothering you?"

"Brant, my great-uncle, loved this song," Icelin said. She let the words in. The lute player's voice enveloped her like a warm blanket covered in needles.

"It's a sad song," Ruen said. "He's lost in the wilderness. Does he ever find his way home?"

"The song doesn't tell," Icelin said. "What do you think?"

"I think a bard should say what she means. Otherwise what's the point of the show?"

"What's the *point?*" Kaelin shouted incredulously from right behind them. The lute player's song ground to a halt.

Icelin sucked in a breath. Kaelin's hand came down on her shoulder; it was ice cold and strangely invasive, as if he had put his hand inside her skin. She could tell by the lack of color in Ruen's face that he'd had no idea the boy had been behind then.

Kaelin patted Ruen on the back before the monk could flinch away. "The point, he wants to know. He wants the full story of the boy lost in the wilderness." Kaelin's eyes sparkled. "But will he want it told, after all's done?"

He looked at Ruen expectantly. Ruen shrugged. "Tell your tale. You're the bards, and it's no difference to me."

"Truly, then, I have your permission?" Kaelin bent in a half-bow, so that his face was close to Ruen's.

"Truly," the monk said through gritted teeth. "Be gone."

"How wonderful," Kaelin said. "It will be a fine tale. Clear the stage! Places!"

The lute player vanished. She reappeared a breath later, without her lute and wearing a black cloak. She flipped her hood over her face and joined the rest of the troupe assembling at the back of the stage. They were all dressed identically, their clothes and features covered by the cloaks.

Kaelin jumped onto the stage, taking his place at the front of the assembly. "Who will play the lead?" he asked. He put his hand theatrically to his ear to hear the response of the crowd.

"Kaelin!" they cried on cue.

"Yes, and don't you forget it," Kaelin said. "Tonight, I will be playing the part of the boy lost in the wilderness, the boy named Ruen Morleth." He swept an arm up, and suddenly he was swathed in black too.

Ruen sat forward, his jaw muscles rigid. "What are they doing?" he said.

Hatsolm answered. "They're going to tell your story," he said eagerly. "You're lucky to be chosen. Most newcomers never get picked until they've been here at least a season."

"How do they know what to say?" Icelin asked, as Ruen lost more color. "They know nothing about us."

"Silence before a performance! We know all we need, just by touch," Kaelin said from the stage. His voice sounded deeper, older. He swept off the cloak. It dissolved into a flurry of crows that flew out over the crowd. The stage transformed in the birds' wake.

The bow of the boat was now a forest glade, draped in dense green ferns. A small, stagnant pond dominated the scene, its watery arms wrapped around the exposed roots of an oak that crawled up the hull.

Icelin's eyes blurred at the sudden appearance of the illusion. She knew it wasn't real, yet she swore she could smell the moss clinging to the pond stones. Unseen, a sparrow chirped its shrill song. Wind rustled in the wild grasses.

"Not natural," Bellaril said. She swiped a hand across her nose, as if she could smell the green too. "Magic can't mimic life, not like that."

"Ah, but death can mimic life. The dead remember." Kaelin's voice echoed from the heart of the glade, though they could not see him. His voice still sounded strange.

Two cloaked figures, male and female by their shape, came from opposite ends of the glade to stand in front of the pond. They faced each other. Only visible were the skin of their hands and bare feet.

"Where is my son," the woman cried, "my foolish, fanciful boy, who runs through the forest like a wild animal?"

"He likes to run," hissed the man. "Loves to run away and worry his mother. What a terrible boy; he thinks the village is not good enough for him. Poor, foolish boy."

"That's not true," Ruen murmured, but only Icelin could hear him above the cloaked woman's wailing.

"Where are you, Ruen!" With her slender arm extended to the forest, the woman dropped to her knees as a blue light fountained from within the green pond. The light cast the ferns and the cloaked figures in glowing relief. The woman shouted, "He is doomed!"

She disappeared. The man crouched to address the audience in a stage whisper.

"But does the boy know why he is doomed? Did his mother never warn him of what lurks in the forest? Poor, poor mother. Poor, ignorant son."

The blue light faded, and the man vanished, his cloaked form revealing a small figure sitting by the pond, his back to the audience. Lazily, he reclined on his elbows and tossed a fishing line into the water. Somewhere, a bird called, and the boy turned his head to stare at the audience.

Icelin felt Ruen stiffen next to her. She made to put her hand on his arm, but he moved away, closer to the stage.

Icelin looked at the boy. It took her a moment to realize that it was not Kaelin sitting there, but an older boy. He lacked Kaelin's mischievous air and had an overly serious demeanor, his mouth twisted in an introspective frown.

His hair was dark, with brambles and grass clinging to its wild strands. But his eyes . . . they were common brown, yet so familiar.

Icelin looked from Ruen to the boy and back again. In her mind she filled in the progression of years—the widening jaw, the added height and musculature of manhood. Ruen was in his early thirties, the boy only thirteen or fourteen, but Icelin could see it. They were not so different, except for the eyes.

The boy was Ruen.

Icelin watched the young Ruen strip down to the waist and wade out into the pond. Up to his elbows in the green muck, he took swipes at the water, coming up with a bright green frog. He put it back in the water and watched it swim.

When the blue light came back, the boy didn't see it at first. He was too absorbed in watching a dragonfly glide in dizzying circles over the water. Its wings touched the edge of the blue light. There was a flash, and the dragonfly disappeared, vaporized by the magic surge.

Seeing the light, the boy waded to the spot, his hand outstretched.

"Don't do it," Icelin said. "Don't touch it, you'll be killed!" Hatsolm and the others were looking at her strangely, but she ignored them. She looked at the adult Ruen. His body was still tight, but he watched the scene with a kind of detached resignation.

The boy stepped into deeper water. The light wrapped around him, flowing up his legs and chest until he had to squeeze his eyes shut against the brightness. Panicked, he tried to back away, but he lost his balance and fell, his head going under the water.

The beggars gasped. Hatsolm murmured, "He's lost now. The plague'll rot his mind."

Icelin knew better. She waited, her hands clutching her skirt.

The boy's head burst from the water, and he was screaming, clutching his face, and thrashing while he tried desperately to find the shore. He crawled onto the bank and collapsed in a snarl of cattails. Their brown heads quivered above him.

The blue light continued to glow, but Icelin could see the pond's surface bubbling. The floating plants and moss shriveled up and turned black, their essences consumed by the spellplague. Soon, the water itself began to recede, pulling away from the bank and leaving behind a jagged shelf of claylike soil.

The boy rolled onto his back, his eyes staring vacantly at the crater where the pond had been. Streaks of blood ran down his cheeks. He climbed unsteadily to his feet and ran blindly into the green glade, away from the empty crater.

He stumbled and fell against the oak tree. There was a loud, sickening crack. The boy screamed and clutched his arm. He stumbled and ran on.

The boy vanished, the glade melted from green to brown, and suddenly a small parody of a village square grew from the ship's hull. The tallest buildings stood to the port and starboard side. Each adjacent building was smaller than these, making the village appear to recede down a long tunnel.

An old woman hobbled across the dusty path down the center of the village, passing in front of a thatched house with no windows. In the open doorway, a sullen boy crouched, playing with the rocks at his feet. A dirty linen bandage covered his left eye. The other was red and swollen. He blinked rapidly when the wind kicked up.

That same wind yanked the old woman's shawl from across her shoulders. The scrap of green fabric tumbled through the dust and tangled with the boy's dirty feet.

Wearing an irritated expression, the boy tore the shawl away and started to hurl it across the square, but he stopped when he saw the old woman. They watched each other—the shawl dangling from the boy's hand—each unsure what to do.

Slowly, the old woman walked to the doorway and stood over the boy. When she stretched out her hand, he put the shawl in it and started to back away, but she caught his hand in both of hers.

"I am so sorry about your eyes, boy," she said. "My sight is failing me, just as yours is. Someday soon, we both of us will have to help each other."

"I'm not going blind," the boy cried. "I don't need any help! Let go—your hands hurt." The boy struggled to loose his hand, but the old woman clutched him tighter.

"It's all right to be scared," she said. "It won't be so bad."

"You're cold," the boy whimpered. His hand had turned blue in the woman's grip. "Your hands are too cold. Get away from me!"

He shoved her. She dropped his hand and fell in the hard dirt. Her cry of pain brought more figures running from the neighboring buildings. The boy ran inside his house, screaming, "Mother!"

The old woman's shawl drifted away on the wind. Icelin's eyes were still following the patch of green when the scene changed again.

This time it was the smoky interior of one of the thatched cottages. The old woman lay on a bed below a dark window. Candlelight illuminated her sunken features. She was clearly dead.

Kaelin's black-cloaked figures stood over the bed, talking in hushed whispers.

"They say he touched her, the day before she died. His hands were red and raw, like he'd been frostbitten. Frostbitten in the middle of Flamerule!"

"I say he made it happen," a female voice whispered. "The spellplague wormed through his fingers and killed poor Megwem. Any of us could be next. Don't let him touch you. He's got death in his hands!"

The black cloaks melted, and the scene changed again. Another cottage, a dirty kitchen, and the boy now sitting on the floor in front of a fire pit. A woman sat on a chair behind him. She had gray hair and bony arms. She cut herbs in quick little chopping motions on a board. Every few breaths, she would look up at the boy. Her eyes were shadowed.

"Where did you go to play today?" Her voice was strained. "I told you not to stray out of sight of the house."

"You mean out of your sight," the boy said without looking at her.

The board clattered to the floor. The woman yanked the boy to his feet by his belt. "You will not defy your mother, do you hear? If they find out you've touched anyone else—"

"I didn't kill Megwem!" He reached up to wrench her hand away, but she released him before he could touch her.

"You're just the same. You think I'm plague-touched!" he shouted.

"Darling, that's not true, I only—"

"She was already dying." Tears ran down the boy's face. "She was going to die anyway. I could feel it." He looked at his hands. They were still swollen. "She was so cold. How could she live like that?"

His shoulders shook. His mother turned him around and wrapped her arms around his waist. She stood behind him, rocking him slowly. The boy continued to sob, but eventually he quieted, soothed by his mother's arms.

Arms which were very careful not to touch his bare skin. Icelin could see the fear in her eyes, the fear she tried to hide from the boy.

The cottage vanished, whisking away the boy and his mother. In their place, Kaelin reappeared on top of a rotting crate. He held a rat comfortably in his lap. The rest of the troupe was gone.

"Well played!" The beggars were on their feet, applauding and whistling as enthusiastically as the crowd at the Cradle. Icelin could only sit and marvel at how quickly the illusion had come and gone. How fast a boy's life could change.

Kaelin slid off the crate, letting the rat run free. He walked over to stand in front of Icelin.

"Did you enjoy the show, false front?" he asked, his eyes alight.

Icelin shook her head. "You should have asked his permission. That wasn't right."

"Oh, but I did ask. He wanted to hear the tale of the boy lost in the wilderness. You should be grateful. He would never have told you himself."

"You still had no right."

"Ah well, then you have my deepest apologies," the boy said. He didn't sound the least bit abashed. "Perhaps I should tell him your tale, to even the ground between you."

"I have no secrets left from any of my friends," Icelin said. "You don't scare me."

Kaelin leaned down. "What about the secrets you're keeping from yourself?" he said, his words for her ears alone. "The tower where you've hidden them all?"

Icelin felt a chill. "I'm not the only one with secrets," she said unsteadily. "You are not truly a boy, are you? You are spirits imitating flesh."

"Of course we are," Kaelin said, sniffing as if he'd just been insulted. "But I remember what a child is, and so do they," he said, nodding at the beggars. "Everyone knows the best liars are children, and the best story-tellers are liars. I am what I am, in service to my craft."

"So all that," Icelin said, waving to where the imaginary glade had been, "that was a lie?"

"To the senses, it was," Kaelin said. "As for the story itself—ask him."

Icelin blinked, and suddenly a sleek crow was sitting on her knee. The bird cawed once, loudly, and took flight. Icelin watched it until it disappeared beyond the wrecked ship.

The crowd of beggars broke up, each going to separate nooks of the ship to sleep or talk.

"We should all be resting," Bellaril said. She stood with Sull off to one side, where the beggars wouldn't hear.

"You two sleep," Icelin said. "Ruen and I will keep watch. I'll wake you in a couple of hours."

"Why should it be you?" Sull said. "You both look exhausted."

"We are," Icelin said. She looked at Ruen, who was staring at the crates and rats. He hadn't said a word. "Yet neither of us will sleep."

A quiet figure crouched in the shadows of two crates and gazed down on the beggar folk. He watched them settle in after their strange audience had concluded.

Imagine, watching a cluster of crows and rats for entertainment. Tarvin shook his head. His job had shown him some strange things, but this was a story for tavern talk if he'd ever heard one.

He stood up and faced the guard who'd come bearing a load of food: bread, dried meat, and a bushel basket of nearly rotting fruit.

"A hardy feast," he said, eyeing the fare. "I trust your master never neglects to bring the food?"

"None have died due to his neglect," the guard said. "Did you find what you sought? My master will require word of your departure."

"He doesn't like having me here," Tarvin said. "Well, there's some satisfaction in that. Tell him I'm leaving directly. I didn't find what I was looking for."

"A waif of a girl, wandering Mistshore; she's likely dead," the guard said.

"You think so?" Tarvin said. "I hope you're right."

The guard looked surprised. "I thought your orders were to bring her in alive?"

"Oh, I'm quite clear on my orders. My wishes are another matter." He crossed his arms. "I have little care whether Icelin Tearn lives or dies in Mistshore. She belongs here with the rest of the outcasts, as far as I'm concerned."

"Well then, I wish you good fortune in your diligent search," the guard said dryly. He pushed past Tarvin and began tying rope to the handles of the baskets.

"Are you judging me," Tarvin said, "when you're tossing food to the diseased with gloved hands and sweating because you don't want to get too close?" The guard didn't respond. Tarvin grabbed his arm and spun him around. "Answer me, wretch!"

The guard shrugged his arm off and put a hand to his sword hilt. "You won't be touching me, little watchman, not out here. You said it yourself: this is Mistshore, and we outcasts don't like to be looked at down the nose of Waterdeep's mighty, especially when he's all alone."

"Alone?" Tarvin said, laughing. "You have no idea how many of us walk in Mistshore this day. Best be holding those threats inside. You never know who might be listening."

"Be off with you," the guard said. He tipped the basket over the side of the ship and lowered the food. "Turn your wrath on the girl. I hope she keeps you running in Mistshore forever."

"You can be sure she won't," Tarvin said. He walked away from the guard, and walked back in the direction of Whalebone Court.

She couldn't hide for long, not with her wild nature. The burnt warehouse was just the beginning. It was only a matter of time before Icelin Tearn slipped up again and got somebody else killed.

Tarvin clenched a fist. Gods help her if she tried to turn her wild wrath on him or any of the Watch. Orders or no, he would bring her back to the Warden on a board before he let her magic kill any more of his friends.

He glanced toward the Court. He should meet up with the patrol to see if they'd gained any ground, but something held him back. His presence obviously irritated the master of the Cradle, so why not take advantage of the situation?

He settled back among the crates to watch the beggar folk a while longer. He found it strangely fascinating to see them from this distance, unobserved. Like watching the rats on a sinking ship. Except these rats were staying on board. Like the rest of Mistshore, they had nowhere else to go.

.:⌢:.

Icelin lay awake as darkness fell. She watched the stars come out, the tiny lights framed by a ship's hull. There were no floating crags tonight. She usually only saw them from her roof, on nights like this when she couldn't sleep. They were often illuminated in purple, their underbellies some kind of crystallized rock.

It had never occurred to her to wonder where the drifting motes came from. They'd been a part of that distant world for so long she'd never questioned what happened to them when they left Waterdeep's view.

Just as she'd never before questioned what her dreams meant, until Cerest, and Kaelin's whispered taunts. Now she wondered about the strange rock crags and the crumbling tower of her dreams. Why did she dream of a place she'd never been to? Why was an elf from distant lands seeking to possess her like an object of power?

"What are you thinking about?"

It was Ruen. He sat a few feet away from her in the dark. These were the first words he'd spoken since Kaelin's strange play had ended.

Icelin shifted so she could make out his profile. "How long did you stay in the village after you'd been scarred?"

"That's not what you were thinking about."

"I was thinking I should read Elgreth's letters. I have all this time to examine them, yet I haven't."

Ruen turned his head. She saw the slash of red in his eyes. "I didn't stay long. After Megwem, the whole village knew. They wouldn't touch me. When the monks came to take me into their training, I knew she—my mother—had arranged it somehow. That was fine. I didn't want to slip and accidentally learn or cause her death, anymore than she did. I'd rather they all died peacefully, without the knowledge of when it would happen."

"Is it such a certainty?" Icelin asked. "It doesn't seem possible to know when someone's going to die, just by touching them."

"Doesn't seem possible for someone to have a perfect memory either," Ruen said.

Icelin had nothing to say to that. "Were you happy with the monks?" she asked instead.

"For a time. The monks understood more than the others," Ruen said. "All things originate from the hands, they said. The ki. It's true. Otherwise Kaelin wouldn't have any stories for his stage."

"What do you mean?" Icelin asked.

"He touched all of the beggars. Not many barriers can keep the dead out, and the mortal mind is exceptionally fragile when it's weakened by illness or infirmity."

"If that's true, how did he know our stories?" Icelin said. "We're not sick."

Ruen looked at her a long time without saying anything, his gaze burning her with its intensity. It frightened her.

"What is it?" she whispered. "What's wrong?"

He blinked and shook his head. "Nothing. Maybe the boy could see through us because somewhere inside we wanted our stories told."

"Yet my letters sit unopened."

"So open them," Ruen said, his voice rough, tired. "Even I can't hide you indefinitely."

But I'm afraid. "Do you already know how all this is going to turn out?" Icelin asked. "Will I . . . die from this adventure?"

"I haven't touched you," Ruen said. "Not your hands, nor any part of your bare skin. I don't know how close to death you are." He looked down at her, and Icelin saw him chewing something over in his mind. When he spoke, it was hesitantly. "If you're afraid for your life, why not stop now? Turn yourself in to the Watch, and you won't have to cast any more spells. I can see how they weaken you," he said when she started to speak. "Why do you hold onto magic, when it brings you so much grief?"

Icelin was silent for a long time. She knew exactly how to answer him, but she couldn't at first, because she'd never admitted it outright to herself. It felt strange to do so now.

"The first time I cast a spell, it was agony," Icelin said. "My head hurt; my stomach felt like it was being yanked inside out. When it was over, my teacher told me not to worry, that the pain would not always be so debilitating. I knew even then that he was wrong. I didn't care. I cast spell after spell; I learned every magic he taught me."

"Why?" Ruen said. "Why put yourself through the pain?"

"Because it made me *forget,*" Icelin said. "In that breath when I called the magic, the pain made me forget everything. Me, who can forget nothing. It was a miracle. All the memories I couldn't bury disappeared when the magic engulfed me. Their weight was gone. For that short time, I was free. Give up magic? I couldn't conceive of it, not until the fire. Even after I killed those people—"

"It was an accident," Ruen said.

"When I swore I would never use magic again, I broke my promise almost immediately. I locked all the dangerous spells away, yes, but even the little magics caused me pain. I kept those spells close, and cast them often. It was the only way I could forget."

"It's not so easy for the rest of us to forget," Ruen said. "The worst and the best memories stay with you. Some things you're supposed to experience, no matter how painful."

"Do words like that aid you, when you touch a man's bare flesh?" Icelin asked. "When you learn when he will die?"

"No," Ruen said. "But I still say the words. It's all I can do."

He turned his head away from her and tipped his hat down over his face. Icelin started to say something else but let it go.

She pulled the letters out of her pack and laid the bundle in her lap. The first she'd already read. She folded it carefully and laid it aside.

The second letter had dirt caked around the edges of the parchment. Icelin fingered the stains. This letter had come from outside Waterdeep. She wondered what it had gone through to make its way to her great-uncle's house.

Breaking the brittle seal, Icelin unfolded the pages.

> *Dear Granddaughter,*
> *I wish you could be with me as I pass through the Dalelands. You would love this country. The sun is rising, the air is crisp, but the dying hints of campfire keep me warm. If I listen closely, I can hear the most remarkable sounds. Brant would call me sentimental, but I imagine I can hear the voices of those who walked these roads long ago. What stories would they tell, these brave phantoms, if they could stop a while by my fire? Would their adventures be of storming perilous castles or tilling fertile fields? Would they slay dragons or raise daughters? All these things I wonder, as I sit by my fire and think of you.*

Icelin clutched the parchment in her hands. This letter and the handful following all came from a different land or city—some she had never heard of. Four years went by in a bell as she read. The only thing she could conclude of her grandfather, besides his affection for her, was that restless was too weak a word to ascribe to him. He never stopped moving.

> *Dear Granddaughter,*
> *Today I looked for the first time upon the city of Luskan. I pray you never have cause to enter this den of depravity and violence. There is no law but that of the thieves' guilds and street gangs.*

Ever at war with each other, they take no notice of a lone man seeking shelter.

I sat upon a rooftop and looked out over Cutlass Island, at the ruins of the Host Tower of the Arcane. The locals say it is a cursed place, and I cannot help but agree. The restless dead walk that isle, sentinels to its lost power. In my younger days, I would have longed for the challenge and promise of treasure to be found in such a forgotten stronghold. I can see the magic swirling under shattered stone. It drifts among the bones of the once mighty wizards who ruled here. The riches tempt me even now, but my strength would never hold out long enough to reach the isle, which seems as distant as gentle Waterdeep. No, tonight I long only for a warm blanket and unspoilt food. Strange how one's priorities shift with age.

Icelin stopped reading. Hatsolm rolled onto his side, bumping against her leg. He coughed once, deep in his chest, then again. A fit overtook him, and he curled upright into a ball, his body shaken by the hacks and wheezes. Icelin pulled his blanket up over his shoulders. He opened his eyes and looked at her.

"I'll get you some water," she said.

"No need." He wiped the blood from his mouth. "It's over." He pulled the blanket over his head and laid back down, his face turned away from her.

Icelin looked at the letter in her hand. Hatsolm had come to Waterdeep seeking refuge from the world, and he'd found it, in a way, through Kaelin and his ghostly troupe.

Elgreth spoke of being old. The tone of this letter was much different from his earlier messages to her. Perhaps he wasn't sick like Hatsolm, but he seemed in no fit condition to travel in Luskan. Her great-uncle had always said the city was not a city at all, but a damned place where only the desperate sought refuge.

She went back to the letters. They continued in Luskan for a year, all written from the same perch on the rooftop. Elgreth had constructed a rough shelter from abandoned slates of tin and wood, in the ruins of a condemned tavern. The more she read, the more Icelin suspected that her grandfather's adventure would not continue beyond the hellish city.

At the bottom of the pile, Icelin found an especially thick bundle. The seal was cracked; the wax had not been sufficient to hold the folded parchment. Was it a memoir? A deathbed request? It was the last letter. Icelin's fingers shook as she unfolded the sheets.

Dear Granddaughter,

The time has come. You are old enough now to be told the truth. But even if you were not, I have no time left to delay this tale. I pray it never happens, but if Cerest comes looking for you, you must be prepared.

CHAPTER FIFTEEN

RUEN WATCHED ICELIN READING HER LETTERS. HER ATTENTION WAS completely absorbed by the writing on the page.

He sat up quietly, slid into the shadows, and climbed the ladder. When he got to the dock he glanced down to be sure he hadn't been followed. He slipped the illusion cloak from his shoulders and moved through the shadows in his own form.

When he was safely out of earshot of the beggars, he pulled the *sava* pawn from his pouch and warmed it between his fingers. He felt the connection at once.

"What is it, Morleth?"

Tallmantle's voice. "Where's Tesleena?" he asked. "Has she tired of me so soon?"

"She walks in Mistshore, seeking Icelin," the Warden said. "Know that if Tesleena comes to harm through your delays, none of the squalor in Waterdeep will be able to hide you from me." The Warden's voice was polite, even conversational.

"Your wizard will be fine," Ruen said. "Icelin is another matter."

"What's happened?"

Ruen hesitated before plunging into the tale. He left nothing out—his battle in the Cradle, Icelin's letters, her unique memory, and every instance of her spells going wild. He gave a detailed account of what Arowall had told him about Icelin's gifts. When he'd finished there was a long silence.

"Are you certain?" the Warden asked. "Certain she is dying?"

"I haven't touched her," Ruen said. "Nor will I, so do not waste breath in asking. "But I see the evidence of my eyes. She needs help. Perhaps Tesleena—"

"Are you saying you're willing to bring her in?"

Ruen clenched the pawn in his fist. "Can you aid her, if I do?"

"Tesleena and I will do everything in our power. Tell me where you are, and I'll send a patrol to get you."

She won't forgive me, Ruen thought. But she'll be alive.

"Not yet," Ruen said. "It has to be her decision."

"Ruen—"

"Thank you, Warden. I'll be in touch. Give my regards to Tesleena." He severed the connection.

In the end, there was no choice. Perhaps, if he let the Watch capture them, the Warden would take pity on him and not reveal his identity to Icelin and the others.

"So it's the coward's way, as always." He shook his head. Soon he would be well and truly hidden in the Watch's skirts, a tamed dog they used for their own amusement. Or was he already there, and he just didn't realize it? If that was so, what more could the opinion of one dying woman matter to him?

Tarvin couldn't believe his luck. Ruen Morleth, expelled from the bowels of the beggar ship by the gods' own sweet blessing.

He considered subduing the man, but thought better of it when Ruen spoke into the *sava* pawn. Tarvin recognized the Watch Warden's voice, though he could make out little of the substance of the conversation.

If Ruen Morleth was here, then Icelin Tearn was somewhere nearby. Tarvin looked down into the ship, but he could see nothing except rag-cloaked bodies.

Odds were she was hiding among the sick. It was brilliant, in a twisted way. The wench must be truly desperate.

There was no chance in the Nine Hells he was going down there to search for her. He could go back to the Court and warn the others. They would come in force and root the beggars out, but in the meantime Icelin might leave her hiding place for a safer one. If she did that, he would lose his chance to capture her.

Tarvin sank low in the shadows, hiding himself again behind the crates—abandoned food cartons, by the smell and the buzz of flies. For now, he would wait.

He watched Ruen Morleth clench his fist and slide the pawn away in his pouch. He looked angry, perhaps at something the Warden had said. Was he upset that he was about to lose his wild little plaything?

Go on and sulk, dog. The Warden will have you both. Tarvin smiled at the thought.

.:⌢:.

Cerest watched Ristlara and Shenan work their magic. Arcane radiance lit up the ship's cabin.

Ristlara had Arowall's hands pinned to his desk with two gold-hilted daggers. Magic pulsed down the blades into the man's skin. The pale blue light ran sickly up his arms, creating new veins while pushing others out of the way.

The man's face twisted in agony. A steady stream of blood and spittle ran down his chin. His eyes were fixed on some unknown distance. He would not look at either of the females while the magic sapped his life energies.

"I don't understand," Shenan said. She sounded like a parent disappointed in the performance of a beloved child. "We never have this trouble with the daggers."

"He's strong-willed," Cerest said, but Ristlara shook her gold tresses impatiently.

"He's human. He should have broken by now."

At her words, Arowall spat blood and a piece of what looked like his own tongue. He collapsed facedown on the desktop, his head between the glowing blades. Ristlara moved hastily out of the way.

"Pull the blades out," Shenan told her. When the magic faded from his skin, she rolled the man over and laid her head against his heart. "Dead," she said.

"Your daggers aren't as effective as you thought, Shenan." Cerest slammed his fist against the ship's hull. A waste of time, all of it. He was no closer to finding Icelin than he was a day ago.

"She's obviously here. Half the crowd saw her, but strangely, none of them know where she went," Ristlara said sardonically.

"They fear Arowall," Shenan said. She ran her fingers through the dead man's thin hair. "He's not so terrifying. Perhaps Mistshore has its own sense of loyalty. Incredible thought, isn't it?"

"Search the ships," Cerest said. "The ones circling the Cradle must belong to Arowall. If she's still here, we'll find her."

The Locks exchanged glances. Ristlara nodded at her sister and went above. Cerest could hear her gathering her men.

Arowall's domain had been shockingly easy to penetrate, despite the guards stationed on deck. Cerest supposed Arowall had put the majority of his resources behind maintaining the Cradle instead of seeing to his own protection. A fatal mistake.

Shenan stayed perched on Arowall's desk. She folded her arms across her chest and gazed at him with that parental expression he loathed.

"Well?" Cerest demanded. "Say whatever is on your tongue. I don't have time to waste."

"Cerest, why not give this up?" Shenan said. "We're all exhausted near to dropping, and we've come closer to the Watch patrols than any of us are comfortable."

"I never took the Locks for cowards," Cerest said.

The elf woman smiled faintly. "Oh, Cerest, sometimes I forget how young you are, how like a spoiled child who never gets his way. Do you believe those sorts of taunts will move either Ristlara or I to action?"

"You've been compliant so far."

"We have, because the chase amused us, in the beginning. Also, we recognized the profit to be made by aligning ourselves with you and the girl. But you're ruled by your impulses, Cerest. That's why you will never make a proper merchant, because your emotion gives you away. People can always tell when you want something so badly it threatens to break you. Isn't that why your father let you live but denied you your birthright, because he knew you valued it more than your own life?"

She knew it would provoke him. Cerest could see it in her eyes. He obliged her. He strode to the desk and backhanded her across the face. She fell over Arowall's body, her hair spreading wildly over the dead man's face.

Sitting up, Shenan put a finger to her split lip. Blood welled against her hand. Her face would swell and bruise, but she smiled as if he'd kissed her mouth instead of punching it.

"In the end, that's why we love you, Cerest," she said. "Allow me to be equally blunt: if you continue to pursue Icelin, you will likely be killed, by the Watch or by the allies Icelin has gathered. Perhaps Icelin herself will be your undoing." She raised a hand to stop his argument. "You may continue to hunt her as long as you like. I don't mind how many of the human dogs we lose—keep them and use them with my blessing—but I will protect my sister and our business interests."

"You would leave me?" Cerest said, and he realized he sounded very much like a bewildered child. But this was how it always ended. Everyone in his life had deserted him when he needed them most: his father, Elgreth, now the Locks.

"Where did I go wrong with all of them," he said aloud.

Shenan slid to the edge of the desk so her knees were touching Cerest's thighs. She put a bloody hand against his cheek. "You don't have any notion of what a conscience is, do you? Of how to trace your actions to consequences?

Your mind doesn't work that way. It's fascinating. You don't realize what you did to them, to Elgreth and the others, do you?"

Cerest pulled away, wiping the blood from his face. He felt unsteady in the knees, but he didn't know why. Was Shenan right? Was there some part of his mind that functioned differently from other folk, beyond the differences that separated elf from human? He'd never considered it before. He'd always taken for granted that he was an oddity, an elf in a swell of humans. But to hear her say it gave him pause. "Icelin is different," he said. "We can start over."

Shenan shook her head. "You killed her great-uncle—"

"Brant is not her blood," Cerest said. Why couldn't they understand? "He lied to her about her family. She owes no loyalty to him."

"She loves him as she will never love you, Cerest. She will act precisely as Elgreth acted. She will resist you, or she will run. That is the truth."

"You're wrong," Cerest said. "I can convince her. I can make her see that it wasn't my fault."

She searched his face, read the conviction there, and nodded. Standing on her toes, she kissed him on the brow, on his scar, and finally on his mouth. When she was done, she put her lips against his good ear so he would hear her whisper.

"I wish you good fortune, my love, and I will mourn you when you are gone to the gods."

Cerest didn't reply. He stood, stiffly, and let her have her way. When she'd gone, he remained at Arowall's desk, staring at the dead man. Ristlara's men, he knew, would be waiting for him on deck. To leave him such resources was more than generous, but he wasn't feeling generous at the moment.

His head ached, and his mind screamed with the implications of Shenan's words. What if she was right? What if Icelin rejected him, as Elgreth had?

Cerest acknowledged that Shenan was probably justified in her concerns. Between Icelin's magic and the sheer number of hunters he'd had after her, they'd been attracting too much attention. Perhaps it was time for a different strategy.

When he climbed the ladder, Ristlara's men were waiting. "We're going separate ways," Cerest said. "The first man who sights the girl and returns to me at Whalebone Court will be paid in more gold than any of you have ever seen. Look, listen, but do not approach her. Follow her to whatever hiding place she's using during the day. Once we know where she goes to ground, we'll have her. Do you understand?"

They nodded. Cerest dismissed them. He looked around the empty Cradle, but he knew he would not see Shenan or Ristlara.

If Shenan was right, he wouldn't be able to keep Icelin from deserting him. But there were options, magics that controlled the mind and made a person's will pliable. Wasn't he the expert in objects of such Art?

Everything would work out this time. Shenan was wrong. He had it all under control.

.:⌒:.

Icelin stared at the words on the page.

> *I pray it never happens, but if Cerest comes looking for you, you must be prepared.*
>
> *I hope you will have no need of the tale I am about to impart. My absence from Waterdeep should dissuade Cerest from searching for you, and if it does not, he could hardly know where to begin in a city so vast. He did not know about Brant.*
>
> *To my sorrow, my brother and I were never as close as we should have been, but perhaps it's for the best. Now, to the tale.*
>
> *You must understand, and not be deceived by the good man Cerest once was. He grew up the third son of the Elenithils, a noble family of Myth Drannor. He was educated at the behest of his late mother's family, because Cerest's father would never acknowledge his son's existence or birthright.*
>
> *There was much evidence that Cerest was the child of an affair between Lady Elenithil and a rival family's eldest son. He was several decades her junior. Cerest's mother died soon after his birth under mysterious circumstances. Lord Elenithil was a prominent suspect, but nothing could be proven; so his reputation survived, while Cerest was publicly shunned as evidence of the fall of a noble lady of Myth Drannor.*
>
> *Cerest took his education, but he left Myth Drannor as soon as he came of age. I first met him in Baldur's Gate. He'd come to the city to establish himself as a merchant. He had a small portion of his mother's wealth to invest but no interest in the common trade in Baldur's Gate.*
>
> *I was an adventurer at the time, wandering out from the city to the ruins of tombs and strongholds and floating motes fallen from the heavens. I made enough coin to survive by selling my findings, but I hadn't the resources or manpower to delve as deeply into Faerûn's changed landscape as I desired. Then I met Cerest.*

He purchased some of the pieces I brought back from the ruins. During the third such of these transactions, he confided that he had been in contact with a newly wedded couple who were interested in cataloging the artifacts to document the changes to Faerûn and its magic, resulting from the spellplague.

Here at last was my chance. With Cerest and the young man and woman, I had an expert team to explore more of Faerûn than I ever could hope to on my own. They would have their research, Cerest would have his profit, and my obsession for the unknown would be satisfied. It seemed the perfect arrangement, and we became quite close.

The young couple, Lisra and Edlend, were of course your parents. We were exploring a tomb in distant Aglarond when Lisra was four months heavy with you. We found a name scrawled on the wall, the only marking in the lonely ruins: Icelin. When you were born, Cerest named you after her. Lisra and Edlend named me your grandfather.

I wish I could tell you all the things your parents longed to give you, Icelin. It was their wish that you would follow in their footsteps. I think Cerest wished this, as well—that we would all continue on together, one human generation replacing the last. We were the closest thing to family the elf had ever experienced in his life.

Considering all this, the happiness that we shared, I can't explain why Cerest brought it all crashing down. He lied to us, but you see, we had no reason not to trust him. He had always told us the truth, so we believed him when he swore it was safe. You must believe me, Icelin, you must! I would have given my life before I saw you or your parents hurt.

Icelin turned the page over, but there was no more writing. The letter simply ended.

"No," she said, her breath coming fast. "That can't be all." She went back over each page, thinking one had gotten out of order. When she didn't find another, she sorted through all the letters. Panic made her clumsy; the pages sailed out of her hands, blurring in a yellow haze as her vision swam. The world seemed to spin.

It was too much to take. Elgreth wasn't her grandfather. Brant wasn't her blood at all. She had always been alone in the world, she just hadn't known it. All because of Cerest.

"How," she said, her voice shrill. "How did it happen? Gods above, tell me!"

"Icelin."

She jumped, but it was only Sull. He looked like he hadn't slept at all. There were great red pouches under his eyes.

"What's wrong?" he asked.

Bellaril was sitting up too. She rubbed her eyes with a fist. "What's all the noise?" she demanded.

"Nothing," Icelin said. She slid the letters away in her pack. "It can wait. I'm sorry I disturbed you all." She looked around. "Where's Ruen?"

She heard footsteps on the ladder. Ruen climbed down to them.

"I've been scouting," he said. "It's almost full dark. We can move around soon." He looked to Icelin. "If you're ready to leave?"

"I've read the letters," Icelin said, aware of Sull and Bellaril listening. "My grandfather, Elgreth, tried to warn me about Cerest. He knew he might come after me." She looked at Sull. "Brant must have known. Even if he'd never read the letters himself, he must have known about Cerest. Elgreth wouldn't have left his own brother ignorant of the danger."

"Of course he wouldn't," Sull said soothingly. "Your great-uncle probably thought, after so much time, the elf had given up lookin'. And what was the sense in frightenin' you if that was the case?"

He had given up, until I saved his life in the street, Icelin thought. The bitter irony of it made her dizzy. She remembered thinking, in the moment she'd pushed the elf to the ground, that she was doing something good—a small act of penance for all the harm she'd done. The gods had a cruel streak in them.

"Why's he so interested in you?" Bellaril asked. "Begging your pardon, but you don't seem worth all the men and coin he must be losing."

"I couldn't agree more," Icelin said. "I thought Cerest wanted revenge, but he said he wanted me for my abilities. He said Elgreth had a powerful spellscar; he thought I shared it. Why he would pursue someone with such unstable magic is beyond me, though Elgreth did allow that Cerest's interest lay heavily with magic."

Kredaron had said the same, that Cerest was fascinated by the Art. He'd thought, just as she had, that the elf's scars were a result of a brush with wild magic. If that was the case, Cerest should want nothing to do with her.

"Is there more?" Ruen asked.

"Yes," Icelin said. "This is the part where things get muddled. Cerest used to work with my parents and Elgreth. They adventured together. But for some reason, Cerest betrayed them."

"Why?" Ruen asked.

"I don't know. The letters end. They were either lost or sent incomplete to Brant. I'm sure Cerest would tell you the tale, the next time he catches up to us."

"Maybe it's time that happened."

It was Sull who had spoken. Icelin looked at him. "You can't be serious?"

"I am," Sull said. "That elf's used to huntin' us, drivin' us to ground. Let's turn the tables on 'im, see how he likes being chased."

"We're outnumbered," Ruen reminded him, "even with Bells."

The dwarf snorted. "I'm not afraid of an elf with a mashed-in face."

"None of you are attacking Cerest on my behalf," Icelin said. "We're not discussing it."

"There's another option," Ruen said.

Icelin waited, but the monk didn't speak. She cocked an eyebrow at him. "This option involves throwing us headlong into more danger and strangeness, doesn't it?"

Sull threw up his hands. "I thought it didn't get any stranger than this!"

"I think it's time we go to the Watch," Ruen said.

CHAPTER SIXTEEN

SILENCE FELL OVER THE GROUP. ICELIN THOUGHT AT FIRST HE WAS JESTING.

"You're mad," she told Ruen. "I'm not giving myself up to the Watch. I'd rather spend my life in Mistshore."

Bellaril regarded her as if she'd just asked what color the sky was on clear days. "You're just as daft as he is, if you mean that," she said.

"She's only a child," Ruen said, which made Icelin want to plant her fingernails in his eyes. "She doesn't know what Waterdeep is."

"Then what is it?" Icelin said, forgetting to keep her voice down. "Open my eyes, Ruen Morleth, to more horrors. I don't think I've had enough thus far."

"He doesn't mean to hurt you, girl," spoke a voice, and everyone except Ruen jumped.

Hatsolm rubbed the sleep from his eyes and regarded them blearily from his curled-up pallet. There was a crust of dried blood at the corner of his mouth.

"I'm sorry," Icelin said, ashamed. "I didn't mean to wake you."

"Doesn't matter, I wasn't sleeping anyway," Hatsolm said. He sat up slowly. Sull put his hand on the man's shoulders to steady him. "The problem is that when we're children we're only conscious of our own suffering."

"I don't understand," Icelin said. She felt like a child, and she didn't like it. Nelzun had never made her feel this way.

"You only know the safe space in which you were brought up," Hatsolm said. "That's a wonderful thing, but it doesn't lend itself well to wisdom, or to understanding why folk do the things they do."

"So to understand why Cerest is after me, I have to go right back where I started?" Icelin said. "Into the hands of the people who think I murdered my own great-uncle, the same people who hate me for killing one of their own?"

"No." This time it was Ruen who spoke. "To understand yourself, you have to put your pride and fear aside. Believe me, I know what that costs a person. But the Watch can help you."

"How?"

"I think you know." He looked her in the eyes. "Your great-uncle would not have you live as a fugitive. More than that, the Watch have wizards, folk who can help the spellscarred."

Icelin felt like she'd been struck in the stomach. "No," she said automatically. "I have never been touched by the spellplague."

"Are you certain?" Ruen said, his eyes boring relentlessly into her. Those red eyes. Spellscarred eyes.

"Of course!" Icelin took a step back from them all. "I grew up in South Ward! Waterdeep is safe from the plague."

"Safe, is it?" Hatsolm said gently. "Waterdeep is a refuge to those scarred by the plague. They may be scorned, shoved into forgotten corners like Mistshore, but the plague is part of us."

"No!" Icelin wrapped her arms around herself. The weeping sores stood out on her arms. Repulsed, she ripped the cloak off, peeling away the layers of rags and rotting flesh. She needed to see her own skin, needed to see it normal.

"Put your cloak back on!" Ruen snatched the cloth and covered her. "You'll be contaminated."

"I'm not plagued or spellscarred. I'm not like—"

"Like me?" Ruen said.

She took a step back. "You know that's not what I meant. Stop twisting my words."

Sull touched her arm. Icelin tried to back away, but he held her fast. "You know I'm with you, girl. But just because you've got gifts others don't, doesn't mean you're not a Waterdhavian. You have the right to be protected. You shouldn't be afraid."

"Why not?" Icelin's chest heaved. "Look what my gifts have done." Her magic brought nothing but disaster, and her memory ensured that she never forgot any of it. Every experience, frozen in her mind, perfectly preserved.

Except one.

"I have the same dream every night." She spoke haltingly. Sull squeezed her arm. "I'm in a tower, surrounded by people whose faces I can't see. There's a bright light, a burning light, and I'm afraid." She looked at Ruen. "There's no such tower in Waterdeep. I've looked."

"If you've been outside the city, why don't you remember?" Ruen asked.

"I don't know," Icelin said. "You've no idea what it's like, to have everything lined up and catalogued in your mind, a vast library of things you can't ever be rid of; yet there's this huge crack in the wall, a terrifying maw, and *that's* the knowledge you'd give anything to have."

"What's the Watch going to do for her?" Bellaril spoke up. "If she's scarred, then that's that. Doesn't help her with the elf."

"There are too many missing pieces," Icelin said. "The rest of the dream, Elgreth and his spellscar. That's what Cerest wants. Bellaril's right. The Watch can't help me with any of that."

"But if you accept the spellplague is the source of your flawless memory, that's a place to start," Ruen said. "Waterdeep has done better than any city keeping the plague at bay. There's a reason for that. You won't find another realm in Faerûn where folk know more about the plague's effects."

Bellaril smiled grimly. "And you think she'll just stride up to them and start interviewing likely candidates to help her, do you?"

"The other choice is confrontin' Cerest," Sull said.

"He won't harm Icelin, but he'll have no compulsion to spare the rest of us," Ruen said. He looked at Icelin. "Do you want to risk Sull's life? Do you want to see the elf slide a blade into him the way he took your great-uncle?"

"Don't say that to her," Sull said sharply. "I can see to myself fine enough, and I don't need a magic ring to do it."

Ruen shook his head. "You're a fool. You claim you want to protect her? You're letting your guilt cloud your judgment. It makes you useless to her."

Sull went pale. His hand slid off Icelin's arm.

Icelin looked at Ruen. He was like a stranger, his eyes bright, almost feverish. "What's wrong with you?" she demanded. "The last place you would ever put yourself is in the path of the Watch. Your instinct for self-preservation is too strong." Her eyes narrowed. "Why is it so important to you to see me safely delivered to them?"

"Because he's finally smartened up to doing what he's told."

The voice rang out above them, and a crossbow bolt twanged into the hull a foot above Icelin's head.

The cluster of beggars, stirred to wakefulness by their argument, sprang into frightened motion at the shot. Filthy bodies crowded toward the ladder.

"Stay down!"

Another bolt stuck in the wood above the ladder. The beggars fell back, knocking each other aside in their haste to get away.

Icelin took an elbow to the ribs. Her feet and arms were jammed in the press of bodies. She tried to look up, but the sky spun wildly as she was pulled in one direction or another. She crouched down, trying not to be hit by the bolts she knew were meant for her.

Ruen slammed into Icelin from the side, knocking her to the ground. Her breath whooshed from her chest, and she lay, gasping, staring up at the sky. She tried to roll onto her back, but Ruen was suddenly on top of her. He threw his disguise cloak over both their bodies. Darkness closed in on her completely.

"Stop! Ruen, we have to get out—"

"Quiet!" he said in her ear. "He can't know which one you are, not after all that uproar."

Their attacker must have come to the same conclusion. The firing stopped, and the beggars gradually wore out their frenzy. Icelin could feel them pressing together and against her. They protected themselves by sheer numbers, blending into one form.

"Come out, lass." The voice, mocking and deep, rang out again. "I've already seen your pretty face. You look much better without the sores, Icelin Tearn."

"Gods, I'm a fool," Icelin whispered.

Ruen put a finger to his lips and listened. "He's pacing the dock," he said. "I can hear his bootsteps. I think he's alone."

"He's had plenty of time to reload," Icelin said. "If you try to reach the ladder, he'll put a bolt in your head."

"I'm not convinced he's that good of a shot," Ruen said. He pitched his voice louder. "Name yourself, friend, and we might invite you down to Eveningfeast. We're having stew and apples with the cores plucked out. Are you coming to us from the Watch?"

"I am. Tarvin is my name, and I won't be sharing your table, Ruen Morleth," the man said. "I'm here for the woman, but I'd just as happily bury a bolt in your eye, if you don't hand her over."

"I would *happily* oblige you," Ruen said, "but I'm afraid she doesn't want to go with you. She's a stubborn, difficult creature. I've almost drowned her a time or two."

"You're a smooth liar, Morleth, but in this I believe you. What of the rest of you, then?" he said, his voice rolling over the heads of the beggars. "You willing to give your lives to protect a fugitive? She's not one of you. I saw her. She wears a mask of disease. She mocks you and your suffering."

"She's fresh air to your foul breath," Hatsolm said, and the crowd laughed, tentatively. "If she wants to stay in Mistshore and deigns to walk among us, she's welcome. She's a lot braver than your Watch friends, who won't come to Mistshore at all."

There was a collective murmur of agreement from the crowd. Icelin closed her eyes. *Gods, he wouldn't kill them, would he? Not for hatred of me.*

The crowd tensed, waiting. Icelin couldn't breathe.

"Ruen—"

"Don't," Ruen said. He tightened his grip on her. "He's bluffing."

He was right. There must have been a spark of decency in Tarvin, for in the end he only laughed. "You're truly a wonder, lady. You've got the freaks lapping at your hand."

"Be silent!" The words burst from her before she could stop them.

"She speaks," Tarvin cried, and his voice moved past them. "Sing out again, lovely one, and show yourself."

"Tell your friends to leave Mistshore," Icelin said. "I'd rather die here than be taken and tried for what's in the past. Your bitterness makes my choice for me, Tarvin."

"How long do you think you can survive here?" Icelin could hear him toying with the crossbow string. "We'll drag you and your friends out of there one by one. Is that what you want for them?"

Ruen shifted, alert again. "Now that's an odd statement," he said. "You haven't yet mentioned your friends. Hard to believe they'd be waiting in the shadows while you have your tantrum. Hardly professional conduct for a Watchman. No, I think you're alone up there, and you can't quite figure out what to do about it. If you leave for help, we escape; and if you stay, you're outnumbered. I don't envy you, truly."

"Shut up," Tarvin snarled. "I can wait you out well enough. How would that be? A tenday with no food, no water, and no one to clean your filth— how friendly will you be to the pretty bitch then?"

"Maybe he's right," Icelin whispered. "If he keeps us here, people could get hurt. You said yourself I should turn myself in."

"Not to him," Ruen said. "Not to that one. He's no Watchman."

"I killed his friend," Icelin said. "He has reason to despise me."

"The beggars have done nothing to him," Ruen said. "No Watchman is so cowardly as to threaten the weak." He didn't realize his voice was rising.

"He thinks he knows so much about us," Tarvin said. "Don't you wonder why that is? You want to stake your chances with Morleth? Maybe you'd be grateful to hear some truth about him, eh?"

"Don't listen to him," Ruen said. There was a note of panic in his voice Icelin had never heard before. Dread stirred in her belly.

"Is she too shy to ask? Are you keeping her silent, Morleth, with the weight of your eyes? If you're innocent, what could you possibly have to fear?"

"What truth is he talking about, Ruen?" Icelin said. His body was rigid. He could have been carved of stone.

"Did you ever ask him how he escaped Waterdeep's dungeons?" Tarvin asked. "It must have been a marvelous feat. I'm shocked he hasn't bragged of it up and down Mistshore. Didn't you ever think it strange that a man like him, a thief, would risk his life to aid you?" Tarvin was pacing again. His voice came from directly above them. "Such men work only in exchange for wealth you've never possessed, my lady. Of course it was easy enough for Morleth to steal the treasure he wanted. He lived like a king, with Hawlace's collection to sell off piece by piece. You get used to that kind of lifestyle, well then you can't stand being put in a cage. Makes a man do things. Maybe make bargains he'll come to regret later."

Icelin twisted, trying to look into Ruen's face, but he pressed her down.

"Don't move," Ruen said tersely. "He wants you panicked. As soon as you throw the cloak off, you'll be staring down his crossbow. Don't be stupid!"

"Let me go," Icelin said. She pushed against Ruen's chest, but she couldn't move him. The cloak and his body were suffocating her. Smells of sweat and fear and sickness mingled together in her nostrils.

"Or maybe," Tarvin said, "the question you should be asking yourself is why a master thief turned Watch agent can't deliver one murdering wench to his betters?"

The strength left Icelin's body. She stopped struggling and lay still on the cold floor.

"Icelin," Ruen said. The guilt in his voice sealed everything. "Listen to me. He's baiting you. He knows your temper; he's using it to paw at you."

"Deny it," Icelin said. "Tell me he's not speaking the truth."

At last, he looked at her. Was it any harder for him now than it had ever been? His red eyes betrayed no expression, as always. Somehow that made it worse.

"What can I tell you that you will want to hear, Icelin?" Ruen said. "That I'm not a Watchman—with fervor I tell you I'm not."

"Are you working with them?" Icelin said.

"Yes."

Unexpectedly, Icelin had the urge to laugh. "It might have been easier if you'd tried a denial," she said. "At least then I would know you regretted it."

He clenched his jaw. "You'll never know how much. There were reasons."

"So many things make sense now," Icelin said. "It's very freeing, you know. You risking your life for so little payment, how easy it was to find you—I should have known my tracking prowess left too much to be desired.

I suppose Fannie was in on everything? I probably had that one coming, though, since I almost got her killed. You should pay her extra for that."

"It was never about coin," Ruen said.

"Actually, that might have made things turn out differently," Icelin said. "On the raft, I should have offered up my virtue after all. It might have been inducement enough for you not to betray me."

"Spew venom at me later," Ruen said. "We don't have time for this."

"You're right," Icelin said. "Don't worry. You thought I should go to the Watch, and now the Watch has come to me. I'm going to give everyone what they want."

"I won't let you," Ruen said when she tried to push against him. "We've danced this dance before. You won't move me."

"Probably not," Icelin said, "but I have other weapons now."

She lifted her head and put her lips against his mouth. It wasn't a kiss, and not remotely romantic. But it was skin to skin contact, and that was all she needed.

For Ruen's part, she might have hit him with a lightning bolt and evoked a similar reaction. He recoiled so fast that, for just an instant, he lost his balance.

Icelin shoved him with all her strength. She couldn't roll him off her. He locked his legs around her knees, but she managed to get one hand free. She ripped the cloak from her body.

Fresh air and startled cries from the beggars swamped her. Icelin blinked in the darkness, trying to adjust her eyes. She heard a clattering on the ladder and looked up.

Tarvin stood halfway up on the rungs, the crossbow leveled at her chest.

"Well met, lady," he said. "I'm glad you could see reason."

Ruen released her and rolled to his feet. He was an easy target, but Tarvin kept the crossbow trained on Icelin.

"I'm not going to bother with you, Morleth," he said, his gaze never leaving Icelin's. "Tales of your weapon-catching skills abound. But I don't think your lady is quite as talented. Step back, please. Give Icelin room to climb the ladder."

He climbed back up, slowly, keeping the weapon level on her. When he was back on the dock, he motioned to her.

"Climb up and keep both hands on the rungs," he said. "Bring your clever disguise."

Icelin picked up the cloak and spared one last glance at Ruen and the cluster of beggars. She made her eyes move unseeing over Bellaril and Sull, who were huddled near the back of the crowd.

They must have been herded there by the others, for protection, Icelin thought. Bellaril gripped Sull's arm to keep him from moving. Icelin inclined her head a fraction at the dwarf, as if to say, *keep him back.* Bellaril returned the nod.

"Thank you," Icelin said to Hatsolm, who stood at the front of the group.

"Be wary, lass," Hatsolm said. His eyes were sad. "Remember what I said. You aren't in a child's world now."

She nodded. She didn't look at Ruen.

The ladder climb was quick, much faster than the descent had been, though she tried to go as slowly as possible. When she was on the dock, she held out her disguise cloak to Tarvin.

"Put it on," Tarvin said. "I want to see what you look like."

The group below stirred angrily, but Icelin didn't react. She unfolded the cloak and draped it over herself. Immediately, the sores reappeared, and her flesh took on the ghostly pallor of disease.

"Is this to your liking?" Icelin said. "It's not a punishment equal to Therondol's death."

"You're right," Tarvin said. "I take my vengeance where I can."

"I understand, but if you march a plagued woman through Mistshore at the end of a crossbow, you're bound to attract unwanted attention. Is your vengeance worth that?"

"Worth my life and yours." He took her by the shoulder and spun her around so her back was to him. He put the crossbow at the base of her spine. "Walk, lady, and don't fret. We aren't going far."

.:⌒:.

Borion was cold, and he didn't like the harbor smell. Not that anyone asked his opinion.

He walked slightly behind Trik, his partner. The elf with the funny face had told them to split up, but Borion never went anywhere without Trik. When Trik wasn't around, things got fuzzy. If the elf was angry, well that was too bad.

"What we doing out here, Trik?" Borion asked. He must have asked this question before, because Trik turned around and made a dirty gesture at him. Borion grinned. He couldn't help it if his memory was short.

They fell into step together, but Trik was quiet for a while. That didn't bother Borion. He knew Trik would answer him before too long.

"You know, Boss, I'm walking here, asking myself that same question. Frightening that I'm starting to think at your level, isn't it?"

Trik always called him "Boss." Borion wasn't any higher rank than anyone else in the band, but he was bigger than all of them, and stronger.

"If you don't know why we're out here, Trik, how do you know where we're going?" Borion asked, not because he was overly curious, but because he didn't want to get lost in Mistshore. He didn't like the place.

He didn't like the city much, either. If they were traveling, he'd be happy. Outside the walls, the air was cleaner, and there weren't so many people. People scared him. They moved too fast, and he had a hard time keeping up with their speech.

It wasn't that way with Trik. Trik had lost part of his leg in a tomb raid, had it chopped off by a portcullis that hadn't stayed up like it was supposed to. So now he walked with a limp. Borion had no trouble keeping pace with Trik.

"We're going to stay close to those whale bones, or whatever they are," Trik said, "maybe go in for some ale. Let the elf rot for a while, I say."

"Boss won't like that," Borion said, referring this time to their actual boss, Rynin.

Trik stopped again, so suddenly Borion almost ran him over. "Have you got maggots for brains?" Trik said. "Rynin's dead. He got himself killed in that fight with Arowall's guards. We're thin in numbers, my dumb friend, and it's starting to make me anxious."

It took an effort, but finally Borion remembered. That's right. Rynin was dead. So were others of his friends. What if Trik was next?

Trik seemed to know what he was thinking. "Don't you worry, Boss, nothing's going to happen to me. I'm thinking the coin's not enough to find this little girl. I'm thinking we go off, round up the rest of the company what'll come with us, and leave the city tonight. What you think of that?"

Trik seemed confident, and that made Borion feel somewhat better. "Where will we find the others, Trik? We're all split up. Trik?"

But Trik wasn't listening to him. He was looking at something behind Borion. Without a word, he grabbed Borion's arm and pulled him behind a stack of barrels.

"What is it, Trik?" Borion asked, but Trik waved a hand for him to be quiet. He pointed across the harbor. On a walkway that ran paralell to their own, two figures stood. One of them, a woman, had a crossbow pointed at her face.

"That girl look familiar to you, Boss?" Trik asked. He sounded delighted.

Borion squinted at the woman. She was shaking out a bundle of rags. She looked tired and underfed. Pretty, though. He would have liked to have a wife as pretty as her. Then, the larger impact of Trik's question hit him.

"Is that her?" Borion said. "The girl the elf wants?"

"I'd lay any amount of coin it is," Trik said. "Looks like someone got to her first, though."

"He doesn't look nice," Borion said.

The man with the crossbow was talking to the girl; they couldn't hear what was said. The girl cast the rags over herself. Her body shriveled and transformed, assuming a horrifying shape.

Borion clutched Trik's arm. "What'd he do to her?" he said, frantic. "He's cursed her!"

Trik shook him off. "No, he didn't. He's no wizard, not a dark god's priest, either. It's just a disguise, so people won't know who she is. Doesn't matter, though, we've already seen her."

"We should tell the elf," Borion said. The elf would come and get the girl, and they could finally leave Mistshore.

"Still trying to think, are we?" Trik said. "Don't you remember, we're supposed to bring the *girl* to the *elf*. Then we get our reward."

"But it's only the two of us," Borion said. "I thought the elf wanted us to tell him so all of us could go after her together."

"The elf hasn't managed to do anything right since we started this chase," Trik said angrily. "We bring the girl to him, we get more coin than the others, and we get out of here sooner. That sounds right to me, Boss. What about you?"

The explanation sounded simple enough, but it still bothered Borion. He tried to put the doubts out of his mind. He could never remember anything properly. Maybe Trik was right, and it would be better to bring the girl directly to the elf. It would save time, and Borion wanted to get out of Mistshore more than anything.

"What's the plan?" Borion asked.

"Well, seeing as that fellow with the crossbow's not one of us, he must be a Watch spawn in disguise. First we take her from him, but we have to make sure he doesn't shoot her, or us. Think you can get the crossbow if I get him?"

"Yes," Borion said. The one thing he was good at was taking things. Lately they were objects from tombs and ruins, but he'd taken people before, for coin or food.

"Let's go, then," Trik said. "There's a lady in distress."

CHAPTER SEVENTEEN

ICELIN WALKED SLOWLY. IT WAS DIFFICULT TO SEE OUT FROM UNDER THE raggedy hood and difficult to think with the tip of a crossbow bolt shoved into her spine. Tarvin wasn't taking any chances. He kept her close, one hand on the crossbow trigger and the other on her arm to steer her in the right direction.

They were headed back to the Dusk and Dawn. It made sense as a meeting spot for the Watch patrols, especially if they were moving around without their official regalia. Would Kersh be among them? Icelin hadn't thought of her friend in days. Her former life seemed nothing more than a distant dream.

They reached an intersection. The pathway to the left ended in collapse, wooden planks floating on the water. The other three paths were intact. Tarvin pointed her to the right. Icelin paused to pick her footing and thought she heard the clicking of boots echoing off the planks behind them.

She tried to turn, but Tarvin twisted her arm painfully.

"No going back," he said. "Face front, keep marching."

"There's someone behind us," Icelin said. "Can't you hear?"

"To get behind us they'd have to swim," Tarvin said. "We're alone out here, and if you stall me again I'll put a limp in your step."

He forced her forward. Stumbling, Icelin went, but she could feel eyes on them. She couldn't hear the footsteps anymore, and that made the sensation worse.

Could it be Ruen? If it was, you'd never have heard him, she told herself. Not that she should expect a rescue from that corner, which meant the eyes behind them were probably unfriendly.

Icelin searched her mind for a spell. There were empty corridors all throughout her mind. She'd spent herself of all but the harshest spells. She couldn't risk her magic going wild now.

"Tarvin, please," she said, "think. What if—"

She angled her head in time to see the board. It was one of the planks from the collapsed walkway. She saw it pass out of her peripheral vision and instinctively dropped to the walkway.

She twisted; Tarvin still gripped her arm. He cried out, but the board silenced him. It smashed him in the side of the head.

Icelin heard a weird, hollow crunch. Tarvin slumped to a half-sitting position on the walkway. She could already see he was dead.

Icelin went for his hands, seeking the crossbow, but it was gone. Two pairs of boots filled her vision, one of the pairs at least two sizes bigger than the other. She looked up to see a man as tall as Sull and twice as round. He held Tarvin's crossbow like it was a toy. He had brown hair and a long shirt that he'd belted clumsily below his gut. His clothes were soaking wet.

His partner was slicker, his dark hair shaved to stubble. He had green eyes above a pointed nose. His clothes were saturated too.

"It's amazing how often, in Waterdeep, the goods change hands," the slick man said. In response, the giant pointed the crossbow at her. "You can take off the cloak, though. We're not so nasty as the Watch."

Icelin slid the cloak off her shoulders. She cast it into the harbor. "So you belong to Cerest?" she said.

The slick man took umbrage at that. "We're treasure hunters. You just happen to be the treasure tonight."

"I see," Icelin said. "How wonderful for me."

The giant looked uncomfortable. "Shouldn't we be going, Trik?"

"Soon, Boss," the slick man said. "Hands in front of you, lady. I haven't forgotten you're a spell hurler."

Icelin put her hands together while Trik tied them. They stood on the walkway, and a breath later they all heard the approaching footsteps. It was something akin to a herd of elephants charging in from the sea.

Icelin turned. Horror crashed over her. "Sull, no!"

The butcher barreled into the two men from behind. He got both arms around the giant, pinning the crossbow against his side. Icelin didn't think the man could be moved, but Sull hauled him off his feet and slammed him to the walkway.

He went for his cleaver, but the giant kicked sideways, sweeping Sull's legs out from under him. The butcher twisted and came down on top of the giant. Part of the walkway splintered and collapsed into the harbor, but the big men didn't notice. They were wrestling each other with a vengeance, punching and kicking and grabbing at hair. They might have been children, but the blows they landed were hard enough to break bone.

"Settle 'im!" Trik said. He started forward to aid the giant.

Icelin brought her bound arms up, smashing Trik in the face. He took the blow in complete surprise, his jaw cracking painfully into her knuckles. He staggered back. She drove him forward, trying to push him off into the water, but he caught himself against a piling.

He hooked an arm around her waist and swept her back. She tripped over his leg and fell on her side on the walkway. Her head smacked the wood, and her teeth clamped painfully together. She bit her tongue and tasted blood. Dazed, she tried to get up, but the world swam in and out of focus.

"Don't worry, lass," she heard Sull cry, "I've rolled bigger hunks of beef than this lout. I'm comin—" He took a punch to the jaw. Plucking the giant's fist out of his cheek, Sull gleefully bit the pudgy fingers.

Icelin saw Trik stand up, his shadow blocking out the torchlight across the walkway. He drew a knife from his belt and waded into the tangle of legs.

No, no, Icelin thought. She lunged for Trik's ankle, missed, and lost her breath again when she came down on her chest. Forcing herself to her knees, she bit into the knots binding her hands. She managed to loosen them enough to slip the rope off, but Trik had moved out of reach.

I'm not going to make it, she thought. "Sull, Sull!" she screamed. "Get back—Ruen!" Where was Ruen? And Bellaril?

"Hold him," Trik yelled.

The giant rolled onto his back, pulling Sull on top of him. He locked his arms in an arrowhead across Sull's chest. The butcher wheezed, his face turning bright red. He couldn't break the grip.

"You want to . . . get . . . 'fectionate . . . with me . . . do you?" Sull jammed his elbow into the giant's gut. The giant grunted, but he didn't let go. Sull drove the elbow in again, and again.

Each blow contorted the giant's face. He coughed, blood dripping down his chin. Both the men panted furiously, but the giant maintained his grip.

"Hurry . . . Trik," the giant moaned. His head lolled to one side. His eyes were black glass.

Icelin tried to call a spell. Ice. Fire. Wind. She couldn't find them. Pain and fear took her down twisting corridors in her mind, places that led to songs and stories and visions of her great-uncle, dead in her arms, and Sull's face, his wild red hair.

Concentrate!

But the magic wouldn't answer. The pain in her head blocked it all out. Her body was trying to protect itself, to preserve the few uncorrupted parts she had left.

Icelin gave up. She was searching blind. Instead she concentrated on Trik's dagger. He held the weapon crosswise in his hand. He wanted a quick slash to the throat. A quick cut, and Sull would be gone.

A quick cut. She repeated it, and suddenly everything crystallized in her mind. The alternate paths fell away, leaving her a clear line to the tower. She ran for the door, threw it off its hinges. The spell was waiting, had been waiting, for her to get past the fear. It appeared as a glowing tome of light in the middle of the room.

"Sull, roll him!" she cried. "Keep moving!" She whispered the spell, her voice cracking.

Over the arcane phrases, she heard more footsteps charging down the walkway. Shouts, Bellaril's voice. So far away. They might have been coming from the other side of the city.

She risked a glance at Sull, but kept her concentration fully on the spell.

He wasn't moving. He knew the knife was coming, but he wasn't struggling anymore. She saw a strange, peaceful expression settling over his face. He gazed over Trik's shoulder at her, and the look in his eyes held such a boundless affection and acceptance that Icelin felt her heart tearing open.

Go, his eyes told her. *I'm fine, now.*

Trik came forward. Icelin screamed the rest of the spell. The words were fire in her throat. She felt the spell hold, and the scene erupted in shadows of torch and spell light.

Icelin's world lost focus. The pain was unbearable. The spell burst from her like something newly born. She could only crouch on the walkway and hope that she lived through it.

Streams of metallic force shot from her outstretched hands. They quivered and solidified in the air. Passing each other, they encircled Trik at the chest and legs, tightening into two confining bands.

His balance gone, Trik pitched forward, collapsing half on Sull and half on the walkway. The magic held him immobile.

"Sull!" She came up to her knees, forcing her body to move. There was blood running down her forehead. She must have hit her head harder than she'd thought. Everything was tilting, the torchlight was too bright, but Sull . . .

The giant let go, freeing one of Sull's arms. The butcher reared back, trying to get a hand on the giant's throat. He didn't see the giant pick up Trik's discarded knife, or turn it toward Sull's chest.

"Sull." The name framed her lips, but there was no sound. The dagger went into Sull's chest and pinned his leather sash to his body. He fell back, and the giant fell on top of him.

In the same breath, Icelin felt the backlash from her spell. There was a distant drumming, the blood forcing its way through her body. Her skull felt tight. Would the vessels burst and her mind go dark? Yes. She welcomed it.

Sull's lifeblood dripped between the planks, crimson on the brown water. The colors were just like Ruen's eyes.

Icelin felt herself fall, half-curled into a ball. She could see Sull's face. He was looking at her, the fear intense in his gaze.

Not for himself, Icelin thought. He didn't care at all that he was bleeding to death from a chest wound. He was trying to get up, to get to her. To see if she was safe.

She could hear Ruen's voice now. He came into view, running full out down the walkway. She saw his floppy hat bobbing. He grabbed the giant, peeling him off Sull like a fly. Before he could raise the dagger, Ruen grabbed him from behind, pushed his knee into the small of his back, and used both hands to pull the giant's head back.

There was a soft popping noise, and the giant went limp.

His spine, Icelin thought, snapped in one movement. Such a small sound on such a big man. But Ruen had known exactly what he was doing. He dropped the giant's body and went for Trik, a bland expression on his face. Same intentions, his course set.

He grabbed the spell bands that held the smaller man. When he was sure they were secure, he dragged Trik to the edge of the walkway.

"No, please!" Trik cried, when he realized what Ruen intended. He kicked and struggled, but Ruen kept dragging him. His expression didn't change. "Not the water, don't!"

"Ruen," Icelin said, but it was too soft for him to hear. He gazed at Trik's frantic expression reflected in the water. "Ruen," she said, louder.

The monk paused and turned to look at her. His face visibly softened. He started toward her but checked himself. He looked from the water to Icelin, as if he were suddenly waking from a dream.

"Leave him," Icelin gasped. The blood pounded a sick rhythm against her temples. "Check on . . . Sull."

Ruen nodded and left Trik at the edge of the walkway, facedown toward the water.

He crossed to Sull and examined the butcher's wound. When he saw all the blood, he turned to the giant's body. He fisted his hands in the giant's baggy shirt and ripped the fabric down the middle. The tearing was loud in the darkness. He stripped the giant to the waist and left the body where it was.

"Help me," he told Bellaril.

The dwarf came around to Sull's other side. Together they hoisted the butcher into a half sitting position. Bellaril put her back against Sull's to prop him up.

Ruen looped the ruined shirt around Sull's middle, tying off the end under his armpit to try to slow the flow of blood. Bellaril gently laid him back horizontal.

"He'll live for a while," Ruen said.

Icelin put her head down to quiet the spinning, the roaring blood. She heard Bellaril's footsteps, a short, heavy tread that stopped behind her.

"She's almost as far gone," the dwarf woman said. Icelin felt Bellaril gently roll her onto her back. She probed her chest for wounds, then started on her arms and legs. Icelin started to tell her not to bother, but she didn't have the strength.

"Well?" Ruen said when she was done. He hadn't come any closer. He used Sull's body as a buffer between them.

"Whatever's hurting her is going on inside," Bellaril said. "She needs healing, and even that might not be enough. Her eyes are strange—glassy, like yours."

"Ruen." Icelin sat up, gripping the dwarf's shoulder for support. "Tarvin's dead."

He followed her gaze to the Watchman's body. "He shouldn't have tried to take you alone."

"Ruen, can you call the Watch?"

He hesitated. The pain twisting his face was all the answer Icelin needed. "What do you want to tell them?" he said.

"Give them our exact location." The tide of pain was slowly leaving her. Icelin felt strangely calm, her body inert. She had no more reserves of strength to lose. This was where everything settled. She had to start the slow climb back up. "I assume they're still searching for me somewhere in Mistshore. Tell them we have wounded and need immediate aid. Go quickly, please."

Ruen stood and walked a little distance away. He removed something from his pouch and spoke a word Icelin didn't hear.

He's been connected to the Watch all this time, Icelin thought. Yet he never brought them roaring down on our heads. He and Sull had followed her, no matter where she went. They'd kept her safe.

The conversation was short. When Ruen returned, the familiar tightness was in his jaw, the only sign of concern he ever betrayed.

"They're not far away," he said.

"Good. Would you help me, Bellaril?" Icelin asked.

The dwarf helped Icelin to her feet. When she could walk steadily, she went to Sull.

He was unconscious, but he still breathed. His face had no color, and his skin was cold. Did it feel worse to Ruen?

"I never touched him," Ruen said, in answer to the unspoken question. "I couldn't know—"

"Of course you couldn't," Icelin said. "And I wouldn't have listened, if you'd tried to tell me. I would have denied it until I was blind to everything else."

Ruen removed his gloves and slid his silver ring off his finger. Replacing his gloves, he picked up Sull's left hand. The ring would only fit on his smallest finger. Ruen slid it snugly into place.

"It'll keep his heartbeat strong until the Watch gets here," Ruen said. "He should live, if they hurry."

Icelin nodded. "How long do we have?"

"Not long."

"Then I need to get going."

She kissed the back of Sull's hand, folded it over his chest, and stood up. Her eyes fell on the bound man hanging over the walkway. The sense of detachment settled over her again as she approached him.

He watched her seat herself on the walkway so he could see her in his peripheral vision. She left him as he was, dangling over the water. The threat was there. She didn't need to tell him.

"He was your friend," Icelin said, pointing to the shirtless, dead giant. When Trik didn't answer, she said, "Sull is mine. You don't know how hard it was for me to tell that man"—she pointed at Ruen—"not to kill you. A tenday ago I could never have conceived such a thought in my mind, but time and hunger and desperation and fear work so many worms into the most pristine thoughts, and mine weren't clean to begin with.

"You can't imagine how much I want to kill you myself right now. It should matter that you're helpless, that you can't fight back. I know it should, but it doesn't. I just want to punish someone, for all of it. Perhaps it's the same for you, and that's why you could kill Sull without even knowing him. I don't care about that either."

She put a hand in the air. He flinched, and she took a gross stab of pleasure in his fear. "I talk too much. It's a curse Ruen warns me against, but I won't waste much more of your time. I'm going to release you. You'll go back to Cerest—you've got no other employment, or you'd have taken it by now. Go back to Cerest, and tell him that I want to talk to him."

Out of the corner of her eye, she saw Ruen and Bellaril exchange glances. She didn't look at them or try to explain. They knew this conversation was as much for their benefit as Trik's.

"Do you know what the Ferryman's Waltz is?" she asked Trik.

For a breath the man didn't answer. Then he nodded, a quick jerk of the head.

"That's good. That will make things easier. Tell Cerest to meet me in the heart of Ferryman's Waltz."

"You're mad," Trik said, breaking his silence at last. "No one—"

"No one goes there," she said over him. "That's why it has to be there. No one to hurt, no more friends to kill. Only enemies. If you come there, Trik, I will kill you, with no words preceding the deed. If Cerest wants me, he'll have to come to the Waltz. Will you carry that message to him?"

Trik nodded again. Icelin flicked her hovering hand. The bands around his chest flickered and melted away. He exhaled sharply and slumped on the walkway. Until then, Icelin hadn't realized how tightly the bands had constricted his breath.

She sensed Ruen stepping toward her. His protective shadow fell across her, seen clearly by Trik as he got to his feet and took off running down the walkway.

When his footsteps receded, Icelin stood and faced the others. Sull was still unconscious, his head tossing fitfully from blood loss and fever. She knelt, dipped her arm in the harbor, and smoothed her cool, wet fingers across his forehead.

"Do you approve?" she asked Ruen without looking up.

"Of your plan?" Ruen said. "I don't know. It's very possible that if Cerest doesn't kill us, the wild magic at the Waltz will do the job."

"I know. I am tempted to wait for the Watch, as I should have done back at the ship. I'll be a long time regretting that." Her voice broke, but she plowed on. "There are some questions I need answered. Cerest has the knowledge, and I think he'll give me what I want."

"I'll go with you," Ruen said, "in case he proves reluctant."

"Thank you," Icelin said. "I know it's more than I deserve, after the way I've used you."

"Don't," Ruen said tersely. "You don't owe me anything."

"I never should have kissed you," Icelin said. "I made you feel my death, and you weren't ready for that. It was a very unromantic gesture." She put her head on Sull's chest. It took several breaths, but when she was strong enough, she looked up at Ruen. "How long have you known? You said you'd never touched me—"

"I haven't," Ruen said. "I only suspected. It was Arowall who confirmed it. He has a power to sense those touched by the spellplague, and how badly they've been afflicted."

Icelin nodded, accepting it. "I hope Cerest can tell me that too—why I'm dying."

"You don't have to rush to your demise so soon," Ruen said, his voice harsh. "You might have years yet, if you stop using magic now."

"But I have to use it, if I'm ever to be free of him," Icelin said. "One last time, that's all I need."

"No. We'll do it another way."

"You think you can change fate?" Icelin said.

He looked away. "Just yours."

"That's not true. You wouldn't have brought Bellaril with us if you didn't believe you could change things. I saw you touch her hands in the Cradle. You wanted her out of there, and not just to be my bodyguard. You knew her death waited in that place."

"She's stubborn enough I wonder if anything can kill her," Ruen muttered, but he didn't deny her words.

"You can't protect me by yourself," Icelin said. "Without your ring, we'll need my magic."

Ruen started and looked at his hand, as if he'd forgotten it was bare. He looked at Sull, at the ring keeping him alive. Defeated, he dropped his hand to his side and clenched a fist.

"Is your raft still intact?" Icelin asked.

"Enough to get us out to the Waltz," Ruen answered. He looked at Bellaril, and a spark of black humor lit his eyes. "What'll it be, Bells? Should I tell the Cradle you were too frightened to take on the fair folk, golden locks and all?"

"You won't be telling any tales when I have your head underwater for the sharks to nip at," the dwarf said, smiling sweetly. "But I'll go to the Waltz, and gladly."

"You don't have to do this, Bellaril," Icelin said.

The dwarf nodded curtly. "I do, but not for you, so don't let your conscience prickle you. After Tarvin led you off the Isle, we got word from the guards that Arowall's dead."

Icelin was shocked. "How?"

"How do you think? It was the elf. The survivors said he had a pair of pretty elf princesses with him." Bellaril looked at Ruen. "Might be you were onto something about my death waiting in the Cradle. I owe you thanks for letting me live long enough to get my revenge on the pretties. But in the meantime, do we leave the butcher here?"

Icelin didn't know what to do. The thought of leaving Sull alone on the walkway was a physical pain. He would be vulnerable to any attack until the Watch arrived.

"I have to protect him," she said to Ruen, half in defense, half in apology. The spell had gone awry the first time she'd used it. For once, that would work to her advantage.

She put a hand in her pouch, grasping the cameo as she'd done in the Cradle. She pictured the woman's face in her mind, the blue curve of her cheek, carved forever in stone. Letting the image float in her consciousness, she wove the spell.

Mist slid off her hands and coiled in the air. It took on the shape and substance of the woman in lace. She stood before Icelin in her vaporous gown, her face impassive.

Icelin didn't know exactly what to do. The last time, the servant had automatically gone where her mind willed it. She remembered that she'd been mentally screaming for something to aid Ruen.

"Can you understand me?" she asked the strange apparition.

The woman didn't answer. Her expression didn't change.

"She has no consciousness," Ruen said. "There's nothing in her eyes."

"So she only has life when Icelin pulls her strings?" Bellaril asked. "Tell her to play guard dog, then."

"It wouldn't work," Icelin said. She raised her right arm slowly out from her body. She concentrated on nothing except moving the appendage. The lady in lace mirrored the gesture until their fingertips were practically touching. "She only does what I directly imagine her to do. Once I'm gone, she won't act independently."

Icelin slowly turned her body until she was facing Sull, who lay a few feet in front of the servant. The lady again mimicked the gesture.

"There," Icelin said. "As long as I picture her standing here, she'll remain. The folk of Mistshore should be wary enough of sea wraiths to stay away from this apparition until the Watch arrives."

Still, her gaze lingered on Sull. She took a step toward him, but Ruen laid a gloved hand on her arm.

"If we're going, we need to go now," he said.

"You're right. I just—"

"I know," Ruen said. "You'll see him again."

She looked at him. "Do you truly think that?"

He shrugged. "You were right. If I didn't think I could beat the odds, I'd never play the game."

They looked at each other for a breath. Then Icelin smiled. "So let's play."

CHAPTER EIGHTEEN

RUEN'S RAFT WAS IN GOOD CONDITION, CONSIDERING IT HAD GONE through a sea wraith attack. Ruen and Bellaril worked the oars while Icelin sank into her thoughts. She kept a part of her mind fixed on the apparition watching over Sull, but she knew she would lose the spell soon. The battle ahead would require her complete concentration.

The Watch would be there by now. They would save Sull. Icelin could not consider any other outcome.

She took inventory of what magic she had left. She had never used so much in so short a time. Some of the spells left she hadn't meditated on in years. They were at the very edges of her consciousness. Her teacher had insisted that she be able to protect herself, but she'd put the harrowing magic as far from her active mind as she could.

Now, mentally, she entered the tower room. The sunlight spilling in the windows had become stygian night. When she entered the room, flames sprang from tallow candles, long unused in their brass candelabras. Black shadows stretched to caress the bookshelves. It was only her fear made manifest, but she was still unsettled at the changes.

Icelin walked to a place at the base of the shelves. A black tome floated down from a high shelf to meet her outstretched hand. Arcane writing was burned into the silver spine. The book opened in her hand, and she read.

The spells were powerful, but she was more concerned with the backlash. She'd been caught completely off guard and made helpless when she'd incapacitated Trik. All the offense she could muster wouldn't be worth anything if she were incapacitated herself.

Icelin blinked, and the tower disappeared. She stared out at an endless stretch of dark water. Ruen didn't have his ring. With his body unfortified, he'd be significantly weakened by any blow that managed to land on him. But she trusted his speed. If they couldn't catch him, they couldn't hurt him.

That left Bellaril. She would anchor all of them, and she would make Cerest's men answer for her master. It worried Icelin that she would be walking into a potential den of spellplague, but she knew the dwarf woman would not be dissuaded.

"What will you do when this is all over?" she asked.

Bellaril looked up from her rowing. "Go back to the Cradle," she said, as if it was a foregone conclusion. "No one to run it, the champion should step in. I don't think he's going to be doing it," she said, nodding at Ruen.

"The title's yours," Ruen said. "I have no interest in the Cradle."

"Don't know what you're missing," Bellaril said.

"What do you love so much about the fighting?" Icelin asked.

Bellaril shrugged. "I like the crowd, like it when they cheer for me. It's what everyone wants."

"She likes to be seen," Ruen said.

"Isn't that what I'm saying?" The dwarf woman looked irritated. "What of it?"

"Bells grew up in a family with eight brothers," Ruen said.

"Eight? Isn't that quite . . . prolific, for a dwarven family?" Icelin said.

"Not so much these days," Bellaril said. "I'm thinking our sire wanted a small army, not a family, so he got all of us on my mother. As far as he was concerned, I would grow my cheek fuzz and be indistinguishable from my brothers. Nine soldiers, nine sons. That's what he wanted. He cut my hair himself, when I refused to do it. My brothers held me down."

"Gods," Icelin said. "Your own family?"

"Blood doesn't mean much. The next time he came for me, I bruised him good before he could get the shears on me. After that, I almost took out his eye. Each time I hurt him a little more, until he stopped coming for me."

"That's when you came to Waterdeep?"

"Not at first. I wandered a little, busied my hands at different jobs before I ended up in Mistshore. But the Cradle." Bellaril shook her head. "They'd never seen a dwarf woman pretty as me who could fight as hard as the boys they bet their coin on."

Icelin smiled at Bellaril's pleased expression. "No one ever tried to make you grow a beard?"

"And they know better than to touch my hair," Bellaril said.

In the distance, Icelin could see the behemoth outline of Ferryman's Waltz. Wraiths circled in an endless dance in the water, occasionally swirling up to curl their bodies sinuously around the broken masts of the inverted ship.

The leviathan's bones twined seamlessly with the rotting greatship. There was no flesh left to suggest what the creature might have looked like in its original form, but the thought of it driving the massive ship straight into the air was boggling. The leviathan's remains kept the *Ferryman* from plunging into the deep by sheer force of an old will, a need beyond death to remain locked in battle.

Bellaril looked unimpressed by the sight. "How you thinking of getting past them?" she asked, nodding at the wraiths.

Icelin closed her eyes. She hummed the familiar ballad to brace herself against the magic. The lost boy, trying to find his way home. She didn't look at Ruen to see his reaction to the song. She couldn't let herself be distracted.

"Find a path into the wreckage," Icelin instructed them. She reached into her pouch for foci, careful this time to make sure they were the correct objects. "When the wraiths scatter, make for it with all possible speed."

Bellaril snorted. "They're not just going to let us glide in—"

"Quiet," Ruen said. "Let her work."

Help me, Nelzun, Icelin thought. The raft drifted closer. One by one, the wraiths slowed their restless circling. They sensed a change in the chaotic usualness of their domain and turned their attention to the small raft and its three distinctly human occupants.

Icelin finished the spell and threw her arms into the air. She released a handful of coin-sized stones, three in each hand. They soared high and burst into orange flame. She pictured them in her mind, the wild, soaring orbs, pulsing with arcane energy.

To the wraiths, arcane energy released from a body steeped in spell-plague was like a bone cast in the path of starving dogs. Their bodies glowed in concert with the flames. They streaked after the orbs in clusters of three and four, leaving a clear path between the only three living souls on the water and a cavernous hole snugged between the wrecked *Ferryman* and the leviathan's bones.

The raft drifted up to a slash of sail draped across the upper half of the opening. Ruen pushed it aside with his oar. He maneuvered the raft between hull and rib and they floated on, into the Waltz.

Cerest listened to Trik's report in fascination. "You're certain it's only the three of them?" he said. Trik looked uncomfortable. Cerest narrowed his eyes. "I'm sorry for the loss of Borion, but if you're lying, it won't go badly for just me. We've lost Cearcor and Rondel."

Trik's eyes bugged out and he half-swayed on his feet. "How?"

"Arowall's guards," Cerest said. "They caught them just after we split up. I underestimated their loyalty. But don't worry, Feston is safe. He's gone to get three more of your fellows to aid us."

"Six of us," Trik murmured. "Six of us against three of them."

"More than passable odds, if Icelin is willing to cooperate."

Trik shook his head. He looked at Cerest in a way that made the elf's skin prickle with anger—disgust swimming in pity. But Trik wasn't looking at the elf's scars.

"You go find her on your own," he said. "Take the others if you want. Hells, they'll all fight 'til they're dead, if there's coin in it."

He turned away, the torchlight burning his profile orange.

"Don't you want revenge?" Cerest asked him. "They killed your friend."

"And I killed hers, or near enough," Trik said. "I'm out of it."

Cerest watched the man walk away. It didn't affect him the way it had when the Locks had left him. He felt nothing now, not in light of what Trik had told him about Icelin.

He'd finally worn her down. She was coming to him, and she was coming angry. He would have to fight to bring her to heel, but he wasn't worried about that. He would have the upper hand, because he had the truth Icelin wanted.

All he had to do was make her give up everything to get it.

Ruen's lantern flickered and went out. Icelin started to cast a light spell when she felt Ruen's hand on her arm.

She knew it was him by the cool touch of leather.

"Save your strength," he said. "I'll get the lantern going. Bells, keep rowing."

The dwarf grunted acknowledgment. Ruen moved away in the darkness. Icelin could only assume he was feeling his way.

She tried to get a sense of the interior of the Waltz by the moonlight filtering through the gaps in the rigging, but the sheer bulk of the vessel and bones prevented much detail from being discernible. The structures had massed together in one hive shape, eclipsing all the individual parts.

The raft bumped against something solid about the same time Ruen got the lantern lit. Icelin thought it was debris floating in the water. It took her a breath to realize that it was a boot, propped against the front of the raft. The boot's owner floated six inches above the water.

Icelin looked up into the most frightening collage of a human face she had ever beheld. Naked above the waist, the man's torso and shoulders were disproportionately wide. Veins and bone bulges stood out from his pale skin. Thin patches of hair grew like scrub grass all over his head. His bottom lip folded over on itself in one corner, giving him a perpetual sneer and allowing a stream of drool to escape from his mouth in a needle-thin waterfall. This type of deformity, the godscurse, Icelin had seen before. But the gods weren't done with their jest at this poor soul's expense.

From the man's neck sprouted a quartet of bulbous gray tentacles. He had them draped across his shoulders like a mane that ended at his belt. The tentacles were moving, seemingly independent of any conscious mental direction on their owner's part.

With his boot on the raft, the man brought forward a long polearm, its tip reaching well above his head. He swung the point down level with her chest. His arm muscles tensed. Icelin thought he was going to drive the weapon through her breast, but instead, he let out a keening whistle that threatened to shatter her eardrums.

Icelin folded into herself, clutching her head against the high-pitched whistle. When it was over, she noticed Bellaril and Ruen had adopted similar protective positions.

"We mean no harm here," Icelin said shakily. "We came here for refuge—"

A howling cry echoed from somewhere deep in the inverted *Ferryman*, cutting off Icelin's words. It rose in intensity, so that it mimicked the man's whistle perfectly. The sound rang out again, nearer, and with it came clicks and rapid pounding on wood.

"Get the oars up!" Ruen shouted. Bellaril was already hauling hers out of the water.

Ruen ran past Icelin and swung his oar. He batted the man's polearm away from her chest and reversed the swing for a swipe at the man's legs.

The deformed man backed off, blocking Ruen's swing with his polearm, but he made no further move to fight back. He smiled, and the expression was horrid, his lips curling like worms around uneven rows of teeth.

Ruen plunged the oar into the water, trying to push them away from the *Ferryman*.

"Beware!" Icelin cried, pointing to the ship. Pinpoints of light were visible from a gap in the hull. There came another howl, and a breath later, two enormous bodies leaped through the opening. In size and movement they resembled stags, but their faces were a cross between canine and badger.

They launched into the air using massive haunches, one and then the other landing on the small raft.

The stink of rotting flesh and gamey fur swelled in Icelin's nostrils. Their craft was not big enough to contain the beasts. Icelin fell to her knees to avoid being slammed off the raft by the weight of the furry bodies.

The beast farthest from her whipped its head around, catching Bellaril by the leg. She fell on her backside. The beast shook her like a playtime doll, and for the first time Icelin heard the dwarf woman scream. Terror widened her eyes, but she fought back, and folded her body up to get at the beast's head.

It lifted her by her leg and swung her, tossing its head and snarling. On the second backswing Bellaril grabbed her belt dagger and planted it beneath the beast's eyes. She missed its burning orb by half an inch.

The beast keened and snapped its head down. The knife came out of its flesh. It bit the blade in half, nearly severing Bellaril's fingers too. The dwarf woman dropped the ruined weapon. Her skull smacked the raft, and she went senseless.

"No!" Icelin cried. She tried to crawl between the second beast's legs. Ruen had his arms around its head. His muscles strained as he attempted to keep the beast's teeth from his neck.

"Get up," Ruen hollered when he saw her weaving between the beast's legs. "They're leucrotta. They'll trample you!"

Icelin lunged forward, but the second leucrotta had already seen her. It dropped Bellaril in favor of a moving target. Curling sideways, it lunged. Its massive weight hit Icelin from the side and bore her to the ground.

She hit the planks hard. The leucrotta's rancid breath was all over her. Bone-ridged jaws snapped inches from her face.

Icelin pushed against the leucrotta's throat. Her hands slipped off the oily fur and down its chest. She had the brief impression of a wild heartbeat and stone-hard muscles. She would never throw the beast off. Her only advantage was the size of the raft. The craft bobbed wildly between the leviathan's bones and the bow of the *Ferryman*. The leucrotta were positioned half on these shores and half on the raft.

Icelin couldn't see Ruen now, but she could hear his punches vibrating along the other leucrotta's body. It squealed in pain, and Icelin heard a splash when its back legs skittered off the raft.

She kicked up, into her own foe's belly. It hacked a foul breath and became meaner. Nine feet of muscle and bone settled on top of her. Icelin couldn't breathe. She flopped back and tried to pull her chest free, but the leucrotta latched onto her wrist and began to shake the appendage in its teeth.

Fire exploded up Icelin's arm. She cried out as the flesh was stripped from her wrist, exposing white bone. The pain was mythic. She felt the blood dribble down her arm and almost passed out. She tried to rip her arm out of the leucrotta's mouth, but that only made the pain worse.

Haltingly, she chanted a spell. Her concentration was in shreds, her attention too caught up in her trapped arm. She imagined how the magic would go wild, but she didn't care. Any pain was better than watching the leucrotta tear her hand off. It was playing with her, enjoying her pain before it ate her alive. She shrieked the arcane words and braced herself for the backlash.

Metal spikes burst bloodlessly from her skin. They were two inches long and curled at the tips. She felt them puncture the roof of the leucrotta's mouth. Willingly she gave the beast her hand, driving the spikes deep.

With a high-pitched wail, the leucrotta released her. The beast pulled its weight off her chest, but more of the spikes were growing from Icelin's skin. She felt each one as a tiny pinprick. They stuck and tore the leucrotta's skin until both woman and monster were drenched in blood. The beast ripped free and retreated, whimpering pathetically. It limped to the edge of the raft and licked its wounds.

Icelin could see the wicked intelligence in its eyes as it re-evaluated her. She stretched out her wrecked arm, daring the creature to come at her and taste more spikes.

It watched her with those frightening eyes like the burning edges of coins, but it came no closer. That's right, Icelin thought. I'm not as weak as I look.

She sat up and looked around, careful to keep one eye on the injured leucrotta. Ruen lay on his back; his beast had worked its way onto his chest, but it couldn't keep him still. He punched the leucrotta in the side of its wedge-shaped head over and over. His fists moved in a blur, delivering quick, alternating punches down either side of the beast's flank. Distracted by the constant stream of hurts, it couldn't bite his fists or sever fingers. He would wear it down eventually, but not before he exhausted himself.

Not far away, Bellaril lay in a wrecked heap. Icelin saw she'd taken a bite to the neck before the beast had grabbed her. Her leg flopped in a blood pool. The stench of copper and oily fur was dizzying.

Icelin crawled to the dwarf's side. Out of the corner of her eye, she saw the leucrotta's deformed master pacing the air among the leviathan's ribs. He was agitated, his tentacles writhing over his chest. He propped the pole-arm on his shoulder, but he didn't throw it.

He won't risk hitting the beasts, Icelin thought. She tore her sleeve, wrapping it three times around the deep gash in Bellaril's leg. The spikes made it take twice as long, but she didn't want to end the spell yet.

When she was done, she tore her other sleeve and wrapped her own wrist as tightly as she could. Blood immediately soaked through the makeshift bandage. She felt light-headed. She prayed she could kill the injured leucrotta before she passed out.

Standing on her knees, Icelin chanted again. The spikes sank back into her flesh and dissolved. On the heels of the dispel, she pushed her arms out from her body, the sweep encompassing both leucrotta.

Blue missiles of magical energy shot from her hands. They hit the injured leucrotta in the chest. The beast howled. The blue streamers sank into its flesh, briefly illuminating the beast's face.

Before the injured one could recover, the missiles rebounded, striking the leucrotta Ruen was fighting in the spine.

In the explosion of pain and surprise, the leucrotta lost its balance at last, its back legs collapsing underneath its body.

Ruen took the distraction and flipped himself onto the leucrotta's back, raking his body across the beast's singed fur. The leucrotta howled and bucked, trying to throw the monk off, but Ruen locked both arms around its head.

The leucrotta turned and charged toward the water. It would force Ruen off one way or another. When the beast turned its head, Ruen sprang up, contorting his body so that his full weight landed on the leucrotta's left flank. With his arms locked around the beast's head, Ruen had the leucrotta disoriented. It tried to twist free, but Ruen pulled straight up and to the right with all his strength.

The leucrotta's neck popped with a stomach-turning crunch. It sagged against Ruen, biting and snapping at random, its senses shattered by the trauma it had suffered.

Ruen grabbed the jagged remains of Bellaril's dagger and plunged it into the beast's throat. It coughed once and expired, collapsing half on top of Ruen. He shoved the body off into the harbor.

The injured leucrotta howled furiously, a cry echoed by the deformed man. He hefted his spear, aiming it at Ruen, while the leucrotta lunged for him.

"No!" Icelin cried. Ruen dodged, but the leucrotta grabbed him by the shoulder, tearing out a chunk of flesh.

He crab-crawled back, putting a little distance between them, but the leucrotta was already tensing to spring again.

Icelin gauged the distance and cast another spell. She twisted her arms together and waited, sweat from the pain pouring down her face, until the deformed man threw his spear. He aimed for Ruen's heart.

Icelin spoke a word, and Ruen and the leucrotta disappeared. She untwisted her hands and instantly they reappeared, but they had exchanged places on the raft.

The deformed man stared, his jaw slack with horror, as his own spear punched a hole in the leucrotta's flank. Its wicked point protruded out the other side, between two of the leucrotta's ribs.

The beast collapsed—dead before it hit the ground—and Ruen was up and moving, grabbing Icelin, hauling her to her feet.

She sagged against him, her strength gone. She'd done too much. Three spells practically at once, and she was losing blood, despite the bandage.

"He's still armed," Ruen said, and as he spoke, the deformed man drew a broadsword from a ratty leather scabbard. He let himself fall out of the air, landing on the raft with a crash that sent Icelin and Ruen to their knees and jarred the leucrotta's body.

Seeing the corpse up close seemed to incense the man more. He came forward, slashing wildly with his blade. Ruen let go of Icelin and rushed him. He ducked under the man's reach just before his slash would have come around and decapitated him. He brought his forearm up and blocked the slash at the man's wrist, leaving his other hand free for a counter attack.

One of the few things Icelin had learned to be true about Ruen Morleth—however much honor he showed as a thief, as a Mistshore fighter he would never fight fair.

So Icelin was not in the least shocked when Ruen brought his other hand up and snagged one of the tentacles writhing at the deformed man's waist. He wrapped it around his fist and yanked.

The man's sword arm flew out wide at the same time his face came down, until he was nose to nose with Ruen. The monk snapped his skull against the deformed man's and released the tentacle.

The deformed man staggered back. He tried to bring his sword up, but Ruen had him this time. The monk took his thick wrist in both hands, twisted and brought the sword point down, driving it harmlessly into the raft. The deformed man released the sword and it bobbed there, a scar in the wood.

Ruen brought his fist around and punched the deformed man in the stomach. He stumbled backward and off the raft. No spell held him as he plunged into the water.

Ruen went back to Icelin's side. "Are you well enough to walk? We have to get to a hiding place. We won't be able to fight Cerest like this."

"I know," Icelin said, "but Bellaril's wound is bad. I don't think we can move her."

A pitiful wail erupted from the water. Icelin and Ruen tensed. Ruen turned, his fists raised to defend against another attacker, but it was the deformed man. He thrashed in the water, his tentacles floating weirdly around his head. It gave the impression an octopus was latched onto his neck.

"Gods," Icelin said, "he can't swim." She took a step toward the edge of the raft.

Ruen latched onto her arm. "Or maybe he's a clever play actor who'll stick you with a hidden dagger when you get close enough to help him."

The cries intensified. Icelin flinched. "If that's so, you'll finish him when he makes his attack. If it's not—I can't listen to him die like that."

"He was willing enough to let us be eaten by his dogs," Ruen said, but Icelin had already shaken off his restraining hand.

She walked to the edge of the raft and got down on her knees. She buried one hand in the strapping that kept Ruen's raft together and extended the other out to the deformed man.

He thrashed for a handful of breaths, his eyes huge in the lamplit darkness. He watched her for sign of a trick, but she just let her hand linger in the air like a bird hovering before a cat.

The deformed man dipped down, catching water in his half-open mouth. He coughed and spat. Panting now, he reached out and grabbed her small hand.

Icelin tightened her grip on the strapping. She felt Ruen's legs on either side of her. He grabbed her shoulders to steady her, and hauled her up by the armpits with the deformed man in tow. Together, they dragged him up and onto the raft.

He lay on his side, in a pool of water and leucrotta blood, coughing up harbor filth from his slack mouth. Icelin stood over him, unsure how far the uneasy truce was going to stretch.

The hairs on the back of her neck prickled, like sudden heat in a cold room. She looked up and saw a man standing in the torn gap of the *Ferryman's* hull. She didn't know how long he'd been standing there, watching them, but the man looked to be about a hundred and ninety years old.

He had a narrow, jaundiced face, but his expression was not unkind. Green eyes peered out from eye sockets that were heavy on top and papery with age on the bottom. His thick, stark white eyebrows were raised in speculation. He was clean-shaven, head and face; and wore a long set of robes, white over gray. A black belt that looked like it had been chewed on by wild dogs circled his waist.

But the feature that demanded the greatest portion of Icelin's attention was the carved wooden staff he held in his right hand. The wood had been notched with arcane markings over every visible surface At its peak, a swirling red mist encircled thin shoots of wood, like foliage on a burning tree.

He had the staff slightly pointed forward. Icelin could imagine a ray of arcane power shooting from the tip and striking Ruen down before the two of them could flinch. This was not a warrior's polearm; this was a wizard's staff. It relied not on human strength, but on a connection with its master. The staff would respond to its wielder's slightest instinct, and it would do so in the space between heartbeats.

Icelin raised her hands, palms out. "We surrender," she said.

CHAPTER NINETEEN

WHEN HE HEARD THE DOGLIKE HOWLS, CEREST MOTIONED FOR HIS remaining men to abandon the boats. At first they hesitated, their eyes drawn to the wraiths circling endlessly above the gap between the *Ferryman* and the leviathan.

The undead creatures did not appear to notice them. They chased and dove at three flaming orbs hanging in midair; but for all their frenzied efforts, they could never capture the arcane energy. Cerest thought the orbs must be Icelin's doing, and wondered for a breath if she had laid a trap for him here.

The dwarf woman's screams rang out in concert with the snarls of beasts. Cerest slapped the boat nearest him with an oar to get his mens' attention. Reluctantly, they slid into the dark water. Stealth was the wisest option for whatever lay ahead of them.

They were only five, but they were the deadliest of the Locks's muck-rakers, in Cerest's opinion. Up to their noses in the water, they swam silently through the gap between the *Ferryman's* corpse and the leviathan's. They carried no light source, trusting Cerest's vision to lead them through the complex tangle of ship and creature. Above their heads, the wraiths continued their oblivious circling.

One leucrotta was dead, and the second dying, by the time they came within sight of the raft and its torn occupants. Cerest watched the monk fighting a hideously deformed man, and then a breath later helping Icelin save the man's life.

So that was how it was between them, Cerest thought. He was her dog, awaiting the command to throw himself into death's path. He felt a strange surge in his chest, a heat that did not diminish, even with the harbor soaking his clothes to his skin.

He didn't like the way the monk touched Icelin, the rough way he hauled her back upon the raft, as if she were so much refuse he couldn't wait to cast off. Yet at the same time he stayed as close to her as polite proximity would allow. Like the dog Cerest had named him, he soaked up the energy of her presence; and his body practically vibrated, begging for more.

Cerest didn't want to see that type of connection between the monk and Icelin. Icelin was *his*.

"Kill the thin man," Cerest whispered to his men. But one of them lifted his hand to his throat, gesturing for silence.

Cerest followed the man's gaze and saw the old man standing on the *Ferryman's* ruins. His staff glowed brightly, illuminating too much of the ruins for Cerest's comfort. The old man looked shrewd, and comfortable in his power.

"Dive down," Cerest said. "We'll swim a safe distance away and watch. If we get the chance, kill the old man quickly and bring me his staff. Do whatever you wish with the thin man, as long as you kill him in the end. By that time, Icelin and I will be safely away."

He sank under the water, knowing the men would follow. The burning sensation remained in his chest.

"Who are you?" the old man asked.

Icelin felt a strange pull on her scalp, as if some invisible hand were tugging at her hair. The strange lifting sensation brought the truth to her lips, like drawing up water from a deep well.

"Icelin Tearn," she answered, and felt strangely calm, unafraid of this powerful stranger. "My companions are Ruen Morleth and Bellaril."

As soon as she'd finished speaking, the calm force shattered, and terror burst free in Icelin's chest.

"His magic compels truth," Icelin said, her words running together. "Don't answer his questions."

"My apologies," the man said. "I only wished to confirm your identities. I won't invade your private space again. I owe you thanks for saving my friend's life."

"It was her doing, not mine," Ruen said. "In thanks, why not tell us your name, friend, and how you know who we are?"

"The wraiths whisper things on the edges of my hearing," the man said. "Lies, mostly, and tantalizing hints about secrets that are better left unspoken. I can't help but listen. They have whispered your names in fear."

"Good," Ruen said. "And your name?" he prompted.

"Call me Aldren," the old man said, "faithful servant of Mystra's memory." He stepped down from the *Ferryman* onto the raft. He never lost his balance, and the raft did not stir in the water. Icelin suspected that like the deformed man, he was hovering inches above the water.

The deformed man was sitting up on the raft, his head dipped between his bent knees. He looked like he was going to be sick. Aldren touched the glowing nimbus of the staff to the deformed man's shoulder. Cast in red, his tentacles basked in the arcane heat. The deformed man looked up at his master.

"It is all right," Aldren said. "Take three deep breaths and you'll be feeling back to normal."

Icelin watched the deformed man do as he was told. The pain creases slowly left his face, and a peaceful resignation descended over his features, as if, for this man, "normal" was simply a chosen level of bearable suffering.

"Who is he?" Icelin asked. The unshakable trust in the deformed man's eyes when he looked at Aldren gave her courage. Surely, no one who could inspire that kind of love would hurt them without cause. "Why are you both here?"

"Darvont has been a friend to me for a long time," Aldren said. "He attacked you in defense of me. It is difficult for his mind to grasp the subtleties between intruder and refugee." He moved his staff back to its upright position beside his head. "Come inside my home, if you will. I can help your friend and give you the answer to your other question."

Icelin looked at Ruen, who shrugged. "He has the upper hand as either a friend or foe." He added, "Bellaril will not survive without aid."

Icelin nodded. Together they lifted Bellaril between them and followed the old man through the wound in the *Ferryman's* hull. Icelin cradled Bellaril's head gently and felt the lifebeat in her neck. She thought of Sull, and a fresh prayer surged within her, a plea for the lives of her friends.

They came through a dark passage and into a chamber of muted spell light. Aldren had cast a light spell on the preserved nests of insects clustered near the ceiling. A dank chill filled the air, creating the unsettling atmosphere of a tomb. Jagged planks and ripped sail gave way to what Icelin could only describe as a nest carved of rotting wood and arcane power.

Planks from the main deck had been stacked against the wall, their ends warped by magic so that they curled back on themselves like wood shavings. The rough chairs had been fastened to the hull for stability. Their curling ends seemed to have been done purely for style.

"Put her here," Aldren said.

Icelin and Ruen laid the dwarf woman in the corner, on a narrow straw pallet stacked with blankets. The crude bed had been stuffed into a wooden frame set six inches off the floor. Icelin saw a mouse burrow into the straw and disappear.

While Aldren moved his staff over Bellaril's body, Icelin surveyed the rest of the odd living quarters. Another chair and a table stood in the center of the chamber, reinforced by more wood to make a crude desk. Like the wizard's staff, the surface had been covered with inscribed symbols, some scratched and some burned into the wood. Icelin couldn't imagine how long it must have taken to carve the symbols so meticulously.

Aldren stood straight. The light in his staff dimmed. His eyes looked more sunken than ever, but he smiled wanly. "She will sleep heavily for a time, but she is healing. There will be no permanent damage."

Before Icelin could speak, he brought the staff up and passed it in front of her face. Briefly blinded, Icelin felt warmth and strength flow back into her body. The terrible pain in her wrist went away in an instant. She didn't realize how close the agony and weakness had been to consuming her until they were gone. When the light faded, she saw Aldren make the same gesture before Ruen.

"I'm in your debt," Icelin said. "I am truly sorry to have brought my burdens to your door."

The old man waved a hand dismissively. "I am not so easily intimidated at the prospect of other people's burdens. I welcome the distraction from my own." He followed her gaze to the desk and its writings. "Wood is the only reliable substance to hand," he explained. "The harbor and the wild magic together are so toxic the ink is eaten and the parchment crumbling before a decade is out."

"A decade?" Icelin said. "You've been here that long?"

"What is that?" Ruen asked. He pointed to the back of the chamber, which was cast in shadow outside the spell light.

Aldren spoke a word, and two candles jumped to burning life from the back of the hold. They sat in brass dishes on another wooden table, this one free of symbols but draped in a cloth runner of purple velvet. Faded gold braiding lined the edges of the runner, and in its center, true gold glinted in the candle light.

"Is that an altar to Mystra?" Icelin asked. As she approached, she thought the glintings were jewels, but when she got close she realized her mistake. They were not jewels, at least not in the sense that a high lady of Waterdeep would value.

They were holy symbols. She recognized Mystra's symbol, and Deneir, Helm, even Mask and Eilistraee. There were several others she didn't know.

"I don't understand," Icelin said, turning to Aldren. "I thought you served Mystra's memory?"

Aldren seated himself on a chair and propped his staff next to him. Darvont sat on the floor across from him. His eyes never left the old man's face.

"I first came here in the Year of Blue Fire," Aldren said. "I was a man of thirty, then. I awoke on a slope of sand with water lapping my face and found that I had been brought to the place by this man," he said, gesturing to Darvont. "I remembered only that I had been caught in an arcane storm of the magnitude you only imagine in nightmares."

"The Year of Blue Fire," Icelin said. "You were there at the beginning of the Spellplague? But that would make you—"

"Over one hundred and twenty years old," Aldren said.

"How is it you're still alive?" Icelin asked.

"Your spellscar keeps you alive," Ruen said. He stood next to Icelin at the altar, but he did not touch any of the pieces arranged there.

"In a way," Aldren said. "I have died several times over the course of these nine decades, but my scar, as you call it, restores me."

Icelin stared at the old man. She thought she'd ceased being surprised at the suffering endured by those the plague had touched, but she was wrong.

She looked at the holy symbols. "You were a priest of all these gods?"

"Over each of my 'lifetimes,' and sometimes more than one," Aldren said. "I served them all, faithfully, not realizing at first that they, like Lady Mystra, had passed on. How could they cease to be when I could not? It was one of the more horrifying truths I've had to face: to accept immortality when the gods were dying around me. When I realized that none of them would be able to grant the long sleep I desired, I dedicated myself to what the Art had lost—to Mystra's memory."

"How does your magic function?" Ruen asked. "From whom do you receive your divine power?"

"The gods are silent to me," Aldren said, "even those I know to be alive and thriving. I don't know why. Fortunately, the magic in this staff has remained strong. It is my only link to the power that once was Mystra's, and so I will watch over it, this small shard of the unbound weave that no longer has a weaver."

"But why stay here?" Icelin asked. "Why not live in the city?"

"Because I feared the day I would be struck down. I imagined awakening in a sealed crypt, enduring a slow death over and over until I descended into madness. And I couldn't leave him." Aldren touched the side of Darvont's head. "He saved me and shares my curse. I suspect part of his mind dwells forever in the heart of that arcane storm."

"So you'll live here forever, custodian of the same magic that scarred you," Icelin said, "venerating gods who won't answer your prayers?"

The old man shook his head. "You should not anger yourself on my behalf. Many others suffer greater trials. You yourselves are touched, are you not?"

Icelin and Ruen exchanged glances. "How do you know that?" Icelin asked.

"Because we are all the same, now," Aldren said. "Weavers—custodians of the Art that was lost."

"Only Mystra could control the weave," Ruen said. "We aren't gods, and we aren't immortal."

"Then what is magic, without its caretaker?" Aldren challenged. "Lost, ungovernable. Yet in some few individuals it finds a vessel. You're quite right: we are not gods, and most of us do not survive the blue flame that burns our flesh and bores our minds. But without the Lady, where can the Art go? It's been too long mastered. I say it cannot survive on its own, so it clings to the mortal realm and threatens to destroy what it loves most."

Ruen snorted. "You can think that, if you find it comforting. The truth is magic doesn't have a soul. There's no beauty left in the Art. The only thing it can do is burn."

"Is that why you gave Fannie the quill?" Icelin asked softly. "Why you stole a collection of magic at amazing cost to yourself? Did you risk your freedom because you believed there was no beauty left in the Art?"

Ruen stared at her. He pressed his lips into a hard line, but his expression wasn't exactly angry. "What has the Art ever done but bring you misery?" he said. "Why would you defend it?"

"I would defend *you*," Icelin said. "I don't know if what you say is true," she said to Aldren, "but my friend and I must leave soon. We're being pursued by a group of men. I led them here, thinking only the wraiths would be disturbed by our presence. I would lead them away—"

"But there is no better place than here for confronting demons, real or imagined," Aldren said, "Please don't fear for my safety. Darvont and I will be protected within the *Ferryman's* hold. You are welcome to share its sanctuary, but I suspect that would defeat your purpose."

"It would," Icelin said. "Yet I would beg sanctuary for my friend Bellaril. I've no right to ask, and I have nothing to offer you in return. But if I live long enough I would find a way to repay you."

"She's true to her word," Ruen said. "Stubbornness has never known a more faithful lover than Icelin Tearn."

Icelin shot him a look, but Aldren said, "Of course your friend will stay. No one will harm her while I keep watch."

"My deepest thanks," Icelin said. She looked at Ruen. "Are you ready, clevermouth?"

Ruen nodded. They made their way to the gap in the hull. Icelin paused by Bellaril's pallet. The dwarf was still unconscious, her skin the color of the moon, but she breathed evenly and deep.

"She truly would have been killed," Icelin said to Ruen, "if you hadn't made her come with us. Cerest killed the master of the Cradle—such a mad action even someone so well protected as Arowall couldn't have predicted it. And Bellaril wouldn't have abandoned her master to save her own life."

"Doesn't mean she'll live any longer than she was meant to," Ruen said.

"Maybe," Icelin said. She looked at Aldren. "Do you think your fate can be changed?" she said. "That one day the plague will allow you to die?"

"That is my fondest hope," Aldren said. "Until then, I will live as best I can."

"You and I are two halves of the same curse," Icelin said. "The plague lives in me. It causes my memory to be nigh perfect, for a price. Ruen says it will take my life before age does. The more I use my own magic, the quicker that fate will come for me."

Aldren's soft green eyes reflected the spell light. "I am sorry for your burden," he said.

Icelin shrugged. "I am sorrier for other burdens—loss and pain done to my friends because of my own fear. I think you're right. We, all of us, can only live as best we are able, and hope to change our fates—" She stopped as something took hold inside of her.

Memory came, this time uncalled. With trembling fingers, Icelin removed her pack from her back and dumped its contents on the floor. The deformed man skittered out of the way.

"What are you doing?" Ruen said. Seeing her face, he crouched beside her and helped her gather the scattered letters from Elgreth. "What's wrong?"

"He tried to live as best he could," Icelin said. "Just like us, like Aldren, retreating to this place."

She found the letter she was looking for and practically tore it in her haste to unfold the old parchment.

"Cerest isn't after a perfect memory," Icelin said. "Elgreth's scar was different from mine. Here!" She read part of the letter aloud. "I sat upon a rooftop and looked out over Cutlass Island, at the ruins of the Host Tower of the Arcane. The locals say it is a cursed place, and I cannot help but agree. The restless dead walk on that isle, sentinels to its lost power. In my younger days, I would have longed for the challenge and promise of treasure to be found in such a forgotten stronghold. I can see the magic swirling under shattered stone. It drifts among the bones of the once mighty wizards who ruled here."

Icelin stopped reading and looked at Ruen. "Do you see?"

Ruen shook his head. "What are you talking about?"

"I can see the magic swirling under the shattered stone," Icelin repeated. "He could detect powerful magic, through stone and earth, just with his eyes. What gift would tempt a treasure hunter more?"

"Cerest will be disappointed when he finds out you inherited a very different gift," Ruen said.

"Yes," Icelin said. "A perfect memory is of little use to him. His hunt was for nothing."

It was all a tragic jest. Icelin was grateful to have the one mystery solved, but there were still missing pieces. "I have to know why he betrayed my family," she said. "If Cerest won't confess it . . . *how* do you remember something you've managed to forget so thoroughly that even the spellplague can't penetrate the defense?"

She'd meant the question rhetorically, and was surprised when Aldren answered, "If your mind has seen fit to bury something so deeply that even the spellplague can't touch it, I would count the power a blessing."

"Blessing?" Icelin said. "I don't see how. If I had this memory, it would explain so much about my life. Why would I want to bury it?"

"You mistake me," Aldren said. "I didn't mean it was a blessing that you be denied a piece of yourself. I meant to say that if you could find within you the same power that pushes the plague back from this one, vital memory, you might find the power to change your fate."

As Icelin digested this, she noticed Ruen looking at the old man intently. "Can you help her?" he asked. "Is there any priestly magic in that staff that can help her remember what she needs to know?"

"There are ways of bringing memories to the surface, if you truly want to relive them," Aldren said. "When dealing with the spellplague, such methods are never certain to work and carry their own cost. I have stored the memories of each lifetime I've lived," Aldren said. "I don't know if I can impart such a thing to your friend, but if she is willing, I would try."

"At what risk to yourself?" Icelin said. "No. We've caused you enough grief."

"Are you afraid, Icelin?" Ruen said.

Icelin could hear the challenge in his voice. "No," she said, "I'm not afraid. But I'm tired of other people risking pieces of themselves for me. I think it's time Cerest was made to answer for what he's done. I will make him tell me."

She stepped to the gap in the hull. She could feel an invisible presence. The old man's magic formed a protective seal over the opening.

"Thank you," she said to Aldren. "Whatever happens, I'm glad to have met you."

"And I, you," said Aldren. "The gods go with you."

Icelin nodded and stepped through the opening. Ruen followed behind her.

She didn't know what she expected to happen once she crossed the seal. An ambush, another monster, or a spray of magic from the elf woman who'd taken her on the shore? She got none of those things, but she sensed the change in the air as soon as the harbor scent hit her nose.

"Look above you," Ruen said quietly.

Icelin looked up and lost her breath. She could see slivers of moonlight through the *Ferryman's* tangled rigging. The skeletal forest canopy swelled with movement. Sea wraiths circled each other and the wreckage. More were floating up from various parts of the ruins to join the mass. The unearthly choir keened softly, as if singing to the moon or some other, invisible celestial body.

"You said there was wild magic here," Icelin said, "that it draws the wraiths. Can they feel it—the three of us here together?"

"I don't know," Ruen said. "But it's possible we're stirring up whatever's been lying dormant here since the *Ferryman* was destroyed."

"Not just us," Icelin said, "him too."

Cerest sat cross-legged on Ruen's raft. He was alone, and looked completely at ease beneath the canopy of swirling wraiths. Icelin knew his men would be nearby, but wherever they were, Cerest had them well hidden. She wondered if Ruen, with his sharper eyes, could detect them. The only illumination came from the lantern on Ruen's raft and a torch Cerest had propped in front of him.

He looked up when they appeared, and smiled in genuine pleasure. "Well met, Icelin," he said. "I received your message. I'm happy to see you are well."

He didn't seem to notice or care that there was a puddle of drying blood—leucrotta and Bellaril's—behind and to his left. The copper scent combined with the leucrotta's naturally pungent stink must have been overwhelming. But like the dying horse that day on the Way of the Dragon, Cerest took the horror completely in his stride. His pleasant expression never faltered.

Somehow, though, the sight of him amid the blood was less intimidating instead of more. Here at last he wasn't trying to hide what he was, the deficiency of mind that had set him on her like a crazed hunting hound. She could see him in this true state and feel pity, though it was a fleeting emotion.

"Greetings, Cerest," she said. "I hope you haven't been waiting long."

"I'm accustomed to being patient. I was more than willing to wait for you," Cerest said. "In the end, I knew you'd come back to me."

Icelin felt Ruen tense behind her. She reached back to touch him, but of course he moved just out of her grasp. She dropped her hand.

"Are we alone?" she asked, deliberately affecting a teasing tone.

"There's at least one in the crow's nest," Ruen said. "Ten feet up." He pointed, and Icelin heard the scuff of boots on wood, a figure hastening to conceal himself in the shadows. Ruen smiled. "I don't think he enjoys heights."

Cerest was not so amused. Hatred came alive in his eyes when he looked at Ruen, an emotion so intense Icelin wondered at its root. "I would be more than willing to dismiss my men, Icelin, if you would send your friend away," he said. His voice was unsteady. He swallowed.

"But that's hardly fair," Icelin said. "I have so few friends left, thanks to you." She reached into her pack and pulled out the stack of letters. "Do you know what these are?"

Cerest stood and walked toward her outstretched hand. Icelin allowed him to approach but kept her body squarely between Ruen and Cerest, noting the irony of her protection of the elf.

Not for long, she thought, as the viper took the letters from her hand. I won't need you for long.

Cerest shuffled through the letters, and Icelin could tell he recognized the handwriting immediately. "These are Elgreth's," he said, handing them back to her. "I never would have credited him with the strength to write them. He was in poor shape when I left him in Luskan."

She thought she'd been prepared for anything, but at his words, Icelin felt a cold kiss on the back of her neck, as if one of the wraiths had drifted down to whisper hateful truths in her ear.

Anger bloomed in place of the cold, and the contrast made her tremble. She felt the letters flutter from her hands. They landed on the harbor's surface and became tiny, worn boats carried away by the rippling current.

She had felt many things upon learning of her grandfather's identity and subsequent fate: grief, confusion, loss, but always a place removed from her heart. It wasn't that she was callous. It was simply that nothing could surmount the pain and anger that lived there after Brant's death—until now.

"Why?" she said. "If you found Elgreth in Luskan, why didn't you bring him home to Waterdeep? You said he was your best friend. How could you leave him in that godscursed place?"

"He was too far gone to walk," Cerest said, "and I didn't have enough men. I never would have made it out of the city with him. We would have been set upon—fresh carrion for the vultures."

"Of course," Icelin said bitterly. "You wouldn't have risked yourself to make your old friend comfortable in his last days."

"Whatever you think of me, Icelin, I *was* Elgreth's friend," Cerest said. "I would have given anything to have brought him home. He should never have gone to Luskan."

"He went to protect me," Icelin said. "He must have been terrified you would find me. What was it, Cerest? What did you do to betray my family's trust in you so completely?"

"I never intended to betray them," Cerest said, "just as I didn't intend for Elgreth to run from me. You are too young to understand. My family was composed of artisans. They had centuries to hone their skills. My father could craft weapons that sang with arcane music. He only made a handful of blades in his lifetime, but they were *named*. If not alive, they were near enough to sentient that men in Myth Drannor craved the bond between sword and man more than they craved a mate. And it was all because my father could sense magic and make it bend to whatever shape he desired. It didn't matter that the Spellplague was ravishing magic all over Faerûn. My father might have been a god. He was master of the unbound weave."

"But his son did not inherit his ability," Icelin said.

"No," Cerest said. "I tried, but the gift never came. There were reasons, my father said. A question of birth."

The naked longing in his eyes was of a kind Icelin had never seen except on a grieving person. Cerest had long ago realized what he could never be, but he refused to come to terms with his inadequacy.

"It was easier after I left," Cerest said. "I comforted myself by thinking that this kind of gift was an aberration. I would never see it again, even in my long lifetime." His voice was ragged, emotion breaking through at last. "I met Elgreth, and your parents, and everything was perfect. We would have continued together, year after year, explorers all"—his face contorted—"if Elgreth hadn't wanted to explore the Rikraw Tower."

These were the words Icelin had waited to hear. Cerest had given the tower a name, and names were power. She felt the bonds around her memories snap.

CHAPTER TWENTY

As Cerest spoke, Icelin felt a kind of stupor descend upon her mind. The fog thickened and deepened. This was not like the other times she'd gone into her mind, seeking a stray piece of lost information. This was not in her control. She was being led down the twisting corridors by a hand that belonged to a person that was her and yet not her. This person was a child and yet possessed of more wisdom than her waking self.

Icelin was only half-aware, in this state, of Cerest moving closer to her and Ruen farther away. This repositioning made no sense to Icelin, but she had no time to consider the implications. The hand pulling her was moving faster, sweeping her along with its urgency.

The corridors turned to aged stone; dust and cobwebs clung to the corners. Was she going backward in time? An appropriate metaphor, Icelin thought. Brant always said her mind worked with the same practicality of a history text. Past was old, present was new.

She came to the end of the passage and found a swathe of green cutting brilliantly across the stone. Stepping out of the passage, Icelin found herself in a vast field.

At first she was afraid. The space was too open. The smells of the city were gone. She could only detect grass and the distant smell of smoke in the air.

This was what outside the city smelled like. This was what *space* smelled like. Gone were the constant press of animals and South Ward wagon traffic and the refuse of so many folk living side by side. She felt—remembered—the grass tickling her ankles, the movement of insects in the living carpet.

She breathed deeply and caught the hint of smoke again. Mingled with the ash and fire was the scent of onions cooking, and fresh game nearby.

A dusty ribbon of road, stamped many times over with hoof prints, snaked out in front of her. It led up a steep hillside and out of sight. She followed it, and when she crested the rise saw the campfire, the stew pot cooling in the grass, and the circle of figures waiting for their meal.

The feeling of familiarity cascaded over Icelin with such intensity that it left her dizzy and unmoored in her own memories. It was like encountering beloved friends with whom she'd corresponded for years but never seen face to face.

Elgreth cradled a spit stuck with flaming venison. He looked young, his dark brown hair showing only a few threads of silver in the sunlight. He had a thick moustache and wide arms like ale barrels. His cloak fell around him in a pool of darker green against the grass. He pulled the venison off the spit, snatching his hand back from the steaming meat. He sucked on his fingers and pulled faces at the child seated across the fire from him.

Icelin recognized her young self only distantly. Her black hair was trimmed short. She looked like a boy, except she was delicately framed and wore a dress of thick cotton and indeterminate shape.

How strange to see herself this way. She was no longer walking through vague half-memories, as she had been in her dreams. Her mind was spinning the completed story, as vividly as Kaelin had staged his play.

A woman stepped into view and dropped a blanket over her younger self's head. The child squealed and crawled out from under the quilt, her eyes staring adoringly up at her mother.

Her mother and father. Icelin saw them more clearly than she saw her younger self. Her father sat behind her mother, pulling his wife back into his lap, trapping her between thin arms. He was not nearly as burly as Elgreth. His back was slightly hunched under the weight of the pack he wore. His spectacles had been bent and repaired so many times they gave his face a misshapen appearance. When he looked at her mother, his face was so full of love. And in that breath he became the most beautiful man Icelin had ever seen.

Her mother looked exactly like Icelin. She had the same dark hair, trimmed short, but there was no mistaking her curves for a boy. She had the full mouth and healthy weight Icelin lacked, but their eyes were the same, their cheekbones as finely chiseled.

How did I keep you away from my memory for so long? Icelin thought. Where have you been hiding? She sat down on the grass, determined to stay forever in the field, content to bask in the presence of the family she'd never met.

When she looked back at the scene, she noticed the tower for the first time. An ugly gray spike that was slightly off center from the rest of the landscape, the tower cast a shadow that reached nearly to the campsite.

She noticed other things. Her father kept shooting glances in the tower's direction, a look of barely contained excitement stretching his face.

Thirty paces from the fire, Icelin saw another figure, small with distance, agile when he moved. The figure had his back to her, but Icelin could see he was male. Two points of flesh stuck out from his golden hair. When the figure turned, Icelin was shocked to see the smooth, handsome features, the lively eyes unmarked by grief and trauma.

Cerest was an angelic blight on the idyllic scene, Icelin thought. She could see how anyone, man or woman, human or elf, would be taken with him. His face, in its symmetry, was more beautiful than any she'd ever seen. He motioned to her family, his face bright with exhilaration.

The camp broke up. Elgreth left the venison smoking in the grass. Her mother scooped her younger self up in her arms and tossed her over one shoulder. Her delighted squeals trailed away down the hill toward the tower.

Don't do it. Don't go. Stay, and be with me always. Icelin got to her feet and followed her family. She tried to run, but the tower seemed always at a safe distance from her footsteps, and no shout would reach the ears of the living memories before her.

She closed her eyes, and when she opened them, she was inside the tower, just as she had been in every nightmare that had haunted her from childhood.

This time, she was no spectator. She resided in the body of her younger self. She could feel the cool ground beneath her bare feet, and the shadows swirling around her had form and substance. They were her family. Her father was taking scrapings from the brittle stone walls and placing them in vials on his belt. Her mother was chanting in an undertone, her hands on the spine of what had once been a massive tome. The spine was all that remained. Her mother's eyes were closed. Yellow light encircled her fingers.

Her mother—a wizard! Icelin couldn't believe it. Her mother had carried the gift of the Art, and Icelin had inherited it. Gods, how much her mother could have taught her, guided her, if she had lived to see to her daughter's tutelage.

"Be cautious," said a voice.

The sudden interruption jarred Icelin from her thoughts. She looked to see who had spoken and saw Elgreth standing next to her mother.

"It's all right," her mother said. She touched Elgreth's arm. "I sense no pockets here. Cerest was right. The plague has abandoned this place. Have you found anything?" she asked, addressing her husband.

"Where's Cerest gone to?" Elgreth asked.

"I think he's putting out the campfire," her mother said. She touched Elgreth's cheek affectionately. "I expect we forgot to douse it in our excitement."

Icelin only half-listened to the rest of the conversation; her attention was caught by the ruined book. She got on her knees and turned her head to see the letters on the spine. They were outlined in blue fire, the edges of the script blurring and fluttering like wings on a dying butterfly.

As she watched, the flames punctured the leather binding, leaving blackened curls in their wake. The smell of charred leather rose in her nostrils. She looked up, and saw that her mother was watching the book too. Her eyes widened, and the color drained from her lovely face.

Icelin, hampered by her younger body, could not get to her mother. She tripped over a pile of wood and fell. Her face caught the sunlight coming from a gaping hole in the tower ceiling. The light beating down was too intense. The ground had been cold only a breath ago, yet everywhere around her she felt heat. It was like she'd stepped into the middle of the campfire.

"Icelin."

She heard her mother's voice. It had never sounded like that before. With a child's certainty and an adult's memory, Icelin knew this was the end.

The spellplague pocket, awakened by her mother's simple magic, swirled to life from the rafters of the ruined tower ceiling. A cerulean cloud that looked like a tiny, confined thunderstorm, it crawled along the walls, finding cracks in the stone and exploding them, spraying shards of rock on the helpless people below.

Someone was at her side, hauling her roughly under a cloak.

"Get her out!" she heard her mother scream. Then her voice faded. Icelin was running, running on legs that didn't belong to her. Elgreth had picked her up. The blue fire was everywhere—in her eyes, her mouth. She was blind. She couldn't see either of her parents.

They broke free into daylight, but the blue fire wasn't done with them. It stretched out hungry tendrils and snared her hair and her arms. Elgreth dropped her to the grass.

She started to cry. The heat was too intense. It was the worst sunburn she'd ever had. Her flesh should be melting from her bones. She heard Elgreth next to her, screaming. She reached for him, but she couldn't touch him. The blue light was everywhere. There were other screams, shouts her young mind couldn't comprehend but that the adult Icelin recognized as the Elvish language.

Cerest was nearby, crying out in agony. His beautiful face was melting and being reforged into something new, a visage that more closely matched his soul. Icelin curled up in a ball on the grass and waited for it to be over. She didn't care if she died, as long as the pain stopped.

Oblivion came, sweeping its cool hand across her body. She was resting in a dark place. She wanted to sleep there forever. To wake was to re-enter that world of horrid pain.

When she opened her eyes again, she was still on the ground. She could see the tip of the tower, weirdly, in her peripheral vision, as she stared up at the sky. Star and moonlight illuminated the scene now, and somewhere, far off, she smelled another campfire burning.

Elgreth leaned over her, adding another blanket to a growing pile on her small body. Her nose was cold. Elgreth's breath fogged in the night air.

"Is she awake?" It was Cerest's voice. He spoke in the human tongue. He sounded weak.

Elgreth didn't reply. He stroked her cheek, and threaded his fingers in her hair to push it away from her face.

He looked broken, the adult Icelin remembered. Gone were the light-hearted smile and the fringes of youth that she'd seen by the campfire. They had been replaced by a tremendous weight and sadness.

She reached up to touch him. His skin was warm, his moustache hair brittle. He smelled like smoke. It was no campfire that burned, only the remnants of the Rikraw Tower—the funeral pyre for her parents.

When Elgreth left her at last, she crawled out from under the blankets and walked to the tower. Elgreth called to her, screamed for her to stop. But she couldn't. Her parents were somewhere in the wreck of stones.

The tower's collapsed wall was a black blemish on the landscape. Scorch marks sprayed out from it in jagged, oily streaks. Viewed from above, the tower might have been a stygian sun.

Elgreth was still screaming. He's injured, Icelin thought, or he'd be running after me. I am wrong for leaving him. But she couldn't make her feet stop walking.

She caught her foot on a rock. When she looked down, she realized the rock was a hand, clutching her ankle. The fingernails were black, the palms blistered and oozing white pus.

Frightened, Icelin jerked away. She followed the arm attached to the hand and found Cerest, curled on the ground. He had one arm thrown across his face. The appendage was out of its socket. His other arm stretched toward her, trying to stop her.

Icelin looked at that blistered, trembling hand for a long time before she turned and resumed her long journey to the tower.

The stones vibrated with a power beyond sun-warmth. Everything was cold now, but she could feel where the energy had been. When her eyes adjusted to the dimness inside the tower, Icelin could see there was nothing left. Her mother's hair, her father's spectacles—the spellplague had burned them to ash.

She touched the blackened stones, caught the ash-falls drifting through the air. Illuminated in moonlight, they might have been dust or the remains of flesh. She caught as many as she could in her small hands and clutched them against her chest. She started to cry and found she was too dehydrated for the tears to form.

Carefully, she got down on her hands and knees and placed her cheek against the ground. The ash stirred and warmed her skin. She stayed there, imagining her mother's arms around her, while Elgreth screamed for her outside the tower.

.:⌢:.

Daerovus Tallmantle was a patient man, and his office demanded discipline, but, as he surveyed the wraiths circling the distant Ferryman's Waltz, he concluded that he'd been patient long enough.

"That's the place," he said.

"Can we trust him?" Tesleena asked.

The Warden thought of Tarvin, his head crushed by a plank. His body had been borne away to the Watch barracks and then to his family.

He surveyed the group of men and women that stood before him in homespun disguises. Their eyes flitted between the Ferryman's Waltz and his face.

"You know what's expected of you," he said. "If any man or woman among you feels he cannot perform his duty, you may accompany Tarvin's body back to the barracks. I look you in the eyes and ask this plainly: will you see justice done?"

A chorus of "ayes" answered him. As promised, he stared each of them in the eyes, hunting deceit. He found none, and was satisfied.

"On the boats," he said. " 'Ware the wraiths, but Icelin is the one you want. Bring her in."

.:⌢:.

"You have to untangle yourself from this," said a voice Icelin did not, at first, recognize.

She looked up, and for some reason was unsurprised to find Aldren standing in the shadows of the tower.

"I didn't think you could weave yourself into memories," Icelin said.

"Only yours, it would seem," Aldren replied. "But I would rather not be here. This is a foul place, and you're needed elsewhere."

"I don't know how to leave," she said. "What if the plague won't let me?"

Aldren made a motion with his gnarled hand, and his staff appeared in the clawed grip, as if it had always been there, invisible.

"To weave magic requires discipline," he said. "At the best of times, anything can go wrong, because the Art runs unchecked. We are its only shepherds now." He held out his staff to her. "To be a weaver requires a focus," he said, "a tool to channel your energy. You should never rely on such a thing completely, but in the worst of times it can help you endure the wildness of the raw Art."

Icelin touched the staff and felt a pulsing energy. The Art ran through the staff like blood in wooden veins. She could feel the contained power, frightening and pure.

"What if it gets away from me again?"

"It surely will," Aldren said. "Such things are inevitable. The only thing you can do is focus on what is most important to you—what's worth saving."

"Ruen." She remembered his name as if he had been the dream, and this her only reality. She stood up, and her body was an adult's, though weak and fragile.

The tower melted around her. The black stones faded, as if all the filth was being drained from her memory. She closed her eyes against the swirling, turbulent cleansing.

She smelled the harbor, but when she opened her eyes, the scene had changed. Her mind couldn't process it at first.

Ruen stood thirty feet away, fighting two men at once. A third man floated in the water, his right arm and chest contorted at an odd angle in the water.

She was lying on Ruen's raft. Cerest crouched over her. His crumpled face showed concern, but Icelin noticed he held a dagger slackly in his right hand.

"Are you well?" he asked.

She licked her lips and tried to speak, but she'd been in her mind too long. The words came out as incoherent mumbles.

Cerest leaned closer. "Say it again, Icelin. I didn't hear you."

Icelin didn't repeat what she'd been trying to say. She brought her knee up and crushed it into Cerest's stomach.

He lurched back onto his right elbow, losing his balance when he tried to bring the knife to bear. He pitched over the side of the raft into the water.

Icelin sprang to her feet and immediately saw that Ruen was in trouble. He held off the two men at his right and left flank, but the man on the crow's nest was frantically cranking a crossbow into position. He propped it on the lip of the nest to steady his aim.

Cerest thrashed in the water. He grabbed for the raft. Icelin kicked him in the face. Blood exploded from his nose; her heel had knocked it out of position. The elf cursed and backstroked, putting a safe distance between them.

Lifting her arms, Icelin chanted a spell and brought her hands together, as if she were cupping them around the crow's nest. The basket of rotting wood burst into flames that rose up around the man with the crossbow.

The man shrieked and dropped the weapon. It landed in the water and sank. The man dived from the nest, fistfuls of flame eating at his clothing. He hit the water belly first.

The men fighting Ruen had their backs to the crow's nest. They tried to turn to see their companion's fate, but Ruen wouldn't give them a respite. He clipped the shorter of the two in the jaw, spinning him half toward the water and upsetting his balance on the bones of the leviathan.

It was all about balance. He kept them both at bay because they couldn't keep their feet. If they'd been on level ground, Ruen would have had several of his bones crushed by now.

While the shorter man steadied himself, Ruen dodged a roundhouse punch from a man wearing a mail vest and thick gauntlets. Built like a brick, this man would be harder to move with simple punches.

Icelin picked her spell carefully, focusing on the chain links pressed tight against the man's body. She could feel the trembling in her fingers as she worked through the complicated gestures.

Two spells, by the gods. Give me two spells without pain, Icelin pleaded. Lady Mystra, I can't pray to your memory. I never knew you. But if any goddess can hear me . . .

She flexed her fingers and released the spell. Her vision blurred. Nausea rose in her gut, and she felt cold, sticky sweat clinging to her forehead. She forced past the sickness and concentrated on the brick man's mail vest.

There was no visible change. Ruen took a glancing punch to his shoulder from the shorter man. He answered with a kick that took the man's right leg out from under him. The short man grabbed an overhanging bone, perhaps a rib of the long-dead creature. The bone snapped off. The man grabbed wildly for his companion and buried his fingers in the mail links.

The brick man roared in pain, and the shorter man cried out as well. Smoke rose from the brick man's clothing where it had pressed against the metal links.

Wide-eyed, the brick man patted his chest, touching hot links wherever his hands rested.

Ruen shot a quick glance at Icelin across the water. He jerked his head in acknowledgment.

"Let me help you with that," he told the brick man. He aimed a kick to the man's midsection. The brick man howled and fell backward into the water. A chorus of snakelike hisses rose from where the hot metal touched the cold water. The brick man sank to his chin, a look of relief crossing his face.

"Get back up 'ere!" cried the short man. He dodged a second kick from Ruen. "Help me!"

The brick man shook his head and swam away. He was obviously done with the fight.

Icelin turned her attention from Ruen to Cerest, who was climbing onto the raft behind her. His knife was gone, but he looked furious enough to kill her with his bare hands. His nose was a red, twisted mass on his face. The blood seeping into his scars made him look like a demon. Icelin remembered the scene outside the tower, when the newly scarred elf had looked up at her young self in agony.

"I remember now," she told him. "The tower. My parents. Elgreth. Did you really think it was safe for us to go in, Cerest? Or was that just what you told yourself? The same way you convinced yourself it wasn't your fault that they died?"

"I had to weigh the risk and reward," Cerest said. There was no remorse in the words. "The knowledge and artifacts we might have found would have enriched all our lives, including yours."

"Oh yes, my life has been enriched indeed," Icelin said.

"I was more than willing to take care of both of you afterwards," Cerest said. "Elgreth could have used his scar to unearth treasures unimaginable. He'd become just like my father, a god of magic—the very aberration I never thought to see again. But he refused to help me. He forced me to look to you."

"And here we are," Icelin said, "in another plague den." She listened to the sounds of fighting behind her, Ruen's muffled cry of pain as he took a blow to some vulnerable part of his body.

"I'm sorry," she told Cerest as she came to a silent decision. "You named me, Cerest, but you were never my family. I thought my family was Waterdeep and a sundries shop. That would have been more than enough for me. But my family is everywhere: Waterdeep, the Dalelands, Aglarond, Luskan—even a burned-out tower. Their footsteps can be heard in the tombs and lost places of Faerûn."

"You can be more than they ever were," Cerest said. "You survived, when Elgreth did not."

"I survived because my gift is different," Icelin said. "Poor Cerest, I share your curse. I don't have Elgreth's sense of magic. I only know memory."

She took a step toward him and lifted her hands, the palms facing each other. Cerest flinched, but only for a breath. His eyes reflected the blue glow illuminating her fingers. He was transfixed, watching the power swirl in the empty air between her hands.

"What are you doing?" he asked.

"Protecting what I have left," Icelin said. She felt the cold touch her palms. She thought it was the first taste of the frost ray forming, but the sensation spread up her arms and lingered around her shoulders.

Icelin looked up and saw the wraiths swirling silently, less than ten feet above their heads. Like Cerest, they seemed transfixed by the radiant glow that was now climbing her arms. Her flesh glowed cerulean, far beyond the scope of the attack spell.

"What's happening?" Cerest demanded. He looked up at the wraiths. Icelin followed his gaze. Beyond the undead, another blue glow was forming on the bones of the leviathan. More of the creatures dived and chased the light around the bones. Like mad fireflies they soaked up the raw spell energy.

"It's the spellplague," Icelin said. Her magic had released the long dormant energy. The wraiths were finally going to have their feast.

"Get off the raft," Cerest cried. He grabbed her arm, trying to tow her toward the *Ferryman*. "If we can make it to some cover—"

Icelin stumbled and fell. On her knees, with one hand on the raft and the other caught in Cerest's grip, she looked up and saw the blue light descending the magnificent bones, a waterfall coming down a mountainside.

"It's too late," she said. "Ruen!" she screamed, and turned to see the monk holding onto one of the rib bones for support. He clutched his chest with his other arm. The short man lay at his feet, a strip of blood leaking from his mouth. His eyes stared vacantly up at the doom working its way down to them.

Ruen jumped into the water. He surfaced five feet from the raft and started to swim to her.

"No!" Icelin waved him off. "Go down," she cried. "Swim down, as far as you can. Get away from the light." She could barely see him now. The light was so bright, she had to squint. "We'll be behind you."

Ruen hesitated. Icelin could almost see him calculating their odds. "I'll try to find an air pocket around the ship," he said. Then he was gone, diving beneath the surface. Icelin crawled to the edge of the raft to follow, when suddenly a heavy weight hit her from behind.

Her breath gone, Icelin fell flat to the raft. She could feel Cerest pressing his body against hers.

"Get off!" she cried, but her scream was lost in the cry of the wraiths. They dived and hovered around the raft, blocking her escape into the water.

"They still smell the magic," Cerest shouted. His strength held her immobile. The blue light fell over them in a curtain.

The glare brightened to a painful intensity, and suddenly everything went black. Icelin thought she'd gone blind.

Blinking reflexively, she felt a warm breeze against her face. She looked up and saw a crescent of sunlight spilling over a pile of stone. It was the remains of a rooftop.

She was back in the tower. The heat continued to build, just as it had in her vision. Her two realities were merging, past and present bridged by the spellplague.

But this time something was different. Icelin rolled onto her side and saw the body lying next to her. Cerest was staring, disoriented, up at the sunbeams and the tower roof.

He doesn't know where he is, Icelin thought. His mind is joined to mine by the plague.

"What happened?" The elf sat up and swung toward her. His face paled visibly. Icelin turned to see the specters of her parents and Elgreth searching the tower. They went about their exploration, smiling and laughing, oblivious to the two figures sitting on the ground.

Cerest's lips formed the name of his old friend, but he couldn't speak. His eyes welled with unshed tears. Icelin couldn't believe the sight.

He's in pain. This pains him. Does he know what's coming? She looked up at the light. It fell in sunbeams and blue threads. Did Cerest know how few breaths stood between his friends and oblivion?

She reached out, against her will, and touched the elf on the shoulder. "Cerest," she said. "Close your eyes."

"What?" He turned to her, gripping her shoulders. "It's them, can't you see them? They're alive!"

Icelin winced at the pressure he exerted. His hands trembled. Half-crazed joy shone in his liquid eyes.

"They aren't real," Icelin said. "This is memory. Everything's going to burn, Cerest." Maybe us too.

"No!" He shook his head. Sweat dripped from his hair. "Not this time. I'll be able to warn them this time. I'll get them out before anything happens."

"They can't hear you," Icelin said. She closed her eyes. She couldn't watch it a second time.

Cerest continued to hold her in a crushing grip as the heat built to a roar in her ears. She heard the screams. Cerest's raw shriek pricked icy needles all over her flesh. She tipped her head forward, resting against his chest while he wept and screamed, over and over.

He was seeing everything as he had never seen it before—from the inside of the inferno. Elgreth had long since carried her young self away, but the memory and Cerest's imagination had taken over. She could hear her mother crying out for her husband and for Cerest. The smell of burning flesh filled the air.

To distract herself, Icelin conjured an image of Ruen, swimming deep in the rotting harbor. She prayed he'd found safe haven from the plague's reach. He'd already drowned in its grip once.

And what about Aldren, Darvont, and Bellaril? Would they be safe inside the *Ferryman*, or would the plague consume the ship and crush them all? She held onto the screaming elf and hoped that one of Aldren's deities would take pity on all of them.

CHAPTER TWENTY-ONE

TALLMANTLE HEARD TESLEENA'S SCREAM A BREATH BEFORE THE EXPLOSION. The keel of the *Ferryman* erupted in blue fire. Debris shot thirty feet into the air. The flames spewed toward the sky in an arcane geyser the likes of which he had never seen.

"Halt the boats!" Tallmantle raised a hand, but the men were already bringing their oars up from the water to watch the spectacle. A shower of blue flame and what looked like humanoid forms were raining down over the harbor.

"Gods above," said Deelia, who was behind him in the boat. "Are those people?"

"No," Tesleena said. She was in the boat adjacent to Tallmantle's. Her voice sounded detached from her body. Her eyes stared, unfocused, at some distant point on the horizon. "They're sea wraiths." A crease appeared in her forehead. "I understand. My thanks."

Tallmantle looked at the wizard. "What does the Blackstaff say?"

"He's too far away to know how much damage was done," Tesleena said. Her eyes shifted, centering on Tallmantle. "Which also means he has no way of knowing if it's safe to approach. He can't return to the city now. He leaves it up to you to decide whether to go in."

"What do you think?" he asked her.

"I will go," she said without hesitation. "But it's likely anyone who was in the wreckage was killed instantly when the spellplague pocket erupted."

Icelin awoke staring into darkness. She flexed her fingers—grateful that she still possessed the appendages—and cast a spell using the least possible amount of energy.

A pinprick glow lit her fingertip and spread to her whole hand. By its light, her eyes adjusted to her surroundings.

She stared up at the sky. It took her a long time to realize that the *Ferryman's* masts and rigging had been incinerated by the spellplague blast. Small fires burned at various points along the *Ferryman's* length.

The entire ship had listed far forward, but by some miracle the leviathan's bones held it stable and prevented their being crushed under its weight. The small chamber created by the wreckage had been reduced to half its size, but Ruen's raft was miraculously still intact. Gaps yawned in the planks like missing teeth. Water seeped freely across the ship's surface, but for now it stayed afloat.

As her vision adjusted, Icelin became aware of the bodies. There was one on either side of her and another draped half on the raft and half in the water directly across from her. She could smell the burning, the singed flesh and hair. Her breath quickened.

The body on her right stirred. Icelin swung her spell light toward the movement. Her wrist stopped in midair, caught in an iron grip.

Icelin's heart lifted. "Ruen," she whispered. She removed his sodden hat from where it had fallen over his face. His skin was wet but unmarked by arcane fire. His eyes, when they opened, were the familiar rust red color. "Are you all right?"

He nodded and released her wrist. "Hat, please," he said.

Icelin helped him sit up and put the hat back on his head. "How did you manage not to get that thing incinerated or lost in the harbor?" she asked.

Ruen looked at her, his expression grave. "Magic," he said.

Icelin had the urge to laugh, but it died in her throat when she remembered the other bodies. She moved the light away from Ruen. Her spell illuminated a face she didn't immediately recognize. The man was beautiful, his face smooth-skinned and symmetrical. His long golden hair fell across ears that were pointed like needles.

"Merciful gods," she said. "This is Cerest."

Ruen looked over her shoulder. The elf's face had been perfectly restored. His eyes were open and staring glassily at something invisible in the distance. The expression on his face was both peaceful and sad.

Icelin put her hand against the elf's cheek. It was ice cold. "He's dead," she said.

"So is this one," Ruen said, checking the man draped across the raft. He put his hand against the man's chest to find a heartbeat, but they both saw the burns on the man's face and torso. His skin was blackened, and his hair was gone. His clothes had been burned to brittle strips that turned to ash when Ruen touched them. His chain vest had melted into his skin.

Ruen met her gaze. Icelin knew they were both thinking the same thing.

"Maybe Aldren's magic protected them," Ruen said.

Icelin shone her light around the wreckage. The entrance to Aldren's chamber was now underwater. The channel they'd used to get the raft into the wreckage was filled in with debris.

"We'll have to swim out," Icelin said. Her gaze strayed involuntarily back to Cerest's face, perfect now in its death pose. "Why did it happen?" she asked. "Why were we spared?"

"I don't know," Ruen said. "We're already scarred. Maybe we're immune to the plague now."

"Cerest was scarred," Icelin said, "in body, if not magically. Why would the plague restore him and then kill him?"

Maybe it hadn't been the plague. She remembered Cerest's anguished screams inside the tower. "He saw my mind," she said. "In that breath we were joined, he saw everything he'd done, for the first time. He was inside the tower with me, watching my parents die."

"A perfect memory," Ruen said. "Maybe Cerest's mind couldn't survive that kind of clarity. To have all the defects of your own psyche laid out for you in a ring of fire—not many people could face it and live."

"So this," Icelin said, touching the elf's smooth face, "this is memory. His last memory." She felt an overwhelming wave of sadness—for her parents, Elgreth, and for Brant. So many lives destroyed.

"We should get out of here," Ruen said. "There's no telling how long the structure will hold."

"The Ferryman's Waltz is over," Icelin said quietly. She turned away, leaving Cerest on the raft, staring peacefully up at the sky.

.:⌒:.

They swam out of the wreckage together, Icelin's bobbing light leading the way. Gray mist clung to the harbor's surface. In the distance she could smell the Hearth fire burning. The orange glow gave the impression of a false dawn.

Out of the darkness, Icelin saw the line of boats coming toward them. Lantern light swayed at each prow. Icelin could see there were at least two men in each boat.

"Think you can take ten of them?" she asked Ruen, who was treading water next to her. "Leaves eight for me."

"Only ten?" Ruen said. His face twisted with a gallows humor smile. "Bring me a true challenge, lady."

The lead boats drifted to a stop practically on top of them. Icelin squinted up into the face of a woman in robes. She wore a tense frown, but she seemed more interested in the wreckage than in the two figures in the water.

A tall man leaned down to Icelin. This man she recognized immediately, though she'd never expected the Watch Warden to come for her himself.

"Warden Tallmantle," she said. "I understand you've been looking for me."

"Well met, Icelin Tearn," Tallmantle said, inclining his head gravely. "Would you care to come aboard?"

"I would, and if you've a spare blanket or two, I'd be weepingly grateful for those as well. But I've a problem. Three of my friends are trapped in the wreckage. We can't get to them."

" 'Ware!" shouted one of the men at the back of the group. "We need more light over here."

Tesleena spoke a word, and the surrounding harbor lit as if a miniature sun had risen.

A single small boat drifted toward the group. Her oarsman was hunched over, forcing the craft through the water.

The Watch officer nearest raised his crossbow. The oarsman lifted his head, and Icelin shouted, "Stop! He's a friend."

The crossbow stayed aimed at the deformed man. His tentacles undulated across his shoulders. He continued to row toward them, undaunted by the stares.

When Darvont got close enough to Tallmantle's boat, Ruen grabbed an oar and hauled the boat in the rest of the way. There were two figures lying side by side in the bottom of the boat. Icelin recognized Bellaril and Aldren, but she couldn't see if they yet breathed.

The deformed man slumped against the side of the boat, exhausted by whatever toil had brought them out of the wreckage. Tears streaked his face. Icelin could see him stroking Aldren's robes. Her heart lurched painfully.

She swam to the boat, but Tallmantle was closer. He bent over the prone figures. "The old man is dead," he said. "The dwarf lives."

"The Art is around her," Tesleena said. She put a hand on the dwarf's shoulder and rolled her onto her back. Clutched between her two hands was Aldren's staff. It pulsed with pale, crimson radiance, but it was clear at Icelin's touch that the item had been drained. It was nowhere near as powerful as it once had been.

"Is he truly dead?" Icelin asked. She saw Tallmantle nod, but she was looking to the deformed man. He met her gaze and seemed to understand what she was asking. He nodded. The sorrow in his eyes pierced her.

"It was what he wanted," Ruen said.

"He protected Bellaril," Icelin said. The Art requires a focus, Aldren had told her. She lifted the staff from the sleeping Bellaril's arms and cradled it in her own. "Thank you," she murmured. "In Mystra's memory, thank you."

"In Mystra's memory," Tesleena whispered. The words echoed down the line of boats.

EPILOGUE

ICELIN SAT OUTSIDE THE WATCH WARDEN'S PRIVATE OFFICE, AWAITING her audience and her fate.

It was strange, to be alone in the small chamber, not to hear the constant flow of the harbor and the people on the twisted walkways. She felt, in some ways, that she'd lived her whole life in Mistshore, and was only now venturing out into the sun-washed world.

She ran her hands over the bodice of her dress, marveling at the softness of a fabric that was not stiff with salt water and grime. All trace of the harbor stink was gone from her body, though her hair had been a struggle. She'd ended up cutting most of the muck out of it. The strands barely brushed her shoulders now, and the shorter locks at her temples were stark white. She ran her fingers through the strands self-consciously.

The forced haircut had yielded another secret of her past. Tesleena had seen it first: a faint, almost indiscernible blue light appeared at the back of her neck when she drew deeply on her memory. Tesleena said the spellscar was a circle broken in two places, the lines so thin she would never have seen them unless she'd known to look.

It was one of many things she was going to have to grow accustomed to in her new life. Another was the staff resting beside her on the bench. The red light had fallen dormant, but she could recall it again with a word of power. She had divined no further secrets from the item, but she was satisfied with her small progress. For now, she used it mainly as a walking stick.

It had been five days since her confrontation with Cerest and her second exposure to the spellplague. Since that night, exhaustion overtook her easily. She found herself leaning on the staff often to maintain her equilibrium.

Her strength was slowly returning. Tesleena had assured her it would, though they both knew she would never again be as spry as a normal twenty-year-old girl.

Tesleena had also told her if she stopped now, she would likely live another twenty years or more. Icelin hadn't asked what the last several days had cost her in longevity. She didn't want to know. She would change very little of what she'd done in defense of herself and her friends. Whatever time she had left was the gods' gift. She didn't intend to waste it on regret.

A door to her left opened, and Kersh came through. Icelin stood to greet him, but he got to her first. The Watchman wrapped his arms around her and lifted her onto her toes.

"Have a care for an aging woman," Icelin said, laughing.

"Not a chance," Kersh said. He pulled back to arm's length and regarded her with mock sternness. "Every time I let you out of my sight you work yourself into more trouble."

"Lucky for you I'm too stubborn to let anyone do away with me," Icelin said.

"Are you well, Icelin?" Kersh looked at her intently, as if he could take her apart piece by piece to find any deficiency. "I don't expect you to ever forgive me, but as long as you're all right, I can be content."

"I'm more than well," Icelin said. "You followed the right course, Kersh. I should have trusted you from the beginning."

"We should have made ourselves more worthy of your trust," said a voice from the open doorway.

Icelin looked beyond Kersh to see Daerovus Tallmantle towering over both of them. He regarded Icelin with an uncertain expression. Icelin had never expected to be on the receiving end of such a look from the imposing Warden.

A memory came to her, with crystal clarity as always, of another time when she had sat in this chamber. She'd been much younger, and Brant had been with her, holding her hand.

When she looked into the Warden's eyes, she knew he was remembering that same day.

Kersh squeezed her hands and stepped away. She felt suddenly adrift. She looked at him imploringly, but he shook his head and smiled. "I'll leave you two to talk," he said. He gave her hand another squeeze, the Warden a salute, and left the room.

"I am truly sorry," Icelin said, "about Tarvin, and any other men you lost these past nights."

"Tarvin was our sole loss, and that was none of your doing," Tallmantle said. He sat on the bench across from her and gestured that she should resume her seat. "I know you're tired," he said, "so I'll be brief. Cerest is dead. What of his men? Are any of them still hunting you?"

Icelin shook her head. "The only ones that might be are a pair of elf women Cerest had working with him. I don't know who they are or what their fates were."

"They are the Lock sisters," Tallmantle said, "well known dealers in antiquities and magic. We believe they hired a portion of the men who hunted you, but we have no evidence linking them directly to Cerest, other than your testimony." His mouth twisted. "They have already lined up several witnesses who will swear they were giving a party the night you were kidnapped."

"I don't want to go after them," Icelin said. "Cerest was the one bent on hunting me. They should have no interest in me now." She thought of Bellaril, master now of Arowall's Cradle and all its men. The dwarf woman had her own score to settle with the sisters. Icelin had no doubt the women would be made to answer for what they had wrought in Mistshore.

"What will you do now?" the Warden asked, surprising her with the change in topic.

"Do the charges against me still stand?" Icelin asked.

"One," Tallmantle said. "The outstanding charge of evading a Watch summons waits only for my signature to dismiss it."

"My thanks. You will not be popular for that decision in some circles," Icelin said.

"You overestimate our enmity," the Warden said. "Tarvin was the exception. Any others who privately held you responsible for Therondol's death have changed their opinion, based on the events that have transpired these past days." A faint smile lit his features. "You've shamed them, my lady, by choosing deadly Mistshore as a safer haven than the Watch." His smile faded. "You shamed me, as well."

Icelin shook her head, unable to believe what she was hearing. "You have more reason to hate me than anyone. Therondol was your son." Her voice cracked. "I know what it's like to lose yourself to that kind of grief."

The world had stopped working the night she'd lost Brant. Right and wrong became concepts that belonged to other people. Perhaps she was more at home in Mistshore after all. At least she could understand the place now, what created and sustained it as well as what kept it apart from the rest of the city.

The Warden put a hand on her shoulder. Icelin couldn't meet his eyes. She remembered that day, sitting in his office with Brant. His face had been gray, lifeless as he read the account of the fire and his son's death.

"I would have been glad of someone to punish that day," Tallmantle said, as if reading her thoughts. "But it wasn't you I wanted. I stopped believing in the gods that day. I didn't care whether any of them lived or died, because I thought they had forsaken this world. They'd forsaken my son."

Icelin did look up then, but she couldn't read his expression. "Do you still believe that?" she asked.

"I don't know," the Warden said. "I've learned to put my faith in this city and the men and women who serve to keep it thriving. I look to them for aid and inspiration when I need it. So far, those forces have been enough to sustain me."

Icelin nodded. She knew that kind of strength. Ruen and Sull and Bellaril had been hers. "What will happen to him?" she asked.

She was speaking of Ruen. They both knew it. "He did bring you to the Watch, as I instructed, though it was after considerable delay," the Warden said. "Unfortunately, it's been made clear that he can't be trusted to act under our direction. That leaves two options, as I see it."

"You can't send him back to the dungeons," Icelin said. "I owe him my life."

"I don't enjoy the prospect," the Warden said, "which is part of the reason I inquired after your immediate plans. Will you take up your great-uncle's shop and stay in Waterdeep?"

Icelin shook her head. "I considered it, but no. My family wanted me to see more of the world than Waterdeep."

It was a desire she'd never found in herself before. But she knew the breadth of her life now, and the urgency and wanderlust in her blood had flared. The time to begin her journey was now or never.

The Warden nodded thoughtfully, as if he'd been expecting her answer. "I suppose I could recommend a period of banishment from the city for Morleth. A man of his resources should have no trouble finding a direction in the world. Perhaps that direction will coincide with yours."

Icelin grinned. "You might ask him about this course of action before you undertake it. He may vastly prefer the dungeons to being saddled with me indefinitely."

"I have already asked him," Tallmantle said. "He has agreed to keep an eye on you for me."

Icelin didn't know how to respond. Her throat constricted around emotions she couldn't begin to handle. "My thanks," she said roughly, "for everything."

"Gods and friends go with you, lass," the Warden said, "wherever you choose to walk."

When Icelin stepped outside the barracks, she didn't immediately see the monk. Ruen stood in the shadow of a building several paces down the street.

"Were you waiting for me?" she asked when she reached him.

"I would have waited in Tallmantle's office with you," Ruen said, uncrossing his arms, "but I can only spend so long in the place. I break out in a rash."

Icelin fixed a look of annoyance on her face. "So the Warden thinks I need watching after does he? What makes him think you're the man for this task?"

"I'm still alive," Ruen said, shrugging. "No small accomplishment, where you're concerned."

"Hmmm," Icelin said. "I suppose you're right. Will you be vexing me the entire journey?"

"At least halfway there and back."

"I see. I suppose I'll have no choice but to pay you back in kind." Icelin took a step closer to him and leaned in. When it became clear she was about to kiss his cheek, Ruen stepped back, his hands on her shoulders.

Icelin smiled up at him teasingly, but he didn't return the humor. His eyes were shadowed under the brim of his hat.

"Don't," he said simply.

"Don't what? Don't kiss me now, or don't kiss me ever?" she said. "You already know the outcome. What can it hurt?"

"I don't know anything," Ruen said. "Nothing is carved in stone."

"Finally, he admits it. His gift is not infallible," Icelin said. She brought his gloved hand to her lips and kissed the back. "Congratulations."

"Mock me if you want, but you're not giving up either," he said. "You wouldn't be leaving Waterdeep if you didn't think there was something to find in the world that could help you."

"I admit it freely," Icelin said. "Aldren's burden was lifted. But if such a cure doesn't exist for me, I'll live the remainder of my life as well as I can. And I'll have my taste of adventure besides."

"Lead on, then," Ruen said.

Icelin nodded, but she did not turn in the direction of the city gates. "I have a stop to make first, to Sull's shop."

"It's closed up," Ruen said. "Going there won't change anything."

"I know," Icelin said, "but I need to go anyway."

They walked in silence, and Icelin was surprised, when she turned onto the butcher's street, to see Bellaril standing in front of the shop. She held the signboard with its painted haunch of meat in her hand.

"I didn't expect you'd get roped into helping him," Icelin said when they walked up.

"Didn't think it myself," the dwarf woman said. She made way as Sull's bulk crowded the doorway. The butcher's bright red hair caught the sunlight. His teeth flashed in a wide smile when he saw Icelin. He dropped the hammer and nails he was carrying into his apron pocket and went to her.

He swept her up in a hug that was ten times as crushing as the one Kersh had given her. Icelin had no breath left to protest.

"Almost done here," he said when he released her. "Just need to board the windows for winter, then we can be on our way."

"She came to make you reconsider," Ruen spoke up.

Icelin elbowed the monk in the ribs. She smiled sheepishly under Sull's black glare. "I'll be fine, Sull. Ruen's coming with me, and what about your shop?"

"Got it all with me," Sull said. He trotted around the side of the building and came back with a small cart and pony. "We need provisions, and I'm goin' to see to it you don't starve on hard rations. Besides, I've got recipes for the road," he said proudly. "There are spices and meats out there in the world Waterdeep never sees. How can I pass up the chance to bring some back? This is research, is what this is, an investment. Got nothin' to do with you," he said, grinning broadly.

Icelin looked at Ruen, who shrugged. "I don't mind eating good food," he said.

She appealed to the dwarf woman next, but Bellaril shook her head. "Nothing to me if he goes or not, but I'm staying. The Cradle's a mess, and I'm still looking forward to dealing with the pretty elves," she said, a wicked light gleaming in her eyes.

Icelin sighed. "Fine. You're all baggage, though, and nothing but."

Ruen bowed. Sull grinned wider.

When they passed beyond the city gates, Icelin silently composed the letter in her head.

> *Dear Grandfather,*
> *I leave today on a new adventure. Faerûn calls to me, and I'm willing to hear what she has to say. Wish me good fortune, and know that wherever I go, I carry all of you in my heart.*
> *Love always,*
> *Icelin*

DOWNSHADOW
ERIK SCOTT DE BIE

INTRODUCTION

I**T'S ALL TOO EASY TO BLOW UP THE MOON.**

It's even tempting, if you have the power—and in a world full of magic, the stroke of a pen can always muster power enough.

Which is why the first of the firm, written rules decreed by Jeff Grubb, the brilliant designer who was the first "traffic cop" of the published FORGOTTEN REALMS®, read as follows: "Don't blow up the moon."

Jeff's last rule was: "Remember: Don't blow up the moon. I mean it."

It's a credit to Jeff's vigilance (and that of his successors in the post, which some have compared to being sheriff in *High Noon*), that the moon still serenely glides along in the night skies of Faerûn. (Which must be a great comfort to the moon goddess.)

Not everyone can resist such temptation. That's why fantasy readers get to read so many multi-book sagas where the fate of the world hangs in the balance as gods grapple, armies march, seas open up to swallow clifftop castles, dragons crash down into cities, and, yes, the moon blows up.

Exciting, stirring stuff. (I know; I've written some of it.)

Not everyone can resist the temptation to read it, either. Yet just like a steady diet of ice cream, or any other culinary treat, it palls after a bit. It should be special, and kept for special occasions.

Which leaves the rest of the time, when we need darned good storytellers to leave the armies unmustered and the dragons slumbering in their lairs and tell us gripping, exciting, fun-to-read stories about this particular character, here, or that one yonder.

Stories that look over the shoulders of people who dwell in Waterdeep and live out their daily lives without ruling it, or leading armies.

Stories that vividly bring to life what it must be like to be a member of the long-suffering City Watch. And a paladin, living by a moral code that places strict limits on what you can do—and that gets sorely tested, all too often.

And to be torn between two loves. Or three. Or four. All under one roof with you.

A story like this one, *Downshadow*, which is a delight of a tale. Full of fights and duels, chases, a splendid revel, long-sought and bitter revenge, sinister secrets, at least one deadly hired slayer, a little dungeon-delving, and faithful love.

Want to really feel what it's like to tramp the streets of Waterdeep? Read this book.

Want to get caught up in a story that really zips along? Read this book.

Want to read another one? Hope this powerful, funny writer pens another Realms tale as delightful as this one.

I created Waterdeep, and just as I felt thirty years ago when I opened a book by Elaine Cunningham called *Elfshadow*, I opened this one and felt right at home. This *is* Waterdeep, brought to life vividly all around me.

Gosh, I wish I'd known these characters earlier.

I'm buying four copies of this book. I know I'm going to wear them out reading *Downshadow* over and over.

Ed Greenwood
November 2008

PROLOGUE

BLACK RAIN LASHED THE CITY, POUNDING AWAY AT RAGGED COBBLESTONES and blurring the glow of street lamps to a haze. Buildings that towered majestically by day became, by drenching night, idols of stone and shapeless mountains. Such a rain dampened the City of Splendors, changing its romantic luster into something much colder—much darker.

Such a rain made the city resemble the world below.

Beneath the slick streets, in the nefarious passages of a legacy of old Faerûn, lay Downshadow. Under the city, under the mountain, sprawled treacherous halls that knew no light except that which men made.

Once, this labyrinth had been called Undermountain, the dream of a mad wizard called Halaster, and the deeper levels still teemed with his warped whims and creations. The shallow stretches, however, had become a home for the cruel, the desperate, and the scarred.

Some said Downshadow tainted its inhabitants; some claimed the reverse. Regardless, what once had been dungeon was now desperate homeland—where once had been monster, now was man.

In one unlit chamber, a man crouched amid a circle of foes, flaming steel in hand. Leering faces surrounded him, half-illumined in the light of his sword. Blood and sweat dripped from his worn leathers. Numbness choked his arms and legs but he gave no sign of it. His left hand held him aloft, and his body was tensed like a cornered wolf. His head was bent and his sword low, but he was not broken. A knight in shadow.

A darkness, he thought. I will make for myself a darkness in which only I exist.

Six men stood around him, growling and glaring. At first, ten had threatened, but now the other four lay crumpled and moaning against the walls.

Shadows flickered among them, cast by the glow of the brilliant sword, which dripped silver fire onto the floor.

He'd given them a chance to surrender, and they'd laughed.

Now, their mirth had faded. The biggest tough—a burly wretch whose hoglike features and olive skin spoke of orc blood—spat on the stone floor at the downed man's hand. The yellow spittle landed on his steel gauntlet.

"Picked the wrong gang to push, crusader," said the half-orc. He slapped the haft of his nail-studded morningstar with his free hand. "Drop the steel and we kill you quick."

The man smiled through the slit in his full helm. Numbness crept through his body, and his lungs burned as though he breathed smoke. But he would not fall.

"Take it from him, Dremvik! Take it!" others of the gang shouted.

Yes, the knight thought as he focused past the pain in his lungs. Take it.

The leader—Dremvik—was a tyrant, the knight knew, but he wasn't stupid. Warily, the half-orc feigned a stomp on the knight's sword hand and kicked instead at the helmed face.

Rather than counter, the knight dropped his sword on the ground and jerked his thick gray cloak over it, stealing its light from the chamber and blinding them all. He shifted toward the kicking foot and pounced, wrapping his arms around the half-orc's leg.

Cries went up in the darkness but the knight ignored them. He wrenched to the side, toppling Dremvik to the ground with a satisfying thump of head against stone, and sprang away.

"Help!" Dremvik moaned. "Kill the bastard!"

"Get 'im!" one of the thugs cried, and they all started stomping and kicking. "Get 'im!"

The half-orc bellowed. "Not me, you bastards, not—" Then a boot crunched his face and ended his commands in a moan.

Deprived of their leader, lost in the lightless chamber, the thugs scrambled, lashing out at anything and everything that touched them. One squealed as a club smashed his head against a wall, and he fell nerveless to the ground. Jabbing knives opened flesh and wrenched forth screams—none of them the knight's cry. Finally one of the thugs managed to jerk the cloak away, revealing the sword and returning light to the chamber. The four remaining toughs looked around, trying to reason where their quarry had gone.

The knight, clinging to the wall just above their heads, whistled. They looked up to see his pale eyes blazing down at them. The eyes seemed to have no color, like diamonds.

"Four left," he said, and he leaped into their midst.

His booted feet took one in the face, and he lunged off the falling man to slam his iron-wrapped fist into a second's face. The two fell in opposite directions, and the knight whirled in the air to land on his feet, knees bent, near his sword.

An axe chopped toward him, but he tipped up his sword with the toe of his boot and flipped it into his hands in time to block the strike. He bent under the force, compressing through his knees—one hand on the hilt, one halfway up the long blade. The axe-man—a gigantic brute whose size bespoke orc and even ogre blood—held him in place, straining.

A blade stabbed the knight through from behind, but he barely felt it. The studs in his leather deflected the thrust just enough that it opened his ribs but missed his lung.

The knight twisted, throwing the axe wide, and slammed the pommel of his sword into the half-ogre's jaw as he stood. The big creature stumbled back and the warrior followed. The blade slid from his back with a splash of blood but not so much as a grunt came from his throat. The knight shoved the half-ogre against the wall and elbowed him in the ear.

The brute went down and the knight pivoted to face the one who'd stabbed him. With a gasp, the man looked down at his treacherous sword.

The knight smiled behind his helm.

As the thug lunged, the knight twisted his sword point down, then stepped forward to thrust from above. His block and his counter were a single movement; every parry was an attack unfolding. The silver-burning blade glided through the man's chest, dropping him to his knees.

The knight had miscalculated, though, for his sword wedged in the man's ribs and resisted when he tried to pull it free. He gripped it firmly and tugged it loose, but too slowly.

A club struck his face. It snapped his head back and sent him staggering. The sword fell from his numb fingers. The club-wielding dwarf sported a wide red mark on his face in the shape of the knight's gauntlet.

Then a larger body crushed him against the wall—the half-ogre. He felt the pressure but little of the pain. Trapped fast against the heavier brute, he could only struggle to no avail.

Two thugs still stood: the dwarf, who clutched a broken jaw, and the half-ogre, who didn't seem much hurt. The man who had caught both feet with his face wasn't getting up, and the backstabber was choking and gasping. All told, he'd downed eight of the gang of ten.

The knight made a note to take more care with those of ogre blood.

"Damn, damn!" moaned the dwarf, his words wet in his mouth. "Bastard done break me face, Rolph. And stuck Morlyn for good an' all."

The enemy he had skewered coughed and moaned. Blood trickled from his wound but did not gush. The knight knew he wouldn't die of that injury, but he wouldn't be fighting any time soon.

"What we do with 'im?" asked the half-ogre. He squeezed the knight's helm against the wall until it started to give.

"Break 'is head off?" suggested the dwarf.

At that moment silence fell and there was a sense of suction from high in the chamber—above and between them. The dwarf opened his mouth but the chamber exploded in blue light, blinding them, bathing them all in a light brighter than the sun.

When the knight could see, he blinked at a woman floating in midair—a woman cloaked in crackling, blue-white flames. They did not burn her, but seemed to clothe her. Her feet trod upon nothing but air, and long hair floated around her. He could make out little in that bright light—everything was blue and white and dazzling.

She blazed like an angel of Celestia, he thought. Like a *goddess*.

She was saying something, but the words were nonsense to his ears. She screamed and sobbed in a tongue that sounded like the blackest whispers from the foulest dreams. Her eyes scanned things he could not see, and she seemed to be fighting invisible demons.

Then, just as abruptly, she vanished. The light died as though it had never been.

"What?" said the dwarf.

At that moment, the half-ogre howled—the bellow started low, then grew in volume and pitch until it became a scream. The beast clutched at himself where the knight had kneed him in the groin. The half-ogre tipped and fell with a tremor that shook the underground chamber.

The dwarf started to cry out but the knight slammed him against the wall and pressed his empty sword scabbard under his chin.

"Don't!" the dwarf gurgled, but the knight just shook his head.

His voice was cold as ice and sharp as lightning. "Run."

"Uh?"

"Run," the knight said. "Leave your friends—they belong to justice now. I have told the City Watch where they will be found. Go, and warn those like yourself."

The dwarf blinked rapidly.

"The Eye of Justice watches Downshadow." He pressed the dwarf harder. "Tell them."

"I don't understand!"

The knight's glare gleamed in the dwarf's terrified eyes like sunlight off ice.

"Tell them Shadowbane waits." He narrowed his eyes. "Tell them I wait for them."

And with that, he jerked the scabbard away and sent the dwarf scrambling with a shove. Without even looking back, the thug vanished into the everlasting night, choking and sputtering.

The world seemed so heavy—and cold. Shadowbane watched the dwarf flee down the tunnel, then turned his head heavenward.

A bowshot above, through thousands of tons of stone, rain would be falling on Waterdeep. Rain that would shatter against his steel helm.

He knew he would barely feel it, thanks to the spellplague.

He felt, instead, only a creeping numbness—the absence of feeling. The surfaces of his thighs and arms had become like natural armor, like frozen leather greaves and bracers. It left his flesh filled with senseless nerves. His fingers, however warm, perpetually felt frostbitten to his touch, and his legs, as much as he pushed them, felt disconnected. His skin felt like dead flesh.

The spellplague had stolen feeling from Shadowbane, as it had stolen so much from the world. In time, it would take his life as well. He could only hope it would give him long enough.

"Long enough," he whispered, "to do what I must."

He thrust the scabbard through his belt, turned down another passage, and ran through the darkness below the world.

CHAPTER ONE

24 Tarsakh, the Year of the Ageless One (1479 DR)

Araezra Hondyl sighed heavily, smiled, and silently counted to six. The ranking valabrar of the Waterdeep Guard despite her tender twenty-odd winters, she exercised the iron-clad control of her passions that had secured her so many early promotions.

Despite her firm grip on the reins, patience was fleeing her. She put her fingers to her temple where, Kalen saw, a vein had risen beneath her skin.

"Once again." Her long tail of braided black hair trembled under the strain. "Slowly."

Kalen Dren, vigilant guardsman and Araezra's chief aide, took notes in his small, tight script, spectacles balanced on the end of his nose. His plume scratched quickly and efficiently, and his face remained carefully neutral. He had his duties as a scribe and fulfilled them scrupulously. Not that they were on official business, exactly, but it was his job.

Araezra's best friend, Talanna Taenfeather, loitered casually nearby. She had bent to examine some of the wares in a shop window. The "fashion" spikes wired out of her orange-red hair bobbed behind her head as she nodded and murmured to herself. She wore the uniform of her office but was off duty, and was present for the same reason as Araezra: to part with coin. They'd stopped after morning patrol out of South Gate, only to find a situation requiring their attentions.

"A fine sun that brings you through my door, lady," said Ellis Kolatch, a greasy, unpleasant man who sold jewelry and fine silks—also knives, flints, and small crossbows, if the rumors were to be believed. "And timely, for I have need of the Watch!"

"Guard," Kalen corrected indifferently, but no one seemed to hear. He continued scribbling down the merchant's words and those of the accused thief: a small half-elf boy.

"I tell you, this little kobold pustule is stealing from me," Kolatch said. "He's been in here twice in the last tenday, I swear—him, or someone like him. Always some half-blood trash that's lashed me with his tongue an' stolen my wares!"

"Blood-blind pig!" The half-elf grinned like the scamp he was. "I've never been in this place afore—you must think all the pointy ears be the same, aye?"

"You!" Kolatch raised his fists threateningly.

"Goodsir." Araezra's voice snapped like a whip. "Have peace, lest I arrest *you*."

Nothing about the valabrar's fine face—widely and fairly thought to be one of the best in all of Waterdeep—suggested impatience. Here was the controlled seriousness that had won her the respect and love of the Guard, the Watch, and much of Waterdeep. One who knew her well, as Kalen did, might see her fingernails straining and failing to pierce her gauntlets as if to draw blood from her palms.

"Aye, my apologies." Reining himself, Kolatch put his hands behind his back and cleared his throat. "I am sorry, gracious lady Watchman."

"Guardsman," Kalen murmured, but kept writing.

The distinction meant less and less, these days. The City Guard had become a division of the Watch, and while the guardsmen might be—as professional soldiers—better armed and trained than the average Watchman, the names meant little to the ordinary citizen. Kalen, who had been an armar in the Watch proper two months before, didn't mind.

Araezra had commissioned him as her aide based on his record as a lion who had to be lectured more than once regarding his "impressive but nonetheless embarrassing zeal."

Now things had changed, though she couldn't have known they would do when she called him to service. His debilitating sickness had been his first confession, and he knew he'd become a disappointment to her: he was a kitten and not a lion.

But Araezra had a great love of kittens, too. He smiled.

"*Sst*—Kalen!" Talanna hissed.

Kalen looked around to find Talanna poking at him. He hadn't felt it, of course—because of his sickness—but he heard her quite well. He raised an eyebrow.

The red-haired lass held a sapphire necklace to her throat. "What of *this*? Aye?"

Kalen sighed and turned back to his parchment booklet.

"And you, boy?" Araezra asked the half-elf accused of thievery. "Name yourself."

He bowed his head. "Lueth is the name my father gave me, gracious lady."

Kalen noted this, recalling that "Lueth" meant "riddle" in Elvish. A false name? The boy was unremarkable, forgettable in face and form, but for the sharp gray eyes that peered up at Araezra with intelligence, wit, and bemusement. Something was not quite right about him. Kalen's neck tingled.

"What have you to say?" Araezra asked.

"Naught but what I said, good lady," said Lueth. "This stuffed puff of a blood-blind don't know what he seen. Was just admiring the baubles and gewgaws, and he done accuse me of stealing." The boy spread his hands. "Why'd I need jewels, aye? They'd better laud your beauty, good lady." He blushed and winked.

Kalen saw Araezra stiffen and recalled the one time he had brought up her looks on duty—and the blackened eye he had suffered. Not that she minded being beautiful, or being beloved of half the Watch (and half the magisters, merchants, and lordlings of the city), but when she ceased to be taken at her word because of her face, it tended to . . . *irritate* her.

Araezra hid her feelings behind a cool, lovely mask. "If there is no evidence," she said, "then I cannot arrest you, boy."

Lueth stuck out his tongue at Kolatch, who glared at him. Then the merchant turned his glare on Araezra. Talanna giggled. Kalen smiled privately.

"On your way, child," Araezra said to the boy. She gave him a little smile. "And in the future, best not to admire gewgaws with your hands, aye?"

Lueth flashed a wide, pleased grin and skipped toward the door, where Kalen stood.

Casually, Kalen swept out his hand and caught the boy's arm. "Hold."

"Ay!" The boy struggled, but Kalen was deceptively strong. "Why stay me, sir?"

Calmly, Kalen transferred his notebook to his teeth, then reached down and tugged on something in the boy's sleeve. A bright red kerchief fluttered forth, studded with gold and silver earrings and a large, dragon-shaped brooch. The fat merchant gasped.

"That," young Lueth said. "I can explain that."

Kolatch blinked as Kalen continued to pull. Tied to the end of the kerchief was another—this one the blue of the sea after a storm—that also sparkled with jewels. Knotted to it was a long scarf, and finally a puffy pink underlinen, such as a lady of the night might wear beneath her laced bodice, had she the coin for silk.

"Ay," the boy said. "That—"

"My jewels!" Kolatch shrieked. "Thief!"

"Hold, you!" Talanna said from where she stood trying on bracelets. "I've got him, Rayse!" She leaped forward, the spikes in her hair bobbing and the half of her orange-red mane left unspiked dancing around her shoulders.

The boy gave an *eep!* and twisted out of Kalen's grasp, shedding his patched and frayed coat as he did. He caught at the red kerchief as he ran, tearing it and sending jewels tumbling across the room. Kalen lunged, but phlegm boiled up in his throat and he coughed instead of grasping the thief. Lueth darted out the door, Talanna in immediate pursuit. Kolatch, puffing and red in the face, stormed after them.

Araezra stepped toward Kalen, eyes worried, and put her hand on his shoulder. "Kalen?"

"Well," he said under a cough. "I'll be well."

He didn't meet her gaze and tried to ignore the pain in his back. He could feel her hand only because it fell on a bruise—it felt distant, far removed from his empty body.

They stepped into the street. A furious Kolatch shouted and cursed after the distant red head of Talanna, who was running westward like a charger after the boy. They turned south along the busy Snail Street, cutting back into Dock Ward.

"Think he'll escape?" Kalen asked softly.

"Unlikely. Tal's the fastest lass in Waterdeep."

"And this Lueth is only a boy," Kalen said. "Short legs."

Araezra smiled and laughed.

Kolatch, hearing their voices, wheeled on them and glared. "Smiling fools! That knave has taken hundreds of dragons from me!"

"The Watch will return your good when the thief is caught," Araezra said. "We know his name and face—have no fear."

"Bane's breath," Kolatch cursed. He stared at Araezra and his lip curled.

Kalen felt a familiar tingle behind his eyes: cruelty hung in the air. Araezra seemed to sense it too.

"Though it's to be expected," the merchant said, wiping his sweat-covered brow in the morning sun. "Those damned pointy ears—can never really trust 'em." He spat in the dirt.

Kalen hid his contempt. Waterdeep was a free city, one where any blood was accepted so long as the coin was good, but there existed some few who held these sorts of views.

"I'm not sure I take your meaning, *goodsir*," Araezra said.

Kolatch sniffed. "One day, thems that buys from pointy-eared, thin-blooded freaks like them, or the spellscarred, what should stay down below in Downshadow," he said. "One day, the taint on that coin'll be seen. And on that day, we'll rid ourselves of the whole lot. Keep 'em away from our homes and our lasses—" he grinned and stepped toward Araezra, who narrowed her eyes.

"That will be enough, goodsir," said Araezra.

Kolatch spread his hands. "Just trying to watch over you, ere you find a husband."

"I hardly need your protection." Araezra fingered the sword at her belt.

"Just a concerned citizen," Kolatch said. "But as you wish. And if a handful of those tree-blooded elves or those spellscarred monsters winds up . . . *uncomfortable* in sight of my dealings, I'll make sure not to protect them either, eh?" He pursed his lips. "All for *you*, sweetling."

Kalen knew the man was dangerous. But he had confessed nothing, so they could do nothing against him. Kalen knew how that would infuriate Araezra—she, who would take good and justice over the law of Lords any day of any year.

The fat merchant gave her a "what are you going to do, wench?" grin.

Kalen heard a roar beginning in Araezra's throat and started toward her. "Araezra . . ."

Kolatch looked over at the unassuming Kalen. He said nothing, but his eyes were laughing—asking what a beautiful woman was doing trying to wear a uniform and sword, and whether Kalen was going to defend her honor.

"The day goes on," Kalen said. "Let us leave Goodman Kolatch to his coin gathering."

The merchant gave a little chuckle, and Kalen could see the arrogance in his eye.

Araezra turned smartly on her heel and started down the Street of Silver.

Kolatch grinned after her. "And of course, sir and lady," he said, "if you catch the thief, I shall lower my prices for your custom—for the service you do me."

Araezra bristled, and Kalen braced himself.

"My thanks," she said tightly. "But bribes tend to insult me rather than flatter."

Kolatch's smile only widened. "Well, have it your own way," he said. "*Lass.*"

Araezra's eyes narrowed and Kalen knew she wanted to say something—loudly—but stopped herself only by virtue of her discipline.

"Come," Kalen said, placing a gentle hand on her arm. "We must let justice work itself at times." He smiled at Kolatch.

The merchant gave Kalen a little nod and the sort of sneering smile nobility-striving merchants reserved for men they thought lower than themselves.

After they had walked half a block down the Way of the Dragon, Araezra uttered a sharp curse that would have startled an admirer of her self-discipline.

"You should have hit him," she said. "Not as a guard, of course, but . . ."

"Araezra," Kalen said.

"Hells, *I* should have hit him," she said. "Not out in the street, of course, but . . . we could have brought someone from the Watchful Order to wipe his memory, aye? No harm done, aye?"

Kalen smiled and shook his head.

She sighed. "You're no help." She looked down the street where Talanna had run. "Reckon we should follow?"

"You know how I am on my feet." Kalen coughed.

"True," she said. "I imagine Tal can handle one little scamp. Aye." She shook out her long black braid and yawned. "Forget the barracks—let's go to the Knight for a quick morningfeast. Feel like a stroll?"

Kalen put out his arm and Araezra, with a smile, took it. They turned back down the Dragon toward south Dock Ward. She leaned her head against his shoulder briefly, almost without realizing it. Kalen was familiar with her habits.

He could feel a cough boiling up inside and bent all his focus to stop it.

Araezra yawned again and stretched. "If Jarthay gives me patrol duty outside the walls one more time, I swear I shall fall asleep in the saddle, or fall out of—Kalen?"

Trying and failing to fight it, Kalen coughed and clutched at his burning chest.

"I will make of myself a darkness," he whispered. He cupped his hand over his ring, which bore the sigil of a gauntlet with an eye. "A darkness where there is no pain—only me."

"Feeling well?" Araezra's face was concerned. "Kalen? Kalen, what's wrong?"

Only me, he thought, and tried not to taste the blood on his tongue.

It subsided—his last meal slowly sank back to his belly.

"Well enough," he said. He reached down, fingers trembling, and found Araezra's hand. Numbness stole the feeling from his fingers, so he squeezed her hand only gently—he couldn't be sure how hard he was clutching her. She didn't seem pained, and that pleased him.

Araezra's eyes searched his face. "These morning duties are hard on you, I can tell," she said. "I'll speak with Jarthay—move us to a less nocturnal schedule."

"I'll manage," Kalen said, as he always did.

Araezra smiled. They walked on, each in their own space this time.

"Thank you, Kalen," she said. "Back there . . . you know how I can be."

"I know," he said absently, and he laid his hand on her shoulder. His touch was brotherly. "Your coin at the Knight?"

"Agreed." She smiled at him. "Come, aide—lead the way."

"Sir," he replied.

As they walked south, Kalen reviewed his mental note of the jewelry—surely cheap, likely fenced—that he had seen in Kolatch's shop. Kalen's sharp eye had noted it all: three earrings, a ruby-eye pendant that would be easily recognized, and the dragon brooch. He studied it in his mind, making sure he remembered it keenly.

They reached the Knight 'n Shadow, at the corner of Fish and Snail streets, after a brisk walk. The bells of Waterdeep's clock (named, by its uninspired dwarven builders, the "Timehands") chimed: one small bell past dawn.

Kalen guided Araezra through the door of the tavern and waved for a pair of ales.

CHAPTER TWO

THE KNIGHT 'N SHADOW WAS A TWO-STORY TAVERN, CONNECTED BY A long, poorly lit staircase that spanned two worlds: Waterdeep above, and Downshadow below.

The Sea Knight tavern, which previously occupied the site, had utterly collapsed in 1425. Whether the result of a wizards' duel or a bout of spell-plague (the accounts of locals differed), no one could ever say for certain. Some enterprising miner had dug out the cellar and discovered its connection to Undermountain. He built stairs, platforms for sitting, and a rope ladder, hired burly, ugly guards with spears to keep the monsters and coin-less hunters at bay, and the shadow—dark half of the tavern—was born. The knight above ground grew shabby and dingy, like a sheet of parchment soaking up blood from below. It absorbed the stink of Downshadow and became the same sort of place: a squatting ground for unsuccessful treasure hunters, coin-shy adventurers, and other criminals.

Men like Rath.

The dwarf savored the tavern's duality. It reminded him of himself: smooth faced, even handsome on the surface, but hard as steel beneath. Perfect for his line of work.

Quite at ease in his heavy black robe despite the moist heat of the shadow below, Rath sipped his ale, ignoring the two dwarves who—like all dwarves who approached him—had come to test their mettle. Like all dwarves in every wretched land he visited, he mused.

They had seated themselves, uninvited, at his table, and had stared at him without speaking for the last hundred count. The first—an axe fighter with a thick black beard tied in four bunches that brushed his hard, round belly—sipped at his tankard. The other—a dwarf with a thick red-gold beard that spilled over his wide chest—was trying hard not to let Rath catch him laughing. He'd cover his mouth so as not to erupt with laughter, but the sounds that escaped his fingers were reedy and almost girlish—grating in Rath's ears.

Finally, when the stench of the dwarves had grown too much for his nose, Rath said, in a mild, neutral tone, "May I help you gentles in some way?"

The two dwarves looked at one another as though sharing some private joke.

Blackbeard smirked at Rath. "Lose a bet?"

It was the smooth face. Dwarves could respect a bald pate, as many went bald at a young age, but to have no beard was practically a crime against the entire dwarf race.

The red-bearded one let loose a loud burst of his childish laughter, as though this was the funniest jest he had ever heard, and slapped the table. Rath's tankard of watered ale toppled, spilling its contents across the grubby wood and into his lap.

Anger flared—hot dwarf anger that was his birthright. Immediately he rose, and the pair rose with him, hands touching steel. Their eyes blazed dangerously.

"Now, now, boy," said the smiling Blackbeard, hand going for a knife at his belt.

Cold swept through Rath, smothering his natural reaction. It was a trick, he realized, so he did not meet their challenge. Instead, he waved for more ale, then sat down and began picking at his black robe, unable to keep the disdain from his face. He'd just had his clothes laundered.

The dwarves watched Rath warily as he sat, and he knew their game. That had been a move calculated to provoke a brawl. Now, though, their trick spoiled, they stood uneasily, halfway to their seats, half standing. Rath found it amusing and allowed himself the tiniest smile.

"You're just going to sit there?" asked Blackbeard. "After I insult you?"

"Obviously," said Rath.

Redbeard chuckled, but Blackbeard scowled and cut his companion off with a hiss. He leaned in close. "What kind of dwarf are you that won't rise to fight?"

"A kind more pleasant than yours, it seems."

Blackbeard's face went a little redder, and his red-bearded friend stopped laughing. The eyes in the tavern turned toward them and Rath could hear conversations subsiding.

Rath wondered if these were native dwarves or foreigners. The dwarves of Waterdeep were few enough, but trade and coin were good in the city. Thus they came, those more accustomed to the merchant's scales than hammer and pick. Plenty of mining went on to employ those with traditional skills, in the bowels of fabled Undermountain or in the new neighborhoods popping up all over the city. In Undercliff, beneath the eastern edge of the old city, dwarves sculpted homes out of the mountainside (illicitly or not). Or in the Warrens, where they could dwell amongst others their own size.

Rath had never considered going to either of those cesspools, and he had no drive to dig or mine. These two did not look like builders or diggers— more like fighters. Foreigners, he decided—sellswords or adventurers, the kind who itched for trouble. He could see it in their bearing and in their confident glares. Besides, had they been Waterdhavian, they might have heard of the beardless, robed dwarf who stalked Downshadow and thus known better than to bother him.

The beardless *dwarf*, for true, he mused. He hadn't thought of himself as a dwarf in some time—not since he had shaved his beard on his twentieth winter solstice, forty years gone.

"I don't like being ignored," Blackbeard said finally, unable to hold back his anger. "You get on your feet, or Moradin guide me, I'll cut your throat where you sit." He drew his knife.

The red-bearded dwarf gave the same wheezing giggle and reached for his own steel.

Rath opened his mouth to speak, but a murmured "sorry" stole the dwarves' attention. The serving lass with her bright red hair and high skirt came and left his ale, sweeping up the coppers he'd set on the table. Rath thanked her without looking up—without paying her the slightest attention. The other dwarves ogled her, as sellswords are wont, and Rath felt queasy.

"You going to say something?" asked Blackbeard. "Or am I going to say it for you?"

At that, Rath had to accept that they weren't going to go away. He took up his tankard and sipped. Nothing for it, he thought, but to deal with the situation.

"Your Moradin," he said softly over his tankard, "weeps for his people."

The dwarves looked surprised at the sound of his gentle voice.

"Care to say that again, soft-chin?" said Blackbeard, his voice dangerous.

Rath set his ale on the table and folded his hands. "Do you know why so many of your gods have faded and died since the world before?"

The two dwarves stared. Redbeard uttered a nervous giggle that died halfway through.

"It is because of faith like yours—that of weak, unquestioning dwarves," said Rath. "The gods thrive upon courage, and when you fear the truth, the gods become weak."

"What?" The black-bearded dwarf was aghast, and the other's face was turning red as his beard. "How *dare* you?"

"You bluster and boast, but I see fear in your eyes—cowardice that would shame your fathers. You have never questioned your heritage, but accepted it without thought, and so you do not know what it is to be a dwarf. I know this, and I choose not to accept it. You . . ." Rath looked at them directly for the first time, "you do not *deserve* to be dwarves. You are nothing."

His speech had exactly the effect he had expected—expected, not merely hoped for. Rath was not a dwarf given to hope.

The black-bearded dwarf drew his dagger and spat at Rath, hitting his tankard. "You beardless thin-blood," he snarled. "You take that back, or you draw and fight me."

Redbeard giggled again—malevolently.

Rath picked up his tainted tankard and looked at it distastefully. He made no move to draw his sword—sacred to his order—from the gold-leafed scabbard at his side.

"It is simply the truth," he replied.

Blackbeard growled low like a murderous dog. "You insult your blood, smooth-face. Take it back!" He prodded at Rath with his blade. "Take it!"

"As you wish," he murmured.

Rath flicked his half-filled tankard in the air to draw their eyes. They looked.

In a blur of motion, Rath twisted the dagger out of the black-bearded dwarf's hand and plunged it—to the hilt—into his companion's right lung. Redbeard looked down at the hilt sticking out of his ribs and his giggle turned into a wet cough.

Blackbeard just watched dumbly as the tankard fell and clattered to the floor, splitting open and sending ale over his boots.

The dwarf looked mutely at his unexpectedly empty hand, then at Rath, then at his companion, who gaped down at his injury. As if on cue, the red-bearded dwarf's eyes rolled up in their sockets, and he slumped in his chair.

"Really," Rath said. "Why would you stab your companion like that?"

The dwarf looked at him again, eyes wide, and they went even wider when Rath smiled. It was not a pretty smile—handsome enough, but cold and sharp as drawn steel. The dwarf didn't bother to catch his ally but turned and ran for the stairs.

Trembling hands pawed at his side. Rath glanced down at the panting, wheezing dwarf and looked at him indifferently. The dwarf, mouthing pleas for help that went unanswered, fell to the floor with a wet burble that might have been a laugh.

Rath waved for more ale.

"Here's for the tankard—and the blood," he said, pressing silver into the terrified serving woman's palm.

In a secluded corner, behind the half-closed velvet curtain drawn for private dealings, a pair of gray eyes set in a feminine half-elf face sparkled as they watched, with some bemusement, the beardless dwarf defending himself against his assailants. A trifle unsubtle, that one, but some matters did not demand subtlety.

"That," said her patron, indicating her breast with one languid, silk-gloved finger, "is a passing fair brooch."

"It pleases?" Fayne ran her delicate fingers over the edges of the dragon-shaped brooch. "I just obtained it today. Had to elude the fastest red-haired chit of a guard, but I managed it."

She went back to watching the beardless dwarf, and she giggled when he drove one antagonist to the ground and scared the other away with a glance. Hesitant tavern-goers stepped forward to recover the bleeding dwarf—Rath did not so much as acknowledge their presence.

That sort of man, Fayne thought, could be very helpful in certain situations. She would have to see about acquiring hold of his strings—coin-pouch or breeches. Either. Both.

"Whence?" Her patron pointed at the brooch.

Time for business, it seemed. Fayne turned to him. "A bumbling old fool of a merchant up on the Dragon," she said. "I've been robbing him blind for two tendays now."

"Different faces?" Her patron's tone was mild.

"What am I, dull? Of *course*." She rolled her eyes. "Art is pointless if you don't *use* it."

"Quite right."

Her patron rubbed at his cheek, where she could see two small scratches that were the only flaw on his otherwise smooth, ever-bemused face. His elf cheekbones were thin and high, his nose sharp without being aquiline, and his eyes a rich gold that matched the soft hue of his skin and his deeper golden hair. He wore a fashionable doublet and coat, rich but not attention grasping, and several rings over his white silk gloves. Each high, pointed ear bore several jewels, and though a great flounce of lace hid it, she knew he wore a thin silver chain around his throat with a locket that she'd never seen him open.

He bore no weapon, but Fayne knew he needed no such thing.

"So to business," Fayne said. "Who shall I ruin this time? Another lordling, perhaps? You'll read about the Roaringhorn girl on the morrow." She smiled at the memory.

He nodded. "Someone more important." Plucking a pink quill from nowhere—it might have come from his sleeve or from the air—he wrote three words, two short, one longer, on a scrap of parchment, without benefit of ink. This he pushed across the table to her.

"Who—?" Fayne furrowed her brow in thought. Then her eyes widened. "You don't mean it." Her hands trembled in her excitement.

He straightened his gloves. "You've prepared for this for some time, yes?"

"Decades," she said. "Suppose that doesn't mean much to you. Just a wink of an eye."

He smiled and handed her a scroll bound with a burgundy leather thong and his seal, a silver shooting star surrounded by a ring of tiny flames.

"I'll do it." She stuffed the instructions into her bodice. "Besha's tits, I'd do it for *free*."

He put a hand up, and she froze as though he'd smitten her with a binding spell. "Have a care upon which goddess's bosom you swear, dear one," he said. "And mind: as much as you've looked forward to this, take care." He slid his fingers along her cheek. "Do not grow careless."

She smiled. "You know me—I am the picture of care."

He didn't look convinced. "I am very familiar with hatred, my little witch," he said. "And I know well the damage it can cause. Do not let it control you."

She closed her eyes and laughed. "I haven't spent half a century sculpting myself to fail now. Don't—" She looked up, but he was gone as though he had never been there.

Fayne sniffed. His abrupt comings and leavetakings had startled her in her youth, but then she'd started to wonder how to do it herself. She hadn't quite mastered that power—yet.

She put her small belt satchel on the table and waved for ale. The serving woman nodded and held up three fingers. Fayne shrugged, took out a small mirror, a quill and ink, and a bit of parchment, and began writing.

When next Fayne looked up, the woman was standing over her, hands folded in front of her apron. "Aye, lady?"

She was a pretty thing, the serving lass, with hair that fell in ruby ringlets to her midback. Fayne liked her looks—had worn such herself, once upon a tenday.

"Take this"—Fayne pressed the note into the girl's fingers, along with a disk of polished platinum—"and a bottle of your best amber brandy to yon beardless gentle."

The young woman looked where Fayne pointed and blanched. "You don't mean . . . Arrath Vir, aye? Oh, lady . . . unwise, methinks."

"What?" Fayne flicked blonde hair out of her eyes. "He's not one for the ladies?"

The serving lass shook her head, then slid into the booth opposite her. " 'Tis said he's a mystic or some such, heartless and cruel. Hails from a temple of some sort of . . . emptiness? Void? Sommat the like. Only"—she leaned closer to speak softer—"only he tired of his brethren, killed 'em all, and now he sells his sword for coin. He'd slit your granddam's throat for a copper nib. Him, or one of the Downshadow folk what worship the ground he treads."

"Mmm," Fayne said. "Sounds perfect." She could feel her heart in her throat and a heat in her belly. "I wonder at his skill with his blade—perhaps I'll sample it myself."

The woman didn't look convinced. " 'Ware, goodlady—his in't the sort you ought toy with. And his taste—" She looked down at Fayne's clothes and bit her lip.

Fayne understood. Beneath her greatcoat, she wore the immodest working clothes—low-cut, high-slit—one might expect of a Dock Ward dancer. The shirt was frilly, the vest cheap, and the skirt revealed more than it hid: the wares of a lady of negotiable virtue at best. In truth, the crass garb did ride Fayne's rather fine curves and lines very well—at least, in the body she'd made for herself with her flesh-shaping ritual.

She'd just come from scandalizing one Sievers Stormont in a Dock tavern, luring him into just the sort of irresponsible play that would cast a pall on his upward-bound older brother, Larr Stormont. Not that she had any idea why—she trusted her patron to keep his own counsel regarding the cut-and-thrust of the nobility (and of those who yearned to join them, like Stormont). This, of course, hadn't stopped her from spending a night in the elder Stormont's bed and acquiring evidence that led her to believe he was a Masked Lord.

Which, of course, only helped in writing her next tale for the *Minstrel*— one of Waterdeep's most caustic, sarcastic, and thus widely read broadsheets. *A lass has to earn a living,* she thought, *and if she did it by ruining the wealthy and self-important, then so be it!*

The serving woman was staring at her, Fayne realized. For a reply, and yet, something more . . .

"I like your *hair*." Fayne leaned across the table and fingered the lass's red curls. Then, impulsively, she kissed the woman on the lips. Then: "Go to, go to! Enough eyes on my chest."

Blushing fiercely, stammering some kind of reply, the serving lass hurried off.

Fayne put the quill and ink away and looked in the silver mirror. She pulled from her belt a thin wand of bone and waved it across her forehead. Her blonde hair shifted into a strawberry red, then a vivid scarlet.

There. Just like the servant's. Only—there. Fayne's hair shortened until it just kissed the tips of her shoulders. Perfect.

Still looking in the mirror, she pressed the wand to her cheek. A scar crept onto her face: not *caused* by the wand, but rather revealed by it. The wand peeled the magic back.

She remembered that day. A thumb to the right, and she wouldn't be sitting there at that moment.

"Oh yes, bitch," Fayne said. "I remember you—I remember you quite well."

CHAPTER THREE

SHADOWBANE CREPT THROUGH A DOWNSHADOW PASSAGE, TAKING great care to attract no notice. He stole past natives as quietly as a ghost, leaving barely a footprint.

Huts and lean-tos crowded Undermountain's stale interior, packed into ancient chambers like the carcasses of freshly cleaned game in a butcher's window. The structures were built mostly of bones, harvested cave mushrooms, and scraps scavenged from above. The folk rarely stayed in one place long, skulking from chamber to chamber to avoid the underworld's inherent dangers. The knight in the gray cloak picked his way between the huts and barriers like a wraith.

Cook fires released greasy smoke into the air and coalesced at the ceiling. There, it escaped through holes and cracks and dispersed into the night above. Visitors to Waterdeep often claimed that the streets smoked, but they did not know why.

Long ago, in the old world, heroes and monsters had struggled in death-dances in these very halls. Now life filled the place: folk too scarred or poor to live in the light above. The last century had seen an influx of warriors, sellswords, treasure seekers, and what many might deprecatingly call adventurers, all of them with more prowess than coin. Waterdeep required coin, so they lived in Downshadow, where the only requirement was survival.

Downshadow was far from healthy, and even farther from pleasant. As he slipped through a chamber the width of a dagger-toss, Shadowbane nudged against something wet and cold near the door, and he stepped quietly back. The corpse of a hobgoblin, its face and snout twisted in terror, sat at his feet, the marks of three dagger wounds livid in its naked chest. The knight stepped over the body and continued stalking through the tunnels, cowl pulled low.

Downshadow was a complex, interwoven system of warrens in passageways and chambers, only one of which held any kind of permanent encampment. The southernmost cavern of the complex, it had once been a breeding and warring ground for monsters, but the adventurers who moved in had cleared most of them out. The newcomers built shacks and shanty huts that huddled against walls or stalagmites until the place resembled a clump of city. Perhaps a thousand souls lived there—the population ever shifting as would-be heroes braved the lower halls of Undermountain, which still held hungry creatures that skittered and stalked.

Shadowbane paused to consider Downshadow "proper." The shanty town was an unpleasant reflection of what Waterdeep could become, were it sacked and burned by a marauding army and rebuilt by bitter, impoverished survivors.

Once he gained the smoky interior of the great cavern, Shadowbane shifted his travel to the walls, rather than the floor, swinging between familiar handholds and stalactites. Downshadow was quiet this night— many of its inhabitants gone to the world above for the hours they thought their due. Climbing allowed him to survey the most dangerous part of the underground world from above—safer and largely unnoticed as he looked for trouble.

Trouble was why he had come—why he came every few nights.

The great cavern was the first area settled in Undermountain, and Downshadow's reach had expanded from there, gradually encroaching on the monsters year by year. Those who lived nearest the surface made some attempt at civilization, forming tribes built on mutual protection. Those who could make food from magic did so for the benefit of their tribes. Other food came from harvested mushrooms, slain monsters, thieves working above, or from trade with the black-hearted merchants who visited below.

The tents and lean-tos hosted exceptionally seedy taverns, dangerous food markets, and shops that traded equally in hand-crafted wares and stolen goods. These establishments sometimes disappeared at a heartbeat's notice. Some of the folk had become sufficiently organized to establish a fire patrol of spellcasters, though residents had to bribe them for protection.

As in Waterdeep above, trade ran the city, but barter in Downshadow took the form of illicit services and stolen goods, rather than hard coin.

Most folk of Waterdeep had never seen Downshadow—they knew it mostly from hushed tales in taverns, and repeated those stories to frighten children into obedience. The Guard ventured down on occasion, but only at need and only in force. Guardsmen hated such assignments, preferring tasks like gate watch or midden duty. More than a few merchants made a killing in these halls—literally and figuratively. When surface folk spoke of "driving the thieves and swindlers underground," they weren't speaking metaphorically.

One of those thieves, Shadowbane meant to visit that night. Ellis Kolatch was his name, and in Downshadow he brought back clothes and jewels he'd sold on the surface a tenday before, then had stolen cheaply. He met with his hired thugs in an alcove not far from the lower half of the Knight 'n Shadow tavern.

"Threefold God," Shadowbane murmured, running his fingers over the hilt of his bastard sword. It bore an inscribed eye in the palm of a raised gauntlet. "Your will be done."

As though in answer, Shadowbane felt that same ancient weakness inside him—the numbness in his flesh that gave him power and stole life from him little by little.

He did not beg for strength, for he would not beg.

Never again.

"I think there's been some misunder—*oof,*" Fayne said, then dropped to her knees in the wake of a punch to her stomach that cut off her last word.

The torchlight flickered, casting wavering shadows against the chamber wall.

"You do this to yourself," said Rath. "Simply give me the gold." He nodded, and the half-orc bruiser who'd put his knuckle prints on her stomach hit her again—with his foot.

Breath knocked out of her, Fayne went fully to the ground, curled like a babe. She cradled her midsection, struggled to breathe, and glared up at the handsome dwarf she'd come to meet, and whom—until two strangled breaths ago—she'd hoped to hire. Her mistake, she supposed, was to trust him to meet her alone in an isolated chamber of Downshadow.

He'd brought four men. One—a bowman—kept watch down the tunnel. A second, a lanky human with pasty white skin and yellow hair, stood impassively at Rath's side. The other two—a half-orc and a very ugly human who might have passed for a half-orc—had gone to work on her shortly after Rath demanded more coin than she claimed she'd promised. She called it a misunderstanding. He disagreed.

"Can we," Fayne panted, "can we talk about this . . . with words?"

Rath stopped them with a raised hand; Fayne could have kissed him. He stepped forward, and the grace with which he moved stunned her. He cupped her chin in two fingers, and her body went cold and rigid as though he pressed steel to her throat. Slowly, he raised her to her knees.

"Until I see the gold," Rath said, "fists and feet will have to suffice."

He stepped away, pulling his hand from her chin so fast she thought he might draw blood. The ugly man, whose arms were wider than Fayne's chest, punched her cheek and sent her into the wall. The punch disoriented her so that she didn't even feel herself hit the stone.

Beshaba, she thought, where do men learn to *hit* women like that?

Before she could ponder that deep and relevant question, a hand grasped her red hair and wrenched her head up, the better to slam it against the wall. The half-orc took his turn as well, kicking her stomach and sides. Stars danced across her vision, and Fayne finally felt the cold steel of a knife against her jaw.

"Getting personal, are we?" she murmured.

"Hold," Rath said, and the thugs did—as obedient as dogs. "Little girl, you must understand—I do not hurt you out of malice. This is merely business."

"Aye," she said, and she spat blood from her split lip. "I understand. And my reply is: Bane bugger you all."

Rath sighed and waved.

Crack.

Fayne didn't even know what they'd done to her. She felt staggering pain, and then she slumped against the wall again. Every part of her hurt.

"You're a pretty thing," said the thug. "Be a shame to peel your face off."

"I agree." Fayne looked right at him, as directly as she could with the dizzying stars in her eyes. "But where I'd grow a new one, I don't think you have that luxury, pimple pincher."

The thug snarled, reversed his blade, and brought the pommel down hard on top of her head. He shoved her to the floor.

Serves you right for antagonizing him, her inner monologue noted.

She made squishing sounds as she tried to rise. Dungeons were worse than gutters. Sludge—mostly dust, mud, and human waste—covered her hair and leathers.

Do business with scoundrels, her patron always said, expect to be dunked in shit.

"Big man," she murmured lazily. "Big arms, big knife . . . little blade, I'm guessing."

The thug's face went red. "This one's keepin' her mouth shut, boss," he said. Fayne knew that look in his eye—that of a man eager to prove a manhood sullied. Mostly by unsheathing it. "Bet I could make her squeal for you, if only—*uhn!*"

Fayne looked up, head swimming, and saw the ugly-faced thug slam into a puddle of filthy water three paces distant. Rath rose from where the man had been standing. The dwarf had thrown him *that* far?

"Do not embarrass yourself," Rath said to him.

The thug sat up, shook his head, and snarled. "You hrasting worm, I'll . . ."

And Rath leaped across the intervening distance and drove his fist down across the man's face. Bone cracked, blood spattered the ground, and the thug curled into a quivering lump.

Fayne blinked. "That's . . . ooh."

Rath turned toward her, and his eyes gleamed in the torchlight without the slightest remorse. He might as well have stared at her with polished emeralds.

The half-orc, Fayne saw, was looking at him with fear in his eyes.

"Give me the coin you promised," Rath said. "Do not, and there will be consequences."

She couldn't help it. "Like punching me to death?"

Rath looked down at the thug, and Fayne saw his lip curl. "His crime was worse than yours and deserved greater punishment. You made a simple error of judgment. He exposed his own cowardice and weakness, which in turn dishonors me, his employer."

"So you won't just kill me," Fayne said. "No profit in that."

Rath shook his head.

"In *that* case . . ." She smiled dizzily. "Piss on the graves of your fathers, beardless dwarf."

With a sigh, Rath waved to the sickly pale man at his side, whose fingers were studded with rusty, iron claws like fingernails. Gauntlets, perhaps? The man stepped forward.

"Your wight is supposed to frighten me? I'm a grown woman, dwarf."

"Hold," Rath said.

The sallow face glared at her.

"You've come to your senses, girl?" asked the dwarf.

"A few more blows and I just might." She coughed. "It's just working so *well.*"

Rath waved, and the half-orc charged forward to kick her in the side.

"That was irony!" Fayne whined in vain.

The half-orc drew back his leg to do it again, but Rath held up a hand and spoke a word Fayne didn't understand. The hobnailed boot didn't meet her belly, so she decided it was her favorite word of the year.

"Rath?" said the half-orc.

"Our sentry approaches," replied the dwarf. "Silence."

"Thank the gods," said Fayne, "that more hitting would be accompanied by further cries of pain."

Rath gestured to her. "Stifle it."

The half-orc kicked her in the stomach. The world blurred.

When her eyes worked again, a stick-thin man with a strung shortbow in hand and a quiver of arrows at his hip appeared in the corridor that led to the larger cavern. His eyes flicked to his dead comrade, but wisely he held his tongue.

"Battle," he said. "Attacked a merchant, downed his guard—didn't kill 'em, though. Probably itchies in Downshadow, looking for coin to scavenge or deeds to do."

Itchie, Fayne recalled, was a term for a sellsword, and most of those brave—or stupid—enough to live in Downshadow were something of the sort. Poor, hungry, and angry. *Itching* for a fight.

"Who?" Rath asked.

"Kolatch," said the sentry. "Awaiting a trademeet, probably." That name swam around Fayne's head—sounded familiar. "The fat merchant hisself is coming this way, wild eyed. Babbling sommat like a shadow attacked him, or the like."

Fayne was about to speak but was spared the commensurate blow by the damnably late arrival of her common sense and the appearance of a figure in the tunnel: Kolatch. When he stumbled into their chamber, she knew him—the merchant from earlier that day. His eyes rolled and his hands shook. Even if he weren't so maddened, he wouldn't have recognized her from the shop—not with a different face and a different gender.

Not seeming to notice the corpse, Kolatch scurried toward Rath and cried, "Save me—the black knight—save me!"

His hands never touched the dwarf. Rath stepped low in a crouch and threw Kolatch into the wall with a shrug. The merchant slumped. Fayne almost laughed at the way his frog lips burbled, but she suspected that making sounds would bring pain.

The thugs looked at one another, seemingly confused at the merchant's ramblings.

Kolatch's eyes focused on the tunnel and he whimpered. "The knight! The black knight!"

Fayne saw a cloaked man silhouetted against the crackling torchlight of the corridor, striding toward them. His worn cloak fell around him like a gray waterfall. She could see no face in his cowl, but she could feel his eyes upon her—upon them all. She shivered.

The figure stalked forward like a great black cat.

"I have no quarrel with you folk," he said in a cold, direct voice, muted only a little by his full steel helm. He pointed at Kolatch, who gasped as though struck. "Only him."

The knight's gaze shifted to Fayne. The torches flickered as though from his glance.

"Leave that woman be and flee," he added.

The self-assurance in his voice made fear—and excitement—rise in her stomach. He might as well have been delivering the words of a god.

The merchant gagged. "I'll pay all the coin I have!" he cried to the men around him. He pointed at his attacker. "Just save me!"

"Bane's blessing." The half-orc left Fayne and drew his steel. "I'll take that offer."

The helm began to pivot as the half-orc charged, scimitar high.

They moved almost too fast for Fayne to follow. The knight raised a scabbarded sword high, caught the scimitar, and stepped around, bringing his pommel down across the half-orc's face. The thug staggered a beat, snorted, and slashed again.

The knight ducked, moving with all the grace of a master tumbler, and punched the flat of his sword into the half-orc's gut. He could have unsheathed the blade and disemboweled his foe, but instead he slammed the pommel into the thug's lowering chin. The half-orc spun senseless to the ground.

Fayne could have cheered to see her attacker thus beaten, but she saw the sentry nock an arrow and draw the fletching to his cheek. " 'Ware!" she cried.

The knight turned toward her, taking the arrow in the shoulder instead of the throat. He staggered back a step, and Fayne's heart sank. The archer laughed—then cursed as the knight, undeterred by the wound, bounded forward. The archer fumbled with a second arrow.

As he charged, the knight shifted his grip to the sword hilt. He closed and whirled, blade coming free of the black lacquer scabbard in a silver blur. The sword slashed the bow in two, and the scabbard took the hapless archer in the jaw. He dropped like a stack of kindling.

The pale-faced man fell on the knight, lunging with his sharp nails stretched forth like knives. He'd been waiting arrogantly for his moment, and now it had come. Blue lightning arced around the man's claws, and Fayne realized—horribly—that they were one with his fingers, and not part of his gauntlets at all. A spellscar, she realized—the spellplague had bound razor steel into the man's hands and enhanced it with magic.

As Fayne watched, the malformed hands closed on her rescuer's steel helm, seeking to wrest it off. The knight wrenched free, but the man caught his left arm. The claws tore into the black leather, and Fayne saw smoke rising from the rent and smelled burned flesh. The pale man's face was rapt in frenzied glee. It was over, Fayne realized—such a wound would stun the knight, and then the spellscarred man would gouge out his throat.

She knew the knight would be in hideous pain, but he did not show it. Instead, he glared into the spellscarred man's face and the ugly smile faded. Then the helm slammed forward, crushing the 'scarred man's nose and sending him moaning to the ground.

The knight whirled back to Fayne. In one hand, he held the gleaming sword, which flared like a wand of silver flame. His left hand thrust the empty scabbard through his belt, then reached up to snap off the arrow in his shoulder. He winced only a little and made no sound. Through it all, Fayne never saw his eyes waver. They stayed cold and solid as ice.

She stood slowly—no sudden dramatics, and certainly not reaching for the knife she kept in her boot. When the knight didn't react, she realized he wasn't looking at her.

"Draw your steel," he said.

Across the chamber, Rath shrugged. He stepped forward from where he had been leaning on the wall—as he had throughout the duel. His smile was easy as he idly touched the hilt of his sword in its red lacquer scabbard. "Another time, if you prove worthy."

Rath moved to the center of the chamber. His posture did not threaten, but neither did he seem cowed.

"Stop," said the knight.

"I have done nothing," said Rath. He pointed to Kolatch, crawling toward the tunnel. "I think you have more pressing matters."

With that, the dwarf turned and—bending low in perfect balance—leaped into the air. He grasped the edge of a hole in the ceiling at least a daggercast above the chamber floor. Fayne blinked as he swung up into a tunnel shaft she had not seen before.

How could a mortal creature *move* like that—jump so high without a running start?

"Ye gracious gods," she said.

The knight looked after him a moment, then turned to the exit corridor. "Kolatch," he said. His voice did not rise.

The merchant squealed, grasped his chest, and fainted dead away at the word.

Then Fayne watched, eyes widening, as the knight in the gray cloak bent low, tensing his legs, as though to follow Rath upward. Magic, surely—she thought. But . . .

She gave a wheezing sort of sigh and stumbled against the chamber wall, sliding down into the ever-present dungeon refuse. "Ooh, my head."

The knight appeared over her and his hand caught her under her arm. He cradled her like the helpless victim she only half-pretended to be. She felt such strength in his hands.

"Are you well enough to stand?" The cold voice broke her thoughts. "Are you bleeding?"

"My pride, perhaps," Fayne said, "and I shall need a new coat." She plucked at the garment, which was more muck than cloth, grimacing.

"Well," the knight bid her, and he turned.

"Wait!" Fayne caught the edge of his cloak and knelt at his side. "It could have gone worse for me. How can I thank you, my hero?"

As she spoke, her fingers brushed her necklace gently and let her illusory face shift ever so slightly. The bruises remained—his eye would stay on those—but her cheekbones rose higher, her eyes became a little larger and softer, and her lips swelled just a bit. She spoke more softly, her words weak and afraid.

In all, she became a bit more enticing—more the grateful damsel. She played upon his need—the need in all men—to protect. To feel strong and in control.

"Not necessary," he said, but she could feel his body relaxing as he considered her.

"How," Fayne pressed, "can I thank you?" She stepped closer—into his arms, should he raise them to embrace her. Most men wanted to, when she plied her charm—and most men did.

Her savior, to her brief disappointment, was not most men. He stepped back, out of her reach, and his sword hand moved toward her, interposing sharp steel. Its fierce glow had dimmed, but the blade still glimmered faintly.

"Does your blade call me dangerous, saer?" she asked, using the form of address for a noble knight of unknown rank. She looked him down and up. "Perhaps you should listen to it." She could see nothing of his face, but she was sure his cheeks would be reddening. Unless he had no shame—which she wouldn't mind either.

"These men." The cold voice startled her—the voice of a killer. "Do you know them?"

Before she could begin the explanation that came naturally, he held up a hand. "You are far too capable a woman," he said, "for this to be random."

Fayne grinned. "You noticed."

The knight's mask was impassive.

"Yes," she said. "I had arranged to meet their ignoble master—the dwarf, Arrath Vir, known to his friends and foes as Rath. Or so I'm told, at least." She kicked the nearest thug—the half-orc—who groaned. "These tripelings I do *not* know."

The knight nodded, once. "And that one?" He pointed at the slain man.

Fayne shook her head. The truth was easy. "Our friend Rath dealt that death with his empty hand. However"—she smiled and stepped closer—"your hands need not be empty this night. My talents are other in nature—but no less moving."

The knight sheathed his sword. "You are rather forward," he remarked.

"Better than backward," she said, and she reached for his helmet.

The knight caught her arm and held it with a grip like steel. "No."

Fayne bristled at being thwarted but only smiled. "How am I to kiss my champion?"

"That would be difficult." He shoved her away, though not hard enough to hurt her. He turned and tensed his legs to leap.

"Wait!" she said. "At least a name!"

He looked over his shoulder.

Fayne shifted her weight and wrung her hands in a way that was very like a demure maiden. "Your name, saer, to remember for my prayers—and to ward off other knaves. A name to call in the night"—she laughed—"when I'm attacked, of course—so that you might save me."

He hesitated. "Shadowbane," the knight said.

She shivered in all the right ways. "Well met," she said. "I am Charl."

Shadowbane paused, and she got the distinct sense he was smiling. "No, you aren't."

Fayne put her hands on her hips. "And why would I lie?"

"I don't know, *Charl*atan," Shadowbane said. "Why would you?"

Fayne licked her lips. True, that had been an easy riddle. "Care to find out?"

He held her gaze for a moment, then jumped, blue-white flames trailing from his feet.

There was magic in his leap—of that Fayne had no doubt. It propelled him up like a loosed arrow. She knew that blue light—had seen it just a moment before: spellplague magic.

Spellscarred, was he? This Shadowbane? How intriguing.

Fayne couldn't help but marvel as he reached the ceiling and pulled himself over the ledge where Rath had disappeared. His movement was athletic—whereas Rath moved with unnatural grace, like nothing human or dwarf or anything like—Shadowbane moved very much like a *man*. Near the peak of human achievement, yes, but a man nonetheless.

Watching him, Fayne found breath difficult. She hated men who resisted her charms, and yet this Shadowbane lingered in her thoughts. She wanted another chance at him, when she could better prepare. He was a man who presented a great challenge.

Gods, how she loved challenges.

She looked to Kolatch, barely awake, who lay moaning and terror-dumb, and smiled.

She loved tricks as well.

CHAPTER FOUR

CORRUPT MERCHANT ATTACKED AND MAGICALLY DISFIGURED!" SHOUTED the boy who carried broadsheets at the corner of Waterdeep Way and the Street of Silver. He held up his wares: copies of the *Vigilant Citizen*. "Vigilante menace spreads in Downshadow—Watch denies all!"

Cellica, who could pass easily for a human girl in her bulky weathercloak, chuckled ruefully and shook her head. The halfling paid a copper nib for one of the long, broad scrolls—printed on both sides with ink that would smudge in the rain—and glanced at it. Apparently, some fool named Kolatch had come away with purple hair and beard yestereve.

She giggled.

"Brainless Roaringhorn heiress caught in bawdy boudoir!" cried a broad-crier for the acerbic *Mocking Minstrel*. "Scandal rocks house; says Lord Bladderblat—'typical'!"

"Undead stalk the nobility!" shouted a third, this one a girl for the infamous *Blue Unicorn*. "You can't see, you can't tell—they survive by bedding the living! Interviews and tales!"

Cellica skipped through Castle Ward, giggling at the worst news that was apparently fit to print. Most Waterdhavians called the drivel in the broadsheets ridiculous, but that hardly stopped them reading it. The printers would never go out of business as long as there was drink and stupidity and nobles to indulge in both.

She strolled west, then north along Waterdeep Way, breathing deeply the refreshing air of the bustling city. Waterdeep grew busy just after the gates opened at dawn, the streets choked with laborers and merchants, commoners and nobles alike. She bought a jellied roll and hopped up on a bench in Fetlock Court—in the shadow of the palace and Blackstaff Tower.

This was one of Cellica's favorite pastimes: watching folk. She watched nobles in particular, because they amused her. She found the way they walked comical: shoulders back, chest forward, staring down their noses at commoners, laborers, merchants, and any they saw as inferior. She giggled at the sharp tongues of lords and ladies in the street, took note of arguments, and laughed aloud when a seemingly delicate old lady seized a younger male relation by the ear and hauled him, flailing and protesting, to a waiting carriage. The gaggle of lordlasses he'd been striving to impress giggled until they saw Cellica also laughing. Then their laughter died and they stared coldly at her.

"Go on, off with you," Cellica said. Her lip crooked. She repeated, more forcefully: "*Go.*"

The young noblewomen stiffened, peering anxiously at one another. Then they shuffled away as though compelled, looking flabbergasted.

Cellica giggled. Folk tended to do what she said, if she said it forcefully enough.

The city raced by day in the warm light, and wouldn't sleep until long after the sun had gone down. Trade was the blood and bile of Waterdeep, as it had been for centuries. And everyone, regardless of country or creed, was welcome in these streets—so long as they brought good coin and a fair hand.

A fair hand was the less consistent of the two, and something Cellica read about every day. Setting aside the remains of her morningfeast, she unrolled the broadsheet—the *Citizen* was the most reputable—and read every tale of news, politics, and commerce in detail. Who was offering fair deals? Who stood accused of dirty trade or slavery? Who might be a spy for the Shades or Westgate or even the defunct Zhents?

This research was largely on behalf of her partner—gods knew he wouldn't do it *himself.* Looking for a target wasn't his firewine of choice; once he fixed on one, though, no man or creature could stand in his way.

So long as he had the right woman directing him, of course.

He would probably be getting back from his nightly ordeal now—collapsing into his bed at their tallhouse, not to wake until evening. She worried that he rested enough, but she also knew that worry was futile. Damned if he would take her advice anyway.

Cellica finished with the *Citizen* and bought a few more broadsheets, including the *Daily Luck, Halivar's,* and even the *Minstrel.* This last (a bitter cesspool about corrupt Waterdhavian politics, lascivious noble houses, and shadowy merchant deals) hardly ever yielded anything of use. That day, its reporting of the Talantress Roaringhorn scandal—as told by the oh-so-noxious Satin Rutshear—curdled Cellica's stomach, so she crumpled the sheet and tossed it aside.

She much preferred the *North Wind*, which featured her beloved illustrations of fashionable garments and easy-on-the-eyes models, in addition to plenty of gossip about circles far above hers. As the *Wind* reported, the annual costume ball was upcoming at the Temple of Beauty on Greengrass, five nights hence.

"Oh, to be noble!" Cellica sighed, clasping the broadsheet to her breast. "Or at least rich."

After fantasizing a few moments, she polished off the last of the watered wine in her beltskin and hopped down from the bench.

With the business of "keeping atop Mount Waterdeep" done, she cut east down alleys and turned north up the Street of Silks, deeper into Castle Ward. These were narrow, less crowded streets—filled with fewer folk and more broken crates, rotting sacks, and other refuse. The people who lived here were poorer, many of them huddled in doorways and beneath raised walks. They looked at her with hungry eyes, and she fingered the crossbow-shaped amulet that hung at her throat. Others waved to her from festhalls just opening for the day.

Cellica pulled her hood lower to attract less attention. Few small folk appeared in this part of the city—gnomes and halflings usually kept their distance. Cellica happened to know, however, that her people were less a minority than the eye suggested. She slipped among the taller people, trying not to touch anyone. No one batted an eye or stayed her.

"Doppelgangers infiltrate houses of ill repute!" cried a small figure who appeared to be a human boy. "Welcomed by festhall madams for their general skills and adaptability!"

Cellica made her way toward the crier, who was not a boy but a round-faced halfling. Anyone who knew Waterdeep might see through his disguise, based on his wares. He was selling *Pleased Toes,* a set of tales written, printed, and sold exclusively by his kind.

"Good to see you, Harravin," she murmured to him. "Mum well?"

"Aye, Cele," he said. "When you coming back to do some more o' that cooking?"

"Soon." Cellica leaned against the wall next to him and took a broadsheet from his stack. She unfolded and began to read. While she did, coin changed hands.

"You can pay me back this month, aye," said Cellica.

"Cheers." Harravin grinned, then called, "Doppelganger whores! Some reported missing—test your husband to make sure he's your own!"

Cellica hurried down the alley. As she went, she heard a sound and looked up at the edges of the roofs above her. Water dripped off split, moss-covered roofs—old rainwater fell on her forehead and she wiped it off. She thought she'd heard . . . but no, of course not.

She gave a little smile and turned to look down the alley. A trapdoor, covered by a heap of dirty cloths and broken crockery, was set into the cobbles. She bent down. A soft thumping sounded from below, like a machine working in the distance.

She pulled open the trapdoor and a dozen bright eyes blinked up at her from smoky candlelight. Farther in, she saw a frame press working, turning out *Pleased Toes* and lurid chapbooks. A halfling turned toward the sudden light and wiped his forehead, removing a thick coating of black soot.

"Philbin," she said, nodding to him.

"Well," he said. "S'bout time th'tyrant of a paladin lets you out. Ready for second print!"

"Celly!" came a cry. The small ones within started cheering and hopping up and down.

"Well met," Cellica said. She climbed down a stout ladder, closed the trapdoor behind her, and joined her adoptive family.

The little halflings crowded around her, cooing and yipping like puppies. She saw their mother, Philbin's wife Lin, cooking a meal over the steaming frame press engine: eggs and sausage and toasted thin loaves. Her stomach growled.

"You've come for more coin, I take it," Philbin said. "And our free food too, eh?"

Though the gruff halfling patriarch didn't look it, he was one of the wealthiest merchants in Waterdeep—partly because he was such a skinflint.

Cellica drew a bottle from her satchel. "I brought wine."

Philbin rolled his eyes.

"Just in time for morningfeast!" said one of the little brothers, Dem.

"Silly!" said a halfling girl—Mira. "*Second* morningfeast!"

Cellica found peace among the halflings of the Warrens, one of the cities beneath Waterdeep. It wasn't home—that was the ruined city of Luskan, far to the north—but for a time, she could pretend.

At least until her tasks called her back.

CHAPTER FIVE

PERCHED ON THE CORNER OF THE DESK, ARAEZRA SAID, VERY CLEARLY, "Ellis Kolatch."

"Ellis Kolatch." Kalen's monotone gave no indication of recognition.

Araezra sighed. Of *course* Kalen would be indifferent. The damned man was a stone.

They'd been taking their evening leisure hour—waiting for the Gateclose bells to sound, signaling the shutting of the gates for the night—before going out on another inspection. They were alone in the room, pointedly not speaking.

Though Kalen seemed calm, Araezra had been boiling with anxiety, wanting to talk but not to be the first to speak. Her nerves manifested in anger that went undirected at either Kalen or herself. Instead, she turned it against their commander.

Damned Commander Jarthay, who'd declined her request for day work. Twice-damned Jarthay, who'd argued so logically that more villainy would be afoot by night than day!

What she wouldn't give for a good invasion or riot to thwart—preferably incited by Shadovar spies or Sharran cultists or any of a thousand enemies of goodness in Faerûn. But no, it was a time of relative peace, and peace meant schemers and conspirators.

She'd take Kalen, of course—and Talanna, if she was at liberty—but she couldn't speak freely with Kalen then. She could now, though, if only he would pay attention to her.

Araezra set aside the locket with the half-done miniature she'd been painting in it: a gilded chamber, with light filtering through a flower-laced window. It was an amusing hobby—one perfectly suited for boring hours at the barracks between patrols.

She fixed her eyes on Kalen—on his hard, grizzled face with the constant layer of stubble, framed in the brown-black hair that fell in spikes. His oddly colorless eyes, like slits of glass, avoided hers, but she was not about to let go now that she'd got a reply out of him.

"Ellis Kolatch," she said again. "The crooked merchant we met yestereve."

"Ah." Kalen pushed the spectacles up his nose.

He'd been looking through Watch ledgers all day, much to Araezra's chagrin. He hadn't told Araezra why, and she hadn't asked.

"I'm told . . ." Araezra shifted her position so Kalen had to look at her. "Kolatch presented himself at the palace today in a frightful state—clothes a mess, eyes puffy—and demanded we lock him up for trade violations and dirty dealing."

Araezra's mouth turned up at the corners in a way she knew her admirers adored.

"You wouldn't happen to know aught of this?"

Kalen shrugged. He moved the ledger away from her and kept working.

Araezra frowned, then draped herself across his ledger, setting her face level with his. "Seems his hair and beard had turned the most frightful shade of purple as well. No?"

Kalen's eyes met hers, and she saw a little flicker in his face—a tiny tic in his lips. Was that anger, or a smile?

"Araezra," he said chidingly, "I'm working."

No one called her by her full name—no one but him, always so damned polite and cold.

She hated his formality when they were supposed to be at leisure. To set an example, she wore her uniform breeches and boots but not her breastplate or weapons. With her hair unbound and cascading in liquid black tresses around her linen chemise, she knew damn well how good she looked, and yet—confound the man—Kalen hadn't even noticed.

She'd never had this sort of trouble with a man. Usually, it was the opposite, and required a stout stick to fend away unwanted hands.

"Who are you looking for so intently?" she asked.

He looked at her over the rim of his spectacles. "Arrath Vir—a dwarf. No beard—turned his back on his blood, I suppose. Suspected of crimes against the city and citizens."

"Why the interest?" she asked.

Kalen kept reading. Perhaps she was irritating him, or perhaps he was simply ignoring her—she had no way of knowing. Kalen kept his own counsel.

She tried again. "That scar, on your arm." She pointed to a long red-and-white mark, as though from a burn, visible out his left sleeve. "How did you come by that?"

He shrugged. "Clumsy with the simmer stew," he said. "At times it burns me and I don't realize, because . . ." He trailed off.

"I'm—I'm sorry," Araezra said. "I didn't mean to mention it."

"It's naught." He adjusted his sleeve over the burn.

Araezra sighed and looked at the ceiling. She wished she could talk to him without putting her boot between her teeth. And his illness . . . she wondered if he would feel it if she hit him in frustration. Likely not.

She tried a third time. "Kalen, there's a costume revel at the Temple of Beauty on Greengrass," she said. "I was hoping—er, I think a guard presence might—"

"If that is your order, Araezra."

Trying to hold in a scream, Araezra tapped her painted nails on the dark-wood desk. Kalen turned back to his ledger, adjusted his spectacles, and scritch-scratched another note. She marked the ring on the third finger of his left hand—with a sigil of a gauntlet—but he turned another page and obscured her view before she could observe it more closely.

Frustrated, she picked up her locket and the delicate little brush and set back to work on painting the light through the window. Kalen's pen scratched. Araezra's teeth clicked.

Finally, she could take it no longer.

She rolled her eyes, threw the locket down on the table, and raised her hands. "Gods, Kalen! It's *Rayse*. How long have we worked together? You can't call me that?"

"If that's an order, Araez—"

"*Rayse*." She grasped him by the shoulder and he winced. "Bane's black eyes, Kalen—after what we've been through? After we . . ."

She cut herself off. Oh gods, had she almost just said that? Talanna was going to *kill* her.

But gods-burn-her, she couldn't help it. She—a woman infamous for her calm, unreadable face—just went to pieces around him.

"Araezra." Eyes calm, Kalen gave her a half-hearted attempt at a smile. "Must we?"

Her heart started beating faster. "Kalen, we should talk about this," she whispered.

"And say what?" He looked back at the ledger. "You were the one who ended it, not I."

"Only because—" Araezra scowled. "Kalen, only because you wouldn't . . . stlaern."

She expected him to correct her language, but he only shook his head. "Rayse, I told you about my illness," he said. "You know I don't . . . I can't. You knew that."

"You wouldn't hurt me." Araezra put a hand against his cheek. "I wouldn't let you."

He gave her a half smile. "It wasn't because I didn't want—"

The door opened, and his hand darted away from hers. Araezra almost fell from her seat but caught herself and stood, straightening her linen chemise and cursing herself for taking off her armor. The silvered breastplate lay on a nearby chair, next to her helm, the five tiny gauntlets denoting her valabrar rank staring at her like five sly, winking eyes.

She composed herself in a flash, exercising her iron self-discipline to the fullest.

Into the room came Talanna Taenfeather, still sporting the wild rack of horns woven out of her vivid hair. On her breastplate, she wore three gauntlets, identifying a shieldlar.

Talanna would have been fine company, but behind her strode an older man—thirty or so winters, brown hair, bright eyes, bemused smile—whom Araezra recognized only too well. Bors Jarthay's badge depicted a single gauntlet clutching a drawn sword—the sigil of a commander.

Talanna froze and looked first to Araezra, then to Kalen. Her smile curled in the way it did when she was about to say something particularly cutting. "Ooh," she crooned. "We're not interrupting aught, are we, Rayse?"

Araezra opened her mouth, but Kalen grunted no without looking up from his work.

"And what a shame that is," Bors added. He nodded to Araezra's breastplate and helm. "Taking our ease, lass?"

"My steel is always near to hand." Araezra smiled tightly. "Do I need to don it?"

"Your breastplate against *me*, Rayse? Nay!" Bors grinned. "I would hardly want to discomfort two of my best lady Watchmen." He nodded to Kalen. "Good day, Vigilant Dren."

Kalen looked up. He started to rise, stiffly, as though to salute, but Bors waved him down. The commander grinned at Araezra, but she refused to look at him.

"Need you aught, sir?" she started to ask, but Talanna rushed to Kalen's side.

"See this, Kalen?" On the forefinger of her left hand she wore a ring of interlocking golden feathers. "A gift of Lord Neverember." She smiled wryly. "The Open Lord's *passionately* in love with me, you know."

"Oh, don't be a dolt," Araezra said. "He knows your inclinations."

Talanna whirled, heat in her cheeks. "But a little banter hurts no one, aye?"

Araezra winced. Jealousy had prompted her tongue, she knew—she longed secretly to marry someone with power like that of Neverember, but *greater*. She wanted to wed one of the Masked Lords; the greatest, if possible. And then, with her husband's power, she could make right all the ills of the city. Rewrite laws to trap the guilty. Put together a secret wing of the Guard, who would reshape Waterdeep into a cleaner, safer, ordered place. Expunge the traitors, slavers, and other evils of which she knew very well. Little things.

She realized she'd lost herself in thought for a breath, and Talanna and Bors were staring at her. Kalen had gone back to work.

"Aye," said Araezra, "what prompted the gift of this ring, Talanna?" The use of her full name—rather than her pet name, Tal—was meant as a warning.

The red-haired woman grinned. "Well, I'm told the spell within is a safeguard if I fall from a great height—some call it 'feather light,' or 'feather float,' or something of the sort—that of course being a jest about—"

"—your last name, aye," said Bors. "But what occasion? Have I missed my sweetling's nameday?" He ruffled Talanna's hair, making the wires in the spikes click. "These are so glim."

"Damn them, then!" Talanna ducked out of his reach and began ripping the wires out. Araezra tried not to wince; Talanna was always so rough with her appearance.

"There," Talanna said when her wavy red tresses fell freely around her face. "As I said, 'tis a gift from Lord Neverember after my accident tenday before last."

Bors and Araezra winced.

Kalen, who looked up when the talking ceased, blinked at Talanna. "What happened?"

"She was chasing a thief from Angette's in Dock Ward," Bors said, "when she fell—"

"Jumped!" Talanna corrected. She indicated the ring on her right hand that gave her the power to jump great distances.

"—*jumped* from a building and broke her ankle," Bors said. "The Torm priests healed her, but not before the story got out. It was the talk of the city—our favorite little flame-haired Watch-lass, having taken a frightful spill."

Kalen nodded slowly. He looked to Talanna. "You caught the thief?"

"Faith!" she cried. "Why do you think I *jumped?* The fall broke more in him than in me."

Kalen nodded casually. "What of the thief at Kolatch's from yesterday?"

"Never caught that one," Talanna admitted. "Damned guttersnipe outdistanced me."

Araezra tapped her fingers on the desk, unhappy at being ignored.

"Getting slow in your old age?" asked Bors, gesturing at Talanna.

"Getting soggy in yours?" asked Talanna, gesturing at his midsection.

Araezra let loose a cough, more exasperation than throat clearing.

"Ah, yes," Bors said. "What brings us to your fine abode this eve? First, I need to borrow Kalen for a late evenfeast and thereafter. In his place, you will take Talanna to visit the walls."

"What?" Araezra asked. "But Kalen's *my* assistant."

"Second," Bors said without pause, "it has come to my attention that you need some aid in asking Vigilant Dren a certain question, Valabrar Hondyl."

Araezra's iron will broke. "What?" She looked wide-eyed at Talanna, who giggled. This was some jest of hers, Araezra realized.

Bors turned his eyes to the ceiling and swept his hands wide. "Can it be that the fair Araezra might be doomed to disappointment and apt to weep herself to a sweet, tender, and no doubt *lonely* sleep this night?" he asked. "Might not I be of some assistance in this—"

Araezra threw back her hair—an impressive flurry—and glared at Bors. "For the last time, Commander, nay. All the poetic words in the fair Realms couldn't get me into your bed."

Bors dropped a hand to the pouch that hung at his belt. "Even if I brought diamonds?"

Araezra glared even harder.

Bors moved his hand. "Well, then, I simply must woo you, lovely Araezra, with prodigious adoring looks." And he got right to it.

"Go on, Commander," Talanna said to Bors. "Tell him, already!"

"Tell him what?" Araezra looked at Talanna and mouthed: *You didn't.*

Talanna beamed innocently at her.

Araezra thought her face might explode. Kalen, gods burn his eyes, seemed nonplussed about the whole situation. He looked up calmly.

"Kalen, son," Bors said, puffing up to his fullest height.

"Commander?"

"I've been told Rayse will be on duty at the costume revel at the Temple of Beauty."

Araezra glared at Talanna, who smirked.

"Regarding the instructions of these lovely ladies," he said, "and knowing as I do that Rayse intends to ask you to go along as her escort, I've come to order you . . . don't go."

Araezra's mouth fell into a perfect **O**. "What?"

Talanna laughed aloud and slapped her knee, her jest completed.

"Sir?" Kalen asked.

"Honestly, if you took Rayse to the ball, it would be disastrous for morale," Bors said. "You can't imagine the number of broken hearts and spoiled nighttime fantasies I'd have to deal with. And no one wants weepy guardsmen." Bors shuddered. "So don't take her, even if she asks. I'm ordering you."

"Ah . . ." Kalen nodded. "Aye, sir."

"Now wait just a breath—" Araezra started, but they ignored her.

"Now that that's settled, Kalen," Bors said, "if you're finished up here, let's go have a drink at the Smiling Siren—just the two of us."

"It's never 'just two' at a festhall," Talanna quipped.

Araezra couldn't manage to produce words. She felt that if she spoke, she might explode.

"Away, good Kalen!" said Bors. "Unless, of course, you lovely ladies care to join us?"

Araezra fumed—at Bors, at Kalen, at everyone. "Mind yourself, Commander."

The commander winked at her. "Just us, Kalen. I'm sure the ladies can amuse themselves without us here. Though"—his voice lowered—"I'd love to watch that, wouldn't you?"

Kalen shrugged.

Araezra plucked up Kalen's discarded ledger to throw, but Bors was out the door—Kalen in tow—before she got the chance.

CHAPTER SIX

NIGHT HAD FALLEN IN THE WORLD ABOVE, BUT BELOW—IN THE TUNNELS
that ran rank with the creations of the mad wizard Halaster—darkness
persisted regardless of the movement of sun or stars.

Shadowbane stalked from chamber to chamber in Downshadow. While
he did not share any of the special visual acuity of elves or dwarves, his eyes
were accustomed to the gloom, and in the presence of even the faintest torch
down a corridor, he could see well enough. He could also, of course, create
his own light by drawing his sword.

Hand on the worn hilt of Vindicator, he paused and listened. He heard
footsteps, harsh breathing, and gentle words ahead, in a chamber that had
once been some manner of living quarters. Who could have dwelt this far
north in the Undermountain of the old world, he did not know—one of
Halaster's legendary mad apprentices, no doubt.

He peered in and saw a single moving figure—a woman in a gray cloak—
among several sprawled, moaning bodies. When her attention turned away
from the corridor, he ducked into the chamber and climbed to a better vantage point. There he crouched, balanced atop a moldering wardrobe, and
watched.

He'd been following the cloaked woman for some time, since she had
entered by one of the northern shafts into Downshadow. He'd glimpsed her
several times before and knew how to anticipate her comings and goings.
This was the night he had chosen to catalogue her doings.

Likely she was a crooked merchant, seeking to peddle stolen goods. But
if so, where were her warders? She could be here for no other reason—why
would a citizen of the world above come down to Downshadow, alone, if it
were not for some vile purpose?

Anyone other than himself, of course.

He watched from the secure, unseen top of the wardrobe as she went about her tasks. Here camped a band of delvers who had seen better days. Two men in armor wheezed pitifully, and a lad in leathers clutched at a torn belly and choked back sobs.

Only three. Shadowbane knew the ways of sellswords: they usually roved in packs of four or five. That meant they had left at least one of their number in the depths.

"Buh-back," the boy murmured. "Back away, lest I . . . I . . ." His hand feebly raised a dagger, then dropped it clattering to the floor.

The two armored men beside him only groaned.

As the woman knelt beside the bleeding boy, Shadowbane tensed, ready to spring to his defense. Adventurers were just as likely criminals as anything else, and his vigil in Downshadow did not include saving those who had brought a harsh fate upon themselves. Still, he would not watch idly while anyone murdered those who were weak or helpless.

She was casting a spell, he realized, but he recognized the words as similar to those of a healing chant his old teacher, Levia, had used many times. He relaxed his grip on Vindicator, though he kept his legs tensed, ready to leap.

Sure enough, healing radiance suffused the woman's body. Shadowbane watched, awed, as she pulled back her hood, revealing a fine-boned face of about forty winters and a forest of beautiful, red-gold curls. Such beauty could touch only a Sunite celebrant, he thought.

The priestess bent to kiss the injured lad on the lips, and healing radiance spilled from her and into his young body. The boy coughed and retched, and Shadowbane saw the wound in his belly close, to be replaced by smooth—albeit bloody—skin.

Jaded as he had become, Shadowbane still smiled at the beneficence of some folk.

The boy looked up in wonder at the priestess who had healed him. "My—my thanks, lady," he said. "I thought for sure, once we lost Deblin . . ."

She shook her head and pressed the boy's shaking hand to her cheek. "Sune watches over us all," she said. "I am Lorien. While I see to your companions, speak: what befell you?"

"A roving spell," the boy said. "It drains your strength away, so you can barely carry your own bones." As he spoke, the priestess healed the first man in armor, who hugged her around the knees, then promptly fell to a snoring slumber. "We escaped that, but then we ran afoul of a pair of those mad panthers with tentacles—the ones who aren't where you think."

Shadowbane knew such creatures: displacer beasts radiated magic that bent the light, making them dastards to strike. And with the lashing tentacles that grew from their shoulders, one needed to strike them quickly.

Lorien nodded as she bestowed a healing kiss on the second of the armored men, who coughed and stammered his thanks. "Are there more of you?" Lorien asked.

The boy's face went pale. "Deblin, a priest of Amaunator—he died when the beasts attacked—and our wizard, a girl called—called . . ." He sniffled, and Shadowbane saw his eyes fill with tears. "I was holding her hand when one mauled me. She disappeared. Can't be far!"

Lorien smiled and cupped his chin. "Never fear," she said. "I shall look for your lady love, and where love shines, there Sune shall guide us."

Shadowbane bit his lip. He'd found little enough of love—or Sune's guidance—along his path. Beauty often surrounded him, he admitted, but he allowed it only so close. He'd made too many mistakes.

The priestess pulled down her cowl and hurried down the tunnel where the boy had pointed.

Shadowbane followed, smoothly and silently. The weary delvers could only blink and question whether they had really seen a figure pass.

The priestess hurried north along a tunnel, heedless of traps. Shadowbane shook his head. What if an accident befell her in these depths? If he weren't following, how long would it be before someone found her?

Lorien paused abruptly, and Shadowbane had only an instant's warning to press himself into a crevice before she looked back, searching.

Impressive, that she'd heard him—perhaps she'd once been an adventurer herself.

A blue light flashed in a chamber at the end of the corridor, and the priestess turned to follow it.

Shadowbane pursued—at a greater distance this time.

As they moved, he got the distinct sensation they weren't alone in the tunnel. Something else was there—something hidden. Several times, he looked over his shoulder but saw no one. He kept his hand tight on Vindicator's hilt.

Finally, Lorien passed into the chamber where they'd seen the blue light. Shadowbane saw her stiffen, then creep cautiously toward something he could not see.

He picked up his pace, heedless of making sounds.

The chamber was wide and roughly square, lit by luminous pink and blue mushrooms. It had partly collapsed some years ago, and great shards of rock stuck out of the formerly smooth floor like stalagmites. A second entrance gaped in the west wall. The chamber was otherwise plain, except for two bodies in the northeast corner. They looked whole, though he could not be certain from his distance.

Strange. Though the room smelled thickly of blood and animal spoor, he saw no beasts, displaced or otherwise, that might have attacked the wounded adventurers. That was odd—why would monsters leave two perfectly good bodies lying in the chamber? Why, if they'd been somehow warded off, had they not chased the wounded and weak adventurers south?

A crude jest around the ante table was that one only needed to run faster than one's slowest delving companion.

He saw his answer, then: against the far wall were two bloody, ashen outlines of creatures like great cats. Shadowbane wondered what manner of magic had done *that*.

"All's well," Lorien was saying. "I'm here to help—not to hurt."

Shadowbane turned, but he could see only that Lorien was approaching someone. He heard another voice—younger, also female—speaking words in a tongue he didn't know. She sounded terrified and, he realized, familiar. He couldn't place the voice.

"Wait!" Lorien said. "Let me help you!"

He saw a flash of blue light, and then the speaker—whatever it had been—was gone. Shadowbane peered closer and saw Lorien kneeling to examine a blood-stained woman, heavy in build and wide of face, who lay in a puddle of blood-spattered robes. Something was odd about her skin, too—it seemed puckered and red as though burned by fire.

Lorien gave her a kiss of healing, and the wizard murmured wordlessly.

Then the back of Shadowbane's neck prickled, and he knew they were not alone.

Lorien looked up, though Shadowbane thought it impossible that she'd sensed him. She looked instead deeper into the cavern, where a short, wiry figure in a black robe perched atop a rock, contemplating her with his chin in his hands. The light of the mushrooms bathed his face in a cruel, fiendish light: Rath.

Shadowbane drew his sword halfway.

"Well," said the dwarf. "Now *that* was impressive. How did you hear me, I wonder?"

"I have a guardian, to serve me at need," Lorien said with a defiant toss of her curls.

At first, Shadowbane thought she must be speaking of him, but then he saw it, finally, in the light shed by the mushrooms. A shadow, unattached to anything else, seemingly of a tall and broad man, flitted across the floor, moving fast toward Rath.

Rath calmly raised a hand and spoke a word in a tongue Shadowbane did not know. Light flared from a ring he wore, bathing the room in a white glow. Lorien shielded her eyes.

The shadow hesitated, then fled into the darkness, and Shadowbane saw it no more.

"Simple enough," the dwarf said. "When one is prepared."

Rath stepped toward Lorien, his hand on his slim sword.

The priestess backed away, spreading her arms in front of the wounded woman.

Shadowbane cursed. He knew revealing himself was unwise, yet he couldn't just stand and watch. He stepped into the room, hand on his sword hilt. "Hold."

Lorien looked up at his appearance and her eyes widened. She gaped.

Rath hardly looked surprised. "Ah," he said. "Come to see if I shall fight you this time?"

Shadowbane drew Vindicator, whose length burst into silvery white flames. "Face me or leave this place," he said. "This lady is under my protection."

Rath eased his hand away from his sword hilt, but Shadowbane could see the violence in his eyes. "Very well," said Rath. Unassumingly, he walked forward.

Shadowbane drew back into a high guard, ready to slash down hard enough to cut Rath in two, but the dwarf just ambled toward him as though unaware of the danger. Shadowbane couldn't help feeling a little unnerved, but instinct seized him and he struck.

Rath stepped aside, fluid as water, seized Shadowbane's grasp on the sword, and elbowed him in the face. The blow would have been hard enough to shatter Shadowbane's nose and cheekbones, if not for his helm.

Stunned, Shadowbane staggered back, empty-handed, and the dwarf admired Vindicator in his hands. The sword's silvery glow diminished but did not go out.

"How amusing," Rath said, as power pulsed along the length of the sword, "that you think yourself worthy of me."

Shadowbane's helmet was ringing, or maybe that was his ears.

"Here," said the dwarf, lifting the blade in his bare hands. "Yours, I think."

Not thinking, the knight groggily reached out to take it.

Rath leaped, twisted over the sword, and kicked him once, twice, in the face. Shadowbane fell to one knee, while Vindicator clattered to the stone near Lorien.

The dwarf barked a laugh, then turned to Lorien. "Now, woman," he said. "We shall—"

But Lorien had seized the sword and tossed it toward Shadowbane.

The knight was already running forward, and he seized the blade out of the air. Rath leaped, and only his speed kept Shadowbane's slash from taking one of his legs. The dwarf landed two paces distant and Shadowbane pressed, slashing and cutting high and low. Rath ducked and weaved and snaked aside, dodging each swing.

Then Shadowbane saw irritation flash across the dwarf's face, signaling that the duel no longer amused him. The dwarf dropped low, knees bent, hands at his stomach. Shadowbane pulled Vindicator back to block.

Putting all the force in his compact, powerful body into one blow, Rath slammed the heels of his palms into the flat of Shadowbane's sword as though it were a shield. The blade slammed into Shadowbane's chest, and the force sent him back through the air and onto one knee. As though with a great maul, the dwarf had knocked him a full dagger toss away.

His face calm, Rath looked down at his black robe, where Vindicator had cut a single slash below his simple wool belt. He fingered the cut, frowning.

Shadowbane coughed and levered himself up on the sword.

"You yet stand." Rath rose, a smile on his smooth, handsome face. "Good."

Calling on the power of his boots to enhance his leap, Shadowbane lunged, crossing the distance in one great step, and slashed down, as though to cut his foe in two.

Vindicator sliced only air and sparked off the stone as Rath leaped. The dwarf wrapped his legs around Shadowbane's head, twisted, and tossed the knight back—this time even farther. Shadowbane rolled as he landed and kicked onto his feet.

The dwarf landed lightly and beckoned with one languorous hand.

Shadowbane obliged. He darted forward, sword reversed as though for a high thrust. Rath sidestepped, just as Shadowbane expected. Exploding out of the feint, he spun toward the dwarf, slashing out and across rather than thrusting.

He had not expected the dwarf to be so fast. Rath ducked and, capitalizing on his low gravity, plowed into Shadowbane, driving him out of his spin and onto the ground.

The knight tried to rise, but Rath leaped onto the flat of Vindicator, which lay across his chest. He shifted his feet, caught the sword between his toes, and kicked it away, where it skittered into the shadows, its light still blazing.

Rath's eyes weren't amused. He bent down, pulling back his fist to crush Shadowbane's head against the stone. "Enough of this," he said.

"I agree," said a feminine voice from behind them.

Rath and Shadowbane looked, and there stood Lorien Dawnbringer, divine radiance shrouding her. If she had been lovely before, she was now truly beautiful—fantastically so, glowing with a force and grace not given to mortals. Shadowbane could not look directly at her.

The dwarf danced off Shadowbane and leaped toward her, but then stopped and lowered his fist, unable to approach her aura of majesty.

"Run," Lorien said, and her words bore the weight of royal command. "Flee this place as fast as you can, and do not stop running until your legs fail you."

The dwarf shivered, fighting against her will.

"*Run!*" Lorien commanded again.

With an angry snarl, the dwarf turned and streaked toward the east tunnel. He moved so fast and with such grace that Shadowbane could hardly believe him a mortal creature.

He looked up. The priestess's figure no longer seemed quite as bright, but she was still almost blindingly beautiful. She reached toward him. "Lorien," she said.

"Shadowbane." He stared at her proffered hand.

"Come," she said. "I shan't hurt you—you just saved me, did you not?"

"You—" he said. "You're not going to command me to remove my helm, or the like?"

She laughed then, and the sound was like cascading water in a nymph's cove. "Of course not," she said. "If you're wearing that helm, then you must have your reasons. Though"—she pursed her lips—"though it isn't horrible scarring, is it? That would almost be a chapbook, right there. The priestess and the masked horror."

She grinned, and Shadowbane realized it was a jest. Warily, he put his hand in hers, and she helped him to his feet.

"You're hurt," she said. She pursed her lips. "I can heal you, if—"

Shadowbane tapped his helmet.

"Aye," she said. "Well then, my good knight." She curtsied girlishly, but thanks to the divine grace that lingered about her, it seemed straight out of the palace court.

"Well done," he murmured. "Though you might have cast some of those dweomers *before* he kicked the piss out of me." His cheeks felt hot. "Forgive my rough manners."

"I can swear like a sailor in my rages," she said. "It's unlikely 'piss' will offend my 'virginal' ears. Speaking of which—" She hugged him tightly before he could elude her.

"Ah, lady?" he asked, confused and more than a little uncomfortable.

"My thanks," she said against his chest. "If you hadn't delayed him so long, I couldn't have cast as many spells as I needed to send him away."

"I delayed him?" Shadowbane said. "You mean—with my face?"

"Aye." She hugged him tighter. "That."

To distract himself from how good she felt against him, Shadowbane looked at the injured wizard, who was breathing regularly, then at the burned shadows on the wall and wondered what might have done that. Could that wizard lass have managed such a spell? It didn't seem likely, if her band had fled from the displacer beasts.

He considered the dwarf and Lorien's shadowy defender. Rath's ring had only scared the creature away, not harmed it. And where had that shadow come from?

Too many questions, and he couldn't decide which to ask.

Shadowbane's ears perked up, and he became aware of footsteps coming toward them. "Lady Lorien?" came a distant, male voice.

"Oh, shush! She'll just *hide* from you." The voice was feminine, closer, and familiar.

"Shush, both of you!" came a quiet command.

Time to go. Shadowbane pulled away, but Lorien caught his hand.

"You saved me, and for that I am grateful," she said. "If I cannot give you a kiss, as the tales demand, then"—she pressed a small, pink scroll into his belt—"my temple is holding a revel a few nights hence, and I should be honored if you would attend."

"Lady," said Shadowbane, but she put a finger to his helm, over his lips.

"It is a costume revel," she said. "Famous heroes of the old world and the new—come as yourself, if you will. The invitations have no names, so even I will have no way of knowing you, saer." She smiled. "Your secret is safe."

Shadowbane wasn't sure what to say. He put his hand over hers.

Then, when he heard a gasp from behind them and reached for his empty scabbard, he realized he hadn't reclaimed his sword from the shadows.

CHAPTER SEVEN

ARAEZRA HATED THESE SORTS OF ASSIGNMENTS, DOWN IN THE DARK AND dank. But the Watch had been doing less and less duty in the sewers and Undermountain, leaving it to the more highly trained—and paid— Guard. She was serving the city, in a way, though she really wished nobles wouldn't get these crazy ideas and go vanishing down into the underworld alone where the Guard had to go fish them out.

She and Talanna trudged along the musty corridors of Downshadow, along with two other guardsmen, Turnstone and Treth. Best that Kalen hadn't come—he'd have been out of his element, and Araezra worried about him in these situations. It wasn't his spirit or his heart, but his body—his illness, after all, didn't permit much in the way of peril.

Not that Turnstone or Treth made her feel much better in a desperate battle. Gordil Turnstone was a wise and stolid guardsman, but well past his prime. His hair and great mustache were white from decades on the streets. Bleys Treth, on the other hand, was a skilled—if overeager and quick to draw—swordsman, but he'd seen well over forty winters. He'd been a hired champion in his youth, called "the Striking Snake" for his speed, and still retained some of his youthful charm and dash, but all the smiles in Faerûn didn't make up for age.

Araezra and Talanna were the youngest and most vigorous of the four. Talanna wore her light "chasing" armor, styled for running and leaping. Her long sunset hair was unbound, in contradiction of Waterdeep fashion, for two reasons, both to do with Lord Neverember. For a first, he liked to point her out to dignitaries by her red-burning curls. Second, he liked to see it tumble when they flirted, which they did shamelessly.

Araezra was glad to have the shieldlar at her side. She valued Talanna's company and her martial skills—in spite of her oft-rambling tongue. As at that moment, for instance.

"Honestly, Rayse, you should be more careful who you wink those lovely black eyes at," Talanna said. "The men of Waterdeep can take only so much, you know."

Araezra groaned. Talanna always thought her choices could be better. Not that Talanna ever advised prudishness in romance—only selectivity.

"I welcome your words, but I shall keep my own counsel as regards affairs of my heart," she said.

"Heart? Nay—I was hardly speaking of such lofty *affairs*. I was aiming a bit lower."

Talanna made a sly and scandalous sort of gesture, and Araezra shot her gaze to Treth and Turnstone. The men seemed, conveniently, not to be looking.

"For true, though," Talanna whispered, "you ought to ward yourself. I have seen how you look at Kalen, and I've told you time and again . . ."

" 'Romancing anyone in the Guard, Watch, Magistry, or Palace is a grave mistake as well as improper,' " Araezra quoted from the Talanna Taenfeather rulebook. She'd learned well the value of dampening jealousies and avoiding entanglements among the city's elite. "I'm well—you needn't worry, *Shieldlar*."

Talanna pinched up her face. "Ooh, citing rank, are we? I see someone's a bit touched."

Araezra ignored that. It wasn't particularly proper, this repartee on duty, but their friendship ran too deep. It was like sisterhood.

"He's just a man, Rayse," Talanna observed.

"Who?" Araezra's blush belied her feigned ignorance.

"Don't try to deny it," Talanna said. "You're still sweet on him."

"Look, it's over, aye?" Araezra said. "Just let it pass."

"Honestly, though—is it him? Poor bedroom play, I think."

"No," Araezra said. Then, blushing more, she added, "I mean, no, I wouldn't know, because we never—"

"Right, right," Talanna said. "And that's why you get so flustered whenever I ask."

She signaled Treth and Turnstone to halt and caught Araezra's arm. She leaned in closer.

"Just tell me one thing, aye? Is it yea—" She held up her hands, about the length of a dagger apart—"or yea?" She brought her hands closer together.

"That's . . . that's none of our business," said Araezra. "Gods curse you!"

"Ooh," Talanna murmured. She brought her hands even closer. "Aye?"

"I am not having this conversation," Araezra whispered. She looked back, where Treth and Turnstone were watching them closely. "Belt up, men!"

Turnstone coughed and looked down, as though interested in his boots. Treth snickered.

Talanna poked her. "So I'll just have to seduce him myself if I want to find out, aye?"

Araezra blushed fiercer than before. "I'll have you flogged in the public square for this."

"Better not have Jarthay do it." Talanna grinned. "He'd enjoy it a bit too much."

"I mean it," Araezra warned.

"Ha! No, you don't." Talanna laughed.

Araezra scowled. "No, I suppose I don't."

Talanna squeezed Araezra's hand reassuringly. "Love is for fools, sweetling!"

"Good thing I'm not a fool." She waved to the men. "Swords forward!"

As they crept through the tunnel, Araezra wondered if Talanna's words didn't hold a ring of truth.

She remembered very clearly when first she had met Kalen Dren, on a raid in Uktar last year, back when he'd been a Watchman on the streets of Dock Ward. In her six years in the Guard, since she had joined at fifteen, never had she seen a man so determined and deadly—at least, not on *her* side of a raid. In his full helm, he'd waded into combat unhindered and unafraid, his eyes cutting through as many men as his sword. During the battle, he had saved her life from a stray arrow by taking it in his own chest.

She hadn't seen his face before the healers had taken him away, but his eyes haunted her dreams for nights after. She learned that Kalen had survived his wounds and was resting at the barracks, healing naturally. When she'd protested, his superiors had explained that letting him heal without magic was a rare reward for valor in the raid; he seemed to loathe anything but emergency magic, and only grudgingly accepted the Watch healers. He preferred to live with his scars, it was said, as a mark of pride.

She visited his bedside and was surprised at his youth: he was hardly older than herself. She'd talked with him for the day and into the night, long after aides had told her to let him rest. Kalen had merely waved them away, so they could speak in private.

In Kalen, Araezra had found someone like herself—someone who burned with the desire to fix the ills of Waterdeep. He wanted nothing more than to find and punish the guilty. He told her of a vow he had made to himself as a child—never to beg. All the while, his eyes had stared through her to the frustrated soul beneath—weighing what they found there, like something more than human. His eyes had made her shiver, but not with fear.

Was her desire really so surprising?

She'd been due for promotion to valabrar—the youngest ever to hold the rank—and she insisted Kalen come with her as her aide. For a time, she thought they could be much more, but he had refused her every attempt in that regard. When finally she confronted him, he told her of his illness, and Araezra's heart broke. She would have stayed with him thereafter, but his eyes were so sad—so frustrated—that she had let their short-lived romance fade.

She remembered his vow and knew that for her to beg would shame him.

As his physical prowess diminished, she'd kept him in service as her aide, thinking that he would want the post but would never ask. She'd thought it would do him honor, but now she wasn't sure. As a caged lion might relax but still see the bars, so might a wild beast waste away at the center of his pride, knowing that he has outlived his days of ferocity.

Nor was she sure that her motivations had been entirely selfless in awarding that assignment.

She had confessed to herself that she still desired him—confessed it every day. It was not love, exactly, but she wanted him to crave her, too—to show her anything but cold distance.

"I see that gleam in your eye," Talanna said. "Honestly—'twas but a simple question . . ."

"This isn't the time," Araezra snapped. "You're sure the boy pointed in this—"

Then she almost jumped out of her mail breeches when Bleys Treth cupped his hands around his mouth and shouted, "Lady Lorien!"

"Shush!" snapped Talanna. "She'll just hide from you."

"Aye, Shieldlar," Treth said sourly.

"Shush, both of you," Turnstone said. "You'll only call monsters or thieves."

Giving a duelist's sneer, Bleys spread his hands. "Let them come—I've my steel." He tapped the heel of his hand smartly on his sword hilt.

"Shush, all of you," Araezra growled. "Did you see yon radiance?"

A bright white light flashed in the chamber at the north end of the tunnel. They heard the clash of steel—a duel, she thought. She put her hand on her sword hilt and nodded. The others did likewise, and Talanna plucked a pair of throwing daggers from her belt.

Araezra waved, and they picked up their steps. She heard two voices, one a familiar soft soprano, the other a rolling bass.

Araezra and Talanna stepped into the chamber. A man in black leathers and a tattered gray cloak stood before them. His face was anonymous, hidden behind a full steel helm. In his arms was the very noblewoman they sought, the priestess Lorien Dawnbringer.

Araezra gasped.

"Away from her, knave!" shouted Talanna, hefting her daggers to throw.

"Hold!" Araezra said, half a heartbeat too late.

The man shoved Lorien down and dived to the side. One of Talanna's blades whistled harmlessly past where the priestess had been, and the other sank into his left bicep. Unhindered and unarmed, he ran toward them.

"Hold!" she shouted. "Down arms—you too, Talanna!"

No one listened. Bleys Treth snapped his blade out and lunged with the speed that had once earned him his moniker, but his target parried with an empty black scabbard. Treth twisted this out of his hands with an expert circle and cut back at his hip, but the man leaped like a noble's stallion over the last fence before the finish.

Araezra watched, gaping, as he soared over their heads and darted down the south tunnel.

"I've got him!" Talanna ran, drawing another blade as she went.

Araezra and Turnstone ran to Lorien. Turnstone searched warily for another foe, while Araezra knelt at the priestess's side.

"Are you well, my lady?" Araezra asked without ceremony. "Did he hurt you?"

"No," the priestess said. "I came here to spread Sune's healing, and yon knight protected me." Her cheeks were flushed. "Shadowbane . . . he means us no ill."

Shadowbane. Araezra shivered.

She considered whether the priestess had been deceived. They might have just saved her from a charming—but very dangerous—attacker. Or perhaps he truly had aided her.

Regardless, he had run, and in her experience, innocent men didn't run.

"Come with us," Araezra said. "We will deliver you safely to the city above."

The guards nodded and Araezra looked to the tunnel, considering what to do next.

"Wait!" Lorien pointed to the north wall. "His sword."

There lay a shimmering blade of silvery steel, a hand and a half longer than a typical adventurer's sword. Araezra's eyes widened and her hand drifted toward it unbidden.

Then she heard Talanna's triumphant cry from down the tunnels and remembered herself. "Confiscate that," she ordered, and Turnstone moved to claim the sword.

Araezra looked between the two guards, frowning.

"Well?" she asked, pointing. "Which of you jacks will go after them?"

Treth ran his hand through his hair. "A snake strikes at short distances, not long ones," he said. "At my age, I'm like to be no faster than Gordil, here. In fact—"

Turnstone, with his grim face and white mustache, shrugged.

Araezra sighed. "Well, *well*." She pulled at the clasps of her breastplate, thrusting it open to the belly. Turnstone's eyes almost popped and Treth just smiled. "Turn, jacks."

They did—though she could swear Treth was still watching.

Araezra shrugged out of her coat-of-plate, revealing her sweat-plastered chemise. It was a thin, short affair that kept her cool under her uniform armor—to which the padding was attached—but it was hardly modest, particularly when sweaty. She rolled her eyes and positioned the straps of her harness where they offered the most cover—and the best support. Sometimes, Araezra wished she'd been born a boy.

"Well," she said, tying her hair back.

The guards turned. Turnstone had the decency to blush, while Treth snickered. Araezra threw her armor at the Snake's chest, blowing the air out of his lungs.

"Ward her well," Araezra said, nodding at Lorien. "Deliver her to the temple, then meet at the barracks. Unless you happen across Talanna or me—in that case, aid."

She seized the silvery sword out of Turnstone's hands and looked to Treth. "Scabbard."

Treth handed her Shadowbane's scabbard.

Araezra sheathed the sword and stuck the scabbard through the straps on her back, securing it with her belt. She made sure that her hips could move freely. She wasn't sure why she needed Shadowbane's sword, but something compelled her to take it. Then, tapping her watchsword hilt smartly in an ironic salute, she sprinted down the corridor where Shadowbane and Talanna had gone.

Talanna would catch him, all right, unless he could outrun the fastest woman in Waterdeep. Araezra wasn't sure, though, what would transpire when she did catch him. Likely, she would need support, and quickly.

This was ridiculous—running through Downshadow so indecently. If this didn't end terribly, she would look into a new suit of armor: a light, balanced harness like the sort Talanna wore, crafted for speed and mobility.

For the moment—well, Araezra only hoped the chase wouldn't take her where any citizens might be.

CHAPTER EIGHT

ARAEZRA RAN SOUTH AFTER THE SOUNDS OF FOOTFALLS. SHE PRAYED TO Tymora that she'd picked the right direction and wouldn't end up a dragon's late-night meal. Fortunately, she saw Talanna's bright orange hair fly around a corner twenty paces ahead, so she ran on.

Shadowbane tried to flee deeper into Undermountain, but Talanna was chasing him back toward the main chamber of Downshadow.

Good, Araezra thought—at least we won't lose him in the tunnels.

Ye gods, but they were fast. Talanna and Shadowbane tore through chamber after chamber, brushing past the injured delvers they'd found, careening through empty rooms, denying Araezra the chance to gain on them.

Not once or twice but *thrice* they startled sentries and adventuring bands in tunnels and chambers Araezra and the Guard had avoided. Every time they caught the eye of a sentry and blazed like hellhounds through the midst of their camp, the sellswords and rogues would scramble up only in time for Araezra to appear. They met her with blades, cudgels, and even spells at the ready, confusion running through their ranks.

"Waterdeep Guard!" she cried for the first such band, and they managed only fumbling swings at her as she ran past, panting, her long tail of black hair flying. "Stand aside!"

She drew her sword but didn't bother to block or parry—she kept running, heedless, and leaped the delvers' cookfire to scramble down the opposite tunnel.

The second such band actually stayed her a moment, where a quick clash of swords and a well-placed kick to the nethers laid low an agile hunter. As she tore open the door Talanna had left swinging, the archer of that group fired an arrow that rustled Araezra's hair and shattered harmlessly off the wall. She had no time to delay.

The third band, composed almost entirely of young noble fops and a single plain-faced lass in the boiled leather of a delver scout, just stared at the flesh Araezra had bared from under her armor. As she ran past, thanking Tymora they had not attacked, Araezra saw the young woman slap one of the lordlings across the face. It didn't break his stare.

As she ran on, the valabrar cursed inwardly, cheeks burning, and wondered how many dreams of the next few nights would star a dark-haired, half-naked swordmaid.

These thoughts stole her concentration. Bursting into a new chamber, panting, Araezra slammed into Talanna, who had halted in her pursuit. Shadowbane, whom she had cornered, darted into an eastern passage as the women fell atop one another.

"Aye, Rayse!" said Talanna. "He's getting—" Her startled eyes drifted to Araezra's all-but-naked torso, and her cheeks went bright red. "Uh. Sorry!"

They fumbled apart and Araezra scrambled up. She forced her legs to carry her after Shadowbane. She saw his gray cloak flick around a corner and darted that way. Talanna, being much faster, caught up quickly.

They sprinted from chamber to chamber. Most were empty but for abandoned lean-tos and rubble, but in some they flew past sword-swingers and spellweavers, packs of monsters and flaming traps. Every time, they barely glimpsed Shadowbane ahead, disappearing around this corner or that. If they slowed even a touch, he would escape.

They crossed through an especially long chamber filled with clashing blades, screams of pain, and trails of sparks and lightning. Half a dozen warriors wielding the various steel of a rag-tag collection of dungeon delvers were fighting a whole horde of shambling, mindless zombies. Blood and limbs spattered the walls—much of it undead, some of it fresh. The adventurers fought and howled against the walking, flailing dead.

The room was outfitted with two rows of thirteen thrones stretching the length of the room. Zombies that stitched themselves together every time they were destroyed would make their way to the thrones. Three of the great chairs had been blasted to rubble over the centuries, and the zombies that approached those only flopped disconsolately to the floor.

Araezra recognized that hall from whispers among the Guard—the Sleeping Kings, it was called. Most sensible folk avoided the room, but few of the sellswords who descended into Downshadow were sensible.

"This is madness!" Araezra shouted to Talanna.

"Look!" Talanna pointed at Shadowbane, who was creeping along the fringe of the room unmolested. The brawl had slowed him, though, and he was only twenty paces ahead.

With a tight nod, Araezra and Talanna plunged into the thick of it, hacking their way through the undead to continue the chase. Swords bright with firelight, blood splashing everywhere, they fought their way across.

They had no sooner stepped near one of the thrones than Araezra heard a grinding of ancient gears. "Rayse!" Talanna cried.

The floor dropped out from under Araezra's feet, and she would have fallen had not Talanna grasped her wrist. Adventurers screamed and tumbled down, draped with the moaning, wrestling corpses animated by the room's fell magic.

Looking around, Talanna could see that most of the floor had dropped away, leaving the thrones on their bases standing like islands around the chamber. From the appearance of the floor and the sounds of the machinery, the trap had been designed as part of the original room.

Araezra dangled over the pit, clinging desperately to Talanna's hand. Her watchsword had slipped from her grip and fallen into the pit along with the trap's other victims.

She looked toward the exit—only two thrones away—where Shadowbane stood watching them. Inexplicably, he had paused in his flight, as though deciding whether to flee or stay and aid them. Araezra tried to catch his eye, but he looked away.

"Ready?" Talanna asked, teeth gritted. The strengthening gauntlets on her wrists glittered, enhancing her natural power.

Araezra realized what she meant to do. "What? No! Don't you even *think*—"

But Talanna strained, swung Araezra back, then threw her toward the next platform. Araezra uttered a tight scream but caught herself at the throne's base. It blew the air from her lungs, but she hauled herself up to discover a zombie shambling toward her, its eyes jaundiced yellow.

Leaping through the air, Talanna kicked it in the head, driving it off the platform and into the pit. Araezra pulled herself up and they stood on the platform, shaking and panting. Shadowbane waited on the opposite ledge, cloak fluttering around him.

"What's he doing?" Araezra asked. "Why isn't he running?"

Talanna shook her head. She gestured at the gap, which was as long as a dagger cast. Araezra nodded. As one, they braced for it, ran, and leaped.

With the aid of her magical ring, Talanna made the jump easily enough, but she slipped on loose rubble and fell with a crash. Araezra's feet faltered on the edge and she reeled back over the pit. Her heart froze.

Then a gauntleted hand caught hold of her arm and steadied her.

She looked up into Shadowbane's face, covered by his helm, but he averted his eyes. He pulled her away from the dangerous drop-off.

The three paused for many heartbeats—Araezra panting, Talanna kneeling and flexing her sore arms, Shadowbane standing aloof. He didn't seem able to meet their eyes.

"Don't run," Araezra said. She felt the hilt of Shadowbane's sword at her hip, slung crosswise across her back. "We mean you no—"

Talanna lunged from behind him, but Shadowbane eluded her hands. He whirled, slapping her in the face with his cloak, and ran into the next tunnel.

Talanna and Araezra looked at one another, then bounded after him.

.:⌢:.

On Shadowbane's heels, they burst into the chamber they had descended to reach Downshadow—a vertical shaft beneath a popular, centuries-old tavern.

Other than the Knight 'n Shadow, this place saw the most traffic into and out of the caves and tunnels. The hounds of Downshadow who stalked the Waterdeep night didn't use such a visible entrance, so the bottom of the shaft was empty.

Shadowbane leaped up, bounced off one wall and then the other, and grasped the harness at the end of a long rope that was used to lower folk into Undermountain—often at the Watch's behest for crimes against the city, but sometimes by request for fools with more greed than sense.

Shadowbane dangled a moment, twenty feet over their heads, then began to climb.

"Tal!" hissed Araezra, but the shieldlar was already moving.

Talanna hurled two daggers into the opposite wall. The fine adamantine edges sank into the stone easily, one at chest level, the other higher. She bounded up one, then the other, then pulled a third blade from her belt and stabbed it into the wall above. She grasped the knife below and snaked it up to jab higher. In this way, wiry arm muscles bulging, the red-haired guard pulled herself up dagger by dagger, as Shadowbane scaled the rope.

It was a bow shot to the top of the well—a long, hard climb.

At the bottom, Araezra shivered, panting at the speed of the chase. She wanted to pursue, but she was helpless without means to climb—or fly.

She seized the lowest of Talanna's daggers from the wall and felt for Shadowbane's sword on her back—still tightly secured. Then she looked up.

Long breaths dragged on, and she heard the click and scrape of Talanna's daggers as she climbed ever higher. The strength of that woman . . .

Shadowbane gained the tavern first, of course, and Araezra heard distant, startled murmurs of patrons at their drink. Talanna reached the top and pulled herself over the lip of the shaft. "Waterdeep Guard!" came Talanna's shout. "Lower the harness! With haste!"

Araezra winced, thinking of the stir she would cause when she appeared, half-dressed as she was. "Tal!" she shouted.

Sounds of a scuffle followed, then a feminine voice swore loudly. A red-fringed head poked over the wall far above. "Rayse! He's going to the street—I'll stop him!"

"Don't even think it!" Araezra shouted. "That's an order!"

Talanna bit her lip, then disappeared back into the tavern.

"Damn it, Tal!"

The harness came slithering down. Grasping the dagger between her teeth, Araezra rubbed her hands together, then leaped to grab hold. She hung on as it was pulled slowly—too slowly!—toward Waterdeep.

As Araezra reached the top, she swung free of the harness and planted her feet on the tavern floor. She ignored the startled and curious looks of patrons as she ran to the door. Talanna was nowhere to be seen, and if she didn't know better . . .

One of the patrons—a white-faced noble lad—gawked at her and pointed out the door. "They—they were fighting, lady, and—and they ran that way!"

Araezra pushed through the door of the Yawning Portal tavern and looked down the dark street—and cursed. "Oh, Hells."

She watched as Shadowbane leaped from one roof to another, running east along the rooftops toward Snail Street. Talanna, her red hair gleaming in the moonlight, sprinted after him.

Araezra darted into the chilly Waterdeep night and streaked after, following along the city streets.

Waterdeep's sky was clear that night, and an almost full moon and Selûne's tears shone down to light the streets. The night was very late—or very early, depending on one's perspective—and drunken lordlings were making their way back to their villas, where servants would aid them (perhaps along with new-met lasses, or possibly other nobles) into their beds. Meanwhile, the common folk—who had to earn an honest living—were rising to begin the day, making dough for the ovens or gathering eggs to sell at market.

Dawn was naught but a small bell distant, and pale light glowed at the eastern horizon. It was still a time for rest before the gates opened and the important business of coin gathering—and spending—began anew.

In Dock Ward, however, there was no such tranquility.

"You stupid, stupid—Tal!" Araezra shrieked as her friend leaped over the narrow thoroughfare between Belnumbra and Snail Street.

Talanna barely made the jump, tumbled, and got up to run again. She turned south to follow Shadowbane, and they ran down Snail Street. Despite its name, nothing was slow about the street that night.

Araezra, heart thundering in her throat from weariness and terror, ran on, panting. The damp chill of Waterdeep clung to her sweat-soaked, bare shoulders.

Talanna leaped from rooftop to rooftop in pursuit of Shadowbane, whose gray cloak streaked behind him like a pair of wings. Gods, the man was fast, if he could outpace Talanna. Araezra knew magic had to be at work, probably in his boots—no living man could run that fast or jump that far. Sure enough, she saw a slight blue glow lingering around his feet.

The few folk on the streets—laborers, mostly—peered at her curiously, but Araezra put her head down and forced her legs to carry her. At least she was in Dock Ward, where frenzied chases and loud drunken disruptions were common in the early hours of pre-dawn. In the finer wards, Araezra would be reprimanded for disrupting the peace, for sure.

Gods, she was tired.

They ran past the Sleepy Sylph tavern on the left. Araezra's heart almost stopped when Shadowbane seemed to fly across the alley between two buildings, and Talanna didn't hesitate to make the jump after him. Still, they continued their chase.

Araezra ran on, narrowly avoiding pedestrians and carts and broadcriers who were just setting themselves to morningfeasts of simmer stew in round loaves. At the sight of her, the older folk gawked and the younger giggled. This, more than anything else, made her cheeks burn.

They passed another tavern, The Dancing Pony, and then Ralagut's Wheelhouse, where Araezra ran up an unhitched wagon and jumped off the other side before pounding her way down the street. Her lungs felt like fire in her chest, but she kept running, her eyes scanning on high.

Shadowbane leaped over the next street, Talanna just behind him.

Surely she was tiring. Araezra thought she could hear the woman panting and wheezing for breath, even from so far away. They were going so fast and leaping so far . . .

At the end of the block, Snail Street curled east and south. At that juncture, a street from the west—Fish Street, named for its vendors, the finest place for a stringer of the morning catch—met Snail Street. It was a broad intersection, much wider than . . .

Gods, Araezra realized. "Tal! Tal, 'ware!"

Shadowbane ran across the roof and leaped—soaring like nothing human—all the way to the other side. The roof was lower there, and he barely caught the edge. Araezra saw him land and roll, and he looked back at his hunter.

"Tal!" she screamed. "*Stop!*"

Too late.

Talanna reached the edge of the building and leaped, and for one heart-wrenching moment, Araezra thought she might make it.

Then she slammed into the edge of the opposite building at chest height, and rebounded to plunge into the open Fish Street, where a few men with their nets were passing. Araezra could only watch, heart frozen, as her friend tumbled like a discarded doll toward the ground.

Then she slowed, and drifted down gently like a fluffy cottonwood seed. Araezra realized Tal was wearing Neverember's ring—the ring the Open Lord had given her to mock her name.

"Tal!" Araezra shrieked, and she pushed herself forward. She slammed into a fisherman rounding the corner, and they both rolled on the wet, grimy cobbles.

Talanna settled gently to the ground and lay there, unmoving.

Araezra cursed, forced herself up, and hobbled to Talanna. She fumbled for a healing potion in her belt, only to prick her half-numb fingers on a shard of glass. Her belt was damp and she realized her potions had broken somewhere in their hectic flight.

The hairs rose on Araezra's neck as Shadowbane dropped next to her, his cloak billowing wide. Two throwing knives—Araezra recognized them as Talanna's—stuck out of his shoulder and forearm, but he appeared not to feel them. Blue smoke wafted from his feet—the remnants of whatever magic he'd used to run that fast and leap that far. His cold eyes gleamed at her—seemingly colorless in the moonlight—then at Talanna. Those eyes looked somehow familiar, but in her terror for her friend, Araezra did not care.

"Away!" Araezra shrieked, falling to her knees at Talanna's side. "It's your fault! *Away!*"

Shadowbane put up a hand to silence her.

Araezra recoiled as though slapped. How dare he—how *dare* he treat her like a child! She remembered Talanna's adamantine dagger in her hand and she lunged forward, driving it toward Shadowbane. He twisted his arm around hers, ignoring the wound along his forearm, and dealt her wrist a slap with his other hand. The dagger clattered to the street.

Then he twisted Araezra's arm, driving her to her knees. His eyes gleamed down at her. He could break her wrist without resistance.

Instead, to Araezra's surprise, he let go. She scrabbled back a pace, cradling her wrist. It didn't seem broken, or even to have suffered serious harm.

Shadowbane bent over Talanna, spreading his hands wide.

"What are you doing?" Araezra demanded. She drew Shadowbane's sword—the only weapon she had left—but the hilt burned her hand and she dropped the blade to the ground. It lay, smoldering bright silver, on the cobblestones.

Shadowbane laid his hands upon Talanna's unmoving chest.

Araezra watched, stunned, as white light flared within his fingers and spread into Talanna. The red-haired woman's eyes fluttered and she curled into a pained ball, coughing.

Shadowbane rose and faced Araezra. She tried to meet his eyes, but he looked away—toward his sword. She stepped protectively before it, daring him to attack.

The man hesitated only a moment, then leaped away into the night.

"Gods, Tal!" Araezra knelt beside her friend and hugged her.

"Geh . . . almost . . . almost made it, eh?" Talanna said. "That jump?"

Then her eyes closed and she moaned, consciousness leaving her.

They were beneath the eaves of the Knight 'n Shadow, Araezra realized. She saw folk standing in the street around them, surprise and concern on their faces.

In particular, a half-elf lady with red hair caught Araezra's eye. She was dressed elegantly in a crimson half-cloak over a gold-chased green doublet, and was staring at them intently. Of all the onlookers, she was the only one who didn't look up. Araezra found her gray eyes unnerving. The woman turned away and disappeared into the tavern.

Araezra cradled Talanna tightly. "Help!" she cried. "Someone *help!*"

A chill rain began to fall.

CHAPTER NINE

CELLICA WAS STIRRING THE SIMMER STEW FROM THE EVE BEFORE, reflecting that it might require a few more herbs, when she heard a thump near her tallhouse window.

Leaving the long wooden ladle in the pot on the fire, she turned toward the sound and saw the latch on the window rise—pushed up by a blade slipped between the shutters. She touched the crossbow-shaped medallion at her throat and waited silently.

The blade teased the latch up, bit by bit, until finally it scraped open. Then the shutter pushed inward and a man in a torn gray cloak tumbled through with a crash. He had clearly been leaning on the window from without, as though injured or weak.

Releasing the nervous breath she had held, Cellica rushed to his side, heedless of the rain blowing inside.

"Are you hurt?" she asked. She ran her hands over his chest and scowled at the knives standing out of his shoulder and his left arm. They stuck mostly in leather, she saw, but there was blood, too. "What passed?"

"You locked the window," Shadowbane said. "I couldn't—" He coughed harshly.

"It was raining. I guess I didn't think," said the halfling. "Curse it, you used your healing on someone else—you *fool*. How many times have I told you? If you need it, you need it." She grasped his helm. "Here. Let me—"

Without meaning it, she let compulsion slip into her voice, but he resisted her influence. He shoved her hands away, then wrenched the helm off by himself. Cellica glimpsed a little blood in the mouth guard before he cast the helmet away to crash, with several loud bangs, off the wall and floor. It rolled to the corner and stopped.

"I can't—I just can't." Shadowbane put his hands to his face as though he would weep. "I made a mistake, Cele. I didn't . . . I didn't mean anyone to be hurt."

"Aye." Cellica didn't know what had taken place, but she recognized the despair in his voice. "I'm sure you did what you could, Kalen."

His colorless eyes gazed at her, wet. He started coughing and retching then, and she could barely hold him up. He'd pushed himself, she knew—running and fighting and leaping. Magic boots or no, strengthening spellscar or no, a man was not meant to push so hard.

"Rest, now," Cellica said. "All's well. All's well."

She could feel his body relax as it bent to her will. Whatever god had blessed her voice with a touch of command, she thanked the fates.

As Kalen coughed and trembled, she held him as she had since they had been children on Luskan's cruel streets. When he'd been hurt or she'd woken with night terrors, they'd embraced each other like this—brother and sister, though not by blood.

After a while, Cellica spoke again. "You don't have to do this," she whispered.

He shook his head and limped to the table. "We'll talk come morn," he said.

"It *is* morn," Cellica said.

He sighed. "Highsun, then."

Cellica gently tugged the knives free and unbuckled Kalen's armor. His thick chest and shoulders swarmed with scars from years of this sort of activity. He wore as much blood as sweat.

"These are bad," Cellica said. "I could fetch a priest, and—"

"No," Kalen said. "Only needle and thread."

She shivered. Of course he wouldn't want magical healing. He wanted the scars to remind him—as though he deserved them. One scar for every drop of innocent blood. Cellica shivered.

Cellica worried at how Kalen didn't seem to feel the needle or thread as she stitched his wounds. He only winced when she touched the deepest bruises.

"You're so stubborn," Cellica said. "Haven't you atoned enough?"

Kalen started to reply, but his words became a coughing fit. He spat blood into his hand.

"You shouldn't worry." He coughed more blood. "Not much longer, I think." He took a mashed scroll from his pocket and handed it over. "Throw this out, aye?"

Cellica took the scroll—which smelled of both perfume and sweat—and frowned. "You shouldn't push yourself like this," she said. "Your body will only fade faster, you know."

"I know." He coughed. "I felt it hard tonight." He winced, but not from the needle.

"What if Rayse calls today?" Cellica asked. She snipped off the thread with her teeth.

He stared at the table a long breath. Such pain marked his face—so many shadows that the halfling knew were only his own.

His eyes closed and he sighed. "She won't," he said finally.

Cellica thought she glimpsed another shadow near the window that couldn't have been his, but it vanished when she looked more closely.

Trick of the dawn light, she thought.

CHAPTER TEN

RATH'S EYES NARROWED.

That was the only sign of unease he allowed himself—a slight squint—at her appearance. Otherwise, sitting back in his booth at the Knight 'n Shadow after a night of drinking, an open bottle of brandy before him, the dwarf might have seemed perfectly at ease. No one could see the conflict inside him, which he drank to pacify.

"You," Rath said.

"Me," she replied.

The red-haired half-elf slid casually onto the bench across from him. She was quite fetchingly attired in flattering black breeches and a green doublet trimmed in gold, puffed at the throat and wrists. The lady threw her legs—long, sinuous, smooth legs—across the edge of the table and leaned back on her right hand. Her left hand, still in view, danced along her knee. Her deep gray eyes appraised him wryly.

Rath couldn't deny a stir in his loins. Strange that she would affect him so. The curve of her hips, the lines of her face—perhaps that was simply her way. Mayhap it was the drink.

The dwarf silently inclined the bottle of brandy toward her.

"No, my thanks," she said with a sweet smile.

He poured himself another. "You're taking an awful risk coming to me."

"What can I say? I'm brave." Fayne waved to the serving lass for wine. "All passes well in Downshadow, I trust?"

Rath only stared at her silently.

When the wine came in a chipped bowl, Fayne raised it to her lips and drank it down greedily, more like a beast than a woman. Rath liked that, too.

"Aye?" Fayne blushed and adjusted her seat. "You're wondering about me?"

"Weighing you." Rath ran his hand across his grizzled chin. He hadn't shaved, he realized, and took his hand away. To look anything but impeccable filled him with self-loathing. "Judging, specifically, whether you purposely arranged matters for me to meet Shadowbane. It seems very much in character."

Fayne put a hand to her throat. "My *dear*," she said. "Certainly not. Why, I would never so much as go *near* that foul creature, even for a thousand dragons. The very idea!" She gasped in mock offense, then went back to smiling. "And have no fear of any tension between us, either: Ours was a legitimate disagreement regarding coin. We are both professionals—I bear no grudges, and I trust you do not either."

Though she smiled broadly, her eyes betrayed nothing.

Rath shrugged. He drained the last of the brandy from the bottle and waved for another.

"You ought take care with such strong drink," Fayne said. "Or does your dwarf stomach ward you from its ill effects?"

Ill effects, Rath mused. It would be worse if he did *not* drink.

The second bottle came, and he snatched it from the tavern wench with a scowl.

He hated this—hated his occasional and inconsolable desire for drink. It reminded him of his dwarf blood, and that heritage was one of the things he most hated about himself. Also failure and his urges. He hated that he could not master himself.

The need for drink had first come before he had shaved his beard and fled his homeland for the monastery hidden deep in the mountain. Training among the monks had suppressed this desire to connect with his hated blood—for a time, at least. He had drunk himself to a stupor just before he killed the masters of the monastery, took their most sacred of swords, and fled to Waterdeep. And for a while, with the blood he spilled almost as easily as breathing, he had not felt the urges.

Until this night—until that thrice-cursed *Shadowbane*.

Was this the third time he would drink to excess?

"Rough eve?" Fayne asked, pointing to the empty bottles—three of them.

Hard as it was—and it was hard, indeed—Rath set the bottle back on the table and pulled his gaze away from it. He still thought about it—craved the sweet fire on his tongue and in his belly, dulling his base impulses—but she could not see his mind.

"What do you know of it, girl?" Rath asked. "I am a master at my art—I have never been defeated, or I would be dead." He was saying too much. It was the liquor in his stomach, saturating his blood and making him weak. Making him into a dwarf, when he should be free.

"And yet," Fayne said, "you look like a man who bears a vendetta. Against a foe who left you alive, perhaps?"

Rath would dance to her steps no more. "What do you want?"

"The question," Fayne said, "is more correctly, do I know what *you* want?"

The dwarf waved. "I want nothing."

"Oh, I wouldn't be so sure." Fayne took a slip of parchment from the scrip satchel she had set on the table and showed it to him. It had a single long word on it. A name.

He read the parchment and his eyes narrowed. "You know this man?" he asked. "Not just know of him, but you *know* him?"

"Indeed!" She nodded. "It's only a matter of time before I have his face, too—and I'm sure that would be worth something to you." She reached across the table and laid her fingers across his wrist. "And perhaps I can think of a few other things, aye?"

Rath looked at her hand on his arm. His face remained expressionless.

"I had thought," he said, "that your inclinations did not match mine." He nodded to the serving lass, who was delivering a heavy tray of tankards to a group of half-orcs. "From your kiss with yon wench of yesterday."

"You noticed," Fayne said. "Would you like to see it again—perhaps in a more intimate setting? Waterdeep is the city of coin, after all."

"You mean—" Rath grimaced. "How disgusting."

"You'd be surprised," she said. "Call me . . . free of mind. I can do many things—even dwarves." She winked. "*Especially* dwarves."

Rath curled his lip. "Offer me coin, or begone—I'll have nothing else of you."

Fayne pouted. "What a pity."

Rath drank his brandy down and poured another. Fayne took out a second parchment, this with two words written on it, and passed it across the table. He looked at the name.

"Interesting," he said. "The first shall be my reward for this? Why?"

"This is personal," she said. "Someone I've hated for a long, long time." Her face and voice were deadly serious. "You are a professional—I do not think you could understand that."

It was Rath's turn to smile—yet it might have been the brandy. "*You'd* be surprised at what I would understand." He chuckled. "I am very familiar with hatred."

Fayne paused at that. "Mmm," she said. "Well. I shall deliver your payment—as noted on that parchment—upon completion. Aught else?"

As quickly as a snake might lunge, Rath reached across the table and seized the lace at her collar, wrenching her face close to his own. Fayne went pale.

"You are afraid," he whispered. "Why?"

Fayne blinked. Her face was calm, but her eyes were fearful. "Release me," she said. "Release me, or—"

"Or you will strike me?" Rath smiled. "I could kill you in a heartbeat."

To demonstrate, Rath gave her face a flick with his fingers, splitting open her upper lip. She didn't wince, and he almost respected her for that. Almost.

He laid his other hand around her neck. "Answer my question."

The woman licked where he had broken her lip. "Dreams," she said.

Rath relaxed his grip. "Dreams?"

"A girl—a girl in blue fire." Her eyes narrowed and her lip curled. "Know one?"

The dwarf sighed and released her to flop back to the bench. He leaned back, drained.

Fayne sucked her broken lip. "So you've caught me," she said. "I suppose I dream of wenches after all—but that isn't a fault, aye?" Discomfited as she was, she winked.

Rath understood something about her then: how she used allurement to fight anxiety. He smiled wryly. So he wasn't the only one who demeaned himself in moments of weakness.

He pulled his hand away. "Within three nights," he said, and gestured for her to depart.

If Fayne had gone then, it would have been well, but instead her eyes held him fast. She reached casually across and plucked up his hand. She rubbed it against her cheek, teasing her lips along his thumb. His arm tingled, and his hand looked blasphemously dark against her skin.

Long after she left the table, her touch lingered.

Rath folded the parchment upon which she'd named his mark and slid it into his black robe. He raised the brandy to his trembling lips, but the cool liquid tasted like ash on his tongue. He threw the bottle aside with a hiss.

Even drink did him no good now. She had ruined it for him.

He needed a woman, he knew, but not *her*. Not that faceless creature.

His sharp eyes fell on the serving lass. She had smallish breasts—well enough—and a strong, rounded backside. He wouldn't enjoy it, he knew, but he had no choice. He wouldn't go so far as to say he wanted her, but he knew that he needed her.

Needed to drive his demons away—to forget.

"Girl," he said across the tavern, and she stiffened. He raised the mostly empty bottle of brandy. "Come. Drink with me."

He laid gold on the table.

CHAPTER ELEVEN

"SHADOVAR ASSASSIN HIDES AMONG CORRUPT MERCHANTS!" CRIED A BOY for the *Daily Luck,* hawking his broadsheet on the Street of Silks as evening fell. "Watch denies all rumors!"

"Shadovar spy rumors stupid!" called a rival broadcrier, a bob-haired girl crying the *Merchant's Friend.* She stuck out her tongue at the *Luck* boy. "*Daily Luck* prints idiocy!"

"Does not!" cried the boy.

"Does *so!*"

A disgruntled Watchman came upon the two and hissed them onto the next street. They ran from him, laughing, hand in hand, and—Kalen thought—likely fell to kissing as soon as they were out of sight. Younglings. He shook his head and smiled ruefully.

"I swear to the gods, Kalen," said Bors. "If you keep on delaying us for words with which to woo yon strumpet—when hard coin will damn well do—I shall declare her the Lady Dren."

Kalen surveyed the chapbooks just inside the shop. "Leleera likes to read."

"I suppose we all have our bedchamber pleasures," Bors said.

"Kindly don't share."

Bors grinned.

Kalen coughed into his hand, though it was mostly feigned. The weakness had subsided since yestereve, but he could still feel numbness throughout his body. As on any other day.

They had stopped on the way up the Street of Silks at a shop called the Curious Past, at which Kalen was a frequent customer. The business—which after more than a century was growing to be an ancient treasure in its own right—sold oddities, antiques, and chapbooks about the old world. Kalen scanned the titles of the books stacked on the table as the anxious vendor looked on.

Both were off duty that day, and as he often did on such days, Bors had invited Kalen to his favorite festhall—the Smiling Siren. Mostly, Kalen knew, Bors did so to interrogate Kalen for intimate information about Araezra. Kalen had not seen his superior that day—she had not reported for duty—but he wasn't about to let his worry show more than was seemly.

Kalen tried to put her out of his mind. He studied the wares laid out before him.

Though all the thirty-or-so-page books were romantic in nature, they ranged from the speculative (*The Chained Man of Erlkazar*, *The Blood Queen of Qurth*) to the historical (*Return of the Shades*, the First and Second of Shadows series), and from the salacious (*Untold Privy Tales of Cormyr: The Laughing Sisters*, *The Wayward Witch Queen*) to the outright naughty (*Adulteries of Lady Alustra: A Confessional*, *Seven Sisters for Seven Nights*, *Torm's Conquests*; this last not a reference to the god of justice, but a lecherous adventurer of the last century).

He also found most of Arita's *Silver Fox* series, up to the eighty-page eighth volume, *Fox in the Anauroch*. Rumors of the upcoming ninth, *Fox and the Blue Fire*, had been the talk of literary circles for some months.

Kalen selected one of the books and handed the vendor five silvers. He slid the book into his satchel and adjusted the thong over his shoulder. The two wore no armor while off duty, but their black greatcoats—hallmark of the Waterdeep Guard—kept vendors from cheating them.

"Well? Which is it?" Bors winked at the vendor's giggly daughter.

"Aye?"

"Which masterpiece shall Leleera be enjoying this night, man?" asked Bors. "Aught with pirates, nay? I've heard the lasses swoon over pirates these days."

"All due respect, sir," Kalen said. "Can you even read?"

"Ha!" Bors clapped him on the back. "Well enough, then."

As they walked to the Siren, a light rain began to fall on what had been a warm day, sending up dust from the cobblestones. It was that time of winter-turning-to-spring when the weather could not choose how to behave. Dust swirled in a breeze that came from the west.

"Sea fog tonight," predicted Kalen.

"Ridiculous!" said Bors. He spread his hands. "You hear this, Waterdeep? Ridiculous!"

Kalen just smiled—and coughed lightly.

With the rain and the approaching eve, business slowed. The street lighters—retired Watchmen, mostly—were about their work, lifting long hooks to hang fish-oil lamps. The streets would grow crowded near the gates, which closed at dusk.

"I don't see," Bors said, munching an apple, "why you bother with lasses of the night, when by all accounts you could tumble a nymph like Rayse for free."

Kalen ignored that. "How are Araezra and Talanna?" he asked quietly.

"You mean yestereve? Bah." Bors sparked a flint and lit his tamped pipe. "Talanna fell—*again*, though at least this time she had the damn ring. Laid up for healing at Torm's temple a few days, but she'll be fine—that girl's tougher 'n bone dragons." He took a deep pull of pipe smoke. "I'm sure the damned *Minstrel* will run a tale in the morn that makes us all look hrasting fools, but no mind."

Kalen nodded. Cellica would tell him about the broadsheets. He never read them himself—he already knew how bleak the world really was. "What of Araezra?" he asked quietly.

"Rayse . . ." He looked down at his hands. "She took yestereve pretty hard, as she always does. Good lass, that one, but hard on herself. Really hard. Thinks she has to be."

Kalen sighed.

"Funny you ask about her, when we're on our way to a *festhall*." Bors clapped him on the shoulder. "Mayhap after we're done there, you'll want to cheer Rayse up, eh?"

Kalen ignored Bors's jape.

They passed under the arms of the Siren—cunningly carved as a blushing, sea-skinned and foam-haired maiden whose gauzy skirts would occasionally billow in the right breeze off the bay. The entry room was cunningly sculpted and painted in a forest scene on one side, a beach on the other. Figures in various states of nakedness seemed to dance off the walls—nymphs, dryads, satyrs, and the like, also knights and maidens reclining and embracing under the boughs of trees.

The images were so lifelike that a small person could blend in by standing still, as was a favorite pastime of Sanchel, the Siren's dwarf madam. Bors and Kalen knew her game, but she startled the Hells out of two young sellswords when she appeared—in thigh boots and a cloak of leaves—from among the trees.

"Sune smile on you." Then, as they almost pissed themselves: "Boy, girl, or common?"

"Cuh-common," said one of them. The other stared at her mostly exposed chest, an impressive edifice considering her stature.

"Love and beauty follow you," said Sanchel. "If you would make your offering?"

The older of the sellswords elbowed the younger, and he drew a purse out of his belt and handed it toward Sanchel. The dwarf shook her head and pointed instead toward a statue of the goddess that stood within a fountain below the stairs. At her gesture, the boy poured the coins into the water, which instantly turned bright gold.

"The goddess is pleased. You are welcome to her hall." Then Sanchel made a bird call and two half-clad celebrants appeared—one lad and one lass. Sanchel pointed each to one of the adventurers. A pause followed, in which the festgirl and festboy appraised the patrons critically, then they nodded and took the young men by the arms.

Sanchel prided herself on knowing the nighttime preferences of her patrons at a glance, and she was right again. The youths looked very pleased at their escorts, and allowed themselves to be led toward the common hall, which would be full of dancing, wine, and song.

Sanchel turned to Kalen and Bors with the smile she reserved for favored regulars. "Good eve, gentles—I see the Watch is treating you well?"

"Hasn't killed us yet." Bors eyed the murals speculatively. "I wonder . . ."

Kalen rolled his eyes. This was one of Bors's favorite games, playing this role.

Sanchel feigned wariness, but her eyes laughed. She knew the game as well and—unlike Kalen—liked it. "Something displeases, honored Commander?"

"I wonder if your practices fall within the scope of the law," Bors said. "Are all your celebrants here of their own will, and given adequate compensation for their arts?"

Sanchel rose to the challenge. "What are you suggesting, sir? All in this place serve Sune—and all want for naught. Or"—she smiled— "did you need to interview one yourself?"

"Mmm, mayhap," said Bors with a grin. He drew out his purse and poured a few coins into the pool. The water glowed. "Clever magic—spares you checking the gold yourself, eh?"

"Just so," said Sanchel. "And yet you pause, my lord. You are uncertain?"

Bors's grin grew wider. "Better make it two," he said, adding twice as many coins to the offering. "Bren and Crin, I think."

Sanchel gave a sweet smile and whistled twice, great trilling bird songs. Kalen wondered if she could speak with birds, if given the opportunity. Two women appeared out of a hidden door in Sune's forest—two dusky-skinned lasses with midnight hair and big, deep black eyes.

Bren and Crin looked identical, though they shared no blood. One, or perhaps both, was a shapeshifter who matched the other. Requests for "the sisters" were common enough—if costly. They smiled at Bors with their full, tempting lips.

"Does this one please you?" Sanchel asked them.

The women looked at Bors Jarthay critically, weighing him with their eyes. Their choosing was the key, Kalen thought. If they did not like the man, no offering was enough, and it would be blasphemy for Bors to coerce or even so much as scowl if they chose "nay."

Oddly, Kalen found himself thinking of Cellica, the only sister he had ever known, and chuckled inwardly at the thought of her in such a situation. She'd probably box Bors Jarthay around the ears, or—failing that, owing to her size—offer him a punch in a more sensitive spot.

Bren and Crin did nothing of the sort. They smiled to one another, then bowed to Bors. "This one," they said together, "half a fool and half a hero—this one always amuses us."

Sanchel nodded.

"Perfect," said Bors with a low bow. Then he smiled boldly and quoted, "Beauty begs joy. The silvered glass smiles, its delight unrehearsed."

The courtesans looked at one another dubiously. Kalen looked at Sanchel, who giggled. Apparently, she understood the private jest.

"Is something wrong, my ladies?" asked the commander, his smile faltering.

"The poesy was not so bad," Crin said to Bren. "Was it Thann, you think?"

"Doubtless," said Bren. "And spoken well, too."

"But my ladies unmake me," said Bors with a small bow. "They have heard this before."

"Of course," said Crin. "It is in *Couplets for Courtiers*, is it not? How does it go, Sister?"

Bren smiled. "Let me see. 'Your lips curve in swift, sweet echo, but this I swear: the mirror smiled first' . . . aye, Commander?"

"Aye, just so."

"Myself, I'd have preferred aught of Thann's 'Gray-Mist Maiden,'" Crin murmured to herself. "'Let years steal beauty, grace, and youth,' or the like."

"Ladies, I bow to your superior learning," Bors said, bowing low.

"But which is the lady and which the mirror?" pressed Bren—or perhaps Crin. Kalen wasn't certain any more. He wondered if he had been wrong all along.

"I should be most pleased to find out." And with that, Bors emptied the rest of his purse into the water, which glowed brightly indeed. "Might we find a place of privacy, ladies, wherein I might—ah? Ladies?"

Bren was looking at the glowing pool. She clicked her tongue and smiled at Crin. "He would impress us with gold where his poetry fails, Sister."

"How childish," agreed Crin. "Hmpf!"

The women stuck out their tongues simultaneously at Bors. They brushed past him toward the commons, seemingly disinterested.

Bors's face fell. "Wait a moment!" the commander cried, and he hurried after them.

Kalen shook his head. The commander was just another man with more coin than sense.

In truth, he did not begrudge Bors Jarthay. Kalen was a man, too, and had the desires of any man. Only the ability . . . Kalen sighed inwardly.

"Sir Dren," Sanchel said. "Have your desires shifted, or is it Leleera again? She has asked for you, should you come around—as you well know."

Kalen turned to her. "Leleera."

"If you wish to marry her," Sanchel said, "that can be . . ."

"No, no," Kalen said. It seemed awkward to claim he and Leleera were merely friends, so he held his tongue. He dropped gold into the pool, which glowed with a radiance more subdued than Bors had wrought with his coin. "As always—an hour longer than the commander stays here. Do not let us leave together."

"As always." Sanchel nodded and gestured to the stairs. "Sune smile upon you."

"Torm bless and ward you." Kalen bowed his head. He paused. "Sanchel—know you a half-elf with red hair, gray eyes, and a quick tongue?"

"If that is your preference," the dwarf said, "we can see if Chandra or Rikkil please you—the eyes would be difficult, but the tongue . . ."

"No," Kalen said, with an embarrassed cough. "Fair eve."

Sanchel nodded and Kalen turned up the stairs, around the image of a great redwood around which dryads pranced.

When he had gone, Sanchel inclined her head to one of the tree nymphs. "Satisfied?"

"Quite."

The dryad pulled away from the wall. It did a pirouette, as though reveling in its sylvan body, and Sanchel frowned. This creature both frightened her and intrigued her with its whimsy.

The dryad plucked a wand of bone from her hair and circled it around her head. A silvery radiance crowned her, then descended to her ankles. Her green tresses turned to bright red curls and her green skin became the particular bronze a half-elf inherits from a gold-skinned elf parent. Her eyes became the perfect gray of burnished steel.

"Which room?" Fayne asked. "From the street, mind—not inside."

"Second floor, third from the north," the dwarf woman said. "When he spoke of the half-elf with gray eyes . . . he meant you, didn't he?"

"Mayhap," she said. "Or mayhap I choose a form to match what he said. It matters little, as you'll say nothing to him—unless you don't care if I tell the Watch certain secrets . . ."

"No," Sanchel said. "Sune smile on you, little trickster."

"Beshaba laugh in your face."

Fayne waved her wand again, and in a blink, she vanished.

Kalen kept his eyes downcast so as not to attract attention or bother other patrons. He would have seen his fair share of attractive sights, but he wasn't there to peruse.

He knocked at Leleera's door and was rewarded. "Enter!" He pushed through.

The room, like most of the pleasure cells at the Smiling Siren, was spacious—sparsely but tastefully adorned to suit the desires of its owner and his or her patrons, whom the celebrant could deny as she wished. Leleera opted for a "queen's chamber," with a stuffed divan, a tightly wound four-poster bed, and even a golden tub. As a full priestess of Sune, she could work the relatively simple magics to fill and heat the bath.

She had a full wardrobe of attire to match the chamber—rich robes, diaphanous silk gowns, and jewelry—along with a fair assortment of martial harnesses, including a thin gold breastplate, greaves, an impractical mail hauberk, and a vast assortment of boots of varying styles and lengths. Warrior queens were popular requests, she had told Kalen—particularly a certain "Steel Princess" Alusair, of late fourteenth-century Cormyr.

The lady herself—who smiled broadly to see Kalen and rose from her divan to embrace him—looked much as a warrior queen ought, with her strong and beautiful features, confident swagger, and honey hued hair, in which she wore dyed streaks of Sune's favored scarlet.

"Kalen!" she cried. "Just in time. I've almost finished *Uthgardt*."

Kalen put down his satchel and sat to remove his boots. "And how goes Arita's debut?"

"Epic," she said. Leleera helped Kalen unbutton his doublet. "I can see why folk love it."

The long-running series, beginning with *Fox Among the Uthgardt*, concerned a heroine from the old world: an eladrin woman called the Silver Fox who couldn't help but plunge into danger with every leap. No one knew the real name of the author—the fancyname "Arita" meant "silver fox" in Elvish—and owing to the volumes' popularity, printers didn't inquire.

"Much wit and banter go with the swordplay, though not *nearly* enough lovemaking. Though"—she pulled the hauberk over his head— "I did enjoy the seduction of the chief."

"Huh." Kalen started unlacing his breeches.

"I suppose there'll be more," Leleera said, slapping his hands away so she could do it. "*Uthgardt* ends in the 1330s, and the Silver Fox is only a young lass. Under forty—but the fey-born age slower than humans, methinks. There are more books, yes?"

Kalen let her pull off his breeches and stood in his linen clout. Leleera looked at his scarred, slightly glistening chest, and he could almost hear her thoughts.

He shook his head. " 'Ware the rules."

"Yes, yes." She pouted. "How many more are there, Kalen? I want to read *more!*"

"I saw *Anauroch* in the shop today, and I believe that's volume eight." He stretched. "Not as many as that other series you like, but each one's twice the normal fifty or so pages."

Leleera wasn't looking at his nakedness anymore, but rather at his satchel. "In the shop?" Her smile widened. "Does that mean . . . ?"

Kalen opened his satchel and produced the book. "One with more bed-play, I'm told."

Leleera gasped. "*Lascivities of a Loveable Lothario*—volume twelve!" She squealed. "Oh Kalen, you naughty, *naughty* knight!" Leleera kissed him on the cheek and plopped down on her divan, feet in the air, to read. She began giggling freely and often.

"I take it that will be sufficient?" Kalen laid the satchel's contents on the bed. Black leathers, a gray cloak—the clothes that fit the man.

" 'You should be flattered, lass,' " she read. " 'Many would give their lives to learn in my bed—many already have.' " She rolled on her back and clasped the book to her chest. "Perfect!"

"Good." He adjusted his sword belt, which felt light without Vindicator. He sheathed his watchsword in the scabbard instead—it was too short, but it still fit, awkwardly.

"Sure I can't tempt you?" Leleera asked. "We could read together." She put her hand on his wrist and if he didn't know better, he'd have sworn she was trying to beguile him.

"Thank you, but no." Kalen kissed her on the forehead and crossed to the window, where he paused. "Leleera—are you . . . are you happy here? In this place?"

She pursed her lips. "When did you start to care about being *happy*?"

Kalen scowled.

"A jest, my friend," Leleera said. "I am content in this place—I serve my goddess, doing that which brings me pleasure. I share her love with the people of this city."

"And that is enough," he whispered. "For you, I mean."

"Kalen." She caressed his cheek, but he could not feel her fingers. He saw her hand move, but felt nothing. "Is it not the same for you?"

Kalen looked away.

"You are a good man, Kalen Dren—but sometimes . . ." She trailed off with a sigh. Then she smiled sadly. "If you want to save someone, why not start with yourself?"

"I don't need saving," he said.

"We'll see." Leleera embraced him and pressed her lips to his. He felt only coldness.

She left him and lay down across her divan. Setting aside the *Lascivities*, she opened *Fox Among the Uthgardt* to the last few pages and began to read silently. Aloud, she murmured, "Oh, *Kalen*—oh, yes—ooh!"

Among other skills, being a celebrant of Sune required substantial acting talent.

Kalen bowed his head to her and she winked.

"Oh, yes—right—*there!*" She flipped a page.

As Leleera moaned, squealed, and read, Kalen donned his helm and opened the shutters. He looked back at Leleera—who writhed in feigned passion as she flipped another page.

Then, without further hesitation, Shadowbane swung out the window into the night.

⠀⠀⠀⠀⠀⠀⠀·:⌢:·

Just below, watching invisibly from an alley just across Marlar's Lane, Fayne smiled.

"I see you, Sir Dren," she murmured. She pinched her nose. "And smell you, too—do you *ever* wash that cloak?"

With that bit of spying managed, she turned her thoughts to the tale she was writing for the *Minstrel*. The life of a scandal-smith was so demanding!

She slipped away, thinking of the japes she'd use. Ooh, she'd prayed for the day she could burn Araezra Hondyl. And it had arrived, with the blessings of the sun god.

Later—perhaps three bells later—Bors Jarthay listened at Leleera's door to a long and loud chorus of her moans. "Yes!" Leleera cried from within. "Oh, Kalen!"

Bors grinned. "That's my boy."

As he made his way down the curling staircase into the garden in the entry hall, he scowled out the misty front windows at the sea fog that had rolled in. "Damn that man—is he ever wrong?"

He whistled a tune as he left, bound for home.

CHAPTER TWELVE

THE CITY STOOD HIDDEN IN GRAY NIGHT. SELÛNE HAD RETREATED behind deep clouds that threatened rain but did not let it fall. A slight breeze came from the sea to the west and broke against the buildings.

Conditions were perfect for the sea fog that rolled through the streets.

Waterdhavians rarely braved such nights, when the fog hid deeds both noble and vile. On a night like that, the creatures of Downshadow would stay below in their holes, denied the clear sky and Selûne's tears.

Wearing the black leathers and gray cloak of Shadowbane, Kalen perched atop Gilliam's haberdashery. He had not come for battle—for such, he'd descend to Downshadow—but rather for freedom in the surface world. Every tenday or so, if clouds hid the moon, he took time from his task to remind himself of that which he defended: a city he could see but not feel.

"Why not start with myself," he murmured.

Were he a man who could feel as other men did, he might have enjoyed the embrace of so wise a woman as Leleera. He might have tried anyway, were it not for his constant fear of being too rough without knowing it—without *feeling* it. Even had the spellplague not stolen his senses in exchange for strength, he was a man of action. Violence was no more easy to leave behind him than was the mask of Shadowbane.

Enough self-pity. It did not become a servant of justice.

"I don't need saving," he repeated.

He and Leleera were both crusaders. But while she served a gentle goddess who craved only her happiness, he obeyed the will of a dead god who demanded action.

He slid off the roof into the night and ran along the rooftops.

A hundred years ago, before the Spellplague had rebuilt the world, the god called Helm was the patron of guardians and the vigilant—an eternal watcher, who once slew a goddess he loved rather than forsake his duty. Then, because of a mad god's trickery, he had fought with Tyr, the blind Lord of Justice, and fallen under the eyeless one's blade.

The night of Helm's death, in a city called Westgate, a boy named Gedrin dreamed of the duel. Helm perished, but his divine essence lingered. The gods' symbols merged: the eye of Helm etched itself onto Tyr's breastplate with its scales of justice. The blind god's eye glowed, and his sight returned. When Gedrin awoke, he held Vindicator, Helm's sword in the dream.

And thus had begun the heresy of the church known as the Eye of Justice.

Later, plagued by guilt and shame, Tyr fell to the demon prince Orcus, but his powers—and those of Helm—had passed to Torm, god of duty. Gedrin dreamed a second time, and watched the three gods become one. The heretical church he had built began to follow Torm, whom they took to calling the threefold god.

Many years after these dreams—almost eighty years later—in the cesspool of Luskan, a famous knight called Gedrin Shadowbane gave a beggar boy three things: a knight's sword, Vindicator; a message, never to beg again; and a cuff on the ear, that he might remember it.

That boy had been Kalen Dren, the second Shadowbane. And his first vow had been never to beg for anything, ever again.

And how sorely that vow had been tested, so many times.

A cough formed in his chest, and he fought it down. His illness—though he pretended it was worse than it was, in truth—would always haunt him. He had the spellplague to thank for that. From birth, Kalen had borne the spellplague's mark: a spellscar, the priests called it—a different blessing and curse for every poor soul who earned or inherited one. For Kalen, it was toughened flesh and resistance to pain. Any warrior would wish for such a thing but for its accompanying curse: a body increasingly losing feeling, one that would eventually perish.

Justice for the sins of a poorly spent youth, he mused.

He watched as the sea fog shifted, taking on color, radiance, and form. Like much of the spellplague's legacy, this was a rare and unexplained occurrence. Soon, the glowing fog would take on shapes and tell a story, though none could say why.

Kalen eased himself away from the banner pole atop Gilliam's and half-ran, half-slid down the domed roof. Using his momentum, he bent low and sprang from the edge. The magic in his boots—one of the few items he'd managed to bring from Westgate—carried him across the alley and up to the roof of the next building, a tallhouse.

He ran along the crenellated edge, leaping over potted plants and a few squatters who sheltered in the corners of the roofs. Running the rooftops was safer than the street. A seagull, borne on the lazy breezes, matched him, and he balanced on the ledge beside it.

He remembered running the roofs of Westgate with his teacher in the church of the Eye: the half-elf Levia, old enough to have borne him, but who looked as young as he. Her skill was not martial in nature, but divine—priestly magic. Healing and the like.

Kalen knew little of such magic. Aside from his healing touch and the protection given a paladin, he asked little of his threefold god—and begged for nothing. He'd once broken a man's nose for calling Levia a spell-beggar, but he was not sure if he'd done it for her honor or his.

He wished Levia had come to Waterdeep. She was family, Kalen thought. Levia, the only mother he'd ever known—and Cellica, his sister in spirit if not in blood.

Not like the rest of their wayward faith. Kalen did not consider such fools to be his kin.

Gedrin had created the Eye, bringing crusaders from the ranks of the Night Masks—a powerful thieves' guild at the time, ruled by a vampire called the Night King. Gedrin had burst forth from the Masks like a hero digging out of the belly of a beast, and aided in ousting the dark masters of Westgate. Thereafter, they had set out to cleanse the world of evil in all its forms. Gedrin was a zealot, and his faith inspired hundreds to worship the threefold god.

But in time, the purity of the Eye faded, its quest tainted by flawed men in the church—men who used their thiefly skills for personal gain, rather than justice. Gedrin left the Eye, after spending so much of his life in the doomed church, and Kalen, years later, had followed in his footsteps. Both had taken Vindicator, hoping to put its power to use elsewhere.

Kalen felt lost without the sword. It had set him on Gedrin's quest to redeem the world. And though a part of him needed it back, another large part of him approved of its loss. If he had not been worthy of it, was it not the threefold god's will that it choose another wielder?

A low sound perked up his ears. Kalen caught a spire, whirled, and pressed himself flat against the stone, closing his eyes. He heard it again: sobbing. A female voice—somewhere near.

He looked and saw a cloud of mists that glowed blue. That was odd—he had seen colors and distortions in the sea fog before, but never blue. And he recognized the hue—a sickly yet powerful azure, like the inner shade of a flame just before it turned white hot. It was spellplague blue, he realized, just like the spellplague that had changed him.

Unease crept into his fingers, but he heard the sob—more like a plea for aid—again and leaped from the roof. If the Eye would claim him this night, then so be it.

The blue fog was close, only two rooftops away. The near building was a squat noble villa with an open-air garden in the center, and he ran along the wall to stay aloft. Blue fog swirled around him, threatening, and he felt a drive to step forward, to face an unknown peril that might be the end of him. Was it not better to fall now, if Vindicator had abandoned him?

He sprang into the alley, rolling with the fall to come up on his feet, watchsword drawn. It occurred to him only then that carrying the blade would be damning if any Watchmen were to see him, but too late.

The mists seemed empty, but he heard the sob again. The blue glow crackled, electric, deeper in the alley, and he stalked forward.

The mist took on shapes, and Kalen fell into guard, both hands on his sword.

Ghosts appeared out of the mist. He saw two figures—slim men who might have been elves—standing together in a room in some distant land. They were arguing—even fighting, waving misty limbs like blades. Then one vanished into the shadows near a leaning stack of crates. The remaining figure turned to Kalen, smiling.

Another figure appeared out of the mist, this one a woman, her features blurred. The mist man turned to greet her. Without warning, he thrust his fist into her chest and she fell, hands clenched.

Kalen felt a surge of anger, but these were just visions. They meant nothing.

The mist man stared at him. "The sword," the mist man said with a too-wide smile.

Kalen had never heard that the visions of Waterdeep could speak. It chilled him.

Lightning crackled again, blue and vivid, and Kalen turned to search for its source.

When he looked back, both mist men were there, looking at him with hunger. They approached him, hands rising, and he realized they meant to attack. He retreated, but his back was against the wall of the alley.

"Away." As Levia had taught him, Kalen let the threefold god shine against them. He began to glow, warding off the walking dead. "Away!"

But either his power was too weak or these were not undead, for they came forward. Kalen saw the woman climbing to her feet, a bleeding hole where her heart should be.

"The sword," the mist whispered. "The sword that was stolen—the crusader has come!"

Kalen thought, for one horrible moment, that they were talking about him. But these were images of long ago, if not entirely random manifestations.

He struck with his watchsword, but the mortal steel passed clean through them, disturbing the mist with its wind. Their hands passed through his guard and leathers as though they were not there. He felt ice inside his flesh.

"Away," he tried again, but his voice was hoarse.

Weakness was taking him, and he could not even flee. The woman in the mist appeared over him, and he thought she was not beautiful but terrible—she was death embodied.

Then the alley was bathed in blue light. Kalen felt the hairs on his neck and arms rise and he threw himself down just as lightning crackled through the air, scorching the stone buildings. A figure stood before him, surrounded in blue electricity and fire. It was the fiery woman he had seen in Downshadow only a few nights before—whose appearance had saved him from death at a half-ogre's gnarled fingers.

He averted his eyes to keep from being blinded, and the mist creatures fell back. He could see them, just vaguely, bowing and scraping like servants, almost . . . *reverent*.

Then the light went out, and the woman—no longer flaming but still glowing—stood shakily in the center of the alley. Her dizzy eyes met his, and he saw they were startlingly blue.

"*Szasha,*" she said in a tongue he did not know. "*Araka azza grazz?*" Then she sagged.

Leaving his watchsword on the cobblestones in his lunge, Kalen caught her just before she hit the ground. She was so light, barely more than a girl, and little more than skin, bone, and . . . blood.

His gauntlets came away sticky. The girl was naked but for a slimy coating of what looked like black and green blood. He searched for wounds but could find none. Her hair, plastered in the sickly gore, was blue. Everything about her was blue: hair, lips, even her skin.

Then Kalen realized her skin was not blue, but rather covered in glowing tattoos. Runes, he thought, though he did not know them. Even as he noted them, the tattoos began to fade, shrinking into her deeply tanned flesh like ink on wet parchment. He blinked, watching as lattices of arcane symbols vanished, little by little.

Kalen didn't know what to do, but he couldn't leave her.

Her arms tightened around his neck and her face pressed into his chest. *"Gisz vaz."*

"Very well," he replied, not having the faintest idea what she'd said.

He took off his cloak and wrapped her in it. Then he held her tightly, looked around for mist figures—the fog had begun to disperse—and started off at a trot.

.:⌒:.

Cellica's stew—left to simmer until morningfeast—was bubbling when he returned to the tallhouse.

"You're back early," the halfling said when he came through the open window. She had risen from her cot, a towel wrapped around her little body, but she didn't look sleepy.

"Did I wake you?" Kalen took care not to hit the strange woman's head against the sill.

"I never sleep when you're—" Cellica's eyes widened. "Who's that?"

"No idea."

Kalen strode into Cellica's room and laid his burden on the halfling's cot.

"She's . . ." The halfling trailed off, touching the sleeping woman's cheek. "She's bone cold! Out! Out! I'll take care of this."

Kalen felt Cellica's will take hold of him and wandered out while she laid blanket after blanket over the sleeping woman. The stranger's uncertain frown became a blissful smile.

Gods, Kalen felt tired. His limbs ached and his armor stank of sweat. The girl was light, but he'd carried her all the way across the city. In that time, her azure tattoos had all but disappeared. Her breathing seemed normal, and she slept peacefully.

"Why lasses run around the night streets naked in this day and age, I'll never understand," Cellica said. "Younglings! Hmpf."

"Mmm," Kalen returned. He was rubbing his eyes. Gods, he was tired.

"Who *is* she?" the halfling asked. Rather than being upset, she was inspecting the woman critically, fascinated. "Your hunting extends to naked ladies in addition to villains and dastards?"

Kalen murmured a reply that did not befit a paladin. He traipsed off to his cot, shedding his leathers as he went, and slumped into bed. He was asleep two breaths later.

It only briefly occurred to him to wonder where he'd left his watchsword.

CHAPTER THIRTEEN

FAYNE SLAMMED HER FIST ON THE TABLE IN THE LITTLE CHAMBER IN Downshadow.

"I should have known." She spat in most unladylike fashion on the array of cards. "Useless. Utterly useless. I should have known you were a perverse little fraud, after you fed me all the drivel about the doppelganger conspiracy."

B'Zeer the Seer—the tiefling who ran this small, illicit "diviner's council" in a hidden chamber in Downshadow, of which only those of questionable honor knew—spread his many-ringed hands. "Divination is an imprecise art, my sweet Satin, and requires much patience."

"Oh, *orc shit*," Fayne said. "Divination hasn't worked right in Waterdeep for a hundred years." She shoved her scroll of notes in her scrip satchel. "I don't know what I was thinking, coming to a pimply faced voyeur like you."

B'Zeer ran his fingers over the cards and furrowed his brow. His milky white eyes, devoid of pupils, scanned the tabletop, and he scratched at one of his horns. "Now wait, I think I see aught, now. Something to do with your father . . . your need to please him . . . perhaps in—"

"I don't need some peeping, pus-faced pervert to tell me about my father, thanks," Fayne said. "I was asking about my dreams—you know, the girl in blue fire?"

"Ah yes, B'Zeer sees and understands. I believe—"

"With all due respect—and that's none—piss off and *die*. I have business to attend to this night, and a tale for the *Minstrel* to deliver to print."

Fayne exploded from her chair, but a hand clamped around her wrist. She looked down, eyes narrow. "Let go of me, or I will end you."

"This may be a touch indelicate, what I ask now," the seer said. "But what of my coin?"

Fayne glared. "No hrasting service, no hrasting coin."

"Call it an entertainment fee," he said. "We all have to eat."

"Piss," Fayne said, "off."

He moved faster than a shriveled little devil man should be able to, darting forward and seizing her throat to thrust her against the chamber wall. She saw steel in his other hand.

"You give me my coin," he said, "or I'll take it out of you elsewise."

She should have expected this. Most women in Downshadow were of negotiable virtue. It was simply part of living coin-shy. Particularly amusing were those monsters that took the form of women and revealed themselves only in a passionate embrace. Justice, Fayne thought.

She smiled at B'Zeer dangerously.

"Hark, Seer—it isn't bound to happen," she said. "I think, if you read your destiny, you'll see only you . . . alone but for your hand."

"So you say, bitch," the tiefling said. "But let us see what—*uuk!*"

The seer choked and coughed, grasping at himself where she had driven a knife through his bowels. Blackness poured down his legs. He mumbled broken words in his fiendish language—harsh, guttural sounds—but he could summon no magic with his life spilling down his groin.

"If it gives you any comfort," she said as he sank to the floor, "I *did* warn you."

Then she left him in his small nook in Downshadow, which to him had become a shrinking, blurry world of heaving breaths, pain, and—quite later—wet darkness.

CHAPTER FOURTEEN

As dawn rose, Araezra sat alone in her private room at the barracks. She slapped the broadsheet down on the table and leaned back in her chair, fuming.

"Watch *fails* to apprehend vigilante in Castle Ward," noted the *Mocking Minstrel*, this particular tale written by the bard Satin Rutshear. "*Clumsy fool* Talanna Taenfeather injured in pursuit while *narcissistic superior,* Araezra Hondyl, parades *half-naked* through streets."

Araezra groaned. The emphasized words were underlined in a girlish hand.

"Open Lord Neverember calls Araezra's actions 'justified,' saying 'I'm sure she acted for the best' . . . in protecting his *bedmate interests* in the Watch," she read. "Neverember was later seen *furtively* arriving at Taenfeather's bedside in the temple of Torm, protected by cloaked men."

Then: "For *misuse* of city taxes to support *nonregulated* religious bodies, see *over*."

Araezra rubbed her eyes. The quotations were accurate if slanted, and the additions infuriated her. Lord Neverember and Talanna's energetic flirtations were well known, but had never been put quite this way. The casual cruelty left a foul taste in Araezra's mouth. She stabbed her nails into her palms hard.

And of course, Satin quoted Lord Bladderblat, the broadsheet's ubiquitous parody noble.

"On young Hondyl's competency as a valabrar, Lord Bladderblat calls Hondyl 'too pretty for a *thinking* woman, but she's got assets; better she find a blade for 'twixt her thighs than one for her belt—though she can wear the belt to *my* bed, if she likes.' "

That Araezra was presented as the bedmate of a fiction rankled. And being described as "young"—true, she was just over twenty, but her rank came from her *success*, not her beauty.

This wasn't new to her, this ridicule. She'd often tried to track down "Satin Rutshear," but it was just a fancyname, of course. The *Minstrel* protected its own, and the Lords' command against punishing broadsheet writers and printers stayed Araezra's hand. Violating it would have led to her discharge— but it would have made her feel much better.

"Watch keeps silent on continued threat," Satin went on. "Hondyl has no comment."

In that private, unheard, and thus safe moment, Araezra finally let vent. "Mayhap you might *ask*, Lady Rutshear," she cried. "I'd give you a comment, well and good—then twist your snobby head off your shoulders, you little *whore!*"

She balled up the *Minstrel* and hurled it across the office into the spittoon. She felt better.

Then she set to repressing her anger into a tight, simmering ball.

Burn her eyes and her waggling tongue, but this "Satin" had the right of it—there was no place for screaming, hysterical lasses in the Guard, particularly not those ranked as highly as she.

This story—and the whole situation it cat-raked with such fiendish glee—was bad enough. If she was going to be humiliated and reprimanded for abandoning her patrol, endangering her men, and landing her second in a bed at the temple of Torm, then at least she could do it with some dignity. The judgmental eyes of the rest of the Watch and Guard, the disapproving glare of Commander Jarthay—they were bad enough.

And where in the *Hells* was Kalen? He hadn't appeared for duty this morn, and she could really use his shoulder to—

Araezra dropped her face into her hands. She wouldn't cry—she couldn't. Crying was for weak-willed women, and she must be strong—for Talanna, if for nothing else.

Don't think about Talanna, fading in and out of life under the hands of those priests.

She looked instead at the sword on the table, and let its silvery masterwork distract her.

It was a bastard sword, well and good, but deceptively light and sharp. Magical, she knew—it had glowed fiercely silver in Shadowbane's hand, and retained this glow even after he'd left it. Now, sitting cool on her desk, it radiated power at a touch—but *balanced* power.

A sword is neither good nor evil, she thought, but that its wielder uses it for either.

Araezra looked in particular at the sigil carved into its black hilt: an upright gauntlet with a stylized eye in its open palm. She'd thought at first it was the gauntlet of Torm, but an hour in the room of records had shown her otherwise: it was the symbol of a long-dead church—that of Helm, God of Guardians.

That god—a deity neither inherently evil nor good—had faded since the old world, like many across Faerûn. She'd read one story of his death at the hands of the then-god of justice, Tyr—who had also perished in the last century. That hardly made sense to her: Why would two such gods make war? And why were they not left to rest?

She found this sword a mystery, a relic of an ancient past. Its symbol—in particular, the eye—stared at her wryly, as though amused by its secrets.

She thought about the gauntlets on her own breastplate—five, for valabrar. Here was only one, for the rank of trusty. But, she noted, the gauntlet adorned both sides of the hilt, making two, for vigilant. And Helm had been called the Vigilant One.

Araezra thought of Kalen, who wore two gauntlets. Something about a ring he wore . . .

But that was ridiculous—with his worsening illness, Kalen could hardly walk fast, much less run. He trained, she knew, and kept his body in excellent condition to stave off the illness he'd told her about—but surely he couldn't outpace Talanna Taenfeather.

She was startled out of her thoughts when a loud knock came at the door. She wiped at her cheeks and was aghast that her hand came away damp. "Come," she said.

The door opened and Bors Jarthay glided into the room, his face solemn. Standing at attention, Araezra felt a chill of terror and grief.

"Talanna," Araezra said. "How—how is she?"

Bors narrowed his eyes. "Well, Rayse—I don't know the best way to say this . . ."

Tears welled up in Araezra's eyes and her lip trembled.

"She'll be . . ." Bors whispered, "perfectly well."

Araezra's heart skipped a beat. "Wait—what?"

"Healing went fine, and she'll be well," the commander said. "A little wrathful, but generally her precocious, loud, and—ow!" Araezra slapped him. "Heh. Suppose I deserved that."

Araezra slapped him again. "Gods burn you! Why do you have to *do* that?"

He smiled gently. "All's well, Rayse."

"You monstrous oaf!" She wound back to strike again. "Damn you to all the Hells!"

Bors caught her wrist, pulled her to him, and hugged her. "All's well," he whispered.

Stunned, she put her arms around him and buried her head in his chest. Tears came—thankful, angry tears—and she didn't stop them.

"You ever want to talk, lass," he said. "I'm here."

"Just . . . another moment." Then she glared up at him. "And don't think this means anything. With all due respect, you're still a boor and won't be seeing me naked any time soon."

Bors sighed. "More's the pity."

He hugged her tighter.

CHAPTER FIFTEEN

KALEN WOKE WITH THE KIND OF SPLITTING HEADACHE THAT COMES after one has slept only moments in the space of several hours. He felt as though he'd never bedded down at all. His nose was stuffy and he coughed and sneezed to clear it.

Worse, he was numb all over. He allowed himself one horrified breath before he tried to move his senseless hands. With some hesitation, they rose, and he pressed them to his cheeks.

"Thank the gods," Kalen whispered.

Cellica stood in the room, a bucket of water in her hands. She looked a touch disappointed, and moved the water behind her back. "Well!" she said. "About time."

Kalen groaned.

"Get up, Sir Slug, and come have aught to eat. Our guest has been at the stew all morning, and if you don't make haste, it might be gone." As he started to sit up, she glanced down, then back up at his face, unashamed. "And put those on." She pointed at a pair of black hose, crumpled at the foot of his bed.

Kalen realized he was naked, which made sense. He hadn't donned aught last night.

"*Try* and be presentable for our guest."

"Guest?" he managed as he plucked up the hose, but the halfling was already gone.

The highsun light filtered through his shuttered window, and deep shadows undercut his eyes in the mirror. His wiry chest, with its familiar scars, gleamed back at him. Stubble gone to an early gray studded his chin and neck. Generally, he looked and felt terrible. Pushing himself too hard, he decided.

"Gods," he murmured.

He paused at the door to his bedchamber and fought down a wave of dizziness. His legs felt beyond exhausted. He still hadn't recovered from his flight from Talanna and Araezra.

"Fair morn, Risen Sun," said Cellica when Kalen staggered out to morningfeast—or highsunfeast. She turned to the table with a brilliant smile. "Myrin? This is Kalen."

Kalen realized someone else was in the room—a tawny-skinned young woman who couldn't have seen more than twenty winters, with shoulder-length hair of a hue like cut sapphire, who seemed more bone than flesh. He remembered her now—the woman in the alley from the night before.

"Oh!" She blushed, casting her eyes away from his bare chest.

Kalen grunted something like "well met"—which sounded more like "wuhlmt."

Myrin wore a ratty, sweat-stained tunic and a pair of loose breeches—*his,* Kalen realized. Being far too big, they made her look even more frail than when he had carried her home.

"I hope you don't mind," Cellica said to Kalen. "None of my things would fit her."

"Huh." Words didn't come easily to Kalen in the morning.

The halfling, however, was at her most garrulous just after sleep. "Nothing fashionable, but at least they're clothes." Cellica winked. "Not like you provided any last night."

Kalen grunted and looked to the cook pot, in which the remainder of the morning simmer stew bubbled warmly. He fished a roundloaf out of the box by the hearth, hollowed it out, and spooned in a healthy dollop. The stew had a sharp, pungent aroma from the many spices Cellica had added—she knew his illness stole his sense of taste as well as touch, so she took pride in making food that he could taste. He limped back to the table, sat on the stool Cellica had vacated, and stared across at Myrin.

Heedless of the tears rolling down her cheeks at the heat of the spices, Myrin was eating like she hadn't eaten in years, and seeing how skinny she was, maybe she hadn't. She licked up Cellica's stew with wild abandon, and Cellica brought her another roundloaf while Kalen sat there, picking at his stew. The halfling was smiling grandly, and Kalen imagined she was thrilled to practice her adoptive mother's recipes on someone who appreciated their full taste.

Kalen nodded at Myrin. "So . . . who is she?" he asked Cellica.

Myrin paused in her eating and looked to Kalen. Cellica sniffed.

"Why don't you ask her yourself?" Cellica's manner was sweet, so her suggestion didn't strike him as a command.

Kalen looked at Myrin sidelong. "You can talk?" He winced at Cellica's glare.

"I . . ." she said. "I can talk."

Cellica beamed. "Go on, peach," the halfling said. "Tell him what you told me!"

Myrin looked shyly at the table.

Cellica clapped her hands. "She's a *mys-ter-y!*" she exclaimed, pronouncing the word in excited syllables, like this was a great adventure. "She doesn't know who she is or where she came from—only her name and a few things from her childhood."

Kalen looked at Myrin, who was staring at her bread. "Aye?"

Myrin nodded.

"Naught else?" Like how I found you naked in an alley, he thought, speaking gibberish?

"Kalen!" Cellica snapped at his tone. "Manners!"

Myrin only shook her head. "I remember a little . . . a little about when I was small." Her voice was thin, and her words were oddly accented—old, like something out of a bardic tale.

"My mother—her name was Shalis—she raised me alone. I never knew my father. I was apprenticed to a wizard—his name was . . . I don't remember." She sniffed. "I can see these things, but they seem far away—like dreams. Like I slept years and never woke."

Kalen eyed her tanned coloration. Her complexion was exotic—Calishite, perhaps, though mixed with something else entirely. A whisper of elf heritage was about her as well—not a parent, but perhaps a grandparent. It was clear she would be quite beautiful when she grew to womanhood, but she was yet on the verge.

"Aught else?" he asked. "Homeland?"

Myrin shrugged.

"Was it city or countryside?" Cellica glared and Kalen added: "If you remember."

"City," Myrin said slowly. Her eyes glazed. "It was always cold . . . cold off the sea. Gray stone buildings, sand on the streets. Nights spent locked inside while terrors waited without. They waited, you see—the creatures in the night. Masks of shadows."

Cellica looked anxiously at Kalen, who only shook his head. "What city?" he asked.

"West, it was called," she said. "West . . . aught else, but I don't remember."

"Westgate?" Cellica suggested.

Myrin shook her head. "Mayhap."

Kalen shrugged. "Could be," he said. "I don't know what 'terrors' you would mean—there haven't been anything but men in the shadows of that city for a century, almost. Not since Gedrin and his knights drove the vampires out . . ."

He trailed off as Myrin looked down, her shoulders shaking as though she would cry. Cellica cast Kalen a sharp look, and he sighed.

They sat in silence for many breaths—perhaps a hundred count—saying nothing. Kalen ate a few spoonfuls of his stew, but it was tasteless to him. He drank his mulled cider and tried not to feel so awful.

As he did so, he gazed at Myrin, exploring the contours of her exotic face, trying to figure out where she had come from. She wasn't exactly *beautiful* without that crown of flames she'd been wearing in the alley, Kalen thought, but there remained a certain girlish appeal to her delicate features. Wearing Kalen's old shirt made her look like a child, too—in a dress or even a real gown . . .

Cellica caught him staring. "You've another question, Sir Longing-Gaze?"

Myrin's head shot up and her eyes went wide in expectation.

"Mind your stew," Kalen said to Cellica, harsher than he intended.

Myrin looked back down, blushing. Cellica's wry smile became a chiding frown.

Kalen ignored them both and turned back to his mostly untouched roundloaf, only to find nothing but his spoon on the table. He looked across to where Myrin was contentedly eating his morningfeast with her hands. Curious—he hadn't thought her reach so long.

"Do you need a spoon, peach?" asked Cellica.

"Sorry," the girl said. "I don't mean to be rude—I'm just so hungry." She looked at Kalen's spoon and murmured something under her breath that Kalen didn't understand.

Cellica reached for the spoon as though to give it to Myrin, but it skittered away, rose into the air, and floated to Myrin's hand. She caught it and set immediately to spooning stew to her mouth. Kalen and Cellica looked at one another, then at her.

Myrin, looking nervous in the silence, blinked at them. "What?"

"Lass," the halfling said. "Was that a spell?"

"Of course," Myrin said. "Can't—" She blushed. "Can't everyone do that?"

Kalen and Cellica exchanged another glance. Myrin went back to eating.

Before anyone could say more, there came a loud knock at the door, and Cellica fell off her stool with a startled gasp. Myrin didn't seem to notice and went right on eating. Kalen reached for Vindicator by instinct, and only then remembered he didn't have the blade any more—or his watchsword, for that matter. Bane's breath, where had he left *that?*

"Hark," he said. "Who calls?"

No answer came.

He seized a long knife from the table and reversed it, the better to conceal the blade against his forearm. Cellica grasped the crossbow amulet around her throat and Kalen nodded. He rose, a finger to his lips, and crossed to the door.

He put his left hand on the latch and lifted it as silently as he could, keeping his body shielded by the wall. Then he threw open the door and raised the knife . . .

A familiar red-haired half-elf, clad in a plain leather skirt and vest over a white shirt, leaped over the threshold into his arms. "Shadow, *dearest!*" she exclaimed.

Her lips found his and he could see only the stunned expressions on Cellica's and Myrin's faces.

CHAPTER SIXTEEN

WHEELING AROUND FOR BALANCE, KALEN MANAGED TO BREAK THE KISS and breathe.

Fayne seemed undaunted. "Shadow! It's been so *long!*" She hugged him tightly and squealed.

He blinked over her shoulder to the table, where Cellica was staring at him in shock. Myrin looked at him, then the newcomer, then down at her stew—she seemed to shrink on her stool. Cellica looked halfway between angry and wonderstruck.

"Oh, Shadow, we'll have such a *glorious* time at the revel," she said, emphasizing her words breathlessly. "I can't *believe* you have an invitation—I can't *wait* to wear my dress! Oh!"

Kalen could hardly breathe, she held him so hard.

"Kalen," Cellica asked slowly, "Kalen, who is this? What revel?"

"I—*urph,*" Kalen said as the woman kissed him again, cutting off any words. This kiss was harder than the first, more insistent, and he tasted her tongue in his mouth.

A little hand tugged the hem of the half-elf's vest. "Pardon, lass," Cellica asked, hands on her hips. "Who . . . who are you?"

"I'm Fayne," the half-elf said, lacing her fingers through Kalen's. "A . . . *friend* of Shadow, here—I mean, Sir Kalen Dren." She winked conspiratorially.

Kalen could only stare when Cellica looked at him. "I don't know her," he said.

"She knows *you*," the halfling quipped. Then, eyes widening: "She *knows?* About—"

"Of *course* I know," Fayne said with a laugh. Then she looked between them and put her hand over her mouth in mock fear. "What, is it a secret?"

Cellica's face turned bright red, and Kalen shivered. "It's not how it looks—"

Kalen saw Fayne glance at Myrin, and she hesitated half a breath. Then she let loose a squeal. "Who's this, Kalen? She's *adorable!*"

Myrin's eyes widened as Fayne rushed to her and hugged her around the neck, then proceeded to fuss over her like a child with a kitten. Myrin stared at Kalen, stunned.

A tiny blue rune appeared on Myrin's cheek, Kalen saw, where Fayne had touched. But before he could comment, a halfling finger poked him insistently and he looked down.

"What's going on?" Cellica looked furious. "Kalen, who *is* this woman?"

"I don't—" Kalen's head hurt even worse than when he had risen. "I can explain."

"Oh." Cellica climbed up on her stool and crossed her arms. "This should be grand."

Myrin looked positively mouselike at the table under Fayne's attentions.

"Better make it *fast,*" Fayne noted, drawing out the word. "Someone *else* is coming up."

Kalen's heart skipped. "Who?"

"A woman," Fayne said. "Very pretty—gorgeous, even. Long dark hair, deep blue eyes. Armed and armored. Five gauntlets on her . . ." Fayne made a gesture across her collarbone and giggled. "Why—" She smiled. "Do you know her?"

"Tymora guard us," Cellica said. "That's *Rayse.*"

"Who's Rayse?" Fayne looked at Kalen jealously. "*Another* lass friend?"

"His superior, Araezra Hondyl!" Cellica said. "You were supposed to report this morn, Sir Snores-a-bed!" Cellica stared, wide-eyed, at Kalen. "What do we—?"

Kalen was in motion, crossing to the table.

Fayne purred at him. "You're quite the man, to have so many—hey!"

Kalen seized her by the arm and hauled her toward a closet, in which hung their spare clothes. He pushed her in, despite muffled protests, and stepped in himself.

"Kalen!" Cellica hissed. "What am I supposed to tell her?"

Kalen shrugged—he couldn't think, except that he knew he couldn't let Araezra catch them.

He shut the door behind them.

Myrin took very close care to stare at her stew the whole time.

She didn't know what was going on—where she was, who these people were, or anything—but just because she remembered nothing didn't mean she was an idiot. She'd seen that red-haired girl—Fayne—and the way she touched Kalen.

Of *course* he's got a lass friend, you fool, she thought. What did you *expect?*

She fancied she could still feel Fayne's fingers on her cheeks—the way the half-elf had prodded at her, grinning all the while. The touch lingered and Myrin felt oddly full, though it was not just from all the stew she had eaten. She felt full in *spirit*.

Maybe it was just Kalen looking at you, she thought. You're such a *girl!*

Cellica looked at her, and her mouth drooped in a sympathetic frown. She threw up her hands. "He's not always so," she said. "Just . . . hold a moment."

Myrin opened her mouth to speak, but she felt a gentle pressure in her ears—a voice that itched at her mind, telling her to remain in her seat. *Magic.* She stayed sitting, wondering.

Cellica got up and started toward the door, which Fayne had left open. In the corridor, Myrin saw with a stabbing curdle in her stomach, stood a very lovely and very angry lady. She had sleek, glossy black hair and liquid eyes bound in a face like that of a wrathful nymph. The woman wore a uniform, but Myrin did not know what sort. Little about this world seemed familiar to her thus far.

"Rayse!" Cellica said. "What a surprise! Won't you come"—the dark-haired woman swept into the chamber past the halfling—"in?"

"Well—" Araezra pulled up short and stared. "Well met?"

After an awkward breath, Myrin realized she was talking to her. "Oh . . . well met."

Araezra looked confused. "I'm sorry—have we met? I don't know you."

"Uh—I'm . . . I'm Myrin." Her fingers curled and her heart thudded. Why did they all have to be so *perfect?* "I'm . . . uh . . ."

Her brow furrowing, Araezra looked to Cellica.

"You probably want Kalen," the halfling said. "He's . . . ah—"

"It's very important," Araezra said. "He was supposed to report for duty this morn, and I haven't seen him." She glared toward Myrin, whose cheeks felt like they might burst into flame. She picked at her blue hair and wished it weren't so straggly.

Myrin wondered if Kalen wasn't some kind of nobleman, or rich merchant, or perhaps the lord of a harem, to have this many lasses flocking to his door. She wasn't certain where she'd heard that word "harem" before—it was floating somewhere in the back of her mind. Elusive, like a shard of a dream that danced just on the edge of her awareness.

Like her mother's face. Like all her memories.

"I'll tell him when I see him," Cellica said. "He's . . . he might be with Commander Jarthay. They were bound for the Siren yestereve. Perhaps they're still there?"

Araezra glanced at Myrin, who tried to shrink smaller. She looked back at Cellica. "You didn't . . ." she said awkwardly. "You didn't happen to read the *Minstrel* this morn?"

Cellica folded her hands behind her back. "No, absolutely not."

"Cellica."

"Well, yes—". The halfling winced. She waved her hands. "But it's horribly unfair! You aren't like that at all. That's just bloody Satin Rutshear."

Araezra smiled and sighed. "My thanks. I—I just have to find Kalen. We need to talk."

Cellica nodded. "I'll tell him when I see him."

The halfling looked at Myrin as though expecting her to say aught, but Myrin had no idea what to say. She couldn't stop staring at Araezra, who was the most beautiful woman she had ever seen—that she could remember, anyway.

Araezra didn't leave. She bit her pretty lip, and Myrin saw her eyes were damp.

Cellica shrugged. "Better have a seat, dear. Would you like cider?"

The armored woman nodded, tears rolling down her cheeks.

Kalen stood inside the closet, hands pressed flat against the sides.

Crushed against the inside wall, every inch of her body just a hair's breadth from his bare chest and loose hose, Fayne blinked at him with her gray eyes. She was about the width of a hand shorter, and he could feel her breath against his bare chest. His lips were level with the bridge of her nose, and he had the unsettling urge to plant a kiss on her forehead. Something about her made him want to kiss her.

She wore a wry little grin.

"Do not," he said.

Fayne smiled and edged a little closer to him, pressing her breasts to his chest and her mouth near his ear. "I wouldn't dream of it." Her tone wasn't girlish at all, but sharp. He felt, uncomfortably, as though all of this was according to her plan.

Kalen bit his lip. "Be still."

"You think your valabrar will hear?" That word confirmed his suspicions—she'd tricked him and knew full well what Araezra was doing there. All of this was her scheme, including hiding with him. "Oh, I promise—no one will hear *anything* we do in here."

A little tingle ran through Kalen. "Why would you fear Araezra finding you here?"

"I've made enough women jealous to know the look."

"Is this a trick?" Kalen asked. "Who are you?"

"Does that really matter?"

"How do you know . . ." He bit his lip. "How do you know who I am?"

"Again, is it meant to be a secret?" Fayne stretched just the tiniest bit, rippling across Kalen's body. Whoever she was, Kalen thought, she knew how to move.

"How did you find me?"

She grinned. "Did you think yourself hidden?"

"Do you answer every question with a question?"

"Don't you?"

Kalen's voice almost broke. "Damn it, lass, I—"

"Hold a moment."

Fayne slid down his chest and belly, startling him. If Kalen hadn't been concentrating on staying quiet, he would have gasped and fallen backward out of the closet.

He heard the rustle of cloth and felt Fayne's head brush his thigh.

"What the Hells?" he snapped.

"Pardon . . . almost . . . ah."

She stretched back up, slowly and languidly, and presented to him a ring of silver, etched with an eye sigil. "Dropped this. So clumsy."

"That's mine," Kalen said.

"Was," she corrected. "Or were you going to take it back?" She pressed her hip against his. "I would love to see you try."

Kalen tried to ignore the threat—and implicit offer. "What could be staying them?"

"Lass talk, I imagine." Fayne shrugged, which made him tingle. "It lets us be alone."

Kalen turned his full attention on her. "Who are you?"

"I told you," she said. "Fayne is my name."

"No, it isn't."

She put her hands on her hips. "And why not?"

"*Feign?* You think me a simpleton?"

"Ha!" she said. "Very well. My true name," she said grandly, "is Feit."

"Really? Counter-*feit*?"

"Damn!" She giggled, a touch of her assumed girlishness coming back.

"Enough." Kalen glared at her. "Unveil yourself, girl, or gods help me, I will burst out of this closet and get us both caught."

Fayne's eyes narrowed. "You wouldn't *dare*," she said.

"I have only embarrassment in front of my superior to fear," Kalen said. "You, on the other hand—I believe you are a thief and a scoundrel and have considerably more to lose."

"Well, then." Fayne dared him with her eyes.

Kalen started to move.

"Wait," she said, throwing her arms around him and holding him back. "Mercy. Gods! Don't get so excited." She held up the ring in the flat of her palm, near her face.

Kalen took it, and while he was distracted, she kissed him again.

He pulled away, thumping his head on the ceiling. Thankfully, Fayne did not follow, just stood there smiling wryly at him.

"Very well, my captor—what would you have of me?" She winked. " 'Ware you don't ask too much—this is naught but our second meeting. I usually wait until the third, at least."

Kalen ignored her and perked his ears—Araezra was still talking, but her voice sounded no nearer than before.

"You call yourself Fayne—very well," he said. "Why are you here? What is your game?"

"My game, dearest Vigilant Dren," Fayne said, "is a mystery by its nature. The hints are in the playing." Still holding him, she pressed her cheek against his chest and purred. "You must be an active man. Not only does it look passing well, but it feels like a *rock*."

"Uh . . ." The numbness in his body wouldn't let him sense her hands.

"Hard as stone." She nuzzled his chest, and he felt a tingle. "I like the scars, as well."

Your chest, idiot, Kalen thought. Keep the thinking in your head!

"Answer my other questions," he said. "You are here for some purpose. Is it coin you want? I have little enough, but it's yours."

"Nothing of the sort!" Fayne looked insulted. "I'm in no such business except"—she shook her hair back grandly—"the business of misery and scandal." Her voice was sweet.

"You must be a writer," he murmured.

"Pique!" Fayne smiled brilliantly. "I don't often tell folk this, but I am, in fact, a writer for a little rag you might know: the *Mocking Minstrel*."

Kalen narrowed his eyes. "Satin Rutshear," he murmured.

"What a guess!" Fayne narrowed her eyes and licked her lips. "Can you read my mind?"

"No," Kalen said. "She's just the only one wicked enough."

"What charm," Fayne purred. "I like you more and more every breath, Shadowbane."

Kalen gritted his teeth behind a hard smile. What was taking Araezra so long? Why didn't she leave? Fayne was looking at him so directly, so boldly with those deep gray eyes . . . he wondered how long he had before his words—or his body—betrayed him.

"I was hoping to persuade you," Fayne said, "to take me to the revel on the morrow."

Kalen frowned. "Revel?"

.:⌒:.

"So that's . . ." Araezra said. She'd stopped crying halfway through her story, in no small part due to the aid of a steaming mug of cider from the fire. "That's what happened. It was an accident. Tal . . . Talanna jumped too far and couldn't make it."

"Mmm," Cellica said, nodding.

Myrin, taking the cue, nodded as well, though she had no idea what they were talking about. Shadowbane, though—that was Kalen. She kept her mouth shut.

"I can't understand it," Araezra said. "This Shadowbane seemed—I don't know. He didn't want to be caught, but he helped me out of the pit when he could have run. And when Tal was hurt, he helped her. Do those sound like the acts of a criminal to you?"

Cellica shrugged. "Not at all."

"Then why the mask?" Araezra asked.

"I'm sure he has his reasons," Cellica said. "It's all very romantic, isn't it? Like something you'd find in a chapbook. But I'm sure"—Myrin noted her glance at the closet—"I'm sure that whoever this Shadowbane is, he feels just as badly about Talanna."

Araezra shrugged.

"Talanna . . ." Cellica sipped her cider and asked, cautiously, "She'll be well, aye?"

Araezra nodded. She seemed to catch Myrin looking at her, and her deep blue eyes flicked to meet her gaze. Myrin hid behind her big cider mug as best she could.

"And you—Myrin, aye? What say you?"

"It . . . it all sounds so exciting," she said. "I can't imagine. Um." Myrin took a mouthful of cider, burned her tongue, and choked.

Araezra shifted uncomfortably. "And how do you know Kalen, Myrin?"

"She doesn't," Cellica said. "She's a . . . friend, from Westgate. My friend. Not his."

Araezra pursed her lips. "But you've *met* Kalen, aye?"

"Oh, aye!" Myrin said, and immediately wished she'd restrained herself.

"And what do you think of him?" Araezra asked, looking at Myrin closely.

"He's so—" Myrin looked at Cellica, who was frantically shaking her head. "Kuh-kind," she said. She looked down at the spoon she was fiddling with nervously. "So very kind. *Yes.*"

"*Kind?*" Araezra frowned at Cellica, who grinned helplessly. "Perhaps you know a different Kalen than I do."

Myrin's mouth moved but she couldn't find words.

"Look—gods above, I'm sure I don't want to know," Araezra said. "Vigilant Dren's life is his own, and he *clearly* intends to keep it that way." She stood, leaned over to kiss Cellica on the cheek, and nodded to Myrin. "Coins bright." She crossed to the rack by the window where she'd left her greatcoat.

Myrin leaned toward Cellica. "What does that mean?" she asked. "Coins bright?"

"Traditional Waterdhavian saying. 'May fortune smile,' or the sort."

"Oh." Myrin cradled her mug. "She's so sweet."

The halfling whispered back. "I believe she thinks you're a doxy or some such."

"A what?"

The halfling blushed and shook her head. "Never you mind."

"Cellica," said Araezra from near the window. "Are these blood stains?"

Myrin and the halfling both looked toward Araezra, where she knelt investigating a pair of red marks on the sill and floor.

"Oh, just me," Cellica said. "I mean—I made a pie and set it there to cool, and it spilled a bit. You know how treacherous balancing at the window can be. You know."

Again, Myrin felt that tickle in her ears that indicated magic was afoot. Cellica's voice had an enchantment of some sort about it, that took hold when she was either angry or concentrating on making her words strike. It was working on Araezra, who shrugged.

"Well, then," she said. "Coins bright. Tell Kalen I came to call." She headed out the door.

Cellica breathed a great sigh of relief. After a moment, she crossed to the closet, grasped the latch, and flicked it open.

Kalen tumbled out, the red-haired half-elf on top of him. The halfling put her hands on her hips and looked down at them both.

.·:^:·.

One breath, Kalen was standing in the closet, practically hugging Fayne, and the next he was on the floor, straddled by Fayne. He blinked up at Cellica, whose face was stormy, and over at Myrin, who looked away.

"Is she gone?" Fayne asked. "*Excellent!*" She bounded up and straightened her skirt. "Well, I should be off. I'll see you at highsun before the revel on the morrow? *Outstanding.*"

"Revel?" asked Cellica. "Tomorrow?"

"Ah." Kalen got to his feet, mumbling. "That scroll I gave you. The one I told you to—"

"You mean . . ." The halfling plucked a small, crumpled scroll out of a pocket and held it up in both hands. "You don't mean *our* revel?"

"*Our* revel?" Fayne asked, mouth wide. She glared at Kalen.

"Please?" Cellica turned her eyes up at Kalen. "The yearly costume revel at the Temple of Beauty on Greengrass—I've been saving coin for just such a windfall. Please—*please?*"

"Ah—" Kalen said. He looked at Myrin, who shrugged.

Fayne put her hands on her hips. "Sweet wee one," she said. "But Kalen's *my* escort."

"Is that so?" the halfling said. Though she reached only to Fayne's belly, she stood just as strong, arms crossed over her breast. "And don't you *ever* call me 'wee.' "

Fayne smirked and crossed her arms. "Well, if you weren't such a *little* thing—"

Kalen was suddenly immersed in the midst of a firestorm that flowed from the women's lips. Their argument was just as loud, just as fast, and just as deadly as any duel he had ever survived—and many he'd run from. The one and only time he tried to step in, they upbraided him so sharply and fiercely that he reeled as though struck.

The situation was a mess. He'd been planning to give the invitation to Fayne just to get rid of her, but Cellica wanted to go as well. If he gave it away, he would never hear the end of it, and if he didn't please Fayne, then gods only knew what would happen.

"Choose one of us," Cellica said, and Kalen felt compelled by that voice of hers. "Choose one of us ladies, right here, right now."

"Aye." Fayne tossed her hair over her shoulders. "That choice should be obvious."

"Only if he dreams of maids half elf, half *giant*," added Cellica.

Fayne smirked. "Unless he prefers lighter fare—girl-children, perhaps?"

Cellica's face went bright red.

The ladies went back to bickering sharply, throwing turns of phrase that would have made the best broadsheet satirists applaud.

Kalen turned his eyes on Myrin at the table, who blushed down at her hands in her lap. She was a buoy of gentle calm in a sea of dueling, querulous words. She saw Kalen looking at her and blinked. Then she smiled gently—demurely—and went back to looking embarrassed.

Finally, head spinning and aching, Kalen closed his eyes and pointed. "I'll go with her."

Cellica and Fayne looked at him, then at his finger.

"You're taking *her?*" Fayne asked, eyes dangerous. "The blue-haired waif?"

Kalen pointed at Myrin. The young woman opened her mouth to speak, but before she could, Cellica grinned widely.

"How sweet! Myrin could use a gown—gods know she can't go on wearing Kalen's things all her days." She sneered at Fayne. "I'm sure we can dress her better than *this* ogre."

Ignoring that, Fayne rounded on Kalen. "Why is she wearing *your* clothes?"

"Better than *you* wearing them," said Cellica. "Though they might fit you, she-whale."

Fayne blushed so fiercely that her face matched her hair. "What?" She investigated her backside. "There's not a drop of blubber there. Unlike certain halflings—"

As they fell to bickering again, Kalen looked at Myrin. Her mouth drooped in a lonely frown and her eyes were cast toward her hands, which were bunched into fists on the table. Kalen watched as she clenched her fists harder and harder.

A splotch of blue appeared on her wrist, then branched into lines of tiny runes—like a sprouting vine of ivy—that spread up her arm.

"Just because I'm not the perfect height for—*cuh!*" Fayne's words ended in a cough.

Grasping her throat, Fayne burbled a cry and slumped, hands clutching her head. She would have fallen, but Kalen caught her. Her hands tightened into claws on Kalen's bare chest.

"What's happening?" Cellica cried, terrified.

Fayne was looking around wildly, a look of sheer rage on her face. She murmured words in a language Kalen did not know and clutched at her forehead as though to smother a fire inside.

Kalen looked to Myrin, who sat at the table staring vacantly at the reeling Fayne. Her skin had sprouted an entire lattice of blue runes growing across her shoulder and down her arm. Her eyes glowed like stars.

Flames leaked from Fayne's hand—dark magic. Her eyes scanned the room as though searching for a foe. Kalen realized she was staring right at Myrin but didn't seem able to see her.

Yet.

"Stop!" Kalen snapped.

Myrin jumped, fell out of her chair, and scrambled against the wall. "Uh?"

Fayne moaned and slumped against Kalen, panting. The agony slipped away from her face, but her anger burned all the brighter. She glared, still seemingly unable to see Myrin.

The hate in her eyes shivered Kalen to his core.

Cellica's eyes darted back and forth between Kalen and Myrin. She seemed not to notice Myrin's eyes or runes—the girl's eyes had been locked on the half-elf. "What was that?"

"Damn," Fayne murmured, touching her head as though it were tender. "Damn me for good and all." She shook her head and looked to the table, where she finally was able to see Myrin. Her lips curled like those of an angry canine, and Kalen half expected to see fangs. But no, her teeth were quite normal.

"Wait," Kalen whispered to Fayne.

She looked up at him, gray eyes slowly draining of rage—and replaced by wariness. "Aye?"

Kalen fell into communion with his threefold god, fingers curling around his gauntlet-etched ring. His hands glowed, attracting Myrin's and Cellica's awed gazes. Healing power flowed into Fayne, easing her breathing.

She closed her eyes and nuzzled her cheek against his hand. "Oh, *Shadow*," she said.

"Kalen," he corrected.

"Hrmm." Fayne moved away—a little wobbly, but that might have been feigned. "If you're taking blue-hair girl, then I'll just have to wait until next time, won't I?"

She winked at Kalen in a way that assured him there would indeed be a next time.

"You don't—you don't have to," Cellica said. "Let me look at you. I've a healer's—"

"No need!" Fayne gave Cellica a winning smile and bent to kiss her on the forehead. "I'll be just fine." She tossed a glare at Myrin. "Just fine."

The half-elf left.

Kalen glanced at Cellica and Myrin. The halfling stood, pale faced, near the door, staring after Fayne. At the table, Myrin looked terrified. Blue runes adorned the left side of her face.

Kalen sighed. "I'll see her home," he said. "Wherever home is."

He grabbed his spare uniform, the black coat of leather and plate with its two gauntlets of rank. Heedless of whether they watched, he pulled off his hose and dressed.

With an *eep!* Myrin blushed and looked away.

Cellica looked hard at Kalen. "Do you know where?" she asked.

Kalen shrugged.

"So you really *don't* know her, eh?" the halfling said brightly.

Kalen laced up his breeches and shrugged on the harness straps.

"You . . . you're still taking Myrin to the revel on the morrow?"

Kalen shrugged. It hardly seemed relevant.

"Well, then," Cellica said. She smiled.

.:⌒:.

Myrin pressed her back against the wall and slid down, trembling and hot in the face.

What had she done?

She stared at her hands and her heart leaped. Little blue marks showed vividly against her left palm. She rubbed at them, as one might dirt smudges, but they didn't come off. She pulled up the sleeve of the old tunic, breathing hard. She found more marks traveling up her arm. She scratched hard at her skin, trying desperately to get rid of them, but she drew blood.

She touched her cheek, which tingled. In the small mirror across the room, she saw a vine of blue runes running along her throat and up her face. She sat, rigid in horror, and tried vainly to stay calm. The marks were moving—shrinking.

Soon, they faded entirely, and she could breathe again.

Fayne had gone, she realized, and Kalen—fully dressed and about to follow—was staring at her. His icy eyes glittered balefully. When Myrin opened her mouth, nothing came out. Wordlessly, Kalen strode into the corridor and banged the door shut.

Myrin looked down at her hands. Tears welled in her eyes.

"Don't mind him." Cellica appeared at her side, smiling. "He's just a glowering bastard."

"Really?" Myrin sniffed.

"Yes," she said. "I know what will make you feel better." Her eyes twinkled. "Dresses!"

CHAPTER SEVENTEEN

WHEN SHE REALIZED KALEN WASN'T IN THE ROOM OF RECORDS EITHER, Araezra slammed her fist on the table. Pain flared and she kissed her wrist to lessen it.

Damn that Kalen—where the Hells *was* he? He wasn't at home, and he wasn't anywhere at the barracks. This, the Room of Records, was his favorite place—it was peaceful and quiet, and he could read. Where could he be?

And who the Hells was that *girl?* Wearing his tunic, with hair like that? Had he brought a girl home from the Smiling Siren?

She felt sick. Everything was going wrong that day—*everything*. Except for Jarthay being so kind, she'd have sworn this was still a nightmare. The commander being sensitive made it seem more a fever dream.

Who *was* that girl? Gods, had Kalen fallen in love with someone else? *Gods!*

In her anger, Araezra hadn't noticed the door quietly opening or anyone entering. Only as she sat there, willing herself not to cry, did gooseflesh rise on her arms. She realized she was no longer alone. "Who's there?" she asked. "Kalen?"

Light vanished from the room and she gasped. The Room of Records had no windows, and with the door shut, it was utterly lightless. Pushing her uneasy shivers aside, she put her fingers to the amulet she and those of her rank wore and whispered a word in Elvish. The medallion glowed with a gentle green light, softly illuminating the room around her.

She made out the desk nearby and anchored herself. The candle on the edge of the desk gave off a little plume of smoke from its too-short wick.

"Fool girl," she said. "Scared by a burned-out candle."

She saw another source of light, then, coming from her belt. She froze and reached down, very slowly, to the hilt of Shadowbane's sword. She remembered that it had scalded her hand before, but the hilt was no longer warm to the touch. Instead, it felt cool and comfortable. *Right.* Light leaked around the edges of the scabbard and she drew it forth, gasping in awe at the silver shimmer that fell from it.

"Gods," she murmured. She cut the blade twice through the air, marveling at the way the light trailed. It felt so efficient—a killing weapon, beautiful and deadly.

Then she thought she saw movement against the wall. "What was—?"

She crept forward, Shadowbane's sword held before her like a talisman. She approached, letting the circle of light creep closer and closer to the wall, until—

Nothing.

Nothing had moved—it was just a Watch greatcoat hung on a peg by the disused hearth.

Araezra loosed a nervous breath.

Then a man was there, leaping inside her guard. She gasped and tried to slash, but he was too fast, batting the sword out of her hands. The weapon spun end over end toward the door and clattered to the floor. Her attacker seized her by the throat and hip and crushed her against the wall. She could see, by the dim, flickering light of the sword, that it was a smooth-faced dwarf. His features were flawless, making him look all the more monstrous to her eyes. She knew his name—remembered Kalen mentioning a beardless dwarf.

"Arrath Vir," she squeaked.

"I am pleased that you know me," the dwarf said. "It means you might be useful." He fixed her eyes with his own. "Tell me—who is seeking me? A name."

"Piss—*urk!*" He pressed his arm tighter against her throat, cutting off air.

"Know that you are mine to slay on a whim." His eyes bored into hers. "You are powerless. The Watchmen in the barracks—all those swords and shields sworn to serve this city. All those men who hunger for your beauty. All of them mean nothing to you now."

Her face felt as though it would burst from the pressure within. As though he sensed this, Rath eased his arm enough that she could breathe.

"All the years spent cultivating your life—everything you learned as a child, all the pointless loves and hates that have defined who you are. All of it ends, here and now, at my whim." He smiled gently. "You will die at my hands, no matter what you do now."

Araezra gasped but could not speak. She could barely breathe.

"Aye," he said. "But you've a choice. Aid me, and I shall make your death a painless one. Do not, and I shall not."

Araezra looked over Rath's shoulder.

"What say you?" The dwarf eased his grasp so she could just choke out words.

"Pick . . . it . . . up," Araezra said.

Rath looked back, and there stood Kalen Dren.

Kalen had trailed Fayne through the streets as best he could, but she was like a devil to follow. She would vanish around a corner and appear elsewhere, a dozen paces to one side or another. Eventually he lost her entirely.

Perhaps it was good riddance—to be free of whatever scheme she'd concocted for the revel—but in truth, no small part of him *wanted* to see her again. To finish what they'd started.

But duty came before beguiling lasses who showed up at his door unannounced, and so he made his way to the barracks. Araezra was not in any of her usual haunts—her office, the commons, the training yard—and Kalen was a little relieved. He didn't feel like facing her, and if duty had called her away before he got the chance, then so be it. After Talanna had been hurt, he didn't feel like he could lie to Araezra anymore.

He reached the unlatched door of the Room of Records—just a little ajar, so he could see inside—and froze. Rath was inside, holding Araezra captive.

At first, neither of them noticed his appearance, so he kept to the shadows and stood, unmoving, in the doorway. He was not wearing Shadowbane's leathers and cloak, but the Guard uniform was black and he could use that to his advantage. He called upon the lessons he'd learned first in Luskan—how to stand still and silent—and thought hard.

Kalen's instinct was to strike, but he suppressed it. Rath held Araezra at such an angle that if Kalen stepped forward, the surprise could prove fatal for her. With his training as a thief, Kalen could kill the dwarf in one, fast blow, but he could not cross the room without one or the other noting him. The silver glow of Vindicator illuminated the room enough for that.

Neither could he cry out for guards—as Araezra would surely die in the confusion. And if he went to get aid quietly, he would be abandoning his friend to death.

He had to do something, though. He had—

He had no sword. The scabbard at his belt was empty.

How had he forgotten that? He had dropped the blade when he brought Myrin back, and never retrieved it. He'd even walked past the barracks armory on his way, coughing and feigning weakness as always. He could reclaim Vindicator, but surely moving the light source would alert Rath.

Think, he told himself. *Think.*

But nothing came. He was the weakling Kalen Dren who could barely hold a sword, much less fight with it. There was so little he could do. The dwarf had been too much for him at his prime as Shadowbane, armed and on even ground. If he attacked now, in any way, Rath would kill them both. If it were just himself, he might take Tymora's chance, but it was *Rayse*.

He felt helpless. He could not attack, could not flee, and if he revealed himself . . .

That was it.

Making sure to hunch as usual, Kalen stepped forward, out of the shadows, and coughed—softly, but distinctly.

Araezra's eyes danced with stars, but she clearly saw a figure step out of the shadows and into the silvery light: Kalen! His hand was not a dagger's length from Shadowbane's sword.

"Pick . . . it . . . up," she said.

Rath looked, and a smile spread across his face, particularly at the stooped way Kalen stood, and his empty belt. He only smirked as Kalen stood over the silver blade.

"Touch that steel," Rath said, "and I snap your commander's neck."

"Valabrar," Kalen corrected, in his damnably precise manner.

What are you doing? Araezra thought at him.

"Speak thus, again," Rath said. "I do not understand."

"She is a valabrar. To explain"—Kalen gestured to the two gauntlets on his breastplate—"two, for vigilant. Araezra wears five for a valabrar. One would be a trusty, three a shieldlar—"

"Silence," the dwarf said. "If you wish this *Araezra* to live, down any weapons you carry, shut the door, and do only as I say."

Kalen inclined his head, the way he did whenever an instruction was given. Not taking his eyes from Rath, he slid the door quietly shut. He spread his hands to show them empty.

"Kneel," Rath said. "There—where you will block the door."

Kalen did so without argument, sinking to his knees.

Araezra wanted to scream at him. Burn him, what was Kalen *doing*?

The dwarf smiled at Araezra, and she could smell the brandy on his breath. "What a finely trained mastiff you have," he murmured.

"Let him go," Araezra said. "Don't hurt him. I'll do whatever you want."

"Such as?" A bemused fire lit in the dwarf's eye, as though she had reminded him of a private jest. "What could you possibly offer me?"

"Me." The word tasted like wormwood in her mouth. "I'm beautiful, did you not say it?"

Rath smirked.

Then he hauled Araezra away from the wall and threw her to the floor near the desk as though she were an empty tunic. Her head knocked against the stout darkwood and her vision blurred. She reached to pull herself up, but the dwarf caught her hand—her sword hand—and twisted it. A crackle of bones sounded and her wrist exploded in pain. She uttered a screech that did not reach any volume, because he kicked her in the belly and blew any air from her body. The scream became a wet sob.

Kalen was saying something.

The dwarf looked at Kalen then. "I did not hear you, trained dog," he said.

"You should flee this place," Kalen observed in his indifferent manner. "You can accomplish nothing here."

The dwarf lunged across the distance between them and stood over Kalen, one hand grasping him by the brown-black hair that hung messily in his eyes. "Why, dog?" he asked. "Do you offer me a threat?"

Kalen's eyes did not leave Rath's, and he shook his head. "Only a fact," he said. "You are in the heart of our barracks, and a cry will call more Watchmen than you can defeat alone."

Araezra realized Kalen was distracting Rath. She flexed her wrist—broken, but she'd trained left-handed as well. She could still wield a sword, albeit poorly. She looked to the silvery blade on the floor. But it was nearer Kalen than herself, and he could not fight, could he?

Would he? She wondered.

"You can slay both of us, but you cannot silence both of us at the same moment." Kalen continued. "Thus, if you kill either of us, the other can cry out and you will die."

The dwarf did not blink, but the look on his face told Araezra he had counted the guards he had bypassed. "Why not call for them now?" he asked.

"Our bargain," Kalen said. "You leave this place and do not harm either of us, and we will not cry out. No one need die."

Araezra gasped and coughed, as her breathing once again became normal. "Kalen . . ."

He ignored her and stared at Rath, who seemed to be considering.

Then the dwarf's fingers touched the edge of Kalen's jaw, caressing it softly and gently—like a lover, and like death. "Very well, dog," said Rath. "But I want to hear you *beg*."

Kalen cast his eyes down.

"Beg for mercy," Rath said with a cruel smile.

When Kalen spoke, his voice hardly rose above a whisper. "Please," he said. "*Please.*"

"Kalen . . ." Araezra couldn't believe it. The Kalen she loved did not beg.

Rath sniffed. "You call yourself a man, and yet you take the coward's path," he said. He looked at Araezra. "Your mastiff is not a hound, my lady, but a mongrel bitch."

Kalen's eyes, gleaming pale at Araezra, seemed very, very cold in that silvery light.

Araezra rubbed her bruised throat. "Choose, dwarf," she said. "I have a good scream in me yet, and weak as he is, I've no doubt Vigilant Dren can muster such a cry."

Rath looked from her to Kalen and back. Then he snorted.

"Very well." He hauled Kalen up, and to his credit, the man barely coughed. "Know that your cowardice falls beneath the weakest pup, for even such a cur can fight when cornered."

Kalen did not answer.

"Have you nothing to say?" asked the dwarf.

Kalen only stared at Rath. Araezra felt a trembling anger build within her.

Then Rath was gone, nearly flying down the hall. Kalen slumped to the floor, but he caught himself before his face struck the stone. Araezra saw his eyes, bright and furious and icy, gleam at her. Then he started to cough.

In an instant, as though that sound had given her strength, Araezra pushed herself to her feet. "Guard!" she cried, loud as she could. "Watch, Guard—to arms! Intruder!"

A great clamor of feet and steel arose in the rooms around them. Folk were coming, summoned by Araezra's cry. Araezra looked at Kalen, so weak and sad, lying there. She reached down. "Up, Vigilant."

He took her hand and climbed up shakily. "Are you hurt?" he asked.

She shook her head, furious words building in her throat.

Kalen coughed. "Gods, Rayse, I didn't want you to get hurt. You know that."

"Spare me." Araezra shook her head, too angry and hurt to spend soft words on him. "I don't need anyone to protect me—especially not a coward."

Kalen cast his eyes down.

Araezra took Shadowbane's sword—it felt warm to the touch but did not burn her—then ran into the hall to muster the Watch.

Kalen stood shaking, wounded deeper than any sword could have cut.

He'd given everything to save Araezra. He had broken his greatest vow to himself, never to beg. And still, she had turned away from him. He had seen the contempt in her eyes.

He was less than a man to her, and he had pulled her low as well.

A coughing fit came upon him then, bubbling up like a cruel reminder of his failure, and he fought it down—in vain. He coughed and retched and spat blood into his hand.

That blood and spit could easily have been Rath's blood on his hands. The temptation had been so strong—to trick the dwarf into vulnerability and plunge a blade into his liver, kidney, or heart. Like a backstabbing thief, or like an assassin. The way he would have done in Luskan. But that would have sullied his vows, and the paladin in him would not allow it.

He lifted his hands to heal himself at a touch, but his powers did not come forth.

He realized why, and the understanding struck him like a slap across the face.

All this time, he had protected Waterdeep—this city of faceless citizens—and protected those he loved and cherished. But he could not do it at the cost of his own principles. He could not compromise the deepest commitment of all: to himself.

So that he might continue in his duty, he hadn't revealed himself after Lorien, or after Talanna had been hurt. The threefold god had not punished him for that. But when he hadn't revealed himself today, he'd chased away his only friend other than Cellica.

Although Araezra was alive, he knew he had acted wrongly. The Threefold God had taken his powers for sacrificing his duty to himself for his duty to others.

He saw that he must do both—fight for the city, and fight for himself and those he loved. He would prove himself worthy.

He swore it.

CHAPTER EIGHTEEN

To prepare for the revel, Cellica took Myrin to a dress salon called Nathalan's Menagerie—named, Cellica explained, for the elf noble who was the owner.

Lady Ilira Nathalan owned a number of such shops across Faerûn, which did their part in supplying—and in many cases creating—the fashions of the day. Patrons tried on styles amid cages filled with exotic birds and flowers. The gowns, sashes, and shoes were rich in quality but low in cost, which, Cellica explained, was the reason behind the Menagerie's success.

"I don't know how she does it," Cellica said as she gestured to gown after gown for the attendant to take for her, "but some lucky goddess must watch over her supplies. Her prices always undercut her competitors. Nobles usually have their own seamstresses as a matter of pride, but Ilira caters to merchants and other wealthy folk who don't have signets stuck up their—heh." Cellica smiled wryly. "Better dresses, too, though don't let the nobility hear that."

Myrin watched as a pair of lovely middle-aged human women draped a series of gowns over their chests, admiring the colors in the mirror. An attendant—whom Myrin realized must be a half-orc, owing to her small tusks and gray skin—watched impassively. Her hair was a brilliant pink that could not be natural. It reminded Myrin of her own blue hair, which she pawed at idly.

"Ninea," said Cellica, tugging at Myrin's arm and pointing to the half-orc. "Just watch."

One of the customers framed a request to Ninea the half-orc, who touched the woman's shoulder briefly. The effect was as sudden as it was impressive:

the woman's skin took on a brilliant golden sheen, astonishing her companion, who gasped and broke into tittering.

"Gods!" Myrin said. "That's amazing!"

"Simple magic," Cellica said. "Ninea has a spellscar that lets her alter colors to match her whims. Temporarily, of course." She continued breezing through gowns. "Certainly you could find cheaper attire elsewhere, but the quality is hard to defeat." She selected her tenth and eleventh. "Perhaps it's goodness rewarding the same."

"Aye?" Myrin hadn't selected a gown—she was remembering Kalen's glare.

"Aye," Cellica affirmed, taking down her twelfth. "Lady Ilira's a patron of the Haven of the Scarred, for those run afoul of spellplague or other magical maladies—a consortium of priests and healers. I'm a member."

The halfling frowned at a conservative brown gown Myrin was looking at and led her away. "It'll be a costume revel," she said. "Most of these are a particular lady from history—that one must be a Candlekeep ascetic. Boring as old rat tails!"

"What?" Myrin was standing shyly to the side, grasping her right elbow behind her back and burrowing her left foot into the floorboards.

"Pay it no mind, dear," said Cellica. "Let's find another that suits you better."

"Oh?" Myrin behaved around the finery the way a mouse must in a hall full of cat statues. She was terrified she would perish under the assault of silk. "Can . . . can we afford this?"

"Of course! We halflings have a way with coin. Just none of the priciest, eh? Ooh!" Her eye fell on a rich cloth-of-silver gown. She spoke with a halfling attendant in a language Myrin didn't understand, winced, then nodded. The gown went into the attendant's already full arms.

The half-orc woman with the bright pink hair brushed past Myrin. While the attendant was dexterous enough, Myrin's inherent clumsiness almost knocked her over. The half-orc had to catch her by the hand and ward her off. Ninea's hand sparked against hers. "Ooh, sorry!" Myrin said.

The woman started to respond, then shook her head, seeming faint.

"Ninea?" asked the halfling attending Cellica and Myrin. "Be ye well, lass?"

"Aye," said the half-orc. Her hair, Myrin saw, was fading from its sharp pink to a dirty brown. "Just weary, methinks."

"Well, ask Ilira if you can go early, aye?" Cellica's voice carried a touch of compulsion.

"Aye." Ninea gave Myrin a curious look. "Aye, I'll do that."

The half-orc wandered to the back of the salon, looking ill.

Hesitantly, Myrin selected three gowns—a gentle, deep blue affair with gold trim, a conservative green with silver chasing at the bodice, and a sleek black garment. She didn't particularly want any of them. She pulled Kalen's worn tunic tighter about her body. She liked how it smelled—it felt like Kalen was embracing her. Why did he have to be so *handsome?*

Stop it, girl, she thought. You don't even know who you are. You shouldn't worry about men—particularly ones who *hate* you!

She hoped Kalen didn't hate her, after what she'd done—accidentally—to Fayne.

But what *had* she done?

As they made their way to the mirror-walled fitting room, Myrin spotted Ninea near the back of the Menagerie. The woman she spoke to was slim and elegant and beautiful, with long midnight hair and delicate pointed ears. An elf, Myrin thought, but there was something . . . otherworldly about her. Looking at her made it hard to breathe.

"Lady Ilira herself," Cellica said, poking her head around Myrin's waist. "Aye—you're thinking she can't be mortal. She's an eladrin, lass—they're all like that."

"Eladrin?" Myrin frowned. She'd never heard this word before.

Cellica shrugged. "High elves, eladrin, all the same to me." She took Myrin's arm. "Come—you'll see her again at the ball, of course."

"She's coming?" Myrin hadn't thought there might be nobles there, but of course there would be. Good thing she would be in costume, otherwise she'd be too afraid to show her common face. Around such a creature as Lady Ilira, she would feel even worse.

"Every year!" Cellica said. "It's a tradition."

Myrin blinked then hurried to follow. She felt self-conscious trying on the gowns with the aid of an attendant, but the way Cellica casually flung clothes around made her relax. The attendants measured them, then waited for a decision. The dresses would be altered later, to be picked up in time for the revel.

"The dance between Ilira and Lorien is traditional," Cellica said. "Every year, she and Lady Lorien dance at the height of the ball. No two ladies are closer friends than that pair, and—so the gossip says—it's more than that." She tossed a slinky green gown over her shoulder, and the attendant barely caught it. "But never we lesser mortals mind."

Myrin blushed, though she couldn't say why.

"And who . . . who will Lady Ilira dress as?" Myrin asked. If she stood on her toes, she could just see the elf woman over the mirrors, surveying her salon.

"Probably no one." Cellica shook her head. "She always wears black, and lots of it," she said. "Dull, I know, but she's so elegant." She leaned in close to Myrin. "Some say she does it in mourning for a lost love, but I rather think it's to hide something. Unsightly tattoos or scars or the like. Some say she has one on her back—and that's why she never wears her own backless gowns—though I think there's a reason she always wears long gloves, let me tell *you*."

"How do you know all this?" Myrin asked.

"One of us has to keep up with the news in the city, and gods-know Sir Shadow isn't going to do it." Cellica shrugged into a silver gown and admired herself. "And I like gossip."

Myrin smiled and looked at her feet—thinking of Kalen.

The attendant returned with a woven basket in which lay two gowns. "If you would be pleased," she said, "the lady suggests you try these."

Cellica frowned at the gowns. "Who—?"

"Lady Ilira," said the attendant. "She saw you in the Menagerie and thought these colors and styles might serve. Fitted per your measurements. Perhaps . . . a happy coincidence?"

Curious, Myrin looked across the room. Lady Ilira was gone. She seemed to have vanished into the shadows. It gave her a chill.

"Ye *gods*." Cellica held up a scarlet gown, human-sized. She eyed Myrin devilishly.

"I don't think—" Myrin started, but Cellica wouldn't accept such an answer. She disrobed timidly while Cellica drew on a gold gown.

Myrin had to admit the red dress looked fine. It was sleek, it was daring, and it was bright without being gaudy. And the cut was perfect—it hugged her waiflike curves in a way that was not at all waiflike, but neither was it loose. She almost thought she looked pretty.

"Perfect for your skin!" Cellica nodded.

Myrin looked at her shimmering skin in the mirrors. In the soft lighting of the salon, it glowed a deep tan like polished betel wood. She blushed.

"The blue doesn't really serve," said Cellica. She stood on a stool, straining up to finger Myrin's shoulder-length hair. Myrin flushed and tried to look away from the mirror, only to remember she was surrounded by mirrors. "It's a lovely blue, and all, but it's . . . blue."

Myrin's insides tingled. "What . . . what *would* serve?"

"Well," Cellica said, "this one's an evening gown worn by the legendary Lady Alustriel of Silverymoon, who—as one of the Seven Sisters—had silver hair to her waist. If we could just get Ninea over here. Shame, as she charges such hard coin for—"

And just like that—as Myrin watched in the mirror—the scraggly blue hair spun and swam like the currents in a whirlpool. In a breath, it turned to rich, burnished silver and fell to her waist.

Cellica's eyes widened. "Now that . . . that's impressive." She looked for Ninea, who had disappeared out of the store, then leaned toward Myrin to whisper. "Can you do aught for me? I'd love . . . I'd love a good crimson, if you wouldn't—"

"I don't even know how I did it for me." Myrin blushed. "I could try—"

"No, no!" Cellica said, turning white. "It looks too glim for such a risk. Keep it that way."

Myrin frowned. Then she realized something. "You wanted crimson? Like Fayne's hair?"

"Ha! Hark—how the day wanes!" Cellica picked nervously at the gold dress. The color flattered her well and the gown was cut with gods' eyes to show flashes of sunbrowned flesh on her slim belly. "This one, then."

She whistled, and their attendant glided over. The halfling didn't seem surprised to see Myrin's silver hair.

"I think we've decided," Cellica said, and Myrin realized she wanted to be away from the salon as soon as possible. Was it something she had said?

"Please, my lady, to have these as well," said the halfling girl, presenting two parcels bound in waxed string. "Less elegant—more practical, but fine. A gift, for gracing the Menagerie."

Cellica blushed furiously. "We can't accept these," she said.

But the attendant shook her head. "Lady Ilira mentioned aught of a debt," she said. "She spoke of a 'shadow that wards'?" She shrugged. "She said you would understand."

Cellica and Myrin shared a long, curious glance. Then the halfling smiled. "Very well, but we pay for these in full." She gestured to her gold gown and Myrin's scarlet.

The attendant shrugged. She looked at Kalen's borrowed tunic and breeches and tried to hide her disdain behind her kerchief.

Cellica murmured a laugh. "Better just toss those out, I think."

The attendant nodded and took up the old clothes, averting her nose. Myrin watched the clothes in her arms and felt Cellica's eyes. The halfling smiled at her mysteriously.

"Cheers, peach," Cellica said, squeezing her hand. "No reason to fret—he did promise to take *you* to the revel, not that other stripling."

"But—"

"Kalen, for all his faults, is a man of his word." Cellica winked. "Don't you forget that!"

When Cellica turned away, Myrin wiped at her cheek and noted in the mirror a tiny blue rune on her wrist, glowing softly. It hadn't been there when she'd entered the salon, but it was there now—a bright little spot that filled her with nervous dread. It felt warm to the touch and didn't fade no matter how long she looked at it.

Myrin looked where Lady Ilira had stood, at the back of the Menagerie, but no one was there. She saw only a shadow on the wall, which flickered away as though someone—unseen—had moved.

"Come, lass!" Cellica called. "Delay too long, and I'll just have to buy another!"

CHAPTER NINETEEN

FAYNE ROSE LATE THE FOLLOWING MORN, IN HER ROOMS ABOVE THE rowdy Skewered Dragon in Dock Ward. She was alone, and every bit of her ached.

Awakening from reverie alone in her own bed was in itself cause for concern. She hadn't spent more than a dozen nights alone in all the years since her mother's death. She normally required only a few hours of the trancelike rest—only half what she had just spent. She must have felt truly awful, to fall into bed by herself and rest the night through.

Perhaps she had even spent some of the time in real *sleep*—ye gods. Maybe she was wearing a half-elf's face too much.

She recalled that the owner of the Dragon had questioned her gruffly when the carriage had dropped her off, but she'd waved him aside, along with the catcalls of patrons. She'd ignored the sneers of the serving girls—saucy wenches who sold their charms as openly as drinks—and managed to climb up to her chamber before collapsing into bed.

She examined the damage in the mirror. That blue-headed snip had muddled her mind, adding worry lines around her eyes and lips. She'd often wondered what it would feel like, being struck by dark magic—gods knew she'd done it often enough herself.

"Hit me with my own power, eh?" she murmured. "*Children.*"

All in all, totally unacceptable, she thought. She set to work. She would just touch up a few details of her appearance.

She caressed the invisible pendant that hung at her throat. It faded into sight and gleamed as she harnessed the magic—complex, powerful things for which her wand was not quite suited. It wasn't that she *couldn't* cast the shaping ritual with the wand—it just didn't feel right to her. It was better for quick castings, particularly illusions and dark, fey-touched art. It had come from her mother, who had been a talented witch of the fey path. The amulet, on the other hand—her patron had built it precisely for this sort of ritual, which was more wizardly than warlock.

She thought she should see Kalen today. Fayne hoped the man was suitably in agony over the wounds she had sustained in his tallhouse. She might suggest that he could make it up by taking her to the revel instead of Myrin, thus furthering her plan.

She left shadows under her eyes, so as to make herself appear a little more vulnerable. She knew Kalen liked the gray eyes, so she made them shine. She slimmed her image slightly, and made her face just a bit more darling—her nose, in particular, seemed a bit too long, so she made it small and delicate.

More like Myrin's nose, she realized, and she stuck out her tongue in disgust.

Her amulet had been a gift from her patron on her fortieth name day (gods, how long ago that seemed!), and coincided with her learning how to change her face. First, she had used the wand's illusory powers, but her patron had taught her how to perform a ritual that would make the changes deeper, harder to dispel.

Finished, she stepped back to admire her handiwork. This was the face she would wear this day—Greengrass, the festival of spring. It wasn't what she'd call beautiful, exactly, but a proper seduction was accomplished according to the desires of the man or woman seduced. She winked at the mirror, glad of her false face. A blessing no one could see the real one—she didn't spend so much effort hiding it in vain.

Her face and body made up, Fayne selected suitable attire for the Watch barracks: mid-calf gray dress with open front, laced black bustier cut with slits on the flanks to reveal slashes of lacy red underslip, matching scarlet scarf for the cold, wide leather hat for any rain, and her favorite knee-high boots with dagger-length heels.

None of them cheap, but none of them rich—quite what she thought Kalen liked.

As she dressed, she smiled at the revel-ready garments hanging in the wardrobe, carefully selected for the occasion. She would have quite the laugh at that private jest—most of her best pranks were personal.

She threw on a weathercloak to hide her outfit, whisked her way out the Dragon around a few highsun brawlers and patrons waving for her charms, and hailed a carriage.

Vainly, Kalen had hoped that by the next day, Araezra would have calmed herself about the Room of Records and they could talk. But he hadn't seen her all morn, and when he'd asked, a gruff Commander Jarthay had told him she was out on duty. Kalen didn't need the subtle, tight pitch of the commander's words to know things would be tense with Araezra.

He hadn't wanted to go home, so he'd spent the night at the barracks and eaten among the Guard. Thankfully, no one bothered him. His notorious indifference was good for that, at least. That morn, he had tried to work in the Room of Records, but every time he looked up from the ledgers, he would see Rath holding Araezra helpless or hear her choked whispers. Eventually, he moved outside to work in the warm, sun-filled courtyard.

Greengrass was the first day of spring, and the weather treated Waterdeep to warm days, cold nights, and frequent rain. Kalen disliked autumn and spring, with their long shadows and false warmth: he preferred the commitment of summer heat or winter chill.

In the yard, he left the ledger untouched and began a letter to Araezra, trying to explain what he had done. He paused now and then, to listen to the sounds of training in the court.

A cluster of Watchmen had gathered to watch a practice match between two of the youngest and most handsome members of the Guard: Aumun Bront and Rhagaster Stareyes. The latter was the more handsome thanks to his elf heritage (the legacy of a scandalous, hypocritical indiscretion on the part of his elf supremacist father, Onstal Stareyes, with a serving lass in Dock Ward). The men circled each other, stripped to the waist and sweaty, padded swords swishing.

They sparred under the unimpressed eye of Vigilant Bleys Treth, whom Kalen had done his best to avoid these last days. He didn't much like the man (the feeling was mutual), and Treth had seen Shadowbane on the night Talanna had been hurt. He might recognize Kalen.

The other guard who might have known him—Gordil Turnstone—was there, too, sitting on a bench. Though he was ostensibly watching the sparring, Turnstone was dozing.

Bront cut over and high and Stareyes replied with a plunging block. It could have become a counter to the belly, but the half-elf held the parry too long. Finally, Stareyes broke the parry and cut in from the opposite line, then reversed again, striking from both directions in sequence. He feinted right and attacked left. In rhythm, Bront tried to parry right, and the half-elf dealt him a sharp rap on the left side with his blunted blade.

The watchers clapped and Stareyes flashed his winning smile. Bront cradled his bruised side and gave Stareyes a rueful grin.

Kalen watched them surreptitiously over his spectacles. A part of him wished he could lord his prowess before an audience, but the needs of his disguise prevented it. He'd learned that lesson in a harsh manner during his time as an armar, before Araezra.

He thought about the flaws in Bront's style, and it must have shown on his face. Treth was watching him with a sneer. Kalen averted his eyes.

"Dren," Treth called. "Care to teach us aught?"

The congratulatory chatter in the courtyard fell silent, replaced by whispers.

Kalen said nothing, only looked at his parchment and quill. He had paused before telling Araezra the truth. He could see the unwritten sentence: "I lied to you, Rayse."

Did he dare? Would she understand? Or would she continue to hate him, not only for humiliating her but for lying to her as well? Not to mention that Araezra would be honor-bound to arrest him as a dangerous vigilante—or would she keep his secret?

He shook his head. He hadn't given her any reason to trust him.

A gloved hand seized his book of notes—with it the letter—and tore it from his hands. He looked up, calmly, to see Bleys Treth gazing down at him with that same cocky smile.

"Come, Dren," he said. "You've not graced the yard in some time. Spar with Stareyes, and show us your style." He winked lewdly. "Now that Rayse's attentions are elsewhere, you've the chance, aye?"

Though Treth was older, almost twenty winters over Kalen, they were the same rank in the Guard: vigilant. But Treth had been a master swordsman for hire, a sellsword for nobles, and he bore an aura around him that had made him quite popular. "The Dashing Jack," the older Watchmen called him—a name he hated. His looks had faded little with the years, but his smile still melted hearts.

He took pride in his charms, and in his skill. And like many warriors past their prime, Treth saw the need to assert his dominance among the "young pups," as it were.

Kalen saw no reason to stand in his way.

"I've work to attend." He refused to meet Treth's eye. "Perhaps when I am at leisure—"

"I'm sure"—Treth dropped the ledger in the dirt—"this can wait."

Kalen looked up at him and around at the silent training yard. The folk—Guard and Watch alike—watched the confrontation intently.

"Vigilant Treth," Kalen said. He coughed. "You know I can't—"

"Fleeing behind your weakness of the flesh, eh?"

Kalen looked around once more, seeing uncertain, expectant faces.

The Watch and Guard knew of his illness only in part. Certainly none knew he pretended it had grown worse than it truly had. It had been months since he had wielded a sword while wearing a uniform. But when he had . . . Those who had served with him knew of his ferocity, and he saw in the eyes of those gathered that tales had spread.

"I must decline," Kalen said.

"Then Rayse told true," Treth whispered in his ear. "And you *are* a coward."

That stabbed into Kalen's chest like a searing knife. It struck not because of his own ego—though he confessed there was some—but because of the truth in Treth's words.

He shouldn't do anything to risk revealing himself, but everything was going so very wrong. And Kalen was angry.

"Very well, Dashing Jack," said Kalen, invoking the man's hated moniker. Treth sneered.

Kalen rose, stiffly, and stepped to the center of the yard. He heard gasps at first, then applause. Rhagaster Stareyes saluted and took a high guard with his padded blade.

Kalen took the weapon handed him by Bront, who smiled. Kalen shrugged.

"Tymora's luck on you," said Treth—mostly to Kalen. "Begin!"

They circled each other slowly, the ring of Watchmen backing away to give them room. The half-elf skipped from foot to foot, keeping himself loose. Kalen flexed his legs. The front of his thighs felt as if they bore heavy pads, but the sensation was merely his numb flesh.

Stareyes came at him with a plunging cut that Kalen knocked aside easily. He coughed and sidestepped, not holding the parry or countering.

Stareyes turned back toward him. "To you, sir," he said.

Kalen shrugged—and attacked high. He didn't move fast—he didn't have to.

From his hanging guard, Stareyes parried high. He could have countered, but as Kalen had expected, he didn't. Rather than pull back, Kalen ran a hand along the length of his own sword, caught the end of his blade, and twisted to set the edge near the hilt at the half-elf's throat.

A gasp passed through the yard.

"You hesitated to reply," Kalen said. "You don't need speed—just readiness." He pulled back a step and set his sword against Stareyes's raised blade. "You just parried. Now stab."

Stareyes, blinking, pushed forward, and the padded blade punched into Kalen's belly.

"A counter in every parry," he said. "Do not hesitate, but commit yourself."

The half-elf shook his head. "But my parry needs to be—"

"Firm, I know," Kalen said. "Trust yourself to set a strong position, and there is no way the other blade can hit you."

He demonstrated, slapping his blade against Stareyes's parry. With the guard wide enough, his blade could not reach Stareyes's arm.

The gathered watchers—who had grown in number, Kalen saw—murmured agreement.

Treth laughed. "Try a master, Sir Dren." He tossed his hat and black watchcoat to a junior Watchman, then unbuttoned his uniform and unlaced his white undertunic to the belly.

"The winner goes with Rayse to the ball tonight at the Temple of Beauty," said Treth.

Coughing, Kalen nodded grimly. He'd known it would come to this.

Treth sneered. Gray-black hairs bristled along his chin and neck.

Kalen shrugged. He handed the sword to Stareyes with a nod, then brought his fingers up to the buttons of his uniform.

Apparently, an attractive form—such as the one she had donned in the Skewered Dragon—was more a hindrance than a help in a barracks filled with wandering eyes.

Fayne had arrived at the barracks earlier, and now wore the illusory form of a junior Watchman whose name she hadn't asked. She could have done so, but why bother? The boy, who had been only too eager to follow her into the stuffy Room of Records, now slumped senselessly under a desk, trapped by magic that bound his mind into a relentless nightmare. Fayne had invoked the power in her wand, taken his face, and gone out into the warm sunshine. She found Kalen in the courtyard, just in time to see him handily defeat a rather handsome half-elf with dark hair and the most beautiful eyes.

Fayne made a mental note to visit the barracks more often.

Then a good-looking man of middling years—Vigilant Treth, she heard a Watchman whisper—challenged Kalen, and they proceeded to disrobe in the middle of the yard.

Fayne had to restrain herself not to squeal. She wasn't a gambler, but she *loved* cockfights.

She shared in the collective intake of breath when Kalen stripped off his shirt. His body was covered in scars—knife cuts, arrow holes, burns. Some of them, Fayne recognized: the finger-shaped lines on his forearm were the spellscar burns he had suffered in Downshadow the night they had met. His tightly woven muscles carried not a drop of fat.

Treth was a whip-wire of a man, like a curled snake, ready to lunge. Kalen, on the other hand, was a wolf. Fayne saw it in his movements and the way he stood—and the way he glared.

Her cheeks grew warm, and she cursed herself for a brainless child.

The men faced each other across the courtyard. Sneering, Treth held his steel low. Kalen held his high, and coughed. Part of his disguise, Fayne realized.

Then Treth lunged toward Kalen, fast as a striking viper, and Kalen caught his spinning, shifting cut with a solid, low-hanging parry. The padded swords thumped.

Treth pulled back and struck again, reversing, and Kalen parried easily. Where Treth attacked wildly, with great sweeping slashes and flurries, Kalen's movements were quick and precise—conservative. It was obvious to Fayne—who knew as little about swordplay as a stray kitten—that Kalen was better. But could he win, and still maintain his mask?

That held Fayne's interest—that, and Kalen's glimmering skin. Mmm.

They came together again, and again. Every time, Treth attacked, lunging fast, and every time, Kalen warded him off. He didn't press—he was holding back.

They broke apart for the eighth time, and Treth, hopping from foot to foot, grinned madly. "Don't say you grow weary yet, youngling," he said. "I'm enjoying this."

Kalen dropped a hand to his heaving chest. It curled into a fist.

Treth came again, his lightning strike harder—more brutal. He hammered into Kalen's high guard, both hands on his sword, and Kalen compressed toward the ground.

Then the older man dropped a hand unexpectedly from his sword and punched at Kalen's face. Fayne bristled at the injustice, but Kalen seemed to have expected it. He grappled his left arm around Treth's and threw their flailing swords wide. They wrestled, each trying to push the other away, and finally half a dozen Watchmen rushed forward to pull them apart.

Fayne saw that the watching horde had grown—sixty or more folk were in the yard. Some commotion arose at the gates, but she couldn't see what it was.

Treth thrust, but Kalen moved so suddenly and quickly that the crowd gasped. He attacked high into Treth's attack, locking blades. The clash of steel rang blasphemously loud.

Kalen punched forward to shift his blade under Treth's and inside his guard. Treth's arm was hopelessly twisted and wide. Kalen grasped the older man's throat.

"Low guard," Kalen said. "Surely you know better than that."

A cry came from the gates and both of them looked, startled.

Fayne saw a girl—she realized, after a heartbeat, that it was Myrin—with a shimmering red gown and a wild, perfect sweep of silver hair that fell to her waist. She was as a magical apparition—so unexpected that the courtyard gaped at her.

Kalen hissed as Treth broke the hold and wrenched away. Kalen tried to follow, but Treth lashed out hard across his unprotected face with his padded blade, making a sound like a hammer on wet wood. Kalen's head snapped back and he fell, like a cut puppet, to the dirt.

"Kalen!" Myrin shrieked. She shoved past black-coated forms as she ran to him.

Treth stood over Kalen. He blew his nose on his hand then spat in the dust. "Well struck, Dren." He jerked his head at Myrin. "Now I see your weakness, Rayse's hound."

Kalen only glared at him, blood running from his nose. As he sat on the ground, coughing and retching, Fayne reflected that he must be as fine a mummer as she.

"What the Hells is this?" shouted a voice. Fayne recognized it from a past misunderstanding as that of Commander Kleeandur. Kleeandur was much like Bors Jarthay—whose tastes in women Fayne knew quite well—but older, harder, and less amusing. She'd crossed him before and come out the worse for it. She retreated behind a pillar as the commander strode into the yard.

Kleeandur grasped Treth by the arm. "What the Hells are you about, Vigilant?"

"Commander," Treth winced. "I can explain—"

"Caravan patrol for two tendays!" Jarthay shouted. "At half pay."

Fayne stuck out her tongue. What kind of vengeance was *that*? She would get Treth much worse than that for daring to hurt Kalen.

Since when do you care? she asked herself. You're just using him, anyway. Aye?

Kleeandur turned on Kalen, who lay coughing in the dirt. "And you, Dren," he said. "Brawling in the yard—goading him like that. Suspension without pay for a tenday."

Fayne almost screamed at the injustice of it, but Kalen only coughed and nodded. Kleeandur strode away, beckoning Treth to follow him. The man sneered at Kalen and went

Myrin arrived at Kalen's side and fell to her knees beside his sweaty, dirty form. "I'm sorry!" she cried, patting dust away from Kalen's head and shoulders. "I didn't mean—"

"Not your fault," Kalen murmured. He smiled at her, and his eyes sparkled.

Fayne shivered. Those . . . that . . . *gods!*

She realized then that her illusion had slipped away. No one had yet noticed, all eyes intent on the duel. Fayne didn't even care, until a small voice beside her asked, "Fayne?" She looked, and there was Cellica, peering up at her curiously. The halfling had entered with Myrin and picked her way through the crowd to Fayne's side. "What are you about?" Cellica's frown was suspicious.

Mind racing, Fayne grinned broadly. "I , . . ah . . ." Then her plans shifted in a heartbeat. "Cellica! Just the lass I was searching for. I have a small proposal for you—a favor that you might pay me, if you're interested."

Cellica's eyes widened. "Aye?"

CHAPTER TWENTY

As they climbed down from the carriage before the Temple of Beauty and joined the fancifully dressed revelers waiting outside, Kalen admitted to himself that he was not pleased.

But when he looked at it honestly, he had no one to blame but himself. He'd known this was a mistake. How had he let Cellica talk him into this?

"Give me one good reason why you *shouldn't* go as Shadowbane," she said.

When Kalen had given her seven, Cellica frowned. "Well . . . give me one more."

In the end, Kalen privately suspected she'd used the voice on him.

"Kalen?" Myrin asked at his side, calling him from his thoughts. "Is aught wrong?"

"No," he said, taking the opportunity once again to admire how the red gown and silver hair suited her. She looked uncomfortably womanly, rather than girlish. He hadn't said anything, of course, but that didn't stop him thinking it.

Mayhap that was why he hadn't argued against Cellica more effectively.

Don't let yourself be distracted, he thought. You can survive the night. It's just a ball.

He hoped there wouldn't be dancing. Graceful as he might be, he was a soldier. He knew nothing of the world of courtly balls or dancing.

They entered through the foyer, decorated with images of the Lady Firehair and her worshipers—beautiful and graceful creatures, all. Fountains shaped like embracing lovers trickled wine. Windows of stained glass depicting scenes from Sunite history let in the radiance of the rising moon. Guests were gathered, laughing and flirting with rose-robed priests and priestesses. This, Kalen could handle. Only a ball, he thought.

"Sorry again," Myrin said. "About yestereve—I didn't mean to hurt anyone."

Kalen shrugged.

"I thought for sure you'd bring Fayne," said Myrin. "She's your . . . ah?"

"No." Kalen looked at her blankly. "I know her about as well as I know you."

"Oh." Myrin held his arm a little tighter. He could have sworn she added, "Good."

"Saer and Lady—if you'll enter the grand courtyard?" A pretty acolyte gestured to a set of open golden doors carved with the visage of the goddess.

"Courtyard?" Kalen murmured, but he couldn't argue with Myrin's brilliant smile. She took his arm and pulled him along.

At least *Myrin* was happy.

Fayne was fuming. Kalen had taken that little chitling—not a real woman like herself.

The carriage started to turn onto the most direct thoroughfare, Aureenar Street, but Fayne wasn't about to lose a single moment of style. Ostentation made her feel better.

"Keep around!" Fayne snapped to the driver. "Up to the Street of Lances!"

The man in his pressed overcoat tipped his feathered hat. "Your coin, milady."

Since she had the carriage already, she might as well prolong her rich procession.

The carriage broke away from the loose train of vehicles and swerved northeast. Fayne smirked out the window, surveying the streets, the jovial taverns, and the folk walking.

Cellica, sitting across from Fayne, fidgeted her thumbs and chewed her lip. Their ride had included a visit to Nurneene's for masks, and the halfling wore a plain white eye mask with her gold gown. She'd added a lute to represent a bard Fayne had never heard of, but apparently halflings knew their own history quite well.

"How long will this be?" She looked at Fayne anxiously.

Fayne laughed. "Enjoy it, little one! Not every day working lasses like us ride in style."

"I appreciate you inviting me along, Fayne." The halfling smiled halfway. "I'm just worried about—" She peered out the window.

"Oh, don't fret!" Fayne insisted with a girlish smile. "I'm sure your jack can handle himself. That little wild-haired girl didn't look so vile." A touch dangerous, mayhap—but that was intriguing, rather than off-setting. If only the little scamp weren't interfering!

"No." Cellica smiled, apparently at the thought of Myrin. "No, she isn't."

Beshaba, Fayne thought, what is it that makes everyone cling to such pathetic waifs?

They continued north on the Singing Dolphin thoroughfare and turned east on the Street of Lances. Fayne grinned at onlookers, whose responding stares she chose to interpret as jealous. They turned south again on Stormstar's Ride. At the end of the street, they saw the Temple of Beauty.

"Ye gracious gods," Cellica murmured, eyes wide. She reached across for Fayne's hand.

"Shiny, eh?" Fayne took Cellica's hand automatically, and the halfling clutched her tightly.

Sune's Waterdeep temple was best approached from Stormstar, Fayne thought, and particularly at this time of evening, when the last rays of the setting sun fell upon its ruby towers and gold-inlaid windows. And from the look on Cellica's face, she was right.

The great cathedral, palace, and pleasure dome towered over the noble villas alongside, shining like a beautiful star of architectural brilliance. Soaring towers and seemingly impossible buttresses made for a façade of true grandeur, which masked an open-air ballroom from which the sounds of revelry could be heard even from far away.

The halfling smiled wanly all the way until the carriage let them off.

"Aye?" Fayne grinned. "Pleased?"

But Cellica said nothing—she looked at her feet nervously.

The iron-faced dwarf attendant at the door looked at their invitation—which Fayne had forged—without any suspicion, then eyed them appraisingly. It was uncommon that two women came to a revel together, but hardly rare. "Who're you lasses supposed to be?"

"Olive Ruskettle!" Cellica peeped, then she went back to staring at the temple.

The guard nodded—he seemed at least to have heard of the "first halfling bard"—then looked at Fayne. He handed back the scroll. "And you, lass?"

"Aye?" Fayne gestured down—black leggings tucked into swashbuckler boots, billowy white shirt and black vest, scarlet half-cape and matching dueling glove—and flipped her magic-blacked hair. She grinned through her scarlet fox mask. "I'm not . . . *famous?*"

The guard shook his head.

"Good," Fayne said, and she kissed the dwarf on the lips. "Tymora's kiss upon you!"

They skipped inside, arm in arm, Fayne pulling Cellica along.

.:⌢:.

"Your names?" the herald asked Kalen and Myrin inside the courtyard. Music wafted across the open space from minstrels near the central staircase.

Kalen hadn't thought about such a question. "Ah—"

"Lady Alustriel of Silverymoon," Myrin said without hesitation. Smiling beneath her gold mask and crown, she took Kalen's arm.

The herald nodded. He peered at Kalen's ragged old armor with a touch of distaste. At least Kalen had let Cellica buy him a new cloak. "Of course, your ladyship."

He stepped forward and called to the assembled, "Alustriel of the Seven, and escort."

Heads turned—apparently, dressing as such a famous lady was daring—and Kalen felt Myrin stiffen. But most of the masked or painted faces wore smiles. There was even applause.

Myrin relaxed. "Good," she said, clutching her stomach.

"Outstanding," Kalen agreed, though he wasn't sure he meant it.

She smiled at him in a way that made his chest tingle.

In the courtyard, Kalen and Myrin looked out over a sea of revelers dressed in bright colors and daring fashions. Kings and tavern wenches mingled and laughed around braziers, and foppishly dressed rapscallions flirted with regal queens and warrior women. Muscular youths in the furs and leather of northern barbarians boasted over tankards of mead, eyeing dancing lasses dressed in yellows and oranges, reds and greens, like nymphs and dryads. The dancers whirled across the floor while musicians struck up a jaunty chorus on yartings, flutes, and racing drums.

The ballroom was open to the night sky, and though the season was cool, braziers and unseen magic kept the courtyard comfortable—teasingly so, inviting revelers to disrobe and enjoy the headiness of Sune's temple. And, Kalen noted, some of the revelers were doing just that.

They had arrived in time to witness the finale of a dance between two ladies. One—their hostess, Lorien Dawnbringer—wore gold accented with bright pinks and reds. The other, a dark-haired elf clad in sleek black, was unknown to him. They whirled gracefully, in perfect balance, arms and legs curling artfully. Most of the nobles were watching their dance, enraptured, and when the women finished and bowed to one another, the courtyard erupted in applause and cheers.

Lorien, panting delicately, bowed to the gathered folk. The elf smiled and nodded. They joined hands and bowed to one another. Then Lorien turned up the courtyard stairs and climbed slowly, turning to wave every few steps, as the elf lady disappeared into the throng of nobles.

Myrin tensed at his side. "The *dance!*" she cried. "We didn't miss it, did we?"

"What?" Entirely too much dancing was still going on, Kalen thought.

"Lady Ilira Nathalan," said Myrin. "And that priestess—Lady Lorien."

Several nearby lordlings and ladies rolled their eyes at her outburst.

"Nay, nay," said a youthful man at their side. He wore the simple but stylish robes of a Sunite priest. "You've not missed it. They dance again at midnight—Lady Lorien will return to dance with Lady Ilira, as the sun with the night. In the middle-time, enjoy yourselves."

"Oh," Myrin said. She smiled vaguely.

The acolyte took Myrin's hands and kissed them. "Let me know if there is aught I might do to aid in this," he whispered with a sly wink. Myrin blushed fiercely.

The priest took Kalen's hands and paid him the same obeisance, to which Kalen nodded.

When the acolyte had gone, Myrin's eyes roved the crowded nobles, as though searching for someone. She found something far more interesting. "Food, Kalen!" Myrin gasped. "Look at all the *food!*"

"Yes—let's . . ." Kalen swallowed. The spectacle dizzied him. "Let's go there first."

Banquet tables around the yard were stacked high with the bounty of the realm. Myrin found sweetmeats and fruits, honey and melon and tarts, breads of a score of grains carved in the shapes of animals, wines of a hundred lands, cheeses of dozens of creatures.

While Myrin piled her plate high, Kalen scanned the party. Merriment filled the courtyard: the murmur of a thousand conversations, laughs, and whispers in out-of-the-way corners where intimate encounters waited.

Damn, Kalen thought, seeing the lovers in their half-hidden alcoves. He glanced at Myrin—at her slender posterior as she bent to inspect some cheeses—and blushed. Amazing what a difference a proper gown made to Myrin—that and the silver hair, which went so perfectly with her skin like polished oak. The red silk forced Kalen to see her for the woman she was, and that scared him as much as pleased him.

A thought occurred, then, and Kalen shuddered. Gods—she might ask him to *dance*.

To distract himself, he tried to recognize the costumes. Kalen was no student of history, and he did not recognize all the masks and manners, but he remembered a few heroes from the chapbooks he had bought and occasionally scanned. Mostly, he knew them by their salacious parodies—little about their true lives—and it made him feel even more awkward.

Kalen stood stiffly, trying to quell a wave of panic that had begun in his stomach and threatened to engulf the rest of him. Too many folk—and too much Myrin.

Were she here, Fayne would have a great laugh about this, he had no doubt.

The herald's next call perked Kalen's ears. "Ladies and lords, the Old Mage and escort, the Nightingale of Everlund," he cried. "Representatives of the Waterdhavian Guard."

Kalen froze at the words and turned slowly around.

"Kalen?" Myrin asked, her mouth half-full, but Kalen didn't acknowledge her.

Instead, he stared at the woman he least expected to see: Araezra, walking the halls on the arm of Bors Jarthay. It was the tradition of Watchmen to wear their arms and armor to costume revels—for instant use if needed—but to alter the garb with a tabard or cloak that could quickly be discarded in the event of trouble. Araezra's tabard depicted a stylized bird in purple embroidery. She carried a shield painted with the same bird, and she'd dyed her hair a lustrous auburn.

He told himself he should be keeping his distance, since she was one of only a few who could recognize Shadowbane. Kalen ducked behind a knot of nobles praying she wouldn't see him.

Fortunately, Araezra was distracted by something Jarthay had said. The commander had shirked tradition and opted to dress as a buffoonish sort of wizard in a red robe and an obviously false beard. He looked more than a little drunk; in fact, as Kalen watched, Jarthay took a swig of something from a flask crudely disguised as a pipe.

"A moment," Kalen murmured toward Myrin. Then he cut into the crowd, looking for a mercyroom or a broom closet or at least an alcove where he could lose the tell-tale helm. He could escape—he could . . .

When a hand fell on his arm, he whirled, thinking certainly it was Araezra.

"Behold, the day improves!" a woman said. "Unveil yourself, man—and don't try to lie about your name, for I'll know."

The noblewoman in question—barely more than a girl, Kalen saw—wore a tattered black gown and must have enchanted her hair, for as he watched, it writhed like a rustling nest of silver vipers. Her gown was cut cunningly and scandalously, with more gods' eye slits than dress. He knew her apparel from stories—the legendary Simbul, the Witch-Queen of Aglarond.

"Choose your words with care!" the girl said with a confident sneer beneath her half mask. "I've been taking lessons from the greatest truth-teller in Waterdeep, Lady Ilira herself! I can hear lies in a voice or read them in a face . . ." She snaked her fingers across his mask. "That is, I *could* read your face if you'd be so good as to unmask yourself." Her hand retracted and she grinned at him—much like a cat grins at a mouse. "For now, a name will do."

Kalen stumbled in his head for a reply. "But lady, my name—"

The girl smirked at his consternation. "I don't mean your *true* name, good saer," she said. She gestured to his outfit. "I mean, who are you meant to *be?*"

That didn't make it better. He didn't have an answer for that, either.

"Lay off him, Wildfire." The venomous lady's voice behind Kalen's back saved him, and he felt something take hold of his arm. "I saw him first!"

Wildfire. He knew that nickname. He didn't remember the girl's true name, but Lady Wildfire, heir of House Wavesilver, was infamous for one of the sharpest tongues in Waterdeep. Kalen remembered Cellica telling him considerable gossip about her, and wished he'd listened more. As it was, he'd heard enough to thank the gods someone had saved him.

Until he looked around.

Kalen gawked at a petite woman dressed in a gown composed of black leather and webbing—not much of either—that barely covered her most precious family heirlooms. Her skin was tinted black and her hair was snowy white. Her skin matched her garments perfectly, especially her thigh-high boots with heels as long as fighting dirks, giving her a height to match his. She fingered the handle of a whip wrapped around her waist.

It took Kalen a breath to recognize her: a drow priestess of the spider goddess, Lolth. He knew she wasn't really a drow, as she'd made no attempt to disguise her human features. This did not surprise him: lordlings and lordlasses were quite vain. The whip didn't match, either—it made her look more a priestess of Loviatar, goddess of pain.

At his side, Kalen heard breath catch and saw The Simbul's eyes light up with fire that was anything but magical.

"Perhaps you saw him first, Talantress Roaringhorn—but I *claimed* him first," Lady Wildfire said in a low, dangerous hiss. "I'm surprised to see you, after last month's scandal. If I recall—the Whipmaster and his . . . *whip?*"

Kalen knew Lady Roaringhorn as well—Cellica had mentioned aught of such a scandal, though he remembered no details. He did recall that these noble girls *hated* each other, and competed in all ways—for the best salons, fashion, marriage, anything that could be fought over. For Waterdeep entire, if it was on the table.

"A misunderstanding," Talantress said tightly.

"Mmm. Aye, you leather-wrapped tramp," Wildfire countered.

"Kindly note my utter lack of surprise," Talantress said, "that you're so crude."

Wildfire hummed—almost purred—at Kalen. "Mmmm. Buck-toothed tease." She shot a glance at Talantress.

"Ah!" Talantress glared. "That will be quite enough, slut of a dull-eyed dwarf!"

"Gutter-battered wick-licker!" Wildfire put her fingers to her lips and licked them.

"How unwashed!" Talantress's wrath had almost broken through her calm face, but she seemed possessed of as much self-control as Araezra. Her lip curled derisively. "I wonder about those tales in the sheets about all those sweaty dockhands that loiter around Wavesilver manor. I'm sure they're very helpful with your . . . *boat.*"

"That's more than enough!" Wildfire's eyes flashed. She looked to Kalen. "We'll let Lord *Nameless* decide."

"What?" Kalen goggled.

Wildfire caught up his right hand and wound herself into his arm; her smile could cut diamonds and her glare was positively deadly. If The Simbul of legend had half that sort of menace, no wonder she'd kept Thay so terrified so long. "Choose," she said coldly.

Talantress curled herself around his left side. Kalen was almost glad he couldn't feel much, or all that magic-black skin would drive him to distraction. "You'd better choose *me,* or you'll regret it," she whispered. "I'll make personally sure."

"Choose *me,*" Wildfire purred in his other ear. "I'm much more fun than she is." Her tone shifted from suggestive to commanding. "And my uncles are richer—and employ more swordsmen to throttle fools who spurn me."

"Ah," Kalen said, his mind racing to match his thundering heart.

"Ninny!" Wildfire said. "You want *me,* aye saer?"

Talantress grasped Kalen's other arm. "He's dancing with *me.*"

"Me!" Lady Wildfire hissed.

All the while, Kalen watched as Araezra wandered toward them. He couldn't get away, not with the ladies fighting over him. He was trapped.

"You should spare yon knight, ladies," said a gentle voice behind them.

The soft and alluring voice—strangely familiar—froze him in place like a statue.

"Ilira!" Wildfire's eyes widened, and she curtsied deeply. Her beautiful face broke into a genuine smile. "So good to see you."

"Lady Nathalan." Talantress gave her a false smile. "We did not ask *your* opinion." Her tone was that of a noble addressing a lesser—an upstart merchant, whose only honor lay in coin.

"Apologies, young Lady Roaringhorn. I only meant to warn of knights who wear gray and walk lonely roads." A velvet-gloved hand touched Kalen's elbow. "Like this one."

Kalen turned. Lady Ilira—the eladrin he'd seen dancing with Lorien—stood just to his shoulder, but her presence loomed greater than her size. Perhaps it was the weight of years—like all elves, she wore a timelessness about her that defied any attempt to place her age. Her face hid behind a velvet half-mask that revealed only her cheeks and thin lips.

Her pupil-less eyes gleamed bright and golden like those of a wolf, with all the tempestuous hunger to match. Those eyes had seen centuries of pain and joy, Kalen thought. Wisdom lurked there, and a sort of sadness that chilled his heart and shivered his knees.

Ilira wore a seamless low-cut black gown that left her shoulders and throat bare but otherwise covered every inch of her body, highlighting and enhancing her skin. Her midnight hair was bound in an elaborate bun at the back of her head. She wore what he thought was a wide black necklace that broke the smooth expanse of her breast. He realized quickly that it was not jewelry—she wore naught of that but a star sapphire pendant looped around her left wrist—but rather a series of black runes inked in her flesh, which gleamed as though alive.

She had asked him a question, Kalen realized. He also realized he'd been staring at her chest, and his face flushed. Not for the first time, he thanked the gods for his full helm.

"Is this not so, Sir Shadow?" Ilira asked again.

Why was her cool, lovely voice so damned familiar? Where did he know it from?

"It is," Kalen said, because he could say nothing else.

Lady Wildfire laughed and clapped her hands, delighted to see Lady Ilira proven right. Talantress scowled on Kalen's other side. "Spare us your poetry, coin-pincher," she spat. "I'm taking him to dance now—unless you plan to steal him yourself?" She sneered at Lady Ilira. Her voice might have been that of a serpent. "But surely you wouldn't be interested—surely you'd not sully yourself with us mere *humans.*"

Ilira smiled and released Kalen's arm, the better to focus on the drow-glamoured girl.

"If I were you, Talantress Roaringhorn," Ilira said, "I should not fight battles that cannot be won—particularly over those whose worth is not measured in *noble* blood." She winked at Kalen.

"You mean—he's not *noble?*" Talantress peered down her nose. "How unwashed."

"Tala." Ilira laid a gloved hand on her arm. "Is not your *precious time* better spent finding a suitable mate for resting 'twixt your nethers? Aye, I believe your *time* grows short." The emphasis she put on the words struck Kalen, but he hadn't the least idea what she meant.

By the way her face turned white as fresh cream—despite the glamour that painted her skin black—Talantress certainly did. Her lip trembled and she gazed at Ilira in shock before she stumbled away. Several lordlings turned to gawk as she scrambled ungracefully through the throng—and thus did those men earn slaps or harsh words from their feminine companions.

Kalen looked back to the ladies, who shared a smug smile. "I cannot dance," he said.

"That hardly matters, saer, if the Lady Ilira partners you." Wildfire laughed. Then she turned her wicked smile on the elf. "If she beats *me,* of course."

"Oh?" Ilira turned to the girl and raised one eyebrow.

"What boots it?" Wildfire put her hands on her hips and set her stance. "I love common men as well as nobles." She smirked at Ilira. "I shall fight you for him! Choose the game."

"Very well." Ilira nodded serenely. "You are a brave and bold student, Alondra," she said. "But let us see how *good* a student you are. You will tell me whether I speak a lie or the truth, and if you are right, he is all yours." She winked at Kalen. "Gods help him."

Wildfire straightened her shoulders. "I accept!"

Ilira closed her eyes and breathed gently. Serenity fell in that moment, and the dancers and gossipers and servants around them grew hushed and seemed far away.

The elf opened her eyes again, and they seemed wet. "I wear this black in mourning," she said. "For my dearest friend, who was taken from me long ago through my own cowardice."

Wildfire looked positively stunned, as though Ilira had smitten her with a mighty blow.

"Oh, my lady," she said. "I'm so sorry—I did not know . . ."

Ilira looked away. "It seems you believed me," she said. "Aye?"

Wildfire nodded solemnly, and Kalen saw tears in her eyes. The rest of her face revealed nothing though, and he marveled at what must be self-discipline like iron. Like Araezra.

Ilira smiled. "What a pity." With that, she led Kalen toward the center of the dancers.

"What?" Wildfire colored red to the base of her silvered hair. "*What?*"

But they were safely protected from any fury she might have wrought, blocked by a living wall of nobility clad in the finest costumes and brightest colors coin or magic could buy. And on Lady Ilira's arm, Kalen could see no one else.

It completely escaped him, moreover, that a dance with her might attract exactly the sort of attention he didn't want.

"Olive Ruskettle and . . ." the herald looked at Fayne, who just smiled. "Escort."

Arm in arm, Cellica and Fayne looked out into the courtyard full of revelers and song. The dancing—the music—the colors—the gaiety! Cellica, in a word, *loved* it.

"I'm so glad you came by an invitation," the halfling said. "Funny you didn't dress as anyone in particular, though. I was sure—"

"Pay it naught," Fayne said, her eye drawn to the dancers in the courtyard. She stiffened, as though she saw someone familiar.

"What?" Cellica asked, straining to see, but everyone was too tall. "Who is it?"

"No one," Fayne said. "No one of any consequence."

"One moment." Fayne let go of Cellica's arm and skipped away through a mass of nobles—roaring drunk and dressed as fur-draped Uthgardt barbarians.

"What? Wait!" the halfling cried. "Fayne!"

But Fayne was gone, leaving Cellica lost in a forest of revelers.

With a harrumph, she started looking for Kalen or Myrin.

Not bothering with the servants' stairs, Fayne made her way immediately to the grand staircase that led to the balcony on the second floor. There she'd find the rooms of worship and splendor—where her mark waited, preparing for her dance at midnight.

On the way, she nestled something amongst the statues of naked dancers that flanked the stairs. The item was a small box her patron had given her—a portable spelltrap—into which she had placed an enchantment of her own, one of her most powerful. The item gave off only a faint aura when inactive, and with a courtyard full of woven spells and the temple wards, no one would notice until it was tripped. And by then, enough chaos would be caused.

Two jacks, descending the stairs hand in hand, looked at her askance, but she just nodded. "Sune smile upon you," she said.

They replied in kind and joined the throng.

Fayne, managing to keep herself from giggling like a clever child, strung the privacy rope between the statues' hands and nodded to the watchmen, who smiled indulgently and knowingly. Just a reveler off to some tryst.

Oh, yes, fools—oh, yes.

Fayne skipped up toward Lorien Dawnbringer's chamber. No guards milled about—why would they, when all were below, at the revel?

Fayne knocked gently, and a womanly voice came from within. "Who calls?"

Then Fayne remembered, and swore mutely. She had almost forgotten—dressed in these ridiculous clothes—a face to go with the attire.

She ripped off her fox mask and passed her wand over her body, head to toe. She shrank herself thinner and a little shorter, her face slimming and sharpening, and she became the elf to whom this outfit belonged—the one Fayne remembered in her nightmares.

Fayne always committed herself fully, throwing herself into danger with wild abandon.

The door opened, and Lorien peered out, blinking in genuine surprise. "Lady Ilira?"

Fayne gave her a confident wink, then she leaped into Lorien's arms. She kicked the door closed as they staggered inside.

CHAPTER TWENTY-ONE

I T WAS A TRICK," KALEN SAID AS ILIRA LED HIM TOWARD THE DANCERS. "What you told her."

"What, saer?"

"It was both true and false," Kalen said. "Your face is covered, and I couldn't tell from your voice or your eyes, but I saw it in your throat. You lied, in part, and told true in another."

"How intriguing, good Sir Shadow." Lady Ilira looked at him with some interest. "When you become more . . . *familiar* with moon elves such as myself, you will note that our ears tell lies more clearly than anything else."

Kalen's heart beat a little faster at the thought of becoming familiar with this woman. "Will you solve the mystery, then?"

"I did lose my dearest friend long ago," she said. "But I do not dress in black for him."

"A half-truth, shrouded in lie." Surprisingly, he could feel her hand—very warm—in his.

"Like a paladin shrouded in night," she said. "Light hidden in twilight, aye?"

A song was ending—a gentle Tethyrian melody, with decorous dancing to match. Kalen knew styles of music—he had once romanced a traveling bard of Cormyr—but dancing was quite beyond him. He hoped he did not disappoint the graceful elf.

As though she read his thoughts, she smiled again. "Never fear, saer—I shall teach you."

Lady Ilira released his hand—he felt the loss of her touch keenly—and presented herself before him. She offered an elegant, deep bow, which Kalen returned.

They waited for the applause to die down and for the lordlings to select new partners. Most of this was according to rote, already long established. Many envious glances fell on Kalen and Lady Ilira, who was clearly one of the most beautiful and graceful ladies in the ballroom. In particular, one sour-faced elf lord was glaring at him. That one wore a long false beard and black robes, making him look like a dark sorcerer. Gloves of deep red velvet gleamed, and Kalen could see his fingers tapping impatiently. Kalen felt unsettled.

"Ruldrin Sandhor," she said. "I imagine he does not like to see me dance with a commoner. But I dance with whom I wish—I always have."

Kalen smiled wryly. "How did you know I was not noble, lady?" he asked.

"The way I know *I* am not." She chuckled. "It is obvious."

"Your husband does not make you noble?" Kalen offered. "Lord Sandhor, mayhap?"

"Oh, good saer." She showed him that she wore no rings over her gloves. "No husband."

Then she took his hands and placed his right on her hip and kept his left hand in her right. "You are fortunate," she said. "As a man, the dance is easier."

The bards played the first few strains of what sounded like a vigorous refrain, then paused to give the dancers a chance to pair off in preparation.

With her left hand on Kalen's shoulder, Lady Ilira reached up for his brow, and his heart leaped at the thought that she might remove his helm and kiss him—but her hand only touched his mask. For some reason, he thought of Fayne, and wondered where she might be.

"Who are you thinking of, I wonder?" she asked as they bowed to one another.

That snapped him back to the ball. "Ah, no one . . ." Kalen floundered.

"Fear not—I am not jealous," Ilira said. "Your face is hidden, but I can see your eyes well enough." She grinned mischievously. "Keep your secrets as you will."

Her exotic eyes—pure metallic gold without iris or pupil—were unreadable, but he sensed her wisdom—and playfulness. "Indeed, lady."

They danced. The steps were foreign, as he'd feared, but not difficult. He credited his movements to the superior skill of Lady Ilira, who was without a doubt the finest dancer he could have imagined. She flowed through the movements, letting her skirts and sleeves trail like wings as though she were flying. Her shadow seemed to dance independently of her, with the same movements but in different directions, but Kalen reasoned that was a trick of the light.

After the first tune, there was applause and the dancers bowed. He seized the opportunity to remove his gloves and stuff them in his belt. Hands shifted and partners moved, but Lady Ilira seized Kalen's arm and held him steady, her eyes like yellow diamonds binding him in place.

With more confidence than the first time, he laid his bare fingers on her hip. Without his gloves, he tried and failed to feel the silk of her gown; all he could feel was the heat of her flesh beneath. Maybe he was touching her too hard—he had no way of knowing—or maybe she was pleased. Regardless, her whole body reacted to his touch, sending tingles up his arm. She was like an immortal creature—not at all human or even elf. A spirit.

They danced again—this time to a Sword Coast tune more forgiving of missteps.

"What was it you meant, touching Lady Roaringhorn?" Kalen asked.

"My good knight, your mind wanders Downshadow, to think of me touching Talantress."

Kalen fought to keep the heat out of his cheeks. "I mean about her 'precious time.' "

"I happen to have heard of a tiny enchantment." She looked at him knowingly. "Secrets are coin, saer—interested in buying one?"

Kalen smirked. "If I'm to keep mine, you'll keep yours."

She nodded serenely.

The minstrels began another song—this one much faster—and rather than let him go, Lady Ilira grasped Kalen harder. It was a Calishite rhythm, he realized—a dance of passion and heat, more akin to loveplay than innocent dance. Watch horns blared in his mind, and he repeated to himself that he could not dance, but his feet didn't listen, and his hands—*well*.

He'd thought her skilled before, but now—with such a tempestuous dance—Lady Ilira was wonderful. Her leg wrapped around his, bringing heat into his cheeks, and she turned around him so gracefully, so expertly, that he might have thought them destined to dance together. He saw her eyes flash; she couldn't have failed to note the steel strapped to the insides of his thighs.

Then she whirled up, pressing herself hard against him, arms around his neck, lips almost against his ear. He felt the whole of her, and he tingled.

The dance lulled, allowing for folk to stand.

"Well, good saer," she whispered in his ear. "You're full of hidden dangers."

Kalen didn't flinch. "Care to search them out?" he whispered back.

She pressed her lips to the mask of his helm: kissing the shadow, not the man. Then she said—aloud for the benefit of the dancers nearby, "Keep your dagger in your breeches, goodsir."

Kalen couldn't help but smile.

The dance built to a furious tempo that he could hardly follow. He felt more and more as though he were merely there to allow Lady Ilira to show herself, and show herself she did. All eyes in the hall fell upon her, and all but the most vigorous dancers stopped to watch.

Kalen wondered about the runes tattooed across her collarbone. What did they mean? He realized they were Dethek, the script of dwarves. Why would an elf wear dwarven runes?

Ilira whirled and met him once more, and he caught her in a fierce embrace. They spun together once, twice—then he held her bent low like a swooned woman as the song ended. Their eyes met, and she smirked at him—mysterious, alluring, *dangerous*.

As the hall erupted in applause, her expression became a wide grin—the first genuine smile he'd seen her wear. Kalen couldn't help but sigh, pleased.

Ilira made him think, oddly, of Fayne—how he wanted to see her smile like that.

Ilira rose and laughed, curtsying to the crowd in an elegant fashion. She smiled and waved, and blew a kiss at the sour-faced silk merchant she'd pointed out earlier, Lord Sandhor. Kalen did little more than stand stiffly and wait for her to return. She did so, bowing to him as was proper.

"What have you lost, Lady?" Kalen asked.

Her smile instantly vanished, replaced by a dangerous cold. Unconsciously, Kalen's hand twitched toward one of those knives he'd been thinking of just breaths earlier, but he reined his impulse.

"Your tattoo." He nodded to the runes inked along her collarbone. "*Gargan vathkelke kaugathal*—Dwarvish, aye? I know only *vathkel*—lost. What does the rest mean?"

He raised his hand toward her chest. He didn't intend to touch the tattoo, but perhaps he did—he couldn't feel anything. His thoughts were suddenly distant—only the warmth of her body pressed against his, the sweet lavender perfume of her hair, the cool velvet of her gloves . . . he wanted—he *yearned*—to know how her skin felt.

But Lady Ilira broke away from him, hand reaching halfway to her chest. Her eyes like burnished gold coins were far away—distant and sad. "No," she said, and he could have sworn before the Eye of Justice that he saw tears in her eyes. "Good saer, my thanks for the dance."

"Wait, I did not mean—" he said.

"Your pardon, boy," said a velvety smooth and dagger-sharp voice behind him. The robed elf—Sandhor—slid past him and seized Ilira's gloved hands in his own. "Does this human offend, my twilight dove?" He glared back, down his impressive nose.

Ilira blinked over Sandhor's shoulder at Kalen, and for an instant, he thought her eyes were pleading. Then she assumed a brilliant smile and put her hand on his shoulder.

"Ruldrin, heart, just in time—" They swept into the dance. "I've been meaning to discuss your latest donation to the Haven."

"What donation?" Ruldrin favored Kalen with a cruel smile over Ilira's shoulder.

"Exactly," the elf woman said sweetly.

They whirled away, leaving Kalen stunned and very alone amidst the other dancers.

He saw, over the whirling gowns, a face framed by red-dyed hair: Araezra. "Gods," he murmured, and ducked away. With that display, she must have seen him and recognized the outfit. Yes, she was coming his way. *Idiot*.

He was making his way back to Myrin when he smelled something strange—something burning. He looked at his hand, and saw—mutely— smoke rising from his fingertips. The tips of his fore and middle finger were blistered and bleeding.

When had *that* happened?

"Hmm-*mmm*," Fayne moaned, lounging in one end of Lorien's golden bathtub. "Perfect."

The priestess, ensconced at her own end, watched Fayne with a serene smile on her face. Her cheeks were rosy in the candlelight reflected off the warm water.

"Dancing next?" Lorien asked. "Our appointed arrival at midnight cannot be far off."

"Just," Fayne said, stroking one of Lorien's long, slender legs. "Just a little longer."

The priestess smiled and closed her eyes. Fayne hadn't been certain this would be the right course—seduction, her favorite method—but it was certainly paying off thus far. And if she enjoyed it a little herself, all the better! Time enough to dispense pain after pleasure, aye?

Careful, she thought. You'll sound like that Roaringhorn girl you humiliated last month.

The memory made her giggle. The *whipmaster*. She had rather liked wearing such a big, muscle-bound form. It had felt stupid and thick, but oh so enjoyable—particularly after.

Lorien saw her smile. "What are you thinking of?"

"A jest—nothing." Fayne in Ilira's form giggled again. "You?"

Lorien stretched and drew herself out of the bath, gleaming and perfect. The light glittered off her soft curves. Fayne told herself to remember that effect, to use some day.

"Many things." Lorien crossed to a divan and drew a ruby red robe around her lovely body. "Things about you—and about us."

"Oh?" Fayne pressed her breasts against the edge of the gold tub and grinned. "What?"

"First—" Lorien lifted from the divan an ornate, golden rod. "Have I shown you this?"

"And what might *that* be for?" asked Fayne, still blissful.

Lorien smiled. "Revealing secrets," she said. "From a false face."

Fayne didn't understand immediately, and that proved her undoing. "What do you—?"

Lorien gestured languidly. "Come." Her word was powerful and inescapable.

The hairs rose on Fayne's neck—a magical attack. Fayne's will hammered at the command, but her body was already caught. She stood, trembling, and wrenched herself out of the bath. Against her will, her body began walking toward Lorien.

"I don't understand," Fayne said. "Heart, what are you—"

Lorien shook her head. "Whatever you are, creature," she said, "Ilira and I love each other well, but you misunderstand our relationship. A pity for you."

Fayne's mind whirled. "I felt . . ." she tried. "I felt it was time to . . . My love, don't punish me for my haste! I only wanted to take us to another ledge, my darling one!"

Lorien rolled her eyes. As Fayne stood before her, Lorien gestured for her to kneel, and Fayne did so. "I can't decide," she said, "whether you are one of my enemies, or one of hers." She shifted the golden rod from hand to hand. "Which is it, child?"

"Dear heart," Fayne gasped. "I don't understand what you mean."

"Show truth," Lorien intoned in Elvish, and tapped Fayne on the forehead with the rod.

Fayne screeched, loud and long, as magic ripped away from her, shattering her illusions and deceptions. They faded in sequence: first Ilira's face, then the conjured black hair, then the alluring features, then—as her skin prickled and stretched—her entire shape began to shift, back to—good *gods*—back to her true self. Something that was certainly not a half-elf.

Lorien gasped. "One of Lilten's creatures," she said. "Ilira warned me."

Those names. Ilira, the woman Fayne hated, but the other. How did she know . . . ?

Fayne looked at herself, at her black-nailed fingers and alabaster skin. Her tail slapped her legs. Not her real body—not now! She pawed at her garish pink hair and screamed.

"Gods." Lorien put out a trembling hand, reaching toward Fayne's head by reflex. "That explains everything. I'm sorry, child. I didn't—"

There came a rush and a snickering sound, and Lorien's head snapped back. Fayne looked at her, confused.

For a heartbeat, Lorien stood there, bent backward, standing erect.

Then she fell in a geyser of blood from her opened throat. The priestess slumped to the floor, twitching and dying.

Rath stood near them. He had struck and sheathed his blade in a single movement.

"What?" Fayne's mind barely functioned. "I thought . . . you said you never use that."

The dwarf looked down at her as one might look at a child. "For those who are worthy," he said. "And those for whom I have been paid."

Fayne stared numbly at Lorien—at the blood spreading around her face—and could not think. The priestess's eyes blinked rapidly, and she tried to speak but only gurgled. Fayne's stomach turned over and she felt like vomiting into the golden tub.

Rath turned away from Fayne in disgust. "Clean yourself. Put your mask back on."

Fayne grasped her head, which was reeling. Magic drained the vitality from her limbs, but those limbs shifted, their deathly pallor replaced by the smooth warmth of her half-elf body. She felt her teeth—normal once more—and sighed in deep relief. It was only an illusion and would have to last until she could perform her ritual again, but it was enough.

She rose on shaky, weak legs. Rath didn't help her.

Finally, her ugly self hidden, she could think clearly again. The enormity of Rath's actions struck her, and she gasped.

"You stupid son of a mother-suckling goat!" she screamed at the dwarf as she wound a white towel around her nakedness. She pointed at Lorien, who lay dying on the floor. "She wasn't supposed to die—I didn't pay you to *kill* her!

Rath shrugged. "You are welcome."

"You beardless idiot!" Fayne's face felt like it would explode. "*Who asked you?* Who asked you to step in? I had everything under my hand, every—*urt!*"

The dwarf seized her by the throat, cutting off words and air. Choking, she could not resist as he forced her against the wall and pinned her there with his arm. Her weak fingers could only flail at his ironlike arm.

"Her, I took coin to kill," Rath whispered in her ear. "You, I slay for free."

Fayne gasped as light entered her vision.

CHAPTER TWENTY-TWO

KALEN FOUND MYRIN SURROUNDED BY A CROWD OF ADMIRERS—young noble lads who were taking turns trying to get the silver-haired girl to dance. She kept giggling at their flattery and answering their increasingly bawdy compliments innocently. While her gold crown-mask hid her face, Kalen thought he saw understanding and bemusement in her eyes.

"Kalen!" she said as he approached, and the noble lads looked around.

Kalen flinched—she shouldn't use his name when he was trying to keep a low cloak.

The lads puffed themselves up against him, but one sweep of his icy eyes and they turned to easier sport elsewhere. At least the damned Shadowbane getup was good for something tonight.

Myrin threw herself into Kalen's arms. "Hee!" she said. "I'm having such a—*heep!*—marvelous time." She ran her pale fingers along his black leathers. "Dance with me."

Newly confident in that regard from his dance with Lady Ilira, Kalen thought at first to accept. Then he thought better of it, owing to the scent of flowery wine on her breath. From that and the slur in her speech, Kalen could tell Myrin was quite drunk.

"There you are!" said a familiar voice. Cellica appeared out from under a banquet table.

"How did—how did you get in here?" Kalen asked.

"Fayne brought me," Cellica said. "Haven't you seen her?"

"Fayne?" Kalen furrowed his brow inside his helm. It was hot and hard to think in there—good thing Cellica hadn't seen him dancing, or she'd start blaming that for any . . .

"Aye," the halfling said. "Little red-headed half-elf dressed as a swash-buckler . . . maybe you didn't notice her while you were dancing with that elf hussy. Who was she, anyway?"

"Uh." Kalen flinched. He remembered Cellica speaking of Lady Ilira, usually in glowing terms. Perhaps it was for the best that she hadn't recognized the woman.

Cellica stared up at him, tapping her foot. "Well?"

"Well what?" Kalen flinched away from Myrin teasing at his mask.

Cellica looked at the intoxicated woman in his arms.

"Eep!" Myrin said, and she giggled.

"Oh." Kalen hitched Myrin up and set her down on the table with a bump that made her giggle. "I wasn't doing—"

Cellica just narrowed her eyes, and Kalen sighed.

At that moment, a scream split the night, cutting through the music of the minstrels. The murmur of conversation, jests, and laughter died a little, and nervous titters followed the scream, as though it were a jape or prank played by some noble lass with more drink in her than sense.

Myrin shivered. "Kalen, I don't think I like this ball any more."

Louder screams followed—screams of someone being tortured in the rooms above—and the revelers could ill laugh it off. "Fayne," Kalen said, recognizing the voice.

Cellica went white.

"We need to get up there," Kalen said.

Kalen saw a pair of guardsmen start up the grand staircase, only to meet a crimson flash. Black, froth-covered fangs appeared in the air, gnashing and tearing at the first guard. The others paused, horror-stricken, and disembodied mouths struck at them, too. Ladies screamed and panic broke around the stairs as the spell struck celebrants and revelers at random. The other guards employed to watch over the revel could not get through the crush of bodies.

"Not the stairs," Kalen said, and Cellica nodded.

The screams died, but chaos was in full bloom. Revelers scrambled this way and that, shouting and shoving. Kalen saw noblemen arguing, terrified, hands on their blades, and he knew a brawl was imminent.

Abruptly, another cry came—loud and wrenching—from the midst of the dancers. Kalen looked, for he recognized the voice: Lady Ilira had backed away from Lord Sandhor, clutching at her throat. The elf merchant stepped toward her, casting the shadow of his cloak around her, but she shook her head to whatever he was saying. She vanished into him, as though she had stepped *through* him. She did not appear out the other side.

Wide-eyed, Kalen looked at Cellica, and the halfling nodded.

"Kalen?" Myrin asked sleepily. "Kalen, what's going on?"

"Have you your murderpiece, wee lady?" Kalen asked, drawing the daggers from their sheaths against the inside of his thighs. Where Lady Ilira's leg had wrapped, he recalled.

Cellica gave an impish smile and drew out her necklace, with its little crossbow-shaped charm. "Always." She spoke a word in an ancient language, and the medallion grew to fit her hand. She wound the crossbow with two quick twists of her wrist. "And don't call me 'wee.'"

Kalen boosted the little woman up on his shoulders and bent his knees.

"Kalen?" Myrin's face was pale. She seemed sober—and frightened. "Where—?"

"Wait." Kalen cupped her chin and rubbed her cheek with his thumb. "We'll be back."

He scooped up Cellica, hopped onto the banquet table, and ran. When he reached the end, his boots gleamed with blue fire and he leaped for the edge of the balcony. He caught it with one hand, hoisted Cellica up, and swung himself over the rail.

Myrin's hair rustled in the wind of Kalen's jump. He and Cellica flew up and away, toward the balcony where the screams had come from. Many revelers looked up, startled, and shouts renewed. Men argued, shouted, and shoved.

She wondered what magic let him jump like that—leaving a thin trail of blue flame.

Myrin only watched Kalen as he flew, and silently cursed herself.

"Of course he didn't kiss you, you ninny," she said, fighting the tears. "You get drunk and throw yourself at him? How pitiful!"

Then Myrin gasped as a lordling slammed into the banquet table beside her with enough force to crack it. The man who had shoved him—a cruel-faced man in a black cloak—turned to leer at Myrin. She gaped and fought for air, frozen at the suddenness of his appearance.

"Kalen!" she moaned.

"Coward!" the nobleman cried. He lunged from the table and punched the cloaked man in the face. The rogue staggered back, snarling, and reached for a blade.

"Are you well, my lady?" the lordling demanded of Myrin.

"Uh," Myrin said. She couldn't think. She didn't know what to do.

Shoving her under the cracked banquet table, the lordling pointed a wand at his advancing foe and fired a blast of green-white light. The spell struck the man hard like a hammer's blow, staggering him, but he only smiled and straightened once more.

"Run, my lady!" the lordling said as he looked at his wand angrily. "Run—"

Then the word became a cry of pain as the rogue ran him through.

Myrin could only stare, horrified, as the man kicked the body off his sword. She knew that the blade would come for her next, but she could only crouch, paralyzed in terror.

The murderer squinted around, as though trying to see her. That didn't make sense to Myrin, who hadn't moved. She was sitting right before him, not a pace away, just under the table.

The sword flashed through the air, prodding this way and that as though searching for her. She cringed as far back as she could.

The murderer growled in frustration. He rose and ran back into the melee.

Myrin was puzzled. Why wasn't she dead? Hadn't the man seen her sitting before him?

Dazed, Myrin looked around, then crawled across the floor to escape her hiding place. She gasped when she looked down—her hands had changed color to match the stone floor. She held them up in front of her and her skin changed tone and pattern to blend with the room. Myrin panicked and grabbed hold of a nearby crimson drapery to haul herself to her feet—and her body immediately flushed crimson to match the fabric.

What was happening to her?

She rubbed at her reddened arms and saw that a trail of blue runes like ivy had crept up the inside of her forearm. She slipped back to the floor and sat, wrapped in the velvet drapery.

She didn't understand—she couldn't think. Why had she had so much wine?

Looking around the courtyard, she saw that at least twenty men and women in black cloaks—like the man who had attacked nearby—had appeared in the courtyard, attacking revelers. Chaos swept the courtyard, leaving cries of pain and terror in its wake.

A chill passed over Myrin, as though a door had opened nearby and let in a wave of cold air. She saw her skin shift again, back to its usual tan, and the blue runes faded from her arms. Whatever that chameleon magic had been, it was leaving her.

A face bent down to peer at Myrin. "Excuse me, young mistress."

Myrin turned where she sat, and a shiver of fear passed through her. "Y-yes?"

The woman was very old, but Myrin wasn't sure how she knew this. The rounded figure standing before her was rather youthful—even lush, with a heart-shaped face surrounded by vibrant gold curls. Her emerald gown, under a jet black cloak, was perfectly in fashion.

Myrin had the distinct sense the woman wasn't alive, though that couldn't be.

"I am Avaereene," said the woman. "Your jack seems to have abandoned you, and I thought you might be in some distress. May I aid you?"

"Oh, no," Myrin said. "Kalen's just gone away for a moment. He'll be—"

But the stranger was raising her hand. Myrin sensed, too late, the pulse of enchantment within the woman's arm, which beat with its own inner heat. Its proximity tickled her senses like the aroma of a steaming platter of hot sweets.

"Sleep," the woman said, in a language Myrin understood without knowing how.

Darkness swallowed Myrin.

The woman who'd called herself Avaereene lifted the girl fluidly. The young body was light, yet she felt a little dizzy—her power diminished around this girl, somehow. She knew the blue-headed waif had power of some kind, but she didn't know what it was.

No matter. She had more than enough strength for this purpose.

She tucked the sleeping girl under her cloak and whispered a spell to shroud them. Her cloak dimmed and bent the light, hiding them from view. A fog appeared in the air, shrouding half the courtyard in mist. In a few more moments, the temple would be one great brawl, and she and her followers could slip away.

Her employer would be most pleased.

Kalen swung up onto the balcony, where Cellica hopped down and they cast about for the source of the screams. Kalen heard loud, harsh words from the half-open door to the nearest chamber. He pointed, and Cellica dashed to the door, crossbow up and scanning for a target. He padded after her, thankful she'd made him wear his leathers after all.

What they found in the chamber, neither of them could have expected.

Lorien Dawnbringer lay dying upon the floor near a great golden tub. She choked and sputtered and tried to speak, but only blood came from her throat. Bent over her, cradling her as she bled, was Lady Ilira. She seemed to blend into the shadows of the golden tub, as though she had melted from them just heartbeats before.

"No," Ilira moaned. "No, no, *no!*"

Her gloved fingers caressed the priestess's face. Lorien did not seem able to see her, and could only cough, sputter, and finally go still.

Ilira, her face in shock, opened and closed her mouth several times but could not speak. Then she lowered her lips, tentatively, to Lorien's forehead. She shook as though from strain at the effort. Then, gently, she kissed the priestess's pale face.

Kalen expected something to happen, though he did not know why. Nothing came to pass but the gentle sound of her kiss.

Then, as if a wave loosed within her, Ilira threw back her head and screamed, loud and long—an elf mourning cry unknown in the lands of men. She bent and kissed Lorien's face again—kissed it over and over, washing it with her tears. She cried out in Elvish, but Kalen could not understand. She tore off her gloves and pressed her hands on Lorien's cheeks as though she'd never touched them before, as though her skin could bring life to death.

All eyes remained on her, but Kalen became aware of someone else in the room. His gaze flicked to the side, where he saw a thick figure in the shadows. It was Rath, pinning a squirming, mostly naked Fayne under his arm. Both of them looked rapt at Ilira's display.

"Hold and down arms!" Kalen cried. "Waterdhavian Guard!"

"Ka—!" Fayne gasped.

Rath slammed her head against the wall and Fayne slumped to the floor, unmoving.

CHAPTER TWENTY-THREE

ILIRA WAS THE FIRST TO MOVE. RATHER, *SHE* REMAINED STILL, BUT HER shadow moved.

Kalen realized, to his horror, that her dark reflection did not match her—it was great and broad, like a hulking warrior. It moved of its own will; though Ilira knelt, still and trembling, her shadow reached toward the dwarf with clawed hands meaning to rend him apart.

Suddenly, Kalen recognized it—from Downshadow, the night he had followed Lorien. The shadow must be bound to protect both women.

Then Ilira was in motion. She screamed a war cry of fury and leaped—not toward Rath, but backward, toward the wall. Kalen watched as she melted into the shadows, then appeared next to the dwarf and tackled him to the floor. Her hands fumbled at his black robes, and the two rolled and bounced across the silk carpets.

"Fayne!" Cellica cried, and she ran to Fayne, who lay unmoving.

Her voice snapped Kalen into motion. He lunged toward Rath and Ilira, daggers wide.

Rath got two feet under Ilira and heaved, sending her flying toward Kalen. He braced himself to catch her, but she twisted in the air, landed lightly on his chest with both feet, and kicked off, turning a somersault and landing on her toes near the dwarf. She lunged at Rath, hissing like a serpent.

Driven backward by the collision, Kalen fell to the floor. He coughed and kicked his legs around, pushing himself to stand. What he saw paralyzed him for a heartbeat.

Ilira's shadow had fallen upon Rath. It stood like a living man—a giant of a man. Its features were blurry, but Kalen could see torturous pain etched on its face. With a soundless cry, it tore at the dwarf with its black claws.

Rath eluded its blows, eyes wide. He danced backward and around the room, running around the tub and leaping over divans and dressers. The shadow pursued, relentless in its assault. Rath ran up a wall, kicked off, and dropped behind it, right hand across his belt on his sword. The creature turned—or rather, turned itself inside-out—and grimaced at Rath out of its back-turned-front. The dwarf began to draw steel.

"*Elie en!*" Ilira screamed, and she pounced on him like a cat. Her bare hand grasped his wrist, holding his sword in place.

Flesh sizzled and the dwarf screamed. Kalen smelled it before he saw the smoke rising from Rath's wrist. His flesh burned under Ilira's touch as though by incredible heat. Great red welts appeared and blood dripped to the floor. Bubbles of skin collapsed into blackening burns.

A spellscar, Kalen realized—Ilira's power was to unmake flesh at a touch. That explained his burned fingers, her dress and gloves, the way she recoiled from contact. Never would he have suspected it of such a lady—so fair, yet so monstrous as well.

Kalen understood, in a flash, what had happened with Lorien—why Ilira had cried out after she had touched the priestess. Lorien's flesh had not burned at her touch because the priestess was dead. Only the living suffered the burns. Like Rath.

The dwarf struggled to escape, but the hand he laid on her forearm scalded in the same fashion, and he cried out in pain. His eyes were filled with horror and his voice turned to a squeal.

"*Elie en, ilythiri,*" Ilira said, her words soft and cold. She leaned in to kiss him.

The dwarf flinched, Kalen saw, sparing his lips. Ilira's kiss fell instead on his unprotected cheek, and the smoke of burning flesh wafted around their faces. Rath cried out and beat at Ilira, trying to break her hold, tearing her black gown. The elf hung on, clinging to him with her arms and legs like a spider as he burned under her touch and shrieked.

"What's she *doing?*" Cellica screamed. She cradled the unconscious Fayne and pointed her crossbow at the duel but did not fire, unable to sight a clear target.

Kalen shivered to watch Ilira's attack. Even the shadow seemed to pause in its fury, standing back to let her kiss the dwarf with her burning lips. The creature recoiled, seeming to cower as though ashamed. Rath cried out over and over, wordless.

"Hold!" Kalen cried, but to no avail. He knew the fury on Ilira's face. This was not a woman who would stop until she killed or was killed herself.

He ran at the pair, daggers held low and wide, and the shadow lunged into his path. He cut at the creature, but as he expected, his knives passed through the black stuff of its body as though through heavy mist, causing no injury. Mortal steel could hardly touch a creature from beyond their world. If only he still had his paladin's powers, he could harm it.

The beast lashed out with its claws, and Kalen knew better than to parry. He danced aside, weaving, trying to get around the creature rather than through it. It was huge and powerful, but as Kalen guessed, not fast or nimble. He could dodge its strikes as long as he stayed fast and low. Cowardly, perhaps, but it kept him alive.

Fight like a paladin, he thought. Prove to the threefold god that you are worthy. Have faith that your strikes will harm it, and they will.

But growing up in the cesspool of Luskan, Kalen had never trusted to faith. The center of his being was wrought of cold practicality, hardened by a thousand strikes and hard blows. Thanking the gods again he had worn his leathers rather than his Guard arms, he moved in the tight, efficient dance of elusion and avoidance that had marked his days as a thief.

Yet he couldn't get past the shadow. It was too strong a guardian—a perfect mate to its mistress, this elf noble with her hidden scars. He pulled back to face it levelly, and held up his daggers to ward it back. The creature ceased its attack and stared at him, and he had the distinct sense that he was gazing at a guardian just as devoted as he.

He hefted a knife to throw. He thought it might pass through the shadow and strike Ilira, distracting her from Rath. He hated the dwarf, but he needed to stop this.

Then Ilira groaned as the dwarf punched her solidly on the ear—at the same instant, the man-shaped shadow drew back as though struck. The elf reeled away and Rath rose, his half-blackened face dripping blood. He touched it and winced. His bare hand came away bloody and sticky.

With anger that was the stuff of nightmares written on his face, the dwarf reached down with his unburned hand and pulled his sword free. The blade glittered with its perfect, keen edge.

Kalen had seen such blades on the Dragon Coast, among tradesmen from the east. Katanas, they were often called—light, efficient, and delicate.

Rath crouched to lunge at the shuddering woman. His grimace calmed a little as he focused himself into the blade. Then he leaped.

Kalen darted in front of him, daggers crossed, and caught the sword high.

The slender sword shrieked against his crossed steel, and Kalen thought for one terrible heartbeat that it would shear through them and into his chest. But the steel held, and Rath pressed only another instant—face wrought in agony and rage—before he pulled the sword back, dropped low, and kicked

Kalen's legs out from under him. Kalen fell back, colliding heavily with Ilira and falling in a tangled heap. Flesh burned—Kalen's own—but he could not stand. He looked up, saw Rath's sword, and knew he could not block.

A crossbow bolt streaked toward Rath and he swept his blade up to slap it aside.

Cellica! Kalen saw the halfling near the door, standing protectively over Fayne, who was coughing her way back to awareness. The shot had startled them all—broken the rhythm of the battle. Cellica glared at Rath banefully and reloaded her small crossbow.

Eyes wild with horror, the dwarf touched a trembling hand to his face and moaned. Not bothering to sheathe his sword, he leaped through the open window.

Kalen grasped Ilira to pull her away, but the bare flesh through her ruined gown burned his fingers. It felt distant, that burning, but still powerful—he felt the death inside her.

Ilira moaned and struggled. "No!" she cried. "You're letting him escape!"

Kalen tried to respond but she slammed a knee into his belly and he slumped to the floor, gasping.

Ilira glared at her shadow, and the creature nodded. Ilira said nothing, only closed her fists tightly. As though in response, the creature melted into the floor and swirled around her feet, joining with her. She stood, panting and heaving, half naked in her torn gown. Blood—Lorien's and Rath's both, Kalen realized—dripped from her hands.

She glared down at Kalen with a fury and a hate that only an elf—with untold ages stretching behind her and ahead—could know. He crawled backward on the floor, inching away from a lioness that could pounce at any instant. She knelt, meeting Kalen eye to eye, considering.

Two Watchmen burst through the door, swords drawn. "Hold!" they cried. "Down arms!"

The swords pointed first to him, as the man with steel, then at Ilira. Kalen thrust a warding hand toward Cellica, and she cradled Fayne against the wall, hiding her. He opened his hands, daggers hooked between palm and thumb. He rose slowly, trying not to provoke Ilira.

"Hold and talk truth!" cried one Watchman. "What happened here?" His gaze roved to the corpse of the priestess, then to Ilira, kneeling with bloody hands and wrists. "Merciful gods!"

The elf turned baleful eyes toward them and they winced.

"Hold!" the armored man said. "Down arms! Down . . . hands!"

Uncaring, Ilira rose and started toward the window, but Kalen moved to block her.

"Stay, Lady," Kalen said. "None of us are certain what happened here."

"Calm yourself," Cellica said with her suggestive voice. Turning against her will, Ilira raised her hands to her ears, her face contorted. "Stay calm, Lady—calm . . ."

With a roar, Ilira threw her hands out wide. "Enough!" She gave Kalen a sharp glare, and words died on his tongue as though her will had struck him a solid blow. Her eyes glowed gold-yellow from within the shadows that enwrapped her like mist. Darkness roiled in her—a cruel, terrible darkness.

Her shadow did not follow her movements. While she stood calmly, it thrashed and clawed on the floor, as though in agony.

Then she laughed—half crazed, half terrified. The mocking cackle—perfect and terrible as the voice of a singer drowning in madness—chilled him to the bone. "You want to pierce me, is that it?" the elf asked, her words wry. She glared at the Watchmen and ran her bloody hands along her hips, pulling the silk gown up past her knees. Her gaze grew alluring and dangerous. "You and any of a thousand men—little boys with your swords."

Shadows lengthened—the Watchmen shivered. Kalen saw them looking at her writhing shadow, their faces white as cream.

"Lady." Kalen lowered his daggers. "Lady, no one will harm you."

Ilira shook her head dazedly, and some of her darkness fell away as though the shadows that surrounded her were tangible.

"I am Waterdeep Guard," Kalen said. "Calm yourself, and we shall—"

"Shut up!" she snapped, startling him. Angry tears burst forth to stream down her face. "Stay away from me. Away!"

Kalen raised his steel once more. "Lady Ilira, please—"

She loosed a strangled cry of rage and pain, then ran toward the window. Lunging forward, Kalen shouted at her to stop, but she ran straight into the wall—or would have, had not the shadows swallowed her. He staggered to a halt, startled and disbelieving. She had cast no spell—used no magic that he knew of.

"A shade," said one of the Watchmen. "Did you see her eyes? Lady Ilira's a *shade!*"

"Gods above," said the other. "No other explanation—hold!"

When Kalen moved, they perked up and leveled their war steel at him.

Kalen put his hands out wide—peaceful. He looked to Cellica and to Fayne, whom the halfling clutched near the wall. An ugly bruise was seeping across Fayne's face where the dwarf had struck her.

He realized Fayne was looking hard at where Ilira had vanished, and her eyes twinkled.

You and any of a thousand men . . .

Kalen shivered. If Kalen didn't get Fayne out soon . . .

The Watchmen were pointing steel at them.

He had no choice.

He raised his hands to the sides of his helm.

CHAPTER TWENTY-FOUR

BOOTS SOUNDED ON THE STEPS WITHOUT, AND CELLICA SAW KALEN shake himself from his stupor. She heard shouts from outside and a great clamor, but her eyes locked on Kalen.

"Hold!" said the Watchman, but Kalen ripped off his helm. Fayne inhaled sharply.

"Vigilant Dren!" They scrambled to salute.

"Care for this mess," he said. "I'm sure she won't be back, but 'ware Ilira's hands—they burn." He started to don his helm, then stopped. He added, "Her kiss, too."

"Sir!" a Watchman cried. "What passed here? Who killed—"

Kalen shook his head, and Fayne realized that he didn't know. When he arrived, Lorien was already dying, and Ilira had been closest to her.

Fayne's heart raced. What did he think had happened?

Kalen gestured to Fayne and Cellica. "These two are with me."

One Watchman stiffened and nodded. "Sir," he said. The other was openly weeping over the slain priestess. "We'll ward this place, as you command."

Kalen returned their salute then pushed past them, out the door onto the balcony. He carried his helm. Fayne opened her mouth to speak, but Kalen's cold eyes froze her tongue. She snatched up her clothes, which lay next to the bathtub, now wet from all the commotion.

Cellica followed Kalen to the balcony, and Fayne held her hand tightly. With the other hand, Fayne tucked the towel around her body with some degree of modesty.

"You showed them your face!" Cellica hissed.

"No choice," Kalen said. "We needed to get out of there before Rayse arrived." He looked pointedly at Fayne.

Fayne goggled. Revealing himself seemed so stupid, yet Kalen had done it for her? Why would he do something like that? Had the world gone mad, or just her?

You're losing your mind, her inner voice noted. Again.

Chaos boiled up in the courtyard of the Temple of Beauty. Brigands had appeared as if from the air and began a brawl that had since turned the place into a mess of shouts and steel. As they watched, noble ladies screamed and ran from hot-headed duelists. The room was half filled with mist, confusing the fighters into hacking at everything that moved.

"Myrin," Kalen and Cellica said at once.

The name was like a knife in Fayne's belly. What use had they for the doe-eyed stripling? Hadn't Kalen compromised himself to protect Fayne, just now? Didn't he fancy Fayne?

Oh, gods, *did* he? Fayne wasn't sure if she was pleased or terrified.

Fayne's head hurt and she grew fearful, as she always did in confusing situations. Kalen was acting on instinct and passion, not cold rationality, and that was unpredictable.

"Where is she?" Cellica asked.

Kalen shook his head. His rumpled hair swayed in front of his eyes.

"Wait—" Fayne started. "Wait a breath—tell me . . ."

But Kalen whisked her up in his arms, naked and all, and shoved her against the wall in an alcove, pressing himself firmly against her. She coughed, sputtering, but then he kissed her to still her lips and she ceased struggling. Then she was *certain* she'd gone mad.

He broke the kiss, finally, parting them by a thumb's breadth.

"Well met to you as well," she managed.

"I did that to shut you up." Kalen's eyes were cold. "What were you doing there?"

"I—" she said. "You don't understand . . ."

Kalen scowled. "Never mind," he said. "You'd only lie anyway. Just . . . just shut up."

"You could kiss me again," she thought of saying, but stopped with a shiver. Kalen's face was hard and his eyes were those of a warrior. Those of a killer.

No use being ingratiating or alluring. She would just keep her mouth shut for now.

A woman in armor ran past, and when they heard the muffled voices inside Lorien's chamber, they recognized Araezra Hondyl.

"Gods," the valabrar said. "What happened?"

"Murder—gods above!" a man said. "Lady Nathalan . . . oh, gods, her closest friend!"

"Did you see it? You saw the murder?"

"Nay, but . . . Vigilant Dren. He was here, you could . . ."

"Dren?" The valabrar sounded shocked. "Kalen Dren, my aide?"

"Time to go," Cellica murmured. She'd wedged herself into the alcove near Kalen's leg, and she darted out.

Kalen, shoving Fayne roughly along, followed her around the balcony to look down into the chaotic courtyard. Cellica was looking for Myrin, Fayne realized. Kalen was just glowering.

"Are those yours?" Kalen demanded, waving at the intruders.

Fayne could only shake her head, completely at a loss. Whoever had sent these men to the temple, it hadn't been her.

Near the entrance, Kalen saw a knot of guardsmen and Watchmen rallying around Bors Jarthay. The commander—whose drunkenness had been mostly an act—knocked one man out with his handflask pipe and drew a surprisingly long blade out of his billowing shirt. Commander Kleeandur was there too, barking orders to cut off exits and trap the chaos inside.

"I don't see her!" Cellica cried.

The more Watch that arrived, the fewer rogues remained. But the nobles began dueling, and that perpetuated the brawl. Lady Wildfire, surrounded by a dozen noblemen fighting over the right to protect her, tired of the commotion, brained one of the lordlings with her jeweled purse, and fled of her own power. Talantress Roaringhorn was conspicuously absent, and dozens of nobles cried out in search of one another amidst the din.

Kalen saw black-garbed figures slipping out of the courtyard, hooded ladies in their grasp. They moved south into the temple plaza.

Cellica followed his gaze and pointed at the kidnappers. "What are you going to do?"

Kalen pushed Fayne roughly at the halfling and took his helmet in his hands. He slid it over his head.

"Kalen, you have no sword," the halfling said. "You can't—"

He pulled the daggers from his belt. He looked across the courtyard as though judging the distance to one of the high windows.

"Wait, Kalen!" Fayne caught his hand, and he glared at her. His eyes burned. She swallowed a sudden rush of fear. "You . . . saved my life," she said.

"You stupid girl!" Kalen slammed his fist, dagger and all, into the wall beside her head. The blade rang against the stone, deafening her. "What the Hells did you think you were doing?"

Fayne was stunned. "Kalen, I—"

"Shut up. I'm tired of it," he said. "You're a spoiled child playing games. Just a stupid fool who thinks there aren't consequences to your pranks—that people don't die."

"Kalen," Cellica said, casting her eyes down, her cheeks reddening with embarrassment.

Fayne trembled. "Please don't," she said. "Please, Kalen—I'm sorry!"

But Kalen's eyes were cold. "Begone," he said. "I want nothing to do with you. Now, pardon," he said as he locked his helm in place, "but I have someone worthwhile to save."

He ran for the opposite end of the courtyard, leaping from table to table around battles, his enchanted boots guiding him. Screams went up in the courtyard from startled nobles, and a few wary Watchmen fired crossbows in his direction. The bolts cut through his cloak and one cut open his left arm, but he did not falter. When he gained the far window, he paused and looked back—his colorless gaze cut into Fayne. Then he turned, cloak swirling, and was gone.

Fayne, shocked, pulled herself away from Cellica. She drew out her wand—the wand she could use to hide herself from the world, as she had always done—and glared.

"I'm sorry," Cellica said. The halfling rubbed her hands together. "Kalen . . . he—wait!"

The halfling staggered as Fayne turned her gaze on her and whispered a word of dark magic. Cellica pawed blearily at her face and seemed unable to see Fayne, who had pulled away and hurried down the stairs toward the brawl. Her longer legs meant Cellica could not catch her.

As she went, she growled. "Didn't warn me about *this*, Father."

Avaereene paused when they had run two blocks, to see how many of her men followed. It didn't matter—she held the wealthiest prize in her own arms—but every noble lass taken prisoner was more coin for the Sightless.

She was pleased to see that a dozen had escaped, carrying half that many girls among them. Not all of her men had made it, but desperate men were plentiful in Downshadow she could always hire more.

The lead man stopped at her side. He carried an unconscious Hawkwinter in his arms, head hooded, moaning up a squall through her gag. Though the face was hidden, Avaereene knew all the nobles in Waterdeep by figure as well as face. She had an excellent memory.

"Where, mistress?" asked her lieutenant.

They were panting from exertion. Avaereene wasn't breathing hard—she wasn't breathing at all, as she hadn't had to for almost a century.

"The sewers—keep a low cloak," she said. "I shall follow with haste."

The man nodded and directed the other stealthy kidnappers to follow him. Downshadow men, all of them, and useful enough, even if scarred and ugly.

"Hasn't the spellplague warped us all?" she murmured. She thought of the horror lurking inside her and grinned. "Some more than others."

Avaereene stepped into an alley, where she found her employer stepping out of a bank of shadows. His cowl hid most of his face, but she knew he was a half-elf. And while he was not dead, neither was he alive. He was something like her.

"Well accomplished," he said, indicating the girl in her arms. "Give her to me."

"The gold, first." The blue-headed girl started to moan in her arms as Avaereene began to draw the life from her like a sponge from a pool of water. "Or she dies."

His face held no emotion. "Very well." He gestured, and a pouch appeared from his sleeve, heavy with coin. His black eyes never left the girl's face.

Instinct told Avaereene to grasp the reward while it was there, but pragmatism stayed her.

"Such a curious thing," Avaereene said. "To pay so much for a girl with no family or connections. I do not even know who she is, and I've spent more than a century in Waterdeep."

Her employer reached out silently and stroked the girl's temple with his gloved hand.

Then he looked up, over Avaereene's shoulder, and she swore she saw his face for half an instant. His lips had drawn back in a hideous grimace, and his teeth seemed very long.

"Shadowbane," he hissed, more like a serpent than a man. "Damn that sword!"

"What?" Avaereene asked, but he was gone as though he'd turned to dust.

He had not taken the sleeping girl, but he had snatched the coins back from her. Avaereene snarled in anger and resolved to slay the first thing she saw.

A pair of her thieves came upon her. "Mistress?" one asked. "Mistress, what—"

Avaereene tossed the first one aside with a flicker of her will—he shattered against the alley wall. That made her feel better, and appeased the hungry magic within.

She thrust the sleeping girl into the arms of the other one, who looked frozen in terror, and peered down the street. Sure enough, a man ran toward them, glittering steel in his hands, gray cloak trailing behind him. He followed on the heels of four more thieves carrying three noble girls.

"Kalen," the girl murmured as she stirred in the thief's arms.

CHAPTER TWENTY-FIVE

WELL MET," KALEN SAID AS HE CAUGHT THE NEAREST THIEF BY THE ARM. The man turned and Kalen drove both daggers into his chest.

The thief stiffened, blinked rapidly several times, then fell with a choked gasp as Kalen—hands free from the blades he left in the scoundrel—caught the woman he carried.

No time. He set her aside, ripped the curved sword from the thief's belt, and ran forward.

Ten paces farther, two men carried a bulky noble lass in a green gown between them. They cursed and fumbled, pushing her back and forth. Finally, the smaller of the men—an ugly, warty dwarf—took her, and the freed thief—a half-orc—turned to face Kalen.

The brute bristled with metal nails that stood out from his skin like ghastly pierced rings or jewels. The half-orc hefted a stout buckler on his left arm and a length of barbed chain in his other hand, and opened his mouth to challenge.

Kalen didn't slow—he leaped to twice the half-orc's height in the air, driven by his boots. The brute looked up as Kalen hissed down toward him, sword plunging, deadly as a hawk.

The half-orc interposed his buckler between himself and the airborne knight. Kalen's thrust, backed by all his weight, shattered the stout wood— but snapped in two as well. The half-orc howled in pain as shards of wood flew into his face, putting more shrapnel in his flesh than before. The broken scimitar blade tumbled away.

The half-orc, infuriated, swung his chain at Kalen, who interposed his left arm. The chain enwrapped it greedily, barbs barely short of striking his helm. The slashing razors would have split his face open like a boiled egg. The barbs sank instead into his flesh, deep enough that he could feel them prickle. The chain-wielder grinned and Kalen realized his misfortune.

"Tymora—" Kalen managed, before the half-orc jerked the chain and slammed him against a building. Pain swept through his stunned consciousness, and he sank down.

The half-orc wrenched him over and he flopped like a limp doll to the cobblestones. The impact ripped through him, but he was still alive and still conscious.

"Stlarning Watchman." He also growled a few Orcish words Kalen knew to be curses.

"Come!" shouted the dwarf, pausing near the half-orc and struggling to hold the kidnapped girl. "No time!"

"Wait," said the bruiser, and he reached down to seize Kalen's neck.

The noble girl, by chance, kicked the half-orc in the shoulder and his attention wavered.

It was just a heartbeat, but it was enough.

With a roar, Kalen rammed the jagged, shorn-off hilt of the thief's scimitar into one half-orc ankle. The creature howled in pain and faltered on his feet. As the brute teetered, Kalen wrenched the hilt upward and jammed it into the half-orc's groin. Black blood spurted forth and the creature gave a high-pitched squeal like a stuck pig.

Kalen rose, the half-orc's discarded chain hanging from his arm, and faced the dwarf thug who held the struggling girl. Kalen looked down at the chain, the barbs cutting into his arm. Without wincing, with barbs ripping out his flesh, Kalen unwrapped the chain.

This second thief looked somehow familiar.

"Wait!" he said, putting up his hands as though to surrender. "It's you! Shadowbane!"

Kalen hesitated. He recognized this one from Downshadow—this was the dwarf he'd let flee. Apparently, he hadn't learned aught.

The dwarf thrust his forearm forward, and a tiny arrow concealed in a handbow in his sleeve streaked through the air. Kalen batted it aside with the barbed chain.

Kalen leaped forward and split the dwarf's chin with a rising right hook. The thief slammed into the wall and Kalen caught him. With an expert twist of his wrist, he wrapped the blood-soaked chain around the dwarf's neck and pulled. The ugly man's eyes bugged, making his face even more hideous.

The noble girl had managed to free her hands and doff her hood and gag. "Thank—" She saw the strangling thief, saw the way Kalen spat and growled like a murderous wolf, and she froze, horror-stricken. "What—what are you *doing?*"

Kalen ignored her. The dwarf fought for breath and Kalen pulled tighter on the chain.

The noble lass put her hands to her throat, found a scream, and split the night with her terror. Then she fled, shouting for aid.

Not all saviors are angels, Kalen thought. And not all killings are pretty—or quick.

The thief sputtered and slapped at him impotently.

"Kalen," came Myrin's voice, whispering seemingly on the night's mists. She spoke softly, yet he could hear her as plainly as if she stood next to him.

Was this truly her voice, or his imagination? Did that matter?

Kalen released the chain, let the dwarf collapse retching to the ground, and ran.

The night had grown misty of a sudden, and Kalen knew magic was at work. The thieves were hiding their escape, trying to throw him off, but Myrin's voice led him.

He saw another kidnapper who carried a barefoot girl over his shoulder. Kalen outran him and dived, slamming into the man's back. Kalen rolled so the thief did not fall on him and hoped he had picked the right direction to catch the captive. Sure enough, she landed atop him, and wild silver-white hair tumbled down.

He pulled off the girl's hood, and the shocked eyes of Talantress Roaringhorn stared into his. The magic that changed her skin black had failed, leaving her flesh very pale, but her hair was still long and white. She managed to spit out her gag, and she blinked at him, confused.

Then a smile spread across her face. "My . . . my hero!"

Kalen growled in frustration and thrust her aside. Her captor had risen and was plunging a rapier down at his chest. Kalen rolled away, then back against the blade, wrenching it out of the thief's hand. He kicked the man's legs out from under him, toppling him to the ground. Kalen rose and put the man out with a kick to the jaw.

"Kalen!" came Myrin's cry—louder this time. Talantress hadn't seemed to hear it. Kalen turned toward the source of the sound and saw a greenish glow: magic.

Kalen seized the thief's fallen rapier. He coughed, opened his helm halfway to spit blood, then sealed his mask. He strode on.

"Wait!" Kneeling, Talantress caught his hand and held him back.

Calmly, Kalen snaked his hand around and unbuckled his gauntlet. It came free, and Talantress hit herself in the chest with it and fell on her overprivileged rump.

"Wait!" Talantress cried from the ground. "Come back right this breath!"

He continued his run, hobbling a bit more slowly after the punishment he'd endured. Young Lady Roaringhorn got up and gave chase, but he paid her no mind. He plunged into the mists, following Myrin's voice and the green glow.

The fog swelled thicker than before, but Kalen pressed on. He was nearing the source, he realized, but he quickly lost his bearing and swam, blind. His body was aching, his lungs heaving, and his heart raced to put him down. He clutched his left arm, which was in agony. He felt as if the half-orc were sitting on his chest.

"Not yet, Eye of Justice," he hissed through clenched teeth. "Not yet."

He channeled healing into himself, praying that he had proven himself once more worthy, but no power came. He gritted his teeth and pressed on.

Kalen stumbled through an empty, gray-black world. Mist swirled around him.

"Myrin!" he choked. He felt that he would fall at any breath.

"Kalen," came her voice, leading him forward. "Kalen . . ."

He staggered ahead, stolen rapier ready for any attack, but found only mist.

"Show yourself!" he challenged. "Cowards!"

As though in response, the mist parted, and Kalen saw a woman from whose cupped hands the mist flowed. A green glow suffused her fingers—magic. Beside her stood a thief who looked more terrified than anything else, and in his arms was a limp girl in a red dress.

"Something's countering my casting," the woman murmured in a deep, rasping voice that didn't match her slim body. She seemed an ordinary human woman, but the voice was that of a beast. "It's the girl. Somehow, even dazed, she's—"

"Then we stop her!" The thief drew a hooked dagger and raised it over Myrin.

"No, you fool!" the woman roared.

Kalen ran forward and stabbed the thief through the chest. Stunned, the man looked down at the blade, then at a panting, heaving Kalen. He toppled, loosing Myrin as he went.

Kalen dived to catch her. She weighed little in his arms and he cradled her tightly.

An arcane word, in a voice like a grinding gravestone, stole his attention. He looked up at the woman to see her gloved, clawlike hand reaching for his face. A finger touched his brow.

Power seized him—cruel power that sucked the life out of his limbs. Lightning arced through Kalen, lashing every stretch of bone and sinew, stealing the strength from his muscles. He fell to his knees.

"Well," the woman said in her corpselike voice. "This is what happens, Sir Fool, when you cross wills with the most powerful wizard in Waterdeep."

She raised her hands and began to chant a spell that Kalen could only imagine would be his doom. Flames and shadow flickered around her hands, like the fires of the Nine Hells.

And so it ends, he thought.

His eyes blurred and he sank toward peaceful sleep.

Myrin's eyes opened and blue light flooded the alley.

CHAPTER TWENTY-SIX

I N THE STRANGE FLASH OF LIGHT, MYRIN SAW KALEN FIRST, KNEELING
and helpless, and then the woman—the dead woman wearing the false
face—looming over him.

"No," she said in a voice she hardly recognized as her own. She lunged
forward and grasped Avaereene by the arm, trying anything she could to
stop the slaying magic. She wanted to steal the magic away, rip it from
Avaereene so it could not touch Kalen.

And she did exactly that.

The fires darting around Avaereene's fingers faded, flowing instead
into Myrin's hands, which lit with fierce blue light. The wizard opened her
mouth and stammered.

Oblivious to what she was doing, lashing blindly, Myrin struck Avaereene
with her will. A flash of brilliant red and black flame erupted, and the woman
slammed backward against the wall with a chorus of crackles and snaps.
Bricks cracked and turned inward.

Myrin stared down at her hands, horrified and awed. Blue runes spread
down her forearms, almost covering her skin. Power electric filled Myrin's
body, making her shiver and shake. The fog boiled away around her, evaporating in the heat coming off her body.

"Damn you!" Avaereene hissed in a voice from beyond the grave. "You
do not know what you do, child. This is my own power! How are you—?"

"Shut up!" Myrin shrieked. The stolen magic punched Avaereene in the
chest, shaking the building behind her. Holes burst in the wall, and Myrin
saw into the common room of a tavern through the cracks.

Avaereene hardly seemed hurt by the blow, but her eyes went wide. Then
they turned blood red and began to leak sanguine tears.

"How are you doing this?" she roared in frustration. "You're just a child!"

Myrin merely pointed her hands, loosing bright, hungry flames like nothing she had ever seen or imagined to tear at Avaereene. The wizard screamed in agony and fear. Her skin shivered, then began to bubble and boil. Around her, the bricks glowed red, sizzled, and shook as though caught between an anvil and a smith's hammer. Her black cloak and gown started to smolder and unravel, and soon she was naked. Her entire body quaked and rotted before Myrin's eyes, but the wizard could not scream against the pressure of Myrin's spell. Her eyes were livid and terror filled.

A smile spread across Myrin's face and a thought came unbidden—a thought in her voice but not hers: *this will teach her.*

Then Myrin heard a new sound: a gagging, rasping sound from the ground at her side. She looked down and saw Kalen coughing and retching. He tore open his helm, and she saw him vomit blood onto the cobblestones. "Muh-Myrin . . . stuh-stop . . ."

He looked up at her and she gasped. His skin shivered like Avaereene's, and his eyes were shot through with red. Tears of blood leaked onto his face.

Myrin looked around and saw others gagging and retching—folk inside the tavern, and some who had come forth to watch or help. Gods—what was she doing?

The force holding Avaereene against the wall lessened, and the old woman sucked air into her lungs. She looked down at her withered hands, then touched her face. She screamed.

Myrin turned and clapped a hand to her mouth, shocked. Gone were the beautiful face and body—they had rotted into a withered corpse. Worse, her form had been crushed against the tavern with such force that she had somehow melded with the building's skin. Bricks grew out of her like massive, chunky warts. The red eyes that glared out were not dead, nor were they alive. Myrin recognized the woman's true body, that she was—Myrin didn't know where the word came from—a lich. An undead horror.

"My face! My body!" Avaereene shrieked. "You will die for this, girl!"

The wizard's form had been a magic-wrought falsehood—the corpse embedded in the wall revealed the truth. Myrin's magic had undone years, perhaps decades of delicate spellwork that had achieved the beauty the lich wanted for herself. Complex castings, and probably painful.

Avaereene barked a sharp word. Myrin recoiled, but it was no attack. Hissing in pain and anger, the lich vanished, taking part of the wall with her—and leaving aught of herself too.

With a sick cry, Myrin closed her eyes and fists. She willed the magic to vanish.

It didn't.

Dark fire rolled out of her, uncontrolled. Myrin screamed for it to stop, but it was alive in its own right. It danced around her, gleefully consuming whatever it touched.

She could not stop it.

"Myrin," came a voice, cutting through the chaos.

It was Kalen, his form blurring as though it fought to maintain consistency. His gauntleted hand grasped her tightly—strange, that the right hand had a gauntlet and the left hand was bare. she reached for his bared hand, but she remembered what her touch had done to the lich. She drew back, horrified.

"Myrin, you have to stop." Kalen's voice was calm, his eyes filled with blood.

"I can't!" she cried, and barely jerked her face away from his in time to send her words into the air and away. The force of her voice struck a spire on a nearby building, which tore free of its mounting and fell—horribly—toward them.

Kalen seized Myrin in his arms and threw them both aside. Sharp stone shattered into the cobbled street where they had been standing. Kalen held Myrin with fingers hard and cold as coffin nails.

"Stop!" he cried. "Stop this now!"

Myrin moaned and the ground began to shake. Buildings trembled around them and began to wrench themselves apart. Blue-white flames burst out of loose stones and bricks, which started rolling as though to put themselves out—or to delight in destruction. Folk screamed around them, gagging on what Myrin prayed were meals and not blood or worse.

"Calm," Kalen whispered. "All's well. You must calm yourself."

"I can't!" Myrin sobbed. Her body was shaking, far beyond her control.

His eyes bored into hers, shrinking her world to the size of two orbs. She saw her face reflected in his eyes, saw that almost every finger-length of her skin was scripted with blue runes. They told her a story, and she could almost read them.

"Calm," Kalen whispered again. His face was close to hers, but not touching. His lips hovered over hers, not kissing. "Please."

Slowly—so slowly—Myrin's heart slackened its race. Her screams and sobs subsided and her breathing slowed. The buildings ceased their shaking and the blue flames flickered out and died.

Finally, finally, the blue haze faded, and they were alone in the street, Kalen lying atop her, holding her, protecting her from the night—and from herself.

He wasn't moving, she realized.

"Kalen?" she asked. "*Kalen!*"

"Uhh," he groaned and rolled off, coughing. "Not so . . . not so loud."

Myrin could have kissed him, but men loomed over her, and she looked up. Thieves and kidnappers had come to harm them. Many were wounded or bruised, attacked by Kalen in his pursuit or wasted by the spell chaos. Kalen's eyes glittered and he closed his helm's faceplate, preparing to fight again.

No. Myrin would stop this. Words came unbidden to her lips.

Kalen knelt on the ground, coughing and trying to rise. "No," he said. "No—don't do it."

"All's well." She touched his helmed face with a loving hand, which yet glowed blue. "This is mine," she said. "It's only magic."

"Only . . ." Kalen coughed and retched. "*Only* magic?"

Myrin spread her hands and began the chant. This time, no blue runes crawled onto her tanned skin. This was a spell, whose words were written on her heart, though she had not known them until now. The power felt pure—untainted by the horrid darkness she had channeled from the lich woman. Somehow, she had drawn Avaereene's power, but it was too much— she couldn't control something so strong.

Never again would she draw powers like that. Never again.

"Begone," she said, magic crackling about her fingers.

The men hesitated.

"Begone!" she cried, and conjured fire arced up and burst from her hands. The thieves didn't have to be told a third time. They turned and fled.

Myrin let the power subside and die, then breathed out in a rush. She felt so tired—so very drained. She sat down next to Kalen. His breath came raggedly and his face was bloody, but his eyes were bright and sharp as diamonds.

She wanted so much to kiss him, but a part of her feared to do so. Instead, she pressed her forehead against his. "I . . . Kalen, I . . ."

His eyes widened and he thrust her away. She saw, as her backside hit the cobbles, his reason.

The thief who'd held her—the one Kalen had stabbed—was crawling toward them, a hooked blade in his hands. The edge dripped with a purple smear that Myrin knew was poison. Kalen's rapier—still inside him— scraped along the stones with a sickly hiss. Blood ran from his mouth. Pain and hatred filled his eyes, from which dripped red tears.

"Bitch," the thief rasped as he limped toward Myrin. "Stick you good, I will—"

His dagger fell. It would have struck Myrin's chest, but Kalen lunged in front of her and grappled with the thief. Myrin watched, stunned, as they wrestled, the knife pressing ever closer to Kalen's unprotected face. Then the knife cut across his cheek and she screamed.

The thief's eyes flicked to her, and the distraction was all Kalen needed. He slammed his open helm against his attacker's face, sending him reeling. He punched out with his gauntleted fist, hitting the man in the same place and shattering his nose. Before the thief could flee, Kalen caught hold of his wrist. He wrenched, and the man screamed as his arm snapped.

"Kalen, stop!" Myrin wept.

At her cry, Kalen looked up, and the thief punched him in the jaw, knocking him down. The man limped away, coughing. Kalen stumbled after him, his hands curled into claws.

"Stop! Please!" Myrin cried, weeping big tears that ran down her cheeks. The man had attacked her, yes, but she had to stop Kalen. He was not a beast but a man—she wanted a *man*, not a monster.

At her words, Kalen turned and caught Myrin in his arms. And though she knew they were both falling down beaten, she felt perfectly safe.

"Shush," Kalen murmured. "It's well—all's well."

"Gods . . ." Then Myrin's heart leaped. "All's *well?* Kalen—you've been poisoned."

She lifted her fingers to touch the slash across his cheek, where the venomed knife had cut him. Greenish black veins had appeared there and spread beneath his skin, the poison working through his blood. They already covered half his face. Myrin had no idea how she could see it—she knew she shouldn't be able to.

Then, as she watched, the poison began to recede. The veins became pink once again, little by little, and the blackness shrank until it vanished entirely from beneath his skin.

He looked as surprised as she felt. "My blessing," he said.

Myrin felt power unlike her own—divine, rather than arcane—fill him. His bare fingers joined hers against his cheek, and she watched as they shimmered white with heat, so bright she could see his bones. The light spread from his fingers into his skin, and the cut turned into a sharp scar. He gasped in relief and surprise.

"I don't understand," Myrin whispered, yet somehow she did understand. A god had saved him.

He shook his head. "Helm—nay. The threefold god," he explained. "He . . . he isn't finished with me yet." He hugged her tighter and his head dipped against her shoulder.

Myrin let loose a deep, terrified breath. She feared Kalen had succumbed, but she could feel him breathing. Tears welled in her eyes.

She and Kalen held each other in the empty street. They would have to move along soon, she knew—before the Watch came—but for now, they could just rest together.

Above them, far above them, a light rain began to fall.

At the top of the cracked tavern, a half-elf woman moved out of the moonlight, trailing a mane of scarlet hair.

CHAPTER TWENTY-SEVEN

"WHAT'S THE MATTER, CHILD?" ASKED HER PATRON OVER ALE AT THE Knight 'n Shadow.

Fayne couldn't tell him the truth—didn't *know* the truth. She didn't understand the source of the discontented hollow in her chest. She thought she'd feel better with it done. But now . . .

They sat in the shadowy lower level, in the last hour before dawn. It would be darkest out now, or so the saying went, but the darkest time in Waterdeep occurred not in the city at all but below it, when the hunters of Downshadow returned from a night spent above, pillaging and raiding and doing what they loved best.

Fayne used to love this time, but now . . . she felt nothing but sadness. And anger.

"That damned dwarf stlarned it up." Her ale tasted sour—like goblin piss—and she pushed it aside. She gestured at a serving girl to bring wine. "I had Lady Dawnbringer—I had the situation fully in control and he just . . . *damn!*"

She slammed the heel of her palm down on the table. The loud bang attracted the notice of a few fellow drinkers, but her patron's magic made them look away. As for the man himself, he merely listened to her without speaking.

"No one was supposed to die," she said. "And *she* wasn't supposed to get any kind of vengeance. Her lover was supposed to leave her, not *die*." She scowled. "I'm glad that hrasting pisshole Rath got scarred—served him well for taking matters into his own hands."

Her patron watched her levelly, his easy smile betraying nothing. If he agreed or disagreed, she had no idea. She hated that about him, at times.

With that face, he could bluff a dragon out of its hoard, or a god out of her powers. The bastard.

She hated feeling so weak when she sat across from him—hated the way he stared at her, weighing her, like both a prized horse and a petulant child.

That was the way Kalen had looked at her—as a child.

"My sweet?" her patron asked. Fayne looked up, startled. "What are you thinking about?"

"Only how I'm better than *her*," Fayne said, as much to herself as to her patron.

Though Fayne hadn't named her, her patron must have known who she meant: the bitch who styled herself Lady Nathalan. After what Fayne had done this night . . . well. At least Ilira Nathalan's anguished face should chase away Fayne's nightmares about that night eighty years gone.

"Ah." Her patron gazed at her closely. "And yet, something is amiss. What is it?"

"Naught." Fayne downed her bowl of wine and waved for another. "Tell me this, though—it was a brilliant plan, aye? If Rath hadn't come, I'd have ruined Lorien for her, right?"

She saw her patron's wry smile—saw his eyes glowing dimly in the light, as though he enjoyed some private jest. Now it was his turn to grow quiet. "What?" Fayne asked.

"Just reflecting," he said, "how like your mother you are."

Any other day, she'd have taken that for a great compliment.

Fayne sniffed. "What do you mean?" she asked, false bravado in her voice. "That I am proud? Regal? Competitive? Perhaps"—she flipped her hair back—"beautiful?"

He waved a gloved hand and laughed once. "Why not?"

She glared across the table. "Speak plain, fate-spinner."

"As you wish," he said. "She was all those things and more, but she was also flawed. You have shown a similar weakness, but rather than frustrating, I find it endearing."

Fayne bristled. "My mother," she said, "had no weaknesses."

He shrugged, and she saw a quiet twinkle in his eye. "As you say."

Those three little words cut her legs out from under her. They reminded her that she was just a foolish child who had never really known her mother—not as her patron had.

Sometimes, she truly and utterly hated this man. Loved him, of course, but hated him too.

"If you're going to mock me, at least be plain," Fayne said. Her lip trembled.

"Very well," he said. "Your mother . . . if all did not go exactly as she had planned, victory was dust to her. I see the same drive in you, my sweet child."

"That's ridiculous," she said, her voice breaking. "I'm pleased. See how I—"

He reached across the table and laid a hand on hers, cutting off her words. She felt a fearsome heat in his fingers, as though fire coursed in his blood. She stared at him.

"In the end," he said, "did you not succeed at destroying her—this Lady Nathalan?"

The name struck her like a blow, but Fayne felt only a deep, irresistible sadness. "I—I suppose, yes, but—" Fayne wiped her cheeks. "Damn you, I'm *pleased!*"

"Then why are you crying?" he asked. She looked down, and there was a white kerchief in his dainty, perfect hand, the runes for L.V.T. stitched into the corner in red thread.

She ignored his handkerchief and wiped her nose with her hand. "It's not relevant," she said.

Illusions could hide tears, anyway.

"As you say." Her patron smiled patiently, his eyes unreadable. "Don't worry—folk do not change. Killer or hero, angel or whore, no one ever changes. We only wear different faces."

Fayne shivered. She fixed her patron with a cold glare. "You must really hate her."

"Who?" he asked, tucking his kerchief into his colorful doublet.

"*Her.*" Fayne ground her teeth. Who else could she mean? The yellow-eyed whore—the woman who had destroyed her life—she who had taken the only thing she held dear in the world.

He was going to make her say it, she realized. Might as well accept it.

"Ilira," Fayne said, the name like bile in her mouth. "You must hate her as much as I do."

"Ah."

Fayne swore under her breath, remembering. She'd seen such pain on that damned face—and yet, it hadn't soothed her. Now she was not sure what to feel.

Her patron reached across the distance between them and laid a lithe hand against her cheek. She felt his awful heat over her scar—felt again the cutting bolt across her face.

"Do I hate her? No." His eyes were burning pits of molten gold. "Quite the opposite."

Fayne opened and closed her mouth several times. "I don't understand," she said.

"No." His eyes seemed very sad for a moment. "No, I don't expect that you do."

He drew away. She felt as if something had been cut from her—as though an axe had taken her arm, leaving a stump that tingled impotently.

"You wouldn't," he said. "Not yet. Not for several centuries, I don't think."

Anger rose from where it guttered in her belly—the rage let her ignore her doubts. She had always used it to protect herself from herself—that and guile.

Her words were cool and sharp as steel. "Treating me like a youngling?"

"No," he said. "Just someone who is missing the relevant experience."

"That being?" Fayne stretched sinuously. "You'd be hard pressed to find something I haven't . . . experienced." She wet her lips in one long stroke.

The casual flirtation made her feel better. She was no child to be dealt a chiding.

He smiled. "Where were we?"

"The next mark." Fayne leaned across the table, putting her nose alongside his.

"No holiday?" her patron asked. "No rest for the misery-maker?"

"Never." Fayne shook her head and kissed him on the tip of his nose.

"Careful," he said. "You've a place, young one. Remember it."

With a sigh, she leaned back and crossed her arms, pouting. "Tell me one thing."

"Yes, dear one?" he asked.

"Who hired the dwarf to kill Lorien?" she asked. "It wasn't me—so who was it?"

He grinned and did not answer.

Fayne scowled. "Well—who sent Avaereene and the Sightless? You must know *that*."

"Ah yes, lovely Avaereene. Heavens save us from spoiled, sharp-tongued girls!" He winked at her. "Present company excluded."

Fayne smirked. Present company excluded, her curvy *backside*.

"It seems an old friend of mine," her patron said, "one with whom I used to play a game of"—he waved as though thinking of the proper word—"*wit*, say, has decided this city holds an interest for him. Something suitably intriguing—and dangerous, for what it can do."

He yawned and waved. The serving lass brought two more bowls of wine. Her patron winked in thanks, and Fayne saw a shiver pass through the poor girl.

"You were saying, old one?" she teased.

He rolled his eyes. "Naturally, I determined what it was—this plaything my friend has discovered."

"And I'm to obtain it first," she guessed.

"Indeed—tonight, if possible." He raised his hand. "You'll need this."

Seemingly out of the air, he conjured a small pale gray stick, about the length of his smallest finger. He squeezed it once and it lengthened to about twice the length of his hand.

It was a wand, Fayne realized. It didn't feel any more powerful than her mother's wand—the one she carried now—and she had no idea what it was for.

"It isn't my fashion," she said. "So this must belong to someone else."

Her patron smiled. He pulled a pink quill and ink bottle from somewhere and was wrote a single word on a scrap of parchment. He contemplated his writing plume for a moment, then released it into the air, where it vanished. "Though I must tell you the sum total of this one's powers."

"Yes, yes, give it here," Fayne said. When her patron frowned, Fayne batted her lashes. "Please?"

He slid the parchment over and took up his wine as Fayne read the name. She stared.

"You—you must be hrasting *jesting* me." Fayne read it again and blinked at her patron.

He chuckled. "I see the irony is not lost upon that clever mind of yours."

"Oh." A sharp-toothed grin spread across Fayne's face. "Oh, no. Not . . . not at all." She peered at him, eyes glittering. "Why the interest—I mean, for your friend?"

"For that, I must tell you a story, dear child, of long ago—of this very city."

Fayne leaned forward, chin on her hands. Her whole body was tingling, her mind racing. This would be fun.

"The story of a great mage who wanted to stop the spellplague driving the world mad—only he had one impossible barrier." Her patron took up his wine.

"He was already mad."

CHAPTER TWENTY-EIGHT

"Unexplained magical disaster strikes Sea Ward!" called a broadcrier for the *Vigilant Citizen*. He was the loudest in the main streets. "Dozens wounded, priests at work."

"Watchful Order baffled as to cause!" shouted another. "Quoth the Blackstaff, 'It could have been worse—*much* worse.'"

"Watch seeks rogue spellcaster! For his protection, and for ours!"

Kalen and Myrin walked south past the criers on Snail Street. She clutched him tighter as they passed the ones who spoke of the spell chaos in Sea Ward yestereve, which seemed to be most of them. Kalen could feel her fingernails even through his glove, which spoke to what a ruin the previous night had left him. He would never tell Myrin that, though—she carried enough guilt already.

"You didn't mean it," Kalen murmured.

Myrin kept her silence, but Kalen saw tears in her eyes.

"Noble daughters kidnapped, ransom demanded!" shouted the broadcrier for the *Daily Luck*. "Watch following all leads—a dozen knaves in custody." Then, because it was a gambling sheet, the crier added: "Place your bets on the search, win fifty dragons!"

"Roaringhorn heir seeks mystery knight," called the crier for the *North Wind*. "Avows true love—offers hand in marriage! Lordlings line the streets."

Horns sounded in the dawn, bidding the gates to open and the day's business to begin. Kalen had come to Dock Ward to search for Fayne. He had treated her unfairly, he knew, and wanted to make amends.

He told himself it was only that—only a matter of honor.

Despite protests for her safety, Myrin had insisted on aiding. Privately, Kalen suspected the girl worried Fayne had been a casualty of yestereve.

"Imposter noble murders Sune priestess!" the broadcrier for the *Mocking Minstrel* called, startling Kalen. The voice was strangled. "Menagerie Salon ruined! Watch declines comment."

"Boy," Kalen beckoned him over. "Speak."

Tears filled the boy's eyes. "Oh, goodsir and lady," he said, pulling off his hat. "No one was a finer friend of us common-born than the poor lady."

"Lady Lorien, you mean?" Myrin asked.

The boy shook his head. "Lady Ilira," he corrected. "She gave coin to folks like me pa, who's hurt by magic and can't work. It's come out"—he pointed to his wares, to a tale halfway down the page—"come out that Lady Ilira was the one *founded* the Scarred Haven, a body of kindly ones who . . ." He shook his head and pointed to the lead article of the *Minstrel*. "Don't read this tale, m'lord—'tis cruel to one who did so much for us all."

"We all do what we must." Kalen handed the boy a gold dragon and took the broadsheet.

"As you will, m'lord." The boy smiled at the gold—far more than the broadsheet cost—then wandered down the street, crying his wares.

"What is it?" Myrin asked. "You saw how upset the boy was—why read—?"

"That's Fayne," Kalen said, pointing to the name on the broadsheet.

"Satin Rutshear?" Myrin giggled at the name, but Kalen grimaced. She blushed. "Sorry."

"At least we know she's alive," Kalen said.

Myrin smiled hopefully.

"Or at least," Kalen murmured, "she was when she gave this to the *Minstrel* to print."

Myrin's smile faded.

Kalen began to read. The boy had told him true—the gossip-ridden tale was sharp and biting, witty and entirely unfair. Exactly like Fayne.

Lady Ilira Nathalan, it reported, was a creature of cruel, murderous depravity. A search of her villa by the Watch had revealed—much as Satin had long suspected it would—evidence that Lady Ilira had been stealing from her competitors and, indeed, was an assassin. Private papers showed she had been in the employ of the Shadovar, under the name Shadowfox, one of their most effective assassins. She'd killed dozens of folk before the turn of the century—and, possibly, more recently as well—and used the bloody coin to build and support her Menagerie and the dummy organization, the Haven for the Scarred, which masqueraded as a charity. The Watch and mercantile bodies were now working to dismantle those bodies.

"That . . . that can't be Fayne's writing," said Myrin. "That's horrible! Lies! That can't . . . that can't *be*, Kalen."

But Kalen remembered Lady Ilira's hands covered in Lorien's blood—remembered the way she'd lunged at Rath and burned away half his face with her kiss, and the cruel passion in her eyes when she'd dared the Watch to *pierce* her.

He shivered, and Myrin put her arm in his as though to warm him. He smiled at her, but he didn't feel the slightest comfort.

They spent the day looking for Fayne—to no avail. Aside from the broadsheet that proved she was alive—or at least had been that morn—they found no trace of her.

As dusk fell, Waterdhavians returned home for evenfast—and though Myrin kept silent, Kalen heard her stomach gurgle. They had eaten little: only a simmerstew at dawn and handpies at highsun. They should go to a hearth-house, Kalen decided.

Likely Cellica was cooking even now, but Kalen couldn't yet return to the tallhouse and face her reproving stare—not after he had been so harsh with Fayne.

He felt every bit as guilty as Myrin did, he realized, but for a different reason—she had simply lost control. What Kalen had said . . . he'd meant every word, and regretted each one.

Kalen took Myrin to the Bright Bell, just south of Bazaar Street on Warrior's Way in Castle Ward. He didn't often eat at hearth-houses, but this one he liked. While not elegant or exotic, the food was good and plentiful and the place was frequented by plain folk—those people of Waterdeep whom he fought every night to defend from shadows they could not see.

Being around these folk let him think and relax, though he did not know any of them. That struck him as odd for the first time: for a defender of the folk of the city, he rarely spent any time with them. Most of his talk and time were spent with the Guard, the Watch, or Cellica, who, like Kalen, was not from the city. Though his looks and speech marked him as blood of the Sword Coast, he was yet a foreigner. Waterdeep, with all its adventures and splendors, was no more home than Westgate had been—or even Luskan, before that. He no longer had a home.

Myrin, for her part, loved the Bell. She stared about its tight labyrinth, crowded nooks, and choked dining alcoves with the innocent wonder of an explorer. She hearkened close to the loud buzz of chatter and jest that vibrated through the walls, and though the thick, smoky air made her cough, she was smiling as she did it. She seemed to have forgotten her worries with the proximity of folk and the promise of food. She seized Kalen's gloved hand and held it tighter and tighter as a servant led them to a table, deeper in the hearth-house.

Several times, Myrin stumbled and almost fell on one of the many trip steps between chambers that changed level slightly from room to room. Kalen caught her each time, as he knew the perils, and each time she lingered a little longer in his embrace before pulling away with a laugh.

They sat in a curtained alcove on the second floor of the Bell. A tall, thin servant wiped the table clean with an ale-stained rag as they sat. Then he stood waiting, and Myrin looked at Kalen awkwardly, out of her depth.

"You have the courses written?" Kalen asked.

The servant smiled and handed them printed menus—grand, elegantly scripted affairs on thick parchment. Myrin's eyes widened at the lists and she began reading immediately, fascinated.

In addition to a thick warming stew and fresh bread, Kalen ordered a pie of fowl while Myrin opted for boiled tahllap noodles with fresh vegetables and goat cheese. She tried a weak mulled wine, and Kalen requested a small glass of zzar for himself. The night was cold, and he felt like strong drink. The taste of almonds was intense enough to touch his numb tongue.

Myrin particularly liked the first-spring strawberries that came before the meal, and Kalen was glad to let her have all of them. He rather liked her little smile and the way she closed her eyes as she set each one against her lips to savor the taste. Once, she caught him looking and blushed.

He looked away and sipped his zzar. It had a bite that warmed his insides.

"You should tell me about yourself," she said. She blushed again. "A little, if you like—I just remember so little about myself, and I'd rather we spoke than sat in silence, aye?"

Kalen shrugged. "For instance?"

Myrin looked at her food. "That woman—Rayse. She's . . ."

"My superior in the Guard," Kalen said.

Myrin colored. "She's . . . she's very pretty."

"Yes." Kalen fell silent.

Myrin was flustered. "I'm sorry—I didn't mean . . ."

Kalen shrugged. "Nothing else binds Rayse and me," he said. "There was once, but that was some time ago."

Myrin shook her head. "I didn't mean to ask—that was improper."

"All's well." Kalen reached across the table to touch her chin.

Myrin looked up, startled, then smiled.

Kalen realized what he had done and retracted his arm. "Never you mind."

She started to speak but the words became half hiccup, half belch, and she covered her mouth, giggling. Kalen looked back at his food. He wished she'd stop doing that—he knew what Fayne meant, now, when she'd called Myrin "adorable."

"Kalen," Myrin said. "About today. About Fayne."

Kalen stiffened and wondered if she could read his thoughts.

Myrin looked down at her empty soup bowl. "I know why I'm seeking her, because she might be hurt, but why are you doing it?"

Kalen sipped his zzar. "Personal business," he said.

"Oh." Myrin bit her lip. She radiated disappointment like light and heat from the sun.

"Not *that* personal," Kalen said. "I . . . last night, I said something to her that was cruel and unfair. I need to beg her pardon." That was at least *part* of the truth.

"Oh." Myrin didn't ask anything more, but her eyes lingered. Kalen ordered another zzar.

"Will you tell me?" Myrin asked. "Cellica told me only a little. What passed, last night?"

He shrugged. "It's not important."

Myrin's eyes fell and she said nothing. Kalen's reply seemed to have displeased her. He might have spoken again, but their food arrived, steaming and delicious. As always, Myrin fell to her plate with relish, as though to make up for years of fasting. Kalen ate only half-heartedly.

"Speak," Myrin said. "Tell me something—anything about you!" She smiled sweetly.

Kalen *wanted* to speak, but there were too many things he did not want to say—either to her, or to himself. About Fayne. About Lorien and Lady Ilira. It left him uncertain.

As she ate, he started speaking. Not of Fayne, or Ilira, or Lorien, or anything about Waterdeep at all. He spoke about Shadowbane.

He told her, in quiet tones that would not be overheard, of his quest. He spoke of his training in Westgate and of Levia, his teacher. He told her of the Luskan of his youth, when he and Cellica had stolen and begged for their meals, or used her voice when she could. How in his eighth winter he had met Gedrin Shadowbane—the Night Mask turned paladin, founder and leader of the Eye of Justice—who had changed his life.

Kalen told Myrin of the oath Gedrin had exacted from him—never to beg again—and he spoke tightly of Vindicator, bequeathed to him and now in the hands of Araezra.

"Perhaps she is more worthy of it," Kalen murmured.

Myrin looked up, wiped her eyes, and laid her hand on his wrist. "You protected me," she said. "You have your powers back. Should you not have your god's sword back, too?"

Kalen smiled. "As the Eye judges," he said. "If I am worthy, it will come back to me. If I am not . . . then may it bring Araezra victory in her aims. I hope she honors it as I tried to."

Myrin drew her hand away. "It must be well," she said. "Having a god to serve. I don't know what god I served—if I even had one."

They sat in awkward silence, and Kalen was aware that Myrin was looking at him from the corner of her eye. She had stopped eating, and without knowing why, Kalen could sense she was upset. Was it something about her memory?

"Kalen," Myrin asked finally, "why do you do this?"

He looked down at his drink.

"If I don't," he said, "then who will?"

Myrin kept her eyes on him. "Who was that man I saw yestereve?" she asked, barely whispering. "When the villain was running and you hurt him anyway—just to hurt him?"

Kalen understood why she was upset. "That man attacked you," he said.

"But he was fleeing," Myrin said. "He would have run away, but you gave chase. You hurt him, when you didn't need to. Why?"

Kalen shrugged. "You wouldn't understand."

"Stop it!" Myrin touched his hand. Kalen felt a little tingle, electric, beneath his skin. Her eyes were very bright in the candlelight. "This isn't you—you aren't so cold."

Kalen opened his mouth, but a delicate cough arose near their table. The servant had returned. He hovered, looking awkward. "I'm sorry, I didn't mean to interrupt."

Kalen loosed Myrin's hand, and the girl looked embarrassed.

"Not at all," Kalen said. He reached in his scrip for coin. "We're finished, I think."

Other diners called for the servant, who nodded to Kalen and Myrin and left.

Kalen turned back to Myrin. He wished he could tell her everything—all the awful things he had done as a younger man—but he knew that would erase her smile. And that . . . he couldn't bear to do that.

"Mayhap we should buy me a weapon," Myrin said on their way back to Kalen's tallhouse. Her arm was linked in his, and any tension from the evenfeast had passed.

"Why?" Kalen examined her critically. Despite having eaten like a ravenous dog for two days, the girl was thin and light, almost frail. She didn't have the muscle or constitution for a duel at arms. "You have *me*."

She blushed. "But when you aren't there—like at the ball," she said. "A weapon for me to defend myself with, rather than with—you know." She waved her fingers.

"Like what?" Kalen asked. "A sword?"

"A dagger," Myrin said. "Small, light, eminently fashionable." She mimed patting the hilt of a blade sheathed at her hip and grinned. "Easy."

"Daggers are more difficult than swords." Kalen shook his head, which was clouded with zzar. He wasn't accustomed to strong drink. "Most of knife fighting is grappling," he said in response to her disbelieving look. "You don't have that sort of build."

Myrin crossed her arms. "I still want one."

Kalen paused in the street and shrugged. He drew the steel he usually kept in a wrist sheath. Myrin's eyes widened when she saw the knife emerge seemingly out of the air, and he passed it to her. As she marveled at it, he unbuckled his wrist sheath and secured it on her belt.

"Take care with that," Kalen said. "I'll be having it back."

"For true?" Myrin sheathed the blade reverently. "You'll show me how, someday?"

Kalen shrugged.

Myrin smiled and held his arm tighter as they walked on.

A cool drizzle began to fall when they reached Kalen's neighborhood, and he covered Myrin with his greatcoat. She wore a canvas shirt and skirt of leather, warm and practical, but no cloak. They reached the tallhouse and Kalen nodded to the night porter, then waved Myrin inside first. She blushed and giggled and picked up her skirt to cross the threshold.

They climbed two flights of stairs to his rooms and found the door unlocked. Cellica sat at the table, working on Shadowbane's black leather hauberk, stitching the rents. She looked up from her work and smiled. No matter what disaster befell, the halfling always smiled.

"About time," she said. "You two love whisperers had a pleasant day? I can tell you mine's been a crate of laughs." She threaded the needle through the leather and pulled it closed.

Kalen colored and Myrin giggled.

"I'm weary," the girl said. "Is it well if I sleep in your chamber again, Cele?"

"Kalen's bed's bigger," Cellica said.

Myrin flushed bright red. "I . . . I, ah . . ."

"Don't get giggly, lass," Cellica said. "I meant that he'd take the floor again." She batted her eyes at Kalen. "Won't you, Sir Shadow?"

Kalen shrugged. The ladies had shared a bed the first two nights, but after the ball—the third night—he'd given Myrin his bed. "Of course."

Myrin hesitated. "I think Kalen needs his bed. He hasn't fully recovered, you know." She bit her lip and looked at the floor.

Kalen didn't understand this at all. He just needed sleep—it mattered little where.

Cellica stared at her a long time, then smiled, as though picking up some subtle jest. "As you will—you're quite warm." The halfling shrugged. "I'll join you in about an hour. Soon as I finish." She clipped the thread with her teeth and rubbed the stitched breastplate with her delicate fingers. "Merciful gods! One would think you'd learn to dodge more blades and arrows."

"I'll remember that," Kalen said, his voice dry. His head ached and he rubbed his temple.

Myrin grinned and winked at the halfling, who winked in kind. Whatever conspiracy they had hatched, it was cemented. Myrin walked toward Cellica's room but did not let go of Kalen's hand, pulling him along. She opened the door but did not go in, nor did she release Kalen.

They lingered for a moment. Kalen looked over his shoulder, but the halfling seemed not to notice them. Myrin was digging the ball of one foot into the floor.

"We'll find her, Kalen," she said. "I know it."

He shrugged. Then, because it wasn't enough, he spoke: "Yes."

Myrin clasped one arm behind her back and looked at the floor shyly, then up at Kalen. Something unspoken passed between them—something that neither could say.

"Good e'en," Myrin said at length, awkwardly. She went inside and closed the door.

Kalen stood blinking for a breath, then he turned to find Cellica's eyes on him. "What?"

"For a man who reads faces and listens for lies every day . . ." The halfling trailed off.

Kalen rubbed his temples and limped toward his room. "Good e'en," he said.

He stepped inside, shut the door, and pulled off his doublet, which he tossed to the floor. He crossed to the basin and mirror and splashed water on his face. Vicious bruises and stitched cuts rose on his muscled frame. The deepest ached, despite his numbness.

Tough as he was, he had to admit the accumulated hurts of the last few days were taking their toll. All he wanted was to sleep until he no longer hurt.

He saw something move in the mirror and turned.

She lay in his bed, blanket pulled up to her nose. Her pale skin glittered in the candlelight and her red hair seemed almost black. Her eyes were wide and mischievous.

"Well met, Kalen," Fayne whispered. She smiled. "Coins bright?"

CHAPTER TWENTY-NINE

"YOU'RE HERE," KALEN SAID, AND HE STRETCHED. THOUGH HE DIDN'T expect a duel, he didn't turn his back on her and checked the dirk at his belt. He made no hasty moves, and didn't let his eyes linger on her curves under the blanket. "Cellica let you in?"

"Yes." Fayne bit her lip, her smile chased away by his cold voice. "And no. She doesn't remember I'm here. I warded us"—she nodded to the door—"against sound."

"You—" Kalen winced at the zzar ache in his head and rubbed his stubbled chin. "Are you wearing anything under that blanket?"

Slowly, Fayne lowered the blanket to reveal a thin white ribbon around her throat, from which hung a black jewel. Then she raised the sheet back to her chin.

"Ah." Kalen coughed and kept his gaze purposefully averted.

Fayne rolled her eyes. She sat up and lowered the blanket to bunch around her. "This is stupid, I know, and I'm a fool to come here, but I just have to say something, Kalen. You don't ever, ever have to see me again afterward, I just have to say it."

Kalen walked near the bed but remained standing. "Then say it."

Silence reigned between them for a moment. They looked at one another.

Kalen had seen Fayne nearly naked at the temple, but that had been different. A battle, when his blood was up. Now, her skin seemed smooth and soft. She was so very vulnerable, deprived of clothing. She seemed younger and lighter—fragile.

Like Myrin.

As though she could read his thoughts and wanted—*needed*—to turn his mind to her, Fayne opened her mouth and the words gushed forth.

"I . . . oh, Kalen, I've made a terrible mistake," she said. "A woman is dead because of me—because of my pranks. And . . . and I wanted to tell you that I'm sorry."

Kalen broke the gaze and looked toward the window. "Don't," he said.

Fayne's eyes welled. "Kalen, please. Please just let me say this."

She sat upright and edged closer to him. When he stepped away, she stayed on the bed, peering up at him.

"You were . . . you were right about me," she said with a sniffle. "I *am* just a silly girl who doesn't think about the hurt I cause. My entire life, all I've done is lie and ruin. I have a talent for it, and the powers to match, and that was how I made coin. All I've ever done is scandalize folk—some honest, most dishonest—for gold." She wiped her nose.

"Sometimes I did nobles and fops, sometimes people of real importance—merchants, politicians, traders, foreign dignitaries. Whatever they believed or fought for, I didn't care. I know—I was a horrible wretch, but I didn't care."

She sniffed and straightened up, looking at him levelly.

"I . . . I was doing the same thing with Lorien and Ilira and I didn't mean anyone to get hurt." She cast her eyes down. "You believe me, right? I didn't mean—"

Kalen kept his silence but closed his hand on the hilt of the dirk he wore at his belt. The dirk was a cheap, brute object without the elegance of Vindicator, but it could kill just the same. He'd spent the day searching for Fayne, but he hadn't realized that it had been equally a matter of anger as concern.

He didn't know how he felt.

"Explain why I should believe you."

"Why would I lie about this?" Fayne asked.

"I do not know—but you *are* lying." Kalen fished in his satchel and pulled out the folded *Minstrel*. He pulled it open and set it on the table. Then he drew his dirk and slammed it through her false name, pinning the broadsheet down. "Explain that," he said.

She bunched the blanket around herself, rose, and padded toward him on bare feet. "Oh, Kalen!" She flinched away from the broadsheet as though from a searing pan on a fire. "That . . . that *creature* killed my mother. I—I just wanted to cause her pain, that's all. But I never meant anyone to die—that was Rath's doing."

"How do I know you didn't hire him?"

"I'm telling you the *truth!*" Fayne cried. "You saw him try to kill me. He would have done so, if you hadn't come!" She sobbed. "I didn't want anyone to die."

"I don't believe you." He put his hand on the dirk—simultaneously gesturing to the broadsheet and offering a quiet threat. "Why write that? You *know* who killed Lorien."

"I . . . I was upset, Kalen!" Her eyes grew wet. "You don't understand! I was there when she killed my . . . I *saw* it happen! I hate that woman, Kalen—I *hate* her!"

She ripped the *Minstrel* off the table, tearing it against his blade, balled it up, and hurled it to the floor. Her scream that followed nearly shook the room.

Kalen flinched and looked to the door, but Fayne had spoken true. Had it not been warded against sound, Cellica would have burst in.

"So why not kill *her?*" Kalen asked. "Why Lorien, and not Ilira?" He stepped closer to her, so he could seize her throat if he wanted.

"I don't—I don't *like* people, aye," Fayne said. "I hate them. I hate everyone, especially her—but I don't hate enough to murder. That isn't me, and . . . and I have to make you see that."

"Why do I matter so much?"

Fayne wiped her eyes and nose. "Because I can't—not with you. I can't lie to you or trick you. You always know—you *always* know." She sobbed again. "It was so, so frustrating at first, but—there's something between us, Kalen. And it's something I can't understand."

Kalen looked into her eyes. How rich they seemed—bright, wet pools of gray cloud in her half-elf face. How earnest and true.

"I have to know, Kalen." She made a visible effort to compose herself, grasping her hands tightly in front of her waist. "Is . . . is what we have real? Can that really happen between two people who meet only for a moment? I've never loved any . . ." She trailed off and stared at the floor. She stomped angrily—frustrated. "I don't understand! It's not—it's not *fair!*"

"Fayne," Kalen said.

"You!" she cried. "The one man I can't have—the one man I should flee—but I can't leave you. Even now, as I stand here naked before you—you, who chastised me, who rejected me, who threatened to arrest me, and I can't leave—I can't just forget you."

Tears slid down her cheeks, and he couldn't have spoken if he tried.

"I need to know if I love you, and if you love me," she said. "I need . . . I need something real in my life of shadows and lies. Does that make any sense? Can't you understand?"

Kalen looked away when she met his eyes. He weighed her words and body language, probing for a lie, but found nothing. This was the truth, as far as he could tell.

Hers was a life of shadows and lies, he thought. Like his own life.

"Oh, Kalen," Fayne said. "Say something . . . say anything, just *please*."

Kalen turned toward her. "It isn't true."

Fayne's body went rigid, as though his gaze had turned her to stone. "What isn't true?"

"That a woman died because of you," Kalen said. "You didn't send Rath to kill her."

Fayne inhaled sharply.

"I believe you," Kalen said. "Your game was thoughtless and wicked and took Lorien off her guard, but it is not your fault—"

Fayne threw an arm around his neck and kissed him hard. It caught Kalen off guard and he staggered back a step. He could feel the pressure and could taste her lips on his, even with the numbness. The blood thundered in his veins, and he could feel his heart beating in his head.

"No." Fayne pulled away. "No. I'm sorry. I just . . . I had to. I'm sorry."

"What is it?"

Fayne went to reclaim the clothes she'd left on his bed. "You love her," she said.

"Ha." Kalen shook his head.

"Ha?" Fayne scoffed. "That girl practically hurls herself at you every moment you're together—it's in everything she does. She adores you—the sight of you, the thought of you. She loves you, you idiot. And you"—her eyes narrowed—"you love her, too."

He shook his head. "I do not."

She paused and looked at him curiously, warily. "You're sure?"

She stepped toward him, and he could feel heat growing within—lust for her and for the duel. It would always be this way with her, he thought.

"What do you feel, then?" she asked. "What do you feel, right now?"

It came to him, the perfect word. Kalen smiled sadly. "Pity."

Whatever Fayne had expected, that surprised her. "You pity her?" Then her voice became colder. "You pity *me*?"

"Myself." Kalen shook his head. "She makes me wish I were a better man."

Fayne flinched as though he'd slapped her. "That sounds like love to me."

She started to turn but he caught her wrist. "No," he said.

"No?"

He shook his head.

"Well thank the Maid of Misfortune," Fayne said, raising her jaw proudly. "I was starting to think you didn't fancy me anymore."

The sheer, unflappable confidence in her eyes—the mock outrage and scornful words, the shameless flirtation—all of it made Kalen smile. The bravado of this woman astounded him.

Fayne was not like shy and thoughtful Myrin, but bold and conceited, utterly convinced of her own allure. And as arrogant as Fayne was, Kalen had to admire her. She was unchanging, immovable, *perfect* in her imperfection.

He told her what he hadn't told Myrin—what he never would have dared tell her. He wanted to stop himself but couldn't.

"I am sick, Fayne."

She stared at him, as though judging whether he spoke true. Finally, she nodded.

Kalen went on. "When I was a child, I felt less pain than others did. My fingers are scarred from my teeth"—he spread his hands so she could see— "as are my lips." He licked his lips and pursed them, so she might see the marks. "I just—I just didn't feel it."

Fayne nodded, and her gray eyes grew a touch wider.

"I would have died, but for the scoundrel who took me in and raised me, among a host of other orphans," Kalen said. "He taught me how to inflict the pain I couldn't feel—how to use my 'blessing' for my benefit. Or rather, his."

"Sounds like my father," said Fayne. When he paused, she waved him on. "But this is your story—pray, continue."

"I found feeling eventually, but long after my skin had hardened. At six, I shrugged off stabs that would have left a man weeping on the floor."

Kalen watched Fayne's eyes trace the scars along his ribs and chest, some of which were very old. Each one, Kalen remembered well.

"I killed my master when I was just a child," Kalen said. "He was a cruel old man, and I had no pity for him. More pity I had for the older orphans he had hurt over the years—though I reserved the most for myself, understand."

Fayne nodded. She understood.

"I was a thief, and a mean one," he said. "Folk had done things to me— terrible things—and I had seen far worse. So when I hurt folk—killed them, sometimes—I didn't think anything of it. I used my blade to get coin—or food. Or if I was angry, as I often was. I was born hard as steel, and I only got harder."

He almost wanted Fayne to say she was sorry—as though she could take the blame for all the world and offer atonement. But she merely watched him, listening patiently.

"Without my master, I was forced to beg on the streets—to sell my services for food or warmth. I met Cellica shortly thereafter, and she became like a sister to me, but my master had done his work and I was stone not only on the surface, but inside."

"Cellica grew up in Luskan, too?" Fayne glanced toward the door. "She seems too soft."

Kalen shrugged. "She was a prisoner," he said. "Escaped the grasp of some demon cult."

"A cult?" Fayne looked troubled. "What kind of cult?"

Kalen shrugged. "Cellica didn't talk about it much, and I didn't ask," he said. "I met her by chance, and she set my broken arm. Healing hands."

"Mmm." Fayne nodded. "She was a good friend?"

"I hated her, too, at first," Kalen said. "As soon as my arm healed, I hit her, but only once." He grinned ruefully. "She put me down faster than you could say her name."

Fayne giggled. "You wouldn't think it, to look at her."

"Tough little wench," said Kalen, and Fayne shared his smile.

Then he paused, not wanting to tell her the story of Gedrin or of obtaining Vindicator, and in truth it did not matter. That would instill a touch of nobility to his story, and he did not feel noble. He was awash in his brutal past.

"When I was eight years of age, I . . . I made a mistake. I did something terrible, and my spellscar returned in full force. I couldn't move at all."

He tried to turn, but she held his hand tighter and didn't look away. Kalen set his jaw.

"I was frozen, locked in a dead body that felt nothing, but saw and heard everything. It was like my childhood sickness, but returned a hundredfold. A man grown would have gone mad, and perhaps I did—not knowing when or if I would ever move again. I couldn't even kill myself—only lie there and wait to die."

His hands clenched hard enough for him to feel his fingernails, which meant they would be drawing blood. Fayne watched him closely, consuming every word.

"I prayed—to anyone or anything that might hear," he said. "I prayed every moment for true death, but the gods did not hear me. They had abandoned Luskan and everyone in it."

"You were a man of *faith?*" asked Fayne. Her voice was respectfully soft—almost reverent. "An odd choice for a beggar boy."

He shrugged. "Cellica didn't follow the gods either—her healing was in needle, thread, and salve. But she believed in right, and she definitely believed in wrong. And though letting me die might have been kinder, as I thought, she told me every day that she would help me, no question. She loved me, I came to realize, though I had no understanding of it then.

"She kept me from starving. She cared for me when anyone else would have left me for dead. I hated her for that—for not letting me die—but I loved her all the same. She would feed me and clean me and read to me—but other times, she would just sit with me, talking or silent. Just be with me, when I had nothing else.

"And eventually—finally—I began to pray for life. Just a little bit of life—just enough to touch her cheek, hold her, thank her. Then I could rest." Kalen brushed a hand down Fayne's cheek. "Do you understand?"

Fayne nodded solemnly. "What happened?"

"Nothing," Kalen said. "No god came to save me—no begging brought life back into my dead body. I was alone but for Cellica, and she could not fight for me. I had to fight for myself."

Fayne said nothing.

"I stopped praying," Kalen said. "I stopped begging. Once . . ." He trailed off.

He breathed deeply and began again.

"After I escaped my master but before my mistake—when I was a boy of eight winters, begging on the streets. Someone once told me not to beg. A great knight, called Gedrin Shadowbane."

Something like recognition flickered across Fayne's face—the name, he thought.

Kalen continued. "He didn't ask me why I begged—nothing about my past, or who I was. He didn't care. He just told me, in no uncertain terms, that I was never to beg again. Then he struck me—cuffed me on the ear so I would remember."

"What a beast!" Fayne covered a grin with her hand and her eyes gleamed with mirth.

Kalen chuckled. "It was the last thing anyone said to me before I fell paralyzed," he said. "And as I lay unmoving, hardly able to breathe or live, I realized he was right. I stopped praying for someone else to save me, and fought only to save myself. Not to let myself die. Not yet—I would die, I knew, but not yet." Kalen clenched his fists. "Then, slowly—gods, so slowly—it came back. Feeling. Movement. *Life.* I could speak to Cellica again. I told her what I wanted—to die—and she cried. If I had begged her, she would have done it, but I would not ask that of her. She pleaded with me to wait—to give it a tenday, to see if it got better."

He closed his eyes and breathed out.

"It did. Slowly, with Cellica behind me every moment, I recovered," Kalen said. "But I knew it was only temporary. When we had the coin to hire a priest, he told us I still bore the spellplague within me—a spellscar festering at my core. Perhaps I'd had it from birth."

He flexed his fingers.

"Some bear an affliction of the spirit, mind, or heart—mine is in my body. The numbness will return—is returning—gradually, over time. And with it, my body dies, little by little." He shrugged. "I feel less pain—less of everything. And though it makes me stronger, faster, able to endure more than most men, ultimately, it will kill me."

Kalen looked toward the window at the rain hammering the city.

"I had a choice," he said. "I could waste my life dreading it, or I could accept it. I followed the path that lay before me. I accepted Helm's legacy, and followed the Eye of Justice."

As though his voice had lulled her into a trance from which she was just waking, Fayne blinked and pursed her lips. "Helm? As in, the god of guardians? The *dead* god of guardians?"

Kalen said nothing.

"I don't know if you know your history, but Helm died almost a hundred years ago," Fayne said. "Your powers can't come from a dead god—so what deity grants them?"

Kalen had asked himself the same question so many times. "Does it really matter?"

Fayne smiled. "No," she said, as she leaned closer to him. "No, it doesn't."

She caressed his ear with her lips, and her teeth. Kalen could just feel it—enough to know what she was doing—which meant she was probably hurting him. He didn't care.

She dipped a little and bit at the soft spot at the end of his jaw. She pressed her cheek to his, letting her warm breath excite the hairs on his neck.

Through it all, Kalen stayed still as a statue.

"I know you can feel this." Fayne's eyes were sly. "I wonder what else I can make you feel. Things that little girl couldn't dream of—things your mistress Araezra doesn't know."

Kalen smiled thinly. "Only," he said, "only if you give me something."

"And what," she asked, kissing his numb lips, "is that?"

"Tell me your name," Kalen said.

Fayne stepped back and regarded him coolly. "You don't trust me, even now?"

He shrugged.

"Very well. Can't blame you, really," Fayne said. "Rien. That's my real—"

Kalen shook his head. "No. It isn't."

"Gods!" Fayne laid her head on his shoulder and pressed herself hard against him, kissing his neck once more. He felt her sharp teeth, which meant they must have drawn blood. She wiped her lips before she drew away to speak to him, so he could not know for certain. "Rien is my true name, given me by my mother before she died."

"And it means 'trick' in Elvish," Kalen said. "No need to trick me."

She swore mildly, still smiling. Then she nibbled his earlobe and breathed into his ear. He knew his senseless skin awakened and went red, but he could not feel it.

Kalen sighed. "You can stop lying," he said.

"Eh?" Fayne clutched his lips hard enough for him to feel—hard enough to draw blood.

"You don't have to pretend to love me," Kalen said.

With a last, lingering kiss on the corner of his lip, Fayne pulled away and faced him squarely. His eyes glittered in the candlelight.

"How dare you," she said, half-jesting and half-serious.

"All this," Kalen said. "This is just an act. Isn't it?"

Her face went cold and angry, shedding all pretense of jest. "How *dare* you."

Fayne snapped up her hand to strike him, but he caught it and held her arm in place.

"That time," Kalen said, "your anger told the truth."

Fayne said nothing for a long time. Kalen put his hand on her elbow and though he held it only lightly, he might as well have bound her in iron.

"It's still that girl, isn't it?" Fayne accused. She raised one finger to point at him. "It's that little blue-headed waif with her tattoos you fancy, isn't it?"

She drew the bone wand from her belt and flicked it around her head. An illusion fell over her, cascading down like sparks to illumine her form, which shrank and tightened, billowed out a scarlet silk gown, and became Myrin.

"Is this what you want?" came the soft, exotic voice. Fayne in Myrin's image knelt and pressed her hands together. "Please, Kalen—please ravage me! Oh, ye gods!" She caressed herself and moaned. "I just can't *stand* the waiting, Kalen! Oh, please! Oh, take me *now!*"

Kalen shrugged. "This is beneath even you."

"Even me, eh? You have no idea how low I can sink," Fayne said with Myrin's voice. "Wouldn't you like that, Kalen? To see your little sweetling as *wicked* as I can be?"

"She's far too good for me," Kalen said. "For any of us."

"And I'm what—a perfect fit?" She flicked her tongue at him. "You disgust me."

"No," Kalen said, "I don't."

"Oh?" Fayne crossed her arms—Myrin's arms—and regarded him with an adorable pout.

She took out her wand again and broke the illusion. Her half-elf form reappeared, wavered over something darker, then settled. It was brief, but it made him wonder . . .

"Why, O wise knight of shadows," she said, "why don't I hate you?"

"Because you're like me," Kalen said. "A lover of darkness."

Fayne stared at him another moment, anger and challenge in her eyes. Every bit of him burned—wanted him to lunge forward and grasp her, wrench the blanket from her body, throw the paladin aside and free the thief at his heart.

"I should go," she said finally. "You and I . . . she's the one for you, Kalen, not I. She is better for you." Fayne made to leave, but Kalen stopped her. This time, his grip was firm.

"I know well what's better for me," Kalen said. "And I want you instead."

Fayne blinked at him, wordless.

"Show me." Kalen ran his fingers along her cheek. "I want to see your face."

He saw the shift in her stance, could almost feel every hair on her body rise. He felt her bristle, the way a lion might just before it pounces. "But you do see my face," she said, her tone dangerous. "I stand here before you, no illusions."

"That's a lie," Kalen said. "I've taken my mask off for you—take yours off for me."

He still held her by the wrist. Could he feel the blood thundering in her veins, or was he imagining it? His grip lessened.

"Run," Kalen said, "or take off your mask. Choose."

"Kalen, you can't—" she said. "Please. I'm frightened."

Perhaps I *am* cruel, Kalen thought. But Gedrin had taught him the value of pain, with that clout on the ear. Pain reveals who we truly are.

"You want it to be real, then choose." He shook his head. "I won't ask again."

Trembling, Fayne looked at him for three deep breaths. He was sure—so sure—that she would run. But then she drew her wand from her belt with a steady hand. He saw the tension in her body, practically felt her insides roiling and tossing like a rickety boat in a god-born storm, but she stayed calm.

She was like the thief he had been, he thought.

"Very well," she said.

She passed the wand in front of her face and a false Fayne slid away like a heavy robe, leaving her naked before him. Her true face took form—her skin and hair and body. All her lies vanished, and she was truly herself. Regardless of her shape, she was just a woman standing before a man.

Kalen said nothing, only looked at her.

Finally, Fayne looked away. "Am I . . ." she asked, her voice broken. "Am I really so repulsive?"

She tried to run, but he caught her arm once more. "Your name," Kalen said. "I want your name."

Fayne's eyes were wet but defiant. "Ellyne," she said. "Ellyne, for sorrow." Her fists clenched. "That's my name, damn you."

"No." Kalen looked down at her, his mouth set firm. "No, it isn't."

Fayne's knees quaked. "Yes, it—"

Then he kissed her, cutting off her words.

He kissed her deeper.

The blanket slipped down to the floor and her warm body pressed against him.

CHAPTER THIRTY

CELLICA MUST HAVE DOZED AT HER WORK. SHE AWOKE AT THE TABLE, needle and thread in hand, to the sound of muffled sobs.

The tallhouse rooms were not large—only a central chamber five paces across that served for dining and sitting, and two smaller rooms for slumber. Cellica's room, from whence the sobbing came, was small by human standards, adequate for a halfling. It boasted a window—Kalen, in one of his rare thoughtful moments, had cut it out of the wall.

Myrin was crying, she realized. But why?

"Kalen," she murmured.

Cellica slipped down from the chair and padded over to Kalen's door. She peered through the keyhole, much as she expected Myrin must have—

She looked just long enough to see Kalen's back, a pair of feminine arms wrapped around it, and knew instantly what had happened. She pulled away and her face turned into an angry frown. "Kalen, you stupid, *stupid*—"

She hurried to her chamber. Sure enough, Myrin was clad in her red gown again, though it was now much rumpled. She sat in the corner, compacted as small as she could manage, and bit her knuckles. She smelled of honeysuckle—Cellica's favorite and only perfume.

"Oh, peach, peach," Cellica said. She crossed to Myrin and embraced her. "It's not your fault. You know that, right?"

Myrin sobbed harder and leaned her head against Cellica's chest. Where their skin touched, Cellica felt a tickle of magic.

It wasn't difficult for the halfling to connect events. Behind the closed door, Myrin had doffed the more practical attire they'd received at the Menagerie in favor of the red gown, which she'd asked Cellica to mend and clean earlier that day. Armed with that—and Cellica would confess readily that she looked a true beauty—and a bit of Cellica's perfume, she'd padded out to Kalen's room.

But Fayne had pounced on Kalen first.

Cellica cursed the man. How could he be so blind? Myrin had been throwing herself at him ever since that morn when they met. No wonder nothing had ever come of Kalen and Araezra. Cellica was surprised Rayse still *spoke* to the dumb brute.

"There, lass, there." Cellica stroked the girl's hair. "Kalen's just an idiot."

Myrin wrenched away. "No, he's not!" she said. "You know he isn't. Shut up!"

The halfling blinked, stunned by her outburst, and leaned away. She tried to speak, but a compulsion in Myrin's words had stolen her speech.

My voice, Cellica thought. She took my voice?

The girl's anger turned to a sob. "He doesn't love me," Myrin said. "I thought maybe he followed me from the ball because he loved me, but . . . but . . ." She sniffed and wiped her cheeks. "He followed because it was his duty, because he was guarding me. That's all."

"But that's not true," Cellica said. "I've never seen him look—"

"Go away," Myrin said. "Take your false hopes and just *go away!*"

Cellica found herself rising to her feet without thinking. Her conscious mind wanted to stay and talk, but her body obeyed without her consent.

It was the *voice*. Cellica's own command, but from Myrin's lips. How was this possible?

"Go away and go to sleep," Myrin said. "Here." She handed Cellica the blanket.

The halfling closed her door softly, leaving Myrin alone in her chamber. She wandered, increasingly sleepy, into the kitchen and main room. She felt so tired, as though she had run fifty leagues that day. Just a little—

She slumped down on the floor and was snoring before her chin hit her chest.

"Mother!" Fayne gasped, waking with a start, that one word on her lips.

Merely a nightmare, she assured herself with some disgust. She'd been sleeping again.

Fayne leaned back, her naked body glistening with sweat, while the world drifted back. A sparse tallhouse chamber. A plain bed. A man sleeping beside her, head nestled in her lap. Her tail curled around him like a purring cat, restlessly flicking back and forth.

Who was this man, and why did she smile when she thought of him?

She remembered the dream. An elf woman screamed and tore at herself to fight off a horror that existed only in her mind. A gold-skinned bladesinger without a heart moaned on the rough, slick floor. Fayne's own mother, dark and beautiful and dead, lay impaled at her feet. The cold, bone wand in Fayne's tiny hand sent pain through her arm and into her soul.

And the girl—Fayne had seen the girl wreathed in blue flames. The girl flickered into being just as Fayne's mother's magic burned her from the inside out.

She looked down at the muscled, scarred man who embraced her naked thighs and slept. Kalen, she remembered.

Then it all returned, chasing the nightmares away once more. She whistled in relief.

Gods, she hated sleeping. So barbaric. It limited more pleasant activities, anyway.

Fayne slipped out of Kalen's embrace and left him on the bed alone. She smiled at him for a moment before shaking her head. "Belt up, lass," she chided. "You're going all giggly."

She emptied the chamber pot out the wall chute—again, a barbaric necessity—and sat on the cold floor for a moment, collecting herself. Then she rose and stretched.

The moonlight that leaked through the window would not last long—dawn was coming, and she had best take her leave soon. She opened the shutters and put her face out into the cool Waterdeep night. She breathed deep the refreshing breezes off the sea and let loose a peaceful, contented sigh. Then she shut herself back inside.

She reclaimed her clothes—plain leathers, slightly shabby and worn. They weren't the ones she remembered wearing there, but she was used to that feeling. When most of one's wardrobe was illusory, one's basic clothes often varied.

Illusion . . .

She realized something and crossed quickly to Kalen's mirror, which hung on the wall over a small basin. The water was tepid when she trailed her fingers through it, but the mirror was more important.

Her true face blinked back at her.

"Gods," she murmured, caressing her pale skin. "Did I really sleep in *this?*"

She ran her fingers across the scar along her cheek—pushed back the rosy pink hair that obscured it. The scar, from a crossbow bolt, ached, as it always did that time of night.

"This just won't do," she said. "Can't go scaring children, now can we?"

She made to draw her wand from her belt, then stopped. That was for cosmetic changes. Her true body—she really needed to hide that.

She invoked her disguising ritual with the aid of her amulet. Her flesh shifted like putty. The pink hair turned back to her familiar half-elf red, her sharp features smoothed, her ears shrank and rounded slightly, and her wings and tail vanished.

"Now, then," she said.

Over this she slid an illusion, one that suited her. Simply because she felt like it, she made herself look like her mother: a beautiful sun elf with eyes like tar pits and lips like rubies. A gauzy black gown spun itself out of the air around her thin limbs.

It was exactly as Fayne remembered her mother, in the few years they'd had together before the crossbow bolt that had given Fayne the scar on her cheek.

Fayne crossed to the door, opened it as silently as she could, and stepped into the outer chamber. She heard Cellica snoring and saw a sleeping bundle slumped in the center of the room. Fayne smiled gently.

Then she heard a whisper of leather on wood, and she looked just in time to see Rath rushing her out of the shadows. She did not have time to speak.

Once again, Cellica awakened to what sounded like Myrin weeping. "Gods," she murmured, brushing away the stickiness of sleep. She'd had such vivid and bawdy dreams, too.

The first light of early dawn crept through the windows. An hour would yet pass before the sun peered over the horizon. The city lay quiet.

Cellica heard shuffling sounds and stifled sobs from her own bedchamber.

Thinking of Kalen, she lifted her crossbow from the table. Mayhap she'd shoot him for being such an idiot and sleeping with the wrong woman.

She paused to look again through the keyhole into Kalen's chamber. She braced herself for what she would see, but he was alone and unmoving on the bed.

Blushing a little, Cellica tiptoed toward her room. She heard a stifled moan, then something crashing down, like a chair, and the hairs on her neck rose.

The halfling slid the door open a crack and stopped dead.

On the bed, illuminated by the moon, was a struggling Myrin in a nightgown, two hands tying a cloth around her mouth to gag her. Those hands belonged to a black-robed dwarf—the one they had seen in Lorien

Dawnbringer's chamber: Rath. Half his face was a burned wreck, but she knew him.

"Don't move," Cellica said, mustering as much command voice as she could.

The scarred face blinked at her, holding Myrin on the bed with one hand. "Child . . ."

"I'm not a child." Cellica aimed at his face. "And if you think this is a toy, you're damn wrong." Her hands trembled. "Kalen!" she cried. "Kalen!" He would hear that, she hoped—unless his wall suddenly blocked all sound, or some such nonsense.

"Calm yourself, wee one," the dwarf said. "I am unarmed."

As if that mattered, Cellica thought. From what Kalen had told her, he could kill them both with his bare hands, if only he could move. Her voice had trapped him.

"Don't call me wee, orc-piss," Cellica snapped. "Take her gag off."

"I wouldn't," Rath said. As he could not otherwise move, his eyes turned to Myrin. "This girl is dangerous."

"Do it!" Cellica hissed. "And where's Fayne?" She raised the crossbow higher. "What have you done with Fayne, you blackguard?"

"Cellica," came a voice.

A shadow loomed out of the corner, and Cellica turned to find—*her*.

Of all the nightmares she might have imagined, she never would have expected this one. A specter from her past—from before she and Kalen had gone to Westgate, from when she had been slave to a demon cult. One she had never told him about, and one who had haunted her every nightmare through all the years in Luskan and since.

The golden elf lady with the eyes of darkness.

"You," Cellica said, terrified.

The woman paused, considering. Then, finally, she smiled. "Me."

A dagger flashed and pain bit into Cellica's stomach. Her legs died and she slumped to the floor. The world faded. She heard only Myrin's muffled voice crying her name.

CHAPTER THIRTY-ONE

K ALEN MUST HAVE BEEN WEARY—AND INDEED, HE HADN'T SLEPT until shortly before dawn. He awoke near highsun—rested, thirsty, and ravenous.

He was mildly surprised Cellica hadn't awakened him—perhaps with an ewer of water, as was her habit. In a way, he was disappointed he wasn't waking up dripping wet. He would have seized Cellica's pitcher and drank the rest of its contents, he was so thirsty.

Kalen felt around the bed next to him, but Fayne was gone. In truth, he wasn't surprised. A woman like that couldn't be kept abed all night *and* half a day. And had she stayed, she certainly would have awakened him in the morning—he knew that for a certainty.

The desires of that woman—that *creature* . . .

"Growing up like that—hated and beaten and unloved," she said, her wide, silver, pupilless eyes gleaming at him. "It muddled you—ruined you for mortal women, did it not?"

"Yes," he gasped. Her magic heightened his senses and her hands burned him through his hardened skin. Her lips, oh gods, and her teeth . . .

Her sharp-fanged grin widened. "Good."

Kalen shivered at the memory.

He pulled himself from his cool, tousled bed and stretched. It smelled like her. Her scent was everywhere, sweet and intoxicating and wicked.

In the mirror, his face had a short forest of brownish bristle, which he would leave to grow. Fayne had giggled when she touched his rough chin.

The previous night blurred in his mind—he had an eye for detail but his awareness had ruptured against her. She existed to him as a forbidding yet alluring ideal—a memory of pleasure and shadowed pain.

"You have to tell me if I'm hurting you," he had told her.

"Why?" had been her reply.

She whispered a word in his ear that filled him with shuddering agony. He fought through the dizziness to kiss her harder. His fingers dug into her flesh, wrenching a gasp from her lips.

"I can't tell my own strength—I can't always feel everything. You have to—"

"You misunderstand." Nothing about her smile was innocent or confused. "*Why?*"

He shivered again and the image faded.

There had been pain, yes, but none of it physical. It had been in their hearts. Things had broken that had needed breaking.

He shook his head to clear it. He wandered, in only his loose hose, to the door.

In the main room, all looked much as it always did. But he saw immediately that the coals that kept the simmer stew hot through the night in preparation for the morn had gone out, yet the pot still hung over them.

Kalen frowned. Had no one eaten today?

And—when he entered the room fully—he discovered an oily red-black puddle spreading across the floor, coming from the other bedchamber.

Instantly, Kalen was on alert and listening. He heard weak, haggard breathing and recognized it immediately. Heedless of an attack, he hurried to Cellica's room.

The halfling lay within. Her middle was a mess of red and she was paler than chalk. Kalen would have thought her dead if he hadn't seen her chest moving, just barely.

"Cellica," Kalen said, kneeling beside her. "Gods. Gods!"

The halfling's eyes opened and her lips parted. "Well . . . met. Coins bright?"

Kalen cupped her face. "Cellica," he said. "Sister . . ."

"Look at this, Kalen." One feeble hand indicated the black mess that soaked the front of her linen shift. "Killed me, Kalen. Knife cut all my insides. Poisoned. Too much for you."

Kalen's fingers lingered over her breast. He knew she was right. The wounds were too deep, and puckered black by poison. He couldn't heal her—not with his meager powers.

But he had to try. He had to.

He cupped his hand around his ring and closed his eyes.

Eye of three gods, Helm, Tyr, Torm, whoever you are—hear my prayer.

"No, Kalen—even if you'd come four hours gone . . . it's too late."

"Shut up." Kalen gripped his ring tightly, driving the symbol of Helm into his skin. He had sworn he would never beg, but he would beg for any god who might heal his sister . . .

"Don't do it, Kalen," Cellica said. Her suggestive voice was cracked, broken, but still made him pause. "Not for me."

He looked into her eyes and tried to speak through a choked throat. "Let me save you."

"You can't." She shook her head. "Save it for her. The dwarf . . . he took her."

Rath, Kalen realized. "Who?" he whispered. "Who did he take?"

"Myr . . . Myrin."

Cellica shook her head sharply, prompting a series of heaving, gagging coughs. Kalen thought she might spit forth shards of glass. "And Fayne."

"What about her?" Kalen coughed, burying his mouth against his arm. "Did you see her?"

Cellica shook her head. "I saw—" Her eyes widened as though afraid. "Not important."

"I don't understand," he said. Anger suffused him.

"I know—" Cellica clutched his arm hard. "I know that look in your eye."

"Cellica," Kalen said. "Cellica, I swear to you. I will find him, and when I do—"

"Please don't," she said. "Don't make me die listening . . . to dark words." Tears filled her eyes. "If it takes . . . me dying to remind you—to save you from . . ." She gestured feebly, as though to indicate the world entire.

"You're not going to die," Kalen said.

Cellica grinned wanly. "Just remember who you are."

Kalen swallowed. "I'm nothing. Just a shadow of a man—not fit for—"

"Shush." The halfling rolled her eyes. She reached for his face and slapped him lightly on the cheek. "You idiot."

Then blood poured from her lips and she gasped for air. Kalen held her tightly, felt her heart hammering in her chest. "Remember," she whispered.

"I—" Kalen squeezed her hand tighter. "I will, but you'll be right here to remind me."

"So charming." She smiled dizzily. "Always so—"

And then her eyes quaked and saw nothing.

CHAPTER THIRTY-TWO

THE WORLD SWAM BACK GRADUALLY, IN LAYERS OF GRAY AND BLACK.
Myrin struggled for several moments to remember who she was, and even longer to reason out where she was: a darkened chamber with a stone floor and walls. A slim shaft of sunlight fell through a high window, lighting the chamber dimly. Overhead and all around her, she heard a great clicking and whirring, as though from some sort of mechanism—grinding stone and metal against one another.

Fayne sat next to her, looking up at the ceiling and murmuring softly. A bruise colored the right side of her face, and something was wrong with her left arm—it hung oddly from her shoulder.

"Fayne?" Myrin tried to ask. Something lumpy and soft filled her mouth.

"Oh good, you're awake," the half-elf said. She was not gagged. "I'm almost . . . there."

Fayne's hand slipped out from behind her. Myrin heard a fleshy pop, and Fayne's arm shifted back into its socket. Her stomach turned over.

Fayne looked around and reached toward Myrin. "Now," she said, "promise not to cry out or try any magic—something the dwarf might hear?"

Myrin nodded.

Fayne removed Myrin's gag. "Kalen will come to rescue you soon, I think," she said. "I left him a note, and I don't think he knows how to give up." She ran her fingers through her hair.

"What's going on? Who was that gold woman?" Myrin asked, hardly daring to speak. Then she struggled against her bonds. "Why aren't you untying me?"

"Don't be silly—we can't *both* escape," Fayne said. "If we do that, Rath will get away—and you want him to pay for Cellica, right?"

"I suppose." Myrin didn't want anyone else to be hurt. "But won't he hurt me when he finds you gone?"

"I don't think so," Fayne said. "He's been paid to take us alive, I think." She patted herself as though searching for something. Her hand settled over her belly. "Here it is."

"What?"

Myrin watched as Fayne drew from her bodice a shaft of gray-white wood about twice the length of a dagger. It didn't look at all familiar and Myrin had no idea what it was.

"Wait." Fayne moved to put it in Myrin's hand, but paused. "I can only give this to you if you promise you'll be careful, and only use it when the time is right."

"I promise," Myrin said. "But what is it?"

Fayne slipped the item into Myrin's manacled hand and she knew its touch instantly, though her mind had no memory of it. A wand—*her* wand.

Fayne slid it gently into the sleeve of Myrin's nightgown. "Remember your promise—only if you think you can defeat Rath." Fayne stood.

"Yes," Myrin said. She longed to feel the wand again, but she could wait. "Hold—"

Fayne had turned to leave. "Aye?"

"Can't you stay with me?" Myrin asked. "Can't we fight him together?"

Fayne knelt down again. "Child—"

"Don't call me a child," said Myrin. "I'm not that much younger than you. Maybe five or six winters—no more."

Fayne's eyes glittered. "Are you sure?"

"Yes," Myrin lied. She wasn't, now that she thought about it. "But what's more important, I know what you said."

"Oh?" Fayne looked dubious.

Myrin narrowed her eyes. "You said Kalen would rescue *me*—and I also know you aren't unbinding me and putting the wand in my hand because you think I might use it against you. Now why would you do that—unless you were afraid of me?"

"Not convinced by my performance, eh?" Fayne smiled and gestured to the manacles she'd discarded. "I'm afraid you're right. I'm an opportunist, Myrin—and I see my chance. It's nothing personal, you understand."

"This is about Kalen," Myrin accused.

Fayne looked genuinely surprised. "Why would you think that?"

"You're leaving me here," Myrin said, "so I won't fight you for him."

"Would you?" Fayne knelt before Myrin, her hands a dagger's length from Myrin's bonds. "Would you fight me for him?"

"Yes." Myrin stared her down, looking right into her gray eyes.

Fayne stared back, that same ironic smirk on her face. "You'd be wasting your time," she said. "Kalen's a killer—a hard, brutal killer. He'd never love a softling like you."

"He's different now," Myrin said. "He's changed."

Fayne shook her head. "Folk never change," she said. "They just wear different faces."

Myrin shivered at the words. Her mind raced. "If fighting you for Kalen is useless," she reasoned, "then you would as well release me. So why don't you?"

Fayne shook her head. "You're a clever girl. But I can't do that."

"Why not?"

"I have reasons, I assure you."

"I'd like to hear them."

Fayne said nothing, only leaned in to kiss Myrin on the lips, in a gesture that was as sisterly as it was mocking. It lingered, becoming warmer, but Myrin felt trapped—paralyzed as though by a spider's venom.

Dimly, she felt Fayne freeze taut as well. Her hands clasped ineffectually, as though she was trying to escape the kiss but could not.

It felt strange. She'd never kissed a woman—that she remembered, anyway—and it stirred odd, tickling feelings on the back of her neck and down deep in her stomach. She wanted more of Fayne—to drink Fayne in, absorb her into herself.

Myrin saw, reflected in Fayne's widening eyes, blue runes spreading across her forehead.

When Fayne's lips touched hers, Myrin saw her clearly—saw *inside* her. She couldn't say how—as with the lich woman and her magic, Myrin simply saw and did not question.

She was in an underground chamber, she realized, smoky with torches and the reek of burning flesh. She could see no more than half a dozen paces around her.

An elf woman in leathers stood a few steps from her. She looked familiar, and Myrin knew her: Lady Ilira, only younger. Young enough that she could see the difference, which for an elf meant seven or eight decades, mayhap ten. She held a crossbow pointed at Myrin—no, at *Fayne*.

Myrin realized she was watching this through Fayne's eyes.

"Where is she, Cythara?" Ilira's voice burned her ears. "Where is the child?"

Myrin felt strong hands grasp her shoulders. "What child?" a woman's velvet-dark voice asked over her shoulder. "I hold none but my own daughter. Why—lost one of yours, did you?"

Myrin saw Ilira shiver in rage.

"By the Seldarine—don't fire!" a man cried from behind Ilira. "You'll hit her child!"

Myrin looked: a tall, handsome, gold-skinned elf, clad in shimmering mail, with a sword that gleamed in the torchlight. The sword should have pulsed with magic, but she felt a pressure she recognized as a magic-killing field radiating from the elf. A spell he had cast. *Bladesinger*, she thought, though she had no idea what the word might mean.

She understood that he had meant her—Fayne. She had a sense of feeling childlike. If Ilira was almost a century younger here, how old was Fayne? What *was* Fayne?

Myrin looked up through Fayne's eyes at the woman holding her protectively. *Mother*, she realized: a gold-skinned elf, half-dressed in a sweaty black robe. She could have been twin to the bladesinger, were it not for her cruel beauty. Shadows danced in her eyes.

"Kill me if you will, slut, only let my daughter live," Fayne's mother said to Ilira, with a cruel smile. "You see, *I* can have a child, while you are barren, no matter how my brother ruts you. I am well pleased with that and can die smiling."

Ilira gave a strangled cry and would have fired, but the bladesinger stepped in the way.

"Twilight, please!" the elf lord begged. "Please—she's my sister, and she has a—"

"That is *not* a child, Yldar," Ilira said. "That is a demon. A *demon!*"

Myrin felt white-hot loathing for Ilira wash over her like a wave and knew it was Fayne's hatred. It suffocated her, and she could not move.

The bladesinger put his arms out. "You'll have to kill me, too. I'll not move."

Ilira grasped his arm to pull him aside, and Myrin-as-Fayne saw smoke rise where their skin touched. Yldar's flesh *burned*, and yet he stood firm. They both looked startled by Ilira's use of her power, and she quickly let go.

"How can you defend her?" Ilira cried. "She murdered your betrothed!"

"That was an accident," he asserted. "She meant to kill—"

"Don't you see?" Ilira cried. "She's controlling you! She's controlled your life since you were a child. She rules you now, though you refuse to see it. She—*Yldar!*"

The bladesinger had fallen to his knees, clutching his chest. Ilira reached for him, then flinched away as though her touch might kill him. She looked at Fayne's mother. "Stop it!"

Myrin looked up to see a bloody mass in her mother's hand. A heart, Myrin knew—Yldar's heart. She realized Yldar's attention had waned, and his counterspell with it.

"Flee," her mother said, "or he dies."

"Do not do this, Cythara," Ilira said. "He is your brother. You saw how he—"

"Only that he stood between us," Fayne's mother said. "Now you owe him your life—don't waste his. *Flee.*"

Myrin heard the imperative—the magical command in that word—but Ilira fought to hold her ground. Myrin saw something move in the shadows behind her—thought she saw a face—but it was only for an instant.

"Flee." Cythara squeezed the heart in her hand and Yldar, still moaning, screamed loud and long. "I won't say it again."

Ilira, tears streaking her face, rose to go. "You win, Cyth." She turned her back.

Myrin could feel Fayne's mother smile.

Then she heard a click and felt a sharp slash across her cheek. She screamed in Fayne's youthful voice and fell. As Fayne fell, Cythara looked down at the crossbow bolt that had sprouted between her breasts. Myrin realized Ilira had fired behind her back, under her cloak.

Blood—bright red blood—trickled from the corner of Cythara's mouth and she fell.

Something caught Myrin: Ilira had appeared, seemingly from the shadows. Their skin touched and Myrin's flesh tingled but did not burn, as had Yldar's. She wanted to speak—Fayne wanted to speak—but the elf only set her down and ran to the bladesinger, who was coughing and trying to sit up.

Myrin looked at Cythara's corpse. Blood leaked around it—hot, sticky fluid that cooled to tacky sludge. Her open eyes stared. Yldar's heart had vanished from her hand, and she lay like some stripped, crumpled doll. Abused by the world, humiliated, and discarded like refuse.

Myrin felt hot inside—Fayne burning with anger, crawled to her mother's body.

Stop, child, came a voice in her head. *You cannot.*

But she didn't listen. She drew Cythara's wand—a shaft of bone—from her mother's limp hand and turned it toward Ilira's back. The woman was fussing over Yldar and wouldn't see the attack.

Stop, Ellyne, commanded the voice—and she knew it was distracted. A battle was going on, somewhere, between the speaker and some shadowy foe. *It is too powerful for you.*

Myrin leveled the wand and uttered syllables in a language she couldn't possibly know. But she recognized them, horribly, as the tongue of demons.

"*Your worst fear,*" she said in those black words. "*Your worst fear to unmake you!*"

Searing pain swept through her, burning every inch of her body. She fell to her knees and screamed as the horrible power ripped from her and struck the woman she most hated.

And Ilira straightened, back suddenly taut as a wire, and turned toward her. She did not see Myrin, but something between them. Her mouth spread wide in a terrified **O**.

"No!" she screamed. "No—I don't need you! *I don't need you!*"

Blood trickling down her face, Myrin—Fayne—Ellyne—whoever she was—laughed.

She saw something else, then, behind them—a girl, clad in blue flames. *Myrin.*

Herself.

.:⌒:.

The vision ended as Fayne wrenched herself away from Myrin. Fayne lay shuddering on the floor, her hands pressed to her temples.

"Lady Ilira," Myrin murmured. "Lady Ilira killed your mother. That's why you wanted to hurt her. That's why—"

"What?" Fayne shook her head. "What are you blathering about?"

"I was there—I saw you get cut. Right there." Myrin looked hard at Fayne's cheek, and sure enough, a scar faded into existence along the smooth skin.

Mutely, Fayne raised her hand to the scar. Her lip trembled. She was afraid.

Myrin understood what Fayne wanted. More than that, she understood what Fayne *was.* She saw the depths of her game—saw the darkness in her heart. "What happened to you?"

Fayne shook her head. She pulled a bone shaft from her belt—the wand from the vision, Cythara's wand—and slid it across her cheek. The scar smoothed out and vanished.

"Whatever you saw, it doesn't matter," Fayne said. "It has nothing to do with you."

"I saw *you.* Saw what you are. Ah"—Myrin shivered—"what are you?"

Fayne laughed—and in that moment, all the tension went out of her. "Oh, stop it—you're so cute when you're scared." She nuzzled her thumb into Myrin's cheek.

Despite herself, Myrin had to smile.

"You don't have anything to worry about." Fayne traced her fingers down her cheek. "This is one of my rare noble moments."

"Noble?" Myrin blinked.

"Indeed," Fayne said. "The very existence of our world is at stake, and you can save it."

Myrin narrowed her eyes. "How?"

"Simple, my dear," Fayne said with a smile. "You can die."

Myrin laughed, but the nervous sound died away. Fayne's face was mortally serious.

"You . . . you're not jesting?"

Fayne shook her head. "No, tragically. Your very existence is a threat to yourself, everyone around you, and perhaps all of Faerûn."

Myrin was stunned. "But . . . but I haven't done anything!"

"No," Fayne said. "But you will."

"You . . . you can't kill me for something I *might* do!"

"Will," said Fayne. "I didn't say might. *Will*."

"Tell me what it is!" Myrin said. "I won't do it—I promise!"

"No. I'm sorry, but it's inevitable. You can't stop yourself." Fayne shook her head sadly. "You might do it by accident, or more likely some villain or other will use you. You come across an archmage or one of the plague-changed . . . sooner or later, you will absorb something too powerful for you to control."

"I don't understand." Myrin's heart was racing. "What do you mean, absorb?"

"Never mind. The point is that the power inside you is simply too dangerous for you to exist," Fayne said. "Thus, I'm going to take you to someone—someone who can contain you safely, without destroying the city in the process." She touched Myrin's cheek, a little more guarded this time, as though fearing another vision. "Don't worry—you might not have to die."

Tears were streaming down Myrin's face. "Why are you saying this? I'm . . . I'm just a girl. I hardly even have any magic! You can't possibly . . ."

"You're a goddess," Fayne said.

Myrin's eyes went so wide they might have popped. "I'm . . . what?"

"No, no, that was a jest." Fayne tried to stifle her laughter with her hand. "Honestly, you should have seen your face."

Myrin wasn't laughing.

Fayne's expression grew grave once more. "To be accurate, you've got a goddess *inside* you—or, more truly, the death of one," she said. "Metaphorically speaking, you're carrying death, little one—the death of the old world. Just like all the other spellscarred. Like Kalen. Like Lady—" Her eyes narrowed. "Like that *whore*."

"I—I don't—what?"

"It's complicated." She pursed her lips. "You're all spellscarred, but you, Myrin, are far more interesting than any of them. Your powers . . ."

"But what are they?" Myrin almost wept. "What do I do?"

"This is delightful," Fayne said. "You really don't know, do you?"

Myrin shook her head, tears welling in her eyes.

"Very well," Fayne said. "I'll tell you, but only because I fancy you well."

"What?" Myrin choked on the word. Tears rolled down her cheeks.

Fayne bent as though to kiss Myrin, then recoiled, thinking better of it. "Let us begin this way," she said, catching Myrin by the chin. "You remember the lich, in the alley, when you were kidnapped, yes?"

"Yes, I—but I chased her away. I didn't—"

"Silly girl." Fayne batted Myrin across the chin, almost playfully—the way a cat might. "You didn't honestly think that power was *yours,* did you?"

Myrin's lungs heaved and she could barely speak. "I . . . I don't understand."

Then Myrin wept for true—terrified, confused, and frustrated. Had the world gone mad? She was just Myrin—little more than a slip of a girl, with hardly any magic to her name. She wanted her mother—whose face she didn't even remember. That made her weep more.

"Oh, sweetling, don't—I'll be plain, I promise."

Myrin was crying, and damn it if Fayne was going to stop her with anything less than divine revelation.

Fayne smiled. "Remember when we first met?" she asked. "I fussed over you, then later, you struck me with that spell? The one that hurt me and stripped my strength?"

"What—what of it?" Myrin asked between sobs.

"That was *my* spell," Fayne said. "Stolen out of my head."

The words froze Myrin, and she looked up, stunned.

Fayne raised her hand, murmured a few words, and Myrin felt the same pressure in her mind as she had used to strike Fayne in Kalen's tallhouse.

Myrin stared, heart hammering, as Fayne knelt and picked up the gag.

"Please," Myrin said. "Please—I need to know more!"

Fayne scoffed. "Only this," she said. "Folk never change. Do not forget that."

"Fayne, plea—!"

Fayne shoved the gag back in Myrin's mouth with enough force to knock her over. By the time Myrin recovered and looked up, the half-elf was gone.

CHAPTER THIRTY-THREE

THE SUN DIPPED OUTSIDE HIS WINDOW. DUSK FELL QUICKLY, AND MIST flowed into Waterdeep once more. No strange glowing patches would appear that night, though—only calm, expectant fog to shroud the city, hiding the unpleasant things that needed to be done.

The faltering light slanted across the blood-stained floor that Kalen had done his best to clean.

Though Kalen didn't feel like eating, he forced himself. However much Cellica had spiced it, the cold stew tasted like soggy paper. In part, it was his curse; in part, it was fate.

The dwarf was giving him some time, and he was glad of that much, at least.

He'd taken Cellica to her adoptive family in a hired carriage. They'd accepted the body with tears and sobs. Kalen hadn't been able to face her adoptive siblings and stood aloof. Philbin, so like a father, had whispered a silent prayer for vengeance. Kalen had nodded silently.

Now, Kalen sat wearing the armor Cellica had repaired, rolling his helm between his gauntleted hand and his bare one. He had only one gauntlet, after that noble stripling had taken his second away. He was supposed to do this alone, weakened, without his full armor or even his sword? Impossible, he thought, and yet, he had no choice.

He looked again at the scroll on the table—the note that had been affixed to his door with a dagger. *His* dagger, that he had given Myrin the night before.

> *Shadow,*
> *Rath is making me write this.*

Come to the Grim Statue at midnight or he will kill us. Come alone.
He says he may just kill one of us and maim the other. He says
you can pick.
　　-E

Kalen ran his hand across his grizzled chin, thinking. Why had Rath spared him? And, above that, did Rath know he was Shadowbane?

The dwarf could be toying with him, but Kalen did not think that Rath was the sort to play games with his prey. He must have known Kalen was in the room, helpless and asleep. If he'd known Shadowbane slumbered nearby, he could have slain him easily, or awakened him so they could duel on the spot. And if he didn't know Kalen was Shadowbane, he would have had no hesitations about killing him in his sleep.

For the life of him, Kalen could not puzzle out why he was still alive.

Then he realized: Fayne.

Fayne must have done something to spare his life. Perhaps she convinced Rath that Kalen knew Shadowbane, and could deliver the letter. Perhaps she *begged* Rath not to kill him—perhaps she offered him lewd favors in return . . .

Kalen grimaced and clenched his fist.

Or perhaps he did not owe Fayne his life at all, but owed it rather to Rath himself. The dwarf came from a monastery—he knew great discipline. Perhaps he would have thought slaying a helpless man to be dishonorable. And leaving Cellica to die hadn't been?

"Twisted sense of honor," Kalen murmured, but in truth, he was hardly in a position to judge. Would his own code make sense to anyone besides himself?

It had made sense to Cellica, he thought.

He shook his head. Thinking with his heart was a weakness he could ill afford.

Surely Rath would have obtained healing, but likely the scars on his wrist would stop him fighting with his sword hand, or perhaps compromise his technique. That was an advantage for Kalen—a strength. He passed the helmet to his right hand, in its steel gauntlet.

Kalen did not have Vindicator—that was a weakness. He passed the helm to his left hand.

Rolling the helm back to his right hand, Kalen thought he was the stronger—strength.

Rath had proven, though, that his skill more than compensated for Kalen's strength—weakness. He rolled the helmet to his left.

Kalen wore armor that allowed him mobility—strength.

Rath did not need armor and seemed not to tire, while Kalen had to carry the weight of his leathers—weakness.

Kalen had the threefold god—strength.

They almost matched for speed, but Rath was just enough faster—weakness.

Rath had Fayne and Myrin, while Kalen had no bargaining power—weakness.

Rath had picked the dueling ground—weakness.

And, most important, Kalen was dying of spellplague—*weakness.*

Kalen was holding the helmet in his unarmored left hand. He hefted it, as though trying to dispel his doubts, then shook his head.

Going into this duel was tantamount to falling on his own blades, but he had to try.

"If I don't," he murmured, "then who will?"

The words he had shared with Myrin.

He felt the familiar chill at the base of his neck that told him he was not alone—someone stood just outside his door. Had Rath chosen to kill him by stealth after all?

He lifted his helm and slid it on, fastening the buckles with distinct, if muted, clicks.

Then he was up, dagger in his hand, facing the door. It burst open, as if by cue, and a woman in black coat-of-plate armor stood before him. In her hands was a hand-and-a-half sword that dripped with silver fire.

"Waterdeep Guard!" she cried. He knew her voice.

Araezra.

Shadowbane turned to the window, but a red-haired woman sat on the sill, hands at the hilts of twin knives—Talanna. "Lost your other gauntlet, have you?" she asked. *"Shadowbane?"*

Kalen pressed his lips firmly together—they would know his voice.

"Down arms and doff your helm," Araezra commanded. "In the name of the city."

He looked for another way out. Cellica's window, perhaps, but that was a small fit. He could try his luck with Araezra, but a dagger would be as nothing against Vindicator. He might escape with a wound, but he could hardly fight Rath while hurt.

"Do it now," Araezra said. "Down arms and unveil yourself!"

He dropped the dagger, which stabbed into the floorboards, there to quiver. He made no move to unbuckle his helm.

"You're making a mistake," he said as gruffly as he could, to hide his identity. "I've done nothing illegal or—"

"The time for masks is past, lad," said Talanna. She hefted her blades dangerously.

He thought desperately but could find nothing. He nodded.

"Slowly, then," Araezra said. "Unveil yourself—slowly."

He put his hands out, showing them empty—his left hand bare, his right hand gauntleted. Then he reached up and opened the clasps of his helm and pulled it off. He watched Araezra's face and saw the hope in her eyes fade. And with it, his own hopes.

"I *knew* it!" Talanna clapped the blades of her daggers together and grinned. She looked at Araezra, who grimaced angrily. "I told you, Rayse— didn't I tell you?"

Kalen blinked. "What?"

"Kalen." Araezra lowered Vindicator, setting the point against the floor. "I tried so hard to believe it wasn't you. Even up until I knocked on your door, I thought there would be an explanation." She shook her head. "I didn't think you would lie to me, but you did."

"I'm sorry," he said. "You were never supposed to know."

Araezra's eyes narrowed. "Never supposed to know? You think me a dull-wit, then?"

Kalen blinked.

"All those stories we heard," Araezra said. "About the gray knight who feels no pain? And the colorless eyes. You think I don't know your eyes, Kalen? We've . . ."

She looked at Talanna, who grinned. Araezra nodded toward the window, as though directing her out to give them privacy, but Talanna only shrugged, feigning ignorance.

With a scowl, Araezra looked to Kalen. "It was only circumstantial, until that night in Downshadow—when you saved first me, then Tal. We were chasing you, and you came back for us anyway. You didn't want to be caught, but you didn't want us hurt. You're always like that—taking care of us whether we want it or not."

Kalen looked at the floor. He supposed it was true. "I never meant to offend."

"And the ball," said Talanna. She grinned. "Rayse told me about the ball."

"What about the ball?" Kalen asked. He thought he'd hidden himself well enough there.

Araezra waved. "When all the panic started, Shadowbane appeared and picked up *Cellica*, of all folk, and leaped up—" She trailed off.

"We're sorry," Talanna said. "That's why we've come—because of Cellica." Kalen opened his mouth, but she continued. "Of course we heard.

Her family was just concerned about you, Kalen. They sent word to the Watch, and we requested to go along for the task."

"So, now," Kalen said. "You've come to arrest me?"

Talanna laughed.

Araezra didn't look so amused. "Aye, or so the ten Watchmen below think," Araezra said. "You're a dangerous vigilante, Kalen. We came up alone to talk to you, and they're under orders to follow if either of us shouts. But since we know you and love you well, we came to see if you would come peaceably."

"What happens now?" Kalen looked at the dagger stuck in the floor. He was fast, he knew—could he knock Talanna to the floor before she could put two daggers in him?

"We arrest you," Araezra said. Then she shrugged. "On the morrow."

Kalen blinked. "What?"

"Assuming, of course, you're still in the city," Talanna said. "But why would you leave? Waterdeep is the city of splendors—everything you could ever want is here, aye?"

Araezra shifted her boots.

"We worked out a wonderful tale," Talanna said. "We found you, agony-stricken, inconsolable. Plying that indefinable charm of yours, you lulled Rayse and I—"

"Mostly *her*," Araezra noted.

"—into lowering our guard," Talanna continued. "Then you sprang from the window and fled!" She grinned. "Naturally, the story will vary around the Watch for months, and I expect you'll have charmed us both into bed and escaped while we were searching for our trousers, but nevertheless!" She sighed grandly. "Ah, such is the legend of Kalen Dren!"

Araezra groaned.

Talanna sheathed her daggers and stepped toward Kalen. "Here," she said. "Take this." In her hand was her golden ring of carved feathers. "I've had my fill of high places."

"It was a gift," Kalen said. "Won't Lord Neverember be offended?"

"He can always buy me another." Talanna shrugged. "I owe you a debt for saving me."

It was pointless to argue. Kalen did not don the ring, but laced it into the sleeve over his bare hand, so he could use it at a heartbeat's notice.

"I am sorry for this," he said. "I love you both well, and I never meant to hurt you." He looked especially at Araezra. "I mean . . . hurt the Guard."

Talanna laughed. "Surely you jest! Your exile from the city will be the cheeriest bit of news the Guard's had in ages." She winked at Araezra. "It means some certain lass has become free game once again."

Red in the face, Araezra looked ready to strangle Talanna.

"What are you talking about?" Kalen asked.

"Are you that dull?" Talanna asked. "For months, Rayse has been free of suitors because everyone thought that you two—"

Araezra's cheeks were burning. "Shouldn't you be going, Kalen?"

He smiled weakly then said, "I have aught to do, first."

"Does this have to do with Cellica?" Araezra asked gently. "If so, let the Watch—"

"I can't," he said. "I'm sorry—I can't tell you. I must do it alone."

Araezra sighed. "You always seem to have to be alone," she whispered.

Kalen donned his helm once more and secured it in place. "Araezra—I'm sorry."

"I know," Araezra said. "Just—one thing."

He turned toward her, thankful for the helm that hid his anxious expression. "Aye?"

"In the Room of Records," she said. "When Rath was holding me prisoner, and you came in. You . . . you did what you did, broke your vow, to protect me, didn't you?"

Kalen didn't trust his tongue, so he just nodded.

She stepped forward, snaked her arms about his neck, and pressed her lips to his cold, shining helm. "Thank you," she murmured.

He smiled inside his steel mask.

Then she slapped him lightly, causing his helmet to vibrate and his ears to ring. "I don't need you making decisions about what is best for me," Araezra said. "I can make those myself."

"Yes, Araezra."

"*Rayse*," she corrected.

Talanna rolled her eyes. "No wonder you two didn't last."

Araezra reversed Vindicator and handed it to him. As she did, her hand lingered on his. She gazed into his eyes, and he into hers. He knew she wanted to say much, but both of them knew she could not say it.

"I will miss you, Vigilant Dren," she finally said.

"And I you," he said, "*Rayse*."

She smiled widely, as though he'd paid her the finest compliment in Waterdeep.

"Now, go do what you must," she said. She straightened and her face turned stony. "Farewell, and remember—begone by the morrow. You have one day."

Talanna winked at him. "One day," she repeated. "Then I get to chase you down."

Kalen nodded, turned, and leaped out the window. He hit the roof of the building across the alley, rolled to his feet, and broke into a run.

He would need only one night.

CHAPTER THIRTY-FOUR

RATH MEDITATED, WAITING FOR NIGHTFALL.

Fayne had sworn Shadowbane would get the note, and that he would be punctual. The woman had subsequently fled—while Rath had gone in search of food for them—but no matter. The human was the more important, and Fayne's absence meant one less distraction.

He'd drunk three bottles of brandy the night of the revel, when the elf woman had scarred him. He'd paid for all the healing he could afford, but the marks were still there. He'd drunk until he couldn't see them in the mirror anymore. And he'd paid for whores who wouldn't wince to see his face. The next morning, his employer had come upon him as he lay aching from liquor and burns and women.

Now, he would wait for the next move in this game. And he would be sober.

He breathed in and out, in time with the ticking. He'd listened to the clock for a long while—it helped him to focus and align his breathing with the world around him. It was off, he thought, but only slightly. Craftsmen would be required to fix the clock soon—on the morrow, perhaps. After this business was concluded.

The girl fidgeted again, distracting him.

He'd brought her food. He'd even ungagged her long enough to pour soup down her throat—slowly, so as not to choke her. He hadn't unbound her wrists—no need. He'd helped with her toilet so that he didn't have to untie her. She'd nearly died of embarrassment, but he'd just stared at her with the same bored expression until she yielded. There was nothing erotic about it.

Even as he meditated, he was aware of her staring at the back of his head. What a curious creature. At least her fear kept her quiescent enough.

Finally, when he found his thoughts settling too much on her, he opened his eyes and turned his head. She quickly looked away, but he knew she'd been staring at him.

He sighed. Feeling the lightness in his ready joints, he rose and crossed to her. "I will not harm you, girl," he said. "I have not been paid to slay you. If you are hurt, it will be accidental and as a consequence of your own actions." He frowned. "Understand?"

She nodded. From the way she flinched when he turned his head toward her, he could tell the mangled half of his face frightened her. That brought a twinge of anger, but he suppressed it.

"I will remove this," Rath said, touching the gag in her mouth. "But you must promise you will not scream or attempt any magic. There will be consequences. Yes?"

She nodded, and her eyes looked wet.

The dwarf sighed, then pulled the gag out of her mouth. She gasped and coughed but made no loud sounds. This was good.

She looked at him, lip trembling. "What—what are you going to do with me?"

Rath frowned. "Just hold you here for a time. Nothing more."

"Are you—are you going to . . . ?" Myrin trembled and edged a little away.

"Humans." Rath rolled his eyes. "I would swear by any god you could name that you are the most despicable, insecure, bastard blood in the world, but I know the ways of my own kind and find them worse." He shrugged. "You have no dishonor to fear from me."

"Why not—" Myrin swallowed hard. "Why not unbind me? Am I a threat to you?"

"No," he said, perhaps faster than he should have.

She pursed her lips. "You fear me?"

"I fear nothing," Rath said. "I have nothing to fear from you."

"Prove it." Myrin puffed herself up as big as she could in her frail body. "Unbind my hands. If you have nothing to fear from me."

"Hmm." Rath couldn't argue with her logic. "Why do you want them unbound? You cannot escape."

"Uh." Her eyes widened. "My wrists hurt."

Rath said nothing, only reached around to do as she asked. She hadn't lied: the ropes had left red welts on her wrists. He pulled away and let her rub her skin.

"There," said Rath. "Satisfied?"

"Yes." Myrin brought a wand of pale wood from behind her back and thrust it under his chint. Rath felt sparks hissing out of it.

"Hmm," the dwarf said.

Myrin stared at him, her eyes very wide. She breathed heavily.

"You should do it," Rath said. "I have slain many—men and women both. And children."

Myrin breathed harder and harder. Rath could feel her heart racing, see the blood thudding through her veins on her forehead.

"Do it," Rath teased.

The girl inhaled sharply.

Then he slapped the wand away and swatted her head at the temple with his open hand, as one might stun a rabbit. She collapsed to the floor limply. Lightning crackled and died.

"Wizards," he murmured, rolling his eyes.

CHAPTER THIRTY-FIVE

ON NIGHTS WHEN SELÛNE HID BEHIND A VEIL OF ANGRY CLOUDS, THE streets of Waterdeep became much like those of Downshadow below. Moon shadows deepened and buildings loomed. Even the drunk and foolish had the sense to lock their doors against unseen frights. Few but the dead walked such nights. Even Castle Ward, protected by the Watch and the Blackstaff, was risky after dark—particularly on a night like this.

But Waterdeep's darkest nights knew something Downshadow never could: rain.

Water cut against Kalen's cloak like a thousand tiny arrows. Every drop was a command to reverse his course—every one a despairing word. His body told him to lie down and die. The spellplague was taking him, he knew.

Kalen took the crumpled note out of his pocket and read it again.

This was surely a trap, he thought, but he had no choice.

In particular, he thought of Myrin. Fayne could care for herself, certainly, but Kalen could not abandon Myrin. Powerful as she might be, she was still a lost, confused girl. And if her powers overcame her control, no one could predict what destruction might follow. He'd barely stopped her that night after the ball.

And Rath had to answer for Cellica's murder—he would see to that.

Kalen knew that even if he failed, Talanna and Araezra would hunt down the dwarf, but that gave him little comfort. The Guard could do little more than avenge him, and vengeance would mean little to his corpse and less still to Myrin and Fayne, if Rath killed them.

No, he would go, no matter the obstacles—no matter the rot inside him. He would not fail. One last duel—that was all he needed. Just this one last fight.

He opened his helmet and vomited into the gutter. Passersby hurried along.

He staggered down the alley near the Blushing Nymph festhall, which led to a tunnel into Downshadow near the Grim Statue and whispered under his breath.

"I will make an emptiness of myself," Kalen murmured against the rising bile in his throat. "A blackness where there is no pain—where there is only me."

He shuffled past rain-slicked leaves and unrecognizable refuse. His head beat and his lungs felt waterlogged. The fronts of his thighs were numb—he felt as though he wore heavy pads beneath his leathers. If he hadn't worn such heavy boots against the rain, he'd have thought his toes frostbitten. His hands were steady, but that was scant comfort. Dead flesh was steady. His stomach roiled.

"A blackness where there is only me," he said again.

He repeated the phrase until the aches subsided. They did not leave him—not fully—but they faded. He would not recover, he knew. Not if he did this.

"Every man dies in his time," he murmured. "If tonight is my time, so be it."

His hands felt dead as he wedged his fingers under the lip of a metal plate, uncovered beneath the alley's debris. The reek did not offend him, for he could hardly smell it. The trap door had been used that night, he knew—it was loose. It awaited Downshadowers who prowled the rainy streets, and would for hours hence. Creatures of shadow risen from below. What was he, but a shadow come from above?

A shudder, worse than ever before, ripped through him, and he curled over, hacking and coughing. He wedged his helm open and spat blood and bile onto the metal door. It dripped onto the cobblestones and swirled with the rain.

When the fit passed—he had half expected it would not—Kalen righted himself and gazed at the rusty ladder that led into the shadows beneath the city.

"Eye of Justice," he prayed. He didn't beg. "Be patient. I am coming soon."

He wiped his mouth and began to climb down.

Downshadow felt surprisingly empty that night. Its inhabitants saw night in the world above as their due, when they could dance or duel at whim, love or murder at their leisure. Those with eyes sensitive to light could walk freely in the streets, and a heavy rain or a mist off the western sea would hide their deeds, be they black or gray.

No space was emptier on such nights than the plaza around the Grim Statue: a great stone monolith of a man on a high pedestal, his head missing and his hands little more than stubs of stone. Tingling menace surrounded the figure, filling the chamber with quiet dread. A careful onlooker would see tiny lightnings crackling around its hands at odd moments.

Kalen knew the legend that this had been an independent and enclosed chamber designed as a magical trap. However, the eruption of the Weave during the Spellplague—as story would have it—caused the statue to loose blasts of lightning in a circle continuously for years. The walls had been pulverized under the onslaught, making the twenty-foot statue the center of a rough plaza.

Eventually, the lightning had subsided as the statue was drained of its magic. In recent years, lightning flashed from the statue only occasionally. The surviving walls, a hundred feet distant from the statue, marked the danger zone of the statue's destruction. The ramshackle huts and tents of Downshadow extended only to that limit, and most of those were abandoned. Only a fool or a fatalist would live so close to unpredictable death.

A favored game among Downshadow braves was to approach the statue as closely as possible, taking cover behind chunks of stone, to see where their courage would fail them.

Kalen stood at the edge of the round plaza, scanning the neighboring hollows and warrens for any sign of his foe. He saw little movement in the dead plaza, but for a pair of figures that stalked through one of the broken passages nearby.

Then he saw Rath step into the open from behind the remains of a blasted column twenty paces distant. His hands were empty, his face calm and emotionless. He wore his sword on his right hip, as Kalen had hoped he might. The dwarf's right hand was wrapped thickly in linen.

"I thought you wouldn't come," said the dwarf. "That her note wouldn't bring you."

"You were wrong." Kalen put his hand on the hilt of Vindicator but did not draw. He knew the tricks of the Grim Statue—knew how its lightning could be random, but it almost always triggered in the presence of active magic. If he drew his Helm-blessed sword . . .

"I am pleased," the dwarf said. He made no move to draw.

Kalen saw that Rath's face, while not as horrible as on the night of the revel, still showed evidence of burn scars across its right side. His left side was unchanged, and Kalen could tell from his stance that he coddled the burned side. Proud of his looks, Kalen thought. He would remember that. If he could find a way to make the dwarf emotional, it could be an advantage.

"Agree to let them go if you kill me," Kalen said. "They mean nothing to you."

A flicker of doubt crossed Rath's scarred face. Then he shrugged. "What is this *if*?"

"Agree," Kalen said.

Rath shrugged. "No," he said. "Your little blue-headed stripling has another use to me."

Kalen didn't like that reply, but it wasn't a surprise. He shivered to think of the possibilities.

"What will you do next, dwarf, after I am dead?" Kalen had approached within ten paces, and the two of them began to circle. "Do you have other vengeance to take?"

Rath sniffed. "I kill for coin—vengeance means little," he said. "But I do know of hatred." He smiled, an expression made unpleasant by his ruined face. "Two guardsmen. Araezra Hondryl and Kalen Dren—they will die as well."

Kalen smiled, reached up, and pulled off his helmet, showing the dwarf his face.

Rath's eyes narrowed to angry slits. His hands trembled for only a moment. He was realizing, Kalen thought with no small pleasure, how deeply and completely he'd been fooled.

"Well," the dwarf said. "I suppose I need slay only one other after you."

Kalen smiled and put his helm back in place. He circled Rath slowly, keeping his hand on Vindicator's hilt and one eye on the statue.

"You should draw your sword this time."

"If you prove worthy of it," said Rath. "This time."

Kalen was so intent on letting the dwarf strike first that when Rath finally moved, it almost caught him off guard. One moment, Rath was circling him peaceably, and the next he was lunging, low and fast and left, where Vindicator was sheathed. Only reflexes and instincts built up over long years on mean streets sent Kalen leaping back and around, sword sliding free of its scabbard to ward Rath away. Vindicator's fierce silver glow bathed them in bright light, making both squint.

But Rath didn't follow. Kalen saw him dancing back, and felt his hairs crackle just in time to see the Grim Statue slinging a bolt of green-white lightning at him. Kalen couldn't dodge and only barely brought Vindicator into the lightning's path. He prayed.

Kalen felt the force of the blast like a battering ram, blowing him back and away from the statue. He tumbled through the air, trying vainly to twist and roll, and landed outside the plaza in a gasping heap. Lightning yet arced around him, and he twitched and hissed as it faded. If Rath had come upon him then, Kalen would have had no defense.

But the dwarf was merely standing over him when Kalen could finally move again, a wry smile on his face.

"What glory would I gain," asked the dwarf, "if I let some relic of another age vanquish you, the mighty Shadowbane? Come. On your feet."

Kalen coughed and spat and started to rise—then slashed at Rath's nearest leg. Laughing, the dwarf flipped backward and waited, a dagger-toss distant, while Kalen rose.

"Draw your steel," Kalen said, brandishing Vindicator high.

"You have done nothing worthy," said Rath.

"Then come to me with empty hands, if you will," Kalen said, taking a high, two-handed guard. "I tire of your child's games."

That seemed to touch Rath, for his neutral smile faded. He streaked toward Kalen like nothing dwarven. Kalen cut down, dropping one hand from the sword.

Steel clashed, followed by a grunt of pain.

Rath danced back, and Kalen coughed and struggled to stay on his feet.

The dwarf reached down and touched a dribble of blood forming along his right forearm. He looked at the cut curiously, as though he had not been wounded in a long time and had forgotten what it was like. Kalen gestured wide with the dirk he had pulled from his gauntlet, gripping it in his bare left hand. He let himself smile wryly inside his helm.

"I underestimated you, paladin," Rath said. "I shall not make that mistake again."

The dwarf reached for his sword in its gold lacquer scabbard and untied the peace bond. He closed his eyes, as though in prayer, and laid his fingers reverently around the hilt.

"You know what an honor this is," said Rath. "To find a worthy foe."

"I do."

The dwarf drew the sword in a blur, opened his eyes, and lunged.

Kalen almost couldn't block, so fast was the strike. Rath's steel—short and curved and fine—screeched against Vindicator, but both blades held. The speed stunned Kalen enough to slow his counter, which might have taken out Rath's throat if he'd been faster.

Instead, the dwarf leaped away, then lunged back, slashing. He did so again and again, moving so fast and gracefully that Kalen could hardly follow him with his eyes and parried almost wholly by touch.

Kalen worked his muscles as hard as he could, bringing the steel around to foil Rath's strikes, trying always to catch his slender sword between his own blades, but to no avail.

They exchanged a dozen passes before Rath fled, down the hall to the great cavern. Kalen gave chase, and might have lost everything when Rath came at him suddenly. The dwarf could reverse his motion as though by will, in defiance of momentum or balance.

Kalen parried the blow with his dirk, but he felt Rath's blade slit open the leather over his bicep. He took a wider guard—a narrower profile. He tried to bring Vindicator around, but hit nothing as Rath flowed away from him, running along the wall of the corridor. The dwarf plunged into the tunnels, and Kalen followed.

They ran from corridor to corridor, slashing and scrambling forward. Their swords sparked, trailing silver lightning through the halls of Downshadow. Rath struck a dozen times with his blade, but Kalen parried every attack—with sword, dirk, or gauntlet. Each time, Rath bounded away and Kalen cursed, panted, and followed. Lurking creatures scurried out of their way as the men ran and fought, roused from hiding by the duel. The combatants ran on, heedless.

"A darkness where there is only me," Kalen whispered through gritted teeth.

Rath vaulted off a nearby wall and slashed down hard enough to break through Kalen's guard and ring his helmet soundly. Instead of following through, he leaped away and continued the chase. Kalen grunted and sped after him.

"Why do you keep fighting, Shadowbane?" Rath's calm voice showed no sign of strain. "I can see you tiring—feel you slowing."

Kalen said nothing, but ran on.

They ran between crumbling chambers. The magic of Kalen's boots drove his leaps high and far, but the dwarf still eluded him. The dwarf seemed able to run along the very walls if he wanted.

They broke into the main chamber of Downshadow, with its tents and huts, lit by the dancing firelight that flowed across the ceiling. Inhabitants clustered around cook fires erupted in curses, then fled the path of the avenger and his quarry. Vindicator's silver glow made them bright, shining warriors as they chased each other.

They plowed through the heart of the encampment, leaping over cook fires and around startled natives. Hands reached for steel or spell but Kalen and Rath flew past without pause. They knocked down tent poles, sent stew pots flying, and generally wreaked chaos across the cavern. Rath struck

Kalen several more times, but his leathers held. He could not land a single blow on the dwarf, but felt certain that when he did, Rath would fall.

"What will it take?" Rath asked as he vaulted up a wall, caught an overhanging ledge, and swung over the side, seizing higher ground.

Kalen jumped after the dwarf, grasped a broken handhold—his gauntlet screeching—and swung himself up. He caught a narrow metal pole that lay between the ledge and the wall—a waste pipe for the Knight 'n Shadow, he realized, which perched in the cavern wall just above their heads.

He swung himself around the pipe like an acrobat, once, twice for momentum, then he let himself soar, feet first, up onto the ledge. He twisted in midair and landed on his feet, panting, knees bent, sword wide. He looked up at a huge stack of crates and barrels, above which hung the low platform of the tavern. Near Rath stood a small shack, balanced precariously on numerous long splints for legs, where workers would clean the tavern's rags and dump the waste water.

As Kalen landed, Rath scurried to the shed, slashed through two of the supports, then climbed up the side of the shoddy building, pausing to look down.

As the dwarf watched from atop the platform, Kalen grasped his left arm, gritted his teeth, and tried to still his raging heart.

"Wait, Helm," he demanded, calling upon his dead god. "They need me."

"Still you refuse to fall," said the dwarf. He stood, in perfect balance on the platform railing. "What admirable valor—foolish, but admirable."

The groan of buckling wood warned of danger, and the supports of the platform splintered and collapsed. The dwarf launched himself again, flipping and sailing through the air—leaving behind a collapsing storm of wood, stone, and water.

Kalen barely threw himself aside before the shack shattered against the narrow ledge, which itself started splintering. Choking on dust, he tumbled backward.

Rath was there, sword dancing like a steel whip, and it was more luck than skill that let Kalen block. He parried with his off hand, but the sword screeched against his blade and wedged the dirk free—it spun off into the cavern. Rath stabbed, but Kalen kicked his feet out from under him. The dwarf scrambled away before Kalen could get Vindicator in line.

"This will end only one way," Rath said.

He leaped out into the cavern and Kalen jumped after him, falling toward a sea of Downshadow folk who had joined in pursuit of the two crazed duellists. The dwarf bore down on one orc-blooded man and raced across the heads and backs of several others. Kalen crashed down in a knot of folk, sending three or four to the ground, then pushed himself up. He shoved his way through the crowd, holding Vindicator high and muscling the folk aside.

"Move, citizens!" he cried. "Waterdhavian Guard! Stand aside!"

That might not have been the best cry, for several lumbering forms—stirred by anger against that very organization—moved to block his path.

"Damn." Kalen bent his aching legs and sprang up.

His boots carried him up and over the intervening figures, following Rath. He landed badly and stumbled to the cavern floor, face first. Vindicator slipped free, but he recovered it in a roll to his feet. He charged after Rath, who was heading along the corridors toward the Grim Statue. Not attacking—just fleeing. Luring him.

Gods, Kalen thought—was he going toward the place where he'd hidden Fayne and Myrin?

Kalen burst into the plaza just as the statue's hands started glowing. He saw Rath standing before the statue, smiling. The dwarf sheathed his sword and spread his hands.

Whatever Downshadowers had been chasing them stopped at the edge of the cursed plaza, loathe to run into a trap.

With a grunt, Kalen charged.

The first lightning bolt was easy enough to dodge by rolling, but the second came too quickly. He tried to deflect it with Vindicator as before. Fortunately, the blast was at a sharp angle, and the bolt bounced from the enchanted steel into the ground, there to be absorbed harmlessly. The force drove Kalen to his knees, and he threw himself behind a boulder, panting.

"Come, then." Rath stood atop the headless statue. "I wonder if you'll be in time."

Rath leaped up, and Kalen watched as he vanished into the air, as though entering a pocket in the darkness above the statue's head. He saw the shadows wavering, and knew the dwarf had found a portal of some kind. But where did it lead, and how long would it stay open?

Though he knew it was a trap, he had no choice.

Kalen darted out from behind cover. He dodged a lightning bolt with a roll, then leaped over a second blast to grasp the statue's wrist. The figure's heat caused his hairs to rise as lightning gathered, but his eyes stayed on the unseen portal above its head.

He jumped and prayed it was yet open.

Lightning flashed.

CHAPTER THIRTY-SIX

KALEN FELT A SENSE OF INCREDIBLE SPACE, AS THOUGH HE HAD BEEN trapped somewhere cramped and now floated in the open sky. His mind reeled and he wavered on his feet.

Something hit him while he was dazed from his journey. He felt it coming only an instant before it struck and grasped the nearby wall by instinct.

Two feet collided with his face like the lance of a charging jouster. The force sent him arching back, and pain stabbed through his arm as he fought to retain his hold. His helm shrieked as it tore free of his head and flew off, out into the Waterdeep night.

Rain lashed him as he hung weightless over empty space. He saw the lights of Waterdeep far below, and what could only be the palace roof. He realized the portal had led to the small chamber at the top of the Timehands, the great clock tower.

The temptation rose in him to let go—to sail off into the night and fall like an angel with broken wings. He was tired and beaten, choking with spellplague. The strength it lent him was fading, and soon, he would die. Why not let go? If he hung on, he would hurt more.

He hung on.

He swung into the tower, both feet leading, and kicked only air. He landed on his back with a crack that sent shockwaves through his insides, below his numbed flesh. Broken and bruised bones, he could feel.

He lay there and listened to the loud, deliberate clicks of the clock mechanisms working all around him. Without his helmet, the noise was so loud he could barely think. His heart beat countless times between each click. He vaguely saw an open stairwell, where candlelight filtered up.

Up, he thought—up. *Up.*

He spat blood onto the floor and hefted himself to a sitting position. He looked everywhere for his assailant, but Rath must have vanished into the shadows. Waiting.

Kalen expected the dwarf to strike at any instant, but nothing happened. He climbed to his knees, ignoring the complaints from every ounce of his flesh, aching for him to lie down.

"Why don't you come?" he murmured. "Here I am. Waiting."

But he knew the answer. The dwarf didn't want to kill him on his knees. Up—*up.*

Kalen swung one foot flat onto the floor. He could feel nothing in his body. His arms and legs were dead wood to him and moved only accidentally. He had nothing left.

"Kalen?" said a voice, cutting through the chamber. *Myrin.* "Kalen, can you hear me?"

He murmured something that might have been "aye."

"I'm here! Please! Come—" Then Myrin seemed to realize, and he heard her strangled gasp. "No! No—go away! Leave me here! Begone!"

Kalen paused, thinking perhaps Rath had seized her, but then he saw the girl. Tiny blue runes glowed like candles on her skin. He pushed Vindicator in her direction and saw that she was alone, curled up against a corner of the clock room. Runes glowed beneath her eyes, which glittered in the sword-light. He stood and limped to her, fighting to move every pace.

Myrin shook her head, pleading with her eyes that he turn away. He kept coming, though it would kill him. When she saw he would not stop, she sobbed incoherently.

He reached her side and set Vindicator on the floor. He wrapped his dead arms around her and rested his bloody chin on her shoulder. She was shivering.

"Peace," he whispered, shocked at how hoarse his voice sounded.

"It was Fayne!" Myrin moaned. "She said—she said such horrible, horrible things." She shivered. "Oh, gods, Kalen! I'm—gods, all those people!"

"Peace."

"But you don't understand. I'm sick! I'm carrying something that—Fayne said—"

"Stop." Kalen put his fingers across her lips. "Fayne lied."

Myrin stared at him, dumbstruck and frightened and wrathful all at once. Her eyes pooled with tears, and Kalen could see blue flames deep within them.

"Truly?" Myrin asked. "Oh, Kalen—truly?"

Even as Shadowbane, Kalen Dren had never lied. Deceived, yes. Left words unspoken, yes. But flatly lied? Would he be lying to Myrin in that moment? He did not know.

"Yes," he said.

Myrin turned in his arms—held him as tightly as her thin limbs could—and kissed him.

To Kalen, she felt like fire—a wrenching, sucking fire that drained his body. He gagged, breaking the kiss, knowing he would die in that instant. Myrin just held him, weeping.

Then, something returned to him. Life, vitality, strength—it was like healing magic, but painful, and it was pain he could truly *feel*. He couldn't speak—couldn't think—just held Myrin as she held him, weeping and sobbing. Everything else faded, leaving them the only beings in an empty world.

Then it was over, and they were just holding one another, alone in a tiny chamber at the top of the grandest city in the world. A great sense of space spiraled around them, and Kalen felt weak and vulnerable and very small indeed. But he was strong enough for Myrin.

Kalen pressed her head against his chest, holding her as she sobbed, and fancied that he could feel her hot tears soaking through his clothes. Or was that only phantom feeling?

"How touching." Rath appeared around the clock apparatus. He held his thin sword wide. "And now that you're on your feet, I can kill you."

Kalen let go of Myrin and directed her back to the wall. She didn't move. "Myrin," he said. He could barely manage a whisper.

"No," she said and rose to her feet. "You're not hurting him."

Rath shrugged. He pulled something from his belt. A grayish white stick of wood. "I told you I would not kill you, girl," he said. "But there would be consequences to your—"

Myrin thrust out her hand and the wand wrenched itself from Rath's grasp. It flew between her fingers and crackled with magic. "Begone!" she cried.

A bolt of freezing amethyst light streaked past Rath as he twisted aside. It slammed into the wall, blowing hunks of stone in every direction and sending lines of frost crinkling across the stone. The dwarf looked at the patch of ice, then at Myrin, his face an arrogant mask.

"No more!" Myrin declaimed words of power and twirled her wand. "No more!"

Rath started dodging, but the bolt of force that shot from her wand stabbed him in the shoulder. The dwarf cursed, faltering in his dodge, and Myrin cried out in triumph.

As though he'd been waiting for just that moment of distraction, Rath lunged at her.

Kalen moved. Vindicator caught the dwarf's blade and pushed it harmlessly wide.

As Rath barreled in, a victim of his own momentum, Kalen whirled and dealt the dwarf a left hook to his burned face. Clutching at his wound, Rath tumbled back.

Kalen drew a circle with the Helm-marked sword, and a ring of silver runes appeared in the air. Their holy radiance sent Rath staggering back, and Kalen saw Myrin's face bathed in his threefold god's light. How beautiful she appeared.

Kalen and followed Rath.

They fought along the floor and off the walls of the small chamber, blades ringing and scraping. Kalen felt new strength—new fury—flooding his limbs. He felt everything, as though the numbness had fled him. He had no need of inner darkness to hide his pain, for it was gone. Rage coursed through him and he fought tirelessly. Vindicator blazed with light as he struck the dwarf's blade, knocking Rath back.

Rath weaved his blade and spun, and Kalen slashed at him. Their swords clashed and sparked, silver fire trailing. Kalen cut wide and punched around a parry, but Rath danced seemingly along the ceiling, flowing along slashes of Vindicator.

They cut through gears and pulleys, and once Kalen slammed into a bell, setting it to ring the dawn. Waterdeep would awaken many hours before dawn this day. In his fury, he didn't care.

Myrin shouted more words of power and multicolored stars burst into being in Kalen's eyes, dazing him. Rath might have struck in that moment, but the dwarf, too, staggered.

"That isn't helping," Kalen hissed, as he and the dwarf recovered in the same breath.

As Rath fell into a defensive stance, Kalen stabbed high. The dwarf ducked and turned a flip backward, kicking Kalen's hand up. The glowing bastard sword spun up into the darkness.

Rath twirled back, kicked off the wall, and lunged forward, sword leading—and hit air where Kalen had been standing.

Kalen leaped after Vindicator, caught it, and slashed down. He cut open the back of Rath's robe.

Kalen landed two paces from the dwarf, and they stared at each other.

Then Rath leaped back, avoiding a beam of frost from Myrin's wand.

"Stop!" Kalen cried, but it was too late.

Myrin's face was drawn and haggard, and she collapsed to her knees. Blue tattoos sprouted all across her skin, as though the runes were taking over her body. Her wand sagged toward the floor. She stood near the room's window, where the portal had deposited Kalen.

As Rath surged to her, blade low, Myrin pointed the wand with her shaking hand.

A burst of flame emerged from her wand and struck Rath's sword. The blade turned red almost instantly, and Rath hurled it at Myrin. The girl gasped and dodged, and the glowing blade flew out the window.

The dwarf's iron hands caught Myrin by the throat and wrist, holding the wand wide.

"Stop!" Kalen said. He held Vindicator level, pointed at Rath.

"Take another step, Shadowbane," Rath said, tapping his fingers on Myrin's cheek.

"Kalen!" Myrin croaked. "Just cut through me if you have to! I'm not important!"

"Myrin," Kalen said. "Myrin, don't be afraid. I'm going to save you."

"What Fayne said, Kalen! I'm not—*gkk!*"

Rath squeezed her throat tightly enough to cut off air. The knight waited, breathing hard, never taking his eyes from the dwarf's face.

"I wonder." Rath regarded Myrin for a single heartbeat then looked at Kalen. "Which is more important to you—justice or her?"

Kalen said nothing. Vindicator dripped silver-white flame like blood onto the floor.

The dwarf grinned. "Let us see."

He hurled Myrin out the window. She screamed and fell away, arms whirling vainly.

Kalen ran and leaped, sword leading. Rath slid a step to the left, his hands raised, but the knight went past him into the night.

Lightning flashed and an awful screech, as of metal on stone, joined the thunder.

CHAPTER THIRTY-SEVEN

Rain tore the night to shreds, and lightning bathed the high clock tower in light bright enough to match the day.

Kalen hung from the tower, his right hand on the hilt of Vindicator—which he'd wedged between two stones. A struggling Myrin hung from his left.

"You idiot!" Tears fell from Myrin's eyes as she beat at him with her free hand, trying to break his grip on her wrist. "Just let go of me!"

"Stop that," Kalen said. He swung her a little one way, then back the other way, like a pendulum—like the amulet on Fayne's breast . . .

Rath's head appeared in the window.

Kalen kept swinging Myrin, wider and wider. Her feet kicked at the rain-slicked tower stones, but Kalen knew she wouldn't find a hold. There was no ledge between them and the palace roof below. Only Vindicator kept them aloft.

Kalen gritted his teeth and pulled. Myrin swung over open air—and back the other way.

"What are you doing?" she cried. "Are you insane?"

Kalen kept swinging her. Wider—wider. "Listen to me," he said.

"Just drop me!" she sobbed. "I don't want to kill all those people—"

"*Listen,*" Kalen snapped. Myrin gaped. "The ring . . . laced in my sleeve. Put it on."

Myrin moaned. "Just let me go!"

"*Put it on!*" Kalen roared over the rain and thunder.

Then Vindicator shook. Myrin bounced and shrieked, and Kalen gasped at the strain. He looked up, and standing on the broad hilt of his sword—and his gauntlet—was Rath. The dwarf had scrambled down the wall nimbly as a spider and perched on Kalen's sword. Rain streaked around him.

"Interesting plan," the dwarf said.

Kalen couldn't spare a glance at Myrin, but he felt her taking the ring from his sleeve. He prayed the dwarf wouldn't notice.

"I don't imagine my standing here hurts you—you can't feel it, can you?" Rath raised one foot, keeping balance. "But even nerveless fingers can't hold you up when they're crushed."

Kalen gritted his teeth against the storm and the pain in his straining arm. "Make an emptiness of myself . . . in which there is no pain . . ." He kept swinging.

Rath stomped.

Kalen felt it—less than he should have, but no amount of spellplague could mask the jolt of a broken forefinger. Just one finger—the dwarf was cruelly accurate. Kalen swung and almost fell, but kept a hold. Myrin gave a cry halfway between a scream and a sob.

"Put . . . it . . . on," Kalen hissed at Myrin.

Rath grinned. And crushed his middle finger. One at a time.

Against the slipping agony, Kalen shut his eyes. "No pain—only me."

He kept swaying, swinging back and forth as though he might hurl Myrin to safety—as though any building was near enough or high enough. He could not reach the palace wall from this angle, and his hand was slipping.

"Kalen!" Myrin cried. "Just drop me! You can—"

"Put it on!" he shouted.

"Put what on?" Rath saw the ring and sneered. "Humans. So romantic, even to the end."

He crushed the third finger, almost sending Kalen down. Only by the Eye's grace . . .

Kalen coughed harshly. "Have you got it?" he managed.

Fear clouded Myrin's face. She was swinging away from the tower. "Yes, but—"

"Good."

And he let go of her.

Myrin swung to the side before she started to fall, her eyes wide and her face startled. Her expression changed to shock, and then heartbreak. She drifted into the rain and vanished without a sound.

The dwarf frowned. "I don't under—" Rath started to say, but Kalen, continuing his swing, hauled himself up and grasped the dwarf's ankle in his free hand. He planted both feet on the slippery tower wall.

"Fly," Kalen dared him.

With a fierce kick, he wrenched Vindicator free.

For one horrible, perfect instant, they were gliding, falling a little as if they had tripped. Vindicator was arcing, end over end, through the air beside them.

Then Kalen's guts rose up into his throat, and the two combatants were streaking down, wrestling in the air. The dwarf punched him soundly across the face and the world blurred. He held on.

They ricocheted off the palace roof—crashing hard, bones snapping—tumbling madly like dolls. Kalen tried to jump but the dwarf held on. Kalen rolled and wrestled and prayed and . . .

Hit.

CHAPTER THIRTY-EIGHT

FOR A LONG TIME, NOTHING EXISTED BUT DARKNESS.

Darkness, and rain like knives.

Then pain—sharp, stabbing agony that came from every broken limb and ounce of flesh. He had survived the fall—somehow, crashing against roofs and shattering almost every bone in his body.

Rath awoke on the cobbles of Castle Ward, in the shadow of the palace, and coughed up blood before he breathed. This magnified the pain a hundredfold. He couldn't feel his body. He was—

Alone.

That couldn't be. Shadowbane had fallen with him. They must have hit something else—some building. Otherwise, Rath surely would have died.

But who had landed on the stone first? Who had borne the brunt of the fall?

Rath saw a silhouette emerge from the mist. No—he saw the sword first. Saw the silver flames rising from it, the fog boiling away. Shadowbane, he thought for a moment, but . . .

It was Myrin. She walked toward him, the sword held awkwardly in her frail hands. Blue runes covered her skin, but they were fading as she strode forward. Her magic was unraveling, leaving only mortal hatred in her eyes.

"Taking vengeance," Rath said. He burbled. "I slew him and you avenge him. Fitting."

His sword lay on the cobbles, where it had fallen from the window. The hilt, still sizzling from Myrin's fire spell, sent up steam as rain fell on it. It was only a hand's length from his grasp.

A black boot fell on the hilt. Rath looked up.

Shadowbane loomed over him—stooped, bent, but not broken. His damp cloak draped around him. His helm dripped black rain.

"Kalen," Myrin whispered.

He reached toward her with his unbroken hand.

Myrin's face softened. "Kalen, no."

He curled his fingers, beckoning.

"Kalen, please. He's a monster, but he doesn't—you don't have to—"

Kalen said nothing—only held out his hand.

Myrin looked at Rath once more, then put the hilt of Vindicator in Kalen's hand.

"Turn away," Kalen said.

Myrin shook her head.

"Turn."

"No!" Myrin backed away. "I want to see what you are. What *we* are!"

Kalen looked only at Rath. He focused on the dwarf silently, ignoring Myrin's heaving breaths. Then she turned away and darted into the mist, vanishing into the night.

"For Cellica," Shadowbane said, as though in explanation.

Rath smiled, tasting blood in his mouth.

Kalen wrapped both hands around the hilt gingerly, reversed Vindicator, and held it ready to plunge into the dwarf's throat. He paused, his eyes unreadable.

"What will it be, knight?" Rath did his best to smile. "Vengeance . . . or mercy?"

Kalen coughed once and steadied himself.

"Justice."

The sword screeched against the stone.

CHAPTER THIRTY-NINE

"LUNATIC SWORDSMEN CAUSE HAVOC IN DOWNSHADOW!" THE BROADCRIER was yelling at the entrance to the Knight 'n Shadow. "Same culprits suspected in damage to Timehands! Watch . . ."

He trailed off and gaped at a gray figure standing before him—bare headed, bare handed, clad toe to chin in black leathers. Bandages wrapped his right hand and a sword was sheathed at his belt. In the dawn light, his brown-black hair was glossy and his chin dark with stubble. His eyes burned like light off snow.

"Boy," he said to the broadcrier. He took a hand out of the scrip satchel at his waist—in it gleamed five gold dragons. "Do you want these?"

The broadcrier had seen so much coin before, of course—this was, after all, the City of Splendors, where coin was king and blood was gold. But never had he owned that much wealth himself.

The boy nodded. The knight handed the coins over, and they quickly disappeared into the broadcrier's belt pouch. Then, his bandaged hand shaking, the knight unbuckled the black-sheathed sword from his hip and held it out as though presenting a gold scepter.

"Hold this for me." The knight nodded to the tavern. "When I collect it from you again, I shall give you twenty more dragons."

"And—" The boy shivered. "And if you do not?"

The knight smiled. "Then wear it well, and do not try to run from it as I did."

The boy nodded and took the knight's sword in his hands. It pulsed with inner strength—neither good nor evil, only powerful. Waiting for a worthy hand.

Without another word, the knight strode past the boy.

Fayne waited for him, legs crossed on the table. She was in a good mood.

She didn't care about being private or unnoticed; she wore her most beautiful red-haired half-elf face and her most revealing black and red harness, which was more leather straps than fabric. A dozen men had come to her with propositions, but she'd casually ignored each of them until they'd gone away. She'd had to fend off one with a charm to make him run away in terror. After her display of magic, no one bothered her.

She was waiting for one man, and one man alone. She hadn't slept that night, and neither had he, she knew. This would be their last meeting.

He came, just as she had anticipated, at about dawn, when the street lamps were being doused and the shadowy dealings in unused alleys gave way to legitimate business in the streets. The Knight 'n Shadow was mostly empty at dawn, though a few Waterdhavians had come for morningfeast before going about the business of the day.

He was dressed in leathers but carried no sword and wore no helm. His brown stubble defined his strong, tense jaw. His right hand was bandaged. His left was bare.

"Last place you expected this, eh?" Fayne asked.

"On the contrary," her visitor said. "Drinks and sly glances are your favored weapons. Why should I expect anything less than your element?"

"Mmm." She nodded to the two goblets of wine on the table, one before her and one before an empty chair. "Drink? 'Ware, though for—"

Kalen seized her goblet—not his own—drained it in a single gulp, then sat down.

Fayne blinked at him, then at the goblets. He'd ruined her game, and it offended her.

"My apologies," Kalen said. "Was one or the other meant to be poisoned?"

"Very well," she said, keeping the anger he'd roused off her face. "We don't have to play this game, if you don't want."

Kalen shrugged, then belched in a way rather unbefitting a paladin.

"So you beat Rath," Fayne said, tracing her finger along the lip of her empty wine goblet.

Again, silence.

"And I suppose you know about Cellica," she said. "I imagine the dwarf told you *I* stabbed her, did he? I thought he might. That *was* the plan, after all."

"He did not," Kalen said. "But I had guessed."

"Poor puppy." Fayne grinned. "Surely you didn't believe all that romantic nonsense about me *loving* you."

Again, Kalen said nothing, but Fayne could see the vengeful wrath behind his eyes.

"Ah, Kalen." She smiled at him. "I knew—I knew the moment you went after the girl instead of me at the revel—that we would never work together."

He spoke, his voice grave. "Threatening to turn you in had naught to do with it?"

Fayne laughed. "No, no, silly boy—in my circles, that's just flirtation. No." Her eyes narrowed. "You just don't understand my very humble needs."

"Needs?" Kalen's bloodstained teeth glittered at her. The look of it intrigued her.

"Yes—your heart, body, mind, soul—everything." She flashed her long lashes and feigned a kiss. "Is that *really* so much to ask?"

"I might have given it," Kalen said. "Before you killed Cellica—I might have given it."

"And what of Myrin, eh?" Fayne asked.

She seemed to have struck him to the quick. Kalen looked down at the table silently.

"Ah, yes, the girl between us," Fayne said. "And how fares yon strumpet?"

Kalen slammed his fist on the table, drawing wary glances. "Don't insult her," he said low. "A creature like you couldn't possibly understand her."

"I'm sure." Fayne didn't bother looking around. "She's not with you now?"

Kalen shook his head.

"You let her go," Fayne said, clasping her hands at her breast. "Oh, how romantic! You really are such an insufferably good man—and an arrogant boor, besides." She sneered.

Kalen did nothing but stare at her.

"You just *have* to make decisions on behalf of those around you, without consulting them," Fayne said. "Rejecting that slut of a valabrar, for instance, so as not to hurt her. Deciding Myrin would be happier without you. Telling yourself it's to protect *them*, and not yourself!"

"I do what I must," Kalen said.

"Gods defend us!" Fayne threw her hands up in the air. "The arrogance! The conceit!"

"I know Myrin," Kalen said. "And I do not deserve her."

Fayne couldn't contain her laughter. This was just too much.

"People never change," she said. "Once a thief, ever a thief. Once a killer, ever a killer. Too much to expect you might stop hating yourself." She blew him a kiss. "But what if Myrin wanted you anyway?"

"I wouldn't let her."

"How perfect!" Fayne said. "Oh, Kalen, the gods endowed you in many ways, but wisdom of the heart was hardly one of them."

"Whoever she is," Kalen said, "whatever she is, whatever folk have done to her—Myrin deserved none of it." His eyes blazed. "She is better than me—better than all of us."

"Spoken like a man who knows nothing of women."

Kalen shrugged.

"Ah, Shadowbane, the arbiter of justice—but you're working without all the evidence, love," said Fayne. "You don't know what that girl is. If you did, and you had the slightest love for good and justice, you'd march right out of here and take her to the Watch—or the Tower." Fayne grinned. "Why not do that now? Or are you afraid they'd take her away from you?"

Fayne saw Kalen's hand clench, but the knight restrained himself.

"But no—you don't need anyone else." Fayne winked. "You're always alone, aye?"

She could see Kalen trembling as he looked down at the table.

"You really do love her, aye?" asked Fayne.

"You know I can't," Kalen said angrily. "She hurts me too much, just by looking at me."

"You idiot." Fayne laughed. "What do you think love *is?*"

A timid barmaid stood at the edge of the room, and Fayne rolled her eyes and waved to her. Soon, tankards of ale came, and they raised them to each other, even toasted and clinked the tankards together and smiled. By all appearances they were merely young companions, dressed in the garb of sellswords, sharing drink and conversation.

Through it all, the goblet of wine before Kalen went untouched.

"What are you thinking about, lover?" Fayne asked.

"I am thinking about how this will end." There was no warmth in his eyes.

"Then you will not object to assuaging my own wonders," Fayne said.

He shrugged with his tankard.

"First question," Fayne said. "Why did you drink my wine rather than your own? Had you decided what manner of wench I am—one who would expect to be trusted?"

Kalen gestured to the full goblet. "I could drink this," he said. "Or shall we talk more?"

Fayne's smile didn't falter—she wouldn't give him a hint as to her scheme. It was far too delicious. "We should talk, and you should answer my question."

"I knew," Kalen said. "Because I know *you*, Fayne."

"I suppose you do at that—in a certain sense." She winked lewdly then composed herself. "Second question—you knew I was crooked. How?"

"Lady Dawnbringer," Kalen said.

"Ah." She nodded. "But that didn't let you save Cellica. So you must not have been certain. You didn't know Rath was mine?"

"I suspected," Kalen said. "I saw the way you looked at Lady Ilira—the triumph in your eyes. Was *anything* accidental about that night?"

"Well struck," Fayne said. "What I told you was true—the whore killed my mother, and nothing pleases me more than hurting her. I didn't pay Rath to kill Lorien, but I don't care that he did. The only part I lied about was whether I would have killed her myself." She smiled. "Yet still you let me share your bed, even after you knew I was bent. I don't suppose you really did love me? Just a touch?" She batted her eyes at him.

"No more than you did," he replied, his eyes never leaving hers.

Good, that was good. All his attention fixed upon her.

"Glad my true face didn't steal your virility," she confessed. "But I'm so terribly curious—make love to many of my kind, do you?"

"I like my lasses wicked." Kalen shrugged. "But I've never known one quite like you."

"Mmm. Good." Fayne laughed lightly. "Not wielding your paladin's sword, I see." She gestured to his empty belt. "You murdered Rath in cold blood?"

"And if I did?"

"Then I can see why Myrin has left you." She reached across the table for his wrist but he drew away. "Ah, Kalen! You and I know too much darkness for a soft thing like her."

"Yes," Kalen murmured. "I suppose we do."

She narrowed her eyes. "Are you—and this is my last question—here to fight me, rather than claim me for your own?"

Kalen said nothing.

Fayne sighed. "Of course. Well—it would have been joyous, saer, but I can't say as I disagree. You and I were not meant for one another. Irreconcilable philosophical differences."

Kalen shrugged. "I suppose this is where I ask how you intend to kill me." He gestured to the wine goblets—hers empty, his full. "I suppose one of those was poisoned."

"Mayhap." Fayne looked him up and down. "You seem to be alive."

"This likely would have been some game of yours," Kalen continued. "You'd suggest we both drink, and let me choose which wine to take for myself. You just had to decide which I would drink—and poison that cup." He gestured to them. "Apologies if I spoiled your plan."

"And I apologize for insulting you earlier," she said. "Mayhap the gods did endow you with some brain after all—just not enough. You've missed one little detail." When Kalen narrowed his eyes warily, she laughed. "I'll tell you for free—a free lesson in Waterdeep, aye?"

"What could you teach me, Fayne?"

"Every thief," she said, "knows that the first rule of thievery is misdirection."

When Kalen frowned, Fayne gestured to his chair. The paladin reached down tentatively, as though to scratch an itch, and felt one of the tiny, poison-coated needles that were stabbing into his legs, buttocks, and back—needles Fayne had placed there an hour gone.

The irony, she hoped, was not lost on him. Because of his sickness, he'd not have been able to feel them pierce his flesh when he sat down, and by then it was far too late.

"Farewell, lover," Fayne said. She gathered her feet off the table and stood. "I would have liked to share a tumble with you again, but . . . we never would have come to pass." Then, dipping low to give him one last eyeful down her bodice, she claimed his wine goblet and drank. When she was done, she licked her lips. "You and I are too much alike, and yet not enough."

She started to go, but Kalen laid his bandaged right hand on her wrist. The hand was shattered—only partly healed—and had no strength to stay her, but she stopped anyway.

"You're sweet," she said. "But with that much poison in you, you won't even be wakeful but for a few more heartbeats—and your heart will stop in a ten-count. Hardly time for—"

He started to rise. He came away from the needles, leaking trickles of blood, and rose before her like a black specter. She saw, in the folds of his stained gray cloak, the edge of a watchsword, which he drew into his bare left hand.

"There's—there's no way you could fight off that poison," said Fayne. "Unless—"

"Unless I managed to restrain myself"—he rose fully to his feet and kicked the table aside—"took Rath to the Watch instead of killing him"—with a flick of his wrist, he laid the watchsword across her throat—"and retained the favor of my three-faced god."

And thus speaking, Kalen began to glow with silver-white light, as though his skin itself was aflame, as though a deity had chosen that moment to smile upon him—and gaze through him. In the face of that divine radiance, the other patrons stared, transfixed.

"Well." Fayne trembled a little bit, then smiled. "Well played, Kalen—you really are a cold-hearted bastard." Her eyes flicked down to the steel he held at her throat, then up to him. "And you saved your soul to spend on me? I'm flattered."

He looked at her impassively.

She smiled bewitchingly. "I've waited many years for someone as clever as you—a foe who could defeat me. I'm glad he was so handsome, too."

Kalen's eyes were cold.

"Come now, lover—don't you want me?" She stepped forward, letting his blade cut a tiny red trail along her throat. She purred. "Don't you want to *hurt* me? I've hurt you, haven't I—killed your little sister and chased off your blue-haired tart?"

Her face was almost against his. Only the sword, keen enough to slit her throat with a twitch of Kalen's arm—one false step—stopped her from kissing him.

"When you think about that," Fayne said, "when you look at me—you don't have even just a *little* hate in your heart?" She tapped Kalen's chest. "That big, strong, *dying* heart?"

Kalen tightened his hand on the sword hilt.

He shoved her back. She fell to the floor and looked up at him, eyes and hair wild, sneering as he stepped forward. Her heart was pounding and she knew this was the end.

"No," he said. He sheathed the sword at his hip and turned his gaze aside.

Fayne trembled. She didn't dare move—he could whirl and open her throat at any instant. But he just stood, silent and still. Death might as well have taken him as he stood—his sickness crept up and slain him. She panted on the floor behind him, blood trickling down her heaving chest from the wound she had inflicted on herself.

Fayne rose. She dusted her leathers and smoothed her hair.

"Well, then—farewell, Kalen, though I don't expect you will." She winked. "Cellica's dead, Myrin has undoubtedly left, and you just pushed away the only other woman who could have made you happy. But I suppose you'll always have the memories."

She started to walk away.

"Fayne," Kalen commanded. "One last question."

She turned. His back was to her. "Yes, lover mine?"

"What's your real name?"

She pursed her lips. "I told you, it's—"

He whirled and smashed her nose with a left hook. She landed on her backside, dazed and dizzy and coughing.

"Just because I don't hate you," Kalen said, "doesn't mean I'm letting you go."

Fayne tried to retort, but her face exploded in pain.

Kalen pulled a set of manacles out of his belt. "You and Rath might just share a cell," he said. "Perhaps you'll have a nice conversation about how you betrayed him—but I doubt it."

Fayne only moaned on the floor, clutching her bloody face.

"No clever quip?" Kalen sheathed his sword. "Fayne, I'm crushed."

Drizzling blood from her broken nose, she smiled up at him with surprisingly sharp incisors. Her eyes drifted up his frame, lingering in places.

"I've had better, you know," she said.

Kalen smiled. "So have I."

CHAPTER FORTY

FAYNE HADN'T STOPPED SMILING ALL DAY.

She'd smiled silently when the Watch stripped her of her possessions, including her mother's wand and her ritual amulet, crippling her magic. She'd pressed herself hard against each of them in turn, inviting with her eyes, but none of them had taken her offer. Pity.

She'd smiled silently when they asked for her name—then again when the stuffed peacock from the Watchful Order of Magists had threatened to call the Blackstaff to interrogate her personally. He didn't realize that the red-haired half-elf was a false face, though, so he had not tried to break her transmutation. Thank Beshaba for small blessings.

She'd smiled silently, regardless of how much it hurt, when the gray-faced priest of Ilmater set and bandaged her broken nose. She did lick his hand once, because it amused her. She loved the look in his eyes—desire warring with faith.

The Watchmen, the mage, and the priest probably got the impression she was laughing at them, but that wasn't true. Granted, she had not the slightest esteem for the Watch, but today, she felt like laughing only at herself.

Only after they led her into her cell, dressed in her blood-spattered doublet and breeches, and after the door had slid shut behind her, did she finally give voice to the laugh that had been building inside her. It was all so amusing. She was the one, after all, who had trusted a paladin.

She laughed loud and long for quite a while, until the other prisoners—cutpurses and swindlers, hungover nobles and the like—slapped the bars, trying to get her to be silent. But it was just so funny, this whole ludicrous situation, and she was the lead comedienne.

"Oh, Ellyne, Ellyne," she mused. "You're such a gods-tumbled fool! Such a *fool!*"

The Watchman on duty thought she was simply mad, and he made the mistake of asking her to be silent. That man—a bulbous-nosed fellow of thirty winters or so—became the target of her lewdest and sharpest barbs. She threw herself into her mockery with a passion, pantomiming the jests and prompting more than a few cheeks around the prison to redden.

For she was Fayne, the Trickster of Waterdeep, and who would she be if she weren't the center of attention?

The Watchman gave up and stopped paying attention to her after a while, and she turned to tease her fellow deviants. Rath dwelt among the prisoners, sitting silently—mostly wrapped in bandages—in the cell opposite hers. He said nothing, no matter how she teased him.

After an unsuccessful hour of teasing anyone and everyone, Fayne grew bored. And thirsty, too. Not for the pond-scum water they'd given her—which she'd emptied on the guard's head—but for good brandy. Enough to make her face stop hurting.

Another hour passed. Having run out of breath to voice her japes and too proud to beg outright for attention, she contented herself with fuming at times, weeping at others.

Then, in the space of a heartbeat, all went silent.

Her sensitive ears could no longer hear the quiet murmur of the Watchmen at the front of the prison. She looked around, and her fellow prisoners all seemed asleep—or dead. Her heart started racing. What had happened?

"Aye!" she called. "Water, sirs! Please, goodsirs?"

No response.

The door swung open at the end of the hall, quiet and calm as soft death, and her heart almost froze. What was coming for her?

She sensed a presence—someone standing not a pace away from her at the door—and she shrieked and fell to the floor. She scrambled backward on her hands and feet and cowered against the wall.

Then came laughter.

"Mercy, child," a familiar voice said out of the air. "You *are* just like your mother."

A figure materialized before her, invisibility fading around it.

Relief flooded Fayne when she recognized her rescuer. "Gods," she said. "Did you leave me here long enough?"

The gold-skinned elf clad in the loud garb of a dandy swept off his plumed hat and bowed to her. He wore a bright rose pink shirt with dagged lace at the wrists, and his ebony overcoat was trimmed with complex gold swirls on the sleeves. Over this he wore a red half cloak that fell to about his waist, below which he wore white leather breeches. The outlandish garb might have seemed foppish or puerile on someone else, rather than dashing. She suspected, though, that he could wear anything and not fail to dash.

"Truly, Ellyne, you do me such dishonor," her patron said. "I was merely seeing to affairs of my own—I was quite unaware of your unfortunate circumstances."

"Hum." She didn't believe that for a heartbeat. "You've the key?"

Her patron lifted a ring of twenty keys. Then, as Fayne knew he would, he selected one completely at random and fit it in the lock. It turned, and he made a show of gasping surprise.

"You're impossible," Fayne said.

He shook his head. "Just lucky."

Her patron swept in as though he owned the city, and perhaps with good reason; privately, she suspected he was one of the masked lords who did exactly that.

"How positively *dreadful*." He pointed to her face. "Shall I avenge your honor, love?"

"No, no." Fayne's voice was made ugly and hollow by the broken nose. It rankled her, not being beautiful. "I prefer to do that myself."

"I thought you might." He leaned across the doorway, blocking her path out the door. "My darling little witch, I really must rebuke you."

"Oh?"

"For breaking the first rule of proper villainy," he said.

"Misdirection?"

"Point." Her patron smiled. "Very well, the *second* rule of villainy," he corrected.

Fayne spat on the floor indelicately. "And that is?"

"Never do anything yourself." He smiled and bowed. "Hirelings and minions, child! That way, you've no chance being caught—and their antics are always amusing."

Fayne crossed her arms and pouted. "Which am I, a hireling or a minion?"

"Oh, *tsch*." He kissed her on the forehead.

She pushed past him and started walking down the corridor. He stepped out and, as an afterthought, wove a bit of magic over the lock so that it would work only occasionally. He grinned at the mischief that particular cantrip would cause.

"Hold," he said.

"Aye?" She turned and fell to her knees as a wave of power struck her, pulling apart her disguising spells one by one. It felt like Lorien's rod on the night of the revel, but harsher. The power was not gentle, and Fayne felt every bit of its intrusive touch.

When it was done, she coughed and retched on the ground, reduced back to her true form, with its pale skin, hair the color of his doublet, and gleaming eyes of silver. She had long elf ears and delicate features, leathery wings, and a long tail tipped at the end with a spade-shaped ridge of bone. She glared at him with her fiendish eyes.

"This is my punishment?" Her bright red tongue darted between her too-sharp teeth.

He shrugged. "No hiding for a tenday," he said. "You allowed that paladin to use you because of your insecurities. I won't have that—not in a child of my blood. So deal with your weakness."

"Well." She stretched and yawned.

He blinked—he truly hadn't expected that. "Already? You are content?"

At least one person thinks I'm pretty, Fayne thought, but she didn't say that.

"Mayhap my true face is not so bad." Fayne rose, slowly, and stroked her hands down her silky hips. "Mayhap you should wear your own—or am I the brave one?"

"Mayhap you're not as smart as I," he corrected. "Who's the one with the broken nose, who spent half a day in a Watch cell crying her eyes out?" He averted his gaze. "Your punishment stands—until you remember your place."

"Hmpf!" Fayne stuck out her tongue.

He laughed. "Gods know I've made mistakes like yours, and mostly for the same reason." He patted her head. "Love is the sharpest sword of all."

Fayne swore colorfully.

Her patron winked. Then he handed her the amulet and bone wand.

"And what did you do," Fayne asked, "to correct those mistakes?"

"Oh. A bit of this"—he waved three circles in the air—"a bit of that." He put his hand on the hilt of his rapier. His white-gloved fingers caressed the starburst guard. Then, as though its touch had reminded him, he looked at Fayne with affectionate, twinkling eyes. "She made the same mistake many times."

"My mother?" Fayne asked. "Cythara?"

He smiled knowingly.

"Not that again," Fayne said, rolling her eyes.

"I speak with all sincerity," he said. "You remind me of your mother at your best—and at your worst. She made many mistakes of the heart—at your birth and at her death. You see?"

Fayne only nodded. She wondered why he wouldn't say her mother's name. He probably found it painful. A weakness, perhaps?

As they left the jail, the binding spell that had frozen the Watchmen expired, and they bolted upright, searching in bewilderment for their prisoner. Fayne almost started to cast a hiding spell of her own, but of course, her patron had prevented that.

She was, after all, his best and most important asset. She could trust him—at least, until her usefulness to him ended.

The bonds of blood, Fayne thought.

As they were leaving, cloaked in invisibility magic, Fayne mused over the one question that she'd been dying to ask—and could, now that this phase of his game had ended.

"Would you permit me to ask a question?"

"I would certainly permit you to *ask*."

"The dwarf," she said. "*You* paid him to kill Lorien."

Smiling, her patron waved one casual, delicate hand.

"*Lilianviaten*," she murmured, speaking his name.

In Elvish, it meant something like "master fate spinner." Lilten, she knew some called him. Also the Last Heir, though he'd never explained that to her. Mayhap he would, in a decade or so—perhaps a century.

It mattered little, Fayne thought. He was the only man she could trust in the world: trust to love her and betray her with equal frequency.

She wouldn't have it any other way.

She pressed. "So Rath was yours all along? Why didn't you tell me?"

"For my play to work, I had to make your reaction *real*, didn't I? And I knew you'd just ruin the whole game." He smiled wryly. "You should have seen your face."

Fayne started to ask, but then she understood it all—all of his plan, down to the smallest detail. How he had used her to manipulate events, and let her think he cared about her vengeance on the Nathalan bitch.

"Myrin," she said. "Myrin's the whole game—always has been."

"And?" Her patron waved her on.

"And now she's alone, undefended . . ." Fayne scowled. "You bastard!"

He flicked a lock of gold hair out of his eyes. "That's me."

Fayne couldn't help but laugh. It was so deliciously obvious—so simple—and so perfect. She could only pray to Beshaba she had half this sort of canniness when she came of age—and that the opportunity to pay Lilten back for his deception would arise soon.

"So . . . the game went according to your desire?"

"Of course." He stretched and yawned. "The next move is mine to make."

"I could help you with the rest of the game." Fayne nuzzled close to him—half like a solicitous child, half like a lover—and purred. "I promise I'll play by your rules."

"That's kind of you, but no." He shrugged. "Luck is with me—as she always is."

Of course, Fayne thought. She should have known—being the high priest of Beshaba, the goddess of misfortune, had its advantages.

And he was treacherous—she must never forget that. He'd served another god before, in the old world: Erevan Ilesere, if she remembered correctly, one of the faded Seldarine. Lilten the Turncloak, the apostate high priest, who had abandoned his god in favor of his bitter enemy.

She wondered when he would betray Beshaba in her turn.

Fayne hugged herself close to his arm, pressing her breast against his side. "You're sure you don't want me?" she purred.

"Quite sure, my little fiendling," he said. "This is *my* game, and I've dealt myself a shining hand at it."

She leaned up to kiss him on the cheek. "You're such a bastard, Father."

"Indeed I am, Ellyne, indeed I am." Lilten winked and returned the kiss. His lips burned like the fires of the Hells. "But you—you are as trueborn as I could make you."

Fayne blushed.

EPILOGUE

MYRIN WASN'T THERE WHEN KALEN RETURNED.

He hadn't really expected her to be, though he had hoped.

Too much had passed between them, and she had seen the cruelest and worst in him, as he had seen it in her. And yet, he had held out hope that mayhap, just mayhap . . .

A parchment letter—wrapped around Talanna's ring—was waiting on the empty, scarred table. That table reminded him of Cellica. How many times had he lain there while his adopted sister stitched his wounds? How many times had they sat together to mend Shadowbane's armor?

But it was Myrin's table, too, where he had first seen her, eating stew. Everything in the tallhouse had her on it—her scent, her smile, her memory.

The letter was brief. There were gaps, where many things went unsaid. It sounded of her and smelled of her, that sweet perfume of her bare skin. She'd crossed things out, and the ink had run in places. The parchment was dry, but he could see water stains. Tears, he realized.

As he read, all he felt was persistent cold.

> *Kalen, I'm sorry.*
>
> *I keep thinking [smudge] this wasn't supposed to happen like this. Mayhap I would wait for you, to be yours and to live out the rest of our story with you. Gods know I wanted [smudge]*
>
> *But life doesn't work like that. I need to find my own way—I can't have you make my choices for me. And until you see that [smudge] Here's your ring back, by the way.*
>
> *Farewell.*

I hope you find what you're looking for—and that I do too.
—M

Kalen sat a long time, looking down at the letter in his hand. He let the aches and sharp reminders of the past days settle. He felt them more keenly, since Myrin had touched him—had kissed him—though he didn't know why.

A tremor of sadness passed through him. It might have been a sob, if he'd not been weighed down by so many years—so many scars earned in service to the memory of a long-dead god—that he could not weep. So much pain, inflicted and suffered. When would it be enough?

He realized, almost immediately, that it didn't matter.

She was asking him to make a choice that went against everything he was, or had ever been. He couldn't make that choice, and she knew it. That was why she had left.

If he followed her now—if he rose and limped out the door and tracked her down—would it be to set things right, or would it be for her? What would he say to her?

He moved to crumple the note and toss it in the bin, but he saw more words scrawled on the back. He smoothed the parchment with shaking hands.

I wasn't going to say this. I scratched it out on the front, but you deserve to know.

I did something to you, Kalen—I can't [smudge] I can't feel my hand well, as I write this.

When I kissed you, I took some of your sickness from you. I absorbed it. I didn't do it on purpose, it just happened.

[smudge] I think you're going to live. Just a bit longer. Some of my life for some of yours. Call it [smudge] a fair exchange, for bringing me to life at all.

You don't owe me.

Kalen blinked. He stared at the letter for several pounding heartbeats. He was out the window before the letter fluttered to the floor.

ACKNOWLEDGMENTS

Blackstaff Tower

No book is ever conceived of or produced in isolation. In a book about heroes rising to the fore, I must acknowledge those heroes who helped bring it forward. First and foremost, I humbly thank my wife for her patience and love; crafting novels is never simple, but this one got easier with your support along the way. Ed Greenwood, as always, you're a far better friend and mentor than you'd ever acknowledge or possibly realize. My thanks, always. Susan Morris, my editor, has my thanks and many huzzahs for making this better. Jeff Grubb, thanks for letting me bring your Osco Salibuck back from the dead. Thanks also go to friends who became heroes with me in D&D many years ago: David Gehring, Alan Holverson, Bob Andrea, and Dave Beaulieu. This book of emerging heroes is for you guys. Last but hardly least, I need to thank Gary Gygax and Dave Arneson for opening up new worlds to all of us through their game Dungeons & Dragons. It's a debt we can never truly repay, save by crafting new stories and sharing that sense of adventure. —S.E.S.

Mistshore

Grateful acknowledgement to my editor, Susan Morris, for abundant patience and sharp eyes. My clothes are on straight only because of her. Much affection goes to Ed Greenwood, and not just for his guidance with this book. He doesn't know it, but fourteen years ago he inspired a shy, awkward girl to keep scribbling in a notebook until she became a writer. Old Mage, how can I ever thank you for opening the Realms to me? —J.J.

Downshadow

This book is the result of a great support network consisting in no small part of an excellent team of Realms scribes. First and foremost, I wish to honor my fellow Waterdhavians Ed Greenwood, Steven Schend, Jaleigh Johnson, Rosemary Jones—thanks in no small part to whose hard work our beloved Realms soldier on. Special thanks to Ed, without whose tireless and prodigious efforts I could not have written even half of this book. Thanks to the many Realmsians who've given me advice, support, and friendship over the years: Bob Salvatore, Paul Kemp, Elaine Cunningham, Richard Lee Byers, Ed Gentry, Brian Cortijo, George Krashos, Brian James, and dozens more.

Special thanks to Elaine for her great poesy—may Danilo Thann ever live on! He will in my heart. My editor Susan Morris deserves a great deal of the credit (or blame) for this novel. She's done an excellent job on the Waterdeep series, and continues to be one of the Realms' best allies. Thanks also to the sages/scribes at Candlekeep—to Alaundo and Sage and Kuje and Wooly and all the rest—without whom even the strongest swimmer would drown in the ocean of Realmslore. Thanks for the faith, guys, and please keep it up. We need you more than we will ever know. Thanks also to an intrepid band of online writers and adventurers—Mari, Laws, RW, Jeggred, Wraith, Grim, Pred, Gem, and Lady C—who give me hope for the future of our genre. And, as always, my lovely companion in arms, Shelley, without whose constant support, unconditional love, and especially fine editing skills I would be lost for sure. —*E.S.d.B.*